LOVE IS ETERNAL

Love
Is Eternal

A NOVEL ABOUT MARY TODD
AND ABRAHAM LINCOLN

by Irving Stone

DOUBLEDAY & COMPANY, INC., *Garden City, New York*

FOR JEAN, MY WIFE

Contents

LOVE IS ETERNAL

Book I

YOUTH IS THE SEED TIME

1

SHE leaned across her dressing table and gazed into the gilt-framed mirror on the wall. Strange, she thought, how much time you can spend studying your own face, and then scarcely know it. Her nose, at least, never altered: it was short and straight: but everything else seemed to change with her mood. Her upper lip was thin, almost prim, her lower lip full and sensual; the lock she combed across the massive brow was blond but the rest of her hair, which fell in waves below her shoulders, was chestnut. Her eyes were large, wide-set, deep blue, clear and penetrating in their outward gaze though not always lucid within; tonight she was happy, and the intruder who sometimes lurked behind them was nowhere to be seen.

She felt herself under scrutiny, looked up into the right-hand corner of her mirror and caught her fifteen-year-old sister Ann's eyes upon her.

"For a girl who's a prude with the boys," Ann commented in her high voice, "you're displaying what Ma calls an unconscionable amount of bosom."

Mary gazed down at the rich blue Afrique silk; she had designed the gown herself, low off the shoulders, the short puffed sleeves overlaid with needle-point. People rarely said she had a beautiful face, though they often said she was lovely; but no one disputed that she had the most exquisite shoulders and arms in Lexington, with no bones or hollows showing, only full-bodied roundness and the warmest of flesh tones.

Looking upward in her mirror, she saw Ann furiously trying to bunch her undergarments.

"Don't be impatient, Ann. You'll blossom forth . . . someday."

"Better make this dining pay, Mary. Ma says it's your last . . . if you don't manage a proposal from Sandy."

Stung this time, Mary whirled about.

"Mother said no such thing!"

Her voice rose from its usual low, self-possessed tone, the color pounded upward in her scrubbed cheeks. More quietly she continued, "What you may have heard her say is that she hopes the party will bring me a proposal."

"That's the same thing, isn't it?"

"Only to you, Ann."

She walked to the window overlooking the rear garden and coach house, the lawn running all the way down to the little stream at the bottom of the hill. In the west an orange sunset flamed, while across the town fork of Elkhorn Creek she could see the slight purplish tinge on the fields which had earned them the name of Bluegrass country.

For a moment she reflected on how uncomfortable it still felt to call her stepmother, Betsy Humphreys, Mother, then pondered on how wide the divergence could be among four sisters of the same parents. Her oldest sister, Elizabeth, who was married and living in Springfield, Illinois, was like their mother had been: warmhearted, of a sunny, unchangeable disposition. Though Elizabeth was only eleven and a half when their mother died she had gathered the younger children to her, lavishing her affection upon them. Her second sister, Frances, who was now living with Elizabeth in Springfield, was reserved, taciturn. Her own face was a weather vane: it was impossible for her to conceal anything she felt. And here was Ann, her roommate, who liked to twist the meaning of people's words just enough to set them against one another.

There was the sound of slow plodding in the outside hall. Mammy Sally opened the door. She was a big formless woman with hair pulled tautly back from a receding brow, a full row of bottom teeth but not one upper one. She had raised not only Mary and her sisters but their mother as well, having been given as a wedding present to Eliza Parker Todd by Grandmother Parker. The old Negro woman wagged her head in approval as she gazed at Mary's gown, the bodice gathered into a V at the waist, then flaring out over the crinoline petticoats in bouffant fashion.

"Neat but not gaudy as the debil said when he painted his tail pea green."

"Glad you like the new gown, Mammy Sally. I think I'll wear the pearls Father brought me from New Orleans."

"Your own true love is downstairs, chile. I knowed you'd want me to tell you. Too bad he so old, or he propose tonight sure."

Mary laughed; some eight years before, when she was twelve, her father had bought her a white dancing pony; a few days later she had galloped the mile and a half out Main Street to Ashland, the home of Henry Clay. Mr. Clay had been at dinner with important political personages, just prior to his leaving for the Congress in Washington City, but he had excused himself and come out to the front steps.

"Look at my new pony, Mr. Clay. Father bought him from those strolling players that were stranded here last week."

"He's spirited as his jockey." Then he had lifted her down from the saddle, saying, "You're just in time for dinner."

They set a place for her between Mr. Clay and John J. Crittenden, Speaker of the Kentucky House of Representatives, a handsome man with dark gray eyes, an aquiline nose and beautifully sculpted head. She had listened to a furious attack on President Andrew Jackson's executive usurpation, his defiance of the Supreme Court, and the weakening of the legislative branch by his repeated vetoes. She had a good background for such discussions: her father frequently brought her in to the dinner table during dessert when he entertained Mr. Clay and other political associates.

During a lull she had exclaimed, "Mr. Clay, my father says you will be the next president of the United States. I wish I could go to Washington City and live in the White House."

Mr. Clay had laughed. "Well, if ever I am president I shall expect Mary Todd to be one of my first guests."

She bowed with a formal nod of acceptance.

"I begged my father to be president, but he said he would rather see you there. My father is a very peculiar man, Mr. Clay; *I don't think he wants to be president.*"

There was a burst of laughter from the men at the table, only Mr. Clay remaining serious. She gazed up and said:

"If you were not already married, Mr. Clay, I would wait for you."

Fastening the strand of small pearls around her neck, she ran lightly down the carpeted stairs and stepped out onto the white limestone gravel walk, stopping under a sycamore tree where she could see the men in the pavilion. Henry Clay was the center of attention; with him were his fellow senator from Kentucky, Mr. Crittenden, young Richard Menifee, who now represented Lexington in Congress, and her father. Robert Todd was forty-eight years old, an attractive man except that he had been vouchsafed almost no neck, his round head being set down between his shoulders. His long black hair was combed over his ears, and he was handsomely gotten up in a bell-shaped blue broadcloth coat, white linen trousers strapped under his boots, with a high collar topping the ruffled lace shirt. He was even-tempered except for an occasional flash of anger; and one of the best-dressed men in the Bluegrass, with superb taste in fabrics and jewelry. To Mary he had bequeathed his temperament and tastes *in toto*, yet they had always been close to each other in spite of this burden of similarity.

Seeing her under the sycamore, he called out in a muted voice which seemed to originate in his mouth:

"Mary dear, come over and say hello to some old friends."

She walked the rest of the path with her eager, vivacious step and found herself held in Mr. Clay's bony hands for a moment before being bussed soundly on either cheek.

"Well, Miss Mary, it's good to see you again," he exclaimed heartily. "You look lovelier every time I come back from Washington. Are you still waiting for me?"

"Yes, I'm still waiting," she replied, her eyes flashing mischievously, ". . . for you to be elected president."

She sat down amidst the men who were so important a part of her father's life and her own here in Lexington, listening to every word Mr. Clay was saying. His voice had the power to penetrate a mountain, yet for her it was ineffably sweet and moving. Seeing the thin reddish hair falling over the sides of his head, the long bony irregular face, the enormously outsized mouth, the dimpled chin, piercing gray-blue eyes and the long skinny figure, it occurred to her how closely he resembled his archenemy, Andrew Jackson, whom she considered to have unfairly kept Henry Clay out of the White House.

Richard Menifee came and sat beside her on the painted bench. She had not seen him since her disappointment two years before at the Whig convention in Harrodsburg when her father had been suggested as lieutenant governor, and Menifee had gone before the meeting to ask that the Todd name be withdrawn.

"Have you forgiven me yet, Mary?" he asked in a pleasant drawl. "It was your father, you know, who made me do it."

"You should never have listened to him."

There was a reminiscence of anger in her voice. Her father put his arm about her waist and said in a tight but affectionate tone:

"You have a hard time with me, don't you, Mary?"

Yes, she sometimes did have difficulty in understanding her father. Son of one of the six founders of Lexington, he had attended Transylvania University, majored in Latin, Greek, logic and history, graduated with honors. Though he had been licensed as an attorney when he was twenty and was considered to have one of the ablest minds in Lexington, he had never cared to practice what his daughter thought to be the most exciting of professions, the law. Instead he was the owner of a grocery establishment in town, woolen and hemp bagging factories in the country, and president of the Lexington Branch Bank of Kentucky, preferring to be a manufacturer and raise sums of money for new ventures, declining to display the intellectual brilliance which fascinated her in men like Clay and Crittenden.

The Todd butler came down the path carrying the ingredients for mint juleps on a large silver waiter. While he began the ritual of pressing the fragrant mint with the back of a spoon against the inside of a sterling goblet, the men plunged into a spirited discussion of the Whig convention that was to be held in the fall, and the candidates most likely to come before it for the presidential nomination: Daniel Webster, General Winfield Scott and William Henry Harrison. As Mary watched Nelson remove the bruised leaves and half fill the cups with cracked ice before adding the mellow bourbon which had been aging in oaken staves in the Todd cellar, she told herself that these three possibilities would quickly be cast aside, and Henry Clay nominated. Was he not the master of the Whig party, its brains as well as its fighting spirit?

Nelson now stirred granulated sugar in chilled limestone water; with the mixture smooth and silvery, he poured it on top of the ice, garnishing the frosted brim with sprigs of mint. Clay took a sip, exclaiming:

4

"There's no disputing it, Old Nelson makes the best mint julep in Kentucky. We'll have to take him with us to the White House."

She flushed with pleasure at Clay's use of the word "us"; that meant Robert Todd would have an important position in the administration. His avocation was politics: he had served as clerk for twenty-one years in the Kentucky House of Representatives, and his home was the unofficial headquarters of the Whig party in Lexington. Yet he had always been content to work behind the scenes as a kind of business manager, neither wanting nor seeking office.

Henry Clay will change all that, Mary thought. We will move to Washington and rent a fine house and entertain high society.

2

THE house was a blaze of light, the satin draperies of the front parlor and family sitting room having been opened and the hanging crystals sparkling from each of the six lighted lamps of the embossed brass chandeliers. In the front and back parlors the tufted green brocade sofas had been pushed against the walls on either side of the fireplace.

Mary walked up the four stone steps that led off the carriage drive and entered the wide front door with its hand-carved panels. In spite of the underlying tension between them, Mary had a deep-rooted respect for her stepmother, Betsy Humphreys Todd. She recalled her saying: "It takes seven generations to make a lady." Mary had to concede that this home and garden were the creations of a lady of taste, doubly so since it had originally been William Palmateer's tavern which Robert Todd had bought at a bankruptcy proceeding. Betsy had converted the spacious brick building into a charming town house with twelve-foot ceilings, the doors set in molded frames, fireplaces with carved wood mantels in each of the downstairs rooms as well as the bedrooms above.

As she had a dozen times between the age of eight, after her father had remarried, and her present age of twenty, Mary asked herself, Might we have loved each other if Grandma Parker had not set us children against her? For years Betsy lived in an aura of not being wanted. Could that not make her look forward to the day when we would be married . . . and gone? Betsy would not come downstairs tonight; she had not yet recovered from the birth of her sixth child, but Mary knew that this was not the real reason. She was remaining upstairs to give Mary the full pleasure of being hostess at her own party.

She heard the musicians tuning up in the back parlor, from which the green velvet chairs had been moved into the hall, along with the carved cherrywood sofa. Reuben, Henry and George, the famous trio that belonged to Colonel Graham and played for the summer season at Graham Springs, were tuning their violin and guitar to the notes of the pianoforte. She bade them welcome, then indicated the number of the newly fashionable waltzes she wanted interspersed among the cotillions, round dances and reels.

"I think it might be amusing to start with a grand march, as though we were an enormous ball at Monsieur Giron's."

"We ready to strike up any time you say, Miss Todd."

There was the sound of a lone horseman riding up to the front door. She heard Sandy McDonald's voice.

McDonald was of medium height, with sand-colored hair and eyes, and a sandy complexion with a myriad of freckles, a few of which spilled down from his cheeks onto his lips. His coloring and his Scotch ancestry had gained him the name of Sandy; only the registrar at Transylvania University knew that his Christian name was Thomas.

"Good evening, Sandy. My, but you look resplendent in that new buff waistcoat and powder-blue coat."

"Made specially for your party, ma'am. Also to take back with me to Mississippi. I'll be the green-eyed envy of every man in the county."

It was now ten o'clock, and the open carriages began rolling into the driveway from Main Street. The first to arrive was her good friend Margaret Wickliffe, wearing a light blue antique moiré and her mother's diamond earrings. With her was her fiancé, William Preston, who had recently been admitted to the bar in Louisville. Next came Isabella Bodley, dressed in heavy white silk, the skirt trimmed with ermine and rows of scarlet bands embroidered in gold. Isabella had boarded with Mary at Madame Mentelle's finishing school from the time they were fourteen until they were eighteen. Her escort was a young French student, Jacques Barye. Catherine Trotter, another former school friend, had just returned from a visit to New Orleans and had her hair piled high on top of her head in the Creole fashion, wearing wild-rose skirts almost twelve feet in circumference. Margaret Stuart, her cousin, arrived with young Thomas Crittenden; the youngest of the three daughters of Dr. Elisha Warfield, the Todd family physician, was escorted by Robert Wickliffe. Most of the young men were Transylvania University students.

The house was filled with laughter and high spirits. Mary felt intensely alive; she loved receiving at formal parties. Her pleasure at being surrounded by these close friends made her eyes sparkle, the magnificently formed shoulders and bosom caught admiring glances from everyone. She knew intuitively how to welcome people: the warm clasp of the hand, the light kiss on the cheek, the interested question, the appreciative word about a new gown or waistcoat.

They stood about in a wide circle in the front parlor while Tom Crittenden told the story he had read in that morning's *Observer* about the man on the way to his wedding who said to his bride-to-be:

"I have not told you all of my mind. I shall insist on three things: I shall

6

lie alone, I shall eat alone, I shall find fault with you when there is no occasion for it." His bride-to-be replied that she accepted the conditions, adding, "If you lie alone, I shall not; if you eat alone, I shall eat first; and as for your finding fault without occasion, I shall take care that you shall never want occasion."

At a quarter past ten the last couple arrived. Mary flicked her handkerchief at Reuben, the music started and she and Sandy led the grand march, winding through the two parlors, the hallway, her father's library and the family sitting room. Then the band went into a round dance, with the guests wheeling and turning, circling the length of the two parlors. Mary moved through the figures with tireless grace and enjoyed dancing with each young man as much as the other.

Promptly at midnight, after the trio had played several encores of the popular Circassian Circle, Nelson opened the doors of the dining room. The red walnut table had been extended its full length, the dining-room chairs with their black satin-upholstered seats were arranged around the walls for the buffet. A dozen candles in silver candelabra illumined the damask tablecloth, and on it the silver bowls of iced melon, preserved meats from France, chilled oysters, trays of sliced turkey and hickory-cured ham; and from the confectioner, Monsieur Giron, meringues and macaroons in filmy sugar webbing. Nelson circulated among the group with a tray of frosted glasses filled with champagne.

After the first pangs of hunger had been satisfied the talk centered upon the following day's Commencement at Transylvania: the girls recalled the debates of the Adelphi and the Union Philosophical Societies which they had attended in a body, the spring races where the boys had bet each other "hailstorms and snowstorms" on their favorite horses, and the plays they had seen: Shakespeare's *Merchant of Venice*, Washington Irving's *Spectre Bridegroom*, such comedies as *The Dumb Belle* and *Family Jars*. The men discussed their days of study, their prospects for the future.

Mary put aside her meringue, her face serious, the bright light fading from her eyes. Tomorrow would be Commencement for her too. There would be no academic procession, no Morrison Chapel filled with admiring relatives and friends, no learned professors making speeches, no president handing her a diploma with her name in gold letters. Nevertheless she was completing her education tomorrow, and no one could say that she had not worked as diligently as any of these young men sitting about her.

No one could say? Of course no one could say . . . because no one knew! For two years after she had left Madame Mentelle's she had followed the academic courses given by Transylvania, doing the assignments, studying the textbooks, writing the compositions, discussing the moot points with her former schoolmaster, Dr. John Ward, who alone knew of her plan.

She looked up, her eyes traveling among the faces of her student friends. Most of them had been flattered by her interest in their books and studies, but several had asked why she bothered, since such matters as logic and history could hardly be worth a pretty girl's time. Well, it was an innocent enough deception; and now it was over.

Sandy, sitting next to her, asked:

"Why so silent, Mary?"

"Just thinking. . . ."

He leaned closer.

"Come outside with me. I'd like to talk to you."

3

THEY stood in the center of the bridge at the foot of the Todd garden, their shoulders touching lightly. Sandy was talking about River View, the McDonald manor house in Mississippi; his father had died at Easter, and as the only son he would be taking over the management of the big plantation.

"It's surrounded by huge oaks, and has elegant Doric columns with deep shade galleries around three sides. The rooms are eighteen feet high, with French windows that lead to the gardens. It needs redecorating: the wallpaper is old-fashioned, and I think you would want to take out the heavily carved mantels. There's plenty of money for the work, and Mother would afford you an entirely free hand. . . ."

She felt a little faint . . . Sandy was proposing to her. How right, she thought, how well he knew her, to offer her the redoing of a stately manor house.

". . . crops are up to the master," he went on, "but everything else revolves about the mistress of the house. The happiness of everyone depends on her, not only her own family but the two hundred slaves as well. She's the chatelaine, carrying the keys to the storerooms, training the pickaninnies, managing the gardens, the cooks, chambermaids, supplying medicines and nursing. It's a life of . . . responsibility . . . but one that you have the talents for."

He turned her around, his hands gripping her shoulders in a gesture containing more ardency than any he had shown in their long friendship.

"Mary, let's be married tomorrow after Commencement. I've already spoken to Monsieur Giron; he says that for you he will stage the most brilliant wedding supper and ball ever seen in Lexington. We'll invite the whole class . . ."

She put her cheek on his and found to her surprise that she was crying. Sandy felt the tears.

"I hope you're crying because you're happy, Mary."

8

She slipped back, brushed her cheek upward to dry it, then stood gazing over his shoulder to where the Todd house stood above them, glowing brilliantly in the night.

"Sandy dear, I think it's . . . gratitude: this is my first proposal."

"The first! But why? You're the most exciting girl in the Bluegrass."

Why indeed? she asked herself. Was it because she had never been seriously interested in the young men? Or because they had not been interested in her? As a Todd she had gone everywhere, been welcome throughout the Bluegrass; for some five years now she had attended all the parties, picnics, dinners, balls, mingled with the Transylvania students and professors. She had liked the young boys she grew up with, they had wonderful times together. She had watched her schoolmates from Mentelle's fall in love, marry. Yet she had never been a genuine belle. Why? Was it because she had remained unmoved . . . unready?

Hadn't that been the case with Desmond Fleming? Though only twenty-six, Desmond had begun to win recognition for himself as a horse breeder; he owned two hundred acres of rolling pastureland and had built attractive white stables at one end of his own track. She had met him at the Grand Farewell Ball given by the gentlemen and their ladies from Texas, Louisiana, Mississippi and Alabama. A few days before, she had gone to Monsieur Giron's to buy some pastries and he had taken her upstairs to show her the decoration scheme for the big ball. She gasped as she walked through the three ballrooms with their polished cherry folding doors opened wide to the frescoed ceiling, for Monsieur Giron had painted his walls with orange trees in bloom. Mary might almost have been standing in the midst of a southern orange grove.

She went quickly to O'Rear and Berkeley's to buy materials, then sent a boy to summon the family seamstress. Her gown for the ball would have a wide orange satin skirt with embroidered green leaves over ruffled petticoats, a large green leaf across the bodice, and at her bosom a cluster of brilliant gold oranges.

Even with the seamstress' help she had to work very hard to complete the outfit in time, but it was worth all the rush and trouble, for everyone was startled at how perfectly she fitted in with the decorative theme. The gown brought her not only compliments but a good deal of fun and a fusillade of invitations to waltz.

But above all, Desmond Fleming was smitten. He was the best-looking man there, with his head of blond curls, the chiseled features with the air of careless arrogance, and the too tight clothes that displayed his lines in bas-relief. He circled around her several times, then took her arm and led her onto the iron-lace balcony overlooking Mill Street.

She did not particularly care for light-complexioned men; she preferred dark-haired men with dark impenetrable eyes and something mysterious to be grappled for. Nevertheless she had known from the way they taunted each

9

other that there was some basis for attraction. At a Wickliffe birthday party a few nights later, in the midst of an elegy about a magnificent mare he had just bought, she interrupted:

"There's no use giving me an anatomy lecture about the mare, Des, I hardly know a forelock from a fetlock."

"The only way you'd be interested in a horse," he had cried, nettled, "would be if I could get him inside the covers of a book. What can you find in a book that's not plainer in life?"

"The odds on Grey Eagle against Wagner in the big race."

He flushed, looking down at the little publication he had stuffed into his coat pocket. Then he laughed.

"All right, I'm horse crazy. But you're house crazy. Just the difference of one little letter . . ."

This time she had been caught off guard, her left eyebrow shot up to give her a puzzled expression, and there it would stay until the disputed point was settled.

"Architecture is one of the great arts . . ."

"Why, Mary Todd, do you think it doesn't take great art to produce a champion? Any carpenter can build himself a house in a few months, but it takes years to build a blood strain in thoroughbreds." He seized her and whirled her about in a long and breath-taking waltz. "It never occurred to me before, but it must have taken quite a few generations to develop that championship form in you, too."

"I see my stock is rising, now that you've entered me in the same category as your beloved horses."

She had seen him every day for the next week: at outdoor dances at neighboring plantations, watching the bringing in of the crops, riding over the bluegrass on his young horses. There had been a few flirtatious embraces, and one fierce kiss as they rested under a group of beeches with the fragrance of wild grapes and crab apples in their nostrils. That same afternoon he asked:

"Mary, my parents are away, and there is an important group of horse buyers coming in from Nashville. Would you be my hostess for Sunday dinner?"

"Why yes, Des, I'd be happy to. Suppose you make a list of the men, with a little bit about their personalities . . ."

She greeted each of the guests by name, asking a question or two about their own farms and stables. From her seat at the head of the table her gaiety was infectious; but by way of preparation she had made certain that each man had the kind of partner he would enjoy: next to the one who talked constantly she placed Susan Blackman, an accomplished listener; to a slim quiet man she had given Fern Hadley, a seasoned talker. From the foot of the table Desmond flashed her a look of gratitude.

Relaxing for the first time as the dessert was being brought in, she realized that she might as well have been dining in a foreign country for all she understood of what was being said: the blood stock of Colonel Buford, the Orange Boy stallion, Sir Leslie by Sir William, dam by Buzzard, the condition of the courses at Harrodsburg and Charleston, the qualities of the water from the limestone springs that gave the Bluegrass horses their strong bones.

It was late when she stood at the open doorway bidding the guests good-bye. Desmond rested his arm lightly upon her shoulder. She had a deep feeling of contentment and tranquillity: this was her home, these were her guests, this was her husband standing beside her.

As her own carriage was brought around from the stables, Desmond took her in his arms, kissed her on the lips.

"Mary Todd, if those men don't buy half my stables tomorrow, it certainly won't be your fault."

His arms tautened, pressing her to him. If she wanted a proposal now, this very moment, she needed only to return his embrace.

Was this the answer to her problems . . . and her dreams? From early childhood she had known what kind of man she wanted; conventional good looks had never had any importance for her. She had worshiped men with first-rate minds, men who knew the inside workings of the civilized world: the prototype of a Henry Clay, yes, and much as she disagreed with his politics, of an Andrew Jackson. She wanted the young version, the beginner, but always and ever she had thought in terms of a fighter, a man ambitious to serve in the broad turbulent world.

For a moment she clung to Desmond, then slipped out of his arms and started toward her carriage. The cool night air was good on her face. She felt the freedom that comes from a decision unalterably made, and resolved not to fall into any more traps, particularly those she laid herself.

She brought her attention back to Sandy.

"I don't know why this is my first proposal, Sandy. Perhaps it is because I have never loved anyone."

"You've been a good friend to me, Mary."

"I've truly liked you better than any boy I've known. But I'm afraid I've been dishonest . . ."

"Now, Mary, I know your faults: those fiery bursts of temper, the witty remarks that are sometimes cruel. But you're never dishonest."

"Sandy, I was hurt and angry because Transylvania wouldn't let a woman inside its sacrosanct portals, and so I took those courses by myself. Perhaps you wouldn't have become so interested in me if you had known why I was seeing you so often."

"Why, Mary, I knew all along."

She stared at him in disbelief, two red spots appearing on her forehead.

"You couldn't have! I've never uttered a word. Don't tell me that everyone else in town knows too?"

"I don't think so. I found the key at the very beginning; if I hadn't known, how could I have been so helpful?"

Her expression was crestfallen, her shoulders sagged.

"Oh dear, I've been so obvious . . . when I thought I'd been so clever!"
Sandy shrugged this off as a matter of no importance, then cupped her face in his hands, gently.

"Mary, you always have gaiety about you: if you can't find it, you create it. I like that because I'm a little on the . . . dull side . . . myself . . ."
She thought, Oh, Sandy, that's what I want too . . . excitement about me!

". . . of course I could hardly blame you for being unwilling to leave Lexington," he added wistfully, "it must be the most beautiful town in the country, set in these soft rolling hills . . ."

Did she love Lexington so much that she would be unwilling to leave it? She took pride in its title "Athens of the West," with its fine university, library, schools, bookstores, debating societies, theatres, musical organizations. Not only was it the social and fashion center of the state but, because of Henry Clay's residence there, it was the political storm center as well. It was a town whose streets were paved with crushed limestone rock, shaded by rows of locusts, filled with carriages, gigs, barouches at all hours of the day. It was meticulously clean. The brick houses were spacious, surrounded by trees and green shrubbery. Visitors from New York, Boston and Philadelphia assured them that in matters of taste, social grace, comfort and the elegance of interior furnishings, Lexington stood up with the finest in the country. Strange how one's birthplace could hold one's roots, yet have no room for the flowering growth.

In the silence there came the sound of clanking metal and soft moaning. It was a coffle of slaves passing in front of the Todd house, separated only by the width of the sidewalk, the men manacled two abreast and connected by heavy iron chains that extended the length of the line, the women tied by the hand two by two, some of them carrying sleeping children. They would have been on the road for some twenty hours, the Lexington slave jails being the next stop before they could find rest. For six years now, ever since they had moved into this house on Main Street, she had watched these slave gangs being pushed along the road. The sight never failed to arouse terror within her; over by the creek there was a mark on the fence so that runaway slaves would know that here was a place where they could find victuals and sanctuary. Her parents knew nothing of this: her father, who traded with the deep south, would have felt obliged to protest. She and Mammy Sally kept their secret well.

She looked up into Sandy's face.

"No, Sandy, I could leave Lexington . . . if there were a force strong enough to draw me elsewhere."

"And I am not that force?"

He was hurt. She leaned up and touched her lips to his cheek. Her voice was low now, and filled with her own bewilderment.

"We've been good friends. But oh, Sandy, mustn't love be more than that?"

4

THE breakfast bell awoke her promptly at eight. She sprang out of bed and pushed aside the red twill hangings; yes, it was a clear day for the graduation. She poured some water from the pitcher into the bowl on the marble-topped stand, washed her hands and face and vigorously brushed her hair to make it light and fluffy. Before slipping into her mousseline-de-laine robe she stole an appraising look at her figure as reflected in the dressing-table mirror. All of the Todds had a tendency toward plumpness, and she frequently had to forgo Monsieur Giron's pastries as well as Aunt Chaney's candied yams in order to preserve her slim waistline. By crouching down a little she could see her face; it was by no means the heart shape which the young gentlemen of the Bluegrass considered the most desirable, but with its pink complexion, her blue eyes large and set off by long silken lashes, it was intensely alive and expressive. She reached into her ribbon box and selected a gold bow to tie to the single gold strand of hair which crossed her forehead.

She enjoyed waking up in this room. Two years before, when she had returned from a visit with Elizabeth in Springfield, her father had persuaded her stepmother to let her decorate it to her own taste. When it was completed as a combination bedroom-sitting room, with deeply flounced twill draperies, the same dark red material at the top of the Sheraton four-poster, the striped gold and blue silk of the tailored bedspread and the chaise longue, Betsy commented dryly that it was too rich for her taste. Mary and her father admitted to each other that the room was perhaps a *soupçon* overdressed; and that they loved it that way!

She went to the big window at the front of the hall to see what excitement might be abroad on Main Street. Across the road, in front of the Maxwell house, she recognized Dr. Warfield's gig. Mrs. Maxwell must be taken again. Her mind flashed back to the Fourth of July that she had gone out to Fowler's Garden to a barbecue and to hear Henry Clay make a speech. She was only six and a half, and had not understood a word of it, but his voice and presence were compelling. Then, just before the barbecue, she had suddenly been brought back to town. The one-horse gigs of Dr. Warfield and Dr. Dudley stood before the door; that in itself was peculiar. Her mother was having a baby, but Mammy Sally delivered all the children.

That night she was put to sleep in her grandmother's house, and awakened to the sound of weeping. She ran to the window and saw that pillowcases had been hung on the clothesline in the back yard. That meant someone was dead. It must be the new baby, like her brother Robert, who had been born when she was two, and then died the following summer. Later, when she went into her own home, unseen, she heard her aunt Maria say:

13

"Nelson, please hitch up the carriage and deliver the funeral tickets."
She wondered, What is a funeral ticket? In the front hall she saw a pile of
cards with black borders, picked one up:

Yourself and family are respectfully invited to attend the funeral of
Mrs. Eliza P., Consort of Robert S. Todd, Esq., from his residence on
Short Street, this Evening at 4 o'clock, July 6, 1825.

From that hour, and particularly after her father's remarriage, everything
had changed.

The doctor came out of Mrs. Maxwell's house, putting an end to her reverie.
She saw Old Nelson coming toward the house, shoving before him a wheel-
barrow heaped with choice meats, fruits and vegetables. She crossed the
hall to the children's bedroom to get two-and-a-half-year-old Emilie out of
bed. Emilie was the beauty of the family; she and Mary were the closest
friends among all the half brothers and sisters. Emilie's blue eyes lighted
up at the sight of Mary. Mary washed Emilie's face and hands with a cloth,
brushed her reddish-blond hair, put a gingham dress on her and then hoisted
the child onto her left shoulder, holding her securely while she walked down
the stairs and into the dining room.

Her father had already left for business, Betsy was not yet down. Seated
around the table were her half sisters Margaret, aged ten, and Martha, aged
six, also her two handsome half brothers, Samuel, who was nine, and David,
seven. Ann never got up for breakfast; her own fourteen-year-old brother
George, in whose birth her mother had died, ate in the kitchen as part of some
secret and unsocial life he had set out for himself, perhaps the better to
conceal his stutter. She was given a robust welcome by the little ones:
". . . beautiful party . . ." "So pretty, Mary." ". . . naughty Mary, we
saw your ankles . . . !"

She helped herself from the queen's-ware bowl of fresh-cut fruits. Despite
her underlying uneasiness with her stepmother, her love for these fresh-faced
youngsters was greater than for her full sisters and brothers, Elizabeth ex-
cepted. The close relationship with her own brothers, which she had yearned
for, had been impossible these past years with Levi drinking steadily and
young George sulking down hallways the moment anyone came into sight.
And so she had turned to bright-faced, dark-haired Samuel, and pert-nosed,
red-haired David for her companionship, going for long horseback rides with
them, and reading stories to them at night.

In a moment Mary heard her stepmother's light yet determined step on the
stair. She thought:

That's the step of a woman looking for information, not breakfast.

Betsy Todd came into the room wearing a purple velvet dressing robe.
Mary had never been able to learn her stepmother's exact age, but she judged
her to be around thirty-eight. Betsy parted her hair in the middle, then
combed it forward in a wave on either side. Mary had never considered her
pretty: her nose was too long and bony, her mouth thin and severe, but she

had to acknowledge that it was a face attractive for its ever present intelligence. A woman of rigid moral character, she never had done anything less than her total duty to the six motherless children she had inherited, even while bearing six of her own.

Betsy Humphreys was an avid reader, well versed in national politics, two of her uncles being United States senators, and was always giving Mary new volumes of poetry for her birthday, such as Robert Burns or the *Elegant Extracts*. Invariably for Christmas she gave her stepdaughter a package of books on European travel, sometimes having to write months in advance to London and Paris for these volumes: a history of Scotland by Sir Walter Scott; volumes about England, Ireland and France; the *Letters* of Madame de Sévigné; Dresden's *The Art of Traveling Comfortably*; and a good many others that now filled her upstairs shelves.

Betsy had barely entered the room when she asked:

"You didn't accept him?"

"No, Mother, I couldn't."

"Frankly, I'm disappointed. Sandy comes from such a fine family."

"You wouldn't have me marry a man I didn't love?"

"There is such a thing as closing your mind to love."

"How does one do that?"

"By insisting upon remaining a schoolgirl. Are you sure you're not waiting for a knight in shining armor?"

"I don't think I'm a foolish romantic. It's just that I'm in no hurry. Need I be?"

Mrs. Todd's eyelids flared, but she quickly regained her composure.

"That's a clever question, Mary. No, you needn't hurry. This is your home and no one will force you out of it."

A feeling of compassion for her stepmother swept over Mary: for six years Betsy had lived in the house and slept in the bed of the first Mrs. Todd. That could never have been easy for her; and Mary knew that it had been made more difficult by being obliged to live these years on West Short Street next door to Grandmother Parker, whose implacable hatred of Betsy for having replaced her dead daughter had poisoned her well of days. Even when Betsy finally had persuaded her husband to bid for Palmateer's tavern, Robert Todd had found it necessary to sell some of his first wife's land in order to have the cash to buy and renovate the new house. Mary put her hand out, covering her stepmother's hand where it lay white and thin on the table cover.

Mrs. Todd picked up the *Observer* to read aloud:

"Mrs. D. Bartholtz, from Baltimore, Maryland, respectfully informs the citizens of Lexington that she proposes opening a seminary for young ladies on the first Monday in May at the schoolrooms of the Reverend J. Ward."

"I'm glad, Mary, for your sake that Dr. Ward is through with teaching. I think he was the last obstacle in your way."

"Of what, Mother?"

"Of taking your place in the adult world."

"But I'm only twenty." Her voice had raised several tones. She tried to quiet it. "The day will come for me. And when it does, I'll rush out to meet it, eagerly."

5

SHE donned a lemon-colored organdy frosted with ruffles, took a pair of linen gloves from her bureau and a new London straw bonnet trimmed with a lemon ribbon, then began the familiar walk to school. First she passed P. G. Smith's store, which sold paints, varnishes, perfumes and cosmetics; across the street was McLear & O'Connell, with their window full of sugar, coffee and spices. She stopped for an instant in front of Chew & Company to look at some French and Indian cloth that had just arrived, then crossed Main and took the slight uphill grade of North Mill Street.

Dr. Ward's Academy was a large red brick building on the corner of Market and Second streets, kitty-corner from the open field called College Lot. As she walked down the deserted central hall she saw on either side the classrooms in which she had spent seven years, from the time she was eight until she had graduated at the age of fourteen. The highly regarded girls' schools in Lexington such as the Female Seminary or the Green Hills Boarding School advertised that "much care and exertion will be used to inculcate opinions, feelings and manners." Most Lexington parents had looked skeptically upon Dr. Ward's experiment of trying to educate young boys and girls inside the same walls, but Robert Todd had seized it as an opportunity to secure a real education for Mary.

Every school morning she had had to rise before five o'clock, dress by candlelight and make her way through the frequently icy streets in order to complete the necessary recitations before breakfast. At the end of the first year some of the parents had withdrawn their daughters, exclaiming:

"Dr. Ward will end by making our girls unwomanly."

In Lexington this was akin to indecency; once she had become unwomanly a girl was lost to all hope of husband and home.

Mary went up the flight of steps to the cubicle Dr. Ward had made available to her for these past two years. She went to the window and opened it from the bottom, letting the warm spring air flood the tiny room with its single table, chair and revolving bookstand. As she pushed the stand around, her mind reviewed her earlier years of study when she had tried so hard to be the best student in the class but had always been surpassed by at least one and sometimes two or three of the boys. She remembered these years with a sense of exhilaration, not only because of the ever present competition and challenge but because Dr. Ward had pushed her fast-growing mind to the outside limit of its capabilities.

When she was thirteen she was graduated from Ward's Academy, her father bought the Main Street house, and her sister Elizabeth married Ninian W. Edwards, a law student at Transylvania and the son of the first territorial governor of Illinois. Robert Todd knew what Mary would be feeling at losing Elizabeth; he quickly entered her in the select boarding school of Madame Victorie Charlotte LeClere Mentelle. Mary had been happy about everything at Mentelle's from the first Monday morning when Nelson had driven her up in the carriage and deposited her bags on the piazza of the low, rambling ivy-colored school located across from the entrance to Henry Clay's Ashland.

Monsieur Augustus Waldemare Mentelle and his wife were refugees from the French Revolution, Monsieur having been histographer to King Louis XVI. Though the Mentelles advertised that "no pains would be spared in developing the graces and manners of the young ladies submitted to their care," Mary had classes in French literature and the French language, English literature and composition, an hour of instruction each day at the piano and another in the spoken drama, through which the Mentelles had skillfully exorcised her southern drawl without decreasing the rich tonal qualities of her voice.

At night, since no guests were allowed, Madame Mentelle sat down at the pianoforte, Monsieur Mentelle took out his violin and there were hours of practice in the latest and most fashionable cotillions, round and hop waltzes, galopades, Mohawks, Spanish, Scottish, Tyrolienne dances and the beautiful Circassian Circle.

Mary's intensive study under Dr. Ward had borne fruit at Mentelle's; she finished the first year with the highest mark of her class. During the following three years she was given the lead in the plays of Molière, Corneille and Racine which were staged for the families and friends of the students, and she was voted the most popular, fun-loving girl in the school.

When she graduated at eighteen and a half, Robert Todd was so delighted with her winning both the scholastic and activities prizes that he gave her carte blanche for a new wardrobe of gowns, slippers, hats, gloves, perfumery, mantles; and a trip to Springfield, Illinois, to visit her married sister Elizabeth.

In the fall of that year she had gone to Dr. Ward and asked if she might use one of his rooms overlooking Transylvania while she tried to follow the university courses.

She heard footsteps on the stairs, as light as falling autumn leaves. Dr. Ward came into the room, both hands extended in greeting, a mist of white hair curled about his head. He always had dressed in a nondescript blue-black suiting, but never on any two succeeding days had he worn the same suiting of the mind, appearing before his students with gaily colored intellectual enthusiasms and fresh approaches to human knowledge.

John Ward, a native of Connecticut, had been an Episcopal bishop of North Carolina before his health failed. He had come west to Lexington in the hope of recouping his vigor. For Mary he was the embodiment of her favorite ancestor, Reverend John Todd, a Presbyterian minister who had organized a school in Virginia of such high scholastic standing that it attracted students from all over the nation; her three grand-uncles and grandfather had been educated there. It was this same John Todd who had gone before the Virginia legislature and secured the original charter that brought Transylvania Seminary into existence, and who had sent a considerable portion of his own books across the Alleghenies in saddlebags to make sure the young college would have a good starting library.

There was the sound of music coming from Morrison Chapel. Mary and Dr. Ward stood by the window, listening. Below her she could see the students of the Class of 1839 rushing along College Lot in their dress suits for the exercises. Noting the hard look in her eyes, Dr. Ward said:

"I'm sorry I have no parchment to emboss with the name of Mary Todd. Had you been born a man . . ."

She stretched her hands in front of her, palms outward as though to close out the view of the campus.

"Perhaps I made a mistake in coming back to Lexington from my visit to my sister in Springfield? I didn't want to become an . . . exile; and yet, in a way, haven't I become a pariah in my own town? Aren't people beginning to say that all this study has made me unwomanly?"

Below them the Lexington Guard in their blue uniforms with red facings, bell-buttons and jaunty red cockades floating from their black hats, the same uniform her father had worn when he marched away with the Fifth Kentucky Regiment in the War of 1812, was beginning to assemble for the exhibition drill which would be held after Commencement.

"Today I will lock my doors for the last time," said Dr. Ward quietly, "and you will step out into the street with no more study or plans to shore up the future." He gazed for a moment at his thin parchmentlike fingers. "For me it's truly the end, Mary, but for you it's the beginning. You must never give up."

"Give up . . . what?" She was more astonished than he at the full volume of confusion so openly confessed in her voice. "Where does a woman turn? Where does she start? Can I become a lawyer, doctor, architect . . . ?"

"I wanted to become a great clergyman, but my health failed . . . and so I filled my life training children. I would rather have been your teacher than your preacher; in the long run I think I shall have accomplished more. . . ."

"You mean that the accidents of fate are not as important as the certainties of character?"

". . . perhaps you will have to create your place in the world through a husband, or a son. Do not despise this approach . . . if it is all that is open to you. You must leave now, Mary, or President Marshall will begin his peroration and they'll lock the chapel doors. You may be a long time finding out what life holds in store for you, but in the final accounting your life will be good, it will be profoundly rewarding."

18

"Thank you, Dr. Ward. You have just presented me with a gold-embossed diploma."

6

WHEN the Commencement was over Mary bade her companions *au revoir* and started toward home, so filled with the emotions of the morning that she made no effort to return by her usual route; it was not until she found that the block on Market between Church and West Short was filled with a row of buggies and surreys with their shafts turned upward that she realized this was the stipulated Monday when the justices of the peace converged on the Lexington courthouse to handle the month's cases, and the population for thirty miles around poured into town for the festivities.

Market Street quickly emptied into Cheapside; she had to wind her way through the improvised furniture stalls selling beds and secondhand stoves, then secondhand plows, axes, harnesses, the menders of glass, tinware and cane chairs, old women selling jars of molasses and sugar-cane sweetening. Almost drowning them out were the medicine men in frock coats and beaver hats rattling off the diseases which could be cured by one bottle of their panacea.

Finding it difficult to move along the footway, she crossed to the clipped lawn in front of the courthouse, but this was even worse because of the jam of cows and their calves, brood mares with colts and hundreds of horses being bawled at the top of someone's voice for trade or sale. She edged her way through the crowd of bargaining men, reached Main Street and was about to turn for home when she saw them.

Her first impulse was to run as fast as she could, but she found her feet dragging her to the large stile block in the southwest corner of the square which had been built originally to help women get on or off their saddle horses, but had been used for as many years as she could remember as an auction block where Negroes were sold to the highest bidders.

Her eyes went first to the auctioneer in his long hammer-tailed coat, plaid vest, calfskin boots and white beaver hat set on the back of his head. Standing in the street to one side of the block was the group of slaves that had passed her house the night before. They were supposedly Kentucky Negroes; six years before her father, Henry Clay, his cousin Cassius Clay and their friends the Breckinridges and Crittendens had succeeded in pushing through the legislature a bill prohibiting the importation of slaves into the state for the purpose of resale. Since that time the slave jails had been largely empty. Now over half a dozen of the town's leading slave traders were standing in the front row, gazing upward at a young Negro girl.

"Step up, gentlemen! What'll you offer for this sprightly wench? She's warranted sound in mind and body. She'll make you a good cook, washer or ironer. Come, gentlemen. What do I hear?"

When the bidding opened low, the auctioneer continued, "Come, gentlemen, this is as likely a wench as we've had on this auction block in many a court day, sound in limb," yanking her dress up, "and sound in wind," ripping the dress down to her waist. "What am I bid?"

Mary lowered her head, remembering that first afternoon she had returned on foot from Dr. Ward's Academy with her satchel of books, and had stumbled across the whipping post of black locust. She had pushed her way to the front of the crowd and seen a sight from which her eyes had never totally recovered: tied by his wrists to the ten-foot locust post was a Negro, his back a mass of bleeding welts. She had stood frozen in her tracks while the sheriff completed the sentence of "thirty-nine lashes well laid on," after which the man was cut down and the young Negro woman with him was stripped of her dress above the waist, exposing a brand on one breast, then was lashed to the post and a whip made of twisted cowhide brought down across her scarred back.

She had heard someone scream; the adult faces were staring at her strangely. Only then did she realize that the scream had come from her own throat. Blindly she struck out of the crowd and ran all the way home, her body jerking convulsively. They had put her to bed at once. Dr. Warfield had been summoned, but it was not until her father had returned home and was sitting on the edge of the bed clutching her tightly to his bosom that she told of what she had seen. Robert Todd gulped hard many times.

"Father, why do they allow such things? Here in Lexington? Why do people do this . . . to other people?"

"Because they're not considered people; they're bought and sold like any other property. They can be branded as horses are, or mules."

"But can't you stop it, Father?"

"We are trying, my darling; not a day goes by but that we work to get rid of this dreadful thing that has been fastened upon us. The American Colonization Society is collecting money to send free men of color back to Africa."

"But, Father, the free ones aren't the ones who need help. It's the ones who can be whipped in the courthouse square . . . why doesn't your society send them back to Africa?"

The father dropped his arms from around the girl; his fingers lay outstretched at his sides in a gesture of futility. When he spoke his words came hoarsely.

"Mary, these slaves are worth millions of dollars. We would have to buy them from their owners. Where could we get so much money?" He rose from the bed and paced the floor. "No one man can put an end to slavery."

"Father, can we get word to them that we don't approve?"

". . . no . . . their owner would take it as a personal affront. Mary, these terrible things don't happen too often; you have to put them out of your mind and remember that the slaves are better treated here in Kentucky than any-where else in the country. No one you know beats his slaves or brands them. Next to the slave trader the lowest of all men is the one who is mean to his Negroes."

Her mind came back to the present. Up above her the young girl had been sold for four hundred dollars, and the auctioneer was crying off the girl's mother, who was bid in for five hundred dollars for shipment to Natchez. The father was sold for the slave markets of Mississippi. Lastly, their eight-year-old son was put on the block and brought two hundred dollars.

The family of four was about to be dragged off to separate jails; their cries of anguish seemed to fill a great hollow inside her chest. She turned away, but her arm was gripped from behind and a voice said sternly in her ear:

"No, wait, and witness it all, then you'll never again be able to live a whole day without striking some blow against this monstrosity."

It was Cassius Clay, one of the Todd family's closest friends.

"Cash, I'm so glad you're here; I was about to faint."

His strength seemed to enter her. She did not know whether it was the sheer physical force of his tremendous hand on her forearm or the having of someone at her side who had the courage to fight slavery out in the open.

Cassius Clay, whose ancestral home was in Madison County, had come to board with the Todds after his dormitory at Transylvania had burned down. She had been only eleven then, and Cassius had been twenty, but he had never treated her as a child. He was by all odds the most attractive man she had ever known, with a broad, powerful torso and a face of unshatterable determination, with defiant eyes, a jutting chin, a fine straight nose and a tremendous thatch of virile dark brown hair. After the year spent at the Todd house he had gone to Yale for two years, returned to Lexington with his diploma, studied law, then decided to devote his life to politics. He had already served two years in the legislature, was beginning to lecture and write against slavery. A lion and a lamb had been born within him; with Mary he had always been gentle but she also had seen him in gargantuan outbursts of fury. When he returned from Yale he had married Mary Jane Warfield. Mary Todd always had loved him, as a growing child loves an adult, but even then she had sensed that this was the one man in Lexington she might have wanted to marry.

As the last of the Negroes was carried off she and Cassius pushed their way out of the crowd.

"Mary, your face is green," said Clay. "Let's go over to Monsieur Giron's for an ice cream."

They passed Riche's Books and Stationery store, with a window full of flutes, fifes and flageolets, then James March's furniture establishment, fea-turing Venetian blinds and spring-seat rocking chairs, and then at the corner of Main as they turned up Mill Street, Thomas Huggins's grocery with the sharp aromatic scents of spices, Turkish smoking tobaccos and Havana segars. Near the corner of Mill and Short Street they came to Mathurin

Giron's two-story brick building, the ground floor containing the most famous confectionery in Kentucky.

A little bell tinkled as Cassius held the door open. On the counter were spiced buns, iced cakes decorated with pink sugar roses, and tall pyramids of meringue. Mathurin Giron had been her friend and admirer ever since she had started at Mentelle's and learned to speak French. He now came through a parted-cloth curtain leading back to his bakeshop, a totally bald man five feet in height and, on the sworn testimony of the Transylvania students who crowded his shop after classes, an exact five feet in girth. He no sooner had laid eyes on Mary and Cassius than he threw an arm up toward the ceiling and burst into an excited greeting.

"*Monsieur Clay! Et Mademoiselle Marie, plus jolie que jamais!*"

"*Et vous, Monsieur Giron, aussi flatteur qu'antan!*" she replied.

"*Quelle joie de vous revoir tous les deux ensemble de nouveau! Et maintenant que puis-je faire pour vous servir?*"

"Could we have a couple of ice creams, Monsieur Giron?"

When the Frenchman left them Mary said, "Grandma Humphreys liberated all her slaves in her will, and Father and Mother are going to do the same. But, Cash, would it be right to let our domestic servants go now? Some of them, like Nelson and Chaney, are old. How would they live? Never has Father punished one of our Negroes. Sometimes they've been quite bad, like that foolish young nursemaid who got drunk and took our little Emilie out in the street and lost her. Even then she only got a scolding."

Monsieur Giron returned. Mary looked at the two heaping glasses.

"Cash, isn't it unfeeling of us . . . to enjoy an ice this way . . . when those poor creatures we've just left . . ."

"Our eating an ice cream can in no way harm them. But what can harm them is your apology for even a limited slavery."

"I, an apologist for . . . why, Cash Clay . . . !"

"You think you can temporize with evil, Mary: just a half dozen house servants, part of the family, really . . . but never free to walk out. No, my dear, there are few absolutes in the world, but slavery is one of them: an absolute evil. Any man who touches its outermost fringe must ultimately find himself involved in its core."

"Aren't you being an extremist?"

He did not bridle at the word.

"Yes, Mary, someone has to be extreme; gradually is too slow. Tomorrow is too late."

Cash was right, she thought, yet there had been a time after the passage of the Non-Importation Act when it seemed as though slavery, which had not proved profitable in Kentucky in any event since there were few large plantations and neither cotton nor rice could be raised there, would slowly disappear from the state. A few slaves had been liberated and sent to Liberia, the Presbyterian Church had begun a plan for the instruction of slaves, her father had joined an organization of fifty slaveholders to start a movement to emancipate all future offspring of slaves.

Cassius Clay had been waiting for her to look up. When her eyes met his again, and he possessed them, he said slowly and sadly:

"Your father, like everyone else, will sooner or later be caught in a situation where he will be forced to do something just as reprehensible as those soul-peddlers who bought and sold that unfortunate family on the block today."

She returned home to find the family in an uproar: a letter had just arrived from her sister Frances telling of her marriage to William Wallace, a doctor and druggist of Springfield, Illinois. Robert Todd was caught between pleasure at having his second daughter at last married and a sense of outrage at having been left out of the matter. He was a man of strong family attachments and there could be no doubt of his profound hurt at being thus casually informed through the mails. Red flushes appeared on his forehead, one above each eye, as he exclaimed:

"I'm sure this William Wallace is a fine fellow. Frances says the customers in his drugstore are urging him to practice medicine; but I can't see why my daughter should marry without even sending me an invitation to the wedding."

"Now, Father," said Mary, placatingly. "It's a three-week trip to Springfield and back, and she knows how busy you are . . ."

"I'm not too busy to attend my own daughter's wedding!" he shouted, as though he wanted Frances to hear it, all the way west in Illinois. "Are all the children of my . . . first wife . . . going to drift off on their own, conduct their business and marriages privately . . . without ever consulting their father?"

Mary tried again.

"It's just that they go about their marrying rather more suddenly and informally in Springfield. A young couple go together for as long as they think they ought to and on the day they decide to be married, they have the wedding. Why, I remember when I was visiting Elizabeth two of the young men didn't get their marriage licenses until they were on their way to the ceremony."

"Seems hasty and barbaric to me." Mollified, he added more quietly, "However, if that's the custom of the frontier . . . But why are they taking a room in a tavern? What way is that to start married life?"

"Again, the approved way, in Springfield," expostulated Mary. "A tavern out west means a hotel, not a drinking place as it does here. The Globe is a newly furbished hotel, the center of the town's social activities."

"I suppose you'll be leaving us next?" he asked *sotto voce*. "Elizabeth gave Frances a home until she married. No doubt she'll be writing to you . . ."

It was Mary's turn to develop mottled patches on the forehead.

23

"I haven't been invited yet. Besides, I'm not seeking desperately for a husband."

She was angry with herself for letting her voice become hoarse, a sure sign that she was emotionally upset. Her father gestured for her to sit beside him on the linen-covered sofa with its bouquets of red and purple flowers, took her hand in his and interlaced their fingers, so alike in their near plumpness. Gazing at him in her hurt pride, she saw with a shock that there were dark circles under his eyes.

"Don't be offended, my dear. It's just that I love you, and Ann, and your two brothers . . . and I seem to be growing farther away from you all the time. Can you explain Ann to me? Perhaps she shares her secrets . . . or her intents? Levi now wants to move to a hotel. And George! What can be going on in the mind of that fourteen-year-old boy? Why do his eyes never meet mine?"

Mary did not want to answer, but her father peered at her intently, waiting.

"When George was a baby folks used to say, 'This is the one poor Eliza died of.' Somewhere deep down in your mind you've also been saying it, and I think George has always known."

There was an unfocused silence before Robert Todd could bring himself to speak. His gaze fell away; his voice was tight.

"Mary, you're not unhappy here? You'll not run away . . . then send me a letter that you've married some total stranger . . . ?"

"No, I am not . . . unhappy."

"I'm glad, Mary. Mother does really love you. She's worked so faithfully to raise you . . ."

He sat there, mutely begging her to reassure him.

When she replied her manner was tender. "It's my good fortune that Mother and I have a great deal in common; so it's really of no significance that we quarrel occasionally. Your house needed a wife to take care of it . . . and you needed love . . ."

He kissed her gratefully. "You've always been my bright one."

"You have lots of bright ones coming up."

He flushed with pleasure.

"We're planning to move out to Buena Vista next week. You studied so hard at your books this winter, you could use some relaxation in the country."

Mary stared out the window at the rosebushes that had just broken into bud. At Buena Vista there would be the large family and a house full of guests as well. There would be no moment or corner in which one could be alone.

She turned back to her father.

"I think I'll stay in Lexington for the summer. I'll be able to look after George, and the house will be running for those times when you have to stay in town. Besides, I have some tall thinking to do."

7

THE hot, dry days of late June descended upon the Bluegrass. The countryside was suffering from drought, with the corn less than twelve inches high, the hemp thin. Lexington people moved out to their country homes, to Crab Orchard or Graham Springs.

Mary spent most of her hours by herself, insisting only that George pass part of each day with her. She lavished all the tenderness of her own lost and needful heart upon him.

In the early mornings when she sat at her dressing table brushing her long hair, or at night as she prepared for bed, she perceived that the intrusive stranger who lived behind her eyes in periods of uncertainty was giving her an expression of opaqueness; a slight darkness of skin shadowed her left eye. She was not beautiful at such times, but how could anyone be beautiful when caught in indecision, with one's eyes staring back a little coldly from the mirror? She had wanted time to think, but what in all truthfulness had she been able to unravel or decide in the days that had already passed?

Tiring of her own company, she sent out notes to a group of her friends, inviting them to a picnic for the following Sunday on Elkhorn Creek at the bottom of the Todd garden. Tables were spread with white cloths under the sugar maples that bordered the creek. There were kegs of iced drinks, cold chicken, fruits, and for entertainment a group of strolling magicians who did amusing tricks of legerdemain.

The day's fun and companionship served its purpose; the intruder within her gates vanished.

The light of morning barely had begun streaming through the window shutters the following day when she received a message that Grandma Parker wanted to see her. She slipped into a simple pink muslin with a small embroidered flower on the skirt, tied a ribbon through her hair and paused on her way out only long enough for a cup of coffee.

Grandma Parker's house was one block along Main, then a block up Spring Street to West Short, immediately next to her own birth house, a trim brick dwelling where she had spent her first carefree years. Grandma Parker's was one of the first brick residences constructed in Lexington, and it was still the biggest: a rococo cake dripping with an overrich icing, and topped by two towers above the bedroom floor, the kind of watchtower built by captains' wives. Grandma Parker stood here for hours on end, scanning the horizon. Mary had asked once:

"Why do you keep watching for a ship, Grandma, when we have trouble with a rowboat on Elkhorn Creek?"

"I watch the city from here, and I know everything that's happening."

The Todd children had reason to believe that this was no idle boast. Mary groaned as she started toward the front door: Grandma Parker unquestionably knew all about Sandy's proposal . . . and her spending the summer alone; brooding, she would call it. There was little she could not divine from the tower overlooking the town that had grown from the tiniest hamlet since she had arrived on horseback from Pennsylvania as the bride of Major Robert Parker.

As Mary walked through the enormous double parlors with their sixteen-foot ceilings, fourteen-foot windows, overelaborate marble fireplaces and ornate cornices of flowers and leaves she chuckled to herself: Grandmother Parker had money, energy, appetite, but no taste whatever.

She climbed the wood-paneled staircase, then wound her way up to the second watchtower. Here Grandma Parker stood gazing out the windows. Mary stood in silence for a moment, studying the broad back and tightly braided hair wound on top of the seventy-year-old head. She had been married only eleven years when her husband died, thirty-nine years before; but no man had been allowed to approach her romantically during all this time.

"A true woman loves only once," had been her declaration when a cousin asked if he might bring an admirer to call. She also believed that this should apply to men; that was why she never had forgiven Robert Todd for falling in love again and remarrying.

The old woman spoke without turning around.

"You did not accept him? That boy from Mississippi?"

"I did not love him."

Grandma Parker turned around. "But he was a companion, and now that he is gone there is a hole in your life."

There was one seat in the tower, a hard black walnut chair. Mary went to it, feeling a little wobbly at the knees.

"You're right, of course. I am lonely. Even a little . . . frightened."

"But why, child? You're a vigorous and attractive young female." The old woman's voice went harsh. "Don't let that Betsy Humphreys woman drive you out of Lexington the way she did Frances."

"She really doesn't drive anybody out, Grandma."

Grandma Parker had not heard.

"Look out this window to where the sun is shining on those fields. I know every blade of grass, every animal, every hill and stream. Heaven can only be another Kentucky. Out there in that wide circle of bluegrass, Mary, is a mate for you."

"Unfortunately the available ones are not advertised in the *Observer*," said Mary wryly, "the way Mammoth Warrior is, or Todhunter's imported stallion. Besides, I want more than that, infinitely more."

Her blood was up; she rose and faced her grandmother, her eyes blazing.

"I want a man who will accept me as an equal. I want a man who will have so much confidence in himself that he will let me stand at his shoulder, instead of pushing me into the wallpaper. I want a man who wants something

26

more than a pretty girl with polished manners; and above all, I want a man with a first-rate brain and spirit, with ambition and courage. . . ."

"But you take these young men too seriously." After a moment Grandma Parker continued with one eye half shut, as though in a wink. "They don't really know what they want in a woman. You don't have to marry any man on his own premises, and that's not meant as a pun. You choose the best of the lot; you let him think you are everything he wants in an ideal wife. Then, after you have him in tow, you slowly change his ideas, oh, without his even knowing it's happening."

Grandma reversed her wink, opening her left eye fully, closing the right one halfway.

"You want to participate in a man's dreams? Then slowly let him discover that you have a ready wit and sound judgment, but slowly . . . in proportion to his ability to assimilate them. By the time you've been married five, ten years, you'll have remodeled your marriage to include the things you wanted. It's the plan that wives have used from time immemorial."

"Is that what you did with Grandfather?"

"But of course, child. He wasn't the perfect husband when I married him. I protected his flank in public, but inside our own home, inside our own marriage, I slowly achieved compromises which made him right for me. Marriage is the longest race of all, and nothing is needed so much as stamina. Throw away your books, your intellectual excitements. You have magnificent eyes, child, light them up; you have the most beautiful bosom in Kentucky, show it. Use your charm, your warmth, the natural gaiety that you seem to have stored away for the summer; pick the man you want and you'll bring him to heel in no time."

As Mary walked slowly home she could only think, So Grandma Parker too is concerned about my not marrying!

Mammy Sally met her at the door with a letter that had just come in on the Lexington and Ohio train from her sister Elizabeth. It was a newsy letter telling all about the white satin gown that Frances had worn for the wedding ceremony, and the five-layer wedding cake that Elizabeth had baked for the guests. Then came a line which Mary gazed at for a moment in astonishment:

Now that Frances is married, Mary dear, and has gone to the Globe to live, there is a vacancy in our household.

What a strange word to use, she thought: *vacancy:* as though it were some kind of position to be filled!

Her mind went back to her visit with her sister two summers before. Springfield had been a village of less than fifteen hundred people, dumped down in the midst of a dreary prairie and laid out with the unimaginativeness of a checkerboard, the settlement running quickly into cornfields with a hard blue sky above and crows sailing through the hot breathless air. The streets were unpaved, there were no sidewalks between the residential district and the business square; it was six miles to the nearest water, the Sangamon River, and she had sorely missed the little creek at the bottom of their garden. The town square with its green lawn was pleasant; around the square she recalled the busy dry-goods, grocery, drug and clothing stores, and the well-stocked bookstore. But after Lexington and the Bluegrass, Springfield and Sangamon County had seemed monotonous and harsh in contour.

Yet she had enjoyed the summer. A surprising part of the Springfield population had emigrated from Lexington and was starved for news and gossip of their homeplace. In addition to her two sisters and brother-in-law she also had three attractive cousins who had moved there to practice law: John Todd Stuart, John J. Hardin, and Stephen T. Logan. One of her favorite uncles, Dr. John Todd, was practicing medicine there. Her brother-in-law, Ninian Edwards, son of the governor of Illinois, had inherited considerable land and wealth from his father; the Edwards house was not only one of the largest and most beautiful in town, but it was also the center of Springfield's social life. Within a few days she had found herself thinking less of the physical discomforts and ugliness of Springfield, turning instead to a wholehearted enjoyment of the vitality of the young prairie settlement.

Hardly a day passed without a reception, levee or ball given in her honor; she was constantly amazed that this crude frontier village contained elegantly gowned women, fine carriages and an intense intellectual atmosphere, with the debates of the Springfield Young Men's Lyceum as stimulating as any she had heard at the Adelphi or Union Philosophical Societies. The two newspapers, the *Sangamo Journal* and the *Illinois Republican*, filled their pages with more brilliant political reporting and editorializing than she had ever found in the Lexington papers. This was the aspect of life in Springfield which delighted her the most: its people ate, drank and slept politics. Though the town was predominantly Whig in its sympathies, the Democrats also were numerous, vocal and highly effective. Four months before her arrival the Illinois legislature had voted to move the capital of the state from Vandalia to Springfield, and even before she had left in the fall of 1837 they had begun to tear up the public square in preparation for building a fine fossil-limestone state house.

Hadn't she seen a story about that state house in the *Observer?* She went into her father's library, in which were stacked files of newspapers from all over the country, *Niles' Register* of Baltimore being the highest stack, and most widely read. She riffled through the *Observer* and found the item, sat at her father's desk beneath the engraving of Sir Walter Scott in his study at Abbotsford, and read:

Magnificent: The new Illinois State House now in progress at Springfield is the future seat of government, is to cost $120,500, occupies center of three acre lot, is 132 feet long and 89 feet wide and 44 in height.

Her brother-in-law Ninian W. Edwards was a member of the Illinois leg-

28

islature, as was her lawyer-cousin John J. Hardin, of the tall, well-dressed figure and fine intellectual face. They had taken her out to hear Daniel Webster speak at a barbecue in a grove of forest trees outside of town, and to a political banquet given at one of the taverns.

She had found the young men, who were gathering from all over the United States, alert and excited about issues, ideas, causes. They were all on the make, determined to rise to the heights of the political world, frank to confess that that was why they had come to Illinois: because it was new and young and there was so little competition.

She remembered with pleasure what an attractive group of men they had been: Stephen Douglas from Vermont, twenty-four years old, with an enormous head and negligible legs, a pyrotechnical thinker and speaker; his two staunch fellow Democrats, James Shields, born in Ireland, already a veteran soldier, with a generous and engaging nature, but also hotheaded and with excessive vanity; and Lyman Trumbull, the quiet, dignified and good-looking lawyer who practiced in Belleville. Then there was Joshua Speed, a Whig, certainly the most handsome young man in town and part owner of a prosperous supply store, but of a nervous temperament, and with a reputation for falling in and out of love; and his Whig companion, James Matheny, who liked to work quietly inside an organization, the way her father did.

Yes, they had been an interesting group and she had enjoyed every hour spent with them. They were too young and eager to draw ideological lines between men and women; actually the town's mores were still unformed: she had been accepted unquestioningly as a companion and an equal. More than that, since all of her family were Whigs, and she had grown up within the friendly aura of their leader, Henry Clay, she had found herself heartily welcomed as an addition to their ranks.

The three months had sped by in a gay whirl; yet there had been not even a suspicion of romance. The men in whom she was interested were striving to establish themselves, and seemed a long way from thinking of the burdens of a wife and children. She had not gone to Springfield with the idea of seeking a husband, nor for that matter had Elizabeth invited her to remain after the summer, and Mary knew why: like the mother who wants her older daughter married before the younger, Elizabeth was determined that Frances should have no competition from her younger sister. At the end of her stay she had bade farewell to her new friends, and had taken the stagecoach for Alton where she caught the first of the river steamers on the voyage home to Lexington.

But now Frances was married. Now, there was a "vacancy."

8

THE Todd family came back from Buena Vista earlier in September than they had expected, owing to a business reversal at the bank. It had been a long time since Mary had seen her father so worried; his usually pink and white skin was a haggard gray. The responsibility fell on her father's shoulders because as president of the organization he had approved the transaction, and now Stevens, a big planter and hemp manufacturer, was dead, his affairs in chaos.

She was in the Western Emporium exchanging some imperial cassimere when Cassius Clay entered to buy a walking cane. He greeted her affectionately, then said:

"I'm sorry about your father's reversal, Mary, but I do think he's taking it too hard."

"I wish you'd come home with me and tell him that, Cash."

"I can't; at the moment I'm feeling personally hostile to my good friend, your father."

"Hostile? But why?"

"He has just given the order for Stevens's slaves to be sold at public auction. No restrictions about families not being broken up. No limitation on the Negroes being sent down the river."

Mary stood quietly, listening. When Clay had finished, she said:

"I'm sorry, Cash. I know how unhappy this makes you."

She set aside the material she had been selecting and started for home.

Her father was not there. She went up to her room and pulled the green blinds against the late afternoon sun. Robert Todd returned at six. He looked tired and harassed.

"Father, I met Cash today. He says you're going to sell Stevens's Negroes on the block."

"We must."

"But you've always been against that method. You said it was inhuman . . ."

Her father wrung his hands.

"We must get the last possible dollar out of the slaves. It's our only chance to cut our losses. . . ."

"Can't you insist that the families be sold together? Don't let the traders buy them."

"That would cut their value, perhaps in half. I protected us against everything except Stevens's death. If it were only my money that was involved, perhaps I could. . . . But it's a lot of people's money, the other men who started the bank with me, depositors . . ."

He sat down heavily, his face in his hands. She came quickly to his side, threw her arms about him.

"Darling, there must be some other way."

He looked up at her, shaking his head sadly.

"No, Mary, I'm caught: Stevens's Negroes will have to be sold to the highest bidder, the same as his horses, plows and carding machines. It's all part of our business structure; as long as I am president of the bank . . ."

"Isn't this too high a price to pay, even for the presidency?"

Todd flashed her a sharp look.

"Mary, you're talking like a child. You've got to grow up and face the realities. I didn't introduce slavery into Kentucky; you know that I've worked to get it abolished. I didn't kill Stevens; I just loaned him a lot of bank money. And I have to live up to my responsibilities, whether I like them . . . or my idealistic daughter does . . ."

They had been so engrossed in their own emotions that they had failed to hear Betsy enter the room. Now she descended upon Mary with her eyes blazing.

"How dare you condemn your father! By what right do you sit there and pass judgment! What entitles you to this holier-than-thou attitude?"

"Betsy, please."

"No, Robert, don't interfere. I'm not going to let this girl make life more miserable for you than it must be." She seized Mary's arm and raised her more by force of will than physical strength. "You ought to be ashamed of yourself, adding to your father's troubles. Don't you think he has enough to worry about, without your schoolgirl moralizing? Are you the head of this household? Do you do the work, or take the responsibility? Oh no, you just interfere when something happens that you don't like! Well, we don't like it either: we don't like Stevens's dying, nor all the worry and loss. But we don't reproach each other for what has to be done. We help each other to bear the burdens. It's time you learned that!"

Her towering anger was spent, and her strength with it. Robert Todd put his arms about his wife's waist.

"Betsy, you shouldn't upset yourself so . . . in your condition . . ."

Mary's ears stopped hearing. Betsy was pregnant again! And with Alexander only six months old. They hadn't told her; but then, why should they? What business was it of hers, really?

She rose, considerably chastened, went to her stepmother's side. Her voice was hoarse, subdued.

"You're quite right, Mother. Father's doing the best he can, I know that."

"He always has, and always will."

Betsy's voice rang out, strong and clear. Gazing at her stepmother's eyes, still burning with indignation, she thought, How wonderful to love a man that much! To put his interests and welfare above her own, frail as she was, and carrying still another child. To fight for him like a tigress . . . against the world.

31

She kissed Betsy on the forehead.

"I was wrong, Mother. I promise it will never happen again."

Old Nelson put her valises and boxes into the carriage. She had a long and affectionate farewell with her half brothers and sisters. Emilie cried, and this pleased her greatly. Margaret and Martha, too, were sad to see her go; Samuel and David demanded to know why Lexington wasn't as good as that old Springfield town she was going to. At the last instant George darted from around a tree in the garden, jumped into the carriage and buried his head on her shoulder.

Her father was far from happy. He knew that she was taking all her possessions, including two boxes of books, that even if she did not stay permanently in Springfield she was not likely to return to Lexington.

Nelson gave a giddap to the horse. Sally and the rest of the servants stood at the door waving good-bye.

They turned south on Spring Street, then drove along Mill and Water streets where the Lexington and Ohio Railroad had its new and freshly painted depot. The little steam locomotive, the *Nottaway*, stood shined and polished on the strap-iron rails which were laid over limestone sills. About a dozen passengers were already seated on the open top of the one-coach train, most of them leaning over the iron railing to watch the late passengers arrive.

George and Nelson handed her valises and boxes to the engineer, who put them with the other luggage on top of the woodpile. At Frankfort she would transfer to a stagecoach which would take her the fifty-two miles to Louisville; here she would catch an Ohio River boat and at Cairo where the Ohio flowed into the Mississippi River she would find a larger steamboat which would carry her northward to St. Louis and to Alton, where she would once again transfer to a stagecoach which, if the roads were good, would require only two days to bring her to Springfield. The whole journey of roughly eight hundred miles would occupy eight or nine days, if all went well.

A few moments more and they would leave the end of Water Street heading west, and she would see her last of Lexington. As she gazed at the forests of sugar maple, coffee bean and hickory trees, their leaves beginning to turn in the early October frost, and the gray squirrels first scolding the *Nottaway* for its intrusion, then scampering away with their long bushy tails turned over their backs, she found not altogether to her surprise that there were tears in her eyes.

The engineer started a tooting of the soprano whistle and the engine made a jerky start. The sound of the whistle reminded her of Ann's high-pitched, staccato voice, and her sister's parting words:

"Don't take too long, Mary, I'm next in line for that vacancy."

Book II

THE BEGINNING OF LOVE FOR ME

1

SHE smiled as she lighted the tapered white candle in its silver holder and set it in the window of the north parlor as a signal to the young men of Springfield that she was at home. How strange Lexington would think this custom. As she looked about the forty-foot parlor in which the Edwardses held their teas, soirees and balls she remarked to herself what an odd combination the room was with its exquisite Sheraton and Chippendale pieces, ornately carved tables, silver bowls and crystal vases which Ninian had inherited from his father along with the family portraits in oil, and the rest of the furnishings in Elizabeth's plain homey taste. The rosewood and mahogany furniture covered with broad haircloth, the patterned wallpaper and white fireplace with low mantel were Elizabeth's choice; to offset these Ninian had installed tall windows with dark polished wood frames, massive chandeliers and a richly designed French carpet from the drawing room of his father's house in Belleville. The combination should have clashed and been insupportable, but like the Edwards marriage it was a comfortable success.

She fluffed out her white bobbinet costume with the black velvet sash and tie and was inspecting the cut-glass bowls of candies and soft-shell almonds when her sister Elizabeth came through the archway triumphantly bearing the first pyramid cake to be seen in Springfield, a resplendent affair of five layers covered with iced frosting. Mary shook her head to dispel the image of her mother coming into the room. Elizabeth was half a head taller than herself, broader-shouldered and slimmer-faced; she parted her hair severely in the middle, completely covering both ears before sweeping it back into a tight knot at the neck, and though she was only five years older than Mary there was already a touch of grayness going in either direction from the part. From her protective manner, and because at the moment she was heavy with child, she seemed to Mary almost a full generation older.

Mary knew how disappointed Elizabeth and Ninian had been at the outcome of the first Whig convention held in Illinois: the Illinois Whigs had named five electors to campaign the state for the next presidential nominee. Ninian had not been included.

"Ninian should be the next governor of Illinois," announced Mary heartily.

"Someone nominating me for high office?"

Ninian Edwards came into the room; at thirty he had already been attorney general of the state and was serving his second term in the legislature. From his father he had inherited tremendous wealth in lands, stores, farms and city buildings, as well as the best-known name in Illinois. He was a handsome man six feet in height with inch-thick black eyebrows and a jutting nose and chin. His father, appointed governor of the new territory of Illinois by President Madison in 1809, had brought the first culture and tradition to the wilderness, building a spacious home, importing the finest of French furnishings.

Ninian held out both hands to Mary.

"As my first act as governor of Illinois, may I officially welcome you to the Mansion and assure you that you are *persona grata* here for the entire reign of Edwards the Second."

His joking was on the pretentious side but there could be no doubt of his affection. Mary knew that he was accused of being an egotistical man, considering himself superior to the general run of new arrivals in the state; in the legislature he had been called an aristocrat who "hated democracy as the devil is said to hate holy water." But she had never seen any sign of aloofness in him; and he was unalterably opposed to the bringing of slavery into Illinois even though a large majority of its early settlers came from southern slave states. The Edwardses employed four free Negroes, paying them a monthly wage; Ninian had spoken out publicly against the indenture system whereby a number of Springfield families had paid free Negroes a token sum of cash in return for signed indentures which obliged them to work for their new owners for the rest of their lives.

"I see you have a light in the window," said Ninian. "I am sure you will have many callers."

"Do you think Stephen Douglas will come?" asked Mary.

"I doubt if that steam engine in britches ever sets foot in this house again." Ninian's lips set grimly. "Brawling in the public square with John Stuart!"

"Now, Ninian, Cousin John was brawling too," said Elizabeth placatingly. "We mustn't carry on other people's fights. Steve is going to be a big man in this state even if he is a Democrat, and I want him to be our friend." She turned to Mary. "I'm sure he'll call, dear; he always asks for news of you."

Even as she spoke there was an imperious pounding on the front door knocker. Stephen Douglas was a little fellow with a massive head topped by thick waves of curly brown hair worn long on the neck and covering both ears. He had a stocky torso, but there the man almost stopped.

Elizabeth went forward to greet Douglas. Then Mary found both her hands gripped tightly in his as his deep blue eyes, set under enormous craggy brows, sparkled brilliantly in their welcome.

"Wonderful to have you back, Mary. I understand you're staying this time."

34

"I hope so, Steve. Come sit down and tell me everything you've been doing since I left. All I know is that you were Register of the Land Office, that you ran for Congress . . . and apparently have had a whopper with my cousin, John Stuart."

They sat close together on a black satin love seat while Elizabeth and Ninian walked through the archway into the family sitting room across the hall. Born in Brandon, Vermont, son of a doctor who died when the child was only a few weeks old, Stephen Douglas had apprenticed himself to a cabinetmaker and managed to secure some education at the Canandaigua Academy in New York state before reading law as a clerk. At nineteen he had set out for the west, taught school and secured his law license in less than two years. He was five feet four in height and weighed only a hundred pounds, but he had a magnificent voice and charming personality and had risen quickly to be state's attorney and legislator.

Douglas laughed *sotto voce*; Mary saw the short neck, so like her father's, the small white ears peering out from under the heavy hair, the pugnacious nose and mouth, the square chin.

"I was debating your cousin John in front of the old market house and I said something he didn't like, so he got a grip on my head and dragged me around the market house. I had to bite his thumb half off to make him let go. We then retired to Herndon's grocery and fought it out until we were both practically unconscious. Only thing I regret is that Stuart was the first to think of buying a barrel of whiskey for the crowd."

From her earlier visit she remembered that "grocery" was a euphemism for barroom. She shook her head bemusedly at the primitiveness of frontier politics.

"Steve, I'm ashamed of you; that's a fine way to decide which of you is the better man for Congress!"

"I am," replied Douglas, his eyes gleaming, "and that's what the voters of Illinois thought, too. Oh, they say Stuart was elected . . . by thirty-six votes out of thirty-six thousand. But they used fraud, threw out the votes I got from the Irish canal builders, put me down as a candidate for the state legislature instead of Congress. But just wait until I take my evidence to Washington City; I'll have John Stuart's seat before he can get it warm. With apologies to your esteemed family, Mary, of all the Whigs about Springfield, Abe Lincoln is the ablest and honestest."

She had heard the name on her previous trip; he had become John Stuart's law partner a couple of months before she had arrived in Springfield in 1837, but she had never met the man and did not know whether he was still her cousin's partner.

"Steve, I'm not trying to protect my cousin, but won't you only hurt yourself by taking your charge of fraud to Washington City? People will say that you're a bad loser. For you to have come so close to winning in your very first start amounts almost to a victory . . . it makes you the most important young Democrat in the state."

He flushed with pleasure.

"Well, maybe I won't go to Washington and cry fraud. It takes so much money . . . and time." His face turned red as the blood of anger ran again. "But when I think how hard I campaigned for two years; I lived with my constituents, prayed with them, laughed, hunted, worked with them, I ate their corn dodgers and fried bacon and slept two in a bed with them. That's why I know that more of them voted for me than would ever have put their mark after the name of John Stuart. Mary, I've been cheated out of the start of my career."

"Steve, you're on your way up. Bide your time, and . . . one day you will make a bid for the White House."

His eyes looked as though she had struck him. Then he perceived that she was in earnest. His expression cleared; he leaned so close that his lips touched her ear.

"Mary Todd, you're the smartest young lady I ever met. I'm glad you're staying in Springfield . . . permanently."

2

THE following afternoon she dressed in her bedroom which was just over the dining room and faced south; from her window she could see the roof of the Levering house, separated from the Edwardses' by half a grove of walnut trees. The room was a complete contrast to her richly decorated bedroom at home, with an ingrain carpeting of subdued pattern, buff-colored moreen curtains on the windows, a severely tailored brown muslin spread on the four-poster. However there was an attractive pier table with marble top and mirror, bookshelves, a small desk and fireplace. She smiled to herself as she remembered how exactly the room was a replica of Elizabeth's bedroom in Lexington. Only the silver-backed dressing set and the books stacked in the bookcase were witnesses that this was now her room, her home.

A trim black gig sped by, the reins held by twenty-three-year-old James Conkling on his way to pick up Mercy Levering to take her to the meeting. Mary had noticed at the gathering the evening before that lawyer Conkling was smitten by Mercy, the daughter of a judge of Georgetown, D.C., who had grown up in Baltimore society and was now visiting with her brother and sister-in-law.

"Mary, we'll be late for the speaking."

It was Ninian's voice floating up the oak-paneled stairs. As she tied the satin ribbons of her bonnet and drew a long black woolen scarf over her shoulders, she realized anew that Springfield was politics-mad; doubly so since the state capital had been transferred from Vandalia. Although the presidential election of 1840 was more than a year away, only Sundays, which were reserved for prayer meetings, were safe from tumultuous debates.

She caught a glimpse of herself in the mirror of the downstairs hallway and thought how well she was looking, her eyes bright, the color high in her cheeks. She was grateful for having inherited her mother's graceful neck, for her head and face were of substantial size and they needed a solid prop to sit upon. Though she had been in Springfield but a few days, her confused thoughts at leaving Lexington and the uncertainty about what she wanted from the future seemed gone from her mind; and with it the darkness from her cheek. She could not remember when she had enjoyed herself so much as the evening before, surrounded by some thirty young folks like herself, with half a dozen rambunctious political discussions being carried on simultaneously.

Elizabeth and Ninian were in their coach as she came out the front door. Its body was painted a bright lemon yellow, a luxurious carriage inherited by Ninian from his father. Elizabeth gathered up the folds of her wool skirts to make room for Mary beside her. Ninian sat opposite them, his back to the pair of matched iron-gray mares.

They drove north on Second, through deeply shaded groves of oaks; this southern part of the town was the most beautiful with open meadows going to the horizon, light with yellow and vermilion flowers. The green sod of the prairies extended to the stands of dark timber, with here and there a farmhouse and forest broken by the plow. These open meadows were particularly beautiful to Ninian because he owned them all.

They crossed a log bridge over the Town Branch. As they passed a newly completed wooden church, Ninian leaned over to Mary:

"Elizabeth's poundcakes are the cornerstone of that Episcopal church."

The carriage continued east on Adams until it came to the square; the brick county courthouse had been torn down and the buff-colored fossil-limestone state house, with its second floor not yet completed, stood surrounded by tool sheds and piles of stone. Many of the early log cabins and wooden shacks around the square had been replaced by fine brick structures. The town was in a frenzy of building: the state officials and their employees had moved in, almost a hundred homes were in varying stages of construction along with new hotels, shops and office buildings.

Their carriage pulled up at No. 4 Hoffman's Row, one of a group of store buildings temporarily being used as the Sangamon County Circuit Court. They entered the small room, lined with benches from wall to wall and already filled with some two hundred spectators. Mary saw most of her callers of the night before: Steve Douglas, James Matheny, Judge Samuel Treat, homely and shy, with the finest book collection in town; James Shields, flamboyant but brilliant Irishman; handsome storekeeper Joshua Speed; John McClernand, assemblyman; her three lawyer-cousins John Stuart, Stephen Logan and John J. Hardin. Her father's brother, Dr. John Todd, with his daughters Lizzie and Frances, were sitting together in the far corner.

The room was stifling, for there was no means of ventilation. Stephen Douglas beckoned to them; he had managed to save three seats on his bench.

The first speaker, Edward Baker, rose on the stand. Mary found herself plunged into the cauldron of national and state politics. Ninian Edwards and the Whigs burst into frequent applause, Douglas, Shields and their fellow Democrats sat on their hands, their expressions growing increasingly grim.

"Wherever there is a land office," cried Baker with a wide oratorical gesture, "there is a Democratic newspaper to defend its corruption."

She felt Stephen Douglas leap into the air; he had been in charge of the Land Office. However Democrat John B. Weber, brother of the man who owned the Democratic *Register*, found his voice first:

"Pull him down!" he shouted, pointing to Baker.

All about her now men were shouting, "Pull him down!" while Douglas and a group of Democrats surged up the center aisle. The Whigs were also on their feet, shouting and moving to protect their speaker.

In the midst of the bedlam she thought she suddenly had taken leave of her senses, for out of a trap door above the speaker's stand a pair of feet emerged, and then a naked pair of calves, then long legs that kept dropping downward into the room, legs that seemed to cover the full twelve feet from the trap door to the stand. As she sat there in a state of shock the rest of the man finally appeared, a long scrawny torso and neck, arms that seemed to her even longer than the incredible legs, a dark, gaunt, bone-ridged homely face and a disheveled stand of thick coarse black hair.

Turning her head slowly she saw that the men in the aisles and on the platform had frozen in their tracks. After a moment of silence which hung in the air even as had the descending apparition, the man began speaking in a high nasal voice.

"Hold on, gentlemen. This is a land of free speech. Baker has a right to speak, and if you take him off the stand you'll have to take me, too."

There was no anger in the voice, not even the tinge of threat: only authority. Mary felt, and gazing at the faces of the men about her, she knew they too felt, that removing this seeming twelve-foot giant would be next to impossible. It was Stephen Douglas who broke the silence.

"All right, friends, sit down and let Baker talk."

Baker continued his speech, though in a less truculent vein. The gaunt dark man sat on the edge of the platform, his knees raised higher than his chin, his long thin arms twined about them. Mary could not take her eyes off the long hollow-cheeked face with its deep-set, burning eyes.

"Who . . . is he?" she whispered to Ninian.

"Your cousin Stuart's law partner. Their office is just upstairs. They rent it out to the court as a jury room during trials."

"That hole in the ceiling . . . how could he . . . ?"

"Oh, Lincoln likes to lie alongside that trap door and listen to the court proceedings . . . or meetings like this."

"Is he a friend of yours?"

"Well . . . no . . . we're in politics together, is all."

"I've never seen him at the house."

"He doesn't go out in society much."

"Have you invited him?"

"He's not in our social set. Lincoln's an amusing enough fellow but he's not the kind of man a Todd would be interested in."

3

MARY recalled the quarrel she had had with her closest friend, Margaret Wickliffe, when they both were fourteen and had made their way to Fowler's Garden where they found beeves and pigs roasting in pits, whiskey being ladled out of open buckets. When President Jackson rode into the garden Mary studied him for a considerable moment before remarking:

"I wouldn't think of cheering General Jackson, but he's not as ugly as I heard he was."

"If you call General Jackson ugly," Margaret retorted hotly, for the Wickliffes were fervent Democrats, "what must you think of Mr. Clay?"

"Henry Clay is the handsomest man in town . . . except my father."

"Andrew Jackson with his long face is better-looking than Henry Clay and your father rolled into one!" exclaimed Margaret.

When they finally had patched up their quarrel it was with the understanding that they would stop arguing politics. She wished Margaret could be with her now, for surely they would both have to concede that Mr. Jackson and Mr. Clay ran a poor second, and that this Lincoln fellow must have the longest face in the whole world.

Following the meeting she walked with her cousin John J. Hardin through the crisp November twilight to John Stuart's home. Cousin John J., as Mary called Hardin, was also a lawyer and a Whig legislator; it sometimes seemed to Mary that the Illinois legislature was composed solely of her relations. It gave her a warm feeling of belonging.

The John Stuart house was a handsome one located in primeval forest. Every room was ablaze with astral lamps and clusters of candles. The party proved to be not only a mighty gathering of blood and collateral relations, but of family friends who had migrated to Illinois from Kentucky. It was ten o'clock before she had finished saying hello and she was able to acknowledge a tiny gnawing of disappointment: Cousin John's law partner either had not been invited or had not bothered to come.

Her cousin John Stuart was a broad-shouldered, heavy-boned, friendly-faced man; he had graduated from Centre College in Danville, Kentucky, read law for two years and in 1828 opened his office in Springfield, then a raw and sparsely settled community. The intervening decade had made him one of the leading lawyers of the town and the head of the Whigs in the legislature. He was in high spirits tonight, for the next day he would set out for Washington City and Congress in fulfillment of his life's ambition. When Mary found herself standing for a moment alone with him, she asked:

"What will happen to your law practice while you are gone, Cousin John?"

"Lincoln will take care of everything, he knows all my clients and all my cases. He may not look like much of a lawyer, but you know how good he is with a judge and a jury."

"No, I don't. I've never seen him in court," replied Mary. "In fact, I've never met the man."

"What, you've never met Lincoln? That's surpri . . . no, I guess it isn't. He goes everywhere with the men but almost nowhere when there are to be ladies present. I invited him tonight, but he's probably sitting around the stove at Josh Speed's store with a dozen of his cronies, spinning yarns and arguing politics."

"You know, Cousin John, he strikes me as being the last man you would have chosen for a partner."

Stuart took her arm and led her out to a side verandah; it was dark and cold but they were away from the deafening noise of the parlors. John Stuart's voice rumbled up from some deep point of his insides.

"I first met him when we were out to the Black Hawk War together back in '32; he was an uncouth-looking lad, timid, sad, very much countrified, but when he spoke I saw that he had a natural mind. He had been elected captain of his company by his New Salem friends; seems he had whipped the leader of a gang of rowdies from Clary's Grove and so they voted him their leader. We never saw an Indian, let alone fought one, but we certainly had a time trying to act like the military. I remember one day when Lincoln led his company up to a fence and didn't know how to get them over. He cried out in his high nasal voice, 'Halt! This company will break ranks and re-form immediately on the other side of that gate.'"

Mary chuckled. "Sounds like a legal maneuver."

"No, no, he wasn't a lawyer then, far from it. He was clerking in a general store at New Salem, but had a keen appetite for books and study. He told me that a few months before he enlisted he had heard there was a copy of Kirkham's *Grammar* owned by a neighboring farmer. He persuaded the man to lend him the book, and studied it for months, then decided that if grammar was rightfully known as a science, he could subdue another. I asked him if he had a mind to subdue the law. He seemed shocked at that idea, said he didn't have enough education. He had never owned a pencil or a sum book until he was fifteen. I told him that if he changed his mind to come see me in Springfield, that the lawbooks were no harder than Kirkham's *Grammar*. Sure enough, the next spring he started walking the twenty miles into Springfield to borrow lawbooks from me. He bought a store in New Salem with his Black Hawk War pay, but business wasn't good and he had all the time he needed to study. It was an amazing thing to me the way he'd read on that walk home; by the time he got there he had mastered thirty or forty pages of a book."

"Did you help him because of the general kindness you show everybody?"

Stuart flushed at the compliment, then shook his head.

"He's a strange kind of fellow, gets under your skin. Just when you think he's in the grip of a hopeless melancholy and about to go into the woods and shoot himself, his face lights up and he'll tell a yarn with such tremendous gusto that you just have to throw back your head and howl."

Stuart was silent for a moment, remembering scenes out of the past. Mary crossed her arms over her chest in an effort to keep warm.

"He had a lot of bad luck. Guess he couldn't have made a living at all without that little post office job and the fact that he subdued the mathematics of surveying and became assistant surveyor. But the people of the neighborhood liked him and they elected him to the legislature in 1834. I suggested he share my room in Vandalia. When you sleep two in a bed with a man you get to know him pretty well; I introduced him to my friends, put him on committees and taught him everything I knew about politics. I never saw a man learn so fast. After he had read all the lawbooks in my office, and all the others he could find in Springfield, he got his license to practice. Just then my partner decided to move, so I asked Lincoln if he wanted to come in with me."

She had been watching her cousin's face during his recital. She said, "You've told me a lot of facts about Mr. Lincoln, Cousin John, but you haven't explained why you love him."

Stuart was startled; he searched her face for several moments.

"How can you not admire a man who starts a hundred miles under the bottom, who has nothing and no one, so ugly you might well assume he would never know the love of a woman? I think that's what his melancholy amounts to: loneliness: and that's what his humor is for too, to make men draw a little closer to him in their laughter."

She thought, I can understand that. In Lexington, even when I was surrounded by family and friends, I sometimes felt that I was going to live by myself all the rest of my days.

The last thing she saw that night as she pulled the covers up over her shoulders and closed her eyes for sleep was an interminable pair of legs descending endlessly from heaven; somewhere in the distance she heard Ninian Edwards commenting that they could hardly be considered socially *comme il faut*.

4

THE next morning she walked to the Globe Tavern, went through the cheerfully decorated parlors and up the stairs to her sister Frances's room. Mary had never seen her sister so attractive, with a fine texture to her skin and her eyes glowing. The Wallace bedroom was of modest size, but it had a comfortable four-poster, an enormous French wardrobe, a small sofa and a fireplace; located at the end of an ell, it had windows facing east and north, with a full view of the square.

"Shall we reserve this room for you, Mary? It's a pleasant enough place to . . . set up shop."

Mary looked at her sister, who was several months with child, then recalled that John Stuart and his bride had also come to this room after their wedding.

"Yes," she murmured, "put my name down since it's now a family tradition. But don't you think you had better leave the date open?"

Frances put her hand tentatively about Mary's waist, the first embrace that Mary could recall from her older sister.

They left the hotel to go to S. M. Tinsley's where Mary bought some cassimere to make a new walking dress against the impending winter, and Frances shopped a pair of kid gloves. Then they crossed the cluttered square where stonemasons were chipping away at the limestone blocks for the state house. In the far corner they came upon a crowd listening to a political debate. Up on the stand was Colonel Dick Taylor, a bombastic orator who was berating the Whigs for being aristocrats and reactionaries, interested only in the piling up of wealth and the conserving of their privileges while he and his fellow Democrats were poor and simple folk interested solely in the welfare of the people.

During the last sentences of the speech a man edged slowly onto the back of the platform, slipped to the side of Colonel Taylor and then, with the completion of the colonel's peroration, caught the edge of the speaker's vest and pulled it open, exposing to the audience an expensive silk ruffled shirt, a gold watch chain with seals and several other gaudy jewels.

Mary joined the rest of the crowd in hearty laughter. She had recognized the man instantly as the one who had dropped through the trap door at the political meeting. He now raised his cranelike arms above the crowd, obtaining their silence.

"Friends, I am humble Abraham Lincoln. While Colonel Taylor was making these charges against the Whigs over the country, riding in fine carriages, wearing ruffled shirts, kid gloves, massive gold watch chains and flourishing a heavy gold-headed cane, I was a poor boy, hired on a flatboat at eight dollars a month, and had only one pair of breeches to my back and they were buckskin. Now if you know the nature of buckskin when wet and dried by the sun, it will shrink; and my breeches kept shrinking until they left several inches of my legs bare between the tops of my socks and the lower part of my breeches; and whilst I was growing taller they were becoming shorter, and so much tighter that they left a blue streak around my legs that can be seen to this day. If you call this aristocracy I plead guilty to the charge."

The crowd applauded, then went about its business. The speaker stood watching their backs as they dispersed. Mary stood unmoving on what had been the outskirts of the group, but was now an open space of square between herself and the tall figure on the platform. Neither looked directly at the other yet both were intensely conscious of the other's presence.

She turned to Frances and said quietly, "Sometime I would like to meet Mr. Lincoln."

The Ninian Edwards home was located on Aristocracy Hill, the only eminence in the neighborhood. Each afternoon Mary was joined on the hill by Mercy Levering, Julia Jayne and her cousins, Lizzie and Frances Todd, daughters of Dr. John Todd, who had settled in Springfield in 1827 as a doctor. It was lithe-figured, reddish-blond Mercy whom she found most *sympathique*: for Mercy too had vowed to be slow and cautious about marriage, and for all her sweetness of nature was surgeonlike in her dissection of the young men of the town.

The sole point of departure between the two girls was politics. Mercy said: "James Conkling drags me to the debates, but I find them tedious and prosy. Mary, I think these are subjects that the narrow capabilities of our sex can understand but little . . ."

"Oh, Merce, no! Not here in Springfield! I thought I'd left all that behind in the Bluegrass."

"I'm not saying that we should be totally ignorant of politics, but by engaging our minds in the things that belong exclusively to the other sex we're liable to become bewildered and lessen our usefulness."

"In what?" demanded Mary sharply.

"Well, in preparing a delicious roast or trimming a bonnet *à la mode*. Once we lose our dependence, cease to become amiable and attractive . . ."

"In short, become unwomanly?"

"Oh, Mary dear, I've hurt you. I didn't mean to."

Mary was silent until they had gone halfway down the hill.

"It was fright, Merce, not hurt. There are so many things I don't like about Springfield: that foul-smelling Chicken Row on Courthouse Square, the garbage in the gutters, the way people drop their refuse into the creek, and the dead hogs lying in the street, things we wouldn't tolerate for an hour in Lexington. And yet I think Springfield is the most wonderful place in the world because it's a political center. Any hotly contested meeting is more exciting to me than that tame play *Theresa* we saw in the dining room of the

American House the other night. Why, I even enjoyed the near riot that Mr. Lincoln quieted by dropping down from the room above."

One morning a rain started. It poured night and day for two solid weeks. Mary was housebound, for the streets were not only unpaved, a quagmire of viscous black mud through which no carriage could move, but there was not a block of sidewalk between the hill and the square. There was plenty of good reading matter in the house, for Ninian had purchased from Birchall's the novels of Maria Edgeworth and the collected works of Cowper and Irving; in addition she sewed new outfits for her niece, little Julia Edwards.

When finally she tired of being cooped indoors she sent a message to Mercy:

Dear Merce:
I have a bundle of shingles, and by dropping them one at a time in front of us in the worst holes I think we can make town without drowning in mud. Are you ready for adventure?

Mercy came flying in a sky-blue flannel walking dress, violet frilled bonnet and the highest boots she could find. Mary too was prepared for the voyage in a silk cloak over a green cassimere dress with full round sleeves, a touch of white lace at the throat and white feathers in her hat. It was not so bad going down the hill because the rain had run into the branch, but once they reached the flatlands they found it a sea of mud and Mary's lone bundle of shingles lasted only halfway to Watson's confectionery. Both girls were splattered with mud up to their knees when they entered Mr. Watson's for an ice cream and freshly baked cakes. They came out on the square to face the long walk home, *sans* shingles. At that moment a two-wheel wagon pulled by a mud-encrusted farm horse came slowly up the street. It was a wagon which Mary had seen carting all manner of commodities about town: crates, bales of hay, pigs.

"Merce," she exclaimed, "there's Ellis Hart with his dray. And sent straight from heaven to us!"

"Mary, we couldn't possibly ride in that old cart. We'd scandalize the town."

"Good. Then maybe they'd put in some sidewalks. Oh, Mr. Hart, could we engage your dray long enough to haul us home?"

Hart whoaed his horse, scratched his red beard stubble.

"Haul you home? Like you was colts? Why sure, Miss Todd, if you could stand it, me and the horse likely can."

Mary clambered in but Mercy hung back.

"I simply can't, Mary. My brother would consider it improper. But you go ahead."

Mary's white feathers flew in the breeze as Hart toured the unfinished state house before starting south for the Edwards home. By now every store had emptied of customers and clerks alike and the second-story windows were filled with openmouthed male heads. Mary could not see what was so interesting about a girl riding home in the only vehicle available to her use.

But by teatime the house was full of young men all come to tease her on her exploit. The first to arrive was Stephen Douglas, who stood in the center of the floor with his hand tucked in his coat like Napoleon, declaiming in mock oratory:

> "As I walked out on Monday last,
> A wet and muddy day,
> 'Twas there I saw a pretty lass
> A-riding on a dray.

> "Quoth I, 'Sweet lass, what do you there?'
> Said she, 'Good lack a day,
> I had no coach to take me home
> So I'm riding on a dray.'"

The moment Douglas finished, James Shields bounded into the parlor as though making for the center of a stage:

> "Up flew windows, out popped heads,
> To see this lady gay
> In silken cloak and feathers white
> A-riding on a dray.

> "At length arrived at Edwards' gate,
> Hart backed the usual way
> And taking out the iron pin
> He rolled her off the dray."

"I didn't roll off," cried Mary, laughing. "I walked off on my own four feet like any other livestock. Who wrote this epic verse?"

Before anyone could answer, a servant ushered in Dr. Elias Merryman, who said from the door:

> "A moral I'll append
> To this my humble lay . . .

"And it really is all my own lay, Mary, these other bad actors simply memorized their parts.

> "When you are sticking in the mud,
> Why, call out for a dray!"

There was an outburst of laughter and applause. Ninian Edwards walked in. Oh dear, thought Mary, have I embarrassed my brother-in-law?

But Ninian was no prig; he kissed Mary and said:

"Well, Miss Todd, you're the toast of the town. You've also succeeded in demonstrating something we've been blind to: we're going to petition our town trustees for a sidewalk starting at Monroe Street, to go all the way to the square. Fact of the matter is, I have a town trustee with me, just taking the

45

mud off his boots on our porch scraper. Josh Speed asked if he might bring him along."

Joshua Speed walked into the room followed by Cousin Stuart's law partner. She did not hear the introduction, neither made nor acknowledged; all she knew was that her hand was in his, not crushed, not even held tightly, yet imprisoned in the most powerful grasp she had ever known. Then she looked up and for the first time her eyes met those of Abraham Lincoln; met, and were drawn deep into their unfathomable gray darkness.

5

HE outstayed the others; more, it appeared to Mary, because he did not know how to leave than because he was determined to remain. Elizabeth and Ninian left for a supper engagement; Mary had been invited to the Leverings', but she sent a note of regret. He spoke almost not at all, and she heard herself talking twice as hard to ward off silence. Apparently Mr. Lincoln had no fund of small talk. He had declined all offers of tea and by seven o'clock she was sure he must be quite hungry.

"The servants have gone up to their quarters, but I know there is some roast quail, freshly baked bread, preserved blackberries and cream out in the kitchen. Won't you come talk to me while I prepare it, then we can set a little table here before the fire . . ."

He sprang up at once, embarrassed, with one hand groping toward the outside door.

". . . no . . . I didn't mean to . . . I'm not at all hungry."

Without waiting for an answer she led the way through the dining room to a large kitchen at the back, connected to the house by a covered portico. There was only one candle flickering on the rough board table. Mary handed it to Lincoln, who lit the big lamp above the stove. The room was scrupulously scrubbed and had the pleasant aroma of good food cooked and eaten. She took two birds from a platter of quail and put them in the oven to warm, then sliced the bread. Lincoln followed her quick vivacious steps with a slow shambling stride, looking for something to be helpful about.

"You were here in Springfield when I visited two years ago," commented Mary. "Why was it that I never saw you then?"

"Well, I was a pretty poor hand at society. Not that I couldn't have used a friend. Living in Springfield was pretty dull business for me. I was quite as lonesome here as I ever was anywhere in my life. I was spoken to by but one woman in those early months and would not have been by her, if she could have avoided it."

"Mr. Lincoln, I'm sure that's not true! As my cousin John Stuart's partner you would have been welcome in every Todd home at least."

He flashed her a look of gratitude, but commingled with it was a cast of doubt.

"Why, Miss Todd, I even stayed away from church in those days because I was conscious I should not know how to behave."

There was no self-pity in his tone nor bid for sympathy; it was a plain statement of fact. Nevertheless she found herself angry with him. She turned her back on the stove, motioned him onto a chair and looked at him reprovingly.

"Now, Mr. Lincoln, that's just contrariness on your part. What is there to behaving in church? You walk in, sit down in a pew, join in the singing, listen to the sermon, bow your head in prayer. It's simple . . . just as simple as it would have been for you to have walked in this front door two years ago along with Steve Douglas or my cousins and joined in our fun. Then we could have been friends all this time, instead of sitting opposite each other tonight as strangers."

He smiled a slow tentative smile which started somewhere way in the back of his mind, filtering through to his eyes first, lighting up their darkness and then spreading to his lips. She found herself wondering why everyone called him an ugly man; he wasn't really, leastways not when he smiled.

"The last time I went to church, deep out in the country, the old-line Baptist preacher announced his text, 'I am the Christ, whom I shall represent today.' He was dressed in coarse linen pantaloons with baggy legs, and a shirt of the same material. He had no sooner begun his sermon than a little blue lizard ran up his pantaloon. The preacher slapped away at his leg but his efforts were unavailing and the little fellow kept ascending higher and higher. Still continuing the sermon, the preacher loosened the top button of his pantaloons, kicking off the garment and, he hoped, the lizard as well. But in the meanwhile Mr. Lizard was crawling under the preacher's shirt. Tortured, but unwilling to stop his sermon, the preacher undid the collar button and off flew his tow linen shirt. At that moment an old lady in the rear of the room rose up and cried, 'If you represent Christ, then I'm done with the Bible.' "

When he started his story his feet had been planted flat on the floor; by the middle of the yarn his right leg was raising slowly, then just as his climax was reached he threw his right leg over the left, his head went all the way back and he laughed unconstrainedly.

She thought: Cousin John Stuart said he tells these stories in order to draw closer to other people in his loneliness, but I think they are his small talk, the coin of the realm by means of which he pays his way in company.

She handed him a tray of food, plates and silver to carry into the parlor, then went ahead of him to put a linen cloth over a small round cherry-wood table close to the fire. When they were seated, she asked:

"Do you like Springfield any better now that you've lived here several years?"

"A man came up to our Secretary of State the other day and asked permission to use one of the state rooms for a series of lectures. 'May I ask what is to be the subject of your lectures?' the Secretary inquired. 'Certainly. They are on the second coming of our Lord.' 'It's no use,' the Secretary replied. 'If the Lord has been in Springfield once he will not come a second time.'"

For a moment she was shocked: Does the man never give a straight answer? Does he always reply with a story? Then she joined her laughter to his.

"Mr. Lincoln, you're the most perfect original I've ever met."

He had begun to eat his quail, but now he laid down the fork with a grimace.

"I've been told that before . . . less gently."

She put out her hand impulsively, found it engulfed in his bony fingers.

"I'm interested in you. That's the beginning of friendship, isn't it?"

"The best," he replied. "Not many young ladies have been interested in me."

"Have you been interested in many of them?"

"Two or three, perhaps. When I was a little codger a wagon with a lady and two girls and a man broke down near us and while they were fixing up, they cooked in our kitchen. The woman had books and read us stories and they were the first I ever had heard. I took a great fancy to one of the girls; and when they were gone I thought of her a great deal, and one day while I was sitting out in the sun by the house I wrote out a story in my mind. I thought I took my father's horse and followed them and they were surprised to see me. I talked with the girl and persuaded her to elope with me; and that night I put her on my horse and started off across the prairie. After several hours we came to a camp, and when we rode up we found it was the one we had left a few hours before. The next night we tried it again and the same thing happened and then we concluded that we ought not to elope. I think that was the beginning of love with me. What was the beginning of love with you, Mary Todd?"

She stared back at him in silence, thinking:

There has been no beginning; not yet, at least.

Following the rains there came sharp cold and snow covered the vast prairie. The carriages were replaced by sleighs. The young people of Springfield went on rides across the moonlit countryside, frequently ending at the Edwards house for hot drinks and an hour of games, political discussion or dancing.

"I'm not sure I understand just what has happened," Mary confided to Elizabeth as, brimming with high spirits, she closed the door on the last of her guests, and took a cup of chocolate up to her sister. "I am excited by everything that is going on here in Springfield as I never was in Lexington. I like everyone and everyone seems to like me. I must have a dozen invitations to parties next week. Part of it is your wonderful kindness, Liz, throwing open your house this way for me to entertain . . ."

"No, my dear," Elizabeth interrupted, "a mere roof and food on the sideboard aren't enough. It's you alone who are attracting the young people here, with the girls as happy in your company as the men. That means there's a joy in you, a radiance for them all. Nor have you ever been more beautiful."

". . . I feel beautiful! Look, the darkness under my eye is completely gone, and my figure hasn't been this slender since I left Mentelle's." She danced over to Elizabeth's vanity mirror. "I do believe that my nose is a trifle retroussé. Why had I never noticed that in Lexington?" The expression of her eyes had softened, mellowed. Her hands were shapely and white; since she had had many compliments on them she was not averse to using them in graceful gestures. Extending them toward her sister, she cried:

"Could I have been like this at home, Liz, if I had let myself, so . . . easy, so . . . tolerant? I never feel . . . upset, even my humor has lost its sting. . . . It's as though the week's trip I took on the steam cars, boats and stagecoaches was not from one town to another but rather from . . . childhood . . . to womanhood."

Elizabeth smiled a little wanly.

"There were restraining influences at home, pressures left over from childhood. When you visited here you had a 'keep at arm's length, I'm green fruit' attitude."

"And now I'm ripe?"

"Oh, quite!"

Mary rose from the side of her sister's bed, walked to the window and gazed out at the snow-covered fields.

"Which one do you prefer, Mary?" asked Elizabeth with a shrewd smile. "The Yankee, the Irishman, the handsome shopkeeper? I'm sure it will never be the Rough Diamond."

One corner of Mary's mouth went up in a quizzical bantering expression.

"The Yankee, as you call Steve Douglas, would be forever arguing against Henry Clay; Jimmy Shields, the Irishman, has too lately kissed the blarney stone; Josh Speed falls in and out of love too fast. . . . As for a rough diamond, that would depend on how clear and flawless it was, under the surface. To polish a perfect diamond could be the task of a lifetime."

Elizabeth's expression shifted to the maternal.

"Unfortunately there's no way of telling what lies under the surface until all the work is done. And then, if you find the stone worthless, it's too late. . . ."

"But isn't there some kind of dependable divining rod . . . such as love? Oh, I'm not referring to Mr. Lincoln now, I know him less well than any of the others. But if you love a man . . . any man . . . don't you have to take a great deal on trust?"

6

A letter arrived from her father bringing bad news for the Todds, causing them to assemble at the Edwards house as though for a funeral: the Whig convention had rejected their hero and leader, Henry Clay, and had nominated General William H. Harrison for the presidency. Her father and stepmother had been among the hundred dinner guests at Ashland awaiting the news of the master's nomination when the travel-stained courier had arrived with the disillusioning information. Her father wrote:

> After Mr. Clay tore open the dispatch his eyes filled with tears and he cried: "My friends are not worth the powder and shot it would take to kill them! I am the most unfortunate man in the history of politics, always run by my friends when sure to be defeated, and now betrayed for a nomination when I, or anyone, would be sure of an election."

Since coming to Springfield Mary had thought little about going to Washington City when her father accompanied Mr. Clay to the White House, but her disappointment was nonetheless keen. She considered it unfair for Henry Clay to be passed by for a weak candidate who had been selected only because he was a popular military hero.

Elizabeth's son was born on Sunday, December 15. The cotillion party at the American House in honor of the new legislature was scheduled for the following day at early candlelight. Elizabeth, in a state of jubilation at having produced a male heir for her husband, insisted that Ninian take Mary to the party.

They set out for the American House shortly before seven. Mary was wearing her hair in curls, shoulder length, but had brushed it severely back off the brow as though to prove that she could wear the highly feminine curls and still not be frivolous. Her dress was of a changeable shot silk of flame color and blue on which was brocaded small bouquets of brilliantly colored blossoms, the wide skirt buoyed out by a dozen stiffly starched petticoats, the bodice cut low across her bosom.

The American House was kitty-corner from the state house, the largest private building in Springfield, with accommodations for two hundred guests. The outside was plain in design but the interior was furnished lavishly with the finest of French wallpapers, furniture and carpeting. The ladies' parlor had been turned into a dressing room. Mary was surprised to find many of the young women carrying bundles. She stood in the doorway wondering what it was she had failed to bring; then the bundles began to kick and squeal. The mothers unwrapped the blankets from around their infants and fed them their supper. No great inconvenience, thought Mary, for all of the gowns, of handsome silk and satin, were cut as low as her own.

In the far end of the dining room, which had been converted into a ballroom, there was a platform with Springfield's recently reorganized band, including a number of brass instruments and a half dozen violins and guitars. The room was brilliantly lighted with candles clustered in side brackets and in three enormous ceiling chandeliers. The floor had been highly polished for the dancing. All of Springfield had turned out; in addition there were many lovely young girls whom she had never seen before, daughters of the legislators, or sisters, assembled from all over the state for the gay social season.

Ninian was her partner for the first quadrille and then in quick succession she danced a waltz, cotillion and reels with Stephen Douglas, James Shields, James Matheny and Samuel Treat. Joshua Speed linked an arm through hers and half turned her toward a young man whom she had seen in the streets in Springfield.

"Mary, may I take the liberty of introducing Billy Herndon? He threatens to move out of the hotel above my store unless I secure a waltz for him."

Mary recalled who he was, the son of Archer G. Herndon, who owned a tavern. Young Herndon had done preparatory work at Illinois College in Jacksonville for a year but, not being admitted to the college proper, had returned home, quarreled with his father over abolition and slavery, drifted through a number of jobs and finally landed with Joshua Speed as a clerk in his general store. He had a thin-bridged nose, small close-set eyes, a boyish ingratiating manner.

"It's certainly a wonderful pleasure for me to meet you, Miss Todd. The band is about to strike up. If it's a waltz may I have the honor . . . ?"

It was a waltz, "He Never Said He Loved," and before she could say another word Herndon had whirled her out on the dance floor. He danced well but deluged her with a cloudburst of words and ideas, each seemed to spring from the last yet none belonging to any focal core that she could discern; by the time the dance was half over, her head had begun to spin conversely to the movement of Mr. Herndon's waltz. As the dance ended he gazed at her with admiration and said:

"I want to compliment you on the grace of your dancing. You glide through the waltz with the ease of a serpent."

She felt the blood pound up to two red spots on her forehead. Her voice was cold as she replied:

"Mr. Herndon, comparison to a serpent is rather severe irony."

She disengaged her arm, thinking:

What *gaucherie!* I never want to be exposed to that one again.

Unwilling to return to her own circle with her indignation flaming on her forehead, she walked toward the end of the ballroom. She was brought up short by an outburst of laughter. From her vantage point behind a potted shrub she was able to look into the midst of a group of men clustered about a table. Sprawled out on the edge of a chair, dressed in a black broadcloth suit, vest and a stock rigged up with a little bow, was Abraham Lincoln. She had expected he would appear somewhere since he was one of the managers of the ball. He was telling a story, with voice and gesture to emphasize the details. When he had finished, her laughter came a little faster than the rest. Lincoln heard it, bolted upright in his chair, saw her through the leaves of the shrub. He rose, withdrew from the circle of surrounding men and came to her side.

"Miss Todd, I want to dance with you in the worst way."

They stood in silence until the music began. A number of figures went through her mind: she was dancing with a broken windmill, with a ship in a storm at sea, with a flagpole waving in the breeze. It was not an unpleasant sensation, merely painful, for he spent half of the dance treading on her feet. When the music stopped she said wistfully:

"Mr. Lincoln, you have achieved your ambition."

He stared at her uncomprehendingly for a moment, then threw back his head and laughed in high glee.

"A good line, Miss Todd. Reminds me of the boy whose teacher asked him why he didn't spell better, and he replied, 'Because I just hain't got the hang of the schoolhouse.' Do you mind if I add your story to my repertoire?"

She thought, How much wiser he is than I. Why couldn't I have laughed at Billy Herndon? Her eyes traveled upward laboriously almost as one climbed a high and precipitate cliff, to Mr. Lincoln's six feet and four inches of height.

"I give you *carte blanche* to use the story, Mr. Lincoln. But if it hadn't amused you I should have apologized."

7

SHE found that the rough diamond, as her sister had called him, was getting less polished by the day, and for his pains had taken a castigation from the press. True, the *Register* was the opposition newspaper, but very rarely did they get as angry with any Whig as they were this moment with Mr. Lincoln. After admitting that he had made some telling points in the presidential-elector debate with Stephen Douglas, the editorial added:

> Mr. Lincoln has a sort of assumed clownishness in his manner which does not become him . . . will sometimes make his language correspond with this clownish manner, and he can thus frequently raise a loud laugh among his Whig hearers; but this entire game of buffoonery convinces the mind of no man. . . . We seriously advise Mr. Lincoln to correct this clownish fault before it grows upon him.

Buffoonery, and the making of laughter: were they the same? Was the pulling up of Colonel Richard Taylor's vest to expose his expensive shirt and gold ornaments the act of a buffoon? Or of a man who knows that laughter is the greatest leveler of pomposity? What an amazing contrast they were, Douglas and Lincoln, each the leader of the young wing of his party: though Douglas had an endless supply of small talk, he was literal-minded, could never make a joke. Lincoln on the other hand tried to reduce every complexity to a folk story or a single essence line, as when Ninian Edwards offered to reply to the *Register's* attack, and Lincoln answered:

"No, thank you, Ninian; every man has to skin his own skunk."

She determined to hear him the next time he made a speech, and judge for herself.

On December 20 the two political factions began a week of debate. The wind blew an icy coldness across the frozen prairie; the dusk was as dark as a cloudy sky and black soil could make it. She was called for in a carriage by the oldest of her cousins and by all odds the strangest-looking: Stephen T. Logan was just a little short of forty, a small skinny man with a mop of curly red hair, a pinched face, narrow-line lips and a rasping voice. When he stepped from the carriage she saw that he was dressed in his usual shabby coat, baggy trousers, old fur cap and thick farmer brogans.

She wrapped her dark blue merino cloak tightly about her and wondered how anybody in her family could help but love beautiful clothes. The mystery was the more unfathomable when she remembered that Judge Logan was immaculately groomed in his legal thinking and had spent a fortune on his imposing brick home set in the midst of a vast park.

They drew up in front of the Second Presbyterian Church which was being used by the House of Representatives until the state capitol should be completed. Franklin stoves glowed red on either side of the rostrum, the floor was covered with a heavy layer of sawdust. All the seats on the main floor were taken. They went up to the gallery and found seats immediately above the lecturer and a roaring stove. Though the church had been built to accommodate three hundred people, five hundred had crammed in and were standing in the aisles when the speaking began. Judge Logan would be speaking later in the week for the Whigs; he said to her in a tight voice, so like her father's:

"Everyone turns out for the best show in town. That McKenzie and Jefferson theatrical troupe will be playing to empty chairs tonight in Mr. Watson's new saloon."

By the end of the week, however, the show seemed to have lost its attraction, for Mary found only thirty people scattered throughout the uncomfortably silent hall on the night Mr. Lincoln was to close the debate. True, it was December 26, and the town was exhausted from having shopped for its gifts all day Christmas and exchanged them at high tea, but this was really a dismal showing. She knew it would be considered improper for her to attend alone and had almost given up hope of hearing Mr. Lincoln when she learned that Simeon Francis, the owner of the *Sangamo Journal,* and his wife were coming to tea before going on to report the meeting.

"Do you mind if I go with you?" she asked, when the Francises were about to depart.

Mrs. Francis threw her a scrutinizing glance.

53

"To hear Mr. Lincoln? Why, of course, dear, we'd be happy to have company."

They sat her between them, Simeon Francis a fat, exuberant, good-natured man of forty-three, and his wife, also big, deep-bosomed. She was a first-rate journalist in her own right but was completely thwarted by the fact that none of the female news she gathered could be printed in the *Journal,* for a woman's name could appear in a newspaper only twice: when she was married and when she died. However her knowledge of what was happening to everyone in the county was not wasted, she was an inveterate matchmaker who had over twenty marriages to her credit. Barren herself, she felt that all the children of her arranged marriages were in a special sense her own.

"You must come home with us for supper, child," she boomed in Mary's ear. "Mr. Lincoln is coming too."

"Oh no, I didn't mean to impose myself . . ."

"Tush, it'll be the best part of the evening. You can help us edit Mr. Lincoln's speech for the *Journal.*"

Mary looked up to the stand. Seeing that no one else was coming, Mr. Lincoln rose, took a speech out of his pocket and began glumly:

"Fellow Citizens: It is peculiarly embarrassing to me to attempt a continuance of the discussion, on this evening, which has been conducted in this hall on several preceding ones. It is so, because on each of those evenings there was a much fuller attendance than now, without any reason for its being so, except the greater interest the community feel in the speakers who addressed them then, than they do in him who is to do so now. I am indeed apprehensive that the few who have attended, have done so more to spare me of mortification than in the hope of being interested in anything I may be able to say. This circumstance casts a damp upon my spirits, which I am sure I shall be unable to overcome during the evening."

"Oh dear, what an unfortunate beginning," said Simeon Francis. "Now, of all times, he could use some buffoonery."

Mary looked at Lincoln's set expression and stiff posture, then proffered tentatively: "Could it have been the editorial criticizing his manners that has frightened him? I bet there won't be a single joke in the entire speech."

She was very nearly right: Mr. Lincoln plunged into a closely reasoned argument on the subtreasury which Democratic President Van Buren had installed to take the place of the national bank whose charter Andrew Jackson had refused to renew, analyzing the reasons why the Whigs wanted the national bank rechartered.

At first she found his voice unpleasantly high, with a twang and an abrasive quality. She was amused by some of his backwoods pronunciations such as Mr. Cheerman for Mr. Chairman. Then slowly as he tightened the skein of his argument, as she became absorbed in the rhythms with which he enumerated his skillfully written lines, she realized that the penetrating voice had gone not through her but into her.

The Francis carriage was rather small for four and she found herself crushed against Mr. Lincoln's heavy black suit; but for all he knew of her presence she might have been back in the Bluegrass. He sat with his eyes sunk and turned inward, his skin gray, his knees folded up under his chin and his hands clasped tight and bloodless about his ankles. She felt uncomfortable before his deep gloom: if there had been any way of getting out of the carriage and making her way back on foot she would have done so.

The Francis home was northeast of the state house, separated by a few lots from the office of their *Journal*, but for all purposes except the actual printing there was little difference between the two buildings; the parlor of the home was littered with dozens of out-of-town papers scissored for reproduction in the *Journal*, long sticks of type in process of composing, batches of uncorrected galley proof.

Supper was ready on the dining-room table, hot turkey stuffed with English walnuts, freshly baked corn bread and coffee. Lincoln would not touch a thing.

"I got the hypo," he muttered without looking at anybody. "That speech killed my appetite deader than it did General Harrison."

Seeing the look of puzzlement on Mary's face, Simeon Francis explained, "Hypo is his abbreviation for hypochondria. Fact, you might almost call it his pet name, he enjoys it so much."

She saw Lincoln wince but the Francises had known him since 1834 when he was the agent for the *Journal* in New Salem and they treated him as a son.

"Besides, Abe," said Mrs. Francis, "you take too much credit on yourself: since when are you important enough to kill the Whig candidate for president, singlehanded?"

A little color came back into Lincoln's leathery face; he managed a small smile.

"Forgive me if I don't join the wake," said Mary in an astringent voice, "but your speech, Mr. Lincoln, was as lucid a statement of the Whig case as I've heard since General Harrison was nominated. Besides," her tone resumed its semi-southern softness, "you made your best effort. What more can one ask of you?"

The man sitting opposite her, who had yet to acknowledge her presence, pulled up in his chair and looked at her with laughter beginning to germinate behind his eyes.

"Answering your question, Miss Todd, I feel like I once did when I met a woman riding horseback in the woods. As I stopped to let her pass she also stopped, and looking at me intently, said: 'I do believe you are the ugliest man I ever saw.' Said I: 'Madam, you probably are right, but I can't help it!' 'No,' said she, 'you can't help it, but you might stay at home.'"

The Francises joined Lincoln in his outburst of laughter; Mary remained silent and a little pale. Why does he tell such cruel stories on himself?

Then she felt a pair of eyes enveloping her. She turned and saw Mrs. Francis holding her and Lincoln together in a fascinated gaze.

She scrambled breathlessly to her feet.

"I simply must be going! Mr. Francis, could you drive me home?"

8

HER father had sent her a generous sum for Christmas, and in the same letter imparted a piece of information: in her mother's will she had been left eighty acres of good farm land in Indiana which was to come into her possession when she married. It was comforting to know that she would not go into marriage empty-handed; but she felt a long way from marriage at the moment, so she spent half of the Christmas gift on silk velvet, Grecian merino and green Italian crepe for new dresses.

Attached to her father's letter was a note from her stepmother and a few scrawled lines from Emilie. Sitting alone before the fire blazing in the grate in her bedroom she felt a strong nostalgia for her family, particularly for the youngsters, and for the house on Main Street. It was her first Christmas away from Lexington, where the holiday festivities were the most ceremonious of the year, starting two weeks before Christmas with elegant dinner parties and formal balls, and extending copiously into the New Year.

The nostalgia was dispelled the next day when a note arrived from Ann asking what kind of progress she was making and how soon there would be a vacancy at Elizabeth's.

New Year's Day was the most social in Springfield; Mary found that she was expected to call on everyone and to leave her card in the ribboned basket which hung on the front doorknob when the hosts were out calling. Ninian had wanted to pass the day by, since Elizabeth was not yet ready to come downstairs, but Elizabeth claimed that Mary could perfectly well do the family's receiving.

"Mary, tell the cook to prepare escalloped oysters, chicken salad and ice cream. And you'd better be dressed by the crack of dawn: the first New Year we were here a bachelor arrived while we were still in bed."

The first bachelor did indeed call at nine in the morning but Mary was prepared: she had placed about the parlor a number of heavy sterling bowls filled with oranges, the greatest of all New Year's treats. By one o'clock she had received almost a hundred callers. When Frances and Dr. Wallace arrived to help Ninian, Mary was free. The streets of Springfield were literally boiling with gigs, coaches, barouches. By two o'clock she had made a dozen stops but had found not a soul at home, for by now the entire town was out passing each other in carriages.

It was not until ten o'clock that night that the last of the Edwardses' guests had departed. She was at the bottom of the stairs with her shoes in one hand, about to ascend, when she heard a faint knocking. She slipped back into her shoes, put the lamp she was carrying on a table and opened the front door.

There, with his big beaver hat pressed against his chest, and a shy constrained look on his face, stood Abraham Lincoln.

"Mr. Lincoln! Last but not least. Won't you come in?"

"Thank you, ma'am. I know it's not what you meant, but just to keep the record clear this is my first visit today, not my last. I waited until I was sure everyone else would be gone so I could have a few moments alone with you."

Mary's eyebrows raised slightly, but she made no comment. Leading him to the parlor, she indicated two armchairs for him to draw up to the fire.

"Would you like a cup of eggnog? Or perhaps of coffee?"

"No, thank you, ma'am."

They sat watching the flames weave ever new patterns, caught in a reverie by the crackling of the logs, then fell into companionable talk, leaning forward with their elbows on their thighs, hands clasped before them, heads almost touching. They were surprised to learn that they had been born less than a hundred miles from each other in Kentucky, that they had lost their mothers at about the same age. His family had moved to Indiana when he was seven and he did not remember too much about Kentucky, so she told him about Lexington and Ashland and Henry Clay, and together they mourned his defeat at the Harrisburg convention. She spoke briefly about Dr. Ward's Academy and Mentelle's, then asked him about his own early life and education.

"My early life? It can all be condensed into a single sentence, 'The short and simple annals of the poor.' "

"That's from Gray's *Elegy*, isn't it?"

"Yes." He smiled a little wistfully. "I went to ABC schools by littles, two or three months here or there, less than a year in all. Blab schools, of course. No qualification was ever required of a teacher beyond readin', writin' and cipherin'. There was nothing to excite ambition for education. When I came of age I didn't know much, still somehow I could read, write and cipher to the Rule of Three. I have not been to school since."

"Yet your subtreasury speech was a trenchant piece of writing. You're certainly as well educated as I am, for all my thirteen years of formal schooling. Where did it come from?"

"Well, we never owned a book except the Bible, but one neighbor had Bunyan's *Pilgrim's Progress*, and the man who owned the nearest general store had Robert Burns. When you have only a few books you read them over and over until you know them by heart. There was a farmer by the name of Crawford a few miles down the road who loaned me his copy of Weems's *Life of Washington*. I read it at night up in the sleeping loft till the candle burned out; once I put it between the logs and the rain got it wet. I pulled corn for Crawford for three whole days to work out the price of the book, but I didn't mind because then it belonged to me. Each year I'd find another book around somewhere in the countryside, *Aesop's Fables*, *Robinson Crusoe*, *The Life of Henry Clay*. By the time I was fifteen I'd walk a mile and a half to the general store every night and read the newspapers to learn what was going on in the world. My stepmother encouraged me and took my side against my father. He couldn't read or write, just barely enough to sign his name, though it wasn't his fault: he was only six when his father was shot by an Indian in the fields and he never got to go to school even by littles."

He was thoughtful for a moment while leaning perilously close to the fire.

"He never had any schooling and so he feared it and begrudged it to others. He used to say, 'I suppose you're still foolin' yourself with eddication. I tried to stop you, but you got that fool idea in your head and it can't be got out. Now I hain't got no eddication but I get along far better than if I had.' But he didn't get along; nothing ever worked out for him; he was a skilled carpenter and cabinetmaker and could have given my mother a good life in Elizabethtown, but he never was content to stay anywhere for long. Mind you, he isn't a stupid or a lazy man, he always owned land and horses, it's just that he had bad luck . . . coupled with bad judgment; each time we moved on to a new farm, Knob Creek in Kentucky, Pigeon Creek in Indiana, Macon County on the Sangamon River here in Illinois, the land turned out to be poor, or the weather was bad, or the title was defective and he lost the fruits of his labor. We'd move on to a new place with our few household possessions piled into a farm wagon. But he loved my stepmother, Sarah, and she protected my right to read and study in my spare hours."

She noted a sharp change in his voice in this last sentence, as though in his mind he were drawing some kind of painful contrast. She asked so softly that if he did not want to hear the question it could not reach his ears alive:

"And he didn't love your mother?"

"It was only when my stepmother refused him and married another man that he took my mother for a wife. My mother could have known; maybe that's why I never remember her as anything but . . . defeated." His words too were so soft that they could never again be brought back as a reality. "When she died . . . and Sarah was widowed, he traveled all the way back to Elizabethtown to get her. She found us living in a dirty cabin, ragged and half starved; my twelve-year-old sister had been doing her best but she was too young. My stepmother turned that unfinished, lonely cabin into a clean and loving home."

He turned his face up to Mary. She found it lighted by an inner radiance.

"She gave us love. We needed love . . . so badly."

"We all do."

They were quiet, but there was communication between them. After a moment she asked gently:

"And your sister, where is she?"

"Dead. Like my mother. Neither needed to die." Melancholy settled over his face. "When my father moved us from Kentucky to the wilds of Indiana all he built was a half-faced camp with a brush roof; one side was open to the snow and cold. We suffered bad that winter but my mother most of

58

all. Even the next winter when he built a real cabin, it had no laid floor. She didn't have the strength to survive the milk-sick."

He paused for a long time before continuing.

"My sister was nineteen when she married Aaron Grigsby. He let her die in childbed, without care. Love . . . marriage . . . so often . . . they kill."

She reached out a hand, compassionately. He pulled back as though touched by fire.

"It doesn't have to be that way, Mr. Lincoln. The world is full of people who love and marry and do only good to each other."

He searched her face for a moment, a dark fever brooding in his eyes. "Could I call you Molly?"

"Molly?" She was mystified. "You mean as a nickname?"

"Yes."

"I've never had a nickname. But why should you want to?"

He squirmed uneasily in his chair, answering without looking directly at her.

"Well, I knew another girl by the name of Mary . . . few years ago in New Salem. I didn't come off too well in that . . . and the name Mary is still a little . . . painful. . . ."

"Then call me Molly, by all means."

"Thank you. I'll have that cup of coffee now, Molly, if I may."

She started for the kitchen with her head cocked to one side wonderingly. Molly, she thought; what next?

9

THE Edwards house was alight with candle clusters and astral lamps as Elizabeth made her re-entry into Springfield society. She was dressed in the full flowing French bombazine gown Mary had made for her when she came downstairs to receive the hundred and fifty guests who had been invited to meet Benjamin and Helen Edwards, Ninian's younger brother and his bride of four months, out from New Haven to settle in Springfield. Ninian had given his wife a Chinese-red piano as a gift for his first son. Mary and Stephen Douglas sat playing duets while the guests arrived.

Sitting next to Stephen on the red piano stool, their shoulders sometimes touching lightly, Mary felt the tremendous warmth and vigor of the man: brilliant, irrepressible, ambition-ridden. Singlehanded he had set up the radically new but effective structure of the Democratic party in Illinois and was leading his party in the plans to re-elect President Martin Van Buren. At dinner the night before she had heard Ninian tell his younger brother, while analyzing the Springfield lawyers:

"In a bad case Stephen Douglas is the best lawyer in Illinois. In a bad case Abraham Lincoln is the worst."

The man next to her with the big head and thick hair, the heavy torso and childlike legs, singing softly in her ear and flirting outrageously with his eyes, was obviously first-rate. He also was obviously enamored of her. She thought of him in Ninian's term as a steam engine in britches, and enjoyed the cyclonic movements of his mind, which certainly had legs long enough to reach the ground in any situation. She liked him, admired him, was excited and amused by him; but did she love him?

She looked around the conservatory in which there were some fifteen young men, singing, talking vivaciously, pleasant fellows with good starts in life. She liked them all and she had reason to believe they liked her. She favored no one of the men more than the other; she rotated both her invitations and her acceptances. She knew that this method of casualness might discourage anyone from falling in love with her, but she did not want anyone falling in love with her until she herself was committed. Here in Springfield she found that many other girls felt the same way; they were not competing for the favor of the men, they were not anxious, worried or preoccupied by thoughts of marriage. They were young, healthy, attractive, and enjoying life. So was she.

Stephen Douglas came to a loud closing crescendo, then sprang up saying, "I'm hot and thirsty. Come along, Mary, and fix me a beaker of wine punch."

As they made their way across the crowded foyer a Jacksonville attorney grabbed Douglas by the biceps:

"Steve! Haven't seen you since the New Year. This is going to be your year, man. We bring in the bacon for Van Buren, and you may see the inside of the United States Senate."

She saw Douglas flush, then realized she too had gone red of face. Stephen Douglas, in the United States Senate! Sitting next to Henry Clay, John Calhoun, Daniel Webster! When they moved on, she asked:

"Is that true, Steve?"

"If the Democrats get a majority in the legislature . . . they're the ones who pick the next United States senator from Illinois. And since I've taken over the leadership of the party . . . it looks like I'll be put on the track."

He placed both pudgy hands on his face, running his fingers along the contour of the heavy nostrils and then down through the dimples in the square-cut chin.

"But, Steve, you're not yet thirty. . . . Are you prepared?"

"Prepared? How can I tell until I get there and try my wings? Young men have to come up, don't they? Do you know who could go to the United States Senate from Illinois if the Democrats lose?"

"No, who?"

"Your absent friend, Abraham Lincoln."

"Abraham Lincoln!" The loudness of her voice astonished them both. "That I can scarcely believe!"

"I'm glad to see you consider me the lesser of the two evils, my dear!"

"Oh, Steve! I was only surprised because you're so young. I'm sure that if you have your heart set on the Senate, you'll end up a United States senator."

"That's better. As a matter of fact the first time I thought I might be elected, I shocked myself out of a week's sleep."

After she had poured his drink and he joined Ninian and a group of men in the library, she remembered a phrase he had used: *your absent friend*.

It was true, she had not seen him. Why? Had he not been invited? Or had he just not bothered to come? Suddenly she felt someone standing close behind her.

"No, he's not here, Mary."

Mary whirled about.

"For heaven's sake, Liz, stop reading my mind."

"Gladly. Just stop smearing your thoughts over your face like blackberry jam. He was not invited because he is in no sense a part of our social life, only a roomer-arounder, sharing a bed above Josh Speed's store, and eating free meals at the Butlers'."

"But you've invited other young men who have no homes: Lyman Trumbull sleeps in a committee room at the state house. Josh is here and he sleeps above his store."

"They have no homes in which to entertain, but they are definitely interested in society, they reciprocate by entertaining in the good hotels and restaurants, thus indicating that they intend to take their place among us. Lyman is the seventh generation of Trumbulls in America, while Joshua Speed comes from a prominent Kentucky family. Socially, Mr. Lincoln does not exist."

"Won't his feelings be hurt . . . ? If it were me I should hate us all as snobs."

"My dear, you just don't know Mr. Lincoln. The greatest favor we could have done him was to leave him off the list. He's made it clear that he doesn't want to become an integral part of Springfield society, and I see no reason to go against his wishes."

It's true, she thought after Elizabeth had turned away, I don't understand Mr. Lincoln. But how do you solve a man you almost never lay eyes on?

The next afternoon company arrived from Columbia, Missouri. Judge David Todd, who was her father's brother, and with him his lovely eighteen-year-old daughter Anne. The family was invited to Dr. John Todd's home for a Todd reunion. For Mary it was interesting to see her two uncles together; Dr. John, who was the oldest of the lot at fifty-two, entirely bald but with thin thatches of white hair combed back over his ears, a heavy-set man with the foreshortened neck of the Todds. He was a graduate of Transylvania and the University of Pennsylvania, who believed in hell-fire for the erring soul, bleeding and blistering for the erring body.

Judge David Todd was younger, a stockily built man with handsome black eyes and black curling hair, known in the family as a lady's man. He had moved from Kentucky to Missouri very early, bought the best of farm lands, set up as a merchant, studied law and sat on the bench for sixteen years.

The great enthusiasm of her uncle David's life was Missouri.

"You made a great mistake, Mary, coming up here to Springfield," he boomed. "We have nothing but the finest out there: the lands are the richest, the men are the handsomest . . . Say, Mary, you haven't got yourself hitched yet?"

"No, Uncle David, I'm still a spinster."

"Good, good, we need young ladies like you out in Missouri. In fact that's one of my reasons for coming here. I plan to inundate Missouri with Todds. How would you like to come back with us? I know at least half a dozen men there who would grab you at first sight. You don't have that kind of man here, I'll bet."

"Frankly, no," she replied gaily. "I haven't been grabbed at all."

"In Missouri we believe in fast action. What would you like, lawyer, doctor, farmer, merchant, judge? Say, we even got a dentist. Think you might like a dentist? Come back with us, Mary."

10

SHE was walking along Sixth Street one February midafternoon when Mrs. Simeon Francis emerged from her house dressed in a full-skirted white cotton apron and thick knitted shawl, carrying a heavily laden tray. Mrs. Francis went down the half dozen steps to the loose planks her husband had laid between his office and home, saw Mary and called across to her:

"Hello, Mary, come along to the shop and help me feed Sim."

Mary picked her way across the rough frozen mud of Sixth Street, saw that Mrs. Francis was carrying hot food in addition to coffee: a broad, flat-faced woman with the nose, mouth, eyebrows and ears all on the identical plane; with deep-clefted breasts, ample, Mary thought, to nourish an entire generation. She had become a familiar figure in Springfield, plodding down the block with hot soup in winter, cold milk and fruit punch in summer.

As they walked past the several intervening lots, Mary asked:

"Why didn't you build your home and shop next to each other, with a connecting door? It would have saved you many trips."

"About twenty a day: Sim left at six this morning before breakfast; I won't be able to get him out of there until ten tonight. I thought I could keep the two parts of his life separate, create a place of rest and relaxation in our home."

Mary pushed the *Sangamo Journal* door inward, following in the wake of Mrs. Francis. Simeon was standing with his back to the door, setting type. He turned his head for a swift look, his plump stubby fingers never stopping in the skillful roaming of the type box. He was forever brushing his hair back off his brow with the heel of his palm, and his forehead had enough ink on it to print an issue of his paper.

"Hello, Mother, suppertime already? Come in, Mary, make yourself comfortable."

She was tempted to ask, Where? for the *Sangamo Journal* office was one large room, containing the rolls of paper, ink, type, boxes and press. There was a desk in a rear corner, but without a chair for either the owner or a dropper-in.

Simeon Francis had been born in Connecticut, served his printing apprenticeship in New Haven, then published weekly papers in New London and Buffalo. He had come west in 1831, wanting to grow up with a new community. He had been unsuccessful at first because most of Springfield's southern settlers had suspected him of being a "damned Yankee." His paper was now the official voice of all the Whigs in Illinois, yet he could by no means support himself on the four-page weekly, and had to keep his press busy with all manner of commercial printing.

"Around this office I am the editor, compositor, devil and man of all work," he explained. "The only chance I get to compose my editorials is standing right here at the type boxes and setting up my thoughts in print as they come to me."

Mrs. Francis said quietly, "Abe helps you all he can."

The Francises were the only ones in Springfield who called Mr. Lincoln by his first name.

"Yes, Abe is a great help," Simeon agreed. "He writes articles and letters to fill the pages."

"Is it true that he could be our next senator if the Whigs carry the state?" She was conscious that she had blurted out the query, but Simeon did not appear to notice.

"He's far and away our best man."

It was her own opinion that Ninian Edwards stood head and shoulders above all other Whigs. She removed her heavy woolen cloak and, holding the voluminous skirts of her dark green walking dress above her ankles in an attempt to avoid the ink-smudged debris on the floor, walked to the front window overlooking Sixth Street.

"Why do you think so? Mr. Lincoln baffles me. Just what is he, really?"

Simeon and Eliza Francis gazed at each other intently, the room cracklingly alive with the groping movements of their thoughts. Eliza was the first to speak.

"When he came to Springfield in April of 1837 he arrived on a borrowed horse, with all his worldly possessions in his saddlebags. He didn't have the seventeen dollars necessary to buy the furnishings for a single bedstead. Josh Speed tells me Abe said, 'It is probably cheap enough but I want to say that, cheap as it is, I have not the money to pay. But if you will credit me until Christmas and my experiment here as a lawyer is a success, I will pay you then. If I fail in that, I will probably never pay you at all.' Josh says he had never seen so melancholy a face in his life and so he offered Abe half of his large double bed above the store. Without saying a word, Abe took up his saddlebags, went upstairs, and came down again in a moment with his face beaming: 'Well, Speed, I'm moved.'"

"Is it true that he's been boarding with Mr. Butler all this time without paying for his meals?"

The Francises looked pained; this was the kind of question one did not ask. Simeon took up the reply.

"You have to understand how things are out here on the frontier, Mary. We're not a settled community like Lexington. Here we take in the young people and treat them as our sons, not only feeding them but giving them any other help they may need. It's the custom. If Abe has never paid any money to the Butlers, it's because the Butlers have made it clear that they would not accept it. They are his friends. You don't take money from friends when they sit down to table. Besides, a lot of his fees are paid to him in vegetables, groceries and poultry and he turns all these over to the Butlers."

Eliza Francis picked up the defense.

"You see, Mary, Abe won't take a case unless he thinks his client is in the right. The other day after listening to a would-be client's statement, he swung around in his chair and exclaimed, 'Well, you've got a good case in technical law, but a pretty bad one in equity and justice. You will have to get some other fellow to win this case for you.' I remember also when one man asked, 'What will you charge, Mr. Lincoln, to go into court for me?' Abe replied, 'Well, it will cost you ten dollars, but it won't cost you anything if you can settle it between yourselves.' They did settle it, so Abe got no fee."

In the intervening pause Mary thought, He's trying to pretend he lives in a world in which there is no such thing as money. But it won't work; my father could teach him that.

Simeon Francis went back to his type box, picked out a few letters, then dropped them back as he returned to the attack.

"When his two stores up in New Salem 'winked out,' to use his own phrase, and his partner Berry took to drink and died, Abe assumed all the obligations, eleven hundred dollars' worth. He calls it his national debt. He's been paying it off ever since. He didn't have to pay Berry's debts, but he assumed full responsibility for his partner."

"That's commendable, but it's no more than my father and his business associates do in Lexington."

"Granted. There's really nothing unusual in anything Eliza or I could tell you about Abe. And yet the young man adds up to something most unusual. He has a kind of wisdom. That's why we think he can go . . . anywhere . . . to the top, wherever that may be."

There was a knock on the street window and there stood Mr. Lincoln in a tall dusty beaver hat and a coat and vest much too loose for him. He smiled at them while those on the inside waved and smiled back. In the moment that it took for him to reach the front door and click the latch, Eliza Francis turned to Mary and asked soberly:

"What about it, Mary: can you see Abraham plain?"

11

THE legislature adjourned and the town emptied almost at once. All of her male relatives and friends plunged into the new election. Lincoln and Simeon Francis fired the first salvo by issuing a campaign newspaper called *The Old Soldier;* two weeks later Stephen A. Douglas and the *Register* issued an answer in the form of *Old Hickory,* also a weekly party organ, and Mary thought it was well done, but when she encountered Mr. Lincoln on the square and asked him his opinion of Stephen's editorial he replied with a crooked-mouthed smile:

"We have adopted as part of our policy to never speak of Douglas at all; isn't that the best mode of treating so small a matter?"

"Mr. Lincoln, that's unworthy of you!" Her voice had risen and two spots of color appeared on her forehead. "No man's qualities should be judged by the accidental height to which he was born, whether he be too short like Mr. Douglas . . ."

". . . or too tall like me?"

"You are as tall as God made you. Mr. Douglas is as short as God made him. I'm surprised at you, Mr. Lincoln, I've never heard you utter a derogatory line about any man."

He went a little pale, then asked in a low voice:

"Would you defend me with equal vehemence if someone spoke slightingly of me?"

"Indeed I would!"

"Thank you, Molly. I'll never speak slightingly of Douglas again; the truth is, he was entitled to copy our idea for a campaign weekly, for I've borrowed his plan of state organization."

Early in March the Sangamon Circuit Court opened a two-week session. A goodly portion of the lawyers of Illinois thronged in, along with clients, witnesses and business associates. With the exception of the time she had gone into court in Lexington in a slave-beating case on which her father was a member of the jury, she never had watched a court session. Yet here in Springfield it seemed most natural that she should go. Ninian Edwards had no case on the docket; when she asked him why he replied that there wasn't anything coming up that interested him enough since the fees were low.

The rooms in the new courthouse were not yet ready, so court convened in the same store building where she had seen Abraham Lincoln drop down from his office above. Inside the railing stood a group of lawyers. Judge Sam-

65

uel Treat was dressed in a well-fitting black suit, as poised and urbane on the bench as he was shy and awkward when among young ladies. Stephen Douglas appeared first and won two cases in a very few minutes. In quick order Edward Baker, Stephen Logan and James Conkling either won cases or had them settled to their satisfaction. It was almost time for dinner before Lincoln was called. She leaned forward in her seat to see what kind of man Mr. Lincoln would be representing. He put his client on the stand and led him through the testimony that he had loaned a sum of money to a business associate, and that he had not had repayment. When the defendant took the stand his lawyer asked him if he had repaid the loan and the man replied that he had. His lawyer then asked him if he had any proof of this and the defendant drew out of his pocket a receipt of payment. She saw Mr. Lincoln turn and walk a few steps to stand face to face with his client:

"Did you know he held this receipt?"

"Yes, Mr. Lincoln, but I thought he had forgotten it."

Lincoln turned and went down the center aisle of the room to the open door. Mary was astonished. What strange conduct! Judge Treat called out:

"Mr. Lincoln, where are you going? Don't you want to finish this case?"

Lincoln's face was pale. He replied:

"Your Honor, I'm going to wash my hands."

Mary relaxed in her seat with a half-amused, half-puzzled gesture. What an inauspicious beginning for Mr. Lincoln; and yet, remembering what the Francises had told her, how entirely in character.

After dinner he was the first to appear at the bar. He was defending a man who was being sued for a large sum of money. The case revolved around whether or not Mr. Lincoln's client had caused permanent injury to the plaintiff. The key witness was a well-known Illinois surgeon who made positive statements about the severity of the damage done. Mr. Lincoln stared at the surgeon, then said with each word spaced distinctly from the other:

"Doctor, how much money are you to receive for testifying in this case?"

The surgeon turned to the judge.

"Your Honor, do I have to answer that question?"

"Yes," replied Judge Treat, "it's proper."

"Well then . . . I am to receive . . . three hundred dollars."

Mary's gasp was caught up in the gasp of the courtroom. Lincoln pointed his long index finger directly at the surgeon, saying in a voice filled with indignation:

"Gentlemen of the jury, *big fee, big swear!*"

The jurors acquitted Mr. Lincoln's client.

It was not until the fourth day that a case came up which excited the whole town. Mary, Mercy Levering and Julia Jayne arrived a little late and had to stand against the back wall. During the previous August a man named Henry Lockwood had been killed at a camp meeting. A witness, Sovine, had gone to the sheriff and given such a detailed account of the fatal shooting that a certain Grayson had been indicted for murder. Grayson's mother had tried to secure older and more experienced counsel but, being without funds, had failed, and so had come to Mr. Lincoln.

The state prosecutor introduced the testimony of Sovine, who swore that he had seen the shot fired by Grayson, had seen Grayson run away from the scene and that he, Sovine, had picked up the deceased Lockwood who had died in his arms.

It seemed a hopeless case. Mary was interested to see that Lincoln did not take a note during the testimony, nor once rise to object. When the state prosecutor had rested his case, Lincoln pulled himself out of his chair.

"Mr. Sovine, you say you were with Lockwood just before and saw the shooting. You stood very near to them?"

"No, not near. In the timber."

"What kind of timber?"

"Beech timber."

"The leaves on the beeches are rather thick in August, aren't they?"

"Yes."

"Did you see a candle up there by the stand or near Lockwood and Grayson?"

"No."

"How then did you see the shooting?"

"By moonlight."

Mary saw Mr. Lincoln reach into his side pocket and pick out a blue-covered pamphlet, find the page he wanted and offer it up in evidence. When the book was handed back to him, he said:

"By the testimony of this almanac, the official one used by the city of Springfield and the state of Illinois, we now have indisputable evidence that the moon on the night of August 9 was unseen by Mr. Sovine or by anyone else, for the very good reason that it did not rise until one o'clock the next morning!"

Sovine broke down and confessed he had fired the fatal shot.

Mary found herself thinking indignantly, What did Ninian mean by saying that in a bad case Abraham Lincoln was the worst lawyer in Illinois? Apparently there were no bad cases for Mr. Lincoln . . . except the ones he thought dishonest; and of these, in his own words, he washed his hands.

The circuit court no sooner had finished its business and closed its doors, accompanied by the exodus of the legal train which followed it from county seat to county seat, than a tempest broke over Springfield in which the Todd family was involved.

At the time Mary had come for her first visit in 1837, one of her Kentucky cousins, Lucy Hardin, and her husband Marcus Chinn, had settled in the adjoining town of Jacksonville, bringing two of her slaves with them. Since the constitution set up for the state of Illinois in 1818 forbade slavery, an abolitionist group in Jacksonville informed the two Negroes that they were legally free and secreted them in their own homes. The Chinns recaptured the man and sent him down the river for resale, but the girl instituted a suit for her freedom under the Illinois law. Since passions were running high in Jacksonville the presiding judge transferred the case to the capital.

Mary refused to believe the news when Ninian told her that Stephen T. Logan had acceded to the plea of their cousin Lucy Chinn to represent them. The next time he dropped by the house she cornered him in the conservatory:

"Cousin Steve, I can't understand your defending the Chinns, even though they are your first cousins. Surely you don't want to make slavery legal in Illinois?"

"No, Mary, that's not my intention; but everyone is entitled to a defense of his person and property at law. If the issue of slavery is to be settled, then both sides of the case should be presented with the utmost precision."

"But if you plead the case for slavery, won't people conclude that you are in favor of it?"

"I don't think so, Mary; lawyers don't have to subscribe to everything their clients believe, in fact they couldn't possibly. The lawyer is an officer of the court, his duty is to see that all of the law bearing on a case is brought forth. I intend to do my job thoroughly and dispassionately."

At supper that night she reported her conversation to Elizabeth and Ninian. Ninian listened thoughtfully, then said:

"Someone has to represent the Chinns, they have a right to counsel, and it is probably better all around that they have the best-trained lawyer in Illinois. Once Cousin Steve and the Chinns are defeated, we will have established a precedent for freedom which no one will be able to overturn."

"But if Cousin Steve wins, thousands of southern families can migrate to Illinois with their slaves and we will become a slave state."

"He's not going to win," replied Ninian blandly. "I'm defending the colored girl."

Mary gazed at him with openmouthed silence. This was the man they accused of being a cold aristocrat! He hadn't gone to trial in the last session because the fees were too trifling, yet he would take this case for which there would be no fee at all. She rose from her seat, walked around the table, heartily kissed her brother-in-law, then turned to Elizabeth and said:

"Sister, you married yourself a man!"

She invited Stephen Douglas and Abraham Lincoln to an early tea. It was the first time she had had them alone together and while the two men discussed a murder case in which they both had been engaged to defend Spencer Turner, she had a chance to study them. They made an almost ludicrous picture side by side in the middle of the parlor rug, Douglas standing with his head thrown back so that he could see up into the face of Lincoln; Lincoln standing with his shoulders hunched forward, his head lowered, so that he could get closer to Douglas. She reported to them her conversations with Logan and Ninian about the Chinn case, then asked:

"Would you two gentlemen take the Chinn case?"

Douglas's thinking processes were as swift as lightning. He said:

"That is a layman's question, my dear Mary; it shows ignorance of the law as a profession. Your cousin Logan is right. I'm totally opposed to slavery. I would not buy, sell, own or accept a slave as a gift, yet if the Chinns came to me and asked me to defend them against the loss of their legal property, I would feel obliged as an attorney to take the case and present it with all of the force I could summon."

She turned to gaze at Lincoln, who was no longer hunched over but standing up to his six-feet-four height, gazing ceilingward.

"What about you, Mr. Lincoln? Do you agree with my cousin Logan?"

Lincoln was as slow a thinker as Douglas was rapid; Mary could almost see the painful process working itself out. Finally he brought his eyes down to room level.

"I would never raise my voice for slavery; in my opinion it is founded on injustice and bad policy. White men can make themselves free, Negroes cannot; therein lies the basic tragedy of slavery. I consider it no part of my obligation as a lawyer to defend anyone who is attempting to bring slavery into a free land."

"If you two abolitionists will excuse me," said Douglas in a high voice, "I must get down to the *Register* and check this week's editorial."

After he left, Mary and Lincoln drew their chairs up side by side before the hickory-log fire. Lincoln said softly:

"I'm not an abolitionist, you know. I believe that slaveowners in slave states have a right to their property. I have read of too many instances where abolitionists have turned master against slave and increased the hardship of the Negro." He paused for a moment, then turned full face to her. "I've never lived with slavery. In fact I've only seen it twice, on trips to New Orleans when I took flatboats down the Mississippi to market. What is it like to grow up surrounded by slavery?"

She paused to organize her thoughts, then said, "Well, as a child it seemed natural and good. Mammy Sally couldn't have loved me more if she had been my own mother; and we loved her. All of our house servants were part of the family, in fact their idiosyncrasies frequently were indulged far more than our own. Throughout our widespread family, even on our friends' plantations, the Negroes were treated kindly, and there was always an underlying affection between the blacks and whites. I didn't know there were cruel masters and evil ones until I was eight and I was sent off to Dr. Ward's Academy."

She told him of how she had stumbled into the courthouse square and had witnessed the beatings of the young colored man and girl; of the coffles of chained slaves being driven past their house on Main Street; of the auction block in the square and the families being torn apart and sold separately for the swamp areas of the deep south; of Mrs. Turner, a huge domineering woman whose house was just beyond the intervening lot, who suddenly had appeared at one of her second-story windows with a small black boy in her arms, and dashed him to the courtyard below. She told him finally of the unhappy predicament her father had found himself in just before she left Lexington, and of Cassius Clay's dictum: "There are few absolutes in the world, but slavery is one of them, an absolute evil; anyone participating in any part of slavery is responsible for the whole of it."

"My father, like you, is against the abolitionists; he's seen them throw over fifty years of work in the south for the betterment of the Negroes. He has been working for colonization . . ."

". . . I favor that too, strongly . . ."

". . . and the freeing of all the children of slaves as they reach twenty-one. We could achieve gradual emancipation that way. We have men down there who are determined to put an end to slavery, as my friend Cassius would say, 'this very day, this very hour, this very moment.' He's a powerful man, with tremendous courage and vitality, brains too, and a determination never to give up as long as there is one human being still held in slavery."

Lincoln lowered his chin, then raised his eyes as though he were peering at her over spectacles.

"You like that man Cassius Clay, Molly?"

"Like him? I'll never forgive Mary Jane Warfield for marrying him before I had a chance to grow up."

12

WITH April and the advent of an early spring the young lawyers of Springfield began their canvassing of Illinois. This year there would be elections to the legislature as well as the presidential election. Two thirds of her friends were out of town, speaking in Jacksonville, Carlinville, Alton, Belleville, Tremont, Bloomington, Pontiac, Clinton, Petersburg, coming home for a few days' rest before starting out again.

Stephen Douglas remained the most attentive and courtly of the young men: whenever he had to leave town for a few days he called on her to say *au revoir*, and upon his return he would bring a little gift, a lace handkerchief or perfume. She did not deceive herself over the nature of these attentions, for she knew that he made the identical calls and brought back similar gifts for Julia Jayne, Sarah Dunlap and doubtless one or two others.

With the men away so much, the girls formed the Pedestrian Club which gathered of a Sunday morning with packed baskets to walk through the prairies picking wild flowers, then finding an elevation in time to sprawl out for lunch with the bright spring sun on their faces. It reminded her of hickory-nut hunting and berrypicking in the Bluegrass. She returned from the day's outing, took off her Florence braid bonnet, green French Thibet frock and plaid buskin walking shoes and slipped into a voluminous flannel robe. Sitting before the pier table with the mirrored back, she loosed her hair and brushed a scented oil into it to give it luster. She had discovered the oil in Wallace and Diller's drugstore and was pleased to see that its constant use was not only turning her hair several shades darker, which she thought furnished a better background for her light skin and high coloring, but that it also had merged the recalcitrant blond lock with the rest of her hair. She never had quite approved of that lock; she had thought it made her look . . . indecisive. . . .

She was about to lie down to rest, with a copy of Smollett's *The Adventures of Roderick Random*, when the serving girl came up to tell her that Mr. Lincoln was downstairs. She slipped into a walking dress, brushed her hair to the back of her head and pinned it there, then took a lace shawl from the drawer. Unlike Stephen Douglas, Lincoln never bothered to tell her when he was going away nor yet when he had arrived back in town. When she held informal gatherings and sent out invitations to the young men of the group he frequently did not come, then at some inopportune moment, when she was busy sewing or helping Elizabeth bathe one of the children, or resting, as now, he would appear at the door.

She came upon him in the family room, sitting in a straight mahogany chair, arms supported angularly on his thighs, his head down nearly on a level with his knees. She stood in the middle of the room waiting for him to look up, to acknowledge her presence, but after a while she realized that he did not know she was there. She coughed politely, walked over toward him. When he raised his head she saw that his left eye had moved up to the top of the socket, giving his eyes an appearance not precisely of being crossed but of functioning on two different levels.

He gazed at her for a moment, apparently surprised to see her, then turned his head slowly, studying the objects of the room like a man trying to place himself.

"Mr. Lincoln, is something wrong? Are you ill?"

"No . . . it's this . . . ferocious headache. I have been almost blind with pain."

"Is it your eyes that bother you?"

He rose abruptly from the chair, demanding hoarsely:

"Why do you ask?"

"Because you said you were almost blind with pain."

"Oh. No, it's not that."

"Have you tried any of the headache remedies I see advertised in the *Journal* and the *Register*?"

He smiled weakly.

"Those remedies are almost pure alcohol; one bottle will cure your headache but it'll be back tenfold the next morning."

"Would you like a cup of tea, then? At home in Lexington when we didn't feel well the first thing we wanted was a cup of tea."

"Tea? Do you know, I've only drunk it once or twice in my life. It sounds like a good idea. I would like some."

She brewed a cup of strong hyson tea and brought it to the family sitting room. He sipped it slowly. When it was finished the pain seemed gone from his face. He thanked her for her kindness, then confessed:

"When you came in the room and I saw where I was, I was completely surprised to find myself in Ninian's house. All I can remember is that I was walking the street with this blinding pain, and I thought of you last Sunday filling your bonnet with wild flowers and weaving a chain of them through your hair. That was the last thing I can remember until I looked up and saw you standing in front of me."

"I'm happy you found your way here. Please come whenever you're in trouble, or in pain . . . but also come when you're happy and gay and when you have laughter you'd like to share with me."

He probed her expression, trying to perceive her meaning. Then he smiled. It was a sweet smile.

"That would only be fair, wouldn't it, Molly?"

The next Sunday was a warm and beautiful day. The Pedestrian Club met at the Edwards house at noon after church and left for a farm five miles away. They were going to be joined by several of the young men.

Lincoln turned up at the Edwards house with his hair freshly cut and washed, looking soft in texture as it was combed back from his high brow and away from his ears. He was freshly shaved as well, and though there were still hollows under the high cheek ridges, his skin seemed softer than she had remembered it. He had on a new suit of broadcloth with a little gray in it, not as funereally black as the garments he generally wore, and a fresh white collar and gleamingly new silk stock. When Mary opened the door to admit him she could not suppress a bright smile of pleasure.

"My, but aren't you the handsome one, Mr. Lincoln! You're going to be the best-dressed man among all the wild flowers."

"Oh, I was just patronizing home industries," he replied apologetically. "A few years ago in New Salem when I was coming home from the end of a day of woodchopping, all fixed up in my jeans and red shirt, I was overtaken by a bright young Negro. He told me he was a barber but out of work and out of funds. I took him to the house where I was boarding and got him enough work among the boarders to take care of him for a number of days. I then sent him down to Springfield."

"An elaborate explanation, lawyer Lincoln," she twitted him. "Personally, I think it's just the spring sap rising in you."

He flushed, patted her arm gingerly.

"Hope you're right, Molly, hope you're right."

The morning was unusually fine and she enjoyed the hours of walking through the fields, all of them dressed in high boots, crossing the prairies of wild flowers and going through stands of maple and elm. The girls avoided Lincoln and shy Samuel Treat, so Mary had one on either arm most of the

72

way. At the farm they covered the table under a great oak with white table-cloths from their baskets, then spread out the luncheon of roasted chicken, smoked ham and cakes from Watson's confectionery.

When Stephen Douglas saw an ax lying in the yard he suggested they bet to see who could pick it off the ground by its handle and hold it straight out in front of him. A half dozen of the men bet, Douglas, Speed, Treat, Conkling, Trumbull, Matheny, and each in turn set the ax straight, bent down, picked up the heavy wooden handle and tried to raise it. The ax head was tremendous; although several got it off the ground and in particular Douglas, who raised it almost level, none could get it up all the way.

During the last trials Mary watched Lincoln, who had a strange expression on his face. When the others were finished, she turned to him.

"Mr. Lincoln, you're the only one who hasn't tried. Do you think you can lift that ax off the ground?"

"Oh, Molly, I spent the first twenty years of my life throwing one of those axes. I must have split enough rails to fence in the whole west."

"You haven't answered my question. Can you lift it off the ground?"

The men urged him on, and so he walked back to the luncheon table, untied his black stock, took off his white collar, then took off his brand-new coat and folded it neatly. He walked over to the ax, buried the head of it ever so slightly in the ground, so that the handle came back to him straight, then, crouching down, took the wooden end of it and with a slow graceful movement lifted the ax until he stood erect with it, his arm straight out.

When everybody applauded he tossed his head a little and said:

"Long as I'm showing off I might as well do a real good job. Let's see if there's a second ax on the place."

A second ax was brought and Lincoln buried the two heads lightly in the ground about a foot apart. He crouched down, took a handle in each hand and, slowly lifting both axes, held them out before him on a level keel.

For Mary it was an exhibition of strength such as she had never seen; through the thin white shirt and the heavier material of his trousers she could see the powerful muscles and the indestructible male strength of him as he stood there almost like the oak tree under which he was accomplishing his feat, his legs and arms sturdy branches on a long, lean and incredibly virile trunk.

He dropped the axes, took a handkerchief from his back pocket to mop his brow. She felt faint, turned away.

SHE had been invited to the Globe Tavern for dinner by her sister Frances and her husband William Wallace. Their table was in a secluded corner of the Globe dining room, yet even now when there was no legislature and no court meeting there were perhaps a hundred men and women having their big noonday meal. The room was noisy with the bustling of waiters and the coming and going of the guests. Mary wondered how Frances had been able to endure more than a year of this living in public; when she asked the question, Frances replied:

"Actually, I've enjoyed it: it's brought me out of myself, made me meet a lot of people and learn to know them and like them. It's surprising how many people you can be happy with, once you are happy inside yourself."

How wisely Frances had chosen! she thought. Dr. Wallace had a deep fund of sweetness and, unlike her young group, was non-political and non-argumentative. Not that he didn't have a mind of his own; he was in total disagreement with the kind of medicine being practiced in Springfield, rejecting the idea of violent bleeding, blistering and physicking. He simply practiced his own way.

At the end of the robust dinner Frances said, "Anyway, we're moving. We bought a charming little house next to Dr. Helm's. We're planning a housewarming for next month, on a Saturday. May I invite Mr. Lincoln as your partner?"

Mary had a spoonful of chocolate mousse raised halfway to her lips. She put the spoon down.

Why had Frances asked this particular question? She was not conscious of having shown any special interest in Mr. Lincoln. Was this Frances's way of saying that she thought Mary ought to favor him? Before speaking she chose a casual voice from her mind as she might have a dress from her wardrobe.

"Why Mr. Lincoln especially, Frances, above any of the others?"

"I would have said she favored Steve Douglas," Dr. Wallace put in.

"Well, Mary, I notice that you have rather more interest in Mr. Lincoln."

Mary chewed on that thought awhile, bobbing her head slightly while asking herself whether her sister were right.

"Yes, Mr. Lincoln is interesting," she replied slowly; "but isn't that because he is the most unusual? There are no personal feelings involved, Frances. I've never considered him apart from the rest. I would like you to invite him to your dinner party, but not especially for me."

Frances's formal entrance into Springfield society was a grand success, with a platform erected in the back yard for dancing and the Springfield orchestra providing the music. Mr. Lincoln invited Mary to walk out to Dr. Houghan's place with him the next day, where as co-chairman of the Whig rally the following week he had to make arrangements for the barbecue and speakers' stand. She agreed to go, providing he would accompany her to church first. He hesitated for a moment, then agreed.

"Speaking of rallies," she continued, "I hear you had a successful time for the Whigs in Belleville."

"No." He shook his head with an amused despair. "I did poorly. I made an elaborate speech about the depression of 1837 into which Van Buren and the Democrats had plunged us. I'd heard about a horse that had been sold that morning for only twenty-five dollars, so I used the sale to illustrate how bad times were. When I finished, the constable who had sold the horse called out from the crowd, 'That horse had only one eye!' I was undone."

"Well, I saw a reprint in the *Register* saying that in your Belleville speech you were 'lucible, forcible and effective.' I remember it because of that word 'lucible.'"

His gloom lifted at once.

"Ain't that a caution!"

As they left church the following morning he confessed that he hadn't been the least uncomfortable, though he had found the sermon a little subdued.

"When I hear a man preach I like to see him act as if he were fighting bees."

Walking together north of the town, they were the long and short of it; yet she felt comfortable with him, she did not have to speed up or half run. He moderated his stride to match hers, and they moved along in unison. She was pleased because he had thought of this for himself; she gathered that he wanted other people to be comfortable in his presence, knowing that he was the one who was outsized, that he must moderate his stride to bring it down to life size.

The Houghan place stood in the midst of fourteen acres of wooded grounds. Corinthian columns held a wide and beautifully proportioned piazza, reminding her of the architectural grace of the homes in the Bluegrass. Dr. Houghan answered their knock in a red corduroy smoking jacket, a cylindrical red cap with a tassel and smoking an enormous tobacco-stained meerschaum pipe. Mary had met him at her uncle Dr. John Todd's. While Lincoln marked the four trails leading into the cleared area, then checked the location of the barbecue pits, she wandered from room to room entranced by the feeling of open spaciousness and freedom of spirit that she had found in no other house in Springfield.

"Dr. Houghan, your home is a work of art!" she cried.

"Yes, we love it . . . but we're offering it up for sale, it's too big for us."

"For sale! This is exactly the kind of house I want to move into when I marry."

Dr. Houghan took a pull at his meerschaum, then glanced out the window.

"Congratulations, Miss Todd. Do I know the fortunate young man?"

She bit a corner of her lip in embarrassment.

"It was a figure of speech, Doctor. I have no plans for marriage."

"Oh! I understand. Well, I'm in no hurry to sell. If and when I get an offer I'll give you a chance to match it."

Bold humor, she decided, was the best way out of the situation.

"Good! That makes two of us waiting for an offer."

On their way back Mary spoke enthusiastically about the Houghan place; Lincoln said quietly:

"But, Molly, it's such a big house."

"Well, I've always loved beautiful houses; don't you like lovely homes, Mr. Lincoln?"

"Truth to tell, I never thought much about them," he replied. "I spent most of my life in one-room log cabins and the last three-four years I've been sleeping upstairs of Josh's store. I never saw the inside of an elegant house until I moved to Springfield and was invited to your cousin John Stuart's. But a home is important to you, isn't it?"

"Yes, very."

Thousands of Whigs from Indiana, Iowa, Missouri and Illinois poured into Springfield. Some of them had been as long as ten days on the road, for they had come two hundred miles and had camped like an army on the march, sleeping in tents and carrying their own commissary. Because a Democratic newspaper had said derisively that General Harrison would be content to live in a log cabin the rest of his life and drink hard cider, this had become the "log cabin and hard cider campaign." The delegates came on foot, on horseback, in farm wagons; Sangamon County contributed a log cabin shaded by a live tree with the eighty delegates perched on the roof and the whole contraption drawn by twenty-six yoke of oxen. There were a dozen bands of music, hundreds of hard-cider barrels mounted on every form of cart and wagon.

Mary moved with the rest of the crowd out to Dr. Houghan's park where she listened to three hours of Whig speeches before going to the barbecue for midday dinner. Mr. Lincoln was preoccupiedly staring down into the pits where hundreds of beeves and hogs were roasting, apparently matching the quantity against the vast crowd.

"Folks got to be buttressed against this flood of oratory," he snorted.

He was the nineteenth speaker to mount the little platform that had been built on Dr. Houghan's porch; it was already eleven o'clock at night, the grounds were lighted by hundreds of torches. Mary, exhausted, wondered what he could possibly say that had not already been said a hundred times over. After helping to manage the succession of speakers and the feeding of the huge throng, he was in a thoroughly rumpled state, his hair standing up straight, his white collar wilted, his tie bedraggled and the grayish suit which had been so new on the walk of the Pedestrian Club plastered to the rough muscle-structure of his body.

Yet despite the awkward gestures and the high nasal voice something shone forth that lighted his face and the speakers' stand and the whole front of the Houghan house with a light stronger than the flaring torches about him. She could not say what it was; she could not even grasp its meaning.

He spoke short, stepped down. There was a scattering of applause. She was willing now to return home, but none of her family would desert the grounds until the last speaker had uttered his final word.

It was past midnight when she went forward with Elizabeth, Ninian and Stephen Logan to shake hands all around with the evening's speakers. No one was congratulating Mr. Lincoln very much; he had risen only to make an appearance. She went to where he was standing rather dejectedly to one side.

"Abraham, I can't remember a single syllable you said, but nevertheless I was moved."

It was the first time she had called him by his first name.

"I didn't hear a word of it, myself." He linked his arm through hers, held it tightly. "But you are very kind, Molly." He took a deep breath, shrugged off his fatigue and said good-naturedly, "I really should be a happy man tonight; I've had hundreds of congratulations on the barbecued beef."

The crowd began filing out of Houghan's park, the trails illumined by people carrying torches. Elizabeth looked back and saw that Mr. Lincoln had Mary by the arm. They were walking quietly and slowly, passed by groups rushing homeward. It was a long walk through the town, all the way from the northern outskirts to the southwest corner. As they reached the Edwardses' porch, Mary held out her hand.

"This is *au revoir* for a while, Abraham. I'm leaving in a few days to visit Uncle Judge Todd and my cousin Anne in Missouri."

"Missouri? Oh. Any special reason?"

She did not think it would be delicate to tell him of her uncle's importuning letters, or of the elegible young men who, according to her uncle, were breathlessly awaiting her arrival.

"It's just for . . . a change . . . during the hot summer months."

"I'll miss you."

"Will you? Then write to me sometime. The best of luck with your campaigning. I know you're going to have a fine success."

They were standing at arm's length. He took her hand in his, then they were no longer at arm's length as they had been during their entire relationship; he seemed to be inclining toward her, almost yearning. Clumsily, yet hungrily, he leaned his face down toward hers. She turned her cheek up to him, and then without knowing how the angle had changed, nor the decision of her mind, nor even when the actual movement began, the space between them was closed, his lips were on hers and they were clasped tightly in each other's arms. All distance, all difference vanished, they were two lonely creatures, united for one instant before parting and going their separate ways.

After a moment he took his mouth from hers, unclasped her from his powerful arms, turned away without speaking.

Book III

MY HEART AND MY FLESH

1

SHE awoke from her nap in the steamy midafternoon Missouri heat. Her thoughts came back slowly. Her eyes rested on the stillness of the trees outside her window; it was forbidding weather, hot and still. She hoped that it would not storm; while she had sat waiting to depart in the stagecoach in front of the Globe Tavern in Springfield thunder had knocked the top row of bricks off the still unfinished state house. She had been afraid of thunder since she was three, when Mammy Sally had told her that it was the voice of the debil booming out in anger at people's misdeeds.

Anne turned over on the other bed, a tiny smile on her heart-shaped face. Mary chuckled as she recalled her uncle Judge David Todd's story the night before of how he had fallen asleep on the bench while one of the attorneys was making a long speech. Waking up suddenly, he had cried out:

"Mr. Clerk, enter up a fine of ten dollars against David Todd for contempt. I'll break up this habit of going to sleep in daylight or I'll break the court."

Anne sat up in bed, awake at once, without any transition.

"What amuses you, Mary?"

She told Anne, then added, "Mr. Lincoln will love this story; he'll add it to his repertoire."

Anne gave her a piercing glance.

"You like Mr. Lincoln, don't you?"

". . . yes."

"More than the others?"

". . . I don't know. Perhaps." Her heart was pounding.

"I remember him. He certainly is . . ." she hesitated, a little perplexed, reaching for the word, ". . . outstanding."

"I'll admit he's not the prettiest man in the world," said Mary, "but he could make a great president."

Anne bounced out of bed. There were furrows between her eyebrows.

"Surely you wouldn't marry a man for just that!"

"Why would you marry your beau?" Mary was angry with herself for having pursued the subject.

Anne flushed. "I'm going to marry him because I love him; what else is marriage?"

"A way of life . . ." She was glad to hear her uncle David's voice calling to them. "We'd better go downstairs."

Her uncle David was the heartiest of all the Todds: a big talkative man who worked hard, ate, drank and slept hard, and had energy left over for a hundred enthusiasms. One of them was the Todd genealogy. After the supper dishes had been cleared and a big lamp set in the center of the table, he spread out his charts and gave Mary a guided tour through her ancestry, the spectacles caught between two humps in his nose, his short chubby fingers tracing their lines of descent back to Scotland in the year 1679, and to the first of the family who had settled in Pennsylvania in 1720.

"You've got some mighty good fighting men in your blood, Mary: your Covenanter ancestors fought the Duke of Monmouth and the established Church of England; your grandfather fought with General Washington, your granduncles fought with George Rogers Clark, not to mention all the young fellows who fought in the Indian Wars and the War of 1812. But fighters isn't all we have: here's one who was first civil governor of Illinois, another was territorial governor of Michigan, another governor of Pennsylvania. We've had lots of other peaceable folk too, but all important in their day: clergymen, educators, senators, judges . . ."

As her uncle rumbled on, her mind recalled the pained silences which had followed her questions to Abraham Lincoln about his background. He had spoken briefly of the Lincolns, though apparently he cared little about them: they had been Quakers originally, who migrated from Pennsylvania to Virginia and then westward to Kentucky. When it came to his mother's family he had sat in a chair with his head down, absorbed in a long chewed-up silence before saying hoarsely:

"They came from undistinguished families in Virginia . . . second families, I should say."

She caught herself up sharply. I'm behaving like a schoolgirl. No matter what happens, I apply it to Mr. Lincoln. By what right has he become my frame of reference? And to what end? Eliza Francis had told her that the few friendships he had had in New Salem had been with safely and serenely married women: Mrs. Bowling Green, who had helped him when he was troubled, Mrs. Jack Armstrong, who made shirts for him and mended his trousers.

"It's time to dress for the ball, Mary."

It was Anne, cutting into her reverie. The girls returned to their bedroom in the rambling two-story wood house. Mary had announced that she would remain for a limited time, but Columbia, a bustling county seat and tobacco center of some seven hundred people, thought differently; there were teas each afternoon, supper parties and now the fourth ball of the week in her honor, for Uncle David had spread the word that she was available for a permanent place in Missouri matrimony. She was being given an exhausting whirl by a half dozen young men, all new to the state and seeking wives.

The two girls dressed in their gowns of sheer white lawn. At eight o'clock they were driven to a brick home at the end of Broadway; the four downstairs rooms and two halls had been thrown open for the reception and dancing. The traditional Virginia reels were played, but much faster than Mary was accustomed to; she felt almost exhausted at the end of each cotillion. Her partner for the evening was a grandson of Patrick Henry, apparently Uncle David's first choice for her husband. David had told her on the afternoon of her arrival:

"Young Henry is an agreeable man and a fine lawyer. Honestly, Mary, I believe he surpasses his noble ancestor in talents. And I do think you should marry a lawyer, you have such a good head for politics."

"Why, Uncle David," she teased, "what happened to that dentist you promised me? I've been counting on him."

"The idiot refused to wait, upped and married just a week ago. But don't you worry, Mary, I've got a dozen fine prospects all strung out for you like nightshirts on a clothesline."

Mr. Henry obviously was smitten. After one of the dances Mary exclaimed, "I can't get over the excitement with which you run your reels. When I get back to Springfield . . ."

"Miss Mary, I simply cannot brook the mention of your return. Don't you like Missouri?"

How could she tell him, this pleasant man with the carrot-red hair and slightly bulging eyes, that she did not like being plunged back into a slave state; that once having lived in freedom the sight of slaves working the tobacco fields, and of their wooden shacks, was like traveling backward in time to another age?

She and Anne left the party at two o'clock, then she waited in the dark of the downstairs hall while her cousin stood outside the front door saying good night to her sweetheart. The girls discarded endless petticoats, brushed their hair, washed their faces with cold water and Boston soap. Anne burst into a romantic ballad.

"It's so glorious to love and be loved, Mary, I can't imagine why anyone should want to live without it."

For all her effervescence, Anne fell asleep the moment her face found its familiar niche in the pillow. Mary lay sleepless. Why indeed should anyone want to live without love? Surely she had never wanted to. She had watched her schoolmates at Mentelle's fall in love with love, and she had set herself resolutely against any such romanticism. She had only one life and one love; she wanted to use them wisely and well. That did not mean she would not one day love as tenderly, yes and as passionately as any of her more sentimental friends; her hand would never be given where her heart was not.

But where was her heart? Not for an instant had it been possible for the music or the gaiety of vivacious Columbia to crowd out Abraham. She was amazed at the tenacity of his hold upon her. Do I love him? she asked herself. It had not been love at first sight, nor even fifteenth sight; her emotions had grown slowly.

Why? What were Abraham's qualities that she should love him? His honesty? A lot of people were honest, in fact nearly everyone she knew. His simplicity? By itself this would not be important; lots of simple people were dull. His courage? A common commodity on the frontier, possessed in as great quantity by Stephen Douglas as by Abraham Lincoln. Physical strength? Brutes also had physical strength. Spirituality? Not in the accepted sense, for he had not been in a church more than a dozen times. Humor? Some of it was good, though frequently of the barnyard type, but rarely was it subtle or intellectual. Profundity? He had little education or disciplined training. Personality, charm, sparkle, magnetism? There were a dozen men in Springfield and a hundred in Lexington who could outcharm and outscintillate him on ten seconds' notice. Incorruptibility? Perhaps, but as yet with little opportunity to prove itself. Humility? God knew he had enough to be humble about!

Whatever Abraham's qualities, certainly no other young lady in Springfield had caught sight of them. Yet there was something unmistakable there: the Clary's Grove boys had recognized it; the Black Hawk War recruits recognized it; the Illinois Whigs recognized it. Her cousin John Stuart had recognized it. Leadership? What did that mean? That he had learned how to handle, bargain, compromise, control? Many men led who should have been in the rear ranks.

As she lay quietly, watching the leaves of the sycamores and birch with the moon shining upon them, she asked herself the most difficult question of all: Does Abraham love me? If I love, will my love be returned?

He was a man who had been frightened by love. "Love destroys," he had said.

But all that was past. He called her Molly, often with affection. When he was tired or sad or discouraged he had made his way to her sympathetic company. He enjoyed being with her, admired the way she spoke, the manner in which her mind worked. True, he had disappeared for days, and when she left Springfield he had said he would miss her, yet there had been no letter from him, only a scrawled greeting on a copy of *The Old Soldier* he had sent.

Yet she had learned many things about him over the months: he went to no other young lady's house in Springfield, he had danced with no one but her at the cotillion; and when he had confided to her, "I would hate to leave the world without having made it a little better place to live in," he had really bared his innermost thoughts. . . .

She would have to judge carefully . . . both herself and Abraham.

2

SHE returned to Springfield on a sunny first of September and talked to Elizabeth of her visit while she hung away her clothes. Her uncle David had been disappointed at her leaving; he had believed she would stay. At the good-bye supper Anne had given for her, many of the young people had placed bets that she would return.

When Elizabeth left to attend a meeting of the Episcopal Sewing Society, Mary slipped into a light blue muslin, rolled up the sleeves, got her garden shears and went out to cut the roses that were growing so profusely beneath her bedroom window. She had gathered about two dozen fragrant blooms when she heard a staccato step coming around the banjo drive, and looked up to see the broad-grinning face of Stephen Douglas.

"Mary, I just this instant heard you were back. Springfield has been a dull place without you. Welcome home!"

She was delighted by the heartiness of his greeting. His lips touched her cheek.

"Steve, it's wonderful to see you again. Even if you did give us a trouncing in the legislature election."

"Oh, you heard about that all the way west in the wilds of Missouri, did you?" His chest puffed out with pride. "That's only half the story, Miss Henry-Clay-Whig-from-Kentucky: we're also going to beat you for the presidency."

She refused to be drawn into an argument.

"Will there be something good for a deserving Democrat, Steve?"

He ran his fingers agitatedly through his long bushy hair.

"There'd better be! I've been campaigning for so many months I'm flat busted broke; in fact I'm being sued for debt." He jingled a few coins in his trousers pocket. "Seems like I still got a few cents left; what do you say we walk down to Watson's confectionery?"

She had been interlacing the stems of her roses.

"I'd love to, Steve, but you must let me put a garland of roses on your head."

They laughed together heartily as she rounded the wreath and placed it on his enormous head; then they set off arm in arm. They reached the square, oblivious to the raised eyebrows. She commented on the interesting changes that had taken place during the past two months: Wallace and Diller had hung a huge eagle over the drugstore as an advertisement; there were dozens of buildings under construction; Grimsley and Levering's store had a display of materials in from Philadelphia, Baltimore and New Orleans, as beautiful as anything she had seen in the Lexington shops.

It did not take them long to eat an ice, nor yet to walk back to the Edwards house. When Mary bade Stephen *au revoir* she found Elizabeth and Ninian in the parlor, pleased looks on their faces.

"We've already had three callers," said Elizabeth; "women who saw you downtown, arm in arm, Stephen wearing your garland of roses, having such a wonderful time . . ."

"We're just good friends who enjoy each other."

"Oh." Elizabeth's voice had gone flat. "We thought perhaps you had decided . . . while in Columbia . . ."

When Mary's expression remained unchanged, Elizabeth dropped into a black satin chair. Ninian went to his cigar box, lighted a cigar and puffed noisily on it. Elizabeth tried again.

"But you do like him, Mary? Given time, it could turn into love?"

"No, Liz, it never could. My feelings are no different from what they were three years ago, when I first met him here."

"Why do you say it never could?" Elizabeth rose, stood over her. "Why have you closed your mind against him? He's a fine man and he's going far. You are the right woman to help him. You could have a good life . . ."

"There are some people who are not meant to love each other. Perhaps they're too much alike, as Stephen and I are; perhaps there's no strong current between them . . . as a man and a woman. Besides . . ."

"Yes?" Elizabeth had caught the change in her tone.

"I love someone else."

"You love someone else! Who is it?"

". . . Mr. Lincoln."

There was a silence.

"That's impossible," cried Elizabeth. "He's the last man in the world for you to love."

"Not the last, Liz, the first: first and only."

"But when could this have happened? You were away several months . . . you haven't seen him since you've been back . . ."

She smiled. "I guess it's been happening ever since that first moment he dropped into my life . . . through the trap door in the ceiling of the courtroom."

"Dropped straight from heaven, eh?" Ninian's voice had a cutting edge of sarcasm. "Well, you won't find him an angel."

"I wouldn't want an angel, Ninian. I want a man. You'll not deny that he's a man?"

"I don't need to deny or affirm anything: I simply say that I wouldn't want him in the family."

She saw that Ninian was angry. She went to his side.

"Forgive me, Ninian: you know that I love you and respect your opinion. Then tell me one thing: why is it that you accept Mr. Lincoln for yourself, as a leader of your party, but reject him to lead me . . . to happiness."

"He's a good state-level politician," pronounced Ninian, "but he'll never go beyond that. He has no real ambition; he lives poorly, won't mix with the right people and doesn't know how to set up his business so it will return him the fees he has legitimately earned. He cares nothing for the good things of life, Mary: clothes, a carriage, a home . . ."

"But, Ninian, these limitations belong to his stumbling and difficult youth. He can go as far as any other man, farther than most."

"Why should you be drawn to the man who has the least to offer you?" There was considerable pain in her sister's voice.

"Because that is the one to whom I have the most to give. Oh, Liz, I know it's best in all things to be practical; but shouldn't I have faith in my own judgment? And gifts?"

The late summer flies were buzzing at the windows; there was a heavy smell of honeysuckle in the house. Elizabeth's manner became quiet, patient.

"Mary, it's not that we dislike Mr. Lincoln or have any prejudice against him, but only that we're sure he's the wrong man for you. He might be right as rain for some other girl, but think of the differences in your background. He's a plebeian."

"That may be true, but again I say it's the past you're talking about. I don't intend to live the past. We will make our own future."

"Since when does the future not emerge from the past?"

"These differences you speak of, they are the accidents of circumstance." She was hurt now and she could feel the two red spots flaming on her forehead. Her voice became hoarse. "His parents were poor . . . they lived on frontiers where there were no good schools . . . he had to work from the time he could lift an ax. Cousin John Stuart says he has a natural mind; and look how far he has come already, in spite of his disadvantages! I don't agree with what you say about his being lazy, without taste or ambition. It's simply that he has lacked opportunities for polish, what we Todds call culture. Well then, I've had those opportunities . . ." One corner of her lip turned up slightly. "I'm a highly polished Todd. Why wouldn't I be the best of all possible helpmeets for a man like Abraham Lincoln? You once called him a rough diamond, Liz; but remember the diamond is the most precious of all stones."

"And you will do the polishing?"

"I have the training. I have the love. I can give him the background he needs: a beautiful home . . . ," the Houghan house came into her mind, "filled with books, music . . . the proper entertainment for the proper people. He has his talents, Ninian has admitted them; I have mine. Why shouldn't they be wedded?"

". . . wedded? Then Mr. Lincoln has asked you to marry him?"

". . . No."

From the way the blood drained from her face they saw that she was vulnerable. Elizabeth studied her eyes as a mother would.

"Mary, has he told you that he loves you?"

She turned away, unable to speak.

"Then how can you presume . . . go so far in your mind?"

"Because he does love me; he has told me so in a thousand ways. . . ."

She did not intend to cry, and she had no advance knowledge that she would, but now she felt her strength spent. The tears came. Elizabeth took her in her arms, stroked her hair.

"Darling, you're not to be unhappy. We had to be honest with you. We'll not oppose Mr. Lincoln openly; you are to invite him to the house just as often as you like. . . . The more you see him the less likely you are to remain in love."

3

NO one in town had the slightest notion where Abraham Lincoln might be, so she was obliged to go to the *Sangamo Journal* to find out. Eliza Francis had abandoned all hope of living at home and had moved a cookstove, table and cot into the printing office. Simeon was turning out not only the *Journal* but the weekly *Old Soldier* and hundreds of political pamphlets with which the Whigs were attempting to inundate the state. Still smarting from their defeat in the state legislature, Simeon was more than ever determined to bring Illinois in for General Harrison.

"We've got an excellent chance, too," he said, leaning wearily against his press while Eliza stood with her capacious back to them, cooking a broth. "After twelve muddled years under Jackson and Van Buren, the whole country is crying for a change. The committee didn't want Abraham to waste his time canvassing southern Illinois, they've always been pro-slave and pro-Democrat, but he's getting results."

So that's where he is, she thought, down in Little Egypt, talking his heart out to people who don't want to hear him. No wonder he couldn't write letters!

"Simeon, could I help?"

"My girl, you're hired. Suppose you address these boxes of *The Old Soldier*, then you can go through this file of out-of-state papers and shear the good articles for us to reprint."

She took off her gray wool cloak, pushed up the cuffs of her walking dress and pitched in. Abraham's chances of being sent to the Senate, or even of being elected Speaker of the legislature had gone glimmering with the Democratic majority, but if he proved the key figure in carrying Illinois for Harrison surely he would play a role in the new federal government?

Each morning she rose at seven, had coffee and fruit, then went into the north bedroom which had been cleared of furniture and equipped with tables loaded with bolts of flannels, linens, silks; ribbons, laces, thread, tape, cords, needles, patterns. The winter sewing had not yet been started; there were warm wool bonnets, coats and dresses as well as flannel underclothes to be made for the children, new curtains and a bedcover against the impending visit of Cyrus Edwards, Ninian's uncle, and his daughter Matilda. Elizabeth had expressed a desire for a full-skirted merino with a cape, in addition to which Mary wanted to make herself some warm winter dresses with lined skirts. Each day she measured, cut, basted, fitted and stitched until noon, then after dinner she went down to the *Journal* to work with the Francises. Every few days they received a clipping from Lincoln, and occasionally a comment on his progress; thus she was able to follow his itinerary.

Despite her tremendous busyness and the sense of expectancy for the future, the passage of the days and weeks involved considerable strain. If only there were some way of knowing what was in Abraham's mind!

At the end of September she stood up at the wedding of her friend Martha Jane Lowry to Sidney Abell. Mary had designed and made Martha Jane's gown of changeable silk that shimmered from gold to blue. The ceremony took place at seven-thirty in the evening because the bridal couple wanted to catch the ten o'clock stage for Chicago. After the ceremony they sat down to the wedding supper of cold boiled ham, prairie chicken, beaten biscuit and Mr. Watson's bridal cake topped by a miniature bride with a flowing veil and orange blossoms.

Mary returned home as happy as she was exhausted. This was exactly the kind of gay wedding she envisaged for herself and Abraham. But she would prefer a ten o'clock service in church, then a noon bridal dinner. She had no desire to go to Chicago or St. Louis on her honeymoon as most Springfield couples did; she wanted to go east to New York, Philadelphia, Boston, the great cities she had read about since she was a child.

She was having evening supper with Elizabeth and Ninian when she noticed that they were studying her with surreptitious glances. She laid down her fork.

"Is something wrong?"

"Then you don't know that Mr. Lincoln is back?" blurted Elizabeth.

A flame shot through her.

". . . when . . . did he return?"

"Early yesterday."

Despite her effort to conceal her feelings from their unsympathetic gaze, her eyes misted. He had been home two full days and had not let her know! Ninian's voice was speaking to her from across the table; she had not heard the opening phrase.

". . . protect you." Her mind cleared. "We don't want to see you embarrassed, or worse yet to waste your years and opportunities. If the man had any sense of the fitting and proper, if he had the requisite feelings of delicacy about you and your relationship, could he possibly be so . . . indifferent?"

"It's his . . . way. A dozen times before when he has been out of town he has waited several days . . ."

87

"Mary, how can you expose yourself to being in love with a man who has never indicated that he cares for you?"

"He cares for me." Her eyes were lowered, her voice hard, resolved.

Elizabeth flashed her husband a reproving shake of the head.

"Of course he does, my dear. You would not have given yourself to love had you not seen it in return."

That night and another whole day went by without a word from Mr. Lincoln. She knew that if she went to the *Journal* office and continued her work she would encounter him there; but in her mind she was past accepting an encounter. Mr. Lincoln must come to her.

He did. At seven the next morning, with Elizabeth and Ninian still asleep after their return from Belleville late the night before. She had on a flannel long-sleeved, high-necked robe, old and a little faded, but warm against the early morning chill of the rooms. Her hair was pushed hastily on top of her head with combs. She was in the hall, a half-finished cup of coffee in her hand, about to ascend to the sewing room, when she heard the uncertain knocking of the front clapper. She opened the door.

There he stood, thin, hollow-cheeked, seedy. They gazed at each other across the threshold of silent and separate months. At length she murmured:

"Well, the absent Mr. Lincoln. To what do I owe the honor of this matutinal call?"

"Matutinal? Oh, it is early morning, isn't it?"

"Rather! Have you had your breakfast?"

"No, I didn't come for that . . ."

"I didn't assume you did, but you shall have some anyway. Does this robe and hairdress frighten you? I could change, if you'd like to wait."

"Don't bother; you couldn't look any worse than I do."

"Now that's what I call backing into a compliment," she replied dryly. "Just the kind of thing I've been waiting all summer to hear."

His eyes looked flagellated. She took pity on him.

"Enough of this joy of reunion; come into the dining room and I'll have Bertha bring you breakfast. It looks as though you haven't had anything to eat since I saw you last June."

"I swallowed a lot of things, including political jibes," he replied, "but you couldn't properly call them food: greasy side meat, soggy saleratus biscuits, ill-smelling coffee made from parched corn, breakfast the remains of supper. What we politicians won't do for votes."

Now she was all contrition. She went into the kitchen, asked Bertha if she would please prepare the biggest possible breakfast for Mr. Lincoln, and brought him a cup of hot coffee to tide him over. A little color came into his cheeks as he sipped the excellent Edwards coffee imported from Havana. She sat in silence while the cook brought in hot platters of ham and venison steak, eggs, biscuits and a bowl of honey. She watched him wolf the food.

He was finishing when Elizabeth and Ninian came downstairs. Ninian forgot that he was greeting a potential brother-in-law, demanding news of the

Whig progress down around Cairo. Mary seized the opportunity to change into a starched cotton and to comb her hair, tying it back with a wide ribbon. When she returned downstairs she found Mr. Lincoln alone in the sitting room, sprawled comfortably in a big rocker. He said with his first easy smile of the morning:

"I would have come sooner but I was too tired to live. I looked forward to waking to it . . . and this morning I did."

"Then I'm glad you came."

"How did you pass your summer in Missouri, Molly?"

She warmed to the use of the pet name.

"Oh, I took the world easy."

"Quite an accomplishment, in so hard a world." He reached over and took her hand. "Your hands are so soft and beautifully shaped. I did miss you . . . though I never wrote. Simeon told me how hard you worked for the election. I was proud."

She was flustered at the two compliments. She let her hand rest in his bony fingers.

"I always helped Father during the Whig campaigns at home. I'm sorry, Abraham, about the Democrats winning such a large majority in the legislature, but you were re-elected . . ."

"With the smallest number of votes of any Whig. This is probably the last time I'll make it. The country folks are beginning to think I've become big city, but the big city still thinks I'm country."

There was no despondency in his voice, only a matter-of-factness. Nevertheless she rushed to his defense.

"Isn't eight years quite enough in a state legislature, Abraham? It's time you moved up to the national scene. And you will, after Harrison's election."

He described the more amusing aspects of barnstorming: the small-town taverns that were little more than high frame sheds, with three double beds in each room, the snoring so loud that he made no attempt to sleep, reading Burns and Shakespeare all night by the light of a wavering wind-blown candle, his legs sticking out of the short beds from the knees down. Then he asked her to tell him what she had observed of the election in Missouri.

She organized the materials in her mind and gave him an analysis of what she deduced locally and from the national press. He watched her with wide glowing eyes, not knowing that she had been steeped in just such clinical analysis at her father's dinner table.

When she stopped, he leaned across the space between them and gripped her shoulders.

"Molly, you are the most beautiful talker I've ever known. It's like pages read aloud from a book. If only I could talk that way when I'm up before crowds."

"Abraham, you come from a lonely background: the log cabin in the woods with the nearest neighbor miles away, the days spent solitary in the forest with your ax, with no one to talk to but yourself and the trees. I come from a highly convivial background where there were always many people around: twenty in a house, thirty in a classroom, fifty at a cotillion . . ." she chuckled, then added, "all talking at once."

He shook his head soberly.

"Molly, why is it you're the only young lady I feel comfortable with? Only one I ever have, for that matter."

"Perhaps it's because we're friends."

He peered at her for a moment. The room was still, the world locked out.

"It's more than that," he said; "but I know so little of what lies beyond friendship. . . ."

Then again their lips were sealed, as tightly and as mysteriously as they had been on the front porch in June before they had gone their separate ways. She could not think, not while Abraham had his arms crushing her to him, but she knew what she felt: that this was good, and right, and forever.

Slowly, reluctantly he unlocked his lips from hers, eased the crush of his embrace, moved back slightly though without releasing her, and looked at her with glazed, awe-filled eyes.

"Is that . . . what I meant . . . we're in love?"

4

SHE awakened early, watching the bright rays of the October sunlight lay across the coverlet. She thought how much she would like to give a big party and let the whole world know of their engagement, plan her trousseau, buy their home and furnish it. But as she had explained to her father in Lexington when he had been upset over the news of Frances's sudden marriage, it was not the custom in Springfield to announce engagements or to fix wedding dates.

She jumped out of bed, gaily humming the words of "It Was a Dream, 'Twas a Dream," and sat in her nightgown before the mirror. She thought, I'm prettier now than I've ever been in my life. My eyes seem to be larger, my skin is clear and glowing, my hair is alive, easy to do things with. But I must stop using that scented oil on my brush: it's darkening my hair too much. Abraham may like it lighter. I must ask him.

She slipped into a dressing gown and went down to breakfast and a new world.

Abraham arrived promptly at noon. She smiled as he unnecessarily ducked his head while coming in the front door, a protective habit that had become ingrained during his years of entering log cabins. He was freshly shaved, smelled pleasantly of cologne water, his hair was cut, washed and plastered immaculately back, his suit had been pressed and the white muslin shirt lightened the darkness of his skin.

She put her mouth up to be kissed. He kissed her full on the lips but did not put his arms about her, for they were behind his back. When he had taken his lips from hers he murmured:

"You're beautiful this morning."

"Thank you, Abraham. I might say as much for you."

"Well, Molly, in the matter of looking at one another I have altogether the advantage."

"Not true: love agrees with both of us."

He brought his arms forward, proffering a small package.

"Mr. Diller said you'd like this lavender water; just came off the *Great Western* that docked at New York from England."

"Why, darling, thank you. That was a sweet thought. I have no gift for you. I haven't even been out of the house."

He hunched down almost to her level and whispered against her ear:

"Except the rarest gift of all. . . . Molly, I am not a demonstrative man: when I feel the most deeply I can express the least. But one thing I want you to know; you are the only woman I have ever loved."

After a moment she said:

"I shall wear that golden sentence around my heart."

Dinner was only a little constrained; the men assured each other of Harrison's victory and the value of a Whig administration in Washington. Mary sat quietly.

Afterward she and Abraham took a long walk, heading south into the brilliantly colored autumnal woods, making a wide circle about the town and coming at length to the Houghan estate. She remembered that he had been marking trails while she had gone through the rooms. Dr. Houghan was out, but a servant made them welcome. Mary pointed out the flow of the rooms into each other, the fine detail of the cabinetwork, the wonderful windows bringing in the light and air, how symmetrically the house had been designed. In her enthusiasm she failed to notice that he was growing glum.

"It's mighty big; must have cost a fortune."

"Not necessarily: good taste and design cost no more than bad."

She slipped her hand into his and led him to a front window which overlooked the graceful porch and the forest beyond.

"My dear, might I tell you something? You won't think me forward? My mother, when she died, willed me eighty acres of farm land in Indiana. It comes to me when I . . . marry." She rushed on quickly, not looking directly at him. "Father says the land has increased in value; it should be worth about as much now as this house with its fifteen acres. It will be . . . my dowry."

He was silent, his eyes downcast. She hoped she had not offended him; all girls of good family carried a dowry, and what harm could there be in telling her fiancé about the *dot* she would bring to their marriage? When he raised his head she saw that he was not offended; in fact there was a quizzical humor about his lips.

"Molly, I've never even owned the bed I slept in, let alone the room or house. To jump from half a borrowed bed to a mansion . . ."

"It's not a mansion, just a brilliantly conceived house. As for the jump, I'll agree it's a long one, but only because it's so terribly overdue. After all, you're past thirty, a leader of our party, and one of the best lawyers in the state. You could have afforded a home of your own before this if you had wanted it."

"With the national debt still hanging over me?"

She smiled a bit plaintively.

"I've had good training in the running of a home. I'll manage it just as economically as your income requires."

"What income?" he interrupted. "With John Stuart in Washington and me away politicking the past six months, our practice has vanished. I have fewer cases for the next circuit court session here in Springfield . . ."

"But both you and Cousin John are building for your future. Your political career earns you new friends, and your law practice will benefit accordingly."

"Now, Molly, if I owned a palatial estate like this, the Democrats would really be able to call me an aristocrat." His eyes were laughing at her. "They'd pull up the blinds of my parlor the way I pulled up Colonel Taylor's vest in the public square. Besides, all young married couples go to a hotel to live for a year or two so the bride will have a period of freedom. Cheaper too, we could save money."

"I'll do as you wish, of course, but I so ardently don't want to begin our married life in a hotel. There's no . . . privacy. . . . I'm not frightened at the idea of undertaking the duties of a housewife; I'd most heartily welcome it."

His eyes roamed the woods about them, then settled on the trim wood structure of the Houghan house.

"But why do you want to start at the top, then have nowhere to go?"

"The Houghan house is by no means the top, it's only a temporary residence. In twenty years we'll be living in a much finer house, in fact the finest in the land, and we'll not have to buy or even rent it: people will pay us to live in it!"

Puzzled, he asked, "What house could that be?"

She broke into a radiant smile.

"The White House."

He joined her laughter.

"I assure you, Molly, my ambitions don't reach that high."

"Really? Didn't you aspire to the United States Senate at the age of thirty? Being the debt-ridden, black-futured tyro you have portrayed yourself, why should you not aspire to the presidency as well? The White House over the Senate is a difference of degree rather than kind."

He was amused but also flattered by her logic.

"It's too bad you weren't born a man, Mary Todd, you would have been a great lawyer, and could have aspired to the White House yourself."

It took a little effort, but she matched her tone to his bantering one.

"Since my being a woman is a *fait accompli*, I shall have to enter its portals on your arm. Do you mind?"

5

OCTOBER was a wonderful month for love. The air was transparent, the sun still carried warmth, the surrounding countryside was a mass of brown and purple foliage.

Each day after dinner she met him at the *Journal* office where they worked side by side on new issues of *The Old Soldier,* or she wrote letters for him. At four o'clock they joined the Pedestrian Club to go nutting or berrypicking. At dusk they gathered at a different person's house for a light supper of prairie hen with corn bread or biscuits and fall garden vegetables; frequently they went on to the Tippecanoe Singing Club which met in the big room above the *Journal.* All the young Whigs in town came to sing the "Song of Tippecanoe, or A Gourd of Hard Cider":

> In the White House, Van Buren may drink his champagne,
> And have himself toasted from Georgia to Maine;
> But we in log cabins, with hearts warm and true,
> Drink a gourd of hard cider t' old Tippecanoe.

Mary played the accompaniment on the piano for the thirty to forty young women who assembled each night, along with the hundred young men. Abraham was in consistently high spirits. Whatever disappointment he had suffered over the Democratic victory in the state legislature was made up by the tremendous ground swell for Harrison. He had few cases and fewer clients; when his politicking was over for the day he made directly for the Edwards house. If their being together so much was noticed at all it was ascribed to the excitement of the political campaign.

One day they rode with Ninian and Elizabeth to Major Elijah Iles's farm for the Fair of the Sangamon County Agricultural Society, where Ninian was proud to win Second Premium for his bull Reformer. Another time they went to the Menagerie and Circus, which was exhibiting the first giraffe and elephant ever seen in Springfield; the poor elephant had to walk all the way from town to town under a heavy blanket because if people saw him on the road they would not pay to come see him in the circus.

In their walks together Abraham made sure they did not pass the Houghan house. She never mentioned it again.

Many evenings they would sit before the fire in the Edwardses' parlor and read aloud from *Tam o'Shanter*, *Cotter's Saturday Night* and *Epistle to a Young Friend*. He liked books on history, particularly the stories of other elections, and she would read to him from these, though often he seemed more interested in the mind of the author than in the events of history. Once he commented quietly:

"That writer can compress the most words into the smallest ideas of any man I ever heard."

Another time when she had read an involved passage from Greek history and thought he would disapprove, he said: "No, no, you cannot fly a kite high unless you have a long string."

She found herself full of a simple coquetry: she slipped her hand into his, patted his arm, said things she knew would please him, took infinite pains with her clothes so that she would always seem new and lovely, used the graceful feminine gestures she had seen other girls use to attract men, and which she had disdained . . . until now, that she was in love.

He was happy in her company. There were no headaches, no bouts of the "hypo." Even when the weather turned sharply cold he, who had said he never once got warm from autumn to spring, had good color in his cheeks and seemed as comfortable as anyone else.

When she complimented him on his ever present thoughtfulness, he replied:

" 'Twasn't always so. Now that other Mary: once a party of us went on horseback to Bowling Green's. We came to a deep stream, and I rode on ahead while the other girls were being helped by their escorts. When she reproved me for my neglect, I told her that I knew she was smart enough to take care of herself. That night she told her sister that I was deficient in those little links which make up the chain of a woman's happiness."

"You just weren't in love, Abraham. You wouldn't let me half drown, would you?"

"Oh, Molly, indeed not! Back in 1830, when my family was emigrating to Illinois in a wagon drawn by two yoke of oxen, and we had foundered across the snow and ice of a prairie stream, I discovered we had left our dog on the opposite bank. It was growing dark and my father said I couldn't return for him. I pulled off my shoes and socks, waded across the icy stream, and returned with the shivering animal under my arm. I loved that bitch."

"Why, Abraham Lincoln, comparing me . . ."

Then she saw the twinkle in his eyes; he had told the story to watch her risibles.

He was a man of contradictions, that she found: the rustic manners against the innate breeding; the melancholy against the insistent humor; the awkward clumsiness against the fabulous strength; the sometime-ugliness against the sometime-attractiveness; the vagabond living against the ambition to rise; the buffoonery against the penetrating logic; the hunger for love against the shyness with women; the Democratic background against the Whig allegiance. He would ever be an extremely difficult man to unravel; no faint-hearted woman would survive marriage with him; but then, she thought, no fainthearted woman would have fallen in love with him.

How strange it was that, having planned to go to Washington City with her father if Henry Clay were elected, a Whig success could send her there with a husband instead. She looked forward to the possibility with joy; she would rent a fine home, entertain widely, gather the elite of the capital and of the international society centering there, create an atmosphere and background against which Abraham would stand forth like the tall shining beacon that he was.

When the time came for him to leave Springfield for the last pre-election campaign he bitterly hated to go. She saw how miserable he was and asked:

"Must you? Haven't you done everything you can over the months?"

"It'll only be for two weeks," he grunted. "I'll come back by way of Lawrence County and bring in their votes for recording. The fee is nineteen dollars . . . it will cover the cost of the trip."

Their farewell kiss was light and affectionate. As she watched him walk around the banjo drive and then down Second Street toward the town branch she thought:

When the election is over and he comes home, we will marry.

6

SPRINGFIELD went politics-mad; all business came to a standstill while both parties made their last frenzied drive to capture votes. The Whigs raised a big log cabin just south of the American House, and here Mary went every evening to hear speeches and exhortations.

By election day, November 2, she and her family and friends were in a state of jubilation, for swift-riding couriers from Pennsylvania and Ohio, where the vote had been cast on October 30, brought the news that these states had gone for Harrison. Within another two days word arrived that Maine and Vermont had gone Whig, as well as such southern Democrat strongholds as Kentucky, Tennessee and Georgia. With Springfield and the surrounding farms giving Harrison a heavy majority, it appeared that Illinois was safe for Harrison too; at last the Whigs would have their great victory.

But down at the *Journal* office a few days later, Simeon Francis was not at all the picture of the triumphant journalist.

"Simeon, what's the trouble? I heard at noon that we took Sangamon County by a two-to-one vote."

"Look at these charts, Mary. We're running a thousand votes behind in Illinois, with many of the pro-Democrat southern counties yet to be counted."

"Abraham spent weeks down there. He must have convinced . . . ?"

"Some, yes, but not enough. We needed a heavy majority in central and northern Illinois to offset the southern counties."

"But will that make a great deal of difference to us, so long as we have a Whig administration in Washington?"

Simeon Francis studied her face for a moment before saying, "I think I'd better let Abraham answer that one."

There was a silence in the printing shop in which the smells of strong black ink and fresh-milled paper dominated.

"Oh, then he has come back?"

"Last night."

She was in no way prepared for the sight that met her eyes when Mr. Lincoln walked into the Edwardses' parlor that evening. His skin was sallow, with a parchmentlike pattern of wrinkles about his eyes; the off-side dimple in his chin seemed to have deepened, giving his face an out-of-focus structure; his Adam's apple stuck out sharply; his thick, coarse black hair lay unkempt over his forehead, while his body sagged at the shoulders, waist and knees. But worst of all were his eyes: opaque, pain-fraught, the left eye high up in its socket in a tortuous imbalance.

She could have wept for him. She wanted to cradle him in her arms as would a protecting mother. Should she say kind and comforting words? Should she kiss the pain away from the dry lips? Was he sunk too low in apathy for humor?

"Well, Abraham, I see the hypo has got you. Where did you annex our charming friend, in Lawrenceville?"

His voice when it finally came was hoarse.

"No, all I picked up in Lawrenceville was ballots."

"With an asp in their midst, no doubt."

"Just Democrats. They carried the state. By less than two thousand votes, but still they carried it. A full year of my life thrown away, my debts piled higher than ever, my law practice gone . . . and Stephen Douglas has beat us again."

"I know. And I know you have a headache. I can tell it from your eyes. But surely that's no excuse for wallowing in self-pity?"

He sank into the sofa and sat with his arms hanging between his legs, clasped hands almost touching the floor.

"I suppose I deserve that."

She smiled sympathetically.

"Never mind about the just deserts. I was only trying to sting you back to life."

His misery so enveloped the room that she could no longer contain herself. She went to him and put an arm about his shoulders.

"Let me get some coffee . . . and food. Abraham, all you need is rest and fun, to get back your perspective. You're the man who in his very first speech in New Salem said to the voters, 'If in your wisdom you see fit to keep me in the background, I have been too familiar with disappointments to be very much chagrined.'"

He seemed to relax a little.

"It's more serious than you think: Stuart and I will have to dissolve our partnership . . . because there is so little law left for us to practice. In our first year we had sixty-six cases in the July term of the Sangamon County Court. In the session beginning Monday I have eighteen. Most of them to be continued, or dismissed."

"I'm sorry about Cousin Stuart. But both of you have been practicing . . . politics. You'll get a new partner. You'll get new clients. You're a good lawyer, you're the floor leader of the Whigs in the legislature . . ."

His body recoiled in a gesture of refusal.

"Do you know how much I have earned in the past six months? Mighty little, aside from the nineteen dollars paid to me by the state auditor for bringing in the returns from Lawrenceville."

She rose and brought him a cup of coffee from the urn in the kitchen, then stood before him and cried out:

"Abraham, for heaven's sake, where is your sense of humor? *Now* tell stories, now!" She mimicked the high, nasal voice in which he had once said to her, "Ever hear about the first time I was in the legislature? I stood up and tried to deliver a short speech. Three times I cried, 'Mr. Speaker, I conceive . . .' Finally someone in the audience called out, 'Mr. Speaker, the honorable gentleman has conceived three times and brought forth nothing.'"

A wickpoint of light appeared in his eyes, but in an instant the tiny flame went out. She stood for a moment in silence and defeat, then turned, walked out of the room and out of the house.

The following morning she dressed early and went to visit her sister Frances. At noon Dr. Wallace came in from his drugstore at No. 4 Hoffman's Row.

"William, what is the cause of hypochondria?"

The doctor rose, went to his glass-enclosed bookcase and took down one of his medical reference books, *Cyclopedia of Practical Medicine*.

"This book calls *hypochondriasis* a disease, but it's really only a nervous condition. Based largely on fear."

"Fear?" His use of the word had surprised her. "Fear of what?"

"Change it to anxiety: about security, success. An attack can be brought on by overwork, worry, setbacks." He handed her Volume II of the *Cyclopedia*. "Here, read for yourself, it's not too technical."

She settled down to read.

Hypochondriasis . . . a disease remarked by lowness of spirits and an apprehension of extreme danger from the most trifling ailments. Every function of life seems in a state of disorder, and the source of acute and almost perpetual suffering. Patients complain of severe and distressing headache with intolerance of light; pressure on the top of the head

97

threatens to extinguish consciousness; the head is as if squeezed in a vice, the eyes are felt as if starting out of the sockets. The patient suffers an intolerable anxiety, a sense of sinking, fainting, trembling, and apprehends that every minute may be his last. . . .

Dr. Wallace returned as she reached the section titled "Treatment." He glanced over her shoulder, then commented:

"The treatment is simple: it requires no foul-tasting medicines, bleeding, blistering or physicking; instead substitute good food, rest, companionship, laughter, love . . ."

"Love? Evidently that can be bitter medicine too, William. How do you persuade the patient to swallow it when he has his back teeth clamped down?"

She had no word from him for a number of days, then late one evening he appeared. She led him into the family sitting room. His body slumped forward on one leg.

"Mary, I've come to . . . break off . . . our . . . understanding. . . ."

"Break off!"

"Actually, I was a coward. I wrote you a long letter, but when I read it to Speed, he tore it up and threw it in the log fire. Said if I had the courage of manhood I must come tell you myself."

She was too stunned to face the significance of what he had said; she attacked his words tangentially.

"You discussed our relationship with Speed? Abraham, how could you?"

"Well, he is my friend, I needed help . . ."

"And I am not your friend?" Two spots of red were blazoned on her forehead.

". . . it's nothing you've done . . ."

"That's extremely kind," she replied tartly, "considering that all I've done is fall in love with you."

"You're twisting my words . . ."

"A fact which seemed to make you very happy in October, and now appears to be making you equally miserable in November. Which Mr. Lincoln shall I believe, the October Lincoln or the November Lincoln? Or will there be still a third one in December?"

He smiled wanly.

"Anger makes your tongue sharp, Mary."

"And hypochondria makes yours blunt. Because you have suffered a defeat do you want to crawl off somewhere and die?"

"Not die, just sleep through the winter, the way bears do."

"But I am not invited to the cave?" More quietly she asked: "Abraham, do you no longer love me?"

"I never said that. . . . Love's not for me. . . . I can't afford marriage . . ."

"Abraham, do you love me?" she persisted.

". . . yes."

Her eyes closed for a moment, she felt faint.

"I can't afford marriage; my prospects are poor."

"If I'm not frightened, why should you be?"

"Because the responsibility would be mine. I would never want to fail you."

"There are other more important ways not to fail a woman."

He winced, then continued in a high, querulous voice:

"In your world there is so much flourishing about in carriages. You would not have the means of hiding your poverty."

"I should certainly not try to hide it."

"Yes, Mary, you have your pride. But you have not been accustomed to hardship. When I think of that huge Houghan place you want so desperately . . ."

It was her turn to wince.

"I was willful about that. I was wrong to try to force it upon you."

"No, Mary," he cried, "you were right to speak your mind. You deserve just such a house. You have the proper background, culture, tradition . . ."

"Fiddlesticks! Let me decide for myself whether I want to be a snob."

He stretched out his hands, palms open, and raised them up and down slowly, as though trying to balance a heavy weight.

"I can't match you in words, Mary."

"Nor in love . . . ?"

"Mary, let me go. I am unhappy. I have uncertainties. I have nothing to offer you."

"If you love me, and still can say you have nothing for me, then it *is* better that we part."

She walked past him to the front door.

"You are free, my dear."

She opened the door without looking at him.

"Good-bye, Abraham."

"Good-bye, Mary."

He took a step toward the porch, hesitated, half turned to face her. And then they were in each other's arms. She heard him say:

"Forgive me, Molly. I didn't mean it. I have everything to offer you . . . all my love . . ."

The hard, dry tension within her snapped. She had not known the intensity of her own strain. She half collapsed in his arms.

7

THEIR relationship was never quite the same as it had been during the idyllic weeks of October. Yet in some ways their love had deepened, intensified because they had caused each other pain.

Because she had spent so many evenings dressing for him, then sitting alone through supper and huddled in the big chair in the parlor until the clock struck nine and she knew he was not coming, they had agreed that he would take Sunday dinner with her and that he would come visiting on Wednesday and Saturday evenings. However, the first Wednesday in December he sent a note that he would not be able to come that evening; and an identical note arrived late Saturday afternoon. When he finally appeared on Sunday for dinner, he explained:

"I've been lobbying."

"Lobbying? What might that be?"

"It's an informal club we have, meets in the lobby of the new state house. Members of the Senate and House get together there. We appoint mock committees and have tremendous debates: get all the things off our mind that we're too polite or constrained to say when the House and Senate are actually meeting. I am a member of the Committee on Etiquette, Politeness and Ceremony."

"They couldn't have chosen a better man," she said acidly.

"We've practically put the faro banks, roulettes and coffee rooms out of business," he continued, ignoring her aside. "We satirize all the silly bills presented in both houses. Makes a lot of fellows behave while we're in session."

"I can see what purpose it serves and how much fun it might be," she commented, "but it looks as though I'm going to have to get myself elected to the legislature to see you once in a while."

Prior to their quarrel the feeling of impending marriage had been substantial between them. Now it seemed to have vanished, as though Abraham were reconciled to being in love but had put the idea of marriage out of his mind.

With the legislature open, the town once again was filled with representatives and their families from all over the state, in addition to many attorneys and businessmen who foregathered for the special bills they hoped to promote. The social life of Springfield gathered momentum. There were dinner parties and dances scheduled for nearly every night in the week. To her amazement Abraham refused to accompany her.

"I'll be proud to take you to the cotillion at the American House on

December tenth," he said; "that's for the whole legislature; but these other parties, that's too much society for me, I'm not used to it."

"It's easy enough to get used to," she said appealingly. "All these good people want you there. Suppose I pick out half of the affairs that mean the most to me, the others we'll discard. Is that a fair compromise . . . or would I have a better chance if I came down to the lobby tonight and appealed my case?"

He grinned: she could always have her way with him when she fastened him on a point of wit.

Icy winds swept the prairies. Elizabeth came down with a heavy cold. Mary put her to bed. When she took a tray upstairs she found Elizabeth reading a long letter from their cousin Mary Virginia Stuart, who had accompanied her husband John to Washington for his second term of Congress.

"Mary," exclaimed Elizabeth, "did you know that Mr. Lincoln is ill?"

"Ill?" Her eyes began ranging the room. "But with what? I saw him only yesterday."

"It seems that he has begged Cousin Stuart to get Dr. Henry the postmastership here in Springfield on the ground that he needs him desperately."

"Oh, that . . . that's his hypochondria. Dr. Henry talks him out of it every few days."

"And why didn't you tell me about going to Bogotá?"

"Bogotá? Where's that?"

"In Colombia . . . Central America. Cousin Stuart sends word that he'll do everything in his power, as soon as President Harrison is inaugurated, to get Mr. Lincoln appointed *chargé d'affaires* down there."

Mary flushed.

"You mean he never told you he wanted to go?"

When she left Elizabeth's room she sent a note to Abraham asking him to meet her at the earliest possible moment at the picture gallery that had just opened in Caffield's new building on the south side of the square. She dressed hurriedly in a warm wool dress and gaiter boots, put a claret-colored scarf about her neck and waded against the high cold winds as though they were breaking waves. At Caffield's she paid her twenty-five cents admission, walked into the big wood-paneled room and was so delighted with Correggio's *The Holy Family in Egypt*, Albano's *Judgment of Paris*, and Graciano's *Diana and Nymphs* that her uneasiness vanished. She forgot why she had come.

She was standing before a huge canvas called *Coronation of Queen Victoria, June 28, 1838*, at the far end of the hall when she felt him close behind her. Without turning her head, she said:

"Do you like paintings? This is as good a collection as ever we had in Lexington."

He had not even glanced at the pictures. She turned. His eyes were asking why she had sent for him.

"So you are planning to see the world?"

"Oh . . . Bogotá. Then you've heard?"

"By the circuitous route of Washington. *Habla Español?*"

"I didn't mention it because I was convinced Stuart couldn't get the post for me."

"How humble you've become: last summer you were dreaming of the United States Senate; now you're aspiring to some dead-alive hole in the jungle."

"It's a competence."

"Since when have you been unable to make a living?" Indignation flared into her voice. She waited for a moment to gain control over herself. "I've conquered my temper in everything except where you're concerned. When I see you quaking in your mud-splattered boots, all six feet four of you, after I had long since decided that you have the finest talent and future of any man I've met . . . what kind of an idiot does that make me?"

"Pulling my long leg, Molly?"

"Oh, Abraham, how can you think of running? What would you have to come back to four or eight years from now?"

"I'd be coming out the same hole I went in at," he said wanly.

"What about your political career?"

"Gone. I'm mousing around for something to fill the future."

"You haven't said yet whether you intended to take me to Bogotá, but I want you to know that I'd go to purgatory with you if I thought it would serve your purpose. I'd refuse to go to heaven with you if I thought it would hurt your future."

Her figure of speech amused him.

"That's blackmail, Molly; you know I couldn't go to Central America without my most ardent admirer. But I *was* running, wasn't I?" The darkness in his eyes dissipated. "Reminds me of one day during the Black Hawk War when we had a brisk skirmish. I got into camp late at night and somebody called out, 'Abe, is that you? Thought you were killed.' 'Yes,' I said, 'this is me—ain't killed either.' 'But where have you been all this time? Didn't run away, did you?' 'No,' I said, 'I don't think I ran away; but I reckon if anybody had seen me going, and had been told I was going for a doctor, he would have thought somebody was almighty sick.'"

She heard his story eagerly.

"Well, thank the Lord: our Richard is himself again!"

His eyes swept the exhibition hall, saw that no one was present. He kissed her once, hard, then released her:

"You're entirely right, Molly. Those horrid doubts had put a damp on my spirit. Bogotá is gone . . . back into its jungle."

8

TOWARD the end of November, Cyrus Edwards, Ninian's uncle, arrived from Alton to take his newly won place in the House: he had come to Springfield determined that the legislature would elect him to the United States Senate. He declined his nephew's offer of hospitality, saying that he would have more freedom to campaign in a hotel room, but he did leave his twenty-year-old daughter Matilda with them to share Mary's room and bed. Matilda was tall and long-legged, in the tradition of her father and Ninian, with corn-blond hair which she wound in a braid around the top of her head.

"She's come to Springfield to find a husband," practical-minded Elizabeth told Mary. "I'm going to give a dinner party for her."

A hundred guests attended, the entire unmarried set of Springfield. The furniture had been removed from the downstairs rooms. After the guests had dined an orchestra took up its position at the rear of the entrance hall. Abraham had come early.

Matilda was the belle of the party, dressed in a tightly laced bouffant black and purple satin, her shoulders bare. Mary remained in the background; she was in high spirits, her face and eyes aglow, her repartee fast and witty. She played Elizabeth's Chinese-red piano when the party wanted to sing, and sang duets with Stephen Douglas.

Without meaning to she garnered a new admirer. His name was Edwin Webb, a short, stocky, prosperous lawyer and legislator from Carmi, descendant of a fine Virginia family, recently widowed and with two small children. His features were blunt, he had a sharp tongue in controversy, but his clothes as well as his manners were elegant. He refused to leave her side, and though he was an old friend of Mr. Lincoln's, made a point of entering into direct competition with him.

Having brought hot rum drinks into the music room for the three of them, and being refused by Lincoln, he asked:

"Wouldn't you like to get drunk just once to see how it seems?"

"Wouldn't that be like sticking your big toe out and letting a rattlesnake bite it just to see how it seems?" retorted Lincoln.

Mr. Webb reached into his vest pocket, pulled out an enormous cigar and handed it to Abraham, saying, "All right then, have a smoke for yourself."

"Thank you, I have no vices."

Mr. Webb took a ruminative pull at his hot rum, his eyes studying the contents of the cup, then decreed:

"It's my experience that men with no vices have plaguey few virtues!"

Lincoln burst into delighted laughter. The orchestra began a waltz. Mr.

103

Webb put down his cup, took Mary by the arm and was whirling her about before she had a chance to open her mouth.

"Miss Mary, I hear you have an understanding with Mr. Lincoln."

Oh, then the town had guessed.

"Don't be hasty. There are other fish in the sea." He shook his head up and down vigorously, his lips pursed in affirmation, as though he were living proof of the point.

"Why, Mr. Webb, I've met you at three or four parties in the past weeks, and you've never noticed me. Besides, that double-width mourning band on your arm: isn't its purpose to tell us girls that we can't make it?"

"Yes, it is . . . or it was, until I got my first clear look at you tonight. I have decided that I shall court you."

"Now then, this party is for Matilda; she's the one you're supposed to court. Even Mr. Lincoln says she has a perfect face."

"Excellent! We'll let Lincoln court Miss Matilda. I assure you, Miss Mary, you're getting the best of this swap. That man's man doesn't know how to appreciate a woman; he ought to marry Joshua Speed and set up housekeeping above the store."

Mary's eyes roamed the room, found Abraham standing in the middle of a group of gesturing, laughing men. She threw back her head and laughed heartily.

The day before Christmas she was shopping in the square when she came across him unexpectedly. The evening before they had been together at the biggest party Springfield had ever seen, a dinner for three hundred and fifty guests given at the Walters'. He had muttered under his breath: "Springfield certainly is becoming a city of dashers. Will you look at the satin and feathers. These ladies must have been kept busy for months making all these dresses."

A smile lighted his face when he saw her; he took her arm, held it to his side and said plaintively:

"Molly, I'd give practically anything I own to spend a quiet evening with you again. It's a long time since we sat before the fire and you read to me from Burns or Shakespeare, and we had a good talk."

"Then we shall have it this very evening."

"Aren't we s'posed to go to supper at the Bakers'?"

"I'll send our regrets; Elizabeth and Ninian are taking Matilda, so we'll have the house to ourselves. What would you like for supper?"

"I don't know one food from another, Molly, even when I'm chewing it. Always loved apples."

She had the cook prepare a roast beef, and had chilled oysters ready to serve in the living room. He arrived with a package in his coat pocket and the warmest embrace she had known in many days. When she told him so, he replied:

"If that's what you like, why don't we stay home more often? We can't go about doing this at dinner parties for three hundred and fifty." He handed her a box. "I know I shouldn't be giving you your Christmas present until tomorrow, but . . ."

She opened the box and found in it a coral necklace with a coral bracelet to match. She admired the depth of the color.

"Put them on me."

First he clasped the bracelet on her wrist, then stood behind her and secured the necklace. His arms were about her and his cheek on hers. She turned easily in his arms and kissed him.

"Abraham, you shouldn't have spent so much money when you don't have any to spend. But I'm happy you did. Is it silly of me to think that it proves you love me?"

After dinner they sat before the fire. He had brought along a copy of Aesop and read several of the fables from it, after which she read a chapter from De Tocqueville's *Democracy in America* which she had bought at Birchall and Johnson's bookstore that afternoon.

He stayed until midnight. The last hour they spent wrapped in each other's arms in the big chair before the fire, quiet and content.

"Molly, I've hurt you sometimes and I haven't meant to. When my spirits flag down and leave me miserable I guess I just make everyone else miserable around me."

"I understand."

"I know how much stock you Bluegrass people take in engagements . . . would you like for us to be engaged?"

"Yes, my darling, I would like that very much."

"When would you want to announce it?"

"Elizabeth and Ninian are having a big family dinner on New Year's Day. When we are toasting each other for the New Year, that would be a wonderful time. . . ."

"We'll announce it then."

Two days later she heard sleigh bells coming up the drive. She put on her heavy cloak with a cape and mitts and he bundled the two of them under the buffalo robe on the little seat. They rode across the white prairies with their black trees wrapped in winter sleep. Abraham had the reins in his left hand, his right arm was about her. The sun was out, clear and cold; when they spoke their breath steamed behind them like frozen white smoke.

After an hour of driving they came to a crossroads inn, little more than a two-room log cabin. Abraham asked for hot food or drink. The innkeeper replied:

"Nobody out, cold day as this. But the old woman got a pot of soup boiling."

"That would be fine," said Mary.

They took off their heavy cloaks, sitting on a split-log bench with their feet stretched to the fire. In a moment two bowls of soup were set down on the table; they took them in their laps, eating as they faced the warmth.

"I should carry you with me on circuit," he said, reaching out his hand for her. "I never fare this well when I'm alone."

"Darling, you've been alone too long. You need someone to take care of you."

"I don't require much caring."

"Then why are you sick so often, a strapping fellow like you? It's because of the bad food you eat, no regular hours . . ."

"Molly, you sound like my mother."

"The Greek dramatists say there is a little incest in all love."

He fell silent, his face darkening. The pain that came into his eyes was unlike any she had seen there before. He tried several times to speak, but could not give breath to the words. What was wrong?

"Abraham, you look as though something is festering . . . deep inside you . . ."

"There *is!*"

The words came like an explosion, startling them by their intensity. But now at least his teeth were unlocked.

"It's . . . my mother. I've said to myself a thousand times it's all so long ago . . ."

He paused, breathing quickly, gathering strength to expose his heart. After a moment he lifted his head heavily.

"It would be an act of kindness not to mention it. Yet if we are to be engaged you have a right to know . . . beforehand . . . from me."

He fell into another groping silence. Her pulse was pounding in her ears. What was this terrible thing he was trying to tell her? At length his eyes went to hers:

"My mother . . . was a natural child. She was born in Virginia. Her mother, Lucy Hanks, brought Nancy to Kentucky when she was two . . . without a father's name. Everybody knew. . . ." He paused for an instant to see what effect his news had had. "I know what my mother endured; I saw the suffering in her eyes. It was something she could never get away from. That's part of my heritage, her suffering: hardly a day goes by but I feel it inside my vitals, eating at me."

The revelation was shocking. She came from high-placed families on both her mother's and father's side, untouched by scandal or irregularities. As she studied the face of the man she loved, watched him sitting on the hard bench, his head low, his hands almost touching the floor, she knew that his suffering was over his mother's unhappiness and his own need to give sound once again to the dreadful words. Surely, she reasoned, no words from her could mean anything unless they contained an avowal as great as his own?

"Abraham, why do we have to wait? Why can't we start our lives together on New Year's? We'll announce the engagement over the champagne, then have the marriage ceremony after dinner."

He raised himself up, love and gratitude in his eyes. Then, as quickly as they had come, they were gone, and another emotion had replaced them. Anxiety? Fear? She could not tell.

". . . more time . . . year or two."

"And what will we have in a year or two that we haven't got now: more youth, hope, courage?"

"Money . . . security."

"Is there security in money? It comes and goes so fast. Isn't our love our only security?"

"That's true, Molly: love is eternal."

"Then, darling, please let us marry now."

He sat in silence, no longer opposing her. She put her cheek on his.

"Thank you, Abraham. You'll never regret it, I promise."

9

ELIZABETH was the major-domo in the kitchen, which was warm and steaming with aromatic scents of turkeys being stuffed with walnuts; ducks, geese, sides of venison; pumpkin pies baking in the oven. Since two of the four Edwards servants were busy scrubbing and polishing the house, Mary worked in the kitchen as an aide to Elizabeth, wearing a calico coverall, her arms deep in the flour for bread and biscuits.

She had not yet said anything to Elizabeth about the engagement or the wedding, but when her sister was ready to mix the batter for the cakes she knew that the moment had come. She walked to where Elizabeth was setting out sugar and spices, put her hand on top of Elizabeth's big capable flour-covered fingers.

"Liz, it was good of you to invite Mr. Lincoln to the family dinner."

"This is your home." Elizabeth spoke without looking up. "Anyone you want is welcome."

"We're . . . we're going to announce our engagement . . . when the champagne is passed and the New Year's greetings are exchanged."

There was a long silence during which Mary could feel Elizabeth reviewing their hopes and dreams, their relationship as sisters. When finally she spoke, all conflicts and concern were gone from her expression.

"Forgive us for opposing you, Mary. But we had to be sure, considering the obstacles, that you were certain in your own mind. We will welcome Abraham into the family. How long will you be engaged?"

Mary broke into a radiant smile.

"The shortest time on record: we'll announce just before dinner, the preacher will arrive just after."

"A wedding dinner? Well, then I'll have to change the plan for these cakes. They'll have to become wedding cakes."

"Liz, be sure not to tell anyone; I want it to be a total surprise."

The day was clear and cold. She came down a little before one, dressed in a new rose-colored painted muslin, her hair parted in the center and pulled back with a gold chain which she looped through the thickness at the nape of her neck. She wore Abraham's coral necklace and bracelet. She inspected the bowls of oranges, English walnuts, candies and winter sweeting apples. Soon the family began to arrive: the Todds, the Wallaces, the Hardins, Edwardses, all with their children. She was tremendously happy and excited and greeted her relatives with extravagant embraces.

She had suggested that Abraham arrive precisely at one-thirty, after the family would be assembled but before the champagne would be served. Elizabeth sought her eye. Mary walked the few steps to the clock in the hall. It was half past one. She nodded to Elizabeth. By the time the champagne was opened and poured, the trays brought into the living room, Abraham would be there. She stood at the edge of the entrance hall so that she would be the first at the door.

But there were no footsteps on the porch, no sound of the front-door knocker. The extra serving girls hired for the day came in with the trays of wine. She refused a glass when it was offered her. What could have happened to detain him?

By now everyone had been served. One of the young Negro women stood before her with a tray. Her cousin Hardin cried out from the other side of the room:

"Mary, you haven't become a teetotaler?"

She gave a quick glance over her shoulder at the clock. It said a quarter to two. Her heart was pounding in her bosom: she accepted a glass, fixed a smile on her face and replied:

"Hadn't you heard, Cousin John J., I've joined the Washingtonians!"

Everyone laughed at this reference to the Temperance Society, then Ninian raised his glass high for silence.

"The best of all possible New Years!"

The family members cried, "Hear! Hear!" drank their champagne. Handshakes and kisses circulated about the big drawing room. To Mary the champagne tasted like vinegar. The clock in the hall struck two. She went to her sister's side.

"Liz, it's all right to start dinner. Abraham must be having trouble getting the license. He'll be here the minute it's issued."

"Oh. Very well, then."

She was grateful for the animated hubbub about the table, and during the serving of the smoked fish and caviar she was able to join in the conversation. But by two-thirty when the roast fowl had been brought in she knew she was lost: the marriage bureau was kept open all day on New Year's and Abraham would not have had trouble securing a license . . . had he gone for one. It was now so late . . . could he be ill . . . but wouldn't he have sent a message . . . ?

She made a show of eating and of talking, holding on by gripping the fingers of her left hand to the bottom of her dining chair. But when Elizabeth rose from her seat at the head of the table to go out to the kitchen to remove the wedding ornaments and decorations from the cakes, she excused herself, went upstairs to her bedroom, locked the door and flung herself face down on the pillow.

The constricting pain around her heart was unbearable. A numbness grew in her arms and legs and chest until her body lay rigid and cold as in death. Each breath was a distinct and painful one. After a while the very process of breathing exhausted her; her body grew limp, her fists unclamped, tears flooded her eyes, first the cold tears of relief from rigidity and then the warm tears of self-pity. She cried hard. Her body shook. Then she lay quietly.

The sun was beginning to go down in its brief winter cycle. The room grew darker and colder. She rose from the bed, poured water into her washbowl, bathed her eyes and her face and the frame of her hair. She took a flannel robe from the wardrobe, slipped it on over her dress, then walked to the fireplace and started a fire going in the grate.

She knew she was in serious trouble. For it was perfectly clear now, as it had not been in the planning or doing, that Abraham never had agreed to their being married today. She had proposed it, argued for it, beat down his objections. Only then, stricken, not knowing what further to say, had he become silent. And she, in her eagerness, in the great surge of her compassionate love, had mistaken his silence for assent.

She had tried to lead him into something which she had thought would be good for him, and had only forced him into an act that was contrary to his whole nature: to fail another human being. She knew how terribly he must be suffering: the remorse, the sense of guilt, the agony of spirit. She felt so sorry for him . . . and for herself. . . . She could have had her engagement, she could have had the knowledge that in the fullness of time, when he was ready, they would be married. Now she had nothing. She had been too strong, too insistent in her plans. She had driven him away, and Abraham would not easily forgive himself for what he had done. It would be a long painful road back . . . if there were a road back.

What was it he had said at their first meeting? "That was the beginning of love for me." It had been the beginning of love for her too: the beginning and the end. And she had no one to blame but herself.

10

THE night was sleepless, the sunless dawn a filtering of fine gray ash through the south window. She had lain still, breathing regularly when Matilda came up and prepared for bed, but once the younger girl was asleep

Mary opened her eyes and lay staring at the dark lining of the canopy. Was Abraham going to disappear from her life?

If he had failed to appear for their engagement, a relationship he had expressly desired, then she would have had to acknowledge that Mr. Lincoln was hopeless, that he did not love her, and even if he did there was no further room for her to love him: her respect for him would be gone, her own self-respect as well. But in the full cycle of the pain-fraught night she knew that he would have arrived for the announcement . . . had she not compounded his obligation a thousandfold.

She was grateful that no one but herself, Abraham and Elizabeth had known that an engagement announcement was to have been made. Elizabeth never would breathe a word of it, not even to her own husband. As for the minister who was to arrive after dinner for the wedding ceremony: she stifled a groan: should Springfield know about that, her humiliation would be too great to endure.

She slipped into a robe and sat before the mirror studying her face. A ridge of darkness had returned high on the right cheek. She scrubbed her face in icy water, brushed her hair, assumed a small smile. She had had four years of dramatic training at Mentelle's Boarding School; Monsieur and Madame Mentelle had been kind enough to say that she had talent. Very well, she would use it now; it was a basic of the Todd heritage that they could endure any pain or defeat that no one knew about.

Elizabeth's expression was unsolicitous, her voice casual.

"Good morning, dear. Cup of coffee?"

"Thanks, Liz, I could use one."

"Me too. I wonder what it is about family dinners that leaves one so fatigued the next morning?"

It was a rhetorical question with no answer expected. As she felt the warmth of the fluid inside her she thought, Springfield is such a small town: a few streets, a few business blocks. If he doesn't come here, we're sure to meet somewhere before too long: a shop, a friend's home, crossing the square . . . Then we'll slip a hand into each other's . . . words won't be necessary; we'll forgive each other our trespasses.

Though buoyed by hope, the days and nights were interminable; her head seemed to be held in an iron band; her hands and feet were always cold. She stayed in her normal routine, shopping, visiting friends, attending the parties to which she had been invited. Edwin Webb, the widower from Carmi, became her partner, taking her to the dinners and balls, flooding her with gifts: kid gloves, a silver thimble, a lacquered fan. No one commented on the absence of Mr. Lincoln; only among the girls of her own set did she catch an occasional glance of wonderment.

For his part, Mr. Lincoln was apparently following his routine, for the papers reported him spending his days in the legislature voting for an act to incorporate the town of Galesburg in Knox County, in favor of commemorating January 8, the date of the battle of New Orleans, even though Andrew

Jackson happened to be a Democrat, opposing investigations of the accounts of the late Board of Public Works. It also was interesting to her that although the circuit and supreme courts were open, Lincoln appeared in only one case, and that, ironically enough, in which he filed a bill for divorce.

It was Ninian who interrupted the interlude, Ninian who was oblivious to the nuances of other people's emotions. He came into the sitting room late one afternoon and said:

"Congratulations, Mary. I knew you'd come to your senses. It's all over town that you've jilted Abraham Lincoln. I've heard that he has had two cat fits and a duck fit since you backed out from your understanding with him."

She sank her teeth into her underlip to stop its quivering. Who had started this story? Had Abraham done so to help her save face? Had people assumed it, since they had not been seen together for this long period? It had been the town's conviction that no one wanted Abraham Lincoln except herself; if they no longer had an understanding, it would be natural to assume that it was she who had abandoned it.

The next afternoon she learned from her cousin John J. that Mr. Lincoln was confined to his bed at Speed's. From a few discreet questions she gathered that it was not the winter fever or ague, but an acute attack of hypochondriasis. She too was suffering, she was sleeping poorly and eating little, but she had nowhere near his capacity for self-torture.

She saw him for the first time a week later, when she was walking to Lindsay and Brother with her sister Frances. She took Frances by the arm and led her into the nearest doorway so that they would not be seen. In a few moments Mr. Lincoln passed, gaunt as a rail, his cheeks and eyes sunk deep, the bones of his body showing skeletonlike through the old black suit. Frances said softly:

"Poor Mr. Lincoln, what has he done to himself?"

She too was stricken by Mr. Lincoln's appearance. To herself she said, My pride has not allowed me to collapse.

The newspaper reported his return to the legislature. Her cousin Stuart wrote from Washington asking what had happened between them, quoting from Lincoln's last letter to him:

I am now the most miserable man living. If what I feel were equally distributed to the whole human family, there would not be one cheerful face on the earth. Whether I shall ever be better, I cannot tell; I awfully forbode I shall not. To remain as I am is impossible; I must die, or be better.

A few nights later James Conkling came to call. He studied her face over the top of his cup of tea and finally exclaimed:

"Poor Lincoln! The fellow can barely speak above a whisper. I've just written to Mercy that his case is truly deplorable." He paused. "Have you decided to accept Edwin Webb, Mary?"

That night as she lay in her bed she was glad Matilda had returned home so that she could have the privacy of her room again. What had James Conkling said about Mr. Webb? Had she decided to accept him? She was grateful for his gallant championing when she so desperately needed someone. But marriage . . . the idea never had entered her head.

"Then your head is the only one it hasn't entered," said Mr. Webb the following evening when he made his formal proposal. "And if I haven't shown it every day for the past month, it has not been for want of trying."

She looked at Edwin Webb head on for the first time since he had been squiring her.

"You've been a good friend . . ."

"I don't want friendship from you," he interrupted. "I'm prepared to offer devotion, marriage, a fine life together; as for my two young ones, they need a mother and they will love you. You need children, not only these two, but many of your own. You will have them."

"Who is caring for your children while you are here?"

"My wife's mother, she lives close by. . . ."

If she had enjoyed any part of Edwin Webb's attentions as a balm to her pride and aching spirit, this reference to the children's grandmother cut it off abruptly. Her lips twitched, her eyes withdrew.

"Why does that upset you?" he asked.

"It's nothing . . . my own grandmother came to my mind. Grandmother Parker, in Lexington . . ."

"Miss Todd, it's my greatest wish that you marry me when the legislature ends, and come back to Carmi as my wife."

She resolved never to seek news of Abraham, but at the beginning of February she heard that he had lost his bachelor home, for Joshua Speed sold his general store and returned to Kentucky to take over his mother's plantation. Lincoln put one saddlebag over each shoulder and walked the four blocks northwest to the Butler home where he was to room now as well as board. He was growing increasingly active in the legislature, guiding his party in the fight to prevent the Democrats from packing the Illinois Supreme Court with five new Democratic justices. When Stephen Douglas called to tell her that he, Douglas, had been appointed a justice she insisted that they open a bottle of wine and toast his success.

"Justice of the Supreme Court! You'll do a fine job, Steve."

"I just about must after what Lincoln said: 'I would not behave as well as *you have to now,* for twice the money.' "

She smiled at Abraham's witticism, for the whole town had followed the political maneuvering necessary to create the new judgeships for deserving Democrats.

Toward the middle of February her cousin Stephen T. Logan invited her to his home at the north end of First Street for Sunday dinner. It was a big house set back on an elevation, with rolling lawns and a split-rail fence. After dinner he asked her into his book-lined study for a drop of sweet brandy; she saw that her thin-lipped, high-voiced cousin was edging slowly toward a delicate subject.

"Edward Baker and I are breaking up our law firm. I need a new partner. I haven't said anything about it yet . . . but it might very well be that Abraham Lincoln is my man. I've been in cases both with him and against him; he's a mighty fine young lawyer, one of the best of his kind."

Cousin Logan had not added in actual words, *What do you think?* but the question was definitely implied. Curious, she thought, how many members of the Todd family want to take Mr. Lincoln into partnership . . . including me!

"What a wonderful opportunity that will be for him," she exclaimed. "Everyone says you're our best student of law."

Stephen Logan nodded vigorously. "I like the man, and I want to have him with me. The legislature adjourns about March first, he could come in with me then."

She rose impulsively from her chair and kissed her cousin's cheek. With the best law partnership in Springfield available to Abraham, surely he would be on the road back to health, confidence . . . and love? She recalled her uncle's phrase about the end of the session: that meant Edwin Webb would be demanding a final answer.

She invited him to tea and told him about the death of her own mother, Grandmother Parker's hatred of Betsy, the tensions and problems it had created within the Todd home.

"Mr. Webb, it will be so much better for you to find someone who has not already gone through such a situation."

"Then you won't consider . . . ?"

"May the Lord forgive me, but I have to start out fresh, a new life with a new man, to make our own new family."

11

THE legislature adjourned. President Harrison died in Washington, D.C., throwing Springfield into profound gloom. Lincoln and Logan announced their partnership. Still there was no word from Abraham. When a spontaneous encounter had not occurred within the first weeks of the New Year she resolved that when they came together again it must be of his doing. She avoided the places where she might meet him: political rallies and debates, the Lyceum meetings, the *Journal* office, even the streets he would have to use to get from the Butler house to his office.

The strain within her caused her nerves to grow taut. She stepped up the tempo of her activity, surrounding herself with young men and women, accepting all invitations that came her way. Though she knew she was forcing her excitement and gaiety from the deep well of her reserves, there was every reason to believe that she was playing the role convincingly.

But the nights were bad. When she crawled into her four-poster, lying in wide-eyed sleeplessness, she could make no further pretense. She shivered in the warm room, was chilled under heavy blankets. Every few weeks she would suffer complete exhaustion; during these intervals her brain seemed to be trying to pulsate against the metal vise that was encasing her head in a tight cage.

Spring came early, the prairies were covered with wild flowers, the earth felt soft and fertile underfoot. But she felt hard and sterile within; not even the growing warmth of the April and then the May sun could lessen the coldness around her heart: for it was apparent now that mere physical and economic recovery were not going to bring Abraham back to her. Her cousin Stuart reported that he had written Secretary of State Daniel Webster at Mr. Lincoln's urgent request, in a renewed effort to get him the job of *chargé d'affaires* in Bogotá. Abraham was out riding the circuit now, to Tremont for the Tazewell Circuit Court, then to the McLean Circuit Court, then to Pontiac, Clinton, Urbana, Danville, Charleston.

His being away relieved some of the pain around her heart. If it precluded the familiar long-legged step in the driveway, a pounding of the front clapper, the opening of a door to find him standing, sad-eyed and sad-smiling, but with his arms extended to her, neither did she have to breathe the same air he was breathing, walk the same streets, face the dreaded prayed-for encounter.

In June the Sangamon Circuit Court opened and a retinue of lawyers returned. The firm of Logan and Lincoln had many cases to try, as well as a good number in the Illinois Supreme Court, which would open in July. Abraham was no longer seeking the Bogotá appointment.

Another ghost laid! He had said to her, "Love is eternal." Ah yes, she thought, if only I can live that long!

The June, Titus, Angevine Circus arrived in town and she received a note from the Francises inviting her to go to the opening with them. She sat on a bench under the canvas tent imprisoned between her two bulky friends. They made her sit through the clowns and the animal acts before bringing up the subject they obviously had come to talk about.

"Mary, we cornered Abe the first moment he came back," said Eliza. "He used a peculiar phrase, 'that fatal first of January.' I asked him whether you had caused the fatality or been the fatality. He said the latter."

Simeon Francis picked up the narrative. "So then I asked him, 'Why did you let the fatal first happen? Was it an act of omission or commission?' He replied, 'Both. I couldn't help myself . . . I was sick.' We thought you'd want to know that he accepts full responsibility."

She sat listening to the music of a Negro singing act, thinking, Yes, it is nice to know, but what good does it do me really?

"Did you ever know of the other Mary?" asked Eliza.

Mary nodded. "Abraham told me about her when he asked if he could call me Molly."

"We brought you a letter we would like you to see. We felt it would ease you. It was written by Abe to Mrs. Orville Browning about something that happened in New Salem."

Mary took the sheets of familiar handwriting and while the circus band blared and the gymnasts tumbled in the sawdust, she began to read:

In the autumn of 1836, a married lady of my acquaintance, being about to pay a visit to her father in Kentucky, proposed that on her return she would bring a sister upon condition that I would engage to become her brother-in-law. I had seen the sister some three years before, thought her inteligent and agreeable, and saw no good objection to plodding life through hand in hand with her.

The lady in due time returned, sister in company. I knew she was oversize, but she now appeared a fair match for Falstaff; from her want of teeth, weather-beaten appearance I had a notion that *nothing* could have commenced at the size of infancy, and reached her present bulk in less than forty years; in short, I was not at all pleased with her. But I had told her sister I would take her for better or for worse.

Through life I have been in no bondage, either real or immaginary from the thraldom of which I so much desired to be free.

After all my suffering here I am, wholly unexpectedly, out of the "scrape." After I had delayed as long as I could in honor do, I mustered my resolution, and made the proposal to her direct; but, shocking to relate, she answered, No. I was forced to give it up, at which I very unexpectedly found myself mortified in a hundred different ways. My vanity was deeply wounded by the reflection, that I had been too stupid to discover that she whom I had taught myself to believe no body else would have, had actually rejected me with all my fancied greatness.

Others have been made fools of by the girls; but I most emphatically made a fool of myself. I have come to the conclusion never again to think of marrying; I can never be satisfied with any one who would be blockhead enough to have me.

Your sincere friend
A. LINCOLN

She sat with her head lowered, mute at the callowness and cruelty of the letter, a callowness and cruelty of thinking about himself and others which she had trouble reconciling with his hypersensitivity.

She folded the sheets and handed them back to Mrs. Francis.

"Thank you for showing me the letter, Eliza. It does help . . . in a strange sort of way: I know more surely now that I am not at the core of his problem."

"Mary, would you like me to speak to him?" Eliza asked sympathetically.

"Thank you, no. As Abraham says, 'Every man must skin his own skunk.'"

The June thunderstorms were the worst she had ever known; peal after peal after peal. Terror-stricken, she ran to her room and got under the covers. Elizabeth followed. She sat on the edge of the bed, took Mary's head in her lap.

"Now, Mary, thunder isn't going to hurt you; it's all sound and fury, signifying nothing."

Heavy sweeps of rain beat across the window. Mary wept in Elizabeth's arms. Elizabeth stroked her hair gently, knowing that it was much more than the thunder her sister was weeping about.

Summer clamped down upon them with a heat so intense that there was no air to breathe; the house and the town and the prairies were stifling. Her father wrote from Lexington inviting her to spend the hot months at Buena Vista; her uncle wrote from Missouri urging her to inspect "the whole crop of new eligible bachelors" he had lined up for her. She refused both invitations.

At the end of August, Stephen Logan came to dinner. They talked of Abraham's success before the state Supreme Court on behalf of a young Negro girl who had been sold illegally as a slave. Mr. Lincoln's argument had won the girl her permanent freedom, and all of Springfield was congratulating him at having struck a brilliant blow against slavery. Logan also reported that Abraham had just left for a visit with Joshua Speed's family at their plantation a few miles outside of Louisville.

She slept well that night, though it seemed to be not altogether a natural sleep. The next morning she had a fever and was unable to get out of bed. Elizabeth summoned their uncle, Dr. John Todd, who wrapped Mary in a blanket, then drove her the four blocks north to his own house, one wing of which was set aside as his medical offices. He put her in a big chair in his examining room, rolled up the sleeve of her nightgown to the shoulder, tied a cord tightly around her arm halfway between the elbow and shoulder and, using a spring lance, stabbed her in the blood vessel and took a full quart of blood.

He then gave her an emetic, followed by successive doses of calomel, jalap, then a portion of castor oil. At this point Dr. Todd took out a small cake of tallow, pulverized it with a case knife and sprinkled large yellow Spanish flies over it. One such patch he placed upon her breast, a smaller one on her leg. She was put to bed upstairs and covered with feather quilts. The plasters caused excruciating pain for eight hours. At the end of this time they were removed and the resultant blisters sprinkled with powdered alum.

Frances and Dr. Wallace came to visit the next morning. Dr. Todd was in the country making a call. William Wallace took one look at the blisters, listened to the account of the bleeding, emetic and physicking, then leaned over the bed and kissed his sister-in-law upon the forehead.

"Mary dear, this isn't good professional ethics, but all of the things that have been done were unnecessary. There was nothing wrong with you, except that your . . . . difficulties . . . overcame you."

12

COUSIN LOGAN had said that Abraham would return about the middle of September. The date became a new goal for her, the days between a moat across which she must fabricate a bridge. However, it was Joshua Speed who knocked on the front door. She took him into the music room, which was the coolest in the late afternoon, brought in a long drink of bourbon and branch water.

"Have you been busy falling in and out of love, Josh?"

Speed smiled a little wistfully, then replied:

"Lincoln claims that I am in love with Fanny Henning, using as evidence the fact that I dragged him all the way into Lexington so that I could visit with her. He keeps encouraging me into marriage and every time he does I return the compliment."

Winter came early, the darkest, dreariest, rainiest, muddiest winter Springfield had seen. The business district became a sea of black mud with planks and barrels and crates being thrown into it in an effort to provide stepping-stones. Many of the nights were so wild with mingled sleet and snow that meetings and parties had to be called off because no one could get through.

She caught a series of colds, her eyes became swollen and red; the worst days she spent in bed. There had been times during her childhood when she had been high-strung, though never during the four years when she was living at Mentelle's, and only occasionally while she was spending the two exciting years of study under Dr. Ward's supervision. Now the feeling of being on edge seemed to be with her always; she had a constant struggle not to be sharp of tongue or bitter of mood. Elizabeth was kind, but running short of patience: why couldn't Mary accept the attentions of James Shields or of Lyman Trumbull, who had been countenancing her quite a lot of late?

With a start she realized that New Year's Day was approaching, and a presentiment grew within her that Abraham would come calling, not in the crowds which began at nine in the morning but just as it had happened two years before; after everyone had gone home and the house was quiet there would be a knock on the door and when she opened it he would be standing there. She would say, "Mr. Lincoln! Last but not least," and he would reply, "This is my first visit today, not my last." She found herself becoming increasingly excited; she planned the new outfit she would wear, made frequent trips into the almost abandoned sewing room.

Dozens of the Edwardses' friends came to pay their respects on New Year's Day. Mr. Lincoln was not one of them.

She paid a high price for her period of near happiness: now she sank into complete lethargy, her headaches returned in a new form, with configurations and black and white designs weaving themselves before her eyes. Only her pride seemed to withstand the torture she was undergoing; it alone generated the strength to go to hear James Shields deliver his oration before the Sangamon Guards in the Methodist meetinghouse, and to try the new railroad to Jacksonville.

Then early in April 1842 she received a letter from Joshua Speed. After many excruciating doubts about his fitness for marriage, he had finally married Fanny Henning and was now confessing that he was "far happier than I had ever expected to be." The important part of his letter, though, was a section he had copied out from one he had just received from Lincoln:

> I am not going beyond the truth, when I tell you, that the short space it took me to read your last letter, gave me more pleasure, than the total sum of all I have enjoyed since that fatal first of Jany. '41. Since then it seems to me that there is *one* still unhappy whom I have contributed to make so. That still kills my soul.
>
> I can not but reproach myself, for even wishing to be happy while she is otherwise. She accompanied a large party on the Rail Road cars, to Jacksonville last Monday; and on her return, spoke, so that I heard of it, of having enjoyed the trip exceedingly. God be praised for that.

When she had finished reading these lines of Abraham's she sat gazing at the paper with tear-blinded eyes. She reread the line "there is *one* still unhappy whom I have contributed to make so. That still kills my soul." She recalled the letter he had written about Mary Owens. That had been the letter of a callow boy; this was the letter of a profoundly suffering man, one who had matured under that suffering. Abraham's character had been tempered, strengthened. This she had helped do for him.

As for herself, she felt her heart beating wildly: *No man who spoke this way could very much longer withstand his own suffering over the separation.* Dear God, this was not how she had planned it but she would take him on any terms. . . .

Spring brought with it a surcease of the cold and mud. In an effort to shovel some content into the succession of empty hours she went to the opening of the Jockey Club races late in May, helped Dr. Wallace move the perfumes from his drugstore across the square to his new and modern shop. From the papers she learned that Mr. Lincoln was "off the track" for the legislature. She had no way of finding out whether he had refused to run again, or whether he simply was not being nominated by the Whig convention, sharing the fate that Ninian had suffered two years before.

Summer came again, the heat and tedium with it.

Then early one August morning she received a note from Eliza Francis asking her to come to supper. Eliza led her into the parlor. It was dark, with the blinds drawn against the hot sun. In the center of the room stood Abraham Lincoln.

13

IT was almost two years since she had seen him. His eyes were clear, the set of his mouth and chin forceful; he was thin, but he was well and whole.

They said nothing, yet silence was not there: half-formed thoughts darted swiftly within her own mind; behind his luminous eyes she could feel similar thoughts swirling. They stood quietly for a long time and then she found herself held in his arms, his lips were passionately on her own.

"I'm sorry for the trouble I caused you."

When she started to shake her head "no" to the trouble, he tightened his grip on her shoulders.

"More than anything else in the world, Molly, I want us to be together. I wanted it then, that New Year's Day, but I didn't have the strength. . . . You must find some way to forgive me."

"I pressed you, Abraham; we have only to forgive each other. Isn't that what love means?"

They had supper with the Francises around the dining-room table, the light from the green-shaded lamp holding them in the warmth of renewed friendship. After supper Abraham began to write for the *Journal* a letter which he would sign with the name Aunt Rebecca, part of a series attacking the policies of James Shields, Democratic state auditor. The four Whigs got fun out of the discomfort they knew this would cause Shields; but everything was fair in war and politics. He sat before the long sheets of blank galley paper and wrote rapidly. As he passed each page to Mary for her approval their eyes met and held for an instant. She read:

> Shields's story was never meant for the truth. . . . With him truth is out of the question, and as for getting a good bright passable lie out of him, you might as well try to strike fire from a cake of tallow.
>
> I seed him when I was down in Springfield last winter at a fair. All the gals about town was there, tied as tight in the middle, and puffed out at both ends like bundles of fodder that hadn't been stacked yet. . . . There was Shields floatin' about just like a lock of cat-fur where cats had been fightin'. He was paying his money to this one and that and sufferin' great loss cause it wasn't silver instead of State paper.

When Simeon approved the letter for publication, Mary rose from the table. Lincoln followed her into the foyer. She put on her bonnet and shawl.

"I'll see you tomorrow, Molly? Shall I come to the house?"

She hesitated.

"No, Abraham. I think it better if we meet here . . . for the time being; there's been so much . . . talk. . . ."

"As you say, Molly. About four o'clock?"

Simeon and Eliza drove her home in their carriage. She ran quietly up the stairs to her room, and once in bed fell into a profound sleep.

Upon awakening she dressed quickly and left the house. Mercy Conkling was busy being a bride, so she confided in her friend Julia Jayne, a tall, lithe, dark-haired girl with a wonderful sense of humor and complete discretion.

"Julia, you must help me. I don't want Elizabeth and Ninian to know, not until I am more certain . . ."

Julia was delighted to become a party to the tryst.

"Then call for me about midafternoon. We'll walk to the square to do some shopping. After that you can come with me to the Francis home. I'm going to need a chaperone so that the town doesn't put two and two together before Abraham and I have established our own total."

Each afternoon Julia called for her about three o'clock. They walked to the square and then made their way by various routes to the Francis home. A week after Abraham's letter was published, James Shields spoke at a public debate. He was fighting mad and spent two hours tearing apart its accusations. Mary said to Julia:

"I'd like to write the reply to Jimmy Shields. I'd have Aunt Rebecca say, when she learned that Shields was threatening to take personal satisfaction of the writer, 'I was so skart that I thought I would quill-wheel right where I was. If you want personal satisfaction come here and squeeze my hand. But if you insist on fighting, I never fights with anything but broomsticks or hot water or a shovelful of coals. I will give you choice, however, when we fight, whether I shall wear breeches or you petticoats.'"

Abraham was waiting when the two girls reached there. He was amused at Mary's idea for the letter and made her write it down at once. Simeon took it over to the shop, for the *Journal* was to come out the next day.

Shields was so insulted at the new attack that he sent his seconds to Simeon Francis to challenge Mr. Lincoln to a duel. Lincoln had gone to Tremont on business. When Mary learned that Shields and his seconds had set out for Tremont, she persuaded William Butler and the two-fisted Dr. Merryman to overtake them and warn Abraham.

She spent an extremely uneasy forty-eight hours until he returned to Springfield.

"Abraham, I got you into this."

"No, you didn't, Molly. I approved the letter. The responsibility is mine. I'm offering Shields a limited apology for all the letters printed in the *Journal,* but if he won't accept it I'm going to suggest broadswords as the weapon."

"For heaven's sake, Abraham, Jimmy Shields only comes up to your armpits," exclaimed Mary, aghast, "and those broadswords must be three or four feet long. How can he fight a duel against you with those?"

"He can't," laughed Lincoln. "It will surely seem too ludicrous to everyone concerned, and the whole thing will be called off."

Everywhere she went she heard talk about the Lincoln-Shields duel. When Abraham finally returned she could see by the expression on his face that there had been no duel; the seconds had gotten together, he had apologized, and Shields had accepted the apology. At the same time his mouth was set in a most resolute line.

"Molly, I've learned a terrible lesson. I've written anonymous letters to newspapers for years, holding up people to ridicule and satire. I'm through with it, it's no way for a man to proceed. The whole thing is now so painful and distasteful to me I'll never again mention it as long as I live."

She found that he had indeed passed a milestone with the Shields affair. In all things he appeared more consistently resolute. At the beginning of October he announced:

"I have to start traveling circuit in a couple of days, and I'll be gone almost the entire month. I'm not looking forward to the separation. When I return around the first of November, I'm going to ask you to marry me."

She showed no emotion.

"Suppose we let that wait until you get back."

"All right, Molly, but remember that although you haven't accepted me, I've declared for you."

She still made no answer.

She told no one except Julia, who offered to help her assemble her trousseau. Mary shook her head, her own lips resolute.

"Julia, I'm not tempting the fates. I have solid ground under my feet this time, but I don't think I could survive another hurt."

He was back on November 1. He had handled a large number of cases in Clinton, Urbana and Charleston, and while in Coles County had bought his parents a forty-acre tract, deeding it over to them with the provision that it never could be sold. He had spent the early hours of the next day at his Negro friend's barbershop; his hair was neatly cut, washed and combed. He had on a shiny new collar and black silk stock. She stood back from him.

"If you were as beautiful as this throughout the circuit you must have made many conquests."

"I'm monogamous by nature. Will you marry me, Miss Todd, tomorrow or the next day?"

"Is it safe for me to accept?" she asked with a tremulous but mock severity. "You're sure you won't vanish into thin air for the next two years?"

"You name the place and I'll be there. In a brand-new suit with my boots blacked."

She gazed down at his dusty and worn boots, then threw back her head in laughter.

"Well, now I have had a real assurance! If you're willing to go to the extremity of polishing your boots, I know that you've made up your mind."

He grimaced.

"Shall we make it tomorrow afternoon, at the Reverend Dresser's?"

Images of Elizabeth and Ninian floated across her mind.

"I know Springfield is a town of sudden marriages, but I'm going to have a little . . . explaining to do."

"All right, Molly, you set the course, I'll steer the flatboat. Any landing you say."

When she broke the news to her sister the following morning, Elizabeth asked matter-of-factly:

"Mary, must you be married this evening? I would like to plan a formal wedding, one worthy of a Todd, such as we gave Frances."

"That would have been fine some twenty-two months ago, Liz," Mary murmured wistfully. "Isn't it pretty late for that kind of thing now?"

"Then you'll have to be married in front of the Episcopal Sewing Society; they're meeting here tonight and my supper is ordered."

"The Episcopal Sewing Society? Oh, Liz, no!"

"All right, put it off until tomorrow. I'll get up the very best supper I can, but as far as the refreshments are concerned, I'm afraid I'll have to send to Old Dickey's for some of his gingerbread and beer."

Julia Jayne was the maid of honor, the bridesmaids were her uncle John's daughter, Lizzie, and Ann Rodney. Dr. and Mrs. Todd were there, her sister Frances and Dr. Wallace, Helen and Ben Edwards, Dr. Henry, the Butlers with whom Lincoln had lived so long, Mrs. Butler in a yellow satin evening gown.

Mary dressed in a white swiss muslin she had made earlier in the summer but never worn; it was fresh and crisp and the only new white dress she had. She wore the pearl necklace her father had brought her from New Orleans. Poor Father, she thought, he's going to miss still another wedding. For her sister Ann, there would be a vacancy.

Abraham arrived early with his friend James Matheny, who was to be his groomsman, and Justice Browne of the state Supreme Court. At five o'clock the minister arrived in his canonicals. The family and their friends formed a circle in the parlor. The Reverend Dresser began the ring-and-book ceremony:

" 'Dearly Beloved, we are gathered here in the sight of God, and in the face of this company, to join together this man and this woman in holy matrimony; which is an honorable estate; and therefore is not by any to be entered into unadvisedly or lightly; but reverently, discreetly, advisedly, soberly, and in the fear of God . . .' "

The rain had started a little earlier. It beat down in powerful onslaughts, wave after wave of it washing against the windows. She knew that rain always depressed Abraham.

"Abraham, wilt thou have this woman to thy wedded wife, to live together after God's ordinance in the holy estate of matrimony?"

"I will."

"Mary, wilt thou have this man to thy wedded husband, to live together after God's ordinance in the holy estate of matrimony?"

"I will."

The Reverend Dresser turned to Lincoln. "Repeat these words, 'With this ring I thee wed, and with all my worldly goods I thee endow.' "

Justice Browne, who had been listening intently, exclaimed:

"God Almighty, Lincoln, the statute fixes all that!"

There was a thin-sliced second of consternation, then everyone burst into laughter, the minister roaring in amazement with the rest. The laughter wiped out the sound of the pounding rain.

The Reverend Dresser handed a gold ring to Lincoln. Abraham placed it on the third finger of Mary's left hand.

"I now pronounce you man and wife."

They had supper, with two beautiful wedding cakes. A small orchestra came, they danced, there was friendship and joyousness, and much of Ninian's excellent champagne.

Shortly before midnight she and Abraham slipped out the front door where there was a carriage waiting for them. They drove to the Globe Tavern.

He remained downstairs to sign the desk register. She went up to the room that had been occupied by John Stuart and his wife, and then by her sister Frances and Dr. Wallace. There was a brand-new spread on the four-poster, bowls of autumn leaves and flowers. She slipped the plain gold band off her finger, walked over to the lamp to gaze at it. It was inscribed:

LOVE IS ETERNAL

A wave of almost unendurable happiness swept over her. Long ago Abraham had said "Love is eternal," and she had thought, If one can live that long. Well, she had endured.

She must always remember that: love ebbed and flowed, now rich and shining, now shabby and disconsolate. One must survive the bad in order to realize the good. Therein lay the miracle of love, that it could eternally re-create itself. She must always be dedicated, no matter what the years held, what the hardships or disappointments, the sorrows or tragedies: she must come through them all, through the most violent and frightening storms; for at the other end, no matter how long it might take or how dark the passage, one could emerge into clear warm sunlight.

She heard his long rangy steps coming down the hallway. His hand was on the door. She turned, her face suffused with love.

Book IV

IT IS ABRAHAM'S TURN NOW

1

SHE sat soaking in the hot water of the round tin tub; out the north window snow hung like a sheet on a clothesline, but the room was bright with the fire on the hearth and redolent of lavender water. Abraham had gone down to the men's bathing room just off the kitchen of the hotel, carrying his soap, towel, razor and comb.

She rubbed the Windsor soap on her slender hips and stomach, then leaned back against the circular rim, her eyes roaming the room which she had converted from a conventional hotel chamber into something peculiarly their own: the shelves of books against the south wall with a vase of evergreen branches flanked on either side by an ivory figurine; the crimson calico curtains she had sewn and hung in place of the mustard velvets; the round table she had bought to put in front of the fire, covered by bowls of oranges and walnuts, stacks of the Lexington *Observer*, the Baltimore *Niles' Register*, the New York *Tribune* and a volume of Bancroft's *History of the United States*. On the bureau next to their four-poster were her silver combs, brushes and scent jars. She had not been able to avoid the Globe Tavern; she would be here a full year, perhaps two, and so she had used one of her cash wedding gifts to buy an oil painting and prints for the walls, a fluffy white yarn hearth carpet on which Abraham liked to stretch out at night and read poetry to her, and a tiny French escritoire which she placed in front of the bookshelves for her papers and correspondence with the family in Lexington.

She stepped out of the tub and onto the warm rug, dried herself with a big towel, slipped into her underthings, stockings, petticoats and low leather slippers, then a swiss muslin lace-trimmed dressing robe. She pulled the bell cord for the servants to come and carry out the tub of water. In a few moments she heard Abraham coming down the hall; he appeared in the doorway dressed in the blue wool robe and buckskin slippers she had given him for Christmas. He was wearing his side hair considerably longer now; it came down his cheeks to a point level with the bottom of his ears. On top, his hair was cut shorter, falling in a wide part on the right side, the main lock covering the rounded forehead.

Marriage becomes him, she thought; he's looking better than I've ever seen him. He has good color, the web of anxiety lines is gone from under his eyes. Love might be eternal, but how nice that it could also be corporeal!

He put the comb and razor on his worktable under the window, then turned and opened his arms to her. She nestled against his bosom while he kissed her shoulder, murmuring, "Ummm, you smell good."

"So do you. It's that castile soap, isn't it? I must get you more." She leaned back a little, studying his face. "Though I says it as shouldn't, I'm good for you." Imitating his high nasal tone, she mimicked, "In this matter of looking at one another, I'm soon going to have the advantage."

He threw his head back and laughed.

"Now that we're both so scrubbed and beautiful, I wish I had thought to have my good suit pressed for Breese's levee."

"You did."

"Did we also remember to have a clean white shirt and collar?"

"Bottom drawer of the bureau. We can't have you getting nostalgic about the good old days above Josh Speed's store."

He stood still for a moment, his head turned to one side, his eyes puzzled.

"Molly, why were Speed and I so mortally frightened of marriage? For a year and a half we exchanged letters, trying to answer each other's anxieties and misgivings."

"And now?"

The seriousness of his mood passed.

"Anything I might tell you in the privacy of our boudoir would not be admissible as legal evidence in court. But I did write a letter to a lawyer, Sam Marshall, and in it I said, 'Nothing new here, except my marrying, which to me is a matter of profound wonder.' It wasn't until I'd mailed that old letter that I realized how fast and irrevocably I had committed myself."

She took his hand, led him to the comfortable rocker before the fire, then dropped on her knees before him.

"You committed yourself even faster and more irrevocably than you know."

"How do you mean, Molly?"

"My dear . . . I'm with child."

His gray eyes were round in astonishment.

"Are you sure? My, that was fast, wasn't it?"

"Instantaneous would be the better word. But then, what should I have expected from a man who can raise two ax heads off the ground?"

A flush spread over his neck and face.

"Why, Abraham," she exclaimed, "you're blushing. I didn't know you could."

He raised her from her knees, cradled her in his arms. She saw that his face did not know what expression his mind was wearing.

"And after I promised you a carefree year . . ."

126

"Oh, I couldn't be more free from care. Married less than two months and already with tangible proof that my husband loves me . . . written in his own handwriting to a client, admissible as legal evidence in any court of law!"

It was only two blocks east on Adams from the Globe to the American House, but fresh snow lay heavy on the walks and so they shared a carriage with their next-door neighbors, Albert T. Bledsoe, a West Point graduate who was practicing law on the Eighth Circuit, and his wife Harriet from New Jersey.

When they entered the candlelit ballroom of the American House Mary was puzzled to see but a scattering of ladies among the three hundred men present. The only folk who had come to Sidney Breese's levee to celebrate his election to the United States Senate were his fellow legislators.

The orchestra began a waltz. Abraham held out his arms. Mary danced away with him, her full lemon-yellow silk skirts swirling against his polished boots. Stephen Douglas claimed her for the next dance. His dark blue eyes were big and burning, the wavy hair combed back pompadour style over the splendid head.

"Steve, I expected to find you glum, since you were expecting to give this celebration party yourself. Yet here you are, bright-eyed and confident."

Douglas's laugh was a deep baritone. "Breese never could have been elected if I hadn't released my people. I made a deal with him: after he serves one term he must support me. When I get into the United States Senate I'll stay there forever because I won't have anybody back here plotting for their turn. Clever, Mary?"

A sudden stir went through the hall; all eyes turned to the entrance foyer. Standing against a background of twelve disciples in white military uniform, she saw a man in a blue dress coat with a black velvet vest and white cravat. She recognized him as the Prophet, Joseph Smith, leader of the Mormons who had built a prosperous community at Nauvoo.

Joseph Smith was mixed into the memories of her secret meetings with Abraham at the Simeon Francis house, for this was the time Simeon had been publishing the letters of John C. Bennett, who not only accused Joseph Smith of having ordered the shooting of former Governor Boggs of Missouri but of setting up a system of prostitution for the benefit of the church officials, of maintaining a band of Destroying Angels to assassinate the Prophet's enemies, and the creation of a western dynasty which he would rule as emperor. Abraham had done his best to persuade Simeon not to publish the attacks, but Simeon had persisted; Governor Ford then issued a belated warrant for Smith's arrest on the grounds of instigating the attempted assassination of Governor Boggs.

Mary left Douglas's side and went to her husband. "Could I meet him, Abraham?"

"Now, Molly, Mr. Smith is alleged to have seven wives, and I have one little one. Surely you wouldn't send me back to the Butlers after only two months?"

"It's a *soupçon* too late for me to send you anywhere. But I'll confess I'm fascinated. Please do introduce me."

Joseph Smith accepted the introduction with dignity. Abraham moved away to join Benjamin Edwards. Mary found herself gazing into a pair of the most magnetic blue eyes she had ever encountered. Was this man truly chosen of God? Had the Lord led him to the hiding place of the golden plates of the Angel Moroni, and then given Joseph the power to decipher them? Could the Book of Mormon be an authentic new Bible? Certainly thousands of good and honest people believed so, and more were being converted every day.

"May I bid you welcome to Springfield, Mr. Smith?" she said. "Most of us feel you are being persecuted."

"Thank you, Mrs. Lincoln." His voice was a powerful throbbing organ. "The Lord has given us friends in Springfield."

"More important, if I may say so, the Lord has kept you on the side of the law. Mr. Lincoln believes there are no legal grounds for Illinois to send you back to Missouri."

Smith flashed her a taunting smile.

"Mrs. Lincoln, if ever you become disillusioned with your chosen church—Episcopal?—Presbyterian?—come to Nauvoo and let me reveal the true religion to you."

"Thank you," she replied with a full curtsy, "it's always gratifying to be wanted."

When he had moved on she joined Abraham where he was standing with Benjamin Edwards and his wife Helen. Helen greeted her excitedly.

"Mary, Ben and I have bought the Houghan house."

Mary forced back the hot stinging tears which came instantly to her eyes.

"I have news too," Benjamin cried. "Your cousin Stuart asks if I'd like to form a partnership with him when he returns from Washington."

"Does that mean Cousin Stuart is not running for Congress again?" she asked after a barely perceptible pause.

"Yes, he said two terms were quite enough." Edwards turned to Abraham. "Is it your turn next, Lincoln?"

"I certainly hope so. If you hear of anyone saying Lincoln doesn't want to go to Congress, you tell him you know it isn't so."

When the orchestra struck up and Ben and Helen had glided away Mary looked at Abraham with high color in her cheeks.

"For your Victory Ball we're going to have a party like this, only all of Springfield society will be here to help you celebrate."

"Yes, indeed, Mrs. Lincoln, I have to look sharply to the future. Election to the Congress takes place next August . . . and my child will be born . . . let me see . . . in August too? Ain't that a caution? He shall be the first to call me the Honorable Mr. Lincoln."

2

IT was pleasant to do one's New Year's calling with one's husband, to leave cards reading *Mr. and Mrs. A. Lincoln* in the baskets hung on front doorknobs.

They returned to the Globe at nine in the evening, walking arm in arm through the cold night air. The Globe was on Adams, next to a blacksmith shop, a two-story building fronted by elms and maples; the tavern had changed hands every two or three years, each new owner adding rooms so that it now looked like an oversized barn. The inside was comfortable; the women's parlor to the left as they entered the vestibule, the big dining room beyond that facing on Adams. A staircase led upstairs to the ell with its six rooms on either side of a narrow hallway for the permanent guests such as themselves, the Bledsoe family, Mrs. Bournedot, a widow and brilliant pianist, such attorneys as Justin Butterfield and Judge Nathaniel Pope. Occupying this upper floor, they were able to avoid the day-by-day confusion of arriving and departing guests. It was needed, Mary thought, to compensate for the clanging locomotive bell placed on top of the main building, which was rung by a pull rope at the desk every time a stage drew up or a traveler arrived on horseback.

She carried easily, as Elizabeth and Frances had. They went out a good deal, to the marriage of Ann Rodney, to Ninian's party for the baptism of his new daughter, Elizabeth, to the band concert at the Hall of Representatives, the fair at Watson's given by the First Presbyterian Church, to dinner parties and cotillions. But she enjoyed equally the quiet evenings in their room with Abraham at his worktable drawn up before the fire, writing with a steel pen and blue ink on long sheets of foolscap an appeal to the Whigs of Sangamon County.

His joy in the written word and the hours he spent at his desk led her to believe that he was basically a literary man.

"From childhood I've had an ambition to master a style," he told her; "that's why I write verses sometimes, to see if I can make words rhyme. But it's discouraging: I still write by ear."

"Yet it's lucible. You state the essence of a matter with the least possible verbiage."

He flashed her a look of gratitude, then began striding the narrow paths between the four-poster, French wardrobe, small sofa and escritoire.

"If only I can convince the Whigs to adopt the convention system for all nominations. What does it matter that the plan was originated by Stephen Douglas; it's been responsible for the overwhelming Democratic victories in Illinois. I've got to convince them that union is strength, and that 'a house divided against itself cannot stand.' "

She wished she could hear him make his speech, but no ladies were admitted to the meeting. For the next three weeks he campaigned through Sangamon County. The Whigs accepted his platform almost exactly as he had written it. Yet he returned from the convention with a glum look. To her repeated questions of what had happened he replied bleakly:

"The people of Sangamon have cast me off . . . our delegation is instructed to go for Edward Baker." He brought his left hand upward and outward, dismissingly. "Things didn't go well for me on the early ballots, my strength was getting weaker, so I dropped out before I lost all my support."

"You didn't!" she cried. "You should never withdraw, never."

He turned away from her, stood gazing out the east window toward the cupola of the state house. She placed her hand on his shoulder:

"Forgive me, Abraham, you did what you thought right. It just wasn't fair of them to reject you altogether . . ."

"Oh, not altogether," he interrupted with a wry smile. "They appointed me one of the delegates to the Pekin convention; so that in trying to get Baker the nomination there I shall be fixed a good deal like the fellow who is made groomsman to the man what has cut him out, and is marrying his own dear gal."

She smiled, relieved to see that he could laugh at his disappointment.

The following day she learned that she had contributed to his rejection: some of Baker's supporters had claimed that since Abraham's marriage he had become "the candidate of wealth, pride and aristocratic family distinction."

"They yanked up your vest, and there was I!" she said to Abraham *sotto voce* that night at supper. "It was our first flight after marriage and I was so sure it would succeed."

She was grateful that the Sangamon Circuit Court opened the next morning, for Logan and Lincoln had a number of cases on the docket, and Abraham would have no time to brood about his defeat. A number of the cases involved fair sums of money so that it should be a remunerative session for them.

She had seen steady growth in her husband as a lawyer since he had become Logan's partner, particularly in the abstract principles of the law in which Logan had been a student all his life. She knew that her cousin was a severe taskmaster, obliging Abraham to write out their long and intricately reasoned briefs; there were times, too, when she sensed that he was smarting at being treated as a perennial junior law student.

"Cousin Logan loves the law as a science," he complained one evening, "but that's all he does read, the law. When he sees me reading history or poetry or politics he thinks I'm wasting my time."

She had expected that Abraham would bring home his important legal associates, state officers, businessmen, as her father had, but with the exception of the Simeon Francises he never appeared with a guest. Her husband apparently preferred to keep his friendships out of his marriage, meeting these men in the lobby of the state house, the *Journal* office, the post office, the drugstores, the street corners where they congregated to talk. He was still, as Edwin Webb had said, a man's man.

Nor did he consider it necessary to reciprocate for the many fine dinners and dances to which they were invited. Aside from the one dinner she had given here at the Globe for her family, he did not want to entertain. Already in the last couple of weeks Mr. and Mrs. Abraham Lincoln had not been included in two or three *distingué* affairs.

She had put off explaining to him about this; he did not like big parties anyway. He would say that one of the main reasons they had come to the Globe, which cost them only four dollars a week, was that they could save their money, pay off his debts, and put away some capital. However when they were quite pointedly not included in William Thornton's party here at the Globe to which Thornton had invited all the doctors, lawyers and honorables of the capital, and rightly so, thought Mary, since Thornton had already entertained the Lincolns at two dinner parties at the American House without being invited back, she decided to broach the subject.

She chose a night when a white hailstorm bombarded their north window, making the night impenetrable and their bright fire the cozier.

"Abraham, since you intend to pay off every dollar of those New Salem debts, and so much of our lives seems to be circumscribed by them, why not let me sell my Indiana farm land? Then we could start out fresh and free."

He looked up from his book, the puzzled expression on his face asking, Now what brought up this subject?

"No, Mary, I can't let you sell your land and use the money to pay off debts that are mine and mine alone."

"I don't follow your reasoning," she retorted, her expression serious. "If you use current income to pay past debts, doesn't that make them equally mine? I understand your need to repay what you owe, but there is an obligation which I have been brought up to consider equally binding: my social debts."

She saw a frown cross his face; he went back to his reading.

In the middle of March her sister Ann arrived to fill the vacancy in the Edwards house. She had changed little in the three and a half years since Mary had seen her; she was still thin of face, sharp-featured and flat-chested. Mary invited her to the Globe for dinner to meet Abraham. After a few minutes he came in with a group of men, stood in the doorway talking. Ann asked:

"Which one is Mr. Lincoln?"

"The one towering over the rest . . . with the mop of black hair."

Ann studied her new brother-in-law, making no attempt to conceal her disappointment. "Not the one with the dark, lined face . . . ? Well, you certainly didn't help my chances in the Springfield matrimonial mart by that unlikely choice!"

Mary gazed pointedly at her sister's bosom and said with kitchen-knife sharpness:

"If you had more of the *milk* of human kindness in you, Ann, you would not think, let alone say, cruel things like that."

Ann's manner was so unresponsive that Abraham soon caught on.

"I'm afraid I've been a disappointment to your little sister, Mary. Guess I'll have to tell her what the state's prosecuting attorney said the other day: An ugly man stands upon his own merits; nature has done nothing for him, and he feels he must labor to supply the deficit by amiability and good conduct. A pretty man, on the contrary, trusts his face to supply head, heart and everything."

Ann chewed on this for a moment, her eyes cast down, then she looked up, saw the grin on Abraham's face, answered his smile. Mary thought, I fight fire with fire; he extinguishes fire with laughter.

At the beginning of April, Abraham and most of the town's lawyers went out on circuit. Mary persuaded him to rent a buggy from the Globe stables rather than make the journey on horseback. His first note told of miserable roads, deep sloughs, execrable bridges, swollen streams; a mile or two beyond the Sangamon River he had plunged into a bad mudhole when the horse fell and the buggy broke a shaft; the next day while rolling rapidly down a hill his wheel had come off. Next time could he please ride a horse, since a horse rarely slipped a linchpin and lost a wheel?

Mary missed him, but she was never lonely. She spent her afternoons at Elizabeth's or Frances's home sewing for the coming baby. On the rare occasions when she felt ill, her neighbor Harriet Bledsoe took care of her. Once or twice a week she invited friends in for midday dinner, Mercy Conkling or Helen Edwards. She paid for these guests with her own money rather than have the meals go on the bill.

One noon Mercy arrived waving a letter triumphantly in the air. Both of their husbands were in Bloomington, about sixty miles north, attending a full week's court session.

"Mary, you certainly have your husband eating out of your hand: look at this letter I just received from James."

Mary took the sheet of paper, read the line that Mercy was indicating:

I reached Bloomington Monday afternoon, and found Lincoln desperately homesick, turning his head frequently towards the south.

Her eyes misted.

Abraham was due to arrive in Pekin early in May for the Whig state convention. She was completely astonished when, dressing to go to Elizabeth's for Sunday dinner, she heard familiar footsteps coming down the hallway. She threw open the door, and there stood Abraham, tired, dusty and disheveled. He picked her up with a tremendous swoop, carried her to the rocker in front of the fire and sat down with her in his lap, burning the tender skin of her face with his rough beard stubble. When she got her breath back she exclaimed:

"How did you manage it? Aren't you due in Livingston?"

"I just couldn't stand being away from you any longer. When court closed Friday I rented a horse . . . thought I never would cover those sixty miles. We have today and tomorrow together before I start out again."

While he was down in the bathing room, and she laid out his fresh linen on the sofa she thought, He's the only lawyer who came home for the week end to be with his wife. May the Lord forgive me my vanity, but I'm going to show him off all over town!

3

WITH the coming of spring she developed a series of headaches, brought on in part by the clanging locomotive bell on top of the Globe. When it awakened her from sleep she sat up in bed trembling. Her hands and feet were cold, she shivered under the blankets at night, holding herself close to her husband to garner warmth. She tried to conceal as much of this as she could from Abraham, but when he came home at midday and found her with the blinds drawn and the covers over her head, she had to explain that it was necessary for her to shun both light and noise because of the intensity of the pain.

When the Globe's chef quit a new cook was installed. Mary did not know whether it was her condition or his cooking but she found the food inedible; he used too much saleratus, making the buckwheat cakes yellow and the corncakes and short biscuits sour.

"It's a good thing our bodies are not glass bottles and tightly corked," she commented grimly, "or we'd be blown to pieces in excessive fermentation."

"Why, Mary Todd of the Bluegrass Todds: that's the first time I've heard you make a barnyard joke!"

She found it increasingly distasteful now that she was big with child to cross the lobby and go through the dining room three times a day under the gaze of changing male eyes. Once when she was passing the men's parlor she overheard a whispered comment:

"Mrs. Lincoln sure must have become pregnant the first time Lincoln dropped his pants across the foot of the bed."

She burned with indignation at the raucous laughter and could swallow no bite of her dinner. She felt worse when she sensed that they were beginning to count on their fingers; the suddenness of their marriage was known, and she imagined these men checking back in terms of time to see if her child were legitimate. The thought of their prying pierced her composure, yet she could utter no word of protest, neither to her family nor to her husband, for her cousin Stuart's wife had conceived and given birth in this very bed, and so had her sister Frances.

She went to see Dr. Wallace and told her brother-in-law her troubles, not omitting the fact that she was upset by conditions which had not disturbed his wife.

"William, please talk to me as a doctor. Tell me what is wrong."

Dr. Wallace had noncombative eyes, a right eyebrow that went upward and a left eyebrow that turned down, giving his face a quizzical look. Unable to achieve robust health for himself, he managed to cure most people of their illnesses; owner of a drugstore out of which he operated as a physician, he urged his patients to stay away from all medication.

"If you're worrying about your physical health, Mary, or about the child, forget it. But let's assume that a man had a leg as badly broken as your nerves were damaged during your separation from Abraham. It would take a long time to get that leg back to its full strength, and if the break were bad enough, there might always be a little limp. Isn't that so?"

"Go on, William."

"What I am trying to say, Mary, is that during that twenty months of extreme tension you suffered an illness, as surely as though you had been stricken by diphtheria. Your reunion with Abraham, and your marriage, put an end to the illness; but that did not mean that your nerves had recovered."

"William, how long will it take before I am completely well . . . as though that separation never happened?"

Dr. Wallace filled a pipe from the bowl on his desk, then put it down without lighting it.

"That's difficult to say, Mary. You must have a long tranquil period."

She walked back to the Globe slowly, letting the bright spring sun warm her face and bathe her tired eyes. She stopped at the desk to ask the attendant to please send Sarah Beck to her. Mrs. Beck was a strapping raw-boned woman with iron-gray hair and severe facial lines; her husband, long dead, had trained her in tavern keeping on the National Road in Pennsylvania and West Virginia.

Mary had no sooner settled in the comfortable rocker than Mrs. Beck knocked and stood in the doorway. Mary explained that she desired certain services which she knew were not customary, but which her health demanded, and for which she was willing to pay.

"A carryin' woman is entitled," replied Mrs. Beck in a deep voice.

Mary then asked that all her meals be served in her room; that she be permitted to use her own linens, and to bring in her cleaning materials and keep her own chamber.

She went through the lobby only once a day now, at a quiet hour when she was on her way to the Edwardses' or to visit with Mercy or Julia. At first she asked Abraham to have his dinner and supper with her, but she soon saw that this was a deprivation to him: he missed the camaraderie of the laughing, arguing, yarn-spinning men; he liked to meet his friends from over the state who brought news of political strengths and developments, of business and of possible cases. She released him to his cronies around the big bachelor table in the dining room.

Nor were they being invited out any more; six months of no reciprocation had cut their social life down to visits with her sisters and cousins and the Simeon Francises, where they were expected every Friday night for supper.

She settled back to await her day, confident that once her child was born their "carefree year" would be over and she would be able to persuade Abraham to go to housekeeping. Then she would establish their rightful place.

Abraham returned from the Pekin convention with a small-boy expression: her cousin John J. Hardin had turned up with more support than Edward Baker, so Abraham had persuaded Baker to nominate Hardin, then had introduced a resolution that the convention recommend Baker as a suitable person to be voted for by the Whigs for Representative to Congress in the election of 1844.

"I understand: the rotation system," she commented, nodding her head up and down vigorously; "Cousin Hardin and Baker will then support you in 1846?"

"If I support them both with all my strength, in all likelihood they will support me the same way."

She remembered that this was the plan Stephen Douglas had worked out for himself.

"Then we must wait four years for our turn?"

He spread out his long-fingered hands before her in a gesture of resignation.

"What else could I do, Molly? I was running a poor third. This way we have an objective to work toward."

"But you end the arrangement, the same as Stephen Douglas does with the Democrats? You won't be obliged to announce for only one term?"

He gulped. "I had to take the same stand as the others. Cousin Logan also wants to go to Congress. . . ."

"Well, I do declare," she said, lapsing into her early southern drawl. "I thought mothers had to be patient, carrying for nine long months, but I'm the merest tyro compared to you. You're going to wait for four years to get one session as a congressman. And after your term is over where do we go from there?"

His eyes were twinkling now.

"I'll throw the question right back to you, Mary: after your baby is born, where do we go from there? Why, we have more babies, of course. And we'll have more offices, too, if we plan ahead. . . ."

"I guess you're right, Abraham, but I'm certainly glad it's not as difficult to become a mother as it is to become a congressman."

4

SUMMER appeared one morning in the eastern sky as suddenly as a flash storm. She continued to clean her room, changing the bed linen every other day to keep it fresh and cool, bathed twice a day in tepid water, took a piano lesson from her neighbor, Mrs. Bournedot, in the evening.

The volume of work had increased so greatly for Logan and Lincoln that they moved to larger quarters at Sixth and Adams over the post office, facing the state house square. Mary could see the offices from the east window of her hotel room. Abraham did all the circuit riding for the firm and in addition most of the office's trial and paper work in Springfield, for Logan was serving in the state legislature. He did not mind, except for the writing of routine deeds, contracts and mortgages which he found dull, but what nettled him was that Logan was paying him only a third of the office income.

"That was a fair arrangement when we started two years ago, most of the cases were his, but I'm pulling my full load now."

This uneven distribution of the receipts was news to Mary.

"Couldn't you speak to Cousin Logan about it?"

"No, I want him to think of it for himself. His son David will be getting his law license next year and Logan wants him in the firm. We'll rearrange everything at that time."

After breakfast the next morning an envelope came to the Globe addressed to A. Lincoln. In the left-hand corner was printed *Important*. She put on her cross-barred cambric dress and Florence braid bonnet and walked the two blocks to the Logan-Lincoln office. She never had been upstairs. She was surprised to see how meager and dilapidated the furnishings were, consisting of a small desk by the front window, a table down the center of the room, half a dozen oddly assorted wooden chairs, a sofa with a raised head at one end, and on the wall alongside the desk some shelves which enclosed a set of Blackstone, Kent's *Commentaries*, Chitty's *Pleadings*, and a few other reference works. Abraham saw her in the doorway, sprang up from the long table where he was working in a nest of papers.

"Why, Mrs. Lincoln, it's a great compliment, your bringing us your law work. Not a divorce action against your husband, I trust?"

"I brought you a letter that just arrived marked Important. I thought you might be needing it."

Stephen Logan rose from the only desk in the room; beside his junior partner he looked as small as Lincoln's shadow in the near-noon sun. A mass of red hair which he wore high over his head to give him added height was now draining of its color and was pale gray near the roots; he was wearing a cotton shirt, a baggy pair of trousers. Abraham showed him the papers

Mary had brought. Logan thanked her, picked up his fifty-cent straw hat, excused himself and left.

At the rear of the office sat a man hunched over a lawbook, his back toward her. At that moment he turned his head, and she saw that it was William Herndon, the young chap who had lived with Abraham and Joshua Speed above Speed's store, the one who had made the reference to her gliding through the waltz like a serpent. They gazed at each other in hostile silence, then Herndon rose, leaned forward in what could have been interpreted as a miniature bow and walked past her, Mary drawing her skirts aside as he did so. When he was gone she asked:

"What is he doing here?"

"Why, Billy is reading law with us."

"Herndon studying in your office! Whyever would you want to take him in?"

"Well, Billy is a nice boy." His protest was gentle, the tone one of paternal affection. "He's been clerking in a store during the day to support his wife and baby, reading the law at night for three years now. When he asked me for the chance . . ."

"But there must be a great many young men who would like to read law in your office . . . more deserving . . ."

"I was even less deserving when your cousin Stuart gave me a chance to come into his office. As a matter of fact, Billy has a very interesting mind. He reads widely, can spout more words and more ideas in five minutes than any five fellows I know. Sometimes it seems like he is trying to drink up all the printed matter in the country."

"Not to mention the bottled goods," she said tartly.

"Yes, Billy drinks a little too much sometimes," he replied tolerantly, "but it's only been because he was unhappy clerking in grocery stores. Now that he is studying with us he's been cold sober; wouldn't be surprised if he joined the Washingtonians."

Mary quieted, recognizing the earnestness in his voice. "I apologize; who you have studying in your office is certainly your own affair."

On August 1 their son was born. She was tired after the travail, and about to fall asleep when she heard Abraham say to the midwife:

"He's a great whelk of a boy! You're sure he hasn't inherited one of my long legs and one of Mary's short ones?"

She fell asleep wondering what a whelk was, and thinking that his joke about the boy's legs wasn't very funny, but what could you expect from a man holding his first-born child in his arms, with beads of perspiration standing out on his forehead?

Elizabeth and Frances took turns caring for her, and when it was not convenient for them to leave their own children Mrs. Bledsoe came in to bathe her and the baby. Eliza Francis visited each afternoon, proud of the thirtieth child for whom her matchmaking was responsible. Her friends came bearing gifts; the room was filled with flowers, candy, fruits, magazines, clothing for the baby. A packet of French books arrived from Paris, ordered by Betsy months in advance. When the boy was three days old, Mary asked:

"Would you like to name your first son Thomas, after your father?"

"No!"

"Then we'll name him Robert, after mine."

"Look, Mary, I promised Speed . . . my first son named Joshua . . . after him."

"Joshua, indeed! Let Speed sire his own sons! Now pick up Master Robert and bring him here; it's time for his dinner."

She was sitting in a chair between the two windows, catching what breeze might come up, when the bell began to toll overhead, announcing the arrival of the Alton stage. Next she heard footsteps in their end of the ell; she rose to her feet . . . her father stood in the doorway, his hair whiter than she had remembered it, his rounded chin set in the flaring white collar, his face wreathed in an enormous smile; and she was in his arms.

"Why didn't you write to tell me you were coming?"

"I used the time to pack instead; caught the very next cars to Frankfort." His voice was muted still, but it was the sweetest possible music after four years of separation. "Can I see the boy? Does he favor the Todds or the Lincolns?"

"Right now he doesn't seem to favor much except his meals. We've named him after you." She took the baby out of his trundle. "After raising fourteen children, I assume you know how to hold him?"

It was a considerable time before Robert Todd put the baby down and asked about his other three daughters and Mr. Lincoln.

"I do hope you will like him . . . though I chose your exact opposite. Odd, isn't it?"

"Remembering the young men of the Bluegrass you declined to fall in love with, he must be very special."

"If by special you mean unique, he's that, all right." Her laugh was a little uncertain after the scene with Ann. "*Sui generis,* I believe the Latins call it?"

Abraham chose that moment to come striding into the room, his coat over his arm, his boots covered with a layer of dust which had sifted upward onto his wrinkled pants, his shirt soaked through with perspiration, his hair standing seven ways to Sunday.

"Behold, the bridegroom cometh," she murmured as the two men stared at each other with something between consternation and disbelief. "Father, this demon handball player is your new son-in-law. Now wouldn't you think he'd have more sense than to spend hours hitting a small ball against the side of a building in this intense heat?"

From his coat pocket Abraham drew a ball made of the ravelings of old stockings and covered with buckskin, gazing at it ruefully as he said:

"I wouldn't mind the heat so much if only I could win a game occasion-

138

ally. By now I must have lost enough dimes to send little Robert to college. Guess I wasn't cut out to be an athlete."

She said banteringly, "Seems I've heard you brag on how you whopped the bullies from Clary's Grove. How do you explain your becoming a champion wrestler?"

Abraham grinned. "That reminds me of a fellow who had better luck in getting prairie chickens than anyone in the neighborhood. He had a rusty old gun, and no trained hunting dog, but he always brought home all the chickens he could carry. 'How is it, Jake,' inquired a friend who often came home empty-handed, 'that you never come home without a lot of birds?' Jake put his mouth close to the ear of his questioner and said in a whisper: 'All you got to do is jes' hide in a fence corner and make a noise like a turnip. That'll bring the chickens every time.'"

The two men laughed heartily, then shook hands. Mary was happy at having cued her husband into a story that was germane and funny.

The next evening Dr. John Todd had a family dinner in honor of his brother. It was Mary's first time out; she found herself filled with excitement at the prospect of getting into a tight bodice again. She wanted to be particularly beautiful, wearing a blue bishop lawn gown with skirts flounced over several starched and ruffled petticoats in taglioni fashion. She wore her pearls braided through her hair. Her eyes were sparkling, there was high color in her cheeks. Abraham offered to carry her down the flight of steps, but she only wanted his arm for support.

She and Robert Todd shared the limelight; her father had not seen his brother or cousins for some fifteen years. They were having a happy time when Ann seized a moment of silence to comment:

"Isn't it wonderful that Mary had a baby? Otherwise Father might never have seen Springfield."

There was a flat silence; no one could have pinned Ann's words to the implication in her tone: that Elizabeth and Frances had had children and Robert Todd had not bothered to come; but her triumph was short-lived: Robert Todd took from his pocket three official-looking documents which he handed to his three married daughters. When Mary opened hers she saw that she was now the owner of eighty acres of wooded land only three miles southwest of Springfield. Each eighty-acre piece was worth about a thousand dollars.

The next evening after supper at the Globe Mary sat quietly listening to her husband and father discuss the coming presidential race, whether the United States would go to war with Mexico over Texas or with England over Oregon. Then she saw two spots of color grow on her father's forehead while he stumbled around for a suitable opening.

"I didn't give you a wedding present as I did Elizabeth and Frances when they married. Abraham, would you mind if I sent Mary a draft each month . . . oh, say for ten dollars? . . . to buy a few pretty and foolish things that give young women so much pleasure?" He rushed on, fearful lest Abraham stop him. "I'm afraid I rather spoiled her . . . with lovely clothes and jewels and spending money . . . because she loved me . . ."

Mary had been watching her husband's skin grow dark, his lips purse out displeasedly. She had not told her father anything about Abraham's debts or their economical living, and so she felt blameless in the matter. Abraham saw this in her face; the tautness went out of his cheek muscles and he smiled at the two Todds across the table from him.

5

AFTER the first week in September Abraham rode circuit to Tremont, Hanover, Bloomington, Clinton and Urbana; he was never gone more than several days at a time, coming in on horseback to spend a day or two with her and the baby. But by the time the child was two months old he stopped taking his milk, began losing weight and cried so much that the guests on the upper floor complained. Mary summoned Dr. Wallace.

"This boy simply isn't getting his rest, Mary. That's why he won't eat. What's keeping him awake?"

"That confounded bell. It rings until midnight and then again at four in the morning . . . I thought he'd get used to it . . . though the Lord knows I never did."

"Why not pack a few things and stay with us until Abraham returns?"

"Thank you, William dear, but I must find a place to live."

She started on the task that very day, leaving Robert in charge of Mrs. Bledsoe. Mr. Britton, the real estate man on the square, had two homes to show her, one a red brick, large and expensive, the other a three-room cottage with a shed kitchen and an open hearth for cooking. And that, Mr. Britton explained dolefully, was all there was for rent in Springfield. Now if Mrs. Lincoln would like to buy . . . ?

We're going to have to buy, she reasoned on her way home. I'll sell the eighty acres Father just gave me. Abraham won't like it . . . we'll quarrel as we did over the Houghan house . . . but mustn't our baby's health come first . . . ?

Her breath came short, a hollow formed in her throat. She knew she would not risk a breach with her husband. Their happiness together was the most important part of her life. If Robert didn't pick up in the next day or two she would accept William's invitation, stay with the Wallaces while Abraham was out on circuit, return to the hotel when he came back. They had been married almost a year now; she had watched her words and acts with scrupulous care to make sure she never caused him anxiety; anxiety could lead to the hypo, the sole threat to their happiness.

The following afternoon she noticed a farm wagon drawn up in front of a small cottage on Fourth Street, in the middle of the block between Adams and Monroe, and a family carrying its personal possessions out of the house. She learned from the woman of the family that the house had been sold, furnished, to Seth Tinsley. Mary went inside; there was a parlor into which one stepped from the street, behind that a kitchen with a small Empire stove; on the other side two bedrooms, the front one furnished with a plain four-poster and a wooden table, the smaller bedroom behind it empty and unpainted.

She walked quickly to Tinsley's store, which sold raisins and molasses in addition to wallpaper and fancy silks twelve days from Philadelphia. Seth Tinsley was the town's banker as well as merchant. Mary breathlessly explained her errand.

"Well, Mrs. Lincoln, I was intending to sell . . . but if it's that important to you . . ."

"Oh, Mr. Tinsley, it is. I'll undertake to improve the place . . . how much would you charge for the rent?"

Tinsley computed figures in his head, said, "Furnished, five dollars a month."

The hours passed slowly; she was in a fever of expectancy; yet when Abraham returned from Urbana she restrained herself until he had enjoyed a soak in the bathing room. Then she told him in one long breath, the welfare of the child intermingled with praise of the little house, and the fact that it would not be expensive . . .

Abraham took her in his arms and kissed her eager mouth.

"That's quite an appeal to the jury, lawyer Todd. We'll move first thing in the morning."

"Thank you, Judge," she whispered.

She sewed scarlet and yellow loose-woven worsted curtains and bedcover for their bedroom. She hung their paintings in the parlor, put the well-filled bookcase against the wall, arranged her desk, Abraham's worktable and lamps and the place was theirs. The baby slept long, ate well, gained weight; his eyes at four months still were not focusing, the left eye had a tendency to turn inward while he watched the movements of his hands, but Elizabeth assured her that this would pass. Though she found herself none too expert at handling the Empire stove, her years of assisting Elizabeth in the Edwards kitchen were a help in struggling through the first few days of strangely scorching pots, burning bread and underdone meat. For once she was grateful that Abraham was not finicky about his food. At the end of a day of cooking, sewing, cleaning, dishwashing and caring for the baby she was tired; it was just as well that she was content to read for an hour before the fire and go to bed: for Springfield adjudged this kind of housewifery in what amounted to little more than a cabin as a social comedown. They were dropped as completely as though they had migrated to Oregon.

She was not offended; when she was ready for society, she would be society.

Robert was growing robust; however her uneasiness grew as she found that at six months he still could not focus on a toy held in his hand. One afternoon she picked him up to feed him and saw that his left eye was stuck in the very corner of the eye socket. Her heart racing with apprehension, she placed him on the bed, got a ball of red yarn and followed the movements of his eyes as she waved the yarn from side to side: the left eye could get no farther than the middle of the socket.

A chill came over her. She dressed Robert as quickly as she could, wrapped him in a blanket, and with the baby pressed securely on her shoulder walked rapidly to the Wallace and Diller drugstore.

Wallace and Diller had a newly installed soda fountain at one side of the store, at the other white jars containing sarsaparilla root, powdered rhubarb, English calomel, asafoetida, morphia, Swame's panacea. In the center of the store was a square black stove, around it half a dozen cane-bottomed chairs for the men who came in at early candlelight to swap yarns and argue politics, Abraham among them.

Dr. Wallace looked up from his desk at the back of the store, surprised to see her with the child on her shoulder. She set the boy down on the doctor's desk.

"William, I must have the truth: there's something wrong with Bobby's eyes, isn't there?"

"Well . . . one of the muscles . . . is in imbalance."

"You mean crossed?"

". . . it gives that effect."

Her heart plunged through her innards. "Oh, William, will it never come right?"

"It's one of those little imperfections, Mary; we don't know how they happen, but it's something you must face and live with."

"You mean Bobby's eye will be . . ." she struggled for words, ". . . like Abraham's when he is under pressure . . . with headaches . . . ?"

"No, no," he interrupted, "the boy will get used to using the one good eye, and it will be strong. Abraham's eyes sometimes cross vertically; it's the changing focus when he is under strain that brings on his headaches."

She sank into a chair, covered her face with her hands and wept unrestrainedly. William stood above her, spoke quietly:

"Mary, you mustn't. Remember, you too must avoid undue strain."

The Reverend Dresser, who had performed their marriage ceremony and baptized Robert, invited them to Sunday dinner. It was a raw, rainy afternoon, but they were comfortable in the clergyman's book-lined study, discussing Abraham's deism while the minister tried to convert him to the Episcopal Church. Mary attended services every Sunday morning, sitting with the Edwardses in their pew; unbeknown to her husband she had paid the full membership for the year.

Abraham was much taken with the Reverend Dresser's house, showing Mary the solidity of the hand-hewn oak construction, the wooden pegs, walnut clapboarding, and shingles. As they walked home, stopping to pick up the baby at Frances's, he asked enthusiastically:

"Don't you think that's a well-built house, Molly? It'll stand for a hundred years."

She had not liked the house, it had seemed narrow, the rooms small and dark, with a cubiclelike effect, but she saw no reason to criticize Abraham's taste. She replied, "Most comfortable."

As she watched her husband move about his own four simple rooms she saw that he too was pleased to be a householder, though he urged her not to spend any more money than she had to. When he rode circuit he spent no penny other than his hotel bill and the keep of his horse; he had no personal indulgences.

Shortly after the New Year she heard him come into their bedroom and stand behind her dressing table. She turned. There was an expression on his face she had never seen there before: his eyes were luminous, his lips parted in a warm smile. He put his arms down over her shoulders, crossed them on her bosom and laid his cheek on hers. She turned her face slightly so that her lips were on his.

"I bought us a home, Molly. Been dickering . . . and hoping. Just landed it today, with our names on the contract."

"You bought us . . . but what house . . . where?"

"The Reverend Dresser's. Always loved it. Remember I asked if you liked it too, and you said you did?"

Her thoughts were reeling: the Dresser house . . . but I don't like it. It's cramped and graceless . . . what have I done, indulged in a politeness . . . and acquired a home?

"It must have cost Reverend Dresser the full fifteen hundred to build," he went on enthusiastically. "I'm to pay seven hundred fifty in cash, plus that lot we own with Logan, it's valued at three hundred . . ."

He lifted her out of the chair, held her lightly.

"I have been saving that money since the day of our marriage for this one purpose: to buy you the home you so ardently want. That's why I didn't want you entertaining or buying things for this cottage. I even stopped playing handball for ten cents a game . . ."

Tears came into her eyes. How unfair she had been, how ungenerous; all the time he had been thinking only of her. What was it that other Mary had said? "He is deficient in those little links that make up the chain of a woman's happiness." But then he had not loved that first Mary; he loved her, and as long as she lived she must never doubt that love.

How could she tell him that she did not like the Dresser house? What a poor reward that would be for his devotion! She would move in and be happy there; it was a beginning.

143

6

•

OF a Sunday afternoon she and Abraham walked to the southeast end of town to their new home. From the front door, which stood three steps above the street, she could see across the open fields to the state house. A servant answered their knock, admitting them to a dark hallway little more than six feet wide and holding a narrow flight of stairs. She turned to her right into the Reverend Dresser's library, which she decided would be the family's sitting room; it was a good-sized room, sixteen by twenty, with a fireplace and four ample windows, two facing Jackson Street, two facing Eighth. Here she would put informal furniture, a comfortable sofa, rockers, their books, desks, the round table in the center for newspapers and magazines. The room opposite which was the same size and shape would be their formal front parlor, carpeted from wall to wall, with heavy draperies, their paintings, *objets d'art* on the black mantelpiece, black sofas, a number of fiddleback chairs.

She explored further: behind the parlor was a bedroom, not large enough for the nine-foot bed she had promised Abraham, but sufficient for a four-poster and a trundle for Robert. The dining room was at the rear of the hallway, behind half of the sitting room; the unbuilt south half was an open but roofed porch. Behind the dining room was a kitchen with porch and storage space to one side. Of the two rooms upstairs, in which Abraham could stand upright only at the center V of the roof, one would be her sewing room, the other his resting room.

At the beginning of May the Lincolns moved in. The house was entirely paid for when they took possession. Before they could get settled politics took over; Abraham had been named as a presidential elector, Henry Clay nominated for president by the Whigs, and an obscure Tennessee congressman by the name of James K. Polk by the Democrats. According to plan, Edward D. Baker was nominated to succeed John J. Hardin for Congress; Ninian was nominated to the state Senate, as was her cousin Logan. When Joseph Smith, Prophet of the Mormons, announced himself as a candidate for the presidency, Simeon Francis became a spearhead for the ever growing movement to eject Smith and his Mormons from Illinois . . . and from the United States.

Before either the summer or the presidential race could get boiling hot, Smith and his lieutenants burned down the building of the Nauvoo *Expositor*, founded by disaffected Mormons, and threw the printing press into the Mississippi River. This act, coupled with the Prophet's drive for the presidency, so frightened Illinois that Governor Ford ordered Smith and all Mormons responsible for the burning to surrender to the sheriff at Carthage, about a hundred miles from Springfield. Without waiting for the due process of law, rioting militiamen broke into the jail and shot Joseph and his brother Hyrum Smith to death.

A pall settled over Springfield. Simeon Francis was confined to bed, prostrate. Abraham was equally stricken, sitting in his rocker before the open door.

"The problem is bigger than the qualms of any one man's conscience," he said grimly. "Do you remember back in 1837 the story of Elijah P. Lovejoy, who moved into Alton to publish an abolitionist paper? His presses were burned and destroyed twice, and when the mob saw they couldn't stop him that way, they killed him. That killing moved me more deeply than anything that had happened in my life." He handed her an old copy of the *Journal*. "I wrote this article and delivered it as a speech before the Young Men's Lyceum."

She began to read. After an opening paragraph in which he expressed the debt of all Americans to the founders of the country for creating a government with a system of political institutions which assured them of civil and religious liberty, he then asked:

Shall we expect some transatlantic military giant, to step the Ocean, and crush us at a blow? Never! At what point then is the approach of danger to be expected? I answer, if it ever reach us, it must spring up amongst us. . . . If destruction be our lot, we must ourselves be its author and finisher. I mean . . . the growing disposition to substitute the wild and furious passions, in lieu of the sober judgement of Courts.

When she praised him for his cogent thinking, he said, "That's why I'm against any war with Mexico over Texas; it would be the same kind of mob violence. Violence can never accomplish anything, it can only destroy: in particular those who originate it."

Summer brought the broiling sun and the acceleration of the presidential race. Each day at early candlelight she arranged for someone to come and stay with Robert while she went down to the Log Cabin in the square to hear Abraham and his fellow Whigs make speeches about internal improvements, the tariff and the bank question. She often had wanted to accompany him when he went stumping the state, and now she got her wish, a week-long trip to Vandalia for a giant rally.

They set out on a Monday morning in a big carriage which they shared with the Logans. There were several hundred in the Springfield delegation, led by the town band and carrying their own glee club, the ladies in white lawn dresses with gay sashes, and leghorn hats. At Hillsboro they were met by the local band and escorted to a grove of maples for a barbecue; after an evening rally at the courthouse, Mary and Abraham were put up by a local Whig family, and in the morning the procession started out again, reaching Vandalia in the afternoon.

Abraham proudly presented her to families from all over the state. Six thousand Whigs had assembled, a thousand of them women. Mary led a parade through town, served beef and pork at the barbecue, listened to tons of speeches in tents and under the trees in the square. She was filled with gay, warm humor; she liked everyone, the women she met liked her. The men found that she was well versed in political issues, her long-time friendship with Henry Clay brought requests to speak about him. She enjoyed her role as one of the leaders of Whig society and decided that when they returned to Springfield she would consolidate her position by giving a series of intimate dinners.

Two weeks later Edward Baker was elected to Congress, Ninian and her cousin Logan elected to the state Senate.

That was all the Whigs did win. In the November presidential voting the Democrats carried the nation, and Illinois as well. The race was close, but Mary recalled Simeon's bitter line: "That's why I hate politics: loser takes nothing." She became anxious: with a Democratic regime in Washington, would there be enough strength left in Sangamon County and the Seventh District to elect Abraham to Congress when it came his turn two years hence? She could not utter this concern out loud, or she would be accused of dwelling on personal ambition. But weren't all wives ambitious for their husbands? It was not a mere matter of personal gain, of rising in the world; it was something more: fulfillment for a man. What was wrong in believing that one's husband had outstanding talents? Or that they should be utilized? Her ambition for Abraham was no greater than his ambition for himself.

But was ambition enough? Was talent enough? They belonged to the minority party in Illinois, with not nearly enough jobs or offices to go around. Might they not spend their whole lives laboring for their cause and never taste anything but the bitter rind of rejection?

It was not until after the presidential defeat that Abraham grew genuinely restive with his partnership. Mary did her best to keep him content, for the firm of Logan and Lincoln had become one of the most respected in Illinois. Toward the end of the year she found an appropriate moment to ask:

"Surely now isn't the time to break up a successful concern, while we've every expectation of going to Washington? You'll want Cousin Logan to carry on the work and keep our income up. When he follows you for his term in Congress you'll run the office as you see fit."

He agreed not to make any sudden decision.

The next development left her gasping. She had bundled up in her brown merino cloak and walked over to visit with Elizabeth, only to find her sister tight-lipped.

"It isn't true, is it, Mary, that Abraham has broken with Cousin Logan and taken William Herndon in as his partner?"

"No, Elizabeth, of course not. Herndon is just a student in Abraham's office."

"Ninian says he got his license last week."

146

Mary felt her insides tremble; she returned home and sat in the sitting room with her chair turned to the window, too upset to think of cooking dinner. At length she saw him come across the fields from the square, walking with a stoop and carrying one hand behind him, a little pigeon-toed, setting his whole foot flat on the ground and lifting it up all at once. She sat motionless until he had hung his hat and coat on the rack in the hall and came into the room.

"Is it true about your partnership, Abraham?" she asked.

"Your cousin Logan wants his son David in the firm. He thought there wasn't enough for the three of us. I needed a new partner . . ."

". . . so you picked the last man in Springfield . . . in all Illinois, who could possibly have anything to offer you!"

"That's not so; Billy has a great deal to offer me."

"What, for example?" Her voice was rising. She made no attempt to control it. "What prestige has he, what position in the legal profession, what place in Springfield society?"

"Billy is a real worker and will make a good lawyer. He's agreed to keep the books, write the routine papers, release me from the drudgery . . ."

"With all of the well-trained lawyers in the state, men with good practices who would have been eager to come in with you, why you should have deliberately insisted upon cutting your own stature . . ."

"My stature, such as it may be, comes out of myself, and will be determined by how I practice the law; it will not come from my partner." His voice too was growing edgy. "I've had eight years of being a junior partner, of being taught and directed; I'm getting too old for that kind of thing. From now on I'm going to be the senior partner. Billy is just the kind of junior partner I want."

She knew she should not persist, that his mind was made up, but she could not control her indignation.

"Out of what kind of perversity can you want him? Only a month ago he was in a public brawl and hauled off to jail for the night. He moves in one of the lowest strata of Springfield society; our two families can never become intimate."

"Why, Mary? I come from a much humbler background. If I'm good enough to have married into Bluegrass royalty, why aren't Billy and his wife good enough for us?"

To this crushing indictment she could only answer, "You think I'm a snob. But it isn't that. I think your position will be damaged. . . ." Her voice when she continued was a wail, and not a rebuke. "Why did you take him, Abraham, when you could have had the best?"

"Why did you take me, Mary, when you could have had the best?"

"You were the best."

"So is Billy. Give him a chance."

There was such affection in his voice when he used the word "Billy" that suddenly she realized her husband's actions were prompted by friendship rather than expedience; that was why her logic had made not the slightest impression on him. "Molly" and "Billy" were the only pet names he used; all other men in Springfield he addressed by their family names, even as he had his partners Stuart and Logan. She resented profoundly being coupled in Abraham's feelings with this gauche young man; yet apparently the friendship was of importance to her husband.

She continued in a quieter tone: "Certainly you are not going to offer him a third?"

"I've already offered him half."

"Half! But for what?"

"If I put Billy on the short end he would soon come to resent the arrangement, just as I did. What I don't like for myself I can't impose on any other man."

She stretched her hands in front of her, palms outward as though to close him out of her sight, then pulled them slowly toward her with clenched fists.

". . . half your income . . . after all your years of work and preparation . . . and for a drunken partner . . ."

The air of the sitting room was flagellated.

"You must let me choose my law partner, Mary; that is the one part of my life in which you cannot intrude. Marriage doesn't give you the right."

"Apparently not," she commented acidly. "I am to be permitted to be ambitious for you, to give my help and counsel in certain fields, and be ignored in others. Just how do I determine the boundaries of where I belong in your life?"

He winced.

"You're being cruel, Mary. You are my full and equal partner in everything; I respect your judgment, I seek it and listen to it at all times. But this is one thing in which you must abide with me. . . ."

They sat in silence, then Abraham went into the hall, put on his hat and coat and returned to town.

This was their first serious quarrel; it took her a long time to regain control of herself. Only then did she remember that he had gone back to the office without his dinner; and she felt ashamed. No matter how mad you got at your husband, he still had to eat.

7

IT was the mildest winter since she had moved to Springfield; the days were as warm as fine April weather. When the legislature convened, Elizabeth and Ninian officially opened the Springfield social season with the biggest dinner and ball yet seen in the capital. Mary was grateful for this party, for it enabled her to renew many important friendships that had lapsed. There were raised eyebrows when the Lincoln-Herndon partnership was announced, but Abraham still carried on many cases with her cousin Logan, and when he went out on circuit he did not ride as Lincoln and Herndon, but had partners in each county capital, usually the best lawyers there, and so it appeared that neither his stature nor his income was hurt. Abraham was more comfortable as a senior partner; Herndon took a great deal of detail work off his hands, leaving him more time for reading and writing.

On the first Monday evening that the legislature met, Abraham fidgeted in his chair, turning the pages of the newspaper much too fast to be reading them.

"You must be wanting to go somewhere," she said; "I never saw anyone's *derrière* hate a chair as much as yours does at the moment."

"Well, you see, Molly . . . the Lobby is having its first meeting tonight . . . and my old earbones ache for a bout of loud laughter."

"Then for heaven's sake be gone; you're no good to me in this condition."

As he bounded down the front steps she smiled to herself, thinking that she really had no complaint about him: he chopped an ample supply of firewood each day for the stoves and fireplaces, milked their cow and groomed their horse, kept the stable clean and the back yard in order, arranged to have walks put in, the well dug deeper, the fence repaired.

For that matter she was proud of herself as a housewife: her storeroom was filled with barrels of flour, pickles, condiments, hams, sacks of rice and raisins and prunes. She was not the best cook in the world, but she was learning how to roast coffee until it was only slightly red, thus getting the most value and flavor for her money; how to make the best cheese by straining it into a cheese tub immediately after the cow was milked; and her family had been eating fresh peaches all winter because last summer she had learned how to cover the ripe peaches with a paste made of gum arabic, and then two coats of varnish. Now when they wanted a fresh peach they simply took the coating off as though it were the shell of a hard-boiled egg.

The house did not lend itself to an elegance of entertaining, the hall and dining room were small and dark, there was no openness or flow between the rooms; but she substituted her Bluegrass graciousness and skill as a hostess, welcoming each guest in the foyer with a warm clasp of the hand, a light kiss on the cheek, an interested question.

In spite of her many duties at home, for she only occasionally had an Irish girl in to help, she became one of the leaders of the Episcopal Sewing Society. Several afternoons a week a large farm wagon drew up in front of the Lincoln home and when Mary came out with her big sewing basket she would find Mercy Conkling and half a dozen other of the club members in the midst of the huge mound of hay. After she got in, the wagon went on to the next house to pick up another member, until the church ladies were stacked in the hay as close as crockery ware.

It was a Thursday, July 3, when she became aware that she was again

149

pregnant; the date was etched on her mind because she told Abraham that night and they talked of their hope for a daughter, in fact talked so long in the friendly intimacy of their bed that they heard the church bells toll curfew before they fell asleep. It seemed to her only minutes later when she was awakened by the firing of thirteen guns. Abraham's eyes popped open at the same moment.

"All this celebration just because I'm going to have another child? How did the militia find out so quick?"

He chuckled sleepily. "That's partly in your honor, Molly; the rest of it is to awaken Springfield to its Fourth of July celebration. All of which reminds me that I have to deliver an oration at the state house."

Just before two o'clock the Lincolns walked to the square. The state house grounds were still unfenced and filled with stones which were being dressed for the porticoes; hundreds of farm wagons and teams hitched up to the stones.

Mary listened to Mayor James Conkling's flattering introduction, and Abraham's "Mr. Chairman." He then launched into a two-hour speech in which he dwelt upon the forces in American life which created unity, carefully staying away from those issues which were in process of dividing the nation: slavery; war with Mexico over the annexation of Texas and California; war with Great Britain over the Oregon boundary. But his caution served little purpose, for her cousin John J. Hardin let it be known that he was once again on the track for the Whig nomination to Congress. Abraham rode his horse to Jacksonville to visit with Hardin, returning the next day not at all pleased.

"Your good cousin is none too fond of me," he said ruefully; "he repudiates any arrangement made for succession to Congress. He has already started his campaign."

Mary looked crestfallen.

"I worked for three years to establish the principle of rotation in office," he continued, rubbing the stubble on his chin. "However Hardin has a lot of friends; if he takes the nomination this time he's going to stay in Congress. That will be the end of the Honorable A. Lincoln."

To complicate things further, her cousin Stephen Logan chose this moment to inform the Lincolns that he too wished to get the nomination for Congress right now. She and Abraham spent their evenings writing dozens of letters to the Whig delegates stating Abraham's views.

"It shouldn't take very much more effort to get nominated for the presidency," she commented dryly.

Stephen Logan, after considerable persuasion, agreed to propose Abraham's name for the nomination at the next Whig convention providing Abraham would not attempt to succeed himself. There remained only her cousin John J. to mollify.

She waited until he came to Springfield on a legal matter and had herself invited to her cousin Stuart's home where he was staying. Hardin was successful, wealthy, the commanding general of the state militia, still the handsomest of all her cousins, with a mass of jet-black hair just beginning to turn gray at the temples, large and strong black eyes, a Roman nose and firm mouth and chin. Stuart tactfully gave them the parlor for their tête-à-tête.

"Cousin John J.," she began, "Abraham waited patiently while you and Baker had your Congressional terms, and now he believes that it is his turn."

"Mary, I've always liked you, and I don't want this dispute to cause hard feelings. There is nothing personal in my refusal to step out of the way for your husband, but simply my conviction that this is an idiotic method of having representation in Congress. No one man stays there long enough to find out what it's all about, nor yet to gain enough seniority to be put on important committees. How is any one of us to get himself known among his fellow members, and hence have any voice or influence? A freshman congressman can accomplish nothing, and by this rotation method we are going to have nothing but freshman congressmen until doomsday."

"I don't dispute your logic," she said softly, "but belonging as we do to a minority party in Illinois, there is nothing available to us except this one Congressional seat in the Seventh District. That forces us into the position of sharing it among our best men."

"Mary, your husband is trying to interfere with the right of the people to select their candidate."

She put her hands up on his broad shoulders and pleaded: "Oh, Cousin, we've waited so long. Please do let us have our chance."

Abraham returned early in December to attend the opening of the Supreme Court. She did not tell him of her conversation with Hardin. He was convinced that John J. would make a fight of it on the convention floor.

Throughout the controversy she had tried to heed Dr. Wallace's warning, worrying herself as little as possible over the outcome. One other concern she had been less able to crowd out of her mind: the fear that her second child too would be born with crossed eyes.

She was pleased when Abraham agreed to let her celebrate the holiday season with a New Year's party; the activity would keep her mind occupied. She sent out word that all friends would be welcome at open house, then ordered from Mr. Watson two great pyramids of brown sticky macaroons covered with a web of spun sugar, one for each end of her buffet table; in the center she put a bowl of oranges with their skins cut in fancy shapes, flanked by silver trays of raisins, almonds and white grapes; as a special treat she made a pink and white calf's-foot jelly; and at the last moment, when Abraham was not looking, spiked the eggnog with Kentucky bourbon.

Mary was considerably less surprised than Abraham when in mid-February John J. Hardin reluctantly withdrew from the congressional contest, leaving the nomination to Abraham.

In the second week of March in her own home and her own bed, her second son, Edward, was born; the disappointment over not having had a daughter vanished when she became convinced that this little fellow's eyes were normal. The bedroom became a nursery, with the tiny washtub before the fire, the wooden rack for warming his clothes also by the fire, the cradle on her side of the bed, set on high legs so that she could put her arm out in half sleep and rock him if he whimpered during the night. Robert was given one of the upstairs rooms as a bedroom.

On May 11, ten days after he was officially nominated, and four days after Simeon Francis set upon the masthead of the *Sangamo Journal:*

ABRAHAM LINCOLN FOR CONGRESS

the United States declared war on Mexico. Illinois went war-mad; there were mass meetings for volunteers, patriotic speeches, parades, all-day sewing bees. John J. Hardin was appointed by Governor Ford to command the First Illinois Regiment; James Shields resigned as commissioner of the Land Office to become a brigadier general of Illinois volunteers, their friend Edward Baker left Congress to raise and lead the Fourth Illinois Regiment; even Stephen Douglas tried to resign to enter the army. But Mary saw no such signs in her husband; he disapproved of Simeon Francis's editorials in the *Journal* crying up the war, and he feared that President Polk's dispatching of General Taylor to the Rio Grande had helped precipitate the war.

"I take it you are not rushing out to form a Fifth Illinois Regiment?" she asked tentatively.

"I went to the Black Hawk War to chase Indians . . . but I'm much older now. I don't like war. I don't understand it. It kills my soul to think of how many of those fine Springfield boys will never be coming back. Our government's attitude reminds me of the Illinois farmer who said, 'I ain't greedy about land, I only want what jines mine.'"

The Democrats nominated Peter Cartwright, circuit-riding Methodist clergyman, one of the candidates who had defeated Abraham in his first contest for the state legislature back in 1832, to defeat Mr. Lincoln all over again. Cartwright was the most magnetic and indefatigable preacher in Illinois, traveling thousands of miles each year to hold revival and camp meetings. He wore his thick hair thatched like the roof of a peasant cottage, his enormous mouth when in action stretched from one jawbone to the other.

When Abraham heard of Cartwright's nomination he exclaimed, "This isn't going to be a political campaign; we don't differ on anything except the tariff. If I know Peter Cartwright, it's going to be a religious revival. I think I'll just try to shake hands with everybody in the district."

One warm Sunday at the beginning of July they went to hear Cartwright conduct his major Springfield meeting. They found seats on the far side in the last row. The Reverend Cartwright preached a hell-fire and damnation sermon against sinners.

"I don't see why he should be looking for sinners here," Abraham whispered, "these are all his fellow Democrats."

At this moment Cartwright spotted the Lincolns. He gazed at Abraham for a moment, then held out his arms and exhorted, "All who desire to lead a new life, to give their hearts to God and to go to heaven, will stand." A few stood. "All who do *not* wish to go to hell will stand." The rest of the audience rose. Mary sank as low as she could in her seat while the crowd turned to stare. The mellifluous voice of the Reverend Cartwright declaimed:

"I observe that many responded to the first invitation to give their hearts to God and go to heaven. I further observed that all save one indicated that he did not desire to go hell. May I inquire of you, Mr. Lincoln, where you are going?"

Abraham rose slowly and said in his nasal Kentucky drawl:

"I am going to Congress."

There was a moment of stunned silence, then the audience broke into uproarious laughter. Abraham took Mary's arm and led her out of the tent-tabernacle. She was chuckling to herself, but he was not amused.

"I think it is bad taste on his part," he said, "to convert a political rally into a religious one."

Mary linked her arm intimately through her husband's, said: "But that little joke of yours is going to do more than any hundred stump speeches to prove to the people that the Reverend Cartwright should be left at home to practice religion, while you should be sent to Washington to practice politics."

She was right: within two days the story had traveled the length of the district; the people were laughing at the way Lincoln had turned the tables on Cartwright. The clergyman retaliated with a public statement that Abraham Lincoln was an infidel, and hence had no right to represent Christians in Congress.

The humor of the situation drained off. For several days Mary watched Abraham write ideas on small slips of paper and put them in his hat; then when he was ready he sat at his desk with the scraps of paper in front of him and wrote trial drafts until he had a short statement that satisfied him. He took it down to the *Journal* to have it printed and distributed throughout the Seventh District:

Fellow Citizens:
    A charge having got into circulation . . . that I am an open scoffer at Christianity, I have concluded to notice the subject in this form. That I am not a member of any Christian Church, is true; but I have never denied the truth of the Scriptures; and I have never spoken with intentional disrespect of religion in general, or of any denomination of Christians in particular. . . . I still do not think any man has the right thus to insult the feelings of the community in which he may live. . . .

Whether it was the penetrating power of the joke, the reverberations of the Reverend Cartwright's bad political manners, or merely that the district was predominantly Whig, Mary was not able to ascertain, but Abraham secured fifty-six per cent of the total vote.

"I don't know why, but being elected to Congress doesn't please me as much as I had expected it would," he said morosely that night as he wandered into the sitting room from a pacing tour of the house.

"That's a normal letdown, Honorable A. Lincoln," she replied, maternally, "like after childbirth. Wait until you are up and on your feet again, you'll be happy about it."

8

STEPHEN DOUGLAS, re-elected to his third term in Congress, came to the house to pump their arms vigorously.

"Congratulations, *tous les deux*, as Mary taught me to say. I wouldn't want to put it in the *Register* that I was happy over your victory, but then I've always said that of all the damned Whigs around Springfield Abraham Lincoln was the honestest."

Abraham laughed. Mary said, "It took us an awfully long time to catch up with you, Steve, but we're glad you're going to be in Washington when we get there."

"Lincoln, I gather you're fainthearted about the war in Mexico? That's no way to become a national hero: a patriot and moralist never slept comfortably in the same bed."

Abraham shrugged. "I've never yet found a bed that my feet didn't stick out of."

Over a glass of ginger beer and some sweet cakes Mary had baked that morning, Douglas told of his plan to move permanently to Chicago, of having bought property in the new lake-front town. He also confided that he had fallen in love with the daughter of a North Carolina planter, and hoped to be married the following spring.

But when the Illinois legislature met next they named Congressman Stephen Douglas to the United States Senate. Mary exclaimed, "He told me several years ago, 'Once I get into the United States Senate, I'll stay there forever.'"

Abraham went out to the hall and took from his hat an invitation he had received the day before.

"Listen to this, Mary:

"Grand fete in honor of the Honorable Stephen A. Douglas. State House. A fine collation will be spread in the Senate Chamber. Dainty eatables, no lack of drinkables. Grand Ball in the Chamber of the House. You and your lady are cordially invited."

"All we caught up with him for was four months," she said, nettled.

"Now, Molly, I'm not running a foot race with Douglas; there's plenty of room for both of us."

154

"For two presidents from Illinois?"

Abraham chuckled. "Seeing how long it took us to get elected to Congress, we'll be as old as Methuselah by the time we're president. Do you keep making these comparisons between Douglas and me because you could have married either of us and you like to see how good your judgment was?"

"I could not have married Steve because he never asked me, and I never loved him." Her voice was astringent. "Physically and mentally we're as alike as peas in a pod; we would have done as well marrying our image in the mirror. So even if he were to become Emperor of China there would be no reason to regret my choice."

"He's not likely to become Emperor of China, but he has the road to the Executive Mansion surveyed as neatly as the engineers put the rails between here and Jacksonville."

She planted her feet resolutely apart.

"Would you like to bet a hailstorm on the outcome?"

She was ready to pack her things and leave for Washington then and there, but it would be a year before Abraham was seated. She resolved to live quietly and spend the long interval preparing for the trip and for a visit with her family in Lexington. She spent most of her time sewing prodigiously, building a fashionable wardrobe, stocking linens for the boys. When Abraham demurred at buying a new suit and boots, she told him stoutly:

"Abraham, you must! I'm not taking any poor relations home with me."

Having re-established herself socially, she had no need to continue her dinner parties. They both wanted to save money: Abraham to pay off the last of his New Salem debts and leave for Washington a free man; she to accumulate enough to rent a fine home, install a staff of servants, set her husband against a brilliant background. She locked up her sugar bowl and other expensive groceries because the Irish girls who came and went were using them prodigally; when the fire died overnight on the hearth, Abraham walked to a neighbor's house with a shovel to pick up live coals instead of buying expensive friction matches.

When Abraham was leaving for his office one morning she asked him for a little money. He told her he would send it home with his new law student. A few minutes later there was a knock on the door; she opened it to find a blond-haired, blue-eyed young man standing there.

"Mrs. Lincoln? I'm Gibson Harris. Mr. Lincoln asked me to bring this envelope to you."

His voice was soft, his manner genteel. She invited him in. He accepted with a gracious bow, then told her that he had been studying with Lincoln and Herndon for several weeks. Mary asked whether he found Mr. Lincoln a good teacher. He cocked his head to one side, a bright gleam in his eye.

"When I want training on the rules of evidence or anything else technical, I go to Mr. Herndon. Mr. Lincoln teaches me about getting to the point. Only this morning he told me that a tree divested of its foliage was more interesting to him than the same tree in its full array of green. The skeleton, he said, was then exposed to view in all its beauty of curved line, and ugliness of knots and gnarls. It was easy then to decide whether it was worthy of one's admiration or not."

That evening she asked Abraham if it would not be nice to have Mr. Harris join them for Sunday dinner.

"By all means. It'll be good to have a new audience to read to."

He turned a chair upside down, sat on the floor, leaning against the back of the chair and began reading with great relish from *The Report of the Exploring Expedition to the Rocky Mountains and to Oregon and North California* by Captain John C. Fremont, which had started a wave of migration westward by its clear maps and brilliant descriptions of trails, terrain and wild life across the plains and the Rockies. The previous spring Mary had seen a party of her neighbors making up for the trip west, headed by two families well known in Springfield, George Donner and James Reed, with its prairie schooners, horses, mules and cows, furniture, food stocks, guns, a group of thirty-four men, women and children.

Young Harris came to the house frequently for Sunday dinner. On two occasions when Abraham had to be out of town and there was an interesting party, he suggested that Harris be Mary's escort. For Mary he became her husband's law partner, taking the place of the man whose name was never mentioned in their home.

Spring came in warm and lovely, with early blossoms on the trees and wild flowers on the prairies; for Mary it was a pleasant spring. Dr. Wallace had been right; what she had needed was to live without pressure, immersed in a simple household routine. She exercised considerable self-discipline, walked away from little worries and aggravations. It was a period of happiness and placidity. Abraham planted fruit trees, she grew flowers in the back yard. What she could not turn away from she tried to bear with a minimum of emotion. One day a thunderstorm broke, crashing about her head in continuous earth-shaking rolls that seemed to get under her skin, then re-explode outward through the pores of her body. She continued with her chores as long as she could, then fled to the bedroom, pulling the covers over her head. A few minutes later she heard the front door slam and Abraham was by her side, clasping her in protective arms.

"Abraham . . . why are you home . . . in midmorning?"

"I know how much the thunder upsets you, and when I heard it getting worse, I came running."

After the noonday dinner she heard a tremendous clatter on the stairs. She ran into the hall just in time for Robert to land at her feet, yowling. Looking up, she saw Abraham standing in his stockinged feet, shaking with laughter.

"He's been trying to fill my boots for some time now, and I guess they finally throwed him. He isn't hurt."

He was tender and devoted to the children, bringing home sweets, hauling them about in their wagon, inventing games to amuse them. He was particularly devoted to Robert, who was bright and talkative; Abraham called him a rare-ripe, and took pleasure in the boy's sturdy build. Her one complaint was that he refused to discipline his sons, saying:

"There's enough unhappiness in the world; let them have happy childhoods."

"But they'll be unmanageable if they're not controlled. We're entitled to happy adulthoods, aren't we?"

He smiled at her joke. "My father held me with an iron hand. My little codgers are going to love me even if I have to let them burn the house down."

But it began to need more than a father's indulgence to bring happiness to Robert: he grew sullen, uncommunicative, then nasty to his brother. When Mary admonished him he started running away from home; she would have to call at the top of her lungs from the front stoop, or go on long searches for him. She punished him when he was found, but that only made him run away more often. Then one afternoon he came in from playing with the older boys of the neighborhood, buried his face in her apron and sobbed:

". . . Mama . . . why do the boys . . . call me . . . cockeyes . . . ?"

Her heart was encased in pain. She crouched down and held him to her, but could not answer.

". . . why do they . . . make fun of me . . . why must my eyes . . . be like this? Mama, can't you fix them . . . ?"

Robert's private hell continued, and he continued to make Edward's life miserable, destroying his toys, slapping him so hard that once the blood came from the baby's nose. Abraham turned to Mary and asked sadly:

"How can one little boy be so mean?"

"He's taking it out on the baby because Eddie doesn't have to share his burden."

There was a growing unhappiness in Springfield too, for the enthusiasm for the war was abating; many Illinois boys had died of fever at Matamoros, James Shields was shot through the lungs at Cerro Gordo, John J. Hardin was killed at the battle of Buena Vista. Equally heartbreaking was the report from California that a portion of the Donner party had perished in the snows of the high Sierras, with charges of murder and cannibalism in the death of several of the smaller children.

Her father wrote that Cassius Clay had been captured by the Mexicans; however he had saved the lives of an entire company of Lexington boys and was considered a great hero. This was in contrast to the revilement with which Lexington had surrounded him two years before when he had begun publishing a newspaper, the *True American*, whose purpose was to fight slavery from inside the slave states. Mary had seen the announcements of the proposed paper in the *Journal* and had sent Cassius Clay a subscription. She read aloud to Abraham Cassius's first editorials, in which they found

Clay announcing himself as an "avowed and uncompromising enemy of slavery," but calling for "the liberation of all slaves by legal means."

"A brave man, your friend Clay," commented Abraham. "I like it all except his veiled threat that a failure to eradicate slavery will lead to the battlefield."

It had ended with a mob moving onto the *True American* office and dismantling the presses. When Abraham told the story to Gibson Harris over the supper table one night, the law student replied:

"My father believes we'll have to fight a civil war to keep the Union in existence, not in his time, he says, but surely in mine. He believes that when the war is over, slavery will be done away with and the government preserved in even greater power."

Mary's hand trembled; she set down her coffee cup. War . . . between Kentucky . . . and Illinois . . . with her sons fighting . . . and killing . . . Betsy's sons . . . ? It was unthinkable!

"Gibson, I urge you not to repeat such things. Abraham will tell you that that kind of talk is dangerous. . . ."

Abraham sat with his big head bowed, dark and brooding. When he spoke his answer was oblique.

"Our form of government is the nearest to perfection of any I know of in the extent to which it represents and protects the masses. The government is the people's: it's in their hands to make or mar. We've marred it with slavery, but to go to war because we fail to find a peaceable compromise . . . That would be a cruel and tragic failure; our Union is the bedrock of our beings; destroy that and you destroy the last great hope on earth."

On the first of July he left by stage for a four-day trip to Chicago to attend the River and Harbor Convention. Much as Mary wanted to see the infant city, she declined Abraham's invitation to go along.

"I want you to be free to make friends. It'll be a chance for you to meet all the big Whigs, no pun intended, so that you will be known by the time we reach Washington."

"Now, Molly, I'm only to make one short speech."

"What about those three days of storytelling?"

"*Touché!* as we used to say in our French class at Mentelle's," he replied, teasing her. "I should bag a new friend or two."

He did better than that; a few days after he returned home, Mary opened a copy of the New York *Tribune* and read in a report by Horace Greeley, one of the most powerful newspaper editors in the country:

The Honorable Abraham Lincoln, a tall specimen of an Illinoisan, just elected to Congress from the only Whig district in the state, was called out, and spoke briefly and happily in reply to Mr. Field.

"I like that word 'happily,'" she commented. "I like it almost as much as 'lucible.'"

158

"Here's more good news, Molly: I've leased our house for a year to Cornelius Ludlum, the brick contractor. I've agreed to take ninety dollars instead of the hundred we spoke of, in return for the north bedroom where we'll be able to store all our furniture. Pleased?"

Ninety dollars would cover a considerable part of the rent for the house she envisaged for them in Washington! She reached her arms around her husband's neck and kissed him.

"I'm very pleased, Mr. Lincoln."

9

THE stagecoach left from the Globe Tavern at four in the morning, the Lincolns walking to the hotel in the dark, Abraham carrying Robert, Edward asleep on Mary's shoulder. She found the road to Alton little improved since she had come over it eight years before, the season's first rains having turned it into a quagmire. The ninety-eight miles took two days; on Wednesday morning they boarded a fast steamboat for St. Louis, but after they had covered seven miles in the first hour they ran onto a sand bar and were stuck fast, all the men being obliged to go ashore to lighten the boat. At St. Louis they changed to a larger boat which went down the Mississippi and there turned into the Ohio River to Louisville, a distance of over five hundred miles. They occupied a small mahogany-lined cabin, with trundles for the children.

As she neared Lexington on the short railroad trip from Frankfort and began to recognize the brown hemp fields and meadows, then the forests of hickory and maple, nostalgia seized her. Old Nelson was at the station to meet them, dressed in his light blue coat with the long tails and silver buttons. It was a raw blustery day; her heart was pounding so high in her throat that she could hardly see the familiar shops on Main Street.

She went into the house first with Edward in her arms, followed by Abraham carrying the constrained Robert. The family was standing near the front door, first Betsy with her arms open, now with gray in her hair and her face a little thinner but with eyes still enormously alert; next came the children, Martha, fourteen, Emilie, eleven, Elodie, seven, Katherine, six, in crimson merino dresses with white kid boots and ruffled white muslin aprons. David, big for his fifteen years, hugged her until she thought her ribs would crack; Samuel had ridden in from Centre College in Danville, tall, handsome, with a set of gorgeous white teeth; lastly there was red-haired Alexander, whom she had carried around on her shoulder, now eight.

Next was her colored family waiting to shake hands and "make a 'miration" over the babies: first Mammy Sally, bigger and more formless than ever, but with a broad grin as Mary kissed her and put Edward in her arms;

then Chaney the cook, who exclaimed, "Miss Mary, you mean to tell me those Irish girls up there don't know how to make beaten biscuits?"

Abraham was in the meanwhile being introduced separately to each member of the family; he recognized Emilie from Mary's description, took her from where she was hiding behind Betsy's voluminous skirts, saying, "So this is Little Sister."

The door was thrown open and she was locked in her father's arms; this was really home-coming for her. He was wearing a suit of blue broadcloth, buff waistcoat and lace ruffled shirt with jeweled buttons. He had turned out in his newest and best for her.

For dinner Chaney prepared her favorite foods, though Old Nelson's nose was out of joint because Abraham refused one of his mint juleps in the tall frosted silver goblet.

Betsy had made Mary's old bedroom available to the Lincolns. As they were unpacking, Abraham said:

"I like this house very much; it isn't as big and costly as I had imagined."

Mary smiled to herself: Abraham could have no way of knowing how expensive Betsy's severely tailored and rigorous good taste was.

Later, while he was in bed reading the Lexington *Observer*, she joined her father in the library. After a moment of strained silence he said:

"You're wondering where your brothers are. I asked them specially to come today, but you see . . . they didn't accommodate me. Levi is living in your birth house, George is staying down at Megowan's Hotel and going to medical school. He is doing well in his studies, but he will have nothing to do with Betsy and the youngsters." He walked agitatedly to the fireplace; when he turned to face her she saw that there were tears in his eyes. "Mary, you're the only connecting link between my two families, the only one of my children who loves both sides. Promise me that you will love your half brothers and sisters and stand by them. I have no one to rely on but you."

"I've always loved these youngsters, Father, and I never think of them as half sisters or brothers. I remember Dr. Ward once saying that I never would be any good at fractions."

The next morning the November sun was out warm and bright. She took Abraham for a walk along the white gravel paths, lined with rosebushes, then down to the bottom of the hill where they stood on the little bridge overlooking the creek. Then she escorted him on a tour of the town, showing him the beautiful manor houses and gardens, the paved streets and sidewalks. Abraham was enchanted by the lawns and flowers, the absence of pigs and garbage in the streets. Monsieur Giron had moved away and Dr. Ward was dead, but College Lot and Transylvania University were unchanged.

As they came to the terrace of the Parker lawn they heard sounds of moaning and weeping. Abraham froze in his tracks; below them across Mechanics Alley they could see through the spiked palings into the yard of slave pens jammed with Negroes of both sexes, some standing, some squatting on damp brick floors. A Negro was tied by his wrists to the top of a post in the corner of the yard. The blood left Abraham's face.

"That's Pullum's slave jail," said Mary quietly. "You look as though you were about to faint."

Betsy gave a formal party for them, inviting their friends for buffet supper and dancing: the Wickliffes, the Bodleys, the Trotters, the Crittendens, the Stuarts, Warfields, Humphreys, Morgans, Clays, Breckinridges. The years vanished for Mary as she watched the servants move the green velvet and gold rocking chairs into the hall, and then the carved cherrywood sofa. The red walnut table in the dining room was pulled out to its full length, covered with one of Betsy's finest damask cloths, her silver candelabra and silver platters of roasted beef, hickory-smoked hams, the chilled oysters so popular in Lexington.

There was the sound of horses on the gravel driveway, and Mary was welcoming her old friends, dressed in their brilliant gowns and jewels, the men in tight trousers, gaily colored vests and coats. Betsy had invited Desmond Fleming and his green-eyed blond young wife. To Margaret Wickliffe's raised eyebrow, Mary giggled:

"He's as proud and handsome as a peacock; but what would I do with a peacock?"

Her brother George arrived late, red-faced and a little drunk. He had remained small of build; the speech impediment had developed into a serious stutter. Mary tried to tell him how happy she was to see him; he was starting to respond when a group of guests came to say hello to him. He became brusque, went into the dining room, poured himself a long drink of bourbon, then disappeared. Levi finally had consented to come, bringing his wife Louisa, a plump-faced young woman who had helped him to become a reliable manager of the family hemp factory in Sandersville.

The party was a glorious success. She received invitations to a dozen formal dinners and balls. Her friends appeared to enjoy Abraham, though Fleming could not resist calling her "Mrs. Congressman."

Abraham began leaving early in the morning with her father to go down to the courthouse and to the brick buildings of Jordan's Row where Lexington's attorneys had their offices. In the afternoons she found him in the little upstairs sitting room in front of the shelves of books, reading in *Elegant Extracts*. One day he quoted to her from Bryant's *Thanatopsis*, the next it was Pope's:

> Know then thyself, presume not God to scan;
> The proper study of mankind is man.

She rarely had seen him so happy or carefree.

One Saturday evening they went to the Market House to hear Henry Clay; Abraham never had heard his hero speak. He was entranced by Clay's resonant voice and captivating manner; he agreed when Mr. Clay declared that "this is no war of defense, but one unnecessary and of offensive aggression." The next day, Sunday, they were invited out to Ashland for a glass of Madeira.

The following Monday was Court Day. At noon Mary and Abraham walked up to Cheapside where she saw the familiar sight of the lawn in front of the courthouse jammed with horses, cows and goats for sale, junk dealers peddling secondhand plows, nostrum venders dressed in high stovepipe hats, green and yellow brocaded waistcoats, their long hair falling over their velvet collars.

In a few moments the public sale of slaves began in front of the courthouse door. Abraham took her arm. They moved in closer to the slave traders, still wearing their hammer-tailed coats and beaver hats, crying out the virtues of "this buck, strong able-bodied, good kennel man; this wench, twenty-three years old, good cook . . ."

Abraham's fingers were bruising her arm. He whispered, "Come away."

They were making their way through the crowd when she heard a raucous voice cry out from the block:

"Next lot, five Negroes belonging to Robert S. Todd and William A. Leavy: for sale to the highest bidder to satisfy a judgment. All hard workers, child-bearing, sound of wind and limb . . ."

They pushed across Cheapside . . . then Mary found herself staring into the eyes of her father, his face chalk-white.

"Mary, you will explain to Abraham that I had no choice? I loaned William Leavy's brother a large sum of money and he failed to repay. These slaves were his only assets; they were put up for sale by the court."

She slipped an arm through her father's, the other through Abraham's. They walked home in silence. She turned her head slightly and stole a look at her husband to see what he might be thinking of her father's responsibility in the matter. But when Abraham spoke it was in the privacy of their room; nor did he mention Robert Todd.

"How easily I've said that slavery must not be abolished where it existed, that slaves are private property and the constitution guarantees that no man can be deprived of his property without due process of law. Are these creatures property, or are they human beings? Which comes first, life or law? What can our constitution really mean if it permits this enslaving of the human soul and the human body?"

She knew no way of solacing him.

10

THEY arrived in Washington late at night with the children asleep in their arms, made their way through the crowd of rough-looking idlers who thronged the dirty and dilapidated railroad shed and emerged at Pennsylvania Avenue and Second Street, to be faced by shouting hackney drivers. It took only a few minutes to be driven over the rough cobblestones of Pennsylvania Avenue to Brown's Hotel where, chilled and exhausted by the week's journey, they put the children in the center of the big bed and fell asleep on either side of them, only half undressed.

In the morning they had a late breakfast, then went out to see the sights. The mud-rutted streets were littered with garbage, with pigs, geese and chickens roaming the thoroughfares, eating the refuse. Open fields separated every two or three homes. They walked through the grounds of the White House and the Capitol at the end of Pennsylvania Avenue; close by was the State Department in a two-story house, the War and Navy Departments also occupied small houses, and a Treasury building was in process of construction.

On Pennsylvania Avenue they saw a coffle of chained slaves coming up the street, chanting a religious hymn. Just before they reached the Lincolns they were turned by their guards and driven into a barnlike structure called the Georgia Pen, a heavy wooden door closing behind them. Abraham said in a voice she barely could hear: "What a dreadful thing to happen in the capital of a free country."

At noon they piled their luggage in a hackney cab and drove to Mrs. Sprigg's boardinghouse, which stood on a hill overlooking Capitol Park. Mary was delighted to find First Street wide and tree-lined, with a well-defined coal-ash sidewalk. The corner house was occupied by Duff Green, one of the country's best-known newspaper publishers, next came two private homes, after these two boardinghouses, then Mrs. Sprigg's.

Ann Sprigg welcomed them at the front door; she was a cultivated woman with a gracious manner. She led them up two flights of stairs and to the back of the house to a good-sized room containing two large beds, two wardrobes, dusty flowered wallpaper, faded draperies and much-laundered bedcovers. Out the rear windows Mary saw an array of privies, next to them pigsties, then a cowshed and other shanties; ducks, chickens, pigs, dogs rooted about the yard. She turned away quickly from the window; after all, this was temporary.

There was a soft knock on the door. She opened it to find a Negro in his mid-forties with gray cropped hair and gentle eyes, standing with a bell in his hand. He introduced himself as Willis, the butler.

"Supper be served, Mr. and Mrs. Linkern."

The dining room was in back of the main parlor, a long narrow room with a long narrow table. The Lincolns were the last to arrive. Everyone rose to be introduced. At the head of the table sat Mrs. Sprigg and next to her Joshua Giddings, a fiery abolitionist from Ohio. Ranged down one side were five fellow Whigs from Pennsylvania. The Lincolns found their seats at this side of the table. At the foot sat Mr. Richardson with a pregnant wife; coming up the other side were Mr. and Mrs. Duff Green, who had their meals at the boardinghouse, and Patrick W. Tompkins of Mississippi; a Mr. and Mrs. Broome, and Nathan Sargent, a witty journalist whose work the Lincolns always had enjoyed; then Congressman Embree from Indiana; a man by the name of French; next, small red-haired Mr. Humpstuffe, an unhappy-looking creature who immediately launched into a clinical description of his latest malady to a young medical graduate by the name of Samuel Busey. Immediately across from Mary sat a hirsute man with black thatches of hair growing out of his ears and nostrils; during dinner he snatched up snuff from a vest pocket and stuffed it into his capacious nose. There were twenty-four altogether at table. Robert and Edward were the only children.

Monday she accompanied Abraham to the Capitol, making her way up the flight of stairs to the visitors' gallery behind the House where she watched the new members draw ballots for seats. Abraham drew just about the worst location in the chamber, in the back row. Willis had pressed his suit and polished his black boots; she had saved a new white shirt, collar and silk stock for this important occasion. She thought him quite handsome, towering above the rest of the House, his hair washed and combed back from his brow, with a clean close shave, and his eyes alight. At the stroke of twelve the Speaker ordered the new members to rise, and she smiled happily as Abraham took his oath of office.

She settled down to the routine of the boardinghouse, knowing that she must remain here a number of weeks until she became acquainted with Washington and found a proper house in a proper neighborhood. The weather being pleasant, she kept the boys out in the park, reading while they amused themselves sailing boats in the fountain. She importuned Abraham to make his maiden flight in the House; after two weeks he replied:

"Since you are so anxious for me to distinguish myself, I have concluded to do so."

Twice she went to sit in the thousand-seat gallery to hear her husband, on December 22 when he asked President Polk to inform the House "whether the particular spot of soil on which the blood of our *citizens* was shed was, or was not, *our own soil*, at that time"; and then his first long speech concerning postal contracts for the carrying of the mail. She was miffed to find how few visitors had come to hear the Honorable A. Lincoln distinguish himself.

She had expected that the conversation at the dinner table would be peaceable, since there were only Whigs present, but Congressman Dickey of Pennsylvania seemed to derive special pleasure from baiting Congressman Tompkins of Mississippi, a gentleman who preferred to keep his boardinghouse opinions to himself. Abolitionist Dickey's booming voice and violent language several times made Robert cry, so that Mary had to take the boy upstairs to quiet him. The next time Dickey started an uproar, saying he hoped Tompkins would be defeated by an anti-slavery Whig, Abraham laid down his knife and fork, rested his face between his hands and said in his highest nasal drawl:

164

"Speaking of defeat reminds me of a man who was nominated for supervisor. When he left home on election morning he said to his wife. 'Tonight you shall sleep with the supervisor of this town.' The overconfident gentleman was defeated; the wife immediately donned her Sunday best. 'Wife, where are you going this time of night?' he exclaimed. 'You told me that tonight I should sleep with the supervisor,' she replied, 'so I was going to his house.'"

His tale told, he put his head back and laughed; everyone at the table joined in, even the puzzled Dickey, who could not figure whether the joke was on him or Tompkins.

She did not tell Abraham of her plan to find a house; the need for such a house would grow: there would be invitations, they would be obliged to entertain in return; there would be important men and well-placed families with whom Abraham would find it desirable to become more intimate.

Snow began to fall, then came heavy rainstorms, turning the city into a swamp, with mud in the streets knee-deep. It was impossible to take the children to the park. Joshua Giddings sometimes would entertain the boys in the parlor, but her most important help came from Willis. She learned that he had been working for years to buy his freedom; in another two years he would have the remaining sixty dollars paid. On those occasions when she wanted to go shopping or accompany Abraham, Willis took care of the children; when he was busy he brought in his sister Willissa, a competent nursemaid.

Mary started reconnoitering in earnest, resolved to penetrate her way into the fabric of the city. Capitol Hill, where Mrs. Sprigg's boardinghouse was located, was one of the favorite residential districts: here Senator Thomas Hart Benton lived with his wife and several daughters, including Jessie Fremont, whose husband had just returned from California under court-martial. A few houses away was General John Adams Dix's family, also Secretary of State James Buchanan's bachelor home. These people were of the highest social standing, the permanent occupants of Washington. However the section she thought most pleasant was the square on F Street between Thirteenth and Fourteenth, where ex-President John Quincy Adams, who was now in the House, resided. She knew that rents would be high, but she was gambling for high stakes.

New Year's Day was the greatest of social days in Washington, with the president, vice-president, secretary of state, and such illustrious widows as Mrs. James Madison and Mrs. Alexander Hamilton holding open house. When Joshua Giddings learned that the Lincolns were planning to go to the White House for the reception he cried:

"You wouldn't really subject yourself to that?"

Nevertheless on New Year's Day Mary dressed in a gown of white silk with blue brocaded flowers woven through it. They hired a carriage to take them to the White House. The grounds were open to the public; hundreds of people were walking about on the lawns. The long line of carriages in front, made colorful by the liveries and cockades of the foreign ministers, showed that the reception was well under way.

The Lincolns surrendered their cloaks to a servant, then entered a room glittering with chandeliers and mirrors. At one end was a group of beautiful women exquisitely gowned, wearing diamonds on their heads and bosoms; at the other, some fifty or sixty gentlemen, standing in silence. President Polk was in the center of the room, on his right hand Mr. Marcy, the Secretary of War, behind him Mrs. Polk seated in a large chair. Mary and Abraham took their places on the end of a reception line. After some fifteen minutes of inching forward, Mary found herself being greeted by Sarah Polk, quietly gowned in maroon velvet; of a religious turn of mind, she forbade cards, dancing or other amusement in the White House.

In a second she had passed onto President Polk, a man of short stature with a high, broad forehead, well-set eyes and a firm mouth. He told her he was happy to receive her, but she merely curtsied, wanting to leave the time free for Abraham. Abraham was even more mute than she had been. A policeman then took him by the elbow and said:

"Gentlemen who have been presented will please walk forward to the East Room."

Before they knew what was happening they had gone through the East Room, were in the foyer where the Marine Band was playing, and out on the street.

"What do we do now?" asked Abraham, not altogether comfortable.

"I don't know; it's the first time I've ever been at a reception where there was nothing to eat or drink. It was kind of grim. Let's go across the street and try Mrs. James Madison's."

She had counted on old friends to launch her socially, but nothing seemed to happen. Stephen Douglas, now a senator, came to supper at Mrs. Sprigg's but never reciprocated. Mary was furious at Abraham when she learned that he had used the occasion to collect a debt owed by Douglas to one of his clients. When Henry Clay arrived to plead a case before the United States Supreme Court she dropped a note to his hotel. He promptly sent a message inviting them to supper that night, talked to them of his own affairs, then told them how glad he had been to see them. That was the last word she had from Mr. Clay.

Senator Crittenden, a lifetime friend of the Todd family, she saved for a special occasion: Sarah Benton was being married on the night of January 16, and Senator Crittenden had been invited to the wedding. Since the Thomas Hart Bentons were at the top of Washington society, Mary reasoned that if she were to be invited to the affair she would be formally launched. Could Senator Crittenden secure her an invitation to the Benton wedding? He could not; and she realized it had been a *faux pas* to ask.

She told Abraham nothing of her disappointments. He loved Mrs. Sprigg's, enjoyed walking to the Capitol with his fellow congressmen each day, sitting in the parlor after meals for an hour of talk. Several times a week he went with the other men to Caspari's bowling alley and here he bowled in graceless fashion, rarely winning but entertaining the crowd by his awkwardness and stories. Twice a week he took Mary out, to Carusi's to the Exhibition of Ethiopian Serenaders, or to hear the Slomans, a family of father and two daughters who played the harp and piano and sang. Several times they attended the Fremont court-martial to listen to its drama.

"Come spring," Abraham told her, "the Marine Band gives concerts on Wednesday and Saturday afternoons on the White House grounds. They tell me it's warm and beautiful, and you can sit out in your shirt sleeves."

He had been appointed to the Committee on Post Offices and Post Roads, and to the Committee on Expenditures in the War Department, which meant expenditures in furthering the war in Mexico. When this second appointment came through, Mary commented:

"That's like the Lobby in Springfield appointing you to the Committee on Etiquette, Politeness and Ceremony."

Her plan of having the need for a house arise out of the nature of their social life having failed, she started to search the group of residential streets settled by permanent government employees, and found a red brick house built in Baltimore style, with white stone steps and narrow white stone framing the windows of the two stories in front. The rent was high, three hundred dollars through the end of the congressional term, which would be in March of the following year; but the furnishings were pleasant, and she could very quickly turn it into a distinguished background for supper parties, teas and dances.

She waited until after Sunday dinner, then led Abraham to the little brick house, saying casually, "I want you to see a charming place." When she had finished taking him on tour, showing him the front and back parlors which could be opened into one big drawing room, the spacious dining room and three upstairs bedrooms, he suddenly stopped in the middle of a flight of steps, turned to her and said:

"Mary, what are you up to? Why have you brought me here?"

She took a deep breath, then let out her plea in one gasp.

"We've been over two months at the boardinghouse. It's time enough to get our bearings. We're going to be here another fifteen months. I think we ought to live as a family in our own home. . . ."

He was completely surprised.

"I didn't know you were unhappy at Mrs. Sprigg's. You said the cooking was good."

"I couldn't think of a possible word to say against Mrs. Sprigg, Abraham. But you know that I am not constituted for boardinghouse life."

"Then why did you come to Washington? Our plan was to stay at Mrs. Sprigg's."

His voice was a little harsh; she knew she had earned the reprimand.

"I came because I wanted to be with you, Abraham," she replied softly; "and because you like to have the children around. I also came . . ."

"But life is so simple and pleasant at Mrs. Sprigg's," he interrupted. "The rates are modest and we are well cared for. Why must you upset all that?"

"Because we didn't come to Washington to be comfortable. We came to be successful, you as a legislator and I as a hostess."

"Oh, so that's it: society."

She resisted the jibe.

"I have a good crew of servants lined up: Willis helped me get them. It would take me no more than a week to have this house running in beautiful fashion." She extended her hands, pleading. "Don't you see, my dear, I want to create a *milieu* for you; I want to invite the best families of Washington and the most important government officials, not only members of the House and Senate, but cabinet officers, foreign diplomats . . ."

"Whoa, whoa, Mary, the hosses have broken loose and left the cart behind. No one has bothered with us socially in the months we've been here, and I suspect you made several stalwart efforts? Then why should they bother with us just because we rent a house?"

She stretched to her full height, her head and shoulders back. "Society will come to us, I give you my promise of that."

"No, Mary, they won't. I don't want to be pushy, to be embarrassed by inviting people who want no part of us. I've heard it said that Washington is run by high southern society, that they're a snobbish and imperial group of women; they'll never let us in."

"I'm as high society as any woman in this town!"

"Granted, Molly, but the Lincolns ain't."

He was laughing at her now. That upset her more.

"Abraham, we've just got to establish you here as something more than a spinner of yarns in the House post office."

"Do I detect a touch of asperity in that description, Mrs. Lincoln?"

She veered to the political side.

"There is a presidential election coming up in November, and Polk has not been a popular president. If we win next time, it would be to your advantage to be known among the permanent senators and congressmen here in Washington. You want to be high in party councils."

"I can't see that I am going to get there by inviting folks to our home to eat dinner . . ." He started down the stairs. "Besides, I like Mrs. Sprigg's; I like the men there, the fun and comradeship."

"Well, I don't." She kept her position, her hands firmly gripping the stair rail. "It's difficult for me to drink my soup with Mr. Dickey shouting vile names; nor does it season the fish or fowl to have Mr. Humpstuffe describing the symptoms of his alternating constipation and diarrhea; nor is the dessert enhanced by the hairy boarder pushing snuff up his nose, then sneezing all over the table."

"Now, Mary, we have to take people as they come."

"But we don't have to," she pleaded. "This is a lovely house."

"Your cousin Stuart and his wife lived at Mrs. Sprigg's when they were here. Mrs. Richardson and Mrs. Coombs seem to be perfectly content. Why can't you be content, Mary?"

"Since you married me instead of any other woman I have a right to assume that the things that make me different from other women are the reasons that you married me."

He held his hand up to her, as though urging her to descend.

"Yes, you are very special, and I love you for all your special qualities, even those I have to argue with. But I'm not ready for a house like this; I'd be uncomfortable here, as though I were aspiring to some place where I didn't belong. Perhaps the next time we are elected to Congress . . . after we're better known . . . I'm not the greatest social asset in the world. Think how badly we would feel if you prepared for a big levee and no one came. That would hurt you pretty deep, Molly. If we do our job quietly and simply, and then we go home after the one session, there will be nothing to regret, no embarrassment or defeat to look back on."

He put his hand on the doorknob, opened the door and waited for her. She clung stubbornly to the balustrade.

"Don't think I'm ungrateful for what you are willing to undertake on our behalf. I admire you for it and I am grateful: but, Molly, my dear, I don't want it . . . not now. Must I have it?"

Rendered helpless by his implication that if he must have it he would perhaps argue no further, she came down to him, lifted his big bony-knuckled hand, laid her cheek on it, wiped away the tears she had been holding back.

"No, my dear, you don't have to have it."

11

RAIN fell again, making the streets impassable. A cold wind whipped in from the Potomac and the marshes. When the boys grew restive she bundled them up in heavy coats and mufflers and took them to the corner to watch the stonecutters at work. It was not possible to sit down or stand still, the cold was too penetrating; Edward came down with a chest cold; Robert followed with a sore throat. Young Dr. Busey attended the children and each afternoon Willis came to their room during his rest period to play games with them. He refused to take money for his services. When he mentioned that the first thing he was going to do when he gained his freedom was to learn to read and write, she saw a way of repaying his kindness.

"Willis, I am sure I could teach you. I have several spelling books here I've already started Bobby on."

Willis left the room without speaking. Each day she gave him a lesson, along with paper, pen and ink to copy it out.

The Lincolns were invited nowhere. Mary made no further effort to establish friendships or to entertain. Staying quietly in her room reading, or writing letters, she could not bring herself to blame the society women of Washington to whom the Lincolns were an unknown quantity; she too would resist the onslaught of *parvenus*. Nevertheless she was unhappy; she was serving no purpose in Washington. She could hardly allow herself to think of spending a whole year in this one little room, with the children underfoot, with no place to play when the weather was bad, and no way to keep them quiet when they were cranky or irritable. It was a mistake to have leased their home . . . it was a mistake to have come. The boardinghouse was not good for the children, and it certainly was not good for her.

She did her best to conceal her feelings from Abraham, for he was having difficulties of his own. When the administration failed to supply the documents he had demanded to prove that the first shots of the Mexican War had been fired on American soil, he helped lead the Whig attack against the constitutionality of the war.

The repercussions were immediate. The Springfield *Register* excoriated him for his failure to support the war effort; the Illinois Democrats held mass meetings against him. In an effort to prove that Illinois was patriotic and loyal, Stephen Douglas rose in the Senate to make a fervid speech against Congressman Lincoln's stand. William Herndon wrote that even his fellow Whigs at home felt that he was failing the troops who were still in Mexico fighting and dying to bring the war to a conclusion; that his political career was ended. It did him little good to explain that he had voted for all appropriations for the armed forces; that it was the principle of aggression to which he was opposed.

In addition, Abraham was now working to secure the Whig presidential nomination for General Zachary Taylor on the grounds that the thrice-defeated Henry Clay could not win. This alienated the Clay supporters in Washington, while back home the *Register* pointed out that politician Lincoln was backing a man who was politically available only because he had won battles in a war which the Honorable A. Lincoln passionately disapproved.

Mary perceived that she could have drawn into her charming Baltimore-style house only those Whig congressmen who had nothing to offer in return except invitations to their own boardinghouses.

She sank into apathy. When ex-President John Quincy Adams died and Abraham offered to secure her a seat in the official reviewing stands, she declined. An iron band clamped down over her head; the bright sunlight stabbed her eyes; she quarreled with Mr. Humpstuffe when he outlined the symptoms of his latest disease at the supper table: he had no feelings whatever in his extremities, he claimed, and would Dr. Busey examine him?

"No doubt you are going to include your head as one of the extremities to be examined?" she asked.

She could have bitten her tongue the moment the sentence was out; nor did the derisive laughter do anything to lessen her sense of guilt.

Abraham took care of his correspondence and wrote his speeches in their room. Frequently the children were noisy, or Robert tormented Edward because the little one was so often in his mother's lap, his arms about her neck. She could not take them downstairs to the parlors because the other boarders would be there, reading and talking, and she did not have the patience to amuse them. Often Abraham brought home gifts for her, bonbons, a copy of a new French novel. It was this formal attention which convinced her that he too wished she had remained at home, as did most of the congressmen's families, so that he would be free to get his work done and to spend his time with the other men.

He never said so. But she knew that the trip had been an error in judgment. She had failed to accomplish any part of what she had planned, and from the way Abraham tore up draft after draft of his speeches or wrote harshly to Herndon and other correspondents about the political situation, it was evident that he was far from happy. She wondered how she would get through the months until Congress adjourned and they would be free to leave for their projected vacation in the east: to New York, New England, Niagara Falls and the Great Lakes. For that matter, if Abraham continued to grow in disfavor with his party at home, their vacation, which had been predicated upon his combining it with a campaign tour, would probably never come about. They would just have to make their way back to Springfield and go to the Globe or rent a house until November, when they could regain possession of their own home.

Toward the end of March she received a letter from Betsy urging her to give the children the freedom of the Todd gardens.

Abraham asked softly:

"Would you like to visit with your family, Molly?"

"Would you like me to go?"

"I always prefer to have you with me, but you seem so unhappy here . . . those headaches . . ."

"I can't find any function for myself, Abraham. I'm not even of any help to you in your writing . . ."

"You have so much energy, so much driving force . . . and I've deprived you of the one field in which you could have applied yourself: that brick house."

It was generous of him to assume the blame. She reached up and framed his face with her hands.

"I'm sure it's for the best. The children will love the brook and the horses. As long as we've made our decision, I will go as soon as possible."

The next morning he took her to the railroad station. They did not speak to each other; each had stayed awake on his own side of the bed most of the night, lying stiff and unhappy. As he brought her baggage to the platform she thought, We have failed. I don't know where or how.

She was sick at heart, and sensed that Abraham was feeling exactly the same. He held the two boys, one in each arm.

"You don't have to stay any longer than you want to, Molly. Rest for a few weeks and then come back. Perhaps you can hire someone to take care of the children, and return by yourself. . . . Then you'd have more freedom here . . ."

". . . freedom to do what, Abraham?"

"To be with me . . . to help me . . ."

It was a heroic effort; but she knew that it had been motivated more by sympathy than by need. There was a moment of silence, then the engineer rang the bell on the locomotive. Abraham was startled by the sound. A pained look crossed his face. His eyes sought Mary's.

"Take good care of the little codgers, won't you? Don't let them forget Father."

She said, "I will take care of them," but she was crying inside herself because he had been able to let her go.

12

BEFORE the stage pulled into Lexington she put on a bright face: the Todds could endure any difficulty that no one knew about. She told interesting stories about Washington, of the red lights in the windows of the gambling houses, of how the entire town turned out on Sunday afternoons to promenade on Pennsylvania Avenue.

She had written Abraham a note en route and a long letter as soon as she reached Lexington, but to her chagrin she found herself constrained with her own husband. For that matter, Abraham's letters too were a little formal, albeit heartening. He did miss her.

Dear Mary:

In this troublesome world, we are never quite satisfied. When you were here, I thought you hindered me some in attending to business; but now, having nothing but business it has grown exceedingly tastless to me. I hate to sit down and direct documents, and I hate to stay in this old room by myself. You know I told you in last sunday's letter, I was going to make a little speech during the week; but the week has passed away without my getting a chance to do so; and now my interest in the subject has passed away too. . . .

All the house—or rather, all with whom you were on decided good terms—send their love to you.

And you are entirely free from head-ache? That is good. I am afraid you will get so well, and fat, and young, as to be wanting to marry again. . . .

She went horseback riding with David, who was teaching Robert how to handle a horse, enjoying once again the faint purplish hue of the fields. She was invited frequently into the countryside for the day or the week end, but most of her time she spent with Emilie and her other sisters, telling them stories of how she had made a hoop skirt out of willow switches when she was twelve, and tried to go to church in it; and how another time she had donned one of Betsy's gowns in an effort to get to the race track. She also spent many evenings with her father in his library.

It was a relief to be out of the boardinghouse, out of the room which had become a cell to her, out of the city where she had been unknown and unwanted. Here in Lexington her vitality returned, she read widely, had long discussions with the important Whigs of Kentucky who were preparing to secure Henry Clay his fourth nomination for the presidency. If they knew that Abraham was working to have General Taylor win the Whig nomination, no one confronted her with the unpleasant fact.

Abraham wrote that if she found herself unwilling or unable to return to Washington, perhaps he would come to Lexington when Congress adjourned in July. Her uncle James Parker was accompanying his oldest daughter to school in Philadelphia, and he offered to take Mary along with him. Perhaps she could join Abraham at the end of the congressional session, if they could still make the tour they had planned?

She reached no decision. In mid-June when the summer heat settled over Lexington, the Todds moved out to Buena Vista, a tall rambling frame house built on top of a beautiful knoll and surrounded by large locust trees. The children spent the days in the woods and fields; no one made any comment about Robert's eyes; Edward, with his open face and fund of sweetness, was soon a favorite of the household. Robert Todd was overjoyed to have her there. Abraham wrote:

Father expected to see you all sooner; but let it pass; stay as long as you please, and come when you please. Kiss and love the dear rascals. Affectionately

When she heard in August that he was about to start out on a speaking tour for General Taylor, whose fortunes were not going too well in the New England states, it seemed too late to join him. Better to remain here quietly until they were ready to return to Springfield and meet him in Chicago at the end of his trip.

Finally, at the beginning of October, she left Lexington with the boys for Chicago and a two-day stay at the Sherman House. She was looking uncommonly well, with the summer's sun on her face. Abraham too looked well, his cheeks filled out, his eyes cheerful. He was to speak at a meeting in the evening; although there had been only six hours' notice the crowd that gathered was so large it had to be moved from the courthouse to the public square. Mary listened to him for two hours; his campaigning through New England had seasoned and mellowed him: he used his humor more sparingly and cogently, and when he came to his major thesis, that the defeat of General Taylor would mean that the American people approved the extension and perpetuation of slavery in newly acquired territory, he made his point without inciting hatred against the southern states. She thought it the clearest address she had heard him make; when she picked up a copy of the Chicago *Daily Journal* the next morning she found that paper agreed with her, describing the speech as "one of the very best we have heard or read since the opening of the campaign." She handed him the paper with her fingernail underlining the praise.

"You do well in Chicago. The last time you spoke here Horace Greeley praised you in the New York *Tribune*. You should come more often."

He grinned. "Several men have urged me to move here permanently; it's a growing city, but they tell me the winter winds off the lake can blow your lungs clean out of your chest."

It was good to be back in their home again, to bring their furniture down from the north bedroom and be among their own possessions, their own friends and associates, where once again the future seemed amenable to their molding. After their separation she found their love totally renewed, as beautiful as in the early weeks of her honeymoon. In her new-found happiness she remembered her wedding night, when she had stood in the center of her hotel room waiting for Abraham to come up to her, telling herself then, with the words of the marriage ceremony still in her ears, that love ebbed and flowed, was now shining, now shabby; that she must always be dedicated, no matter what the hardships or the disappointments: for no matter how dark the passage, ultimately one would emerge into clear warm sunlight.

Abraham had said: love is eternal. So was marriage; for marriage was the earthly and adult form of love. In her mind the two always had been synonymous; that was why during those twenty months of purgatory, when her love was gone from her, she had turned deaf ears to all pleas to forget Mr. Lincoln and marry someone else. In her own mind she already was married to Abraham; she had been from the moment she knew she loved him.

After ten days at home he went to Petersburg, Jacksonville, Tremont and Pekin, determined to bring in the district for the Whigs and Taylor. No one knew what General Taylor stood for, or what kind of president he would make, but this did not distress Abraham; the Whig campaign was fought on the basis of David Wilmot's Proviso that no form of slavery could at any time be introduced into new territories acquired from Mexico.

She had feared for Abraham's influence in Illinois because of his unpopular stand on the war, but he was attracting enormous crowds wherever he spoke. As the lone Whig congressman from Illinois he represented the administration which would come into being if the general were elected. For the first time in several campaigns he genuinely believed that the Whigs could carry Illinois.

During his absence she had the ceilings whitewashed and the brick hearths repaired.

He returned home the evening before the election so that he might cast his own ballot, exhilarated by his swing through the north. Since he had trouble crowding his long limbs into the washtub placed before the kitchen stove, he put fresh linens under his arm and went down to the City Hotel to the men's bathing room, then stopped at Billy's barbershop on his way back for a haircut and shave. Watching from the front window, she saw him striding up Jackson Street, an amused expression on his features. He looked young and vigorous.

From the *Journal* office he brought news that New York was going two to one for Taylor and that her thirty-five electoral votes put the election securely in Whig hands. They lay awake long into the night, comfortable and companionable, discussing what the future held for them.

General Taylor carried the election . . . but not Illinois. The change of some seventeen hundred votes out of a hundred and ten thousand cast would have brought Abraham his great victory. Where he had campaigned, Taylor had won. His swing through New England also had been effective; and hadn't he been one of the first to tout General Taylor for the nomination? Hadn't he written letters and worked for months, then helped at the Philadelphia convention to get Taylor nominated? Could there be any question but that General Taylor would be grateful?

There were a little over two weeks between the election and the day of Abraham's departure for Washington to attend the second and shorter session of Congress. The question of whether she would accompany him had not yet come up. When she was in Lexington it was her opinion that Abraham would not want her to return; now he gave every indication of wanting the family with him despite their former failure. Many things would be different this time: the Whigs would be returning in a triumphant mood, great plans would be on foot for taking over the administration. Abraham had had a remarkably good press during his tour; he had had important conferences with Vice-President-elect Millard Fillmore and with Thurlow Weed, the political boss of New York. He could no longer be considered an unknown. The doors of official Washington would not be bolted against the Lincolns. The Democrats would fade from office, their southern-belle wives with them. There would be a new society in Washington, and she could help set its tone.

Abraham had stood up and been counted; by all rights he should become one of the inner circle. But would he?

She went about her housework with her eyes turned inward: it was a long and expensive trip for the four of them. Should she risk it? With what would she fill the three months of loneliness when she was without him? Couldn't this first Whig victory be an important turning point?

Yet there was the fear of rejection: a return to Mrs. Sprigg's . . . political uncertainty . . . the tension of close quarters . . . these would be too costly surely for the help she could give during the three months of which they were certain.

She joined Abraham in the sitting room where he was reading the papers before the fire.

"Abraham, I'm not going to Washington with you."

He raised his eyes, looked at her as though peering over the top of spectacles. She watched him closely to see if he were pleased or relieved. He gave no sign. He put down his paper and held out his arms to her.

". . . if you're doing it for my sake, Molly . . ."

She kissed him determinedly. "This will be best for all of us. After the inauguration, when we know what's going to happen . . . then we will be together again." After a moment she asked: "What do you think will happen to us? Is it possible . . . you might get . . . a cabinet post . . . ?"

"Not a chance!" he blurted; then his embarrassed laugh admitted that such a random thought had entered his mind too. "I could get the Land Office, since that always is given to Illinois, but Ninian's uncle Cyrus has made me promise to get it for him. I'm going to propose Edward Baker for a cabinet post."

"After you get Edward the cabinet post and Cyrus the Land Office, what do you intend or hope to get for yourself?"

He fluttered his eyebrows, shook his head from side to side before replying. "You got me there, Molly. I do want to be in government; I think it's the greatest of all sciences, helping people to govern themselves. But just what I can ask for myself . . . where I could best fit in with my limited background and talents . . ."

She threw up her arms in a Mammy Sally gesture of mock despair.

"I don't mind your being modest in front of me, but please don't ever let me hear you utter such words in public!"

He left for Washington on the four o'clock stage from the Globe on Sunday morning. Mary had gotten up at three to feed him a hearty breakfast. He did not wake the boys, kissing them in their sleep; and when it came time for husband and wife to say good-bye they did so casually, as though he were going up to Tremont or Pekin. There was every reason for them to be hopeful.

13

EACH day's mail brought her a letter, a copy of the *Congressional Record* or a Washington newspaper giving an account of the activities in Washington. Very early she learned that there would be no cabinet post for Edward Baker; nor could Abraham get the Land Office for Cyrus Edwards.

I think I could easily take the General Land Office myself, I fear I shall have trouble to get it for any other man in Illinois. McGaughey . . . of Indiana, will be hard to beat by anyone who is not personally known here.

They had imagined that the election of Zachary Taylor on a Free Soil program, which would not disturb slavery where it existed, would bring peace to the country; but in the House Abraham was finding the opposite to be true: new territories like California and New Mexico, which were petitioning for entrance into the Union as states, were being bitterly opposed by southern Representatives on the grounds that they would give the anti-slavery forces added voting weight in the Congress. A number of southern legislatures passed resolutions to secede if their slavery rights in the new territories were not protected. Abraham wrote her of his votes in favor of the Wilmot Proviso, and of drawing up a bill which would abolish the slave trade in the District of Columbia.

As to what lay in their own future, he sent no word. He would remain for General Taylor's inauguration, then appear before the United States Supreme Court in a case involving an Illinois client. If the president had an appointment for him which meant they were to settle in Washington, Mary could sell their house and come on with the children. However, he warned, "There is nothing about me which would authorize me to think of a first-class office; and a second-class one would not compensate me for being snarled at by others who want it for themselves."

She ignored his pessimism.

General Zachary Taylor was inaugurated on March 5, 1849. Abraham was a witness to the ceremony. Then he pleaded his case before the Supreme Court, and arrived home on the last day of March. He was thoroughly perplexed.

"Not one man recommended by me has yet been appointed to any office, little or big. I recommended Simeon Francis as secretary of Oregon Territory, Allen Francis as consul to Glasgow, Hart Fellows to a federal judgeship here in Illinois, Dr. Anson Henry for secretary of the Territory of Minnesota, Archibald Williams as the United States district attorney for Illinois . . . The loss of Illinois for the Whigs has made us little more than poor relations, to be kept sitting in an anteroom. Judge David Davis says that if I can get the Land Office for myself, I should take it. After these seventeen months I have no practice left; Billy has barely eked out a living."

"What does the Land Office pay?"

"Three thousand a year. It's a job I'd like to have, setting policy for the distribution of public lands."

Two incidents brought encouragement: his recommendation for postmaster of Springfield, Abner Ellis, was acted upon; Dr. William Wallace was appointed pension agent in Springfield. Then Abraham received a message from Washington which told him that Justin Butterfield was making a serious bid for the Land Office job. He looked up from the letter with his complexion a gray-green.

"Now that is the most outrageous piece of chicanery I have ever heard of! Last winter and spring when I was sweating blood to get General Taylor nominated, Butterfield did everything in his power to further Mr. Clay. Yet when the election is secured by other men's labor, he is on hand for the best office our state lays claim to. I'll write immediately to every Whig congressman I know, and everyone else that has any chance of getting to President Taylor's ear."

She was glad to put their nervous energies into action.

"Good. And I'll write to my father. He can persuade some of the Kentucky Whigs."

At the end of May the appointment to the Land Office had narrowed down to Butterfield and Lincoln; the cabinet had postponed the appointment three weeks for Abraham's benefit.

"You just have to go to Washington, Abraham, and be on the ground to plead your case."

"You're right," he said emphatically, "but first we must get out another batch of notes urging people to write me letters of support so that I can have them in Washington. You write some of them. Start off by saying, 'Dear Sir, It is now certain that either Mr. Butterfield or I will be Commissioner of the General Land Office. If you are willing to give me the preference, please write me to that effect at Washington, whither I go in a few days. Not a moment of time to be lost. Yours truly, A. Lincoln.' And sign my name."

A few days later he left on the week-long journey.

She received no word, nor did she expect any. She waited anxiously on the twenty-first and twenty-second of the month when the appointment was scheduled to be made; if Abraham won, he would telegraph. No message came.

When another week had passed and there still was no word, she grew uneasy. Then she saw him trudging up Eighth Street from the square, carrying a bag in either hand, dripping melancholy. She ran to the front door and threw it open; his skin was gray, the parchment pattern of wrinkles coruscating under his eyes, his Adam's apple sticking out scrawnily from his neck, his cheeks sunk, his eyes opaque, pain-fraught, the left iris fastened high in its orbit.

She led him into the sitting room and to his favorite chair, brought him a cup of strong black coffee, waited until he had swallowed several gulps. Then she could restrain herself no longer.

"Why did they turn you away?"

He reached out a long arm to place the cup and saucer on the table, looked up at her and said in an empty tone, "Many reasons; I stayed with the Cyrus Edwards nomination too long. . . . When I went up to the Land Office on the twenty-first and learned that the Butterfield appointment had been made, I stumbled back to my room, threw myself down on the bed and stayed there for an hour. I tell you, Molly, I have never been so thwarted . . . or had such a monumental headache."

"From the look of you, you haven't slept since."

"No, nor eaten, that I can remember. . . . I could only think that I wanted to get home. . . . I must be a magnet for defeat."

She sat in a chair opposite him, gulping. Neither could think of another word to say.

She spent the next weeks trying to bring him out of the private hell into which his full-fledged hypo had plunged him. He sat for endless hours staring into the empty fireplaces, a silence which was more impenetrable than the thickest wall. She managed to get him to eat a little and to sleep a little.

Toward the end of September Simeon Francis came running up the street, his fat face dripping perspiration, waving a dispatch high over his head. When he had gained enough breath, he exclaimed:

"Abraham . . . you've been appointed . . . governor of the Oregon Territory. Congratulations!"

Abraham took the dispatch from Simeon's hand, scanning it quickly. Oregon! thought Mary. The farthest and wildest reaches of America! Two thousand miles away, across vast plains and vaster mountain ranges, a wilderness on the Pacific Coast that no one knew anything about except what had come back by way of reports from Colonel Fremont and letters from early settlers. A place filled with Indians, with no towns, no roads, no stores or theatres or concert halls, with none of the appurtenances of civilization.

Abraham remained motionless. Simeon asked, "Will you take it, Abe?"

"I'll have to think about it, Simeon."

When the door had closed behind him, Abraham put his arm lightly about Mary's shoulder; together they walked into the sitting room, sat side by side on the little sofa and held hands. After a long time he began to speak, but in the middle of a sentence as though his thinking had at last reached some point that might be expressed.

". . . first governor of the Illinois Territory . . . he got to be governor of the state . . . where all of Ninian's wealth comes from . . ."

"Ninian Edwards?"

"Illinois was a wilderness then, the same as Oregon is now."

"But not two thousand miles away, not cut off from the rest of the country by months of dangerous travel."

"Then you don't like the idea, Molly?"

"I think it's an effort to placate their conscience."

"The offer has to be considered on its own merits. They could have written me off the books: I have no power or influence here in Illinois."

"You underestimate your future."

"What future?"

"Abraham, we're in the trough, I understand that; so deep that when we look up there is hardly any sky to be seen. But I don't think we want a helping hand from those that pitched you down there in the first place."

"I don't have that much bitterness in my heart."

"Oh, don't you? Perhaps that is because you could not see what you looked like when you came home: how disillusioned and filled with melancholy. I know what I had to go through to nurse you back to health, to put the iron in your soul . . ."

"It's three thousand dollars a year, Mary, the same salary as the Land Office. It's a chance to escape from our predicament . . . from the fact that I have to build up a practice . . . If those letters from California about the discovery of gold are telling the truth, the migration to the Pacific Coast will multiply a thousandfold . . ."

"Abraham, is this job something you genuinely want?"

"No. I never wanted it, but at a time like this . . ."

"My father taught me to lead from strength, not from weakness. If we take this appointment it will be because we are afraid to start over. You are too good a man, Abraham, to make an important move when you are weak. Wait until you are strong before you move again."

"There's a chance to come back to Washington as the first senator from Oregon, once it becomes a state."

She shook her head.

"This is just another Bogotá; to use your own phrase, you could very well come out the same hole you went in at. What do you do then?"

He was silent for a moment, his toe tracing the pattern in the rug, his head lowered.

"I don't know, Molly, I can't read the future."

She rose and stood facing him, her hands clenched at her sides.

"No, but we can read the past; the past tells us that we can't run away. This is our homeplace, this is where we have to make our stand."

He looked up at her. There was a tiny smile playing about the corners of his mouth.

Book V

DESCENT INTO PURGATORY

1

NOW that they were to be nailed down as securely as these oak planks with their wooden dowels, the time had come to convert what she had regarded as a temporary cottage into a permanent home. Abraham had not earned anything for six months, but she had the savings she had intended to invest in the Washington adventure.

She sewed red draperies of corded silk for the sitting room, hanging them from high cornices, then made brocatel hangings for the parlor. She discarded the scattered rag rugs, covering the entrance hall and sitting room with an ingrained carpet. The parlor she painted a dark green; for the sitting room she found a bright wallpaper patterned in blue and white flowers. She bought two high-backed Boston rockers for in front of the sitting-room fireplace; between them she put small rockers for the boys. Their big round table from the Globe still dominated the center of the room, piled high with newspapers and books; between the windows overlooking Eighth Street she placed a French marble-topped table on which she kept her mending basket, with low tables on either side of the fireplace for ferns. She replaced her dining set with a fold-top table big enough to accommodate a large dinner party, bought a set of cane chairs with rung backs, a high sideboard for candelabra and silver platters.

She traded her Empire stove for a new Buck and brought up from the basement the big roaster, waffle iron and presser iron which stood on the back of the stove, the spider frying pan which hung on the chimney, the deep iron kettle to make soap. Abraham installed a new pump on the cistern, promising to build her a brick wall and white picket fence as soon as he found some clients.

Then she tramped from Bunn's to Lamb's to Edwards's, stocking her larder with baskets of potatoes and onions, sacks of flour and rice, stone jars of jam. She was a fanatically clean housekeeper, but had neither talent nor love for the job. She spent the better part of her days in the kitchen; when Abraham returned from the office he left his coat, stock and boots on the hallway rack and joined her there, washing his hands and face in the pans which sat on the long wooden table, one containing hot water to use for the soap-scrubbing, the other filled with cold to rinse. Then he called the boys and stood over them to see that they scrubbed their ears and elbows.

Their meals were domestic; there was no talk of politics. The Springfield Whigs were disheartened and disorganized. His legal life also was non-existent. She had no wish to quarrel about William Herndon, but since he had turned over no fees for almost two years, she thought it might be a propitious time to establish a new firm.

"Billy's been loyal," Abraham replied noncombatively; "kept my lawyer-name alive while we were away. If I was going to make a change it would be of towns rather than partners. I thought Springfield was going to be our great city, but Chicago stole the march on us. I had an offer for a partnership there, from Grant Goodrich, but with me tending to consumption . . ."

"Abraham, you're strong as an ox."

". . . if I went to Chicago I'd have to sit down and study hard. That would kill me."

Fortunately for their depleted pocketbook the Illinois "Suckers" loved litigation. Mary occasionally accompanied Abraham to nearby court towns and watched the litigants crowd about the lawyers as they arrived in the public square, each choosing the lawyer he had heard about or liked the look of. On the opening Monday of the Sangamon County Court's fall session, Lincoln and Herndon had had three clients, the following day sixteen. Many of the matters were disposed of in a few minutes, the largest fee being five dollars. They had one client whom they pleaded guilty to a charge of keeping a disorderly house.

"*Sic transit gloria mundi*," she groaned.

Robert was ready to start Mr. Estabrook's pay school, but she was reluctant to expose him to new playmates. When she insisted that there must be something that could be done about his eyes, Dr. Wallace recommended that she see Dr. Sanford Bell, formerly a surgeon at the New York Metropolitan Medical College. Dr. Bell referred to a big German book, *Ueber das Schielen und die Heilung*, by a Dr. Dieffenbach who had originated an operation on crossed eyes, showed her in the drawings how the overactive eye muscle was cut so that the eye could be released to the normal position.

"And if the operation fails, Doctor . . . what then?"

"Then, Mrs. Lincoln, the iris goes to the outside corner of the eye and stays there. But why dwell on failure?"

Dr. Wallace went with her on the morning she took Robert for the operation. When she saw the two doctors tie the boy with a stout rope against the high leather-covered chair, his face green with terror, panic gripped her. Wasn't it better to endure a known hardship . . . ?

William called another doctor from across the hall. The two men held Robert steady while the surgeon forced the eyelid apart with double hooks. Working fast, he cut the mucous membrane and exposed the muscle.

Blood spurted out of the cut eye; Robert writhed in pain. She was in agony. At last Dr. Bell got his scissors in position, cut the muscle. The operation was over. A surgical bandage was applied, the ropes untied and Robert ran to her. As he reached her, Mary's knees gave way.

She was sitting by the boy's bedside trying to reassure him when a letter arrived from her father, bringing the news that Lexington had been stricken by cholera. Robert Todd had moved the family to Buena Vista and was spending his time riding the railroad cars to Lexington to take care of business at the bank, or on horseback speaking at crossroad hamlets in an effort to be re-elected to the Kentucky Senate on the unpopular program of gradual emancipation. When he had to remain in town overnight he was kept awake until dawn by the death carts on the cobblestones; he would fall asleep around five, only to be awakened by the firing of field artillery which the Transylvania scientists had said might rid the air of the disease. He assured her he was not coming into town again until the plague had passed.

It was the last word she heard from him. Betsy wrote next, in a black-bordered envelope, telling her that her father had been seized by chills, become prostrate, and despite the doses of calomel, rhubarb and opium administered to him, had grown steadily weaker. Mary would be comforted to know that, since the plague had filled the cemeteries, her father had been buried on the slope above the spring where his father and a party of Kentucky hunters had lighted the first campfire of Lexington.

She sat in the rocking chair before the unlit fireplace, Betsy's letter fallen to the floor. Her father dead! The enduring love that had lighted her life like a second sun, strengthening her in dark and discouraged hours, gone from the world. A thousand memories flooded back: Robert Todd taking her to table with the Clays and the Crittendens, bringing her a Mama doll from New Orleans, telling her stories of his march through the snowdrifts to Fort Defiance during the War of 1812; their evening walks along the limestone paths of their formal garden, their Sundays riding in the fields around Buena Vista; instilling her with confidence that she was a talented girl, worthy of the best.

There was a dull ache in her bosom: an ache for this good and decent man who had loved life and lived it so capaciously: music, theatre, books, politics, foods, houses; his hair had grown white and his step slower, but inside himself he always had been young.

Calling to the day girl to stay with Robert, she selected a black dress from her wardrobe and went to Elizabeth's house. In the parlor with the blinds drawn, sitting in a little circle on black chairs facing each other were Elizabeth, Frances and Ann, who had just arrived from Carrollton with the black-bordered letter in her hand. She pulled one of the chairs into the circle and sat with her hands in her lap. She looked at her sisters: Elizabeth, now thirty-five with a touch of gray at the temples, a strong face, maternal, capable, her eyes masked, her lips set in a tight line; Frances, reverting to her childhood, reflecting all its pain and withdrawal, sitting still and cold as a marble headstone; Ann, sharp-featured, ferret-eyed, twisting nervously on her chair.

Mary wanted to talk, to weep, to console and be consoled; yet she discerned no genuine grief in this dark formal parlor. Why? Weren't they sad to know that their father was gone? All four of them, she realized, had come away from Lexington . . . she alone had carried love for her father with her.

She could not let him go like this, an unwanted ghost at a silent wake, attended by the four daughters of his flesh. She began to speak of Robert Todd, quietly, affectionately, recalling good times of their childhood, of trips on which he had taken them, of birthday parties with cakes and candles and pretty gifts. But after a few moments she stuttered, fell silent; for it was not only the tongues of her sisters that were stopped, but their ears as well. In a little while she rose from the tight circle and silently left the room.

2

IN the dullness of her daily routine she mourned her father. A letter from Lexington aroused her: George, learning that their father's will, which left his entire estate to Betsy and her children, had been signed by only one witness, had objected to its legality on the grounds that the law required two witnesses to the signature. The probating judge ordered Robert Todd's estate distributed equally among the children of both marriages.

"But that would deprive Betsy of half her resources," cried Mary. "I'll return my share, so will Elizabeth and Frances. Ann . . . well, I'll handle Ann."

"It's more serious than that," explained Abraham. They were sitting on the porch overlooking Jackson Street. "That court order will oblige your stepmother to sell everything she owns and get cash: the houses, horses, Negroes, the businesses . . ."

"They wouldn't do that! It's cruel and stupid."

"But legal. The money will be divided among the fourteen children. At public auction things bring about a quarter of their value. . . ."

She ran into the house, came out with a straw bonnet on her head and murder in her eyes. She returned in an hour bearing Elizabeth's and Frances's word that they would join in a fight to prevent their brother from bringing the roof down over the widow's head. She sat at the desk in the sitting room and wrote her brother a scathing letter. But when Betsy tried to dissolve Oldham, Todd and Company, George filed suit against his stepmother accusing her of "attempting to defraud him of his rightful share of the estate."

Mary planted her feet firmly on the flowered carpet of the parlor and announced, "Abraham, the sisters want you to represent them in settling Betsy's estate. We must go to Lexington at once."

He looked down at her, his hands locked behind his back, his eyes amused and respectful.

"Agreed."

They traveled directly to Lexington and found George at Levi's house. His eyes were pugnacious. Only by the intensity of his stutter was she able to perceive how confused were his feelings.

"Mr. Lincoln, you're a la-la-lawyer, you know ab-b-bout legal ri-ri-rights."

"He knows about human rights too, George."

George ignored her.

"The court ordered her to l-l-list all . . . es-estate assets . . . but . . . but she's conce . . . conce . . . hiding sil-sil-silverware, p-p-pp-platters . . ."

"For heaven's sake, George, those were birthday and anniversary presents from Father to Mother."

"She's . . . she's not my . . . mother!" He turned to Abraham, said coldly, "She sold one slave and pock . . . pock . . . kept the money."

Abraham took some papers from the family packet:

"According to the record, your father found Bill impossible to handle, and asked that he be sold, the proceeds to go against a debt at the bank."

He rose, put a hand on the younger man's shoulder.

"George, Betsy has eight children, she's grief-stricken over the loss of your father; don't you think her burdens are great enough already?"

"She's r-r-rich."

Abraham's voice grew stern.

"Speaking for Mary and her three sisters, I'm kinda the family lawyer this trip, we will not participate in any suit."

"Then I'll file t-t-two suits, the second against y-y-you!"

Their next stop was the Todd home on Main Street. The house was dark and unendurable. Though evaluated at five thousand dollars, the bids were under three thousand because everyone knew it was a distress sale.

It was not only the house that had changed, but the town as well: all gradual-emancipation men such as her father and Cassius Clay had been defeated in the election, and the pro-slavery men were in control. A curfew bell rang at seven and any slave found out after that hour was sentenced to thirty-five lashes; no free Negro was allowed within the state's borders. Because so many large slaveholders had died intestate during the plague, hundreds of slaves were being sold on the block; the legislature had repealed the Non-Importation Act which Robert Todd had worked so hard to get passed. The terrorized Negroes were running away, many committing crimes in their flight. Shootings of Negroes had grown apace. Violence between white men of opposing viewpoints had replaced political debate.

They went to the Phoenix Hotel for a light supper, then called on Cassius Clay, who was living in his elegant town house, nursed by his wife and mother. He had been contesting with a slavery man by the name of Turner a seat to the Kentucky Constitutional Convention when a son of his opponent had rushed forward, crying at Clay, "You're a damned liar!" Cassius had jumped off the platform and punched the young man, then had been hit over the head with a club and stabbed in the left breast. In turn Cassius had buried his bowie knife in the Turner boy's abdomen. Cassius was given up for dead. Young Turner had died.

Cassius received them in bed, his face thin and pale, his eyes enormous under the rounded brow.

"Everyone thought I would die, Mary, but I relied on my natural vigor. Turner was elected, and now we have a new constitution which holds that the right of the slaveholder to his slave and increase is higher than any human or divine law. Tell me, Mr. Lincoln, much as the Union is to be loved, is it to be loved more than a national conscience? If slavery is to be extended forever, I prefer dissolution of the Union to that!"

Mary always reacted faster than Abraham.

"But, Cash, surely you don't think the Union is in danger?"

"No, Mary, the south will raise the cry of dissolution merely to carry a point, the way boys muddy the water to catch lobsters. The north will cede any point rather than risk the Union; but time will show you that liberty and slavery cannot co-exist." He turned in bed to ease the sharp pain that had misted his eyes. "We have twenty million men spread from sea to sea, without one man of greatness among them: this is the cause of my tears, Mary."

She leaned over the bed, kissed Cassius on the forehead.

"Perhaps you are that man, Cash."

Cassius's eyes were riveted on Abraham.

"Mary, your husband doesn't agree with me. He believes the Union must be preserved at all costs. The south knows how you feel, Mr. Lincoln, and will make the north and the cause of freedom pay those costs."

Clay's wife Mary Jane came into the room to quiet her husband. The Lincolns murmured their adieux. As they walked along the dark and now menacing streets Mary waited for Abraham to comment. He remained silent.

Abraham reported to Mary that Robert Todd, instead of owning a large portion of the bank's assets, was in debt for cash he had invested in various enterprises. Had he lived, he would have brought most of them to culmination, but now . . .

They started for Buena Vista with heavy hearts.

As they came up the road in the carriage they saw that the tall summer house already seemed run down. Betsy came out; the two women were in each other's arms. Mary said: "George is a mighty twisted and unhappy boy, Mother."

"Thank you for protecting our interests," said Betsy. Then she asked in a tight voice, "What have I done that they should grow up hating me?"

Mary went through a swift sorting-out process.

"It wasn't you, Betsy, it was the situation; we first children were a noisy, demanding brood . . . feeling that we came first, so were the most important . . ."

Betsy's gaze softened. "I was always a little jealous of you, because you were your father's favorite."

186

"I knew how lonely he was. I wanted Father to have you, to have love . . . that's why he loved me more than the others."

The next morning a group of neighbors collected, the Tuckers, Hamiltons, Clearys, Youngs, Stuarts and several members of the Humphreys family from Frankfort, come to buy in some of the things Betsy valued the most; and many strangers looking for bargains.

The auction started in the kitchen, the auctioneer standing on a stool hawking each item. Mary stood with her stepmother, holding her icy hand, while her most intimate possessions were sold. When a pile of bath towels was set up for bidding, Mary felt a shudder go through Betsy; these were towels the children used after their baths.

"Bid them in, Betsy," Mary whispered, and her stepmother did, paying six dollars and thirty cents for the lot; then she burst into tears and left the room.

The auctioneer moved into the dining room where the good china set went to Thomas Gibson for twenty-eight dollars, the dining table for seventeen-fifty. The Humphreys family could stand it no longer and bought in Betsy's preserve dishes, her extension table, vases, rocking chair, astral lamp. Mary bought for Betsy the two oil paintings that hung over the sideboard, several silver and glass dishes she knew Betsy loved. But neither she nor the Humphreys family could keep up with the relentless stripping process: the draperies, carpets, furniture, bric-a-brac. Mary was prepared to buy the fifty-one volumes of *Niles' Register* which her father had cherished, but one of the Humphreys rescued that, so she bought Betsy her favorite leather-bound volumes of poetry and travel.

All of the Todd personal possessions brought nine hundred dollars: the beautiful furnishings, glassware, linens, books, art objects that had been brought from all over the world for thousands of dollars. Mary figured in her mind that as his compensation George would receive a little over sixty-five dollars! She groaned aloud.

The farm implements were auctioned under the locust trees, then the horses, hogs, geese and sheep. Wagons drew up to the back door, cash was paid, a long line of possessions began making its way down the dirt roads to other homes. The years that Robert and Betsy Todd . . . and Mary Todd . . . had lived in this house were irrevocably gone.

3

THE operation on Robert's eye was a success; his eyes were moving normally in both directions. His features were good, and now he was quite handsome. When she enrolled him at Estabrook's school she watched him edge toward a group of boys, none of whom ever had seen him before. She thrilled to the happiness on her son's face.

Then Edward came down, though it was hardly more than a lassitude at first: his eyes dulled, his face was drawn. As she snuggled him on her shoulder she noticed that he was having difficulty breathing. When Abraham came home for dinner she asked him to drop by the Wallace home. William depressed Edward's tongue, examined his throat.

"His tonsils are red and mottled. Make a weak solution of chloride of lime and have him gargle frequently."

The next morning the boy had trouble swallowing. Dr. Wallace was there at seven. He said, "Abraham, go for Uncle Dr. Todd. I'd like him to look at Edward's throat."

Fear zigzagged through Mary's insides.

Their uncle came puffing up the steps, divested himself of his greatcoat, put on his spectacles. She heard the doctors exchange phrases, ". . . swollen fauces . . . inflamed surface . . ." Then her uncle said:

"Looks like diphtheria, just starting. There have been several cases in town."

"Diphtheria!" She felt herself pale.

William dissolved twenty grains of nitrate of silver in an ounce of water, attached a sponge to a whalebone and applied it to Edward's throat. Mary was to do the swabbing every four hours.

By nightfull the diphtheria had taken full possession; the disease raged for five days. Mary and Abraham hardly bothered to get out of their clothes, catching two or three hours' sleep when the boy did not need their ministrations. She was a tireless nurse, carried out the medical regime intelligently, turned a calm face to her son. Her task was lightened by the boy's sweet nature.

The crisis passed. Abraham had been planning to buy Edward a regular boy's bed for his fourth birthday in March. Mary exclaimed, "Why don't we get it now? I'll clear out my sewing room upstairs and give him his own room like Bobby has. He would like that."

Abraham went down to buy the bed. By the time it was delivered she had moved her form and patterns and bolts of material.

Christmas and the New Year holidays went by without their knowing. Except when he had to appear before the courts, Abraham spent all his time with the boy. When after an eighteen-hour stretch Mary persuaded him to leave Edward's side and come to bed, she would awaken in the blackness of the night to find that he had gone back to the sickroom, sitting on a hard chair with his eyes on his son's peaked face.

They were deep into the second month of convalescence when it again became difficult for Edward to swallow. Dr. Wallace found the child's soft palate and pharynx paralyzed; the following day his sight was affected, and in spite of the half dozen doctor friends who offered their aid, the paralysis spread to one whole side of his body. On the rainy morning of February 1, after fifty-two days of vigilance, Edward was dead.

Shaking as though she had the ague, Mary got into bed and pulled the blankets over her head. Lightning cracked and thunder rolled into the house and into the bedroom, inside the bed and inside her body. She wept, broken-heartedly, as she never had wept in her life.

"Our little fellow is gone. Oh, Abraham, what have we done that he should have suffered so?"

"The Lord giveth and the Lord taketh away. He took our sweet little codger. He'll give us more children."

The funeral was set for Sunday. Abraham awakened her early by bathing her face with a dampened towel, then holding her up in bed and pressing a cup of strong black coffee to her lips.

"Drink this, my dear, it will give you strength. You must dress now. Reverend Dresser is out of the city, but Reverend Smith will conduct the services. You remember I was reading a copy of his book at your father's house in Lexington. He's a fine minister; you'll draw comfort from the sermon."

She fell out of his arms. His own cheeks were sunken, his eyes buried deep under crags of suffering.

"Mary, you must get up. The carriage is waiting."

"I . . . can't . . . go."

She closed her eyes. Silence came. When she opened them he loomed there, dark and brooding.

"You must come, Mary, You'll want to say good-bye to Eddie."

"I've already said good-bye . . . ten thousand times. Oh, Abraham, please don't make me go . . . to see them put him in the ground . . . I couldn't bear it."

He persisted no further. She heard the front door close, a carriage drive away.

She fell into a fever in which nightmares mixed with delirium. She slept, then would spring up, thinking she had heard Edward call. Chills swept across her, raking her body with cold fire.

At the end of a week she took her first faltering steps; by the end of the second she was in the kitchen doing a few salutary chores; and on the next Sunday morning she went with her husband to the First Presbyterian Church to hear the Reverend James Smith preach. The minister was a large stalwart-looking Scotsman. He spoke with tenderness about death, particularly of little ones, and of the solace to be derived from faith.

The pain eased, the grief crumbled at the edges.

4

IF their outside interests had vanished, she was at least grateful that Abraham could spend his evenings at home. He would return early, carrying a piece of beefsteak in brown paper, hang his coat on the hatrack, exposing the galluses that held up his trousers, divest himself of his heavy boots. She watched him stalk through the house and sit down to supper in his stockinged feet; her efforts to improve his domestic manners had fallen on infertile soil, the log-cabin habits refusing to be polished out of the rough diamond. Afterwards he turned a chair upside down, sprawled out on the sitting-room floor with his back against it and read the newspapers. When she asked him why he read aloud, he replied:

"It's because I learned to read in a blab school. I don't understand what I'm reading unless I speak it out loud and hear it in my own ear."

Each week he would bring home a new book of humor, such as *Joe Miller's Jests*. He would call across the room:

"How many legs will a sheep have if you call a tail a leg?"

"Five."

"Wrong; calling a tail a leg don't make it so."

He brightened many a lonely hour.

She turned to Robert, hoping to get from him some of the affection Edward had given so spontaneously. But Robert had established his independence. Had he never forgiven them for his crossed eyes and for the humiliation that had scarred his early years?

Once when Robert was defying her in cold, hostile fashion she picked up a stick she had been using to stir her ash barrel and brought it down across his behind. When Robert had run out into the yard, Abraham said with sadness:

"Mary, Mary." Wanting to lighten her burden, he added, "Corporal punishment is wasted on the young."

When they bought the Reverend Dresser's house they had stood almost alone on the outskirts of town; now some twenty homes had been constructed on Eighth and Ninth, Jackson and Edwards streets. Just across Jackson Street lived the sheriff, Charles Arnold, and next to him Abner Watson, the county constable, so that she figuratively could look into the kitchen window of the law. Behind them, across the alley, were two lively families each with a number of youngsters, the Sam Graveses, whose little boy Hobart had been Edward's playmate, and William Billington, a civil engineer. Benjamin Moore, the city surveyor, had built a house close by.

There was a group of children who played together. Mary cleared out the barn and let it be known that it could be used as headquarters for their club. Robert converted the barn into a theatre. Mary's heart sank when she saw him taking valuable materials and furniture from the house to be used as props, but she was determined to pay any price to win the boy's acceptance.

One afternoon there was a howling of dogs from the barn; the noise was maddening; she bit her lip, did nothing to interfere. A little while later she heard hurried steps in the street, saw Abraham vault the tall fence, run through the yard, pick up a stave of an old ash barrel and speed across the yard to the barn. There were frantic sounds of running and one short cry.

In a few moments he came onto the back porch, carrying the barrel stave in his hand, an outraged expression on his face.

"Why didn't you stop them, Mary? Why did a neighbor have to make me come all the way home from the office? How can you be so indifferent as to let them hang dogs in the barn?"

"Hang dogs? Whatever are you talking about?"

At that moment Robert came in, pulling a friend by the hand. The little fellow was crying. He ran to Mary.

"Everybody was bigger than me . . . they got through the hole in the wall. Mr. Lincoln hit me."

Robert protested: "We were putting on a dog act is all, teaching the dogs how to stand up on their hind legs. They didn't want to learn so we had ropes around their necks and we were helping to hold them up. Then Papa came in screaming, 'What do you mean by hanging dogs?' "

Mary looked sideways at her husband and, imitating his voice, murmured, "Abraham, Abraham! Corporal punishment is wasted on the young! Shoo now, Mr. Lincoln, you've spoiled the dog act, so you can't stay for the taffy pull."

That afternoon while Robert was helping to clean out the taffy tubs, his cheek brushed against hers in a gesture of friendliness. Happiness warmed her heart. And that night, for the first time since Edward had been taken, she was able to embrace her husband with the fullness of her love.

Within a few weeks she discovered she was pregnant.

"Abraham," she asked, "you've been reading Euclid's *Geometry* lately, what are our mathematical chances of getting a daughter this time?"

She gave a small dinner party for the Simeon Francises, who were trying to sell the *Journal*, for Julia Jayne, who had married Judge Lyman Trumbull and was living in Alton, for the Orville Brownings, who had been trying for ten years to get elected to Congress with no success. Abraham still carried his office in his tall stovepipe hat; when she asked him a question about their personal affairs he would dump dozens of letters and scraps of paper out of the hat onto a table and go looking for the information. She rarely asked about their income; no books were kept in the office, Abraham seldom knew how much they were earning. When money came to him for legal fees he would divide the cash, wrap half in a piece of paper for his partner, put the other half in his pocket. When he wanted to visit a neighboring county seat for a few days he was obliged to write to a friend asking him please to collect a fifty-dollar fee that was owed to him as, "I am short of money." When the fifty dollars did not arrive he told her:

"If you run short you can always go down to Billy Herndon, and he will give you my half of whatever fees came in."

She grimaced.

The next morning while the house was sunk in predawn sleep there was a pounding on the front door. Abraham answered it in his yellow flannel nightshirt, which was held together by one button at the neck. When he returned he began to dress hurriedly.

". . . a client . . . apparently tried to suck all the whiskey barrels in town . . . broke up a grocery . . . I got to keep him out of jail."

He returned at eight o'clock.

"Who called you down in the middle of the night?" she asked as she handed him a plate of eggs and sliced smoked ham.

He fastened his eyes on the food. ". . . there were four of them . . . your cousin Logan's son, for one."

"Why didn't cousin Logan get his son out of jail?"

Abraham's Adam's apple moved up and down in his scrawny neck while he tried to get himself to tell another half-truth. It wouldn't work. Lifting up his eyes, he said dryly, "It wasn't young Logan who sent for me. It was Billy."

"Billy! You mean Mr. Herndon? He was in this drunken brawl?"

"Yes."

"I hope the judge gives him six months in jail!"

"Oh, I got them all out . . . by putting up enough to repair the grocery."

She brought her eyebrows together.

"Where did you get the cash to bail out four drunks?"

"I called on Jacob Bunn, he owed me a hundred dollars for a case I settled for him. Since he's become the town banker I told him to hold it for me."

He laid down his knife and fork.

"I wanted to leave it there . . . for an emergency."

She was angry now. "And Billy Herndon's brawls are to be the emergencies for which our money is saved?"

"We all have weaknesses. If I got into trouble through one of my weaknesses, Billy would pay my costs. That's what friendship means, Mary."

She sank into a chair at the kitchen table, tears of exasperation in her eyes.

"There are times when I think you love him more than you do me."

"Now, Mary, I love Billy as my partner; I love you as my wife. I try to be a good friend to both of you." He grinned weakly. "If you got drunk and broke up a grocery store, I'd bail you out too."

She shook her head at him in despair, high spots of color on her forehead and cheeks.

"That's a mighty Christian sentiment, Mr. Lincoln!"

5

SHE knew that he went to visit his family in Coles County once a year, and wondered why he did not at least invite to Springfield his stepmother, to whom he seemed devoted. She remembered how upset he had been in Washington when he had received two letters, one from his father and one from his stepbrother John Johnston, Sarah Bush Lincoln's son by her first marriage, both asking for money. To his father he had replied that he cheerfully sent him the twenty dollars which sum Thomas Lincoln said was necessary to save his land from sale, even though he knew the story to be untrue; but to his stepbrother he wrote that he did not think it best to comply with his request for an eighty-dollar loan, proposing instead that Johnston go to work "tooth and nails for some body who will give you money for it," promising that for every dollar he earned Abraham would give him another. When his stepbrother wrote that his father was dying from a lesion of the heart, she was hard pressed to understand why he did not leave at once for the Coles County farm; the explanation came three days later in another letter which explained that Thomas Lincoln had simply had a lot of phlegm on his lungs, from which he was now entirely relieved. She thought of her own brothers George and Levi: what family was not complex, obliged to carry its members from station to station as a living cross?

Nor had he once since the painful revelation of his mother's illegitimacy spoken of her. While they were in Washington he had communicated with various Lincolns, trying to find out if they were related to his grandparents; but on the subject of his mother's family and the question of her totally unknown father he maintained silence.

The original joy with which she had welcomed her pregnancy turned to ennui. Did her backaches and constant awareness of the child result from fatigue, or were they due to fear that forces beyond her control might strike her down again?

Abraham was enveloped in his own anxieties. The spring of 1850 was a mild one, wild flowers splashed the prairies with color, the local life of Springfield was peaceable, yet the threat of disunion completely dominated the air. His fearful forebodings filled the house as he read to her the heightening of the slavery conflict as reported in the Washington *National Intelligencer*, the New York *Herald*, *Congressional Globe*, Charleston *Mercury* and Richmond *Enquirer*. True, the best minds of the country were working for compromise: if the south would vote to admit California as a free state, then the north would vote for a fugitive slave law with the federal government returning runaway slaves to their owners; if the south would vote for the admission of New Mexico and Utah as territories without constitutional sanctioning of slavery, the north would admit the new territories without slavery being legally prohibited. But John Calhoun, parental voice of the south, denounced compromise, urging the southern states to withdraw from the Union; the abolitionist voices of the north, even that of Horace Greeley in the New York *Tribune*, were equally shrill in their demands that the south be severed from the Union.

He gazed up from the sea of newspapers surrounding him on the floor and cried:

". . . I failed in Washington . . . if I could be there now I could raise my voice . . . help bring the north and south extremists a little closer together. As it is, I have no place to make myself heard . . . and President Taylor is going to bring on civil war, my life upon it! Did I do everything in my power to see that General Taylor was put into the White House so that President Taylor can bring the country to the verge of dissolution?"

With the widely published statement that it was not merely the southern politician who wanted disunion, but the southern people as a whole, and the calling of an all-southern conference in Nashville with the avowed intent to set up an independent Republic of the South, a dead-ash winter sky seemed to lower over the horizon, blotting out the bright spring sun. This aura of dread tightened the cocoon of her nervousness. Dr. Wallace ordered her to bed.

For her, the conflict over secession was no academic dispute: her roots were in Kentucky, and Kentucky was a slave state, its legislature dominated by pro-slavery men. Any attempt by the north to hold the southern states in the Union by force meant that Kentucky would be in the war, her brothers Levi and George, her half brothers Samuel and David, the hundreds of her blood kin fighting against the Todd, Logan, Stuart, Wallace, Edwards and Lincoln boys of Springfield. Having grown up with many planters who were protective to their slaves, and who faced ruin without them, she understood the blind fury of those who were in danger of being stripped of their lifetime earnings by outsiders who knew little of their problem; while at the same time, having been raised by a father who favored emancipation, having been moved from childhood by Cassius Clay's determination that slavery must go, she understood the spiritual abhorrence of the abolitionists who felt that in helping sustain slavery by federal law they were in turn personally responsible for it.

Her only source of comfort was that she and Abraham agreed on the slavery issue; with the congressional storms beating about their heads, with their friends agitated and quarreling, with her own omnipresent physical fears, she did not know how she would have endured had she and Abraham been split on this basic moral problem.

At the end of three weeks she insisted that she had to cook a few digestible meals for her family, clean the house of the dirt left by the three servants, each of whom she had kept one week.

On the Fourth of July Abraham left for Chicago to attend the United States District Court. A few hours after his departure word reached Springfield that President Taylor was down with cholera. Abraham once had asked, "How do we save ourselves from a man who doesn't understand that he's president equally of all the people, of all the sections and all the states, and as the father of all his children he cannot help one by destroying another?"

One answer came when President Taylor died. Millard Fillmore, a moderate man, was inaugurated. Mary learned with satisfaction that former Congressman Lincoln, who had withdrawn from politics, had been invited by the Whig party of Chicago to deliver the eulogy on the dead president, and had not felt free to decline.

By the time he returned, toward the end of the month, a new political climate had settled over the country. Henry Clay's Compromise Omnibus bill had been defeated not only by the Democrats but by Whig President Taylor, who feared that a victory for Clay meant that the senator from Kentucky would be the next president of the United States. Wanting to preserve the peace, President Fillmore now declared in favor of the Compromise. There was lacking only a new leader to come forth and take command. Out onto the stage stepped the chairman of the Committee on Territories, none other than their old friend and adversary, Stephen Douglas.

"It's funny how that little man always lands on his feet," exclaimed Mary, her expression caught between admiration and puzzlement; "there's never been another time when the Committee on Territories was of great importance, yet today the chairman of that committee holds the fate of the Union in his hands. How does he do it, Abraham?"

"The Little Giant has a genius for being at the right place at the right moment . . . just like me!" He gave an ironic toss of his shoulder. "I'll wager you this: if Douglas is successful in bringing out of his committee a series of bills which will get California, New Mexico and Utah admitted peaceably, he'll be the biggest man in our country. It will make him number one with the Democrats, and put him in line for the presidential nomination in '52."

"Abraham, you can't be serious!" She was aghast. "He's been in the Senate only three years. How can he have taken over the party so quickly?"

She was glad that Abraham did not answer; the question she really had wanted to cry out was, How could he have come so far when we have come up so short?

Swiftly Stephen Douglas took control of the Congress: organizing, whipping recalcitrant factions into line, stripping Clay's Omnibus and separating its parts into individual measures, each of which could pass by mustering friends behind it. The sum total of all the passing was a compromise which could satisfy the majority of both the north and the south and once again, as with the Missouri Compromise of 1820, give them a chance to live without strife. The only shocking aspect was the harsh fugitive slave law. Abraham spread his arms wide, then dropped them hard against his sides, like a man who had pondered these matters long and fruitlessly.

Peace descended upon Springfield, and upon the United States. Wise and moderate men had prevailed. Standing in the center of the landscape, bigger than life, bigger even than the Executive Mansion, stood Senator Stephen Douglas of Illinois: the single greatest cohesive force in Washington. In the streets, in the shops, in the homes of her friends, Mary heard the same remark:

"Stephen Douglas will be the next president of the United States."

"He picked up the pieces the old giants couldn't assemble," agreed Abraham; "he saved us from disunion. That talent for organization is what kept beating us Illinois Whigs for the past ten years."

He left again for the circuit swing. She was in her seventh month, with a great sense of heaviness. The kitchen became the sitting room, she and Robert eating their meals before the warm stove, remaining there until bedtime with spelling book and sewing basket. Since Abraham's defeat for the Land Office he had been lethargic about national affairs and the debates in Congress; now with the passing of the Compromise measure he sank back once again into political apathy. The trip would be good for him. He was happy with his fellow lawyers. She knew the excitement of court days in the Illinois towns when the county folk came to foregather and foreclose. The taverns and coffeehouses would be filled, whole families coming to see the traveling carnivals, revivals and minstrels who followed the courts.

Abraham still was happiest with men. It was not only the excitement of the courtroom, the spontaneity of cases he had to organize by a few moments' reading of the papers, but the hilarity as well, with nearly three-hundred-pound Judge David Davis leaning down from the crude bench saying, "Mr. Lincoln, how does that strike you?" and Abraham, as befitted the official humorist of the Eighth Circuit, giving back a story which would send the court into gales of laughter. The night sessions in the hotel room of Judge Davis, always the best in the tavern, Abraham relished even more; here the lawyers held their mock court, satirizing what had happened in the day's cases, with the stories, the bottle, the singing going the rounds until midnight.

There was the time Abraham refused to join the firm of "Catch 'em and Cheat 'em": upon arriving at Danville, one of his young partners brought him the case of a demented girl with property valued at ten thousand dollars, who was in need of being saved from what the town described as a "designing adventurer." Abraham won the case for the girl in twenty minutes. Upon learning that his partner charged her a $250 fee, he obliged him to return half of the money. Judge David Davis summoned Abraham to the bench, and said in a rasping whisper which could be heard to the other end of the public square, "Lincoln, you are impoverishing this bar by your picayune charges of fees, and the lawyers have reason to complain of you. You are now almost as poor as Lazarus, and if you don't make people pay you more for your services you will die as poor as Job's turkey."

That night the lawyers assembled while the judge tried Abraham before his orgmathorial court, found him guilty and fined him two dollars for his "awful crime against the pockets of his brethren at the bar."

Nor did the hardships faze him: the muddy roads across the prairies, the uneatable food, the two or three men in a bed. Sitting in the shabby buggy behind his bay horse, Buck, he would study Euclid and books on invention in the jogging silence. He enjoyed the handling of hundreds of cases, winning for his clients, counseling the young lawyers who came to him for advice, taking Judge Davis's place on the bench for a day or two when the judge could not preside.

The house was silent during the day, with Abraham on circuit and Robert away at school. There were times when, resting in bed, browsing or daydreaming, it seemed as though she were a young girl back in her bedroom in Lexington, excited at being voted the most popular girl at Mentelle's, living in an atmosphere of fun and gaiety. Everything that had happened in the interval had been a dream: she had never come to Springfield, never met Abraham Lincoln, never married, borne two sons and lost one of them, aspired to the heights, fallen. Then the child within her would stir, the dream recede before the movement of life and the reality of eleven years.

6

THEIR third son was an amazing replica of Edward. She contracted childbed infection, ran a fever of 104°; it was a full month before she was able to get out of bed. In gratitude for Dr. Wallace's constant care, they named the boy William Wallace Lincoln.

She found Abraham pacing the house, his head down, hands clasped behind his back.

"It's my stepbrother again: he's written me two letters telling me that my father is desperately ill, and that I must come at once. Here's a third letter, accusing me of being uninterested in my family. You know that's not true, I desire that neither Father nor Mother should be in want of any comfort in health or sickness, and I'm sure they have not failed to use my name to procure a doctor or anything else that my father might need."

He wrote to his stepbrother:

I sincerely hope Father may yet recover his health. Say to him that if we could meet now, it is doubtful whether it would not be more painful than pleasant.

A few days later, when Abraham received news that Thomas Lincoln had died, she saw that he was not so much distressed by the death as by the fact that he could feel so little over it. She was surprised to find her husband, like her sisters, unforgiving.

At the end of January she left the house for an Episcopal fund-raising supper in the Supreme Court. She had baked as her contribution a three-layer jelly cake, which Abraham carried on a silver platter to the church ladies. In celebration of the birth of their son, he took her to a ball at the courthouse, and to see the Robinson Family in *Maid of Munster*. Much of the odoriferous Chicken Row had been torn down, with three-story brick buildings going up in its place; Jacob Bunn had opened Springfield's first private bank; and it was now illegal for hogs to run the streets.

"Apparently the hogs are taking that law seriously," Mary commented as they made a tour of the square and did not once have a pig brush against her skirts.

Abraham's business was slow, though he was retained by the Alton and Sangamon Railroad to attend the legislative sessions and watch any railroad bills that might be introduced. He came home for supper at five, washed in the basin on the back porch, ate his shrimp creole or Susquehanna shad, played with the baby.

"We must not show too much of our love for William," Mary cautioned; "Robert is too young to understand that part of our feeling is gratitude. . . ."

Abraham no longer read the new books being published, but when Robert led his class in Latin, he started studying with the boy. In the evenings he was restless, more and more often ended his pacing by putting on his boots, stock and coat and going downtown to the Supreme Court library where the lawyers and legislators congregated. She thought it inconsiderate of him to go out night after night, leaving her alone in the house with the two children, but she was too proud to tell him so. Instead she bought tickets for the Washington Birthday ball which was held in the new ballroom over the post office, as well as for the Robinson Family in *What's in a Name?* Her friend Julia Jayne Trumbull came in from Alton and Mary invited thirty couples to dinner. When return invitations were received Abraham groused about getting too much social life; she ignored his grumbling.

At the end of March when he prepared to leave on his ten-week ride around the Eighth Judicial Circuit she was reluctant to have him go.

"Abraham, why can't you split the circuit with Mr. Herndon?"

"Billy is just no good at circuit riding; I get four times the amount of business. Besides, he's miserable on circuit; he insists on staying home with his family."

She thought, And you don't; that's why I'm left without any husband six months out of the year.

The town was filled with wagon trains heading for California; she grew timid about being left alone in the house. Frequently she thought she heard prowlers on the back stairs. She asked Howard Powel, twelve-year-old friend of Robert's, if he would sleep upstairs in Robert's room until Mr. Lincoln returned; he agreed to do so for five cents a night.

She expected Abraham for a visit at the end of the second week, or the third at the latest, but these week ends passed and the fourth and fifth as well. She ran out of money. When Abraham did not come in by Friday afternoon of the sixth week she was forced to go down to the office.

She dressed to the teeth in her newest, a striped pink alpaca falling over large hoops, with a deep rose knitted shawl, and climbed the stairs to the

Lincoln-Herndon office. William Herndon rose from the lone desk by pushing himself upward on his hands. They stood staring at each other over an unbridgeable chasm, he with one eye closed as though to see her better. In the passing instant she noted that his hair and half-length eyebrows still were jet black.

She turned away and looked at the office: the two dilapidated worktables arranged in a lopsided T, well carved by a jackknife, the four or five cane-bottomed chairs and long rickety sofa propped against the wall, the rear windows thick with dirt, the floor unswept, plants growing in a corner where Abraham had dumped the seeds he had brought back from Washington.

She pulled in her lips with a gesture of distaste, remembering how her father's office had been scrubbed every morning before he reached it, how beautifully decorated it had been with its French wallpaper, hunting prints, desk and chairs tooled by Lexington's finest furniture makers. She sighed; that was another world, another civilization, really. Reluctantly she brought her eyes back to Mr. Herndon.

"Mr. Lincoln told me to come here for money belonging to him." She had not known her tone would be icy until she herself heard it. "You have some, no doubt?"

Herndon opened the bottom drawer on the right-hand side of the desk, indicating a number of paper packages, a few of them tied with string.

"Each package is Mr. Lincoln's half of a fee. Help yourself."

She stared at him for another moment, strongly tempted to turn on her heel and go out through the filthy office and down the stairs without taking the money for which she had come. Red in the face and furious at herself, she reached down, picked up a handful of the little packages, dropped them in a shopping bag, swept aside her full skirts and strode out in silence.

Abraham appeared at noon the next day, bringing with him two hundred dollars in cash. She was smarting from the painful scene of the day before, and from the fact that she had had no word from him for nine weeks. When he leaned down to kiss her she turned her cheek sideways.

"This makes me a little impatient," rebuked Abraham. "I did not make the long journey just to argue the week end away."

Each lay rigidly at the far side of the bed; Mary so close to the edge she thought she would fall out. After a while he said, "Now, Molly, let's not stay in a pet." They made it up.

Summer began early, hot and sticky. Cholera struck, with several quick deaths. Mary tried to keep Robert in the house, but his cries rocked the walnut planks of the walls. The only pleasant part of the oppressive season was that Abraham was doing well in the Springfield session of the United States Circuit Court; he had a number of important cases of a business nature, with correspondingly higher fees. He loaned out three hundred dollars to Daniel E. Ruckel at ten per cent, and took a mortgage for six hundred dollars against the Thomas Cantrall eighty-acre farm.

"Abraham, why don't we buy land with our savings?" she asked. "You've told me about Judge Davis and Leonard Swett buying land in all these new townships and getting rich off it."

"Ah well, getting rich . . ." He tousled his hair. "I am not a speculator, I prefer to play it safe."

"But if we had money coming in from investments, you wouldn't have to stay out on the circuit the full three months. A lot of the lawyers are riding only half the time," she added plaintively.

"In order to make money, Mary, you have to think of it pretty constantly. I'd rather not tie myself down. I'm a lawyer, I should make my money from the law. I have no talent for business."

There was nothing more she could say.

By the second week of September he was gone again for the swing which would last until the end of November. He assured her that he would get home when he could, but a number of the lawyers of the county seats were now saving their most important briefs for him to write when he arrived, and this meant working straight through the week ends.

She found a tall red-haired, blue-eyed, freckle-faced Irish girl who had just arrived in Springfield and was looking for a home. Mary cleared out her sewing room and installed young Sarah, who was a good worker. It was comforting to have another adult in the house.

She received no letters from Abraham, only an occasional message carried by one of the Springfield lawyers returning home for a week end. When he did not return by the seventh week end and she knew by actual count that every other lawyer touring the Eighth Circuit had returned at least once to be with his family, she not only missed him but grew ashamed. Nor was there any possibility of keeping her humiliation a secret; the lawyers who traveled the circuit were close friends, their families knew of each other's doings. She could not conceal the fact that she alone had not received a visit from her husband; there certainly was no chance to keep the embarrassment from her sisters. Was he too busy? tired? indifferent?

In the early months of their marriage Abraham had been the only lawyer to ride the sixty long miles for a Saturday afternoon and Sunday with his wife; then she had been proud. Was this the penalty for her pride?

The three weeks of November were a torture; her headaches returning, she lay awake wide-eyed and miserable, spelled out each of the remaining hours: Abraham was in Shelbyville, some fifty miles away, perhaps too long a trip to make, but on the following week end he was only thirty-five miles away in Decatur, not too far to come home had he wanted to.

At the end of the tenth week she came to the conclusion that her husband had been cruel to her and to their sons. If he had been sensitive, if he had been kind, he would have made the journey home for their sakes.

He arrived just before noon of a washday, with the house smelling of soapsuds and steam. She saw him drive through the back-alley gate, the buggy, the horse and Abraham covered with the same dust gray. She was in her morning dress with her hair piled on top of her head. She made no effort to change or pretty herself. When he walked through the yard and up the back steps she said from one of the tubs:

"You couldn't have arrived at a more opportune time . . . for soiled linen."

He stared at the rear outline of a huge girl with red arms and parboiled fingers hanging out wash on a flapping clothesline. Mary commented simply that Robert was in school, William in bed with the colic.

"He's contrary that way, never gets the colic except washdays. What have you got in that brown paper, Abraham, a string of pearls for me?"

"A beefsteak."

The beefsteak came out raw at one end, burned at the other; the tea tasted bewitched; and when she sat down at the table she saw that the tablecloth was wrong side out, the bread had too much saleratus and the milk was sour. She felt there was a kind of rudimentary justice in all this.

7

SOME part of her husband had not returned, or at least was not present in the Eighth Street house. There was little joy in him, or excitement. The dozen or so newspapers lay unopened; he did not bother to read Stephen Douglas's big speech before the United States Senate. She told him about the new books she had bought during his absence, read him what she thought to be interesting paragraphs; he nodded gravely and sat in silence. When Harriet Beecher Stowe's *Uncle Tom's Cabin* was published in book form Mary gulped the first of the two volumes in a single sitting; when she handed it to Abraham he merely glanced at the frontispiece, a woodcut of a Negro cabin, then put the book aside without turning a page. When she attempted to bring him up to date on the news of Springfield he listened with one ear open to her, the other opened inward to his own competing voice.

Could it be disappointment with the results of the trip? He assured her that he had had no failures aside from a case or two which he was confident would be reversed in a higher court.

Then what had caused him to turn to some dark winter cave of disenchantment? Certainly it was no sense of guilt at not having come home during the ten weeks; apparently it never had occurred to him that she might be aggrieved by his staying away. Could it be that he had been gay and vital during the ten weeks of the thousand-mile circuit ride, and that coming home seemed dull or meaningless? But why should this be true? He loved his wife, he loved his children, he loved his home . . . or so he said. How did she treat a husband who seemed perfectly well, even affectionate when affection was asked of him, but whose paddle wheel apparently had stopped turning?

The following Sunday morning as she was returning from church she saw Abraham ahead of her, pulling a wagon with year-old William in it. As she crossed Market Street, William fell out of the wagon, landed on the hard-packed dirt walk and set up a tremendous howling. However it was not loud enough to break in on the thoughts of his father, for Abraham continued to pull the empty wagon to the corner, his head down on his chest.

She ran as fast as her steel-hooped skirts would permit, picked up the child, quieted him. By the time she accomplished this Abraham had turned at the corner and was coming toward her. When he came to where she was standing, legs apart, blocking his passage, he was astonished to find that William was in her arms and not in his wagon.

"Mr. Lincoln, if I had a shillalah, and I could reach up that high, I'd break it over your head to wake you. How far away do you go in your mind that you don't know your own baby has fallen out of the wagon?"

"It's a hard world, Mary," he said sadly, "people are forever falling out of wagons. Willie might just as well get used to it."

He was busy in one Springfield court or another, had won a case for banker Jacob Bunn as well as two cases for the Alton and Sangamon Railroad, but his mood remained subdued. When he sat in absolute silence at the supper table, eating mechanically, and she commented, "A little sprightly conversation might improve the taste of that roast beef," he looked up at her blankly, as though he had forgotten that she was sitting across the table from him, or that he was home at the family board.

She realized anew the enormous hole that was left when politics dropped out of their lives, how much of their waking time had been devoted to study and discussion of the current issues. Though he was appointed a member of the Whig State Committee on Resolutions, and was asked to help select delegates to the Whig national convention, his participation was dispirited. When Ninian Edwards bolted the Whig party and aligned with the Democrats, the first apostate in their circle, Abraham was too disinterested to become upset. Where he used to take her to meetings two and three times a week, now the only one they attended was Orville Browning's lecture on the dignity of labor, at the Presbyterian church. It was a bitterly cold night, nineteen degrees below zero; after the lecture he invited the Brownings back to the house for a hot drink while they continued their discussion of wage scales and protection against unemployment and old age.

He would have to leave again during the first week of April. If she did not tell him how hard the separation was on her nerves and health, could she consider him neglectful? But could she handle it with humor? He must not become resentful, feel put upon.

"Abraham, I hope you're not going to work so hard you'll come home that terribly rich businessman you tell me you don't want to be?"

"Small fees, small change."

"Why not arrange to take off two or three half weeks? You'll be able to use some fresh linen . . . and a digestible meal . . . ?"

Her voice had a bantering note; he rose to it.

"They tell me home cooking is the best." His voice became flat again. "But sometimes the cases go over to Friday or Saturday; I can't ride fifty miles just for a Saturday night and a Sunday."

"Poor dear, now I know why they call you 'Old Abe.' "

He flushed, turned his eyes away from hers.

"Do something daring, Abraham, skip one whole court, say at Danville or Paris. That'll bring you home for a week in the middle of May. We'll not miss the few dollars."

"It isn't only the money . . . people are expecting me . . . lawyers, clients, it wouldn't be fair to disappoint them."

"Would it be fair to disappoint me?" Her voice had risen. "Or your two sons?" She waited until the emotion in her chest moved downward. "I'm sorry I spoke sharply, but I don't believe you know how difficult it is for us to have you gone so long; what can I tell Robert when he says, 'Cousin Stuart or Logan is home, or Ben Edwards, why doesn't my father come?' Can I tell him we're poorer than they, or that you love us less?"

He flinched. She reproached herself; yet he had been so unmovable.

"Very well, Mary, I'll come home. I can't say just when . . . whenever there's a short calendar."

She turned away, weary from the encounter.

"If you feel you must stay out, do so; we'll manage to survive."

And so he left, in the shabby buggy behind Buck, the green umbrella on the seat beside him, his plug hat on his head, the old blue circular cloak from Washington over his shoulders, one trouser leg tucked into the boot. She did not have to wait to know that there would be no short calendar, no week or even day rescued from the passing spring months.

8

HE returned toward the middle of June, walking up from the square late one afternoon with a carpetbag in his hand, having left the horse and buggy at a downtown stable. Mary was in her rocker by the sitting-room window helping Robert work out arithmetic sums, William was playing on the floor with an india-rubber air ball. She was pale and thin, the two lines on the right side of her face had deepened, the stranger behind her eyes was her constant companion. She saw him coming up Eighth Street, his long thin figure moodily morose as he moved slowly toward the house. She sat quietly for a moment, thinking, This must be the gloomiest man in the world! Can there be anything harder for a wife to bear?

She waited in the hallway for him to come up the front steps. As he reached for the knob she opened the door. Standing before her was the Abraham Lincoln of November 1840 who had returned with the election ballots from Lawrenceville, as composite a picture of misery as ever she had seen. Now as then his left eye was high up under the eyelid, his face a pattern of twisted torture lines, his skin sallow, his lips dry and ash gray. Then, he had been out for weeks campaigning for Harrison for president, high with hopes that the Whigs would win, that he would gain an important place; a few nights later he had come to her house to tell her that she must release him. Now, as he stood before her in the open doorway with deep blue rings and intricate ridges of wrinkles under his eyes, sagging at the hips, fatigue and despair carved in every line of him, she asked herself:

What terrible defeat has he suffered this time? What has he come home to tell me?

After supper, when he had read a story to Robert, and played with William before putting him to bed, they sat side by side in their big rockers before the unlighted hearth, no communication between them. A question lodged in her throat:

Why do you look this way?

Finally she started to talk; she told him how she had taken the sacrament and joined the First Presbyterian Church, but did not reveal how sorely she had needed the consolation of the church. She told of buying Dr. Jayne's chest of family medicines, of giving the children Carminative Balsam for colic, but did not add that little William had been sick and in pain for a number of days, that the boy had called for his father. When she told him that she had taken the children to every entertainment that came to town, to the Older Circus which featured Mademoiselle Marietta the first lady equestrian, to see the Fakir of Siva who gave a magic show at the courthouse, she did not add that she was trying to compensate for their father's neglect. When she related that she had bought a fourteen-day French mantel clock from Seth Thomas, gilt china dishes and pickle shells from Wright and Brown, cashmeres and silks from Ninian Edwards's store, she did not trouble to justify her extravagance on the grounds that there were times when she had been so despondent that she had rushed out of the house to shop, buying anything and everything in sight to relieve the heaviness of heart. When she told him that she went to a ball with Helen and Ben Edwards and to a sing with the Wallaces, and had been very gay, she did not tell him that it was because the whole town was buzzing with the gossip that Abraham Lincoln did not come home any more.

The Todds had no real defense against a defeat that everyone knew about.

Ironically, for the first time he was earning sizable sums of money, enough for them to be comfortable. What had caused this depression, this full-fledged bout of hypo that could not be cured by rest, good food, a comfortable bed and financial security?

When she worked in the kitchen he tilted a chair against the wall, his feet on the lower rung, hands clasped about his knees, eyes sad, the picture of gloom. Thus absorbed, he would sit for hours defying interruption. Then suddenly he would throw back his head, tell her a story. At other times he would bolt out of the chair, stalk out of the room . . . or out of the house.

She began to see little of him; Sundays he spent at the office playing chess, coming home only when she sent Robert to tell him that dinner was ready. She did not resist this, for in his absence he seemed more vivid to her than in his presence. When he came home at the end of the day he sat stony-silent before the hearth for four hours at a time, his head sunk deep on his chest, as immobile as a man withdrawn into death. He was taciturn, shut-mouthed, projecting nothing outside himself, alive by such a remote spark that often she could not hear or feel him when he came into a room. She had no clue to what he might be thinking during these long stretches of abstraction; for that matter, she asked herself, was he thinking at all, or simply plunged into a morass of melancholy?

When it was time for sleep she put down her book or sewing but he kept his candle lit and read all night: in Burns, or a philosophy book William Herndon had loaned him, or poems of despair: Holmes's *Last Leaf*; *Mortality*; the third canto of Byron's verse about Childe Harold. Strange, she thought, how one can sleep in the same bed with a man, yet have him be a thousand miles away.

Early one morning she was awakened by strange noises: Abraham was sitting on the edge of the bed mumbling to himself. She listened closely, but his words were incoherent. After a few moments he rose from the bed, put on his trousers, socks and shirt, then dropped into the little chair before the hearth and sat gazing abstractedly into the cold fireplace. She sank back onto her pillow, her heart pounding in her chest.

She cried to herself, Why? Our failure has not been that great! Our end is not in sight! We have committed no unpardonable crime!

She ached as she had during the twenty months after Abraham had abandoned her. Now she had a husband, two children, a home, but her suffering was more intense, the failure cut deeper, the impending tragedy loomed greater. Then she had been a young girl, in danger of losing her love. Now she was committed. Should she lose the love of her husband she was doomed to a fragmentary existence.

The hot airless summer days were much like that earlier period, but she was eleven years older; there were accumulated fatigues, scars: the death of Edward, the end to their public career and ambitions; she no longer could pull the blankets over her head, hide herself from the world. Abraham was not being intentionally unkind, he tried sometimes to take certain burdens from her, but the basic burden, himself, he could do nothing about. How did she avoid being smothered by the oppressive weight?

She shook her head in despair. Wasn't this what she could have expected from a man who was capable of deserting her on an engagement-wedding day? Such a man must have other periods when he would be unable to accept the situation into which he had worked himself, and flee into melancholia. She had imagined that her troubles had arisen from his fear of marriage . . . Yet a man's basic nature did not change; where there was need in him to flee to some tragic tower within himself, the changing fortunes of life always would create the milieu.

Though unable to fathom the why of what he was doing to himself, she did not question the extent of his misery or lose sympathy with him. But they were young, energetic, able. Why had he created this unhappiest period of their marriage because they were momentarily stranded in a backwash? She did not care how long she had to wait; but to be planning and working toward nothing . . . that was living death.

Nor was it much consolation that he was treating the rest of the world as he did his wife: on the street he would look directly at friends without seeing them, shake hands without knowing whose hand he shook; even in court he seemed centered in solitude.

In former times when he had been depressed she had made a conscious effort to compensate for his grimness, keeping the house cheerful, putting a smile on her face, preparing special foods such as the sweet-potato waffles he liked so much, or buying a new vase or picture. But now she had no such expendable strength. When she could no longer stand the hours of bleak silence she would shout at him and then he would walk out of the house without a word and be gone the entire day. Once when she was thoroughly upset he commented in a dry voice:

"Mary, there are times when you make this house intolerable."

"I make the house intolerable!" she cried. "What do you think your charming insouciant manner contributes to the happiness of this household?"

Their home became a grim place, weighed down by Abraham's bleak silences and by her own harshness of manner. There were brief respites, moments of desperate loneliness when their need for each other was greater than the distance and obstacles fate had put between them. But they passed quickly in the unrevealing dark, not to be recaptured when the sun rose and the problem-laden world took over again.

She knew she was hurting herself in giving in to her temper, but she no longer had the ability to control herself. Also weighing on her was the galling knowledge that in the contest for Abraham, waged for years by William Herndon and herself, she had lost. Previously Abraham had spent as little time in his office as possible; now he ran from his home to spend his time with the man he so affectionately called Billy. Was Abraham finding peace with his law partner? Perhaps enjoying himself?

She was shattered by the experience; all reserves of serenity were used up. She asked herself, How long can I last? If I must be destroyed, why can't it be on the plane of high tragedy, where I might sacrifice my happiness for some great or noble cause? But to be caught in the strained silence in the kitchen, the misunderstanding in the sitting room, the quarrel in the bedroom: what a terrible way to waste a life! What an ignominious end.

HER former admirer Edwin Webb was nominated by the Whigs for governor. Mary announced that she would help him because she admired his stoutheartedness in making a fight under such hopeless conditions. Henry Clay died and all the Todds along with Springfield went into mourning; Abraham was nominated to preside over the Clay ceremonies and to give the eulogy. His only comment while they were dressing was that although he admired Mr. Clay for the last heroic stand he had made for the Compromise of 1850, "I do feel that Clay's personal ambitions may have wrecked the Whig party."

When on June 16, 1852, Stephen Douglas was beaten out for the Democratic presidential nomination by Franklin Pierce, an unknown New Hampshire politician, Abraham raised his eyebrows . . . in relief? Later when he read Douglas's first major speech of the campaign, delivered in Richmond, she saw him go red in the face and then a dusty ash gray. She was not surprised therefore when she learned that he was going to answer Mr. Douglas before the Scott Club, named after General Winfield Scott, who had been nominated by the Whigs. He did not write his speech at home. She did not even know whether he wanted her to accompany him but when he came into the sitting room and said, "Aren't you dressed yet?" she took it as a tacit invitation and got into a dark blue summer linen as quickly as she could.

The courthouse was dimly lit by tallow candles. Mary slipped into one of the rear rows alongside her cousin Logan, using a fan to stir the hot air. Abraham rose to tell the Whig club that he was there at his own request because:

"When I first read Douglas's speech at Richmond I was reminded of old times, when Douglas was not so much greater man than all the rest of us as he now is. Believing that the Richmond speech though marked with the same species of 'shirks and quirks' as the old ones was not marked with any greater ability, I was seized with a strong inclination to attempt an answer to it. . . ."

It was the first time she had known Abraham to be querulous in a public talk, and it was obvious to her now as it had been at the moment when she watched him read Douglas's speech that he was consumed with jealousy. Much of the speech she found dull and badly integrated; when he went into a thin falsetto voice to elicit laughs the stories were unfunny and in poor taste. She sat there in humiliation; not even in his earliest days when he was fumbling for means of expression had she seen him put on such a poor performance.

The cauldronlike summer dragged on; the gloom in the house was thick enough to bury in the back yard. She found herself flaring up at situations from which she would have turned away a year before. She quarreled with the man driving Watson's ice wagon because she was convinced he was giving her smaller blocks of ice than she was paying for. She quarreled with an old Portuguese gardener who brought her wild strawberries all summer for an agreed price of twenty-five cents, but toward the end delivered such small and hard berries that she felt ten or fifteen cents was enough for the basket. She refused to give one of the Irish girls, Katy, a raise from $1.25 to $1.50 a week, so the girl quit. A few moments later she found Katy and Abraham in conference on the back porch.

"Now what were you two whispering about, if I may ask?"

"Oh, I persuaded Katy to stay on."

The following Saturday night after she had paid Katy her $1.25 she tiptoed into the kitchen where she saw Abraham give the girl a coin and pat her on the shoulder. She went back into the sitting room and waited for Abraham to reappear.

"Just what did you give Katy?"

"A quarter."

"A quarter? For what?"

"So she wouldn't leave you. It's too hot for you to be doing the heavy work."

"You have no right to go behind my back with the servants. No wonder she's been laughing at me."

"She hasn't been laughing at you. It's just that she's happy because she is getting the wage she thinks she earns."

"I hire the servants for this house, and I know what they are worth. You will kindly go to Katy's place and tell her that I will no longer need her services."

She drudged from day to night through a thousand household tasks, but it was difficult to get Abraham to take care of his chores. The wood box was frequently empty, and she had to cry, "Fire! Fire!" in the hopes of routing him out of his lethargy. Once when she had supper to prepare and he was sitting in a chair tilted against a wall, ignoring her requests for firewood, she picked up the last stick from the scuttle and blazed away with it, hitting him on the nose. It cut the skin, which she fixed up with court plaster and apologies. The next day the story was all around town. She was convinced that it was Herndon who had spread it. However he could not have done so if Abraham hadn't revealed what had happened on his domestic hearth.

She knew too that there was talk going around blaming her for Abraham's unhappiness. His friends were saying, "Poor Abraham Lincoln, married to Mary Todd." How could she answer in rebuttal that Abraham was disenchanted with his life because his ambitions had come to nothing and the future looked meaningless, with little left in it beyond making a living and following a profession he only half enjoyed? If they knew the full facts, if they had to live with him, might they not rather say, "Poor Mary Todd, married to Abraham Lincoln"? For there were others who saw Abraham walking the streets dripping melancholy, who understood what she must be undergoing; she had friends and sympathizers as well as detractors.

Then, just two days before his departure for the fall circuit, she found that she was again with child. She accepted the knowledge with apprehension. How would she fare, carrying under the great burden of their disjointedness? Perhaps if she told Abraham it would help pull him out of his self-concentration; knowing how much she had suffered while carrying William, he might come home frequently. The news might make the difference. . . .

But she did not want his pity. Nor would her pride allow her to use her condition to gain an advantage. She would utter no word; when he returned he would see for himself, and that would be time enough.

The next morning she awakened severely nauseous. She barely made the back porch. Here Abraham found her. He stood behind her, asked sympathetically:

"Mary, what has happened to make you ill?"

She did not reply. Her hands were trembling; in the early morning sunlight her face was a mustard green. He stared at her for a long moment, then said:

"Mary, are you . . . is this another child?"

She nodded her head. He crouched before her, touched her cheek with his fingers. After a moment he said:

"I promised to go to Peoria from Pekin next week and the following week end I must take care of some work in Bloomington, but I can ride in at the second week to make sure you are well. . . ."

She rose, poured some cold water into a basin, rinsed her face and patted the water through her hair.

"I'll be all right. What would you like for breakfast?"

He had not heard her question.

"In any event I'll be home in little more than a month. Stephen Douglas is going to speak for Franklin Pierce at the courthouse here and I'm going to answer him."

She thought, Steve Douglas is apparently the only one who can arouse him any more . . . even bring him home from the circuit.

She bit her lip and said nothing; fried his eggs and sausages in the long-handled spider.

There was little of the impromptu in her nature; she enjoyed giving parties, but preferred them to be for a set time, with the food well prepared, the house ready to receive guests, the hostess dressed in a beautiful gown. Never having encouraged friends to drop in spontaneously, she was almost totally alone.

Eliza Francis came to see her, not so much to cheer her as to make a common bond of their difficulties: for the only other man in Springfield who was as totally unhappy and seemingly a failure as Abraham Lincoln was Simeon Francis. With the splintering of the Whig party, its constant defeat in Illinois, Simeon finally had let the *Journal* slip until it had become a much inferior paper to the *Register*, containing little but agricultural news. Simeon wanted to establish a nursery, raise plants, because, "though plants might be destroyed in frost or hurricane, they could not be blighted by annual elections"; but he found no takers for his paper.

As she and Eliza sat in the parlor desolately having a cup of coffee together, Mary wondered if what had happened to Abraham and to Simeon was the universal pattern of the man who reached middle age and found his aspirations unachievable? Abraham was only forty-three, yet universally known as "Old" Abe. Her father, when he was stricken at fifty-eight, was a member of the Kentucky legislature, president of a bank and of various mills and other businesses, young in his love of the good things of life.

For that matter she considered herself a young woman at thirty-three. Her faith in Abraham was indestructible: she had loved him on that faith, married him on that faith, endured the years of patient waiting on that faith. But for some reason indigenous to his own needs Abraham was driving himself ever downward through Dante's Purgatory to the bottom of the abyss, where the last of his aspirations would be ground to dust on the hard rocks of the pit. And the more his future closed down, the more he turned away from her. This sense of rejection was painful; everything he had done he had done by himself. Where then was her responsibility?

Being well read in the world's romantic literature, she had thought that when a man had disappointments in the outside world he would turn to his love partner for solace, for renewed vitality. But when a man lost his passion for life, did his passion for love also fade?

She had grown up believing that marriage was a rock, the high ground where a couple could stand safe on the lee side of each other's love while the storm lashed itself out . . . a sanctuary rather than a whipping post. Love could leaven failure, give life durable meaning when its youthful hope had fled or its ambition been crushed.

One midafternoon her sister Ann, who recently had moved to Springfield with her husband, Clark Smith, came to the Lincoln house, her plump little figure hurrying up Eighth Street as though every second saved was of crucial importance.

"Ann, you're all palpitating, it must be mighty good news."

"I wish it were good news, Mary . . . but it's always the wife who's last to find out."

Mary's knees began to quake.

"Would you like a cup of coffee to sustain you while you impart the bad news?"

". . . it's that Lois Hillis woman, one of the Newhall family of singers . . . it seems that Abraham goes to every one of her concerts, alone, won't even sit with Cousin Stuart or his friends . . ."

"He likes to be alone at entertainments."

"Well, maybe; but that's not the story Clark heard in his store this morning. Seems like everybody on the circuit noticed and warned your husband not to get involved . . ."

"Now, Ann!"

"Seems last week they were staying in the same hotel and Abraham asked this Mrs. Hillis to sing some of his favorite songs, and she did, then she said he must give her some entertainment, and he stood in the parlor and recited all the verses of *Oh, Why Should the Spirit of Mortal Be Proud?* When it was over this Lois Hillis went up to Abraham to tell him how beautiful it was, and could she have a copy. Abraham said, 'That's the only woman that ever appreciated me enough to pay me a compliment.' Then Judge Davis said, 'Why, Lincoln, I thought you was an universal favorite with the "fair sex!" ' and all the men laughed uproariously."

Mary burned; hadn't she paid him the compliment of falling in love with him and marrying him? Ann, seeing that she had struck fire, hitched her chair closer.

"The next morning, this lawyer who told it to Clark, he got up before dawn, and when he went down to the dining room there was Abraham standing behind Mrs. Hillis's chair while she was reading the poem he had written out for her! Now what do you think of that?"

She had a glimmer of what Ann would have liked her to think, so she replied obliquely, "Abraham doesn't sleep much on circuit; I'm sure he enjoyed writing out the poem. They say women are gossips; if that lawyer hadn't gossiped to Clark, and Clark had not gossiped to you, just how would you have been able to rush here with this luscious morsel?"

She fed her sister coffee and cake; but once she was gone she threw herself down on her bed and lay breathing heavily. It was inconceivable. . . . She would not allow herself to be hurt . . . or torment herself with jealousy.

Yet the next morning she was too miserable to drag her limbs out of bed. She sent Robert over to Frances's to ask Dr. Wallace to stop by. When he came she poured out the tortured story of the past two wretched years.

"Why do I have so little control, William? Why am I stricken, when other wives must have suffered as much, perhaps more, and yet have managed to remain stable . . ."

"Only seemingly," replied William Wallace in a bland tone. "You don't know the anatomy of their suffering quite as well as you do your own. Considering the weight and unacceptability of your burden, Mary, I would say that you are doing pretty well."

She raised herself on her elbows, staring at him in disbelief.

"Do you really think so, William?" Her voice had picked up in tone. "Here I have been despising myself for being so weak!"

"No, I think you are hardy. Things are difficult for you, and I know how sorely you are tried."

"Oh, William, if only I could be stolid . . ."

"Then you wouldn't be Mary Todd Lincoln, you would be several other women, none of whom you might enjoy. If I were you I would settle for being yourself. I've been reading quite a little about genetics lately; that's the science of heredity. It might help you to understand yourself better if you would realize that you weren't given the best chance for a phlegmatic nature: your mother and father were second cousins; and your grandmother Parker married her first cousin."

"I know the Bible forbids cousins to marry, but I always thought that had something to do with morals?"

"It has to do with blood lines: if two different blood lines are crossed they have a tendency to mix their strengths and weaknesses; but if the same blood lines are crossed they build up the identical strengths and weaknesses. If your parents and grandparents had been stolid people, you would probably be so unemotional you would feel nothing. But if they were a touch on the emotional side, you can see how that would intensify your sensitivity."

She nodded, understanding.

"William, it seems like all bad times now. It's been another twenty-month period like that one before we were married."

He pursed his underlip, his eyes gently reproving her.

"You survived that first twenty months when Abraham took to the woods; I don't mean merely that you stayed alive, but that you kept your love and loyalty alive. Anyone who could have been as staunch under those circumstances is not going to be destroyed by a passing irresolution on the part of her husband."

"No, William, not if it is passing and not if it is irresolution. But what if it is permanent?"

"Nothing is permanent, every hour finds a shifting in the million fragments of circumstance. There are no medicines for worry or aggravation, Mary. Now get out of bed and go about your duties, until what Shakespeare called the 'slings and arrows of outrageous fortune' stop hailing down upon you."

She did what the doctor ordered.

10

WHEN he returned at the end of October she needed only one look to know that the thought of the impending child had done nothing to recoup his spirits. He seemed, if possible, thinner and darker and bleaker than before. She saw no sign of animation in him until she brought up the name of Lois Hillis, with only a tiny hem of her seriousness showing.

"I've heard all about that romantic breakfast at dawn with the pretty young singer, Lothario Lincoln."

"That wasn't a romantic breakfast, Mary, in fact it wasn't a breakfast at all. I just copied out the poem I had recited the night before and brought it to her before her stage left."

"It's hard enough for me . . . the malicious talk about my husband never coming home. Now to have them flinging another young woman's name . . ."

He broke into a wide grin, put an arm about her shoulders.

"Mary, that's the highest compliment you can pay a homely man, to be jealous of him. When I was in Bloomington I looked into the glass and I resolved should I ever see an uglier man I would shoot him on sight. The next morning I took one look at a new lawyer in town and said to him, 'Halt, sir; I made a note that if ever I saw an uglier man than I am I would shoot him on the spot. Make ready to die.' 'Well, Mr. Lincoln,' said the man, looking me squarely in the face, 'if I am any uglier than you, fire away.'"

He threw back his head and laughed. She smiled wanly.

"No one would believe any gossip about me and a pretty young girl, Mary. They all know I'm a bad bargain. But if I had known you would be jealous . . ."

"I'm not jealous. I'm just possessive! You're my husband. You belong to me. God knows I've earned that much from all my misery."

"Yes," his face became solemn again, "you have; but it is a small compensation."

They had a tenth anniversary coming on November 4, 1852. She was determined not to let it go by default. She arranged for supper at the American House, going to the hotel to select the menu with the new chef. She then invited Elizabeth and Ninian, Frances and William, Eliza and Simeon Francis, Helen and Benjamin Edwards, Julia and Lyman Trumbull, her cousins Stuart and Logan, Dr. Todd and his two daughters, Elizabeth and Frances, and Ann Rodney Cushman, also a bridesmaid, the William Butlers, James Matheny, Abraham's best man, still clerk of the circuit court, Mercy and James Conkling, now a successful real estate man. She discussed with the manager the hiring of a troupe of choral singers for after-supper entertainment.

She did not confide her plans to Abraham until everything was settled, then told him of what she had done. She could see by the wordless way he looked at her that he had totally forgotten they were to have a tenth anniversary; this fact kept him in the silence that had no choice but assent. She pushed her advantage by insisting that he buy a new suit and a pair of soft black leather boots for the affair.

She resolved to make the dinner party a success: it would be her answer to the gossips of the town. She dressed in a new brocade with a round point lace collar, wrapping her hair extravagantly with a wreath of French flowers.

The dining room at the American House was gaily lighted. Everyone except Abraham drank a lot of the iced champagne with the *hors d'oeuvres;* there was laughter and gaiety at the long table. The only unpleasant moment was caused by Simeon Francis, who arrived with the news that Franklin

Pierce had been elected president by a landslide: the Democrats in Illinois had made such an unprecedented gain that no one could any longer dispute that the Whigs were finished. Abraham took the news easily; he had made only two or three desultory speeches for General Scott, anticipating the defeat. The choral singers rendered "Come Dwell with Me," and a new song, "My Old Kentucky Home." Nostalgically she wondered what her life would have been like had she married Desmond Fleming and remained in the Kentucky Bluegrass.

The party did not break up until midnight. Everyone thanked her for the delightful affair, expressing the hope they would be invited to the Lincolns' twentieth anniversary.

Wistfully, she hoped so too.

When they reached home and were standing in the hall, she turned to him.

"Did you enjoy your tenth anniversary party?"

"Yes, I had a fine time."

All of her rigorous gaiety vanished. She walked into the dark parlor, sat on the edge of a fiddleback chair and held her face in her hands. Abraham lit a lamp, then came and stood in front of her. She raised her head, asked:

"Abraham, what have I done?"

He stared at her for a moment, uncomprehending.

". . . you mean the dinner? But I was confoundedly well pleased."

"Even a criminal must be told the nature of his crime before being convicted. What is the nature of my crime, Abraham? What law of love or marriage have I broken?"

Sadness settled over his face.

"You haven't done anything, Mary."

"Then why do you no longer love me?"

He took the lamp off the mantelpiece and brought it close, peering at her intently.

"Why do you ask that question?"

"Because I've asked it of myself a thousand times in this past dreadful year when you stayed away or when you came home only to move through the rooms like a ghost."

"I never realized you felt this way."

"Tell me, Abraham, have I forced you into activities you did not want? Were my ambitions in directions opposite to yours or unsympathetic to you? Have I judged you unworthy for any task you were called to?"

". . . no, it isn't any of these things . . . it has nothing to do with you . . ."

". . . but it must or you would not have put me out of your life." She sat rigidly in the chair with her hands clasped between her breasts. "What has happened to the closeness of our relationship that you turn away from me, stay out on circuit for months at a time . . . when you don't have to?"

". . . this is terribly painful to me."

"Painful!" Her voice was a supplicating cry to the heavens. "What do you think I've been suffering?"

He put a hand on her shoulder.

"I didn't realize you were suffering, Mary . . . because I was so blinded by my own melancholy, I guess."

"I know I've made mistakes, Abraham: I should never have quarreled with those men at Mrs. Sprigg's boardinghouse; I shouldn't have flares of temper with the servants, or speak harshly to tradesmen. I don't keep house as easily as Mammy Sally; I'm sometimes penny-pinching, but it's you who trained me to be economical so you could pay back your debts. I love fine materials and I spend more money on them than I should, but I'm not buying expensive gowns from New York, I'm only buying materials and spending my own time sewing the costumes . . ."

"Please, Mary . . . don't shrive yourself before me."

She rose and walked to the whatnots on either side of the fireplace, running her hand over the oval frame boxes containing hair flowers.

"Why do I humiliate myself this way? I've never been an ugly woman, I'm not ill formed, I'm not ignorant. I never lacked for friends . . . or suitors. I made up my mind what I wanted in life, and in you I found what I wanted. I loved you. I was never able to understand that dreadful twenty months when you ran away from me; nor why you should have wanted to put us through such misery. Perhaps it is only your children and sense of obligation that keep you from vanishing from my life now . . ."

He hung his head, answered in a hoarse tone, "I deserve that."

"I'm not interested in your just deserts. I only want to know why I am no longer attractive to you. You found me bright and intelligent . . ."

"I've always respected your judgment," he interrupted.

"Then have I become dull-witted? Do I no longer understand the issues that face us?"

He turned away from her, gazed sightlessly into the mirror on the table between the street windows, started speaking in a low tone.

". . . my feelings for you have not lessened in any way, Mary. Nor has any of my . . . gloom . . . been caused by you. Everything that has happened to me comes from outside our home: my falling into disfavor, into a meaningless life because there is nothing to look forward to. There are times when I cannot endure the thought that I have nothing to give to anyone, not even my wife. But you can't know the hell I have suffered. You've never hurt me; certainly you've never been too ambitious for me; mine has always been the greater ambition. . . ." He was silent, winding his watch unknowingly with a brass key. "I have been wrapped up in my own dejection. It never occurred to me to ask what effect all this would have on my wife. I didn't know you were unhappy, Mary; I know nothing about women."

"Are you telling me that you don't know how deeply you have cut yourself off from your wife and children?"

He made fumbling gestures with his hands, his shoulders stooped, his big, long-faced head leaning forward toward her. His answer was oblique.

"Out on circuit I am a practicing lawyer, moving from town to town amidst the bustle of my fellow lawyers and the flurry of the courts and clients and young lawyers coming to me to write their briefs. I am an active and successful man, doing all that any man needs to do . . ."

"And when you're at home?"

"Here in Springfield . . . I realize that the practice of the law can never fill anything but a small part of my life . . . that the rest of it is empty." He gripped her shoulders so hard she could feel the pain of her flesh under his grasp. "Try to understand me, Mary: it's only when I come home that I realize I've been a failure. That's when I feel I would rather be any place in the world than here."

Her voice became lower, gentler. "I have never turned a face toward you accusing you of failure."

He stood so close that the rough material of his baggy knees brushed against the brocade of her dress.

"No, Mary, the sense of being remiss has come from inside me. We started out with such high hopes, you gave me your one and only life when you could have gone elsewhere to greater advantage: men better born, better educated, certainly with better prospects . . ."

"My feelings have not changed . . ."

"It's too late now. When I realize how completely I've let you down, how I have become the least of all the men we know, it's hard for me to come home. . . . It's not that I no longer love you, Mary." His voice too was a lonely cry in the night. "It's that I no longer love myself! The years have put a damp on my spirit."

There was silence in the cold dark parlor. Then she spoke.

"Why have you lost your perspective, Abraham? Everyone knows that politics is a sometime thing, that defeat in an election is no measure of a man's worth."

"I'm no longer interested in politics, Mary."

"Isn't this just another flight?" Her voice was soft, for she did not mean to hurt him, yet the tone was insistent.

"A steaming jungle of despair?" He smiled wanly. "I don't think so. It's just an acknowledgment that I've been barking up the wrong tree."

"You told Gibson Harris that you like a tree better in the winter; that then you can see it in all its stark truth. The only reason you're now saying that you've been barking up the wrong tree is that the tree hasn't borne fruit for us. But if you like it when it is in full fruit, then you have to like it in the winter. This is winter for us; but that doesn't mean the tree of politics is dead."

He grinned ruefully.

"I always felt I could be needed and serve a purpose. But the kind of man needed today is a Stephen Douglas."

"You are the one who has said that there was room for both of you."

"If by his methods he can succeed and become dominant, then my methods can get me nowhere."

"Times change, needs change. May I quote one of your favorite passages from Julius Caesar: 'There is a tide in the affairs of men, which, taken at the flood, leads on to fortune.' I'm still a young woman. I feel that my life lies before me. Politics is in my blood. We must hold our heads high, read and study and think until the day comes when we can find our rightful place."

He took her in his arms, murmured, "You never lose hope for me, do you?" and kissed her tenderly on the mouth.

Someone came running up the steps, pounded sharply on the door. Abraham admitted a young man.

"Mr. Lincoln, old lady Westly is dying. She sent me to ask you to come write her will."

Abraham turned to Mary. "Would you keep me company?"

It was an hour's ride in the cold autumnal night, the fields lying in dark stubble. When they reached the farmhouse Abraham asked Mrs. Westly a few simple questions, and wrote the will. She asked in a feeble voice if he would read from the Bible. One of the woman's sons offered him their copy, but he shook his head, reciting from the Twenty-third Psalm:

" 'Though I walk through the valley of the shadow of death, I will fear no evil, for Thou art with me . . .' "

As they were riding home in the predawn darkness, sitting close under the blanket, Mary said, "Pastor Lincoln, you did real well for a man who is not supposed to have a religion."

Abraham looked up. The heavens were full of stars. He called off a few of their names.

"I can see how it might be possible for a man to look down upon the earth and be an atheist, but I cannot conceive how he could look up into the heavens and say there is no God."

They rode in silence for another moment, then she felt his hand reach out and take hers.

11

IT was what the old settlers called "a good tight winter," with plenty of snow, rain and cold. When Abraham had to leave for three more weeks of circuit, then to take evidence in the Illinois and Michigan Canal dispute for the legislature, he assured her he would be home at every opportunity.

One morning when she felt distress she summoned Dr. Wallace. He said: "Mary, not letting a doctor take care of pregnant women because of the question of delicacy is profound nonsense. There is a man in town, a German doctor by the name of Wohlgemuth who is a surgeon and *accoucheur*. I'd like to have him take care of you during these months, and deliver your baby . . . instead of calling in a midwife at the last minute. Do you think Abraham would approve?"

"He might. . . ."

When Abraham returned in mid-December he gave Dr. Wallace permission to call Dr. Wohlgemuth, who wore a beard as long as Michelangelo's *Moses* but who knew precisely what she was undergoing, and wrote a prescription which did away with most of her pain. Abraham had had a successful trip; he loaned one of the local blacksmiths five hundred dollars on an interest note, and when Ninian Edwards overextended himself, was able to help him out of his difficulties with a substantial amount of cash. He had bought two lots in Bloomington as a gift for her, and also brought the story of the proprietors of an area in Logan County who had asked permission to name their new town Lincoln, in his honor.

"I told them they'd better not do that for I never knew anything named Lincoln that amounted to anything," he said with a laugh, but she could see that he was pleased.

If there was no great fire within Abraham, neither was there the intense melancholy of the past twenty months. The driving force of the early years, that he must somehow leave the world a better place than the one he had come into, was nowhere apparent; if there was a vestige of despair in the quiet corners of his heart, he now shielded it from her and from the world. He was attentive and friendly, spent more time with the boys, playing marbles with them on the front street, going with Robert to Estabrook's Academy to hear the boy recite. Though he refused to join the large crowd going to the Hall to see Governor Matteson sworn in, or to attend the open reception at the governor's home, he volunteered to go to her Bell Society banquet in the Senate chamber to help her group raise money for a new church bell. He also took her to Stephen Douglas's levee at the Capitol in honor of Douglas's re-election to the United States Senate for another six-year term; as part of his recovery he had put aside his feelings about Senator Douglas, pushing through the jam of fifteen hundred celebrants to congratulate him.

When on the morning of February 12, 1853, the Illinois Senate, as a birthday present to Abraham, unanimously passed the bill making the new town of Lincoln the county seat of Logan County, Mary quickly set to work constructing a papier-mâché model of a state capitol which she placed in the middle of the dining-room table, then sent out messages to their family and friends to come to a buffet supper. There was no need for her to play a role at this party, to fix a smile on her face; she was content. At the height of the fun about the supper table Abraham leaned over and said, "This time I think I'll accept your offer. . . . Now that my father is gone, I'd like to name a child after him."

"Frankly, I'm boning up on names like Emilie and Eliza."

"Reconcile yourself, Mary, the science books I've been reading say that like ingredients always bring forth like results."

Her fourth child was delivered by Dr. Wohlgemuth in the early morning hours of a bright April day. She heard the doctor say, "A boy," then noted idly that the baby's cry had a strangely hollow sound.

She slept straight through the next twenty hours, awakening in time for the first feeding. To her eyes the baby seemed the fairest of the four, with a good stand of blond hair and small features. Abraham stood over her, chuckling:

"He looks like a tadpole, with a big head on such a small body. I'll bet it's crammed with brains. I think we'll make a poet and philosopher out of him, like Mr. Emerson." He ran his fingers through the child's fine hair, saying, "You're going to have too much sense to be an ambulating country lawyer, aren't you, Tadpole?"

She smiled; it was good to hear him make a joke on himself. She lay back among the pillows gazing down into the baby's eyes while he nursed. After a time she noticed a tiny but steady stream flowing through his nostrils. She pushed herself up among the cushions, shifted the baby's position, then resumed the feeding; but the strange and somewhat frightening procedure continued.

She told Dr. Wohlgemuth about it. He hesitated, then said:

". . . yes, I know . . . there's a little deviation, nothing too serious . . ."

The hollow-sounding birth cry came to her mind.

"What . . . what . . . do you mean by . . . deviation?"

"Well, a small aperture in the roof of the boy's mouth. Most of his milk he swallows, but at the moment he breathes, it goes up through the opening into the nasal passages."

Too stunned to think, she struggled forward on her elbows, her eyes devouring the doctor's face. Then she started to open the boy's lips. The doctor stopped her with a dismissing dip of the hand.

"There's nothing to see, and nothing to worry about, Mrs. Lincoln. Once he is eating solid food there will be little interference."

"Why did it happen?" she cried in anguish. "We're both healthy, normal people. He looks such a beautiful boy . . ."

"He is, Mrs. Lincoln. Divergences happen. It cannot in any way affect his health."

"But when he cries . . . he doesn't sound like other children . . ."

"Yes, he may have a little trouble with his speech because of the cleft palate. He'll have to be trained; but not until he's in school."

"Does my husband . . . know about this?"

"I told him immediately. He asked me not to say anything to you until you had gotten back your strength."

When Abraham came in she wept in his arms.

"Abraham, what have we done that God should make our children suffer?"

"Now, now, that little Tadpole isn't going to suffer from anything. I'll wager you my law license against your last year's bonnet that he is the smartest member of the Lincoln family. I fell crazy in love with him the moment I laid eyes on him."

"I remember a child in Lexington with a cleft palate: he couldn't talk at all, just a lot of strange sounds. His mother and father said they understood him, but the children taunted him, called him an idiot. . . . Oh, Abraham, they'll make our boy even more miserable than they did Bobby!"

She buried her head against his bony chest. He stroked her hair.

"You should be thanking God that you and the boy are well. Mrs. Dallman around the corner gave birth same time you did, but she's dangerously ill, and not able to nurse their son. They have been searching all over town for a wet nurse."

Mary pulled back slowly, gazed at him, then exclaimed in a voice from which all self-pity was gone:

"Abraham, go get the child and bring him here."

Abraham jumped up from the bed and stalked out of the room. He was back in a few moments with a tiny mite wrapped in a blanket. He stooped over, laid little Charles Dallman in Mary's arms. He was all skin and bone, tugged hungrily, then closed his eyes and fell asleep. Abraham wrapped him in his blanket and walked him back to the Dallman house.

Every four hours he brought the infant to her. She watched him grow strong and lusty, even as her own child was strong and lusty. By the end of the week when Abraham had to leave on circuit, Mrs. Dallman had recovered sufficiently to feed her son. Mr. Dallman came to visit with a huge box of candy, and tears of gratitude in his eyes.

"Without you I would have lost my son, Mrs. Lincoln. How can I thank you?"

"God is good," Mary replied.

She had not meant to say it; she had not even known she said it; yet somehow the tragic imperfection of their own child had been alleviated by her ability to help Charles. This was what Mr. Emerson had meant by the law of compensation.

Somehow the troubles of the past two years seemed well behind her.

She made a fast recovery, without any of the illnesses she had suffered with William. Abraham was convinced that this was due to Dr. Wohlgemuth's excellent care. She went through the house with fresh eyes; saw that during the bad time the place had run down, the fence needed repairing, the front yard was full of brambles and locust shoots.

Abraham was back at the end of three weeks, having ridden an extra eighty miles to spend the days between the Pekin and Clinton courts. He was wild about the new child, constantly picking him up and walking the length of the house with him. They never mentioned Thomas's cleft palate; Mary had found by experimentation the best position in which to feed him; Abraham settled down to the names of Tad or Taddie.

When he returned again early in June he advised her that her brothers Levi and George had filed a claim against them in the Lexington court for $472.54, alleging that he had collected this money from people who owed it to the firm of Oldham and Todd, and never paid it over. It was the first time she had known anyone to question Abraham's integrity. During the past two dreary years the only heartening stories to reach her were that Abraham was maintaining a fortress within himself, that his basic integrity was being preserved intact, a redoubt which no man and no external circumstance could pierce. People called him a fair lawyer; judges said publicly that he seemed innocent of the art of deception or dissimulation; lawyers said that he refused to misstate the law even to his own advantage; clients felt they could follow him without going wrong, that he would abandon a case rather than bolster up a false position; juries said they would take his exposition of the law and the facts of the case without scruple, for they knew he never had misconstrued the law or perverted the evidence.

The fact that the suit had been filed by one of Lexington's leading attorneys and was a matter of public knowledge in Kentucky had Abraham thoroughly indignant. The only money he ever had collected for her father had been a fifty-dollar debt which they had paid over to Betsy's estate.

"If your brothers will name any living accessible man as one from whom I received their money I will go to that man and disprove the charge."

She helplessly swallowed her fury at her brothers. What could she say?

Summer temperatures were so high that when the courts opened in July the judges and lawyers agreed to put the cases off until cooler weather. Abraham told his boys that the weather made him feel like taking off his flesh and sitting in his bones, which literal-minded Robert said was silly, but sent fun-loving William into gales of laughter. By mid-July the temperature was up to ninety-four degrees, sultry and oppressive, with only an occasional evening shower to cool the air. Yet for Mary it was a pleasant summer, and in spite of the sustained heat Springfield was bustling; Illinois wheat was bringing a high price in the new markets opened by the railroad lines; the merchants and farmers were prospering, as were the lawyers: including Abraham.

"I've just been offered the largest law question that can be got up in the state," he confided to her. "Champaign and McLean counties are assessing for taxation the lands owned by the Illinois Central and they want me to represent them. However, the railroad is also asking me to take their case, and they are willing to pay a $250 retainer fee. I'm somewhat trammeled by what has passed between me and the clerk of Champaign County, he has the prior right to my service, but I have to tell him to make sure he can get me a fee somewhat near what I can get from the railroad. I can't afford to miss such a big fee."

Fall came, and Abraham started on the long trek. She was sorry when the Powels moved to a neighboring town and she could no longer have their son Howard to stay at night, but she found a new Irish girl who was willing to sleep in.

Her major preoccupation was with young Tad. When he reached six months she started him on solid foods and learned to distract him with songs and toys so that he swallowed fast. When it came time for him to feed himself she would find ways of teaching him the same technics. William was completely devoted to the baby, watched over him in the yard while he slept, played with him on the floor of the kitchen. As for Robert, she explained to him as best she could the handicap with which Tad had been born, thinking he would sympathize with the youngster since he himself had suffered a hardship. Instead Robert took it as a personal affront that there was something wrong with his brother, acting as though his parents had injured his position among the other boys. When he walked past Tad he did so with eyes averted.

Like Abraham, she loved the boy madly; his affliction sat like a stone on her heart.

12

THEY had a beautiful fall, the weather warm and mellow. She took the children to hear the Swiss Bell Ringers, to see P. T. Barnum's circus with Tom Thumb. In the evenings she left them with the Irish girl while she, Mercy and Helen went to Robinson's Atheneum with its corps of Dramatists and Danseuses, and to a series of lectures by Professor Palmer on Phrenology. Abraham sent her messages: the clerks of the counties had released him; he had been paid his retainer fee by the Illinois Central; his lawyer in Lexington had obliged Levi and George to name the individuals involved in their suit, and he was taking depositions from them at Shelbyville and Beardstown.

Three or four afternoons a week she went to Dr. Jayne's, where Julia had moved her husband so that her father could supervise his recovery from a lung ailment, and tried to cheer her old friends whose fortunes were being blighted by this lingering illness.

In mid-November she had a letter from Betsy saying that Emilie would like to come to Springfield for a visit. Mary invited her to stay with the Lincolns, and spent the next two weeks sewing fresh white sheer curtains for the sewing room. Abraham returned in time to receive Emilie of the long reddish-blond hair, deep blue eyes, soft peach skin and fine features. She reminded Mary of herself when she was eighteen. Abraham held out his long arms to her, saying, as he had in Lexington, "So this is Little Sister."

"I don't have my mother's billowing skirts to hide behind this time," Emilie replied; "besides you don't seem so tall now, Brother Lincoln."

Mary helped her sister unpack.

"The first night I was in Elizabeth's house we put a candle in the parlor window, so that all the young men in town would know we were at home. But Springfield is a big city now, seven thousand people, and it wouldn't do us a bit of good. I've arranged for a buffet supper and dance at the American House."

"That's thoughtful of you, Mary," said Emilie. "But I wouldn't want it said that I came here looking for a husband."

"Very well, I promise not to put a card in the *Journal* advertising for one. But I hope you will settle here."

A month went by in a happy whirl. Mary gave parties for Emilie, took her to formal balls at the Odd Fellows' Hall or in the new saloon of the Ives and Curran Jewelry Building. For their New Year's Eve party she had all the furniture moved out of the parlor and sitting room, spread rice dust on the floor, engaged a four-piece orchestra. The two women received hand in hand.

The New Year was only three or four days old when all hell broke loose. It was their friend Stephen Douglas who was responsible for the outburst: as chairman of the Committee on Territories, Senator Douglas had brought to the Senate the report on the vast Indian-occupied Nebraska country, announcing that it:

". . . *shall be received into the Union with or without slavery*." They were sitting in their rockers before a blazing log fire. Puzzled, Mary asked:

"All of the Nebraska country lies north of the Missouri Compromise line, doesn't it? Wouldn't that fact automatically exclude slavery?"

He gazed at her for a moment, his eyes troubled. When he spoke it was in a slow, absorbed manner.

"There never was any thought . . . in anyone's mind . . . that slaves would be allowed into Nebraska. The freedom character of that country is as unalterably fixed by the Missouri Compromise as our own home here in Illinois."

He picked up the *Register* which contained the report.

"When Douglas talks about moving property into the territories he's talking about slaves. Under his reasoning the Missouri Compromise could be declared illegal, and there would be no territory anywhere in America which would not be open for slavery. He's the one who fought so hard for the Compromise of 1850, but this bill will open the whole conflict again! What is he hoping to gain by it?"

"The White House."

It was as though her three words had struck him across the face like the thongs of a rawhide whip.

223

"But the slavery road is not the road to the Executive Mansion: it splits the Democrats on the north and south line."

He began pacing the floor, brows knitted, body tense. She had not seen him so agitated since he had been deep in politics himself. Her eyes followed him, her own body became tense, her lips pressed tight. The debate in Congress over this Nebraska bill would be a long and heated one; would Abraham remain aroused? He had sworn that he was no longer interested in politics; but certainly the picture of him now as he paced up and down the floor of the sitting room was anything but the portrait of a disinterested man.

During the next three weeks they read all the newspapers they could lay their hands on, the Boston *Post*, the Philadelphia *Argus* and the New York *Tribune* from the north, the New Orleans *Bulletin*, Charleston *News* and Macon *Messenger* from the south. As Abraham pored over the reports he kept asking himself how far Douglas would dare to go in his tampering with the Missouri Compromise.

Their answer came on January 23, 1854, when Stephen Douglas brought onto the floor of the Senate his revised Nebraska bill in which he divided the Nebraska lands into two territories, Kansas and Nebraska, stipulated that when the territories were admitted as states they would be received with or without slavery as their own constitutions prescribed; *and that the Missouri Compromise of 1820 was now null and void*.

Mary no longer had to ask herself whether Abraham would remain aroused; she never had seen him more profoundly disturbed. Was this a strategic move on Douglas's part to consolidate his party? Was he trying to get Nebraska admitted quickly because he wanted the steam railroad across the continent to take a northern route, with Chicago as the eastern terminus? Try as they might they could find no satisfactory reason for the shocking act; nor was Abraham's overpowering wrath any longer a matter of personal jealousy: the issues here were greater than one man's ambition or resentments. If Douglas's bill became law the whole of the unsettled American continent would be open to slavery.

Abraham stood before the fire reaching out his cold hands to the flames.

"Douglas declares that he is the dictator of Congress, and that's the truth: he controls large majorities in both Houses. Singlehanded he is going to plunge this nation right back into its bitter sectionalism and clamor for disunion . . . from both sides. I can only think of the line in Julius Caesar: 'He doth bestride the narrow world like a Colossus; and we petty men walk under his huge legs, and peep about to find ourselves dishonourable graves.'"

Mary fell asleep the instant her head touched the pillow. When she awakened at dawn she saw Abraham sitting on the side of the bed in his long yellow nightshirt, his chin on his chest. He heard her sit up, turned, and with a piercing expression asked:

"Mary, can this nation continue to exist half slave and half free?"

13

IT was as though the years of lassitude had never existed: before, Abraham had been interested in politics as a means of rising in the world, though his ambition had been leavened by a fascination with self-government. Now that he was fired by the determination that slavery must not spread, his self-interest dissolved in a dedication to principle. Evenings found him knee-deep in newspapers and magazines, stretched out on the floor of the sitting room. No longer did he go to the state-house library for fun and companionship; he went instead to study the actual intent of the Constitution on the subject of slavery, the first Ordinance written for the Northwest Territory in 1787, the economics of slavery, the debates which arose out of the Missouri Compromise of 1820 and the Compromise of 1850. When he left the house he told her what he was going to search for; when he returned he told her what he had found. More than ever as he ceased to confide in his men friends she became his confidante and assistant.

Their love blossomed, deep and strong in understanding. Their lives had been compounded of a common faith in accomplishment; without it their relationship had lacked spiritual succor. Now that she was again a full participant he shared with her the slow painful process of his growth.

"If all earthly power were given me, Mary, I should not know what to do as to the existing institution of slavery. But to extend it, that I know to be a crime against God and man."

She was no longer the mirror of his failure, but the reflection of his vitality and his dedication. He was able to face his wife and to respect her because he respected himself.

The wretched months had taken their toll; she could not pretend that she looked young for her thirty-five years; her figure had grown solid, her face was beginning to assume a rigid aspect, her lips taut, her eyes harder. . . . Yet Abraham was ardent. As he came back to life his skin took on color, his eyes sparkled, the whole animated cast of his face became attractive. The moment he entered the house his vibrancy could be felt. No one could set Abraham Lincoln down as absent; once again he was present, ready to stand up and be counted.

She went to the Hall of the Illinois House of Representatives and took a seat in the semicircular balcony under the dome to listen to the debate on the Nebraska bill. Of the seventy Democratic members of the House only three were in favor of Douglas's bill, yet word had been received from Senator Douglas that he wanted his bill backed by the Illinois legislature, and it was approved by a large majority exactly as he had written it. When she took this report home to Abraham, he exclaimed:

"What amazing power that steam engine in britches has acquired, that without even being present he can make a body of men go against their principles!"

By March 4, 1854, in spite of the fact that Douglas was opposed by Horace Greeley in the New York *Tribune*, Henry Raymond in the New York *Times*, William Cullen Bryant in the *Evening Post* and a hundred other northern newspapers; in spite of the mass protest meetings held in nearly every city outside of the south, the thousands of resolutions adopted and sent to the administration and Senate; in spite of his being burned in effigy from town to town, Senator Douglas whipped his Nebraska bill through the Senate. In the ensuing weeks, with the hurricane mounting in furor, with three thousand New England clergymen protesting against the bill, with the lawyers, physicians, architects, engineers, authors giving full time to the defeat of Douglas and his bill, with exhortatory pamphlets flooding the country, with the merchants of Boston, New York, Chicago and Philadelphia circulating petitions and raising money to oppose it, Senator Stephen Douglas pushed his bill through the House and made it the law of the land.

"Law is an improper word," cried Abraham agitatedly when the news was telegraphed to Springfield. "That enactment is a violence: it was conceived in violence, it was passed in violence, it will have to be maintained and executed in violence. There will be violence in Kansas and Nebraska, and if they try to bring those states in as slave states the violence will spread to the rest of the nation. We've been totally defeated, literally millions of us, and we've been defeated by one little man who looks more like Napoleon every day. He has got to be stopped!"

Mary had been stitching in the sleeves of a cotton shirt for three-year-old William. She dropped her work and sat gazing at him, wide-eyed.

"How?"

"I don't know how. But I know the beginning step: Richard Yates from our district is a strong anti-Nebraska man. I've got to persuade him to stand for re-election to Congress, then stump for him with all my might."

A soughing movement swept through her. She tried to keep her voice calm.

"What about yourself? Shouldn't you be in Washington to prevent Kansas and Nebraska from coming into the Union as slave states?" When she saw him looking at her out of the corner of his eye she added hurriedly, "No, Abraham, I'm not speaking from personal ambition: if you can change, I can change; if you can grow, I can grow."

"I don't want to run for office any more," he answered. "I want to be free to stand with the right wherever I find it."

"Could Steve do any part of the damage if he weren't in the United States Senate? Couldn't you do a thousand times more good by being in the Senate to oppose him?"

"Douglas has a genius for getting himself elected. I have yet to discover that genius in myself."

226

They became involved in an election on a more local level: William Herndon was running for mayor of Springfield, and Abraham was out campaigning for him. Mary was convinced that Herndon would make the worst mayor Springfield ever had had, but to her amazement he not only got himself elected, but cleaned up the town, graded streets, put in sidewalks, got rid of the mud, gave out contracts for the installation of gas lamps for street corners, passed ordinances that no more refuse could be dumped in the public streets, ordered all offensive privies removed from the city limits and, to cap the climax, pushed an ordinance through the council prohibiting the sale of liquor within the city limits.

"I'll make a grudging admission, Abraham, your partner must have some ability after all. And I'm so grateful he has banned liquor: you won't be awakened at dawn to bail him out of jail."

"Now, Puss, it's been four years since Billy broke up that grocery!"

During the bad years he had abandoned her nickname, Molly, and she had missed it; now he called her Puss whenever he was feeling affectionate. She did not know where he had picked it up, but she liked the intimacy of it.

The summer brought Cassius Clay to speak at the state house. Since his disastrous campaign for the governorship of Kentucky he had been retired to his farm. Stephen Douglas's Nebraska bill had brought him galvanically out of retirement.

When Abraham came home for his midday meal he brought news that the Democratic Secretary of State had refused permission to Cassius to speak in the rotunda of the state house, the first public lecturer to be rejected. At five o'clock therefore she accompanied Abraham to an open grove where a thousand people had gathered and a wooden stand been improvised. They stretched out on the cool grass, gazing up at the sartorially perfect Cassius, his big head of hair, enormous burning eyes, massive features; a pillar of strength. Abraham picked up some branches lying about on the ground, took out his pocket knife and began whittling away at them. Cassius, amid shouts of "Take him down!" began a two-and-a-half-hour attack on the repeal of the Missouri Compromise. His powerful voice filled the grove, not only with the volume of sound but with the grandeur of his moral indignation.

"So long as slavery continues a local institution," Clay cried with his arms wide-extended, "it should be left to itself. But when slavery becomes aggressive and proposes to extend itself over free territories, I shall rise and stigmatize it as it deserves."

"Would you help a runaway slave?" shouted a heckler standing behind Mary and Abraham.

"That would depend on which way he was running!" retorted Cassius.

At the end of the speech Cassius received an ovation. Abraham said admiringly, "He is still a Jeremiah!" Mary led him up to the platform. When Cassius's eyes lighted upon her he jumped to the ground and embraced her.

"Cash, you tell me this instant where you are staying, so Abraham can go get your bag."

They had supper out on the porch, with pitchers of lemonade to quench their thirst. Mary sat in a corner listening and watching the two men with the moon on their faces, while Abraham asked where they would find an organization of free men who would bury their past political animosities and strike at slavery wherever it could be reached under the Constitution; and Cassius asked him what he thought of the new Republican party which had had its first meeting in Ripon, Wisconsin, in February, and another in Jackson, Michigan, a few weeks later.

"I have no objections to fusing with anybody," Abraham replied firmly, "providing I can fuse on ground which I think is right; but this group is composed of so many radical abolitionists that I don't see how I can stand with them without encouraging a split with the south."

Early the next day Lyman and Julia Trumbull called, hoping to meet Clay, who had left for his next speaking engagement. Lyman had been too ill to go out to the grove, but after reading the speech in the *Journal* he had come to inform Clay and the Lincolns that he was bolting the Democratic party and was going to work to get the Kansas-Nebraska bill repealed. For a man as thin and ravaged by illness as Lyman, this was a heroic decision. Mary told him so. She also invited them to stay for supper. Julia pressed her husband to accept. Julia Jayne had been Mary's greatest admirer, saying, "You're the prettiest talker I ever met." The girls had come really close during the secret meetings with Abraham, and doubly regretted the fact that the Trumbulls had moved first to Belleville and then to Alton, so that they saw each other only during court sessions in Springfield. Julia, who always dressed in black now, had been a witty girl, but she had lost a son in infancy, and the years of living with staid, laughterless Lyman had drained much of the gaiety out of her. To some people Lyman seemed a little cold; he was a good student, an intellectual really, who wore gold spectacles and rarely smiled. However he had a rapport with the Lincolns, and now that he was convalescing, the two families spent many of the warm summer evenings together. Toward the end of the summer Lyman announced that he was going to run for Congress in the fall. He urged Abraham to return to active politics.

"I'm already back in," replied Abraham; "Yates has said he will run for re-election to the Congress if I run for the state legislature and help bolster the ticket."

Mary exclaimed, "But, Abraham, you said it was too late for you to go back to the state legislature."

"That was under totally different circumstances. I promised to get out and help get Yates re-elected, and if he thinks my name on the ticket will be a help, I certainly am going to run."

After Julia and Lyman had gotten into their carriage and driven away, Mary asked, "Have the Whigs a chance of winning a majority in the state legislature?"

"We might get an anti-Nebraska-bill coalition."

A flame of hope shot through her. "Doesn't the new state legislature elect the next United States senator?"

"Now, Puss, I've barely got one toe in the water . . ."

"And here I am pushing you into the middle of the ocean! But Jimmy Shields can't get it again. And if at long last we have a set of circumstances which will put the voting power in the hands of the Whigs . . ."

He smiled, shook his head up and down with pursed lips.

"That random thought has flicked across the open spaces of my mind too. If it comes round that a Whig may be elected to the United States Senate, I shall certainly consider the chance of being that man."

She drew up to her full height, her head high and cocked to one side.

"So we petty men are no longer going to walk under the legs of the Colossus and peep about to find ourselves dishonourable graves. We're on the track again!"

14

ABRAHAM had to go to Bloomington for some legal work, but Stephen Douglas would be there, and he hoped to lock horns with him. He returned with sparkling eyes and a jaunty step.

"Douglas refused to debate me! He said, 'This is my meeting; the people came here to hear me, and I want to talk to them.' But when he finished the crowd called for me to speak. I told them to go home and get their supper, then to come back and I would speak, and I would give Douglas a chance to answer me. I felt confident the Democrats would return for the fun of hearing him skin me."

"Only you skinned him instead?"

He made a head-down, left-shoulder-up gesture of bewilderment.

"That banty rooster is a hard critter to keep skinned. You'll see for yourself: he's speaking here at the Fair Grounds on opening day."

On Tuesday morning, October 3, 1854, she had the family up, dressed and breakfasted by eight.

"We'd better see the exhibits early, remember last year the rainstorm turned the Fair Grounds into a sea of mud. Don't Bobby and Willie look nice in their new broadcloth suits?"

Abraham hitched up the carriage and the five Lincolns drove west of Springfield to the Fair Grounds. There were already hundreds of people abroad, looking at the exhibits of prize cattle, horses, sheep, poultry. At one end of the grounds were the wooden stands that had been erected for five thousand people to hear Stephen Douglas that afternoon. Abraham and Robert were fascinated by the displays of newly invented mowers, reapers and threshing machines; Mary took William to see the fruit and flower displays and to find the quilt which Elizabeth's daughter Julia had submitted in the prize contest. By ten o'clock the children were hungry. Abraham bought them hot roasted corn, cakes and sweet drinks. A sprinkling of rain started; they ran for their carriage, reaching it just as the downpour began.

"That'll be the end of Douglas's out-of-doors speech," said Abraham mournfully; "I hate to lose those ten thousand ears. . . ."

That afternoon they jammed their way into the state house, finding seats at the rear of the long semicircular hall. When Douglas mounted the dais Mary craned forward to get a close look at the man who had become in these four years of Abraham's eclipse the undisputed master of the Democratic party and of the federal government. He had grown heavier than when she had seen him last; she took in the elegantly tailored cutaway coat, silk vest and trousers; the mop of wavy brown hair brushed heavily backwards and grown a little gray over the ears, the wide-set burning eyes, big bony nose, the wide mouth and tremendous chin. She could feel the outpouring power of the man as he stood there, short arms outstretched as though to embrace the crowd of two thousand souls, captivating his audience before uttering a single word. When he started speaking his deep, booming voice served not only as a spear but as a net; the inner fire that flamed forth scorched the listener's mind, burnt away hostility or doubt; the closely integrated arguments led the listener onward from one point to another with almost lethal certainty.

She did not know when Abraham left her side, but after a time she saw him out in the lobby pacing back and forth. He could hear Stephen out there; that voice coming from the platform could be heard all over Illinois. At five o'clock, when Douglas finished, he was given an ovation. All around her she heard people cry, "Magnificent! Unanswerable!"

She made her way to the lobby. In a moment the crowd started streaming out. Abraham mounted the stairway leading to the balcony, and called out over and over: "Come back tomorrow, same time, I will reply to Senator Douglas. Tomorrow afternoon at two o'clock, come to hear the answer to Senator Douglas."

When Douglas appeared in the lobby, flushed with triumph and surrounded by admirers, Abraham called out, "Mr. Douglas, I invite you to be here tomorrow to hear my answer and to correct me in any matters of fact."

"Accepted!" Douglas cried.

They went directly to the *Journal* office where Abraham drew up a handbill announcing his reply to Douglas. Simeon said he would print the handbill after supper and cover the town and Fair Grounds with it the next morning.

Then they went home, had a supper of cold tongue and salad and hot raised rolls. Mary put William and Tad to bed and rejoined Abraham in the sitting room where he had dumped dozens of torn and irregular scraps of paper onto the desk from his hat, as well as a quire of rough and interlined pages of the speech he had been trying experimentally in such towns as Winchester, Carrollton and Jacksonville.

"Help me weave all these notes, Puss. I've been scribbling them for weeks. What would you say was the nib of Douglas's reason why it was good to pass the Nebraska Act and declare the Missouri Compromise null and void?"

"Nib? Well, let's see: that the Compromise of 1850 repealed the Missouri Compromise because it provided for the admission of Utah and New Mexico without prohibiting slavery; that slavery is an economic issue and not a moral one; that it isn't feasible in the vast new lands being opened to the American public, and hence won't exist there; that slavery never has been a matter on which Congress could legislate or impose its will upon a free people; that the question of slavery must be left to popular sovereignty in each new territory and state."

"Good nibbing: now let's see if I can do as well with my own thinking: the Missouri Compromise kept this country at peace for over thirty years; slavery is morally wrong, repugnant to the concept of democracy, and holds us up to the scorn and ridicule of the rest of the world; while it may not be disturbed where it exists because there is no legal way so to do, not one further rod of American earth must ever be exposed to the dread institution; both the Constitution and the Congress have had the legal right throughout our entire history to limit the extension of slavery."

They worked until two in the morning, Mary bringing in coffee and chocolate cake around midnight. They slept for five hours, then had breakfast and went back to work, correcting and revising until noon, at which time they had a clean copy.

The day was sultry. They walked to the square. As they reached the state house Senator Douglas arrived in an open carriage flanked by Governor Matteson and Senator James Shields. Everyone nodded formally.

A seat had been saved for Mary in the front row but she preferred to sit in the rear so that she could watch the crowd. The Hall seemed even more jammed than it had been for Douglas because a large group of Fusionist Republicans were meeting in Springfield in order to form a state central committee, and had come in a body to hear Abraham speak.

When the applause had quieted, she heard Abraham say, "Mr. Cheerman: Yesterday I gave Senator Douglas the privilege of correcting me in any facts which I shall state, but not the inferences which I shall draw from them, as they are the nib of the whole question."

Every few moments Douglas jumped to his feet to make a correction. After a time the crowd began calling out, "You're taking advantage! Sit down, Senator Douglas!" Abraham grew angry, thrust his long arm and index finger down at Stephen Douglas, sitting under him, and cried:

"Senator Douglas, I withdraw the privilege of correcting me. Friends, the facts which I shall hereafter state I shall state on my own responsibility."

The crowd applauded. Abraham plunged into his speech, his manner impassioned, his voice quivering with emotion. The Hall had grown stifling hot. The sweat poured from his brow. She watched him stop to discard his stock, then his coat, then his vest, standing in his shirt sleeves and galluses . . . with the Hall alternately still as death or ringing with applause.

"The repeal of the Missouri Compromise is wrong: wrong in its direct effect, letting slavery into Kansas and Nebraska, and wrong in its prospective principle, allowing it to spread to every other part of the wide world, where men can be found inclined to take it.

"This declared indifference, but as I must think, covert zeal for the spread of slavery, I cannot but hate. I hate it because of the monstrous injustice of slavery itself. I hate it because it deprives our republican example of its just influence in the world, enables the enemies of free institutions, with plausibility, to taunt us as hypocrites, forces so many really good men amongst ourselves into an open war with the very fundamental principles of civil liberty: criticizing the Declaration of Independence and insisting that there is no right principle of action but self-interest."

For Mary, her husband's speech was so loaded with incontrovertible fact and at the same time so filled with moral grandeur that it turned Stephen Douglas's structure of popular sovereignty into a heap of ruins.

Early the next morning Abraham hitched up old Buck to the buggy and left for court at Pekin. He explained that he might have remained at home another day but that the Fusionists planned to call on him to speak at the Hall of Representatives that night and to join their party.

"They're dominated by abolitionists, and I can't go along with their thinking. Besides, if I become known as a Republican I'll lose the support of the old-line Whigs and the bolting Democrats."

The next afternoon her cousin Stephen Logan came to inform her that the ruse had not worked: the Fusionists, fired by Abraham's speech, had named him to their Republican Central Committee. Cousin Logan's red hair had faded white, but his eyes were brilliantly alive; a little man, all bone and sinew and brain. This public embracing of Abraham, her cousin explained, could considerably lessen Abraham's chances of being named to the United States Senate.

Her ears stopped: this was the first time she had heard anyone put their own hopes into words; if Cousin Logan felt that way, must not there be others? She brought her attention back to Logan's high shrill voice.

". . . frankly disappointed, these past few years. I had such high hopes for him. He's been a good lawyer, but the promise of bigness I saw . . ."

"And now, Cousin Logan?"

He stood shaking his head up and down at her.

"Abraham's speech yesterday was the finest I've ever heard. Half a dozen times through it I was choking with emotion. I saw the power and the courage in him that I once thought possible, and then watched crumble away. He is our strongest voice now. I'm going to nominate him myself for the United States Senate."

The weeks that followed were engrossing: when Abraham answered Douglas in Peoria his full speech was printed in the newspapers and widely distributed over the state, becoming the rallying point of Whig, Republican and anti-Nebraska Democrat. Then she learned that he was on his way to Chicago. He arrived home the day before election; though he hadn't been able to concentrate on the law, his campaigning had gone robustly, particularly the address in the Market Hall to an overflowing crowd. He brought her a copy of the Chicago *Journal*, where she read:

> His speech was as thorough an exposition of the Nebraska iniquity as has ever been made and his eloquence greatly impressed all his hearers. Born of parents who could only give him faith in rectitude and virtue, he has become what he is through the trials of poverty and by the sweat of his brow.

"Never thought my 'humble origin' would do me any good," he commented wryly, "but now everywhere I'm introduced: Urbana, Quincy, Jacksonville, Peoria, the cheerman calls me a 'man of the people.' Guess I've made progress since Edward Baker's supporters called me a candidate of wealth and aristocratic privilege. But what does that really mean, a man of the people?"

"It means a man who can lift two heavy axes in front of him at one time."

Abraham and Logan were elected handily to the state legislature; Abraham promptly resigned in order to become eligible for the Senate seat. Lyman Trumbull was elected to Congress on his anti-Nebraska stand. It was a stunning repudiation of Stephen Douglas. When all the state legislature returns were in, Abraham said: "Let's draw up a list, and we'll see how we stand."

She helped him make a chart on a large piece of brown wrapping paper: in the combined House and Senate there would be forty-one Democrats, thirty-seven Whigs and nineteen anti-Nebraska Democrats, bringing the sum of anti-Nebraska men in the combined Houses to a robust total of fifty-six votes.

"It looks good, doesn't it?" she asked eagerly. "You need only fifty-one votes: the Whigs will stand by you, the anti-Nebraska Democrats have nowhere else to go."

"Things look hopeful, Puss, but we're going to have to work hard while treading lightly, picking up votes without offending the fifty-odd others who want the post. We have a rash of letters to write, just as we did when we wanted that nomination for Congress; we must suggest to our friends that we will be very grateful if they could make a mark for me among their members."

Some two weeks later they learned that the first election in Kansas had not gone so peaceably as had the one in Illinois; hundreds of armed Missourians had crossed the river and forcibly stuffed the ballot boxes to elect a pro-slavery delegate. The enraged north cried, "Protect yourself! If you don't have the arms, we'll send them to you!" And so Stephen Douglas's theory of popular sovereignty in the Kansas-Nebraska Territories had broken down the first time it was tried.

By New Year's Day Abraham had been established as the favorite for the Senate election. A letter from Galena assured them, "You are my choice above all others," one from Peoria said, "All the good Whigs are for you," another from Knoxville promised, "I am for you against all others," while another from Peoria said, "A large majority of the people who voted for me expect me to vote for you." A Mr. Strunk wrote from Kankakee, "I'd walk a hundred miles to vote for you."

Mary once again made Julia her confidante, telling her of their election strategy, of the letters of support that were coming in, and the number of pledged votes.

"Julia, I'm overjoyed that you and Lyman are going to be in Washington with us. How much easier it would have been for me that first time, if I had had you there to confide in and discuss my problems with. We must go house hunting together so that we can find homes within egg-borrowing distance."

"We're going to a boardinghouse," Julia replied soberly. "You know how conservative Lyman is about money."

On January 1, they had twenty-six votes assured them; by the beginning of the second week their chart showed thirty-five; and by the middle of the month, forty-four, just seven votes short of the number necessary for election. James Shields would receive the forty-one Douglas-Democrat votes; Lyman Trumbull was the first choice of anti-Nebraska Democrats, but Lyman was content with his election to the Congress. Her cousin Logan assured them:

"No one has a chance but you. We'll have those last seven votes corralled by the end of the week, and you'll be elected on the first ballot . . . second, at the latest."

That night Mary was so happy she could not sleep. The next morning she learned that Mayor William Herndon refused to come out for Abraham Lincoln on the ground that his friend Richard Yates, who had been defeated for re-election to Congress, also wanted the office; that as individuals he owed them both a peculiar friendship: "But not one above the other. I stand for both and against neither."

She flew into a rage.

"That ingrate! He owes you nothing! That fine partner you've clasped to your bosom. 'Billy's loyal,' you said. He's not loyal, let alone dedicated to you."

Abraham took her in his arms, kissed away her righteous indignation, said wistfully, "Only a wife can be dedicated."

15

THE new network of railroads linking Illinois cities was making conventions popular, and on Friday, January 19, the legislature adjourned in fine weather to take the train for the conventions being held over the week end in Chicago. Abraham did not go, but Stephen Logan and Simeon Francis went along to hold the Lincoln structure together. The balloting for United States senator would begin as soon as the legislators returned.

When Julia came in for tea that afternoon Mary confided excitedly:

"There's a wonderful caterer in Chicago who brings in all the food already cooked, as well as the china, table linen and coffee urns. I've ordered a banquet for three hundred; they'll bring it on the same train with the legislators. I'll have my victory dinner ready the moment the balloting is finished."

Julia was quiet for a moment, then asked tentatively, "Mary, mightn't it have been safer . . . elections do sometimes go awry . . . to wait for the result?"

"Oh no, Julia, then I would have had to use one of the local hotels, and we're all so tired of their set dinners. They tell me this Chicago caterer serves the most delicious foods . . . with French sauces we've never tasted in Springfield."

Snow began to fall, the wind whipping it down with hurricane intensity. By the time it stopped, at five o'clock Sunday afternoon, the town was closed in. Most of Monday was spent digging paths from the houses to the square. All trains had been brought to a dead stop in the drifts . . . and the legislature turned up missing. Mary was uneasy; what would happen to her banquet installed in the baggage car of the legislators' train?

It was three days before a train limped in from Alton; a telegraphic dispatch informed Springfield that their legislators in seven passenger cars were still marooned on the prairies, twenty miles from the nearest town, and that they would have to be brought in by teams. On the evening of January 30, after another storm had increased the height of the drifts, Mary and Abraham went downtown to the Masonic Hall to hear Boothroyd Emmett read *Richard III*, seeing the first gas-lighted stores and street corners. The Lincolns were planning to have gas installed in their home if the experiment proved successful, and not too many people extinguished the light by blowing it out.

The legislature was ten days late in getting back to Springfield. The first one to reach the Lincolns was Eliza Francis, who plowed her way up from the station bursting with news.

"My dear, we had a perfectly harrowing time; none of the snowplows could get through. Everyone was starved. On Monday morning we saw the smoking chimney of a farmhouse about half a mile away and four men volunteered to go on a foraging expedition. They returned with a wash boiler filled with coffee, bread, butter, potatoes and eggs. By nightfall we were hungry again, and that's when I learned that your caterers were in the baggage car with all that wonderful food. The men put up their cash and we bought your dinner. They tore out the woodwork and the seats of the cars and split it into firewood, and we had a fine meal. You saved our lives, Mary. We all want to thank you. . . ."

Mary felt a little strange. "I'm delighted the food was there for them. But I'm not sure I like the idea of their eating my victory banquet in advance of the balloting."

"That's another reason I rushed up here. Sim wants Abraham to know that Governor Matteson's people have started his political pot boiling; they think that once Jimmy Shields is through, the Democrat ballots will go to the governor, and the anti-Nebraska Democrat vote as well."

When she reported this to Abraham he flared with the kind of anger she knew so well in herself.

"Matteson would be an impossible choice," he cried. "He has no political convictions. He refused to commit himself on the Nebraska bill. He would stand for nothing in the Senate."

"The legislature was stalled for over a week," she said lightly, "what better way to occupy their time than by caucusing?"

That evening Elizabeth came over to tell Mary that she wanted to give the celebration party for the Lincolns in the Edwards house. She did not mention Mary's already-eaten banquet.

"We can't handle fifteen hundred people the way they did for Steve Douglas's last levee at the state house, but we can take care of several hundred. . . ."

Election day dawned cold but with a little sun and some thawing. The two Houses of the legislature were scheduled to be called to order at two o'clock. At one o'clock Abraham put on a fresh shirt and collar, hugged Mary for a moment while they wished each other good luck, and then was off for a final conference with Logan at the state house.

Eliza Francis called for her a little before two, as excited about the prospects of the election as Mary was. Julia was waiting for them in the lobby. While they were exchanging greetings, Governor Matteson's wife walked by with her two daughters, who had recently completed their schooling at Monticello Seminary. Mrs. Matteson was a tall and stately woman, beautiful of feature and figure. The women went up together to the gallery overlooking the Hall, which was filled with members of both Houses and, beyond them in all the available space and through to the lobby, hundreds of well-wishers and political managers.

It was three o'clock before the Assembly settled down to business. James Shields, the incumbent, was nominated first in a speech which drew sustained applause from the Douglas Democrats; Abraham was nominated by Stephen Logan in an impassioned appeal to the legislature to strike a death blow

236

against the spread of slavery; Lyman Trumbull was nominated in a quiet and dignified speech by Senator Palmer; Governor Matteson was nominated in a short speech which was received with perfunctory applause.

Mary was too excited to keep the tally, so Julia took the pencil and paper from her and during the first roll call marked down each vote as the legislator signified his choice. Every one of Abraham's pledges came through with a vote; at the end of the first ballot he had the forty-four votes promised him, James Shields had the forty-one regular Democrat votes, and Lyman Trumbull had five votes from the anti-Nebraska Democrats. Eight votes were scattered. The Speaker added his vote for Abraham.

Feeling in the Hall was intense; Julia put her hand out to grip Mary's and give it a reassuring shake. Around her the voices in the gallery were saying, "Lincoln needs only seven more votes . . . surely he can pick them up from the anti-Nebraska Democrats . . . there are no extra votes possible for Shields . . ."

Julia's second tally showed Abraham losing four of the men who had supported him the first time, though he picked up two others. Cousin Logan had been confident Abraham would be elected on the second ballot; what had happened? He lost two more votes on the third count.

During the roll call on the fourth ballot Mary began to grow cold; three more voters switched, bringing his total down to thirty-eight. She saw her cousin Logan rise from his seat and move for an adjournment; the vote went against him. On the fifth ballot Abraham lost four more votes from among the Fusionists, with Lyman Trumbull getting ten. There was not one vote cast for Governor Matteson. On the sixth ballot Abraham lost two more votes, Lyman Trumbull lost three.

Evening had come. The gas lamps were lighted in the Hall. There was a commotion on the Democratic side of the chamber, and Mary watched the color rise in Mrs. Matteson's cheeks until the alabaster queenly expression was noticeably flushed. From this she knew that they were in for a flank movement: on the opening of the seventh ballot Mr. Strunk, the man who had written that he would walk a hundred miles to vote for Abraham, abandoned him, the entire Democratic strength of forty-one votes went for Governor Matteson, and three other non-Democrat votes as well. Abraham picked up votes, getting back to his thirty-eight of the fourth ballot, while Lyman Trumbull had the inconspicuous total of nine.

Mary and Julia both were too stunned to keep a further record, for it was evident on the eighth ballot that Matteson was gaining strength while Abraham was losing it. The clerk announced that Governor Matteson now had forty-six votes, Abraham twenty-seven, Lyman Trumbull eighteen. Mary felt that the fight was between Abraham and Governor Matteson but she soon found that she was wrong: Governor Matteson rose to forty-seven votes, just four away from election, Abraham fell to the bare count of fifteen, Lyman Trumbull picked up practically all of Abraham's defaulting votes and rose to the surprising total of thirty-five. Mary saw Abraham look up into the gallery, gaze at her for a long moment, then walk out of the Hall irresolutely. Before the next count he came back from the lobby, his hair severely mussed. He walked up to her cousin Logan. The two men had a conference. When Logan turned she saw that he was crushed. Abraham put his hand for a moment on Logan's shoulder, then walked back slowly out of the Hall. During the next roll call Stephen Logan rose, saying:

"The demands of principle are superior to those of personal attachment: I cast my ballot for Lyman Trumbull."

Pandemonium broke as the other fourteen of Abraham's bedrock supporters rallied to Trumbull's banner; and when the tally clerk read the results Lyman Trumbull had fifty-one votes. He was the new United States senator from Illinois.

Mary jumped up without looking or speaking to Julia, made her way out of the gallery, down the long flight of stairs and into the street.

Alone in the house she paced from room to room, torn between rage, self-pity and despair: all of their plans of the many months, all of her hopes had come tumbling down, as they had so often in the past. Once again they were totally defeated.

It seemed a long time before Abraham came home, came into the back bedroom where she lay face down on the bed, raised her in his arms and kissed her cheek. When she looked up she saw that his face was a battlefield with deep lines of retrenchment and the corpses of destroyed hopes; but his eyes were resigned.

"I see you have assimilated your defeat?"

"Yes. But it wasn't easy." He smiled gently. "Young Henry Whitney, he's one of my associates in Urbana, came in the office and said he'd never seen me in deeper depths of melancholy. But I worked the disappointment out of my system. And so must you."

"Oh, Abraham, I'm so mortified; every man in that legislature knows about that celebration banquet I ordered from Chicago. In fact they ate it in high glee on that snowbound train! And I was so positive with Julia about the results. I also was considerably indiscreet: I kept her informed of every move we were making, of every promise and pledge that came in. You don't suppose I hurt you? That Lyman used the information . . . ?"

He sighed. "Assuredly not. Trumbull is the soul of honor."

Her good sense returned. "So is Julia. She did try to warn me against ordering the banquet. But, Abraham, is it fair that a man who has only five votes to start with, against your forty-four, should win the election? Couldn't you have hung on longer instead of giving Lyman your votes?"

"I became satisfied that it was the only way to prevent Matteson's election. That's why I determined to strike at once and advised Logan and my friends to go for Trumbull. I couldn't let the whole political result go to ruin on a personal point. I regret our defeat, but I'm not nervous about it. Matteson's defeat gives me more pleasure than my own gives me pain. It's a great consolation to see the Douglas men worse whipped than I am. Lyman will fight as hard against the spread of slavery as I could. This is not an end for us, it is a beginning."

"Another beginning," she commented. "Are we never to know fulfillment?"

"Perhaps in the next world." He patted her shoulder, then said, "You have to dress. I know you're going to be the most beautiful woman at the party in your satin and feathers."

"The party! What party? It will be canceled now. . . ."

"Not a bit of it. Ninian sent me word that the party will be given exactly the same except they've canceled the orchestra because the Trumbulls don't approve of dancing."

"Abraham, you certainly don't think I am going to any celebration party for the Trumbulls!" Her eyes were wide with amazement.

"Why not? They were planning to come to the celebration for you. We've got to be good sports."

"Do you think this was a handball game we played today?"

"The same rules apply to losers."

"Sorry, but everything in my background is pointed toward making me a good winner."

"Just smile and tell them you're happy for them. Your friends will admire you for it."

"You mean those loyal friends who stuck their knives in your back this afternoon? The ones who would walk a hundred miles to vote for you?"

"Now, Puss! As a matter of fact I've already invited every one of the anti-Nebraska members of the legislature to a dinner party a week from tonight, even those who abandoned me."

She put on her décolleté blue brocaded silk with lace ruffling the upper edge of the bodice, then brushed her hair back on one side, piling ringlets on top of her head. She wrapped herself in a blue wool cloak, carried a lace handkerchief scented with lavender.

They got into their carriage and went to Elizabeth's reception. The front porch was draped with flags. They were late. As they reached the parlor, people stepped aside and left an opening to Julia and Lyman Trumbull, who were in the center of the room receiving congratulations. Mary felt Abraham grip her arm; he brought her up to the Trumbulls and, putting out his free hand, said:

"Not too disappointed to congratulate my old friend, Trumbull."

Trumbull's expression was bland as he gripped Abraham's hand. He said in a voice loud enough for everyone in the room to hear, "I should be congratulating you, Lincoln. You led the fight, you defeated Douglas, you persuaded Illinois to repudiate the Nebraska bill."

Julia's face had been flushed with happiness, but when she saw Mary she turned pale and lowered her eyes. Had Julia known all along that she would be the victor? Mary became cold inside. Julia finally looked up and met Mary's gaze head-on. Her eyes said:

I'm sorry, Mary.

Mary's eyes said, No, you're not, Julia. You're happy.

With that she turned away, feeling the two flaming spots on her forehead. She fixed a bright smile on her face and passed among her friends, receiving their condolences. As she crossed the foyer to go into the sitting room her cousin Logan came in the doorway. His pale face clouded over when he saw her. He took her hand in his, and said, nearly choking with emotion: "We were permitted to make a race for senator just fast enough to lose money. Once again we Whigs have been rode and rode and rode to death."

When Mary and Elizabeth finally came face to face in front of the buffet table with its sumptuous food and iced champagne, Mary checked her sister's sympathy by exclaiming, "Looks like I'm filling the United States Senate with men who once countenanced me. For Abraham's sake maybe I should have passed him by? He'd be in the Executive Mansion by now."

"More likely he'd still be living in the loft over Josh Speed's store . . . with Billy Herndon."

Abraham was kind, he made her stay only an hour, then they slipped away. As they got in the carriage and drove around the banjo drive to Second Street, Abraham shifted the reins to his left hand and put his right arm about her shoulders.

"I've been doing Mentelle's an injustice; you're a good actress. You convinced everyone."

"Everyone but Julia: I couldn't dissemble with her. Hurt pride, I guess. But every time I saw her I turned cold inside. She felt it, I'm sure."

"Julia will understand. She has a forgiving heart."

"Abraham, what do we do now?"

"This is where we have to make our stand," he said, repeating the words she had used when he had wanted to run to Oregon. "We wait . . . until Stephen Douglas comes up for re-election . . ."

"But that's four years from now!"

". . . then we carry the fight to the people of Illinois, to the tiniest hamlet and crossroads store. That will be a great and deciding election, because by then people will know they have to choose between slavery and freedom."

"Wait . . . as we did in 1843, wait four years to get one term in Congress . . . four years of saying, 'It's Abraham's turn now.'"

"Yes, Abraham's turn . . . to work. There never has been a time in our lives when work was so needed, or could accomplish so much. You saw what happened in Kansas last November: that's only the beginning of the bloodshed. . . ."

They had reached home. She went in the front door while Abraham drove the horse and buggy to the rear alley and put them in the barn. She was standing in the hall, surveying the rooms of her domain and hating them with all her emotional intensity, when he came through the kitchen and the dining room and then into the hall to stand behind her. She whirled about.

"How can we defeat Stephen Douglas? He has this state tucked away in his wallet. He hasn't been beaten since Cousin Stuart defeated him in his first election in '38. We'll work and wait four years . . . for defeat in '58."

"This time it will be different: Douglas is wrong, terribly wrong. The years and the bloodshed will prove it. We will be standing with the right. We will win."

He had drawn up to his full height. To Mary he seemed nine feet tall, dwarfing her. He was like a dark pillar of fire standing there, his head thrown back, his eyes ablaze, his mouth, hollow cheeks and dimpled chin resolute. And before his fire, which warmed her; before his stature, which made her feel petty; before his strength to stand by principle, which gave her the inner fortitude to stand by whatever life might vouchsafe them; standing deep in the shadow of her husband and her love, she knew that she was at long last in the presence of the man she had divined him to be.

She slipped her hand into his, smiled up at him, her eyes clear, her own mouth set in courage and acceptance.

Book VI

A LITTLE WOMAN ON EIGHTH STREET

1

AN impeccably garbed and groomed eastern attorney by the name of Watson called to see Abraham on business. A very few minutes later she heard the front door close; Abraham came into the bedroom holding a fistful of money.

"Look, Mary: four hundred dollars in cash as a retainer, against a thousand-dollar fee. Don't that cap the whole? For a case about mechanical reapers. I figured I'd have to spend this year picking up the crumbs of my lost practice, but this looks like a loaf of bread."

He immediately became absorbed in the case, going back to his early studies of inventions. Then he traveled to Rockford to spend several days in the Manny factory to learn at first hand the differences between his client's machine and the reaper of Cyrus McCormick, who had brought the infringement suit.

In September he left for Cincinnati where the case had been transferred from Chicago. When he returned at the end of ten days she asked if his argument had gone off well.

"I didn't . . . give . . . my argument. When I reached Cincinnati . . . they asked me to withdraw."

"But why?"

He chewed one corner of his lip.

"Seems they hired me because the case was supposed to be heard before Judge Drummond up at Chicago, and they wanted a local lawyer who might have influence with him."

"But what about the brief you wrote?"

He shook his head.

"I gave Mr. Watson my roll of manuscript, told him it was for any use he might care to make of it. They never opened it. But the case was a revelation to me: the finest exhibition of accomplished lawyers conducting a great trial. When it was all over I told them, 'I'm going home to study law.'"

"Abraham, you have the humility of a saint, staying in that courtroom for a whole week after they had turned you out."

243

"They made my argument seem elementary. The way they practice law is hardly the same thing as the way we practice here in Illinois."

A few weeks after the reaper suit had been decided a letter arrived at the house from Mr. Watson containing six hundred dollars, the balance of the fee. From the accompanying note she gathered that an earlier check had been returned by Abraham on the ground that he had not earned it.

"Did you really return the money?" she asked. "That's adding injury to insult! I shall spend part of it on a new gown for the reception at the Governor's Mansion. Those high-toned Yankee lawyers may not think you are the smartest attorney in the west, but your wife is going to be the most brilliantly accoutered woman this side of New York."

The newly completed Governor's Mansion was set back on a knoll, amidst tall trees, with a driveway circling through lush green lawn. Governor Matteson was entertaining all of Springfield that night. From the moment she entered the reception hall on the ground floor and saw before her the magnificent broad staircase, the large high-ceilinged rooms with their crystal chandeliers and floor-to-ceiling windows reminiscent of such Bluegrass houses as Ellerslie and Ashland, her heart was lost.

"Abraham, maybe you should have run for governor?"

He laughed, took a firm grip on her arm.

"I ought to have bought the Houghan house for you, Puss: then we wouldn't have to become governor . . . or president."

"We wouldn't have to, but it might be nice."

At dawn she entered her own cramped hallway and small rooms, waited until Abraham had taken off his coat and vest and sprawled out in a big chair to rest his feet, then spread her satin-skirted hoops about her in a circle on the floor.

"Abraham, I have a plan to enlarge our house: we'll take off the roof, turn those two dormer bedrooms into full-sized rooms, add several more bedrooms behind for the children . . ."

". . . whoa, Mary! I should never have taken you to that reception."

"We can afford it now; we are the only ones left in our whole circle of family and friends who are still living in a cottage."

He pulled his knees up under his chin.

"I'm comfortable here."

"Well, I'm not. I don't think we ought to be sleeping in a bedroom behind the parlor; I need a maid's room and a guest chamber so that when my sister Emilie comes up on her bridal tour with Ben Hardin Helm, we'll have a proper place to put them."

"But, Mary," he groused, "we're just getting on our feet."

"Why don't we ask a price?"

Armstrong and Connelly submitted a bid of twenty-five hundred dollars. "Abraham, you put in thirteen hundred dollars, and I'll put in the twelve hundred I got last year for the eighty acres Father gave me for a wedding present."

"No, Mary, I don't want you to spend your own money. I'll give you your second story, but not just now, costs are too high."

A few days later he left for the circuit. That afternoon at Frances's house she learned that Hannan and Ragsdale would take a remodeling job. She returned home and drew up a rough plan of what she wanted, then sent for the contractors.

"I have twelve hundred dollars. We can use the old shingles for the new roof; the ground-floor windows can be preserved as they are. For the additional bedrooms upstairs it won't be necessary to run a hall all the way through, we'll put a small stairway out of the kitchen to serve the back quarters. Do you think you can do it at that price?"

A carpenter spent two hours crawling around the basement, then inside the walls of the dormer bedrooms. Hannan and Ragsdale reported:

"We can do it at your price, Mrs. Lincoln, excepting for the tin roof on the rear extension: that must be done by a metal man. We guarantee the job won't go beyond thirteen hundred dollars."

"Agreed," exclaimed Mary. "I'd like it finished before my husband gets home, he'll be away two months."

The workmen arrived at seven the next morning and began removing the roof.

"It's about time we had a proper house, Mother," said Robert in a cool, imperious tone. "I always thought this cottage was beneath us."

She moved William and Robert onto cots in the sitting room while the carpenters removed the shingles and rafters, then framed the second-story wall to twelve feet, with new siding to match the original walnut clapboards. As soon as the roof was put back on and the new windows glazed, she moved all three of them upstairs so that the workmen could take down the kitchen chimney, remove the rear wall and throw a beam across the opening to carry the wall of the second floor. During this time she cooked over the fireplace in the sitting room or, if the weather was warm, in the back yard.

The plan included wood stoves where formerly they had gotten their heat only from the fireplaces; a doorbell over the tall clock in the dining room; bookcases for Abraham's law library in what would now be the rear half of the double parlor. At the last moment she decided against the installation of gas for lighting. She had the roof extended over the front edge so that the house would have the look of a Swiss cottage, painted the building a pale chocolate and the outside shutters a dark green. On the front door she put a black plate, on it in silver Roman characters:

A. LINCOLN

Now Abraham could have his own room in which to read most of the night without keeping her awake. She moved their bed from the back parlor up to the new bedroom, immediately behind Abraham's, then went into town and bought him the biggest mahogany framed bed she could find; it was not the nine-foot one she had promised him, but lying cater-cornered he could stretch out full length and sleep with his feet under the blankets.

When the job was finished she stood out in the street gazing at her handiwork; the house had architectural unity, a certain authority arising from the massiveness of the two floors and high roof in front, and at the same time a touch of charm. She thanked the carpenters for their good workmanship, paid the bill of almost thirteen hundred dollars in cash. The entire job including the selection and papering with wallpapers had taken seven weeks. Abraham sent word that he would finish his court work on the following Wednesday and arrive sometime after dark.

She fed the children early, cleaned the kitchen, lit the oil lamps in the parlor and sitting room and the two big upstairs bedrooms facing the street, then took up her seat by the window where she could watch him walking home from the railroad station.

It was a pleasant evening; most of the neighborhood was out, some of the men working in their gardens, others standing around at the corner chatting, the women on the porches knitting or visiting.

She saw Abraham coming up the street carrying a blue cotton umbrella. She was faint with excitement. Would he approve? Would he think she had been shrewd in getting so much accomplished for so little? Or would he be angry with her for going ahead without his consent?

Abraham stopped halfway up the block and cocked his head to one side at the new building. Slowly, very slowly, he continued along the sidewalk. Once again he stopped. The men standing in groups, the women on their porches fell silent. He left the sidewalk, went out into the middle of the street, came to a point opposite the house and stood studying it, shaking his head in disbelief. Then he started walking up and down in front of the house, his hands under his coattails. Finally he stopped, crossed to the opposite side and approached a group of men standing there. His voice came high through the quiet night.

"Excuse me, friends, but I'm Abe Lincoln. I'm looking for my house. I thought it was across the way, but when I went away a few weeks ago there was only a one-story house there and now there is a two. I think I must be lost."

The neighbors burst into laughter. Mary's face burned. She stood concealed behind the curtains. Abraham left the group and came slowly across the street, headed for the front door, then stopped with one foot on the sidewalk. Through the open window she said in a low tone:

"Come in, you old fool. Don't you know your own house when you see it?"

2

HE loved his big north bedroom with the windows on both sides, his lawbooks in their new shelves in the back parlor, the semi-enclosed south porch. He asked if they could put the guest room into immediate use: their neighbor, the Reverend Noyes W. Miner, was holding a Baptist Sunday school convention and several of his delegates had no place to sleep.

Abraham ordered a supply of bricks, extended the wall the length of the house, and on top of the red bricks built a white picket fence. He was still in such a good mood on Sunday morning that he wrote out a check for thirty-six dollars for their annual rent on pew number twenty at the First Presbyterian Church. When he saw that his friend Benjamin Fox, directly across from them in the fifth row, had fixed up his pew with new carpet and cushions for his bride, Abraham whispered:

"As a reward for the admirable job you did in enlarging our house, I shall buy you a new carpet and some cushions for your pew, then everyone will think you are a bride too."

Benjamin Fox owned a store in town where Abraham went to read the abolitionist newspapers to which he would not subscribe himself. After services young Fox said, "Mr. Lincoln, the postmaster is refusing to deliver abolitionist newspapers to my box. Are postmen only supposed to deliver material they agree with?"

Abraham laughed. "I'll take care of it for you."

The following evening Mr. and Mrs. Fox came to report.

"Thanks to you, the postman is delivering my papers, only he refuses to put them in my mailbox. He throws them over the transom."

"He must be afraid of catching something," said Abraham; then added seriously, "You must overlook it, friend; feelings are running high over anything that touches slavery."

The proof of this came a few days later when Mary was in the kitchen making custard, and her cousin Stuart walked peremptorily through the hall waving an ink-fresh copy of the May 10, 1856, *Journal* under her nose.

"Mary, have you seen your husband's name at the head of this abolitionist call?"

By abolitionist, Mary surmised, Stuart would mean the new party known as Anti-Nebraska in certain parts of Illinois, Fusionist-Republican in others. She took the paper from her cousin, saw the name of Abraham Lincoln leading a list of over a hundred names calling for an Anti-Nebraska convention in Bloomington. She was puzzled.

"I don't believe Abraham signed this, Cousin Stuart. He's told me lately that the political atmosphere is such just now that he fears to do anything, lest he do wrong. He did attend that meeting of Anti-Nebraska editors in Decatur last February, but that was in the hope of confining their platform to the non-extension of slavery."

"But these Black Republicans will plunge the country into war. Mary, who had the audacity to sign Lincoln's name?"

One corner of her mouth made an in-sucking gesture of distaste.

"Herndon, probably."

"Herndon! Without authorization? Then he has ruined him! Mary, you must go down to the office at once and force him to publish a retraction."

"Sorry, Cousin Stuart, but I don't talk to the . . . gentleman. I'm afraid you'll have to do it yourself. Cup of coffee before you go?"

Stuart studied her face, then said quietly:

"Mary, you're not in sympathy with these Republicans, are you? They're a dagger pointed straight at the heart of the south. We're southern by birth, we don't want to help precipitate a war. Abolitionism means violence; that hysterical book, *Uncle Tom's Cabin*, has the north so whipped up they'd be glad to burn down the entire south."

"I agree with you, Cousin Stuart. And I believe Abraham does too."

Apparently she was behind in Abraham's thinking, for when Stuart obliged Herndon to get express approval for his act, Abraham telegraphed back:

ALL RIGHT: GO AHEAD. WILL MEET YOU—RADICALS AND ALL.

Had Abraham abandoned the sinking remnants of the Whig party and committed himself to these new Republicans? She knew that when he had attended the meeting of the Anti-Nebraska editors and they had toasted him as the next governor of Illinois, and after that the next United States senator, he had replied:

"The senator part of that sentiment I am highly in favor of, but I should really favor the first, as my wife wants us to move into the Governor's Mansion."

She had exclaimed, "Abraham, you didn't say that!"

Now she wished he would come home for a few days before attending the convention so that she could discuss the matter with him; but he was in Urbana, from there he would go on the cars to Danville and then to Bloomington. It was difficult for her to be alone during these days of violence: Massachusetts' Senator Charles Sumner's vitriolic attack against the south; the beating of Sumner on the Senate floor by Congressman Brooks of South Carolina; the sack of the free-soil town of Lawrence by pro-slavery forces in Kansas; the murder of pro-slavery Kansas settlers by a free-soil zealot, John Brown. When Abraham finally returned home on the second day of June she was in a state of high tension.

"So is the rest of the country, my dear, if that's any comfort to you. I've never heard so much disunionist talk. But it's as I told the convention, 'We won't go out of the Union, and the south shan't.' "

"What happened at the convention, Abraham? Half your friends here in Springfield came out against it: Cousin Stuart, James Matheny . . . they're mighty angry with you and the Republicans. . . ."

"We simply must consolidate everyone who is against Douglas and his supporters. I've made up my mind I'm going to support anyone nominated by the Republicans unless he is platformed expressly on some ground I think wrong."

The picture of her cousin Stuart's face as he cried, "Black Republicanism: the party is a dagger pointed at the heart of the south!" crowded her mind. She held her emotion under control.

"You haven't spoken in public for seven or eight months; how was your speech at the convention?" she asked quietly.

"Privately, between you and me, it was the best I ever made." He blushed. "You remember Jesse Dubois, a staunch Whig from southern Illinois? He came to the convention under protest but when I finished he said, 'That is the greatest speech ever made in Illinois; it puts Lincoln on the track for the presidency.'"

She dropped into one of the rockers, gazing up at him with big eyes.

In Cincinnati, in June of 1856, the Democratic convention surprised the Lincolns and Stephen Douglas by nominating James Buchanan, who had been minister to Great Britain during the Kansas-Nebraska contest. It was felt that many Whigs of conservative feelings who would have rejected Douglas and the Democrats would go for Buchanan. Millard Fillmore, now a third-party candidate, she remembered as the man who had thrown the full weight of the White House behind the Compromise of 1850.

Two weeks later in Philadelphia, where the first Republican national convention was meeting, John Charles Fremont, the glamorous trail blazer and author of the western reports which had sent great migrations to California and Oregon, was nominated for the presidency amidst wild enthusiasm. Then to their astonishment some of their friends who had been at the Bloomington convention began a movement to have Abraham Lincoln nominated for the vice-presidency, and with only one night in which to caucus had run up a total of one hundred and ten votes for Abraham on the first ballot.

"It must be some other Lincoln," murmured Abraham, "there's a fellow up in Massachusetts by that name. . . ."

On the second ballot William L. Dayton was nominated. Abraham set out to campaign through southern Illinois, even as he had during those days in 1840 when she had haunted the *Journal* office to keep track of his movements; then he had been trying to convert Democrats to Whigs; now his aim was to change many of these same converts into Republicans.

The severest blow the Republicans suffered was Senator Thomas Hart Benton's public repudiation of his son-in-law, John C. Fremont, on the grounds that the Republicans were a geographical party and would split the nation in two, that a vote for Fremont and the Republicans was a vote for civil war.

"Families!" snorted Abraham. "If they can't support each other, why can't they at least keep decently still?"

All right, Abraham, she thought, I'll keep decently still. But that doesn't mean I don't have serious misgivings . . . in my woman's heart.

Though she kept open house, though there was coffee and cake and sandwiches for the men Abraham brought home or invited for consultation, for the first time since they were married she remained totally outside his political activities. He did not perceive that she was troubled.

3

RETURNING from a swing through the center of the state, Abraham paced the floor and asked exasperatedly, "Why can't the Whigs understand that Fillmore has no power beyond dividing Republican strength?"

She looked up from the book she was reading.

"These are not easy days in which to see the right, Abraham. People are frightened at the implication of Fremont's election, they want to make sure above all else that they are not casting their vote for disunion. . . ."

"I'm glad to have them take their time . . . right up to the dawn of election day! If only they could know what Douglas just wrote to Ninian: 'In spite of everything that has happened, I am still right about the Kansas and Nebraska bill.' Think of that, Mary: he will destroy the Union, and stand there above the carnage and cry, 'I am right!' That's why we must elect Fremont: Buchanan has no choice, he is committed to let slavery spread into the territories."

She was not convinced.

As the campaign progressed, the feeling on both sides assumed a religious fervor. Even in Springfield, which was largely free of northern abolitionists and southern secessionists, friendships were strained, families were managing to preserve their relationships only by concerted effort. Cousin Logan was fighting alongside Abraham, but Cousin Stuart had become a powerful voice for Fillmore, while Ninian Edwards was a Stephen Douglas Democrat. Though she had lived through exciting political jousts since she was ten, and had witnessed the Jackson-Clay contest of 1828, this was the first time an election had alarmed her.

Springfield was plastered with pictures and posters of Fremont. The Republicans were making progress under the banner of:

FREE SPEECH, FREE PRESS, FREE SOIL, FREE MEN, FREMONT AND VICTORY!

Giant crowds were gathering all over the north to hear speeches about him; torchlight processions throughout thousands of small towns turned the night streets into streams of fire. A flood of speakers covered the north like grasshoppers, trying to leave it bare of any plant except the Republican ideology, while Longfellow and Walt Whitman, Washington Irving and Edward Everett Hale contributed stirring poems, such articulate journalists as Horace Greeley and Charles A. Dana made their presses thunder with biographies, pamphlets, special editions of newspapers. Half the northern preachers filled their churches on Sunday morning with the new political religion of freedom. Fremont the pathfinder was going to find a path through the impenetrable wilderness of slavery.

Or was he? Mary sat with the newspapers of the south in her lap; under her very eyes were the deep-seated fears and threats of secession if he were elected. The Washington *Union,* Richmond *Enquirer,* Charleston *Mercury* told her that instant dissolution of the Union would take place if Fremont won. One report of a mass meeting addressed by Robert Toombs, who had been in the House with Abraham, read:

> The election of Fremont would be an end to the Union, and ought to be. The object of Fremont's friends is the conquest of the south. I am content that they should own us when they have conquered us, and not before.

Senator James M. Mason of Virginia maintained that Fremont's election would mean "immediate, absolute, eternal separation." Senator John Slidell of Louisiana declared that if Fremont were the victor "the Union can not and ought not to be preserved." Nor were the threats originating only in the south, they were coming from Democratic meetings in Philadelphia where the speakers and the crowd alike clamored for disunion. Even the London *Daily News* reported that everywhere its correspondent found talk of the "catastrophe" of a Republican victory.

Mail arrived from her family in Kentucky, sorely distressed messages asking why Abraham had joined the Republicans, and when he had become an abolitionist. She wrote back to assure them that Abraham was not an abolitionist, that in every speech he made the point that slavery must not be interfered with where it existed.

As she lay in her new bedroom and heard Abraham pacing in the room in front of hers, she finally allowed her mind to consider another painful prong of her dilemma: If the Republicans were victorious they would replace the Whigs as one of the two big parties of the country. Should Abraham receive the nomination for the United States Senate in the fall of 1858, he would for the first time in his life be at the head of a majority party. The thing she wanted most was for him to go up to the United States Senate.

In addition she had William Herndon to reckon with. He had emerged as the organizing executive behind the Republican activity in Springfield. Had he not literally forced Abraham's hand by putting his name at the top of the call to the Bloomington convention? Everywhere she went she saw Herndon's tireless work behind the scenes; repulsive as she found the comparison, he had become the kind of executive secretary for the Republicans that her father had been for so many years for the Whigs and Henry Clay. The deeper Abraham got into the Republican movement the closer he was tied to Herndon, who at last had insinuated himself into the position of seeming to direct Abraham's fortune and future.

Yet here was she, pulling away.

The town became quiet after Buchanan's election. When the New England Society gave a banquet just before Christmas all the family opponents, Stuart, the Edwardses and Abraham accepted invitations to speak together. It was a mild day, just cold enough to be fun, so Mary invited all the children down to the square where most of the town's youngsters were shooting off fireworks. As she watched them play she congratulated herself on her discretion, for not once during the long and feverish months of the campaign had she let anyone know how she felt about the election.

Only Abraham seemed morose; he grumbled:

"I did the labor and got thunder for my reward. Please don't mention the election, it plagues me some. I can't help reflect how miserably things seem to be arranged in this world. It's not my tendency to melancholy, it's just that everything now is as clear as mud, with an old and sick man going into the White House, without the strength to stand up to the moral issues."

She consoled him by pointing out that there was a crumb of comfort for everyone: the Republicans had elected William Bissell as governor, and for the first time the state administration would be in the hands of Abraham's friends instead of his opponents. This was of extreme importance, he agreed, for the '58 senatorial race, particularly since Stephen Douglas's whirlwind campaign through Illinois had carried the state for Buchanan by a few thousand votes.

Though Abraham went to Chicago for the Republican banquet at the Tremont House at which everyone congratulated each other on the state and local victories, he continued to be troubled. People everywhere still were synonymizing Republicanism with abolitionism and war. The name had to be avoided, he declared, until the members could convince the country that they too were a peace party.

One of his supporters chose this precise moment to start a new paper, the Springfield *Republican*.

"I think the establishment of the paper is unfortunate," he complained to Mary; "the time is not yet ripe. I just can't subscribe to it."

A few weeks later the first issue of the Springfield *Republican* was delivered to the house. Remembering how strongly Abraham had not wanted the paper started, and resenting it because of her own fear of the Republicans, she sent the editor a reprimanding message, returning the paper to him.

To her astonishment he commented on her message in the newspaper. The town buzzed. Abraham said wanly:

"Mary, Mary, corporal punishment is wasted on adults as well as children. Now we've succeeded in making an enemy of a man who only wanted to be our friend."

"But you told me you had not directed the paper to be left!"

"I meant I could not subscribe to the idea of a Republican newspaper, or help him with money to start it. But I had to patronize it to the extent of taking and paying for one subscription. The Democrats are saying that if we Republicans can't keep peace in our own family, how can we keep it in the nation?"

After her many months of discreet quiet she had by a single outburst exposed herself. Yet through the incident she made one of her dearest friends: Hannah Rathbun, a young widow of twenty-nine who had moved with her two sons from Rhode Island at the death of her husband, to live across the street with her brother, the Reverend Noyes Miner. Coming upon Mary consumed with anger at herself, Hannah countered with a tale of how her own combustible temper had embarrassed her husband by an act a hundredfold more gauche.

"The whole town was laughing at me, and my husband was furious, but at the end of a month the others had forgotten and it became only a humorous story between my husband and myself."

Mary took her hand.

"Thank you, Hannah, that helps me."

She and Hannah were amazingly alike, Mary thought, with their quick tempers, lively conversation and repartee, their love of beautiful clothes. When Abraham was away, Hannah and her boys came to stay with Mary, keeping the house filled with the goodness of her friendship. Mary was able to confide in Hannah her heartbreaking efforts to teach four-year-old Tad how to compensate for his cleft palate. There was such a large part of the alphabet he could not conquer: he said hoak for soak, abhunt for absent, papaday for papa dear. The boy was happy and unaware of his handicap, a lovable imp with a fast-moving mind, but unintelligible to outsiders.

From the moment of Governor Bissell's inaugural in January, there were parties and entertainments almost every night. Mary asked Abraham to take Hannah with them, for she wanted her to meet that part of Springfield which might not be accessible to Hannah through her brother's church work. This was not always easy for Mary because Hannah was prettier, her humor more gentle, and having been left a fair fortune by her husband, Hannah was exquisitely gowned; but she gritted her teeth and continued to invite her.

After a series of fires had burned down whole sections of the square, she and Abraham contributed twenty-five dollars to a fund to buy a fire engine from Boston. Two volunteer fire companies kept the town amused with their bright uniforms, parades and picnics. Elizabeth and Ninian gave a dinner party, Benjamin and Helen Edwards hired a large, horse-drawn omnibus to bring their guests to the Houghan house for a musicale, then Mary and Abraham each wrote out their own invitations for five hundred guests, including the new state officers, most of the legislature, the judges and lawyers to a party. Brown's Hotel, which had just opened, provided the food and a small orchestra.

Heavy rain fell all day. Only three hundred guests appeared. Mary stood in the hall, brilliantly gowned in clear white cockled décolleté organdy marked with a shamrock embroidered in bright green, receiving her guests. The food, music and company were sufficiently good to make up for the liquor which Abraham refused to serve. Mary's friends assured her it was a brilliant affair. To her own surprise she found herself asking people to drop in for a visit any time.

They did. Not only the guests come to tell her how pleasant the party had been, but some of those who had been kept away by the rain, and a number who had been obliged to go to Jacksonville to a wedding that same night. She was happy to see them, even though she was not formally attired, or her hair dressed, or the house immaculate. She wondered why she had not given herself this easy freedom long ago.

Abraham was vexed at the Illinois Central, for whom he had won a major tax case, and spent hundreds of hours defending suits over the Eighth Circuit. With the exception of the first $250 retainer, he had not received a dollar from them. He told Mary that the next time he went to Chicago he would collect the money; but he returned empty-handed, his face red with embarrassment.

"When I presented them with my bill for five thousand dollars their official said, 'Why, we could have hired a first-class lawyer for that figure.'"

"By the Eternal!"

"They refuse to pay. I'm going to have to get affidavits from the leading lawyers in the circuit testifying that it's a fair fee for the work done."

She became angry.

"Abraham, why do these people think they can insult you with impunity? First the lawyers on the reaper case, and now the Illinois Central?"

"Guess I don't have an imposing front, so they kick me in the rear. Judge Davis once accused me of trying to beggar the whole legal profession by my paltry fees. This is the first big fee I've ever felt justified in charging . . . and we'll collect it, even if I have to go all the way to the main office in New York."

"We could go by way of Niagara and Canada," she said dreamily. "That trip the Honorable Abraham Lincoln promised me back in 1848, when we were going to campaign through New England and help elect General Taylor. Remember?"

4

ONCE again Abraham began writing at the worktable in the sitting room. He explained that what he wanted to put down on paper was a new prospectus for the Republican party which would prove that it was not abolitionist, but was the natural successor to the Whigs and the only place where freedom men could go. But such Republicans as William Lloyd Garrison cried, "No Union with Slaveholders!" Wendell Phillips of Boston said, "The Union is accursed of God, away with it!" The Reverend Samuel J. May wanted New England to secede by itself if the rest of the north would not; the Reverend Thomas Wentworth Higginson of Worcester, Massachusetts, cried, "Disunion is destiny." Other ultras of the north claimed, "We are essentially two nations."

The work on the sitting-room table stopped.

Then on March 7, 1857, three days after President Buchanan in his inaugural address had prophesied peace and union, Chief Justice Roger B. Taney of the United States Supreme Court read the five-to-four opinion of that court on the Dred Scott case which all of Springfield had followed: Dred Scott was a slave who had been taken to the Territory of Wisconsin, and there had married another slave, subsequently purchased by his master. Returning to St. Louis, the master had brought Dred Scott and his family with him; but when the master died, Scott sued for his freedom on the basis that, having lived in a free country, he had become a free man and could no longer be remanded to slavery. Chief Justice Taney announced that Dred Scott and his family had not become free by moving north of the Missouri Compromise line for the reason that Congress never had had any right to prohibit slavery in the territories.

Mary and Abraham read the Springfield newspaper accounts of the decision in the austere coolness of their parlor. Chief Justice Taney decreed that Negroes were not included in "that part of the Declaration of Independence which asserted that all men are created equal," and therefore under the Constitution Negroes "had no rights which the white man was bound to respect."

Into Mary's mind flashed the picture of the public square in Lexington, with Negro families being sold and torn apart. She would not be guilty of believing that the Negro had no rights which the white man was bound to respect; that would make him little different from the beast of the jungle. She felt deeply sad, yet in a sense, purged. Never again would she temporize, whatever the consequences, for now the issue stood out in all its naked ugliness for even the morally blind to see.

Slowly she raised her head and looked at Abraham. He had been right when he said of the Republican party that there was no place else for freedom people to go. She was for freedom; and now she too had found the right. She stood by Abraham, shoulder to shoulder, even though her shoulder only came up to his floating rib.

Next year it was probable that Abraham would be the Republican nominee for the Senate. Stephen Douglas, as the Democratic incumbent, would have to stand for re-election. For the first time in their twenty years of intense rivalry the two men would be pitted against each other for the same office. Thanks to the Dred Scott decision, which upheld Douglas's popular sovereignty, people could now take their stand.

She stood by Abraham. Would Illinois?

She was to have her trip to New York; they were going east to collect the Illinois Central fee that had been awarded them by the Illinois court. Hannah Rathbun moved into the guest room with her two children to watch over William and Tad. They were taking Robert with them.

She always had known that she would like life in a big city, but New York was an unending source of delight. Nor did the town seem strange: she had been reading New York newspapers for so long that she knew most of the theatres, shops and news of local happenings. They stayed at the Astor House and Abraham took them in a carriage for a sight-seeing tour from Central Park, which was being transformed from a wild and rocky tract of land to a pleasure ground, down to the Battery Park which had become the city dump. After a ferryboat excursion to Staten Island they walked along the piers; at the foot of Canal Street they found the S.S. *Atlantic* and were given permission to go through the big steamship which was loading for Europe. When they came down the gangplank Mary turned to Abraham, saying with a wistful laugh:

"You can't know how I long to go to Europe. I am determined that my next husband shall be rich."

"Then I'd better start by collecting that five thousand."

The next morning the Illinois Central officials received them with cold courtesy but no cold cash. On the way out Abraham asked:

"Would you like to own a railroad, Mary? Then you could have a chalked hat and ride free over the line, like I do. If we don't receive the money by the time we reach home I'm going to have the sheriff in McLean County attach their railroad."

"Does the Illinois Central have a spur to Europe?"

They had two more days in New York. Mary spent the afternoon hours at Bowen, McNamee and Company's new store at 320 Broadway buying printed muslin delaine, at Nesmith's lower down on Broadway, where she found beautiful seamless hose and purchased a pair of Ontario blankets, at Lane and Porter's on Canal Street where she bought herself a three-flounced organdy robe. Abraham took her to Niblo's Gardens for the vaudeville and ballet and the following night to Wallack's Theatre to see *The Merchant of*

Venice. The next morning they left for Niagara Falls where they put up at the Cataract House. For Mary the Falls were a matter of scenic beauty, but Abraham brushed off the aesthetic concept by asking:

"Where can all this water come from? I've never seen any answer in my science books."

When they reached home there was still no money from the Illinois Central, so Abraham had the sheriff seize a part of the railroad property to satisfy the judgment. The forty-eight hundred dollars reached them at once. It was more money than either of them had seen in a lump sum before. Mary held the check out in front of her.

"I feel very rich. I think I will build us a beautiful Bluegrass house. Forty-eight hundred dollars should go a long way toward paying for it."

"Twenty-four hundred dollars. The other half belongs to Billy."

She held the check against her bosom.

"Abraham, that isn't fair! You've spent the better part of your working hours for two years earning this fee. Mr. Herndon never rode circuit, never tried any of the cases. He just hasn't earned any part of the money."

"I can't divide small sums and walk out with big ones."

"Oh, Abraham, this partnership makes less sense all the time."

He ignored her comment.

"I'm going to invest our half of the money in land out in Iowa. We'll be rich yet."

Her sister Emilie's husband, Ben Hardin Helm, to whom Mary was also related through the Hardin family, arrived in Springfield to try a case. He was a young version of her handsome cousin Hardin, over six feet tall, with penetrating blue eyes, rich brown hair, an open genial face which managed to be both sensitive and strong. He had graduated from West Point, served for a time in the Second Cavalry, but after attending law school at the University of Louisville and going for one term to the Harvard Law School he had returned to Kentucky and gone into partnership with his father, a former governor of Kentucky. Mary installed Ben in the guest room; they found him bright, with quiet manners and a moderate attitude toward the politics that were agitating the nation.

When Abraham asked about the feeling of the people in Kentucky on the subject of slavery, he replied:

"I think the border states will adopt gradual emancipation." He looked at Mary, adding, "Your father did good work in that field, Cousin Mary." Then turning back to Abraham, "But I don't think the cotton states can accept emancipation in any form, even if guaranteed payment. You see, Cousin Abraham, it's not only their investment they're afraid to lose, it is a whole way of life. They're frightened that everything they value will be torn from them."

In the fall of 1857 Kansas drew up its state constitution at Lecompton, written after a series of pro-slavery election frauds. Under the new constitution it became a felony to deny the right of a slaveowner to hold his human property in bondage. When President Buchanan urged Congress to accept the Lecompton constitution so that Kansas could become a state, Senator Stephen Douglas broke with the administration . . . and denounced President Buchanan. Abraham exclaimed:

"This is excellent for us: we were split last year in the election, that's what defeated us; if Douglas and the administration are split in '58, the chance is we shall win."

His jubilation was short-lived: because Douglas was opposing Buchanan and the effort to bring in Kansas as a slave state, many of the Republican newspapers which formerly had fought him now maintained that Stephen Douglas should be nominated as the Republican senator from Illinois. The opposition papers in Illinois grew caustic, poking fun at Abraham as though he had been outmaneuvered. The Urbana *Constitution* said:

Honorable Abe Lincoln is undoubtedly the most unfortunate politician that ever attempted to rise in Illinois. In everything he undertakes, politically, he seems doomed to failure. He has been prostrated often enough in his political schemes to have crushed the life out of any ordinary man.

"Good thing you are not an ordinary man," Mary murmured.

His gray eyes lightened, thanking her for the help of humor.

The Lincoln home became the scene of a wake as their friends filed in with dispatches from Washington and the north, reporting that more and more Republican leaders were going over to Douglas's side: Senator Seward of New York, Simon Cameron, Republican boss of Pennsylvania, the party leaders of Massachusetts.

Abraham wrote ruminatively on the backs of old envelopes the talk he was to make to the Republican convention of 1858, with an observation to Mary that the speech would be built around the sentiment he had expressed to her during their days at the Globe when he was writing a circular for the Whigs: that "A house divided against itself cannot stand." When he returned from the state library on the evening of June 15, where he had rehearsed his speech at the head of a round table of his party leaders, he confessed:

"My friends scolded me a good deal about the 'house divided against itself'; they wanted me to change it, but I believe I have studied this subject more deeply than they have, and I told them I was going to stick to my text whatever happened."

They were in the rear parlor where he had found her sitting in a low chair by the table reading a new French novel under the light of an astral lamp. She sat immobile, watching his dark face and troubled eyes.

"I'd like to read it to you out loud, Puss, just as I did to them. I have a lot of words underlined for emphasis:

"Mr. President and Gentlemen of the Convention:

"If we could first know *where* we are, and *whither* we are tending, we could then better judge *what* to do, and how to do it.

"We are now far into the *fifth* year, since a policy was initiated, with the *avowed* object, and *confident* promise, of putting an end to slavery agitation.

"Under the operation of that policy, that agitation has not only *not ceased*, but has *constantly augmented*.

"In *my* opinion, it *will* not cease, until a *crisis* shall have been reached, and passed.

" 'A house divided against itself cannot stand.'

"I believe this government cannot endure, permanently half *slave* and half *free*.

"I do not expect the Union to be *dissolved*—I do not expect the house to *fall*—but I *do* expect it will cease to be divided.

"It will become *all* one thing, or *all* the other."

His voice was low, deeply moving, filled with intense sincerity. She was silent, the sentences ringing through her head, taking her back to their honeymoon at the Globe, to Abraham saying, "I want to acquire a style, but I still write by ear." He had his style now, as lucible as anything she had heard. She recalled her early observation that basically Abraham was neither a lawyer nor a politician but a literary man.

"It's beautiful, my dear. How can they object to the 'house divided' line? It comes from the Bible."

"One man said it was ahead of its time, another that it would drive away voters fresh from the Democratic ranks, a third declared it a 'damn fool utterance' because it sounds like I'm advocating disunion and war."

"But you're only analyzing what has gone before, and what you believe may happen."

"Precisely what I said to them. I said, 'The time has come when this sentiment should be uttered and if I have to go down because of this speech, then at least I go down linked to what is just and right.' "

"Surely they won't repudiate you?"

"It's the election they're worried about, not the nomination. That should come in tomorrow."

She accompanied him to the state house the following evening to hear him read his speech to a Hall full of shirt-sleeved, perspiring Republicans who at the end gave him a unanimous endorsement for the Senate . . . his election depending upon the Republicans winning a majority of seats in the legislature. After much handshaking they walked up to the *Journal* office to read proof and make sure the friendly Chicago *Tribune* representative sent in his report free from error.

Walking home through the darkness, Abraham informed her that there would be little money available for the grueling campaign: he would not only have to pay all of his own traveling expenses but would have to contribute to the state-wide fund as well; and since he would be campaigning too hard to appear in court there would be short income in the ensuing months.

She let her servant go, spent money only for food. He converted their sitting room into campaign headquarters, spreading out before him on the worktable the vote tabulations of the 1856 campaign, estimating how much pressure would have to be exerted in each district to bring it into the Republican camp.

In spite of Mary's efforts to find Hannah a husband, her friend chose her own time for falling in love. Dr. John Shearer was a thirty-one-year-old Pennsylvanian, muscular and genial. Mary acted as matron of honor at the wedding in the Miners' parlor, then helped Hannah move into a new house immediately across the street on Eighth and Jackson.

At the end of the first week in July Abraham held Mary tightly to him, picked up his carpetbag and set off for Chicago to hear Stephen Douglas make the opening speech of the campaign; and to answer him. Walking back through the sitting room from the front window where she had followed his progress down the street, she saw some writing spread out on the sitting-room table. Her eye caught the opening sentence of the paper which he had headed: *Struggle Against Slavery.*

I have never professed an indifference to the honors of official station; and were I to do so now, I should only make myself ridiculous.

She could not resist picking up the paper and reading on:

Yet I have never failed to remember that in the republican cause there is a higher aim than that of mere office. I have not allowed myself to forget that the abolition of the Slave-trade by Great Brittain, was agitated a hundred years before it was a final success; that the measure had it's open fire-eating opponents; it's stealthy "dont care" opponents; it's dollar and cent opponents; its negro equality opponents; and its religion and good order opponents; that all these opponents got offices, and their adversaries got none. But I have also remembered that though they blazed, like tallow-candles for a century, at last they flickered in the socket, died out, stank in the dark for a brief season, and were remembered no more, even by the smell.

There were tears in her eyes, a lump in her throat. How beautifully he expressed his belief in the right. He had started out on this new campaign only a few moments before; was he already reconciled to another defeat?

5

THE Chicago newspaper accounts of Abraham's first entanglement reached Springfield before he did. His friends had been accurate in their prophecy; because of the "house divided" speech Douglas accused him of being a disunionist plumping for war. Stephen, Mary knew, had come into Illinois under the severest handicap of his political career, attacked by President Buchanan and the administration forces, abandoned by many Democrats who had been repulsed by his repeal of the Missouri Compromise. But now he had an issue, one provided to him ready-made by Abraham.

She sat on the floor and, surrounding herself with the two newspapers and her three sons, read to them first from the Douglas paper, the Chicago *Times*, and then the Lincoln paper, the Chicago *Tribune*, trying to explain to the boys how in politics two diametrically opposite versions of the same thing could appear true, when there was a ringing of the bell above the clock in the dining room. She opened the front door to find Helen Edwards standing there.

She led her into the parlor, which seemed cool and unused after the cluttered sitting room. Helen said:

"Mary, I have unpleasant news . . ."

". . . nothing about Abraham?"

"Oh no, nothing personal." She spoke more quickly. "Ben has gone over to Stephen Douglas. I know that will hurt, your husband has been kind to Ben."

Mary could feel the blood rush to her head. Could Abraham have been so wrong about his speech that even his friends hurried to desert him?

"What I came to tell you," Helen continued, "is that Ben is planning the Springfield welcoming reception for Mr. Douglas at our house. The train bringing him will stop alongside our grove. Douglas will make his major Springfield speech right there."

Mary winced: the Douglas rally to be held at her beloved Houghan house! Helen put a fingertip solicitously on her arm, then started for the front door. "Now I have to go home and write a letter to my Republican family in New York, trying to explain why my husband, after saying in '56, 'I'd rather shake hands with the devil than to hold Douglas's hand on his slavery issue,' has switched to the Democrats."

Abraham returned the next day; when she told him about Benjamin Edwards and the Houghan grove rally he swallowed scrawnily a few times, then said, "Every man must go his own way." He added, "You read about Douglas's triumphal entry into Illinois? That is all bombast, Mary. Judging by the strong call for me to speak when he closed, I believe we could have voted him down in that very crowd."

The following morning he took the cars for Bloomington where Douglas was scheduled to speak.

"I don't know if there will be any opening for me, but I want to be on the ground to take the chance."

After the Bloomington meeting he would board the campaign train that was coming into Springfield with the Douglas enthusiasts, and join the other members of the train when it stopped at Benjamin Edwards's grove.

Late that night as she lay sleepless in bed she heard the faint sound of rain on the roof, then a heavy downpour. This would turn the Edwardses' grove into a vast field of mud. She murmured gleefully, "Lord, forgive me for my uncharity, but I hope You rain out the whole meeting!"

She was awakened at daylight by cannon fire. With a flush of anger she realized that the cannon had been fired by the Douglas Democrats. The cannonading continued all day; by midmorning she heard the sound of the bands assembling in the square and the Democratic marchers beginning their cheering and parading. The speaking would take two hours, perhaps three; it seemed a long wait until Abraham would be home again.

She went to the front window to see if the rain had stopped; there, coming down Eighth Street, a carpetbag in one hand, an unopened umbrella in the other, with his coattails flying in the breeze and his head craned forward, was Abraham.

She led him into the kitchen where he took off his wet shoes; she got him dry socks and brought the crocheted slippers on which she had beaded A.L. He leaned his chair against the wall and sat with his heels locked into the lower rungs, his knees on a level with his bemused and twinkling eyes. She poured him a cup of strong black coffee, then put more wood into the stove and cooked him a fresh lake fish she had bought at Smith and Mc-Candless. Neither of them referred to the fact that he had changed his mind about hearing his opponent speak that day.

By the time the meeting was over and the crowd had thronged back into Springfield the town was agog with the news of Douglas's private railroad car. Robert asked if he could go down to the station to see it. An hour later he was back, wide-eyed, describing the mottoes and flags running the length of the car, the plush parlor chairs, the lounges where people could sleep, the tables for writing and eating, the brass band, two stenographers, a sculptor, a man to take down his speeches in the new method called short hand . . . and the flatcar which carried two cannon.

"Father, when you go out again on the Douglas-Lincoln campaign, are you going to have a beautiful car like that?"

"Why do you call it the *Douglas*-Lincoln campaign, Robert?" asked Mary. "In this family we speak of the *Lincoln*-Douglas campaign."

Robert kept his eyes on his father's face. Abraham replied:

"The Illinois Central appears to be providing this private car to Douglas without too much charge; apparently they think he is going to be re-elected."

"Why do you have to ride in a day coach? Why can't we have a train called 'The Lincoln Special'? We're just as good as Douglas, aren't we?"

"Perhaps, but not as rich. Our friend bought up half of Chicago when it was a wilderness."

Robert drew himself up, stuck his chin in the air, and announced, "When I get to be a man I'm going to be as rich as Senator Douglas. I'll have my own car when I travel, and no one will ever be able to look down on me."

"Then you'd better grow another couple of feet in stature, son," commented his father dryly.

Abraham had announced that he would speak that evening at the state house. They dawdled over supper, then he bathed, put on fresh linen and his lightest-weight black alpaca suit. Mary was curious to see the new Mrs.

Douglas, Stephen's first wife having died in childbirth almost five years before. Abraham brought the carriage around to the front door. Because they were a little early they rode their buggy around the square. As they came to the St. Nicholas Hotel where the Douglases were staying, their horse was brought up with a start by a tremendous cheer; from her vantage point high in the carriage Mary saw Stephen Douglas emerge from the ladies' entrance on the west side of the building with Adele Cutts on his arm. Mary had heard a good deal about the new Mrs. Douglas: the grandniece of Dolly Madison, she had been raised in the highest Washington society; it was rumored that she always had had a great many men at her feet and could have married anyone she chose. She was reputed to be the most charming hostess in the capital. Her home had taken away the social leadership from the White House as run by President Buchanan and his niece, Harriet Lane.

In the strong light of the gas lamps Mary saw that the reports of Adele Cutts's beauty were true: Mrs. Douglas had an exquisitely shaped oval face with large brown eyes, a Grecian forehead, with heavy braids of glossy chestnut hair entwined on her head. She was elaborately gowned in silk taffeta with a tunic of embroidered white Italian gossamer, showing off her tall, well-proportioned figure.

Sitting above the scene, her eyes devouring the handsome, prosperous, enormously successful couple, strong emotion welled up in Mary's bosom: frustration, envy, hatred? She did not know; she knew only that she could hardly breathe, her heart was pounding so fiercely in her throat.

"Drive on, Abraham. It's time for your meeting."

The Hall of Representatives was barely full; Senator Douglas was not coming to hear his opponent, and so the Democrats remained out in the square. Abraham had been speaking for only a moment when a gigantic rocket went off near the window. He said, "I expect we shall have as much of that as we can conveniently get along with," which brought a laugh from the solid Republican assembly, then went on with a recounting of the disadvantages under which the Republican party was working, including the unfair representation in the legislature which had been apportioned years before when the population was greater in the south:

"Senator Douglas is of world-wide renown. All the anxious politicians of his party have been looking upon him as certainly, at no distant day, to be president of the United States. They have seen in his round, jolly, fruitful face post offices, land offices, marshalships and cabinet appointments, chargéships and foreign missions bursting and sprouting out in wonderful exuberance ready to be laid hold of by their greedy hands. On the contrary nobody has ever expected me to be president. In my poor, lean, lank face nobody has ever seen that any cabbages were sprouting out."

She did not enjoy the laughter that followed.

When they reached home, and Mary had changed into the robe she had bought in New York, she brought iced lemonade up to Abraham's bedroom where he was sprawled cater-corner on his bed, his hands under his head. Without bringing his eyes down from the ceiling, he asked:

"What did you honestly think?"

"The end was good."

"And the beginning?"

"When you spend half your time answering Steve you are giving him half your platform. I think you ought to fly your own kite. People are saying that your crowds are small; might not that be because you're trailing Douglas instead of going out on the stump yourself and initiating the issues of the campaign?"

"You think I'm hanging onto Douglas's coattails?" He sampled the flavor of that thought for a moment, working his lips up and down. "Several friends have said I ought to go on the offensive. What about Greeley's suggestion in the *Tribune* the day after Douglas and I spoke at Chicago: 'We trust Messrs. Lincoln and Douglas will speak together at some fifteen or twenty of the most important and widely accessible points throughout the state'?"

"You mean a series of debates? Excellent!" Her eyes glowed at the suggestion. "There's no more exciting theatre in the world than two men pitted against each other on a platform. Every newspaper in the country would report it."

He sat up abruptly.

"I'll have to propose it to Norman Judd and other friends on the Central Committee in Chicago. I'm sure they will concur."

"But will Steve? What does he gain?"

"Look at it the other way. Can he afford to refuse?"

6

ABRAHAM left to consult with his advisory committee and to issue the challenge to Douglas. Stephen's answer came in the form of a letter. She could not resist opening it. After reprimanding Abraham for not inviting this arrangement while they were both in Springfield and Douglas was drawing up his campaign, he then agreed to debate him in Freeport, Ottawa, Galesburg, Quincy, Alton, Jonesboro and Charleston.

She danced around the sitting room waving the letter above her head. When Abraham returned the next morning she asked:

"Abraham, could I come along for the debates? I think I could be as much of an asset to you as Adele Cutts is to Steve."

"No question of that, Puss, but the Douglases can afford to spend a great deal of money on this campaign. We're spending our meager savings. I'm going to have to be on the move every day. You'd have to spend hours in dirty railroad stations, travel in crowded day coaches . . . sometimes sit up in the cars all night . . ."

"I won't mind. Remember our trip to Vandalia for the big Whig convention? I made a great many friends there."

He moved his head from side to side.

"It would be better if you met me at the strategic points. I'd have the freedom of mind to slog on day by day."

She was disappointed.

They had a quiet two weeks preparing for his swing through the smaller villages prior to opening the formal debates at Ottawa. Then on a hot Friday morning toward the end of August she boarded the cars. It was a rough jolting journey; she half suffocated for lack of air, breathing in draughts of black soot. By the time she reached the halfway mark her traveling dress of dark blue muslin was covered with dust and ash. She had prepared herself a small lunch but was too hot to eat.

It was midafternoon by the time she reached Morris, a tiny village with houses nestled among green shade trees. Abraham was at the station to meet her. They stayed with friends overnight, and the next morning went down to the station to board the seventeen-car Republican special, jammed with their supporters. It was shortly after noon when they reached Ottawa. They were escorted from the train to a carriage which had been decorated with evergreens and mottoes by the young Republican ladies of the town; in front of them were bands of music and behind them military companies. The procession circled the square to the sound of cheering, then made its way to the residence of Mayor Glover, who was standing on the porch of his two-story red brick house ready to give them an official welcome to this northern and hence predominantly Republican town.

A holiday mood prevailed over the town, the stores and streets were scrubbed, banners and streamers hung. The square was a seething mass of humanity, some ten thousand people who, the mayor told Mary, had poured into the town the night before on horseback, in carriages, farm wagons, special trains and canal boats up the Illinois and Fox rivers, the town being surrounded by campfires of those who had come in for the great show.

In the middle of the square was an improvised stand with a plank covering to keep off the merciless sun; no one had remembered to keep a lane available to the stand, and so a military company leading the Lincolns fought its way inch by inch, taking a half hour to get through. From another direction Mr. and Mrs. Douglas and their Democratic entourage were undergoing a similar ordeal. Finally they were all seated on the platform, she and Abraham on one side with their delegation, Douglas and his wife on the other. Across the stand Mary saw Adele Cutts Douglas gazing at her.

Below them was a table filled with reporters from most of the important newspapers of the east, as well as short hand writers.

Douglas had the opening speech and the rebuttal. He was dressed in a ruffled silk shirt and dark blue coat with shiny buttons. He talked steadily in a rushing unbroken stream, his voice heavy and rich; he shook his long black hair, walked back and forth across the platform with the springing grace of a panther. Mary remembered him as she had known him in the early days of Springfield; what power he had developed, what amazing qualities of leadership. His questioning of Abraham about the Springfield Republican platform was greeted with cries of "Hurrah for Douglas!" "Hit him again!"

She stole a glance at Abraham's face. He was upset. A number of times he shook his head in confusion and denial.

When he rose, wearing a coat with sleeves too short, and baggy trousers, he was greeted with protracted applause; this cheered her, though it did not lighten Abraham's expression. His voice was nasal, with an unpleasant timbre; the confidence and good nature of the night before were gone, and so was the speech he painstakingly had written at home, tried out and revised in the public squares of small towns between Springfield and Ottawa. Douglas's attack had thrown him off balance. He failed to answer Douglas's questions, did some patchwork rambling, then stopped speaking altogether after only thirty or forty minutes.

She was too apprehensive to hear anything of Douglas's rebuttal; she could tell from the tone of the audience that he had had the better of the day's argument.

She was tired; she wanted to get off the platform, back to Mayor Glover's house and into the quiet and privacy of the bedroom that had been made available to them. Then she saw Mrs. Douglas moving toward her. She turned her face, tried to make her way to the steps at the side of the platform. The crowd was too dense. She felt a gentle hand on her arm, and turned. There was no sense of triumph in Adele Douglas; instead she wore a friendly smile.

"You won't remember me, Mrs. Lincoln, but I was introduced to you once a number of years ago in Washington."

Startled, Mary asked, "In Washington?"

"At my aunt's house: Mrs. Madison. You came in for the New Year's reception. I was only fourteen then, but I remember thinking what exquisite shoulders you had. I can even recall your gown; it was white silk with blue brocaded flowers woven through it."

Mary flushed. "Yes, I did wear my white silk that day. Remarkable that you should remember."

"I don't think so, Mrs. Lincoln. Anyone meeting you for the first time certainly could never forget you. Do tell me, how are you faring on this trip with your husband? Frankly I would have preferred to remain home. My main task seems to be keeping Mr. Douglas in clean shirts. I'm not altogether sure I'm contributing anything to the campaign, though I do my best with the women of the town."

Completely thawed now, Mary held out her hand to the younger woman.

"I'm so glad we've met, Mrs. Douglas. Do let us be friends. I love to travel, and I must say I envy your being able to make the whole trip."

That evening the short hand man brought in Abraham's speech, transcribed to long hand for the newspapers. Abraham read it, turned to Mary with a wry smile.

"I say, as the old man did when he saw his daguerreotype: it's most horribly like me!"

He laughed, then sprang up from his chair and exclaimed:

"I've got it! Douglas played us double. That set of abolitionist resolutions he outlined never was passed in Springfield, and never was the Republican party platform. They were passed by some abolitionist county group up in the north. That's what had me so upset. It was probably an honest mistake, but I'm going to confront him with it at Freeport."

There was no sleep in him that night. He paced the floor of Mayor Glover's upstairs bedroom overlooking the deserted street and sleeping village.

"I've used a lot of Douglas's ideas in the past, now I think I'll use another: he asked me a series of embarrassing questions today; next week I'll ask him some, and with one of them I think I can embarrass him right out of the election."

"Truly? We've been trying to dispose of him for twenty-two years without the slightest success. How can you find such a thrust *fatale?*"

He went to where his stovepipe hat was sitting on a marble-topped table, bottom up, and dumped out some old envelopes.

"This is roughly how the question should read: 'Can the people of a United States territory in any lawful way exclude slavery from its limits prior to the formation of a state constitution?' "

She repeated the sentence to herself.

"Douglas has been upholding the Dred Scott decision; therefore in all legal logic he has got to answer in the negative: that the citizens of a territory cannot exclude slavery, because with the Missouri Compromise dead, slaves cannot be excluded anywhere."

"If Douglas answers 'No,' " said Mary ruminatively, "he loses every vote in Illinois except the ultra-slavery votes in the southern counties. Is that it?"

Abraham was pleased at his stratagem; he went to the front window, took several draughts of air, then got into bed.

"I can sleep now."

She was cutting out the first newspaper reports of the debate in Freeport when her cousin Logan came to call, his face a series of contorted whorls.

"Mary, what happened to us at Freeport?" he cried in a high shrill voice. "Why did Abraham ask Douglas that question?"

Mary thought the Freeport debate had gone well in spite of the wind and showers: Douglas had apologized to a crowd of fifteen thousand listeners for quoting the wrong platform at Ottawa; all the important newspapers of the country had carried their speeches in full. It was the first time Abraham's words had had a national audience.

"Abraham had Douglas locked tight in that Kansas cavern, and now he has willfully unbolted the door and let him out. They're saying all over town we had the election won, and now we've got it lost."

"Sit down for a moment, Cousin Logan, I'll get you some coffee."

She deliberately took her time, for she could hear her cousin pacing nervously in the sitting room. She poured two cups of very thick black coffee. Logan pushed his aside.

"I hear some of our best men advised Abraham against asking Douglas that question. Why does he go contrary to good advice?"

She recalled his refusal to withdraw his "house divided" sentiments from the Springfield speech.

"I don't know, Cousin Logan; but he has to do what he thinks is right."

Logan took up the Freeport clipping and ran a jagged fingernail under the lines of Douglas's answer:

" 'The next question propounded to me by Mr. Lincoln is, can the people of a territory in any lawful way . . . exclude slavery from their limits prior to the formation of a State Constitution? I answer emphatically that in my opinion the people of a territory can, by lawful means, exclude slavery from their limits. . . . The people have the lawful means to introduce it or exclude it as they please, for the reason that slavery cannot exist a day or an hour anywhere, unless it is supported by local police regulations.' "

Logan held her in a troubled gaze.

"How clever that answer is: it'll win him every old-line Whig vote in the state!"

As she stood looking at her cousin she remembered how he had wept when Abraham had been defeated by Trumbull for the Senate seat three years before. What could she say to him? That Abraham had been wrong? That he had made a tactical blunder? She who had watched his slow, troubled awakening, lived side by side with the impetus of his growth and maturing, seen and heard him reach the selflessness of dedication to a humanitarian cause? Should she now doubt his judgment?

She put her hand on her cousin's shoulder, fondly.

"Abraham knows best, Cousin Logan. We must have faith in him."

A few days later, on September 1, he was home, his face bronzed from exposure to the sun, his voice strong in spite of the fact that he had been speaking in open-air groves every afternoon, and in town squares in the evenings. If the election were already lost, certainly no one could find any sign of it in Abraham. He had a number of stories for her and the boys as they gathered about him in the kitchen while she prepared a beefsteak for supper: of how the caboose of the freight train he was riding had been side-tracked in the hot sun for several hours to let the Douglas special go by; how the French harp he had learned to play on the long day-coach journeys had become known as the rival of Douglas's brass band.

Robert brought out the brilliant uniform which the Springfield Cadets had had made to wear on the excursion train which would go to Alton for the last debate.

"You must come too, Mary," said Abraham. "You saw the beginning of the contest; I want you to be there at the end."

After supper he settled down at the worktable beneath his law shelves. When Mary asked in surprise if he were still writing out every speech in advance, he gazed at her over his spectacles.

"Now, take your old friend Douglas, he has a theory that the popular sovereignty speech is the one he is going to win on, and the audiences whom he addresses in each town will neither know nor care whether he is making the same speech elsewhere. For my own part, I can never repeat a speech a second time. Everything about the subject keeps enlarging as I go from place to place, and what seems to me like new truths come crowding in on me."

The next two weeks, while she followed him by the newspaper reports, he traced a pattern across the valleys and prairies of Illinois, on horseback, in carriages, on railroads or canals or riverboats, speaking in rapid succession from Monticello to Mattoon, from Hillsboro to Edwardsville, from Highland to Greenville. The third in the series of their debates, held at Jonesboro, deep in the south of Illinois, went badly for both of them, since the county was dominated by Buchanan Democrats; however in Charleston, the capital of Coles County, there was an enormous banner across the main street which read OLD ABE THIRTY YEARS AGO, showing Abraham driving two yoke of oxen. The papers estimated that some ten to twelve thousand people had come to hear their adopted candidate; chief among them, Sarah Bush Lincoln, his stepmother.

Her other newspaper reading was not as pleasant: the Lexington *Observer and Reporter*, which she still received by mail, informed her that the Kentucky Whigs, which meant her entire Kentucky family, were unanimously in favor of Douglas over Lincoln. Such old family friends as John J. Crittenden and James B. Clay, son of Henry Clay, also favored the election of Douglas.

At the end of September Abraham managed to get home for a week end, coming in late of a Saturday afternoon. She had no sooner freshened the upstairs bedroom and heard him thumping around in his slippers, than the Republican Club came marching down the street headed by a band, assembling almost a thousand strong in front of the house. Since it was obvious that the crowd would not go away until he had made a speech, Abraham linked his arm through Mary's and the two of them went out on the front porch to acknowledge the cheers. The three boys looked on from the upstairs windows. Abraham thanked their friends for the reception, assured them that the prospects were good for the triumph of the principles that were so dear to all of them.

Mary watched the faces of the people as they followed his words, felt the warmth of the community as it flowed upward toward Abraham and herself. She was tremendously moved, it was almost like repatriation; once again she felt close to the town where so often she had thought herself unhappy and unwanted.

7

ON the morning of the Alton debate she was up at five, building a fire in the stove and heating the bath water for herself and Robert. At the station hundreds of people had collected, enough to crowd the eight cars of the half-fare excursion train. The trip took four hours; eleven years before, they had ridden the stagecoach from Springfield to Alton and the ninety-eight miles had taken two full days.

When she alighted from the cars one of Abraham's friends led her to where Abraham was sitting in a closed carriage; he had come down from Quincy on the riverboat *City of Louisiana* the evening before. He reached down both arms to help her into the carriage, kissing her heartily.

"I thought it better not to come into the station, or it would take us hours to get to the hotel. Where's Robert?"

"With his cadet company. They plan to parade about the city before going for their dinner. Did you rest well last night?"

"Went to my cabin after supper and slept till dawn. I wish the Rock Island and the Illinois Central would put boats on their tracks."

The carriage stopped at a side entrance of the Franklin Hotel. Abraham led her up to their suite on the third floor. He had been receiving political friends all morning, but now they were to have a couple of hours of rest and privacy.

At one-thirty they left the hotel.

"We'll be before an audience which has strong sympathies southward," said Abraham. "I'm sure Douglas is going to try to place me in an extreme abolitionist attitude."

When they reached the stand which had been erected in front of the tall ground-floor windows of the new city hall, she was disappointed to find in the space between the city hall and the Congregational church little more than a third of the number who had assembled at Ottawa for the opening debate. In Ottawa the crowd had been filled with families, mothers carrying children in their arms, young girls as well as grandmothers; here it was mostly men. Then she saw that the windows of the city hall and all other windows of the square were filled with women gazing down upon them.

Promptly at two o'clock Stephen Douglas rose and began his speech. His face was bloated, his voice strained and hoarse. He seemed nervous as he strode up and down the platform, nevertheless his argument was well organized: the government had been established by white men for the benefit of white men and their posterity; the signers of the Declaration of Independence had no reference to Negroes when they declared all men to be created equal, they were alluding to white men and none others; there was no power under our system of government which had the right to force a constitution on unwilling people, and if the people of Kansas wanted a slave state, they had a right to form such a state, and he would let them come into the Union with slavery or without because it was their business and not his; and that when he brought forth the Kansas-Nebraska bill its intent was to leave the people there free to regulate their domestic institutions; that Lincoln, in declaring the "house divided" doctrine, had insisted that the government could not endure permanently divided into slave and free states, and consequently he invited disunion; his election would be an invitation to war, resulting in the destruction of the constitution and the government set up by the founding fathers.

Half the crowd cheered him lustily when he finished and took his seat. Mrs. Douglas handed him a clean white handkerchief to wipe the perspiration from his brow.

Abraham rose, took off his coat. A young woman in the audience threw a bouquet of dahlias and roses at his feet. He picked up the flowers and handed them back to Mary, who held them on top of his coat. She strained forward to catch every word he uttered.

He quickly went to the heart of the conflict:

"At Galesburg the other day, I said in answer to Douglas that three years ago there never had been a man, so far as I knew in the whole world, who had said that the Declaration of Independence did not include Negroes in the term 'all men.' I believe the first man who ever said it was Chief Justice Taney in the Dred Scott case, and the next to him was our friend Stephen A. Douglas. When this new principle is brought forward I combat it as taking away from the Negro the right of ever striving to be a man."

He accused Douglas of reviving the slavery agitation in 1854 by demanding the repeal of the Missouri Compromise, and asked why, since the "troublesome thing" was on its way to extinction, Douglas had felt driven to the necessity of introducing a new policy in regard to slavery; whereas "we might, by arresting the further spread of it and placing it where the fathers originally placed it, put it where the public mind should rest in the belief that it was in the course of ultimate extinction." He maintained that all troubles in relation to slavery arose from an endeavor to spread it.

A number of scattered voices cried, "Hear! Hear!" Abraham held his arms out in a wide, encircling gesture.

"The real issue between Douglas and myself is the sentiment of one class that looks upon the institution of slavery as a wrong, and of another class that does not look upon it as a wrong. Judge Douglas says he 'don't care whether slavery is voted up or voted down.' Any man who can say that does not see anything wrong in slavery, because no man can logically say he don't care whether a wrong is voted up or down.

"Douglas contends that whatever community wants slaves has a right to have them. So they have if it is not a wrong. But if it is a wrong, he cannot say a people have a right to do wrong. You may turn over everything in the Democratic policy from beginning to end and everything that Douglas has said, and it everywhere carefully excludes the idea that there is anything wrong in slavery. That is the real issue. That is the issue that will continue in this country when these poor tongues of Stephen Douglas and myself shall be silent. It is the eternal struggle between these two principles, that have stood face to face from the beginning of time and will ever continue to struggle. The one is the common right of humanity and the other the divine right of kings. It is the same spirit that says, 'You work and toil and earn bread, and I'll eat it.' "

Dusk had fallen. Abraham stood above the crowd, every line of his angular body yearning out toward the people who were standing in silence, gazing up at him, not really knowing he had finished, and then when they did, too caught up emotionally to give anything but quiet applause.

When the crowd had melted away Mary and Abraham went back to the Franklin House for an early supper before catching the train to Springfield. Robert and the cadets were still parading in front of the *Courier* office.

At supper, on Mary's right, sat Horace White, reporter from the Chicago *Tribune*, while opposite her was Robert Hitt, the pioneer of verbatim short hand reporting. The dining room was filled with Republicans, the Democrats being with Douglas at the Alton Hotel. There was an exultation in the air, a feeling that Abraham had brought the campaign to a fine close. It was true also, Mary thought as she looked about the table, that everyone except Abraham was exhausted. Horace White and Robert Hitt fell to comparing notes on their relative amount of work and the meager amount of sleep they had had in the past two months. Mary asked:

"Why don't you young men come home with Mr. Lincoln and myself and rest for a few days?"

Robert Hitt put his elbows on the table, leaned toward her and said with mock severity:

"Thank you, Mrs. Lincoln, but I will never visit your home until you live in the White House."

There was laughter around the table. Mary answered wistfully:

"Young man, there's not much prospect of such a residence very soon."

There was no dawn to election day. Leaden skies poured down torrential rains. Abraham commented that the rain and mud would keep a good many Republicans among the country farmers away from the polls. When she accompanied him downtown, just before noon, they found everyone thoroughly drenched and dispirited, with a surprising amount of drunkenness and fist fights taking place in the streets, the constables hauling off the belligerents to city prison.

Late that night they walked home from the *Journal* office where they had been tabulating the telegraphic results: although Abraham and the Republicans had received a majority of the popular vote, the unfair apportionment giving more legislators to the southern counties would unquestionably result in a Democratic victory and give Douglas his re-election to the Senate.

They were silent as they slogged through the mud. While making their way up Eighth Street Abraham became so immersed in his thoughts that one foot flew out from under him and he very nearly fell. Seeing a flash of pain on his face, Mary asked:

"Are you all right?"

He smiled wistfully.

"It was a slip, not a fall."

"Then you think there is some chance for us in the future?"

He was silent for a long time.

"I'm glad we made the race, Mary: it gave us a hearing on the great and durable question of the age. Don't ever believe that all the work was wasted: even though we sink out of view and be forgotten, we've made some marks which will tell for the cause of civil liberty long after we're gone."

She thought of the writing she had found on his worktable the morning he left for the first speech of the campaign, and once again tears filled her eyes. She slipped her hand into his, felt the return pressure as he laced his fingers through hers.

"From now on, Mary, we'll be fighting in the ranks."

8

THREE weeks later they were almost blasted out of bed by a thirty-two-gun salute fired for the early morning arrival in Springfield of Senator Stephen A. Douglas.

"Hail the conquering hero," said Mary acidly once the ground-shaking barrage had ended.

"Oh, he's the hero all right," replied Abraham. "Singlehandedly he crushed President Buchanan and the administration machine; they'll have no influence in the 1860 Democratic convention. Douglas will control it, and this time there will be no possibility of his being put aside for another candidate. The emotions of defeat are fresh upon me, but we shall have fun again."

She rose, poured cold water into the basin, washed her face and put on a starched ruffled morning gown. Then she turned back to the bed, her eyes questioning him sharply.

"Fun again?"

"The fight must go on. Douglas managed to be supported both as the instrument to break down and to uphold the slave power. No ingenuity can keep up this double position. I have an abiding faith that we shall beat them in the long run."

She brushed her hair, braided it and pinned it at the nape of her neck. When she had quite finished she asked:

"Who is the 'them' we are going to beat? And in which fight? 1860? '62? '64?"

He grinned.

"It will come as no surprise to you that I entertain a personal wish for a term in the United States Senate."

"There's one available in 1860."

"Lyman Trumbull's? No. He is doing a magnificent job for freedom. I am anxious that he be sustained. I shall go out and campaign for him over the state . . . also for whomever the Republicans nominate for the presidency. In 1860 we're going to win; though I fall early in the contest it is nothing if I have contributed in the least degree to the final rightful result."

"You make everything sound so posthumous," she replied mournfully, "like that phrase you used in the letter to Dr. Henry, 'though I now sink out of view.' It seems to me there's an awful lot of you just to plain sink out of view . . . as though you had been swallowed by the cat."

"Oh no. Only a couple of days ago I wrote to the Chicago *Tribune* asking if they could send me two copies of each number of their paper that contained the debates so that I could put them together in a scrapbook and have them published. But from now on I must stick to the courts or we will go to the wall for bread."

And so she went back to her housewifery, Abraham to his lawyering. Since he had refrained from personal invective his campaign had made him no enemies; by the same token it had made him a great many new friends and spread his name widely on the national scene. Business came to him almost at once, not merely personal cases, but important business matters from the Illinois Central and manufacturing companies. Although it would take long hard hours, the heavy accounts they had piled up at a number of the stores presently would be paid off. The pressure never to spend a dollar except for food was removed.

Mary turned her attention to the subject of Robert's education, for he was going on sixteen and Abraham seemed content to let him attend the infant Illinois State University, in which the Lincolns had bought a scholarship some years before. Having been raised within the purlieu of Transylvania University and having a basis of contrast, she was determined that Robert must not be obliged to confine his higher education to what the four ministers who composed the Illinois faculty could impart. Abraham seemed surprised.

"You'll want something better than that for your sons," she said quietly.

"It's already better than anything I had."

"That's hardly a test, is it? You want them to have the best in comparison to what is available: Brown University, or Yale where Cassius Clay went; Boston is the greatest seat of our culture, and I would prefer Harvard."

He flinched.

"From blab school to Harvard!"

"Now, Abraham, don't behave like a self-made man. Your sons start from where you leave off, not where you began. Those eastern university lawyers frightened you half to death in Cincinnati."

"You're right," he said seriously. "I can't pull Robert down by the same bootstrap I pulled myself up with. Would my father be surprised to see his grandson in Harvard! He always told me, 'I never had no eddication, and I got along fine without it!' But he didn't. Say, do you think Bob will talk to us after he's a Harvard man?"

The prospectus from Harvard indicated that, come spring, Robert would have to take tests in sixteen separate subjects; since some of these were only sketchily taught at Estabrook or Illinois State, she gathered the textbooks around her and instructed him herself. The studies brought them close together.

After the one discussion she and Abraham had had about the campaign on the morning of Douglas's thirty-two-gun salute, the subject of politics was not mentioned in the house. She was grateful that she had the work with Robert to absorb her time. Abraham seemed grateful that every day brought new law cases to keep him occupied.

Then one day in December he returned from the courts at Bloomington with a bemused expression on his face. Over dinner he told her the story.

"Mary, you remember Jesse Fell, he owns the Bloomington *Pantagraph*, maybe the smartest man I ever met. He said to me, 'Lincoln, I have been east, as far as Boston . . . New York, New Jersey, Pennsylvania, Ohio, Michigan and Indiana; and everywhere I hear you talked about. Very frequently I have been asked, "Who is this man Lincoln, of your state, canvassing in opposition to Senator Douglas?" I told them we had two giants in Illinois instead of one: that Douglas was the little one, as they all knew, but that you were the big one, which they didn't know. I have a decided impression that if your efforts on the slavery question can be sufficiently brought before the people you can be made a formidable, if not a successful, candidate for the presidency.'"

She laid down her fork, raised her glass of water in the air and cried, "Hallelujah!"

"He thinks that what the Republican party needs to ensure success in

1860 is a man committed against slavery aggression, with no record to defend, and no radicalism; he says he should be a man of popular origin. One day an old Democrat from down around Egypt said to me, 'Abe Lincoln, they say you are a self-made man.' I answered, 'Well, yes, what there is of me is self-made.' 'Well, all I got to say,' observed the man, after looking me over from head to foot, 'is that it was a damn bad job!' "

It was the first joke he had told since his defeat; she long ago had noticed that he had a tendency to tell self-deprecatory jokes at those moments when he was relating the highest compliments that had been paid him.

"Fell asked me to write him the story of my life so he could send it east and have it published."

"Good! You write him a fine interesting piece. I can conceive of no better way of fighting in the ranks than by being the commanding general."

"Now, Mary, I'm not going to write the article."

"Why not?"

"In all candor I had to tell Fell that I don't feel myself fit for the presidency."

She raised her eyebrows in disbelief.

"That weak, obtuse, third-rate county politician Franklin Pierce was? And surely 'Old Obliquity' Buchanan is; using his full time and power trying to crush Stephen Douglas instead of governing the country."

"I wasn't thinking of Franklin Pierce or James Buchanan, Mary, but of Thomas Jefferson."

"That's a bootless activity! Today Stephen Douglas is the national hero. Is he a Thomas Jefferson?"

"I'd certainly like to come to grips with him again," he replied pensively. Then he continued in a humble tone, "Fell paid me a handsome compliment, and I'll admit I'd like to be president, but it is only horse sense to keep our ambition within attainable limits."

When by dint of great effort they got together a set of the debates they spent their evenings at the worktable cutting out the columns and pasting them in sequence in the scrapbook. She was not sure the activity was good for either of them: as he sat across from her, his gray eyes, which had been so light and clear during the campaign, became dark and confused. He had felt keenly disappointed but not disheartened by his defeat, and had told his friends over and over:

"I have no regret for having made the struggle."

Now a weariness set in: it was not merely that he seemed of two minds, but more nearly of two hundred. Was he convinced that he would have to fight in the ranks? When he wrote to Dr. Henry did he sincerely think he was going to sink out of view? Now that his days were quiet and removed from the excitements of the fight, now that he had returned to the practice of law, was he feeling the impact of fatigue and discouragement arising out of still another defeat? Would he be content to wait six full years before again trying

276

to get himself elected to the Senate? Could the satisfaction of blows struck for civil liberty sustain him? Already he was moping that he expected everyone to desert him except Billy Herndon.

Did he genuinely believe that he was unfit for the presidency? Then why was he planning this scrapbook, writing to his friends that there was some chance the debates soon would be published when actually there had been no reference to it outside the Lincoln household? He seemed to be inching slowly toward a resolution that if the nomination were available he would go out and work for it; then he would write to political friends:

"I really think it is best for our cause if no concerted effort for me be made."

When the unrest and lethargy, the post-election doldrums set in for him, what would the tension demand of her?

Abraham did not want a party for his fiftieth birthday, muttering something about there not being anything very much to celebrate, but she declared it an occasion she could not let go by. She sat down and began writing out invitations:

Mr. and Mrs. Lincoln's compliments for Wednesday, at seven o'clock.

She had not meant the party to be large, but in the end she invited over a hundred couples. The day was cloudy and remained dismal straight through to night. She swore that all she had to do was announce a party in advance for the weather to turn bad; but by eight o'clock when she stood in the entrance to the double parlors where there was a bright and animated hubbub of people talking and dancing, and began counting heads, she saw that there was a couple present for every invitation she had issued. Abraham came to her side, slipped an arm gently about her waist.

"It's the nicest fiftieth birthday I ever had."

He kissed the lobe of her ear exposed below her heavy braids. She was happy she had made the effort.

Toward the end of February he went to Chicago to take care of some law cases and parenthetically to be on the ground for the first big Republican meeting to be held since the last campaign. He was doing better at the law than ever before, there was money for her to buy whatever she wanted, to employ the new seamstress who had just opened a shop in Springfield; but neither she nor Abraham drew much sustenance from their financial success.

With spring, her headaches returned. She kept her malaise to herself, gritted her teeth and went about her tasks, knowing that this was the penalty of recurrent defeat. When the pain became severe or she felt temper welling up within her, she tried to hide for a few hours in her room, lying on her bed; but there she was overwhelmed by questions, doubts, pictures out of the past, and sensitivity to Abraham's depression. How much of their lives had been spent in vain hoping and exhausting repulses! Abraham said that

Stephen Douglas had a genius for attracting victory; could it be they had a genius for attracting defeat? Surely they had had their fill of it. And this time they had lost with all the signs and forces in their favor.

Jesse Fell was talking about Abraham's running for the presidency; but under what conceivable set of circumstances could he triumph over such men as William H. Seward and Salmon P. Chase, nationally famous and respected leaders of the Republican party? These men had been governors of great states, United States senators for many years, with a vast national reputation and body of public service behind them, with unlimited supplies of money and groups of supporters.

In the southern newspapers she continued to read editorials and reports of meetings which maintained that if a Republican president were elected in 1860 the gulf states would secede. Should any person in his right senses aspire to the White House under such conditions?

She became restless, the room seeming to close in upon her. She would jump up, bathe and dress, return to her routine.

9

SPRING settled early into a long hot summer. Abraham wrote letters, made an occasional speech, followed Douglas's movements closely.

They received shocking news from Cambridge: Harvard University reported that Robert had failed his examinations in fifteen out of the sixteen subjects! This was not only a critique on Springfield's educational facilities but a devastating comment on her own months of tutoring the boy. She felt crushed: the humiliating fiasco was her own doing, for Abraham had not wanted the boy to apply to Harvard in the first place.

Tad too filled her with apprehension and dread, for he had never overcome his speech impediment; no one outside the family could understand him, the children of the neighborhood were beginning to say unkind things about him. It was impossible to send him to school . . . he would not be accepted. What would happen to him when he had to earn a living in an adult world? He was bright, courageous, but who would know it if no one could understand him, if people hearing him for the first time thought he had a defective mind? The younger boys ran wild.

Hearing them wailing in the back yard, she cried:

"Abe, what is the matter with the boys?"

"Just what is the matter with the whole world," he replied sadly, "I've got three walnuts and each wants two."

Robert ran into the sitting room with Tad clinging to him like a burr, demanding the pocketknife Robert had in his hand.

"Oh, let him have it, Bob," his father said, "to keep him quiet."

"No," replied Robert, "it is my knife and I need it to keep me quiet."

Sometimes Abraham would take William and Tad down to the office; he refused to exercise any control over them, and they would scatter the legal papers over the floor, pull books out of the shelves, spill the ink . . . with Mr. Herndon spreading a tale of ill-mannered youngsters.

When she and Abraham went to church and she was dressed in her beautiful gowns and bonnets trimmed with blonde and flowers, Tad would come into the sanctuary, his face sweaty, and stand in the aisle trying to persuade Abraham to come out and play ball with him. One Sunday morning when Mary insisted that the five Lincolns go to church together, Tad acted up in the middle of the sermon and his father had to sling him across his left arm like a pair of saddlebags.

"Heep your eye on Wiwie, hittin' hood a pie," Tad cried out as Abraham started to carry him down the aisle. ("Keep your eye on Willie, sitting good as pie.")

Mary's face flamed. When she got home she said sternly:

"Thomas, I am going to have to punish you."

"Pwea hon' haw me Hawma, Mamaday," Tad pleaded, for not since his christening had anyone called him by his proper name. "Hat he moh huniment I know. I hit in hur hood a pie, if owney you haw me Had."

"If you don't want me to call you Thomas, and it's the most punishment you know," translated Mary, "then you jolly well better sit in church good as pie!"

She did not have the heart to punish him.

Nor could she draw comfort from her only woman confidante, for Hannah Shearer's husband had come down with tuberculosis, and Hannah had taken him back to his home in Pennsylvania.

She suffered a second great loss when Eliza Francis called to say good-bye, her face folded in layers of despondency. She and Simeon were going out to Portland, Oregon, not as pioneers or seekers after a new life, but as though to Bogotá: the farmers' newspaper which Simeon had started after selling the *Journal* had not been successful; it seemed to Eliza that everything had turned to dust, that they had come to this late stage in their lives having accomplished nothing. To Mary they appeared sad and old and beaten; but had the Lincolns been more successful than the Simeon Francises?

She knew how important it was, when Abraham was discouraged, to make a show of good cheer for her husband, but to her chagrin her nerves blew up in her face and then she was guilty of an outburst of temper against whoever might be present. She scolded Abraham for riding on the railroad cars with one elbow sticking out of his coat, for returning with his finely tucked shirt bosoms crumpled into hard balls in a corner of his carpetbag, for walking through the streets in his flapping carpet slippers and single gallus when he wanted to borrow something from the Gourleys or the Graves family. When she asked him to shovel the snow from the walks and came across him an hour later sunk in a chair before the fireplace studying a German grammar, she cried:

"Abraham, you are of no account when you are home. You never do anything but warm yourself and read."

He looked up with an absent expression.

"Mary, here is a curious thing, the Germans have no word for thimble, they call it a finger hat; they have no word for glove, they call it a hand shoe."

"Do they have a word for house chores?"

They sold their cow because Abraham would not take care of her; each day she had to send William or Tad with a bucket to find some milk . . . and a half hour later send Abraham to find his son.

One afternoon, when she was dressing to receive the vice-presidents of her church society, Abraham answered the bell and said:

"Make yourselves to home, ladies, Mrs. Lincoln will be down just as soon as she gets her trotting harness on."

She thought this bit of social manners as shocking as his dishabille. When she grew angry at him he would lower his head like a lamb into the storm, and leave the room. With the hiatus from politics the period of understanding between them, the unity of purpose, of a good team working together, ground to a halt.

She was caught in outbursts over which she had no control. She hired fifteen-year-old Philip Dingley to keep the firebox filled, the walks clear of snow, the buggy greased; but when she caught him sprawled in a chair in Robert's room puffing amateurishly on a pipe she dumped his belongings out of the second-story window into the street. She learned of a new shipment of organdies, went quickly to the store to select six choice patterns, then was furious when she found that the proprietor's wife had already made the best selection, demanding it in return for her own.

When one of the boys got some lime in his mouth, she rushed out screaming for help instead of merely rinsing the child's mouth; when some fat caught fire in a frying pan, she cried, "Fire! Fire!" The Reverend Miner's wife removed the pan and plunged it into a basin of water. She was hiring and firing so rapidly that she could scarcely remember the faces. When she went down to her cellar storage room and found it permeated with a sour smell because of an unwashed mop left standing there, she discharged the maid, then commented tightly:

"If Mr. Lincoln should happen to die, his spirit will never find me living outside the boundaries of a slave state."

She was sitting slumped on a hard kitchen chair before the unlighted fire, feeling immeasurably sorry for herself, when she heard a knocking on the back door. She opened it to find a dark-haired, dark-skinned young girl standing there. She recognized her as Frances Affonsa, the Portuguese girl who worked for the Miners. Mrs. Miner had suggested that she help Mrs. Lincoln, who was poorly.

"Eu sou uma boa lavadeira," Frances said. "I wash clothes, Mrs. Lincum."

Frances was a determined worker, boiling the big tubs of water, scrubbing the sheets, rinsing at the outside cistern. She did a slow but relentless job of the ironing. At the end of the day Frances stood triumphant by the piles of pressed shirts and linens, her face agleam. Mary said:

"Frances, they say in Springfield that I am a hard woman to please. I've had lots of girls come to work for me, but they don't stay long."

"Se o trabalho for bem feito, Mrs. Lincum *nao e dificil?* If work good, Mrs. Lincum is not difficult?"

"No, Frances, but why is it that you don't hate the job, and me, and the fact that you have to be here instead of somewhere else?"

Frances puzzled over this for a time.

"At Madeira where I born, everybody work. You work good, you content. Sunday I free . . . you like I come, make house clean?"

The next morning she received a letter from Harvard saying that if they would send Robert to Phillips Exeter Academy in New Hampshire for a year of special training, the boy could likely pass his university entrance examinations. She would discuss it with Abraham at dinner, and write to Exeter Academy that very day.

Sunday was Easter; out of her bedroom window when she awakened, the sky was bright. Her niece, Julia Baker, married to one of the men who had bought the *Journal,* was having a christening for her baby at the church. She smelled coffee: Frances Affonsa was already in the kitchen working. Abraham came into her bedroom cleanly shaved, his eyes crinkling in a little smile.

"Come to the front window of my room, Mary."

She followed him through the two bedrooms; in front of their house stood a shiny black carriage covered by a black leather top, the carpet-covered steps unfolded, a sleek black horse standing between the shafts. She gazed up at him in bewilderment.

"An Easter present for you, Puss. I knew you wanted to go to church for the Baker baby's christening, and so I decided to take you there in style."

He also had bought a new kind of shirt which apparently had reached Springfield only in the past weeks, with a soft rolling collar attached to the shirt itself. He had a wide black silk tie to go with it.

"You look like a new man," she exclaimed.

"You need a new man. I started playing handball again yesterday too: we've made a new ball alley next to the *Journal* office: the end of it is the solid wall of a three-story building, so we had the ground leveled and a high board fence put up along Sixth Street. I won three games at a dime apiece and used my ill-gotten gain to buy the horse and buggy and these new shirts."

His high spirits were infectious; she slipped an arm about his waist. He returned the embrace. They stood looking at each other, humor playing about their features, the sunlight dazzling on the windowpane.

She woke the three boys, piloted them through warm baths. Frances served breakfast in the dining room, where she had set the table with Mary's best silver and dishware. William observed:

"One of us must be getting christened."

The younger boys were enchanted with the new carriage; Robert wanted to know why they got it just as he was about to leave for Exeter.

After services they went to Elizabeth's and Ninian's home for the reception and dinner. At midafternoon, after they had visited with the family, Abraham whispered:

"Mary, I've told Robert to walk the boys home when they're ready. Let's go for a ride over the prairies."

It was a beautiful afternoon. The rain of the past few weeks had brought out the wild strawberries and tall grasses, brilliant flowering weeds rippling in the wind. Abraham fastened the reins, letting the horse pick his own way while they sat filled with happiness for themselves and love for each other: or were they one and the same?

Abraham began to talk. His voice was clear and resonant. He was going to buy a German-language newspaper, the *Illinois Staats-Anzeiger*, in order that he might have a steady voice among the large German population of Illinois; in two weeks he would be going up to Bloomington where the Illinois Central Republican Committee convention was meeting; he had decided to write the autobiography that Jesse Fell wanted to publish; he was going to write a letter to Salmon P. Chase, head of the Republican party in Ohio, urging that the Ohio Republicans not adopt their proposed plank: "To repeal the atrocious fugitive slave law," on the grounds that such a plank would explode the convention.

He did not say in actual words, I am going after the presidency, yet he made it clear to her that he was resolved to work for the nomination in a constructive fashion: he would try to hold together the disparate parts of the party, urge them to avoid errors of strategy which would alienate blocks of the voters; in particular it was his hope that the Illinois delegation, which would have some twenty votes in the national convention, would not only nominate him but stand steadfastly by.

She plunged into the job of getting Robert ready for Exeter, sewing for him a dozen fine linen shirts, having him fitted for broadcloth suits and formal dinner clothes. She gave a dinner party at the beginning of June because Abraham wanted to entertain a number of colleagues who had been helpful to him during the '58 campaign. A few days later she began a series of teas for the Republican ladies of the town.

Jesse Fell had said Abraham would make a formidable candidate for the presidency, if not a successful one. Such as it was, this was her vineyard. Season after season there was work to be done.

BY the middle of June the strawberries came ripe, with strawberry-and-ice-cream parties every night. Toward the end of the month Mary gave a similar party for seventy. She also invited the young people of the town to a farewell dinner for Robert and a friend who was leaving with him for Exeter.

The next time Abraham had to make a quick trip to Chicago, Mary suggested he take William with him. In a few days William wrote to a friend:

> This town is a very beautiful place. Me and father went to two theatres the other night. Me and father have a nice little room to ourselves. We have two little pitcher on a washstand. The smallest one for me the largest one for father. We have two little towels on a top of both pitchers. The smallest one for me, the largest one for father.
>
> We have two little beds in the room. The smallest one for me, the largest one for father.
>
> We have two little wash basin. The smallest one for me, the largest one for father. The weather is very very fine here in this town. . . .

Tad was hilarious over the letter, making Mary read it to him until he had memorized it.

In July the Lincolns were invited, along with the Logans, the Dubois' and other state officials, to ride the full length of the Illinois Central lines in a private car such as Senator and Mrs. Douglas had had during the campaign, reviewing and assessing the property holdings of the railroad. July 14, the day they left, was the hottest of the summer; they were bundled down with carpetbags, bandboxes and baskets. Each day they covered the distance between towns, at night they put up at a hotel; sometimes the beds were hard and the food bad, but Mary was fascinated by the changing scenes, endearing herself to the railroad officials when she told them she thought "railroad riding the most delightful thing in the world."

After their return Abraham kept the political pot boiling with letters to Republican leaders of other states, suggesting, "In every locality we should look beyond our noses and at least say nothing on points where it is probable we shall disagree. The great problem is to consolidate the conflicting elements in the anti-slavery ranks; everything that leads to disagreement, enmity and factionalism is bad."

But neither was their friend Douglas idle: he had just completed a fiery tour through Ohio, and the leading Republicans of that state urged Abraham to come and answer him in Cincinnati, Dayton, Columbus. Ohio was a critical state; if it went Democratic in the local election of 1859 there would be little chance for a Republican regime to be elected in 1860.

Abraham did not want to go into a neighboring state.

"People always resent it, it causes defeat."

"But that isn't true in this case, Abraham," she argued. "They expressly invited you. Ohio is an eastern state; isn't it a good omen if they turn to the west and ask a Sucker to be the spokesman for their party?" She paused. "Besides, now that you took Willie to Chicago, we've got to take Tad with us on a trip. The boy is fairly bursting to live in a hotel room with two little pitchers on a washstand."

That clinched it.

Once again they were railroad riding. A friend in Columbus showed them the capital, then took them out to the Franklin County Fair. They returned to the hotel for dinner and at two o'clock Abraham made his speech from the east terrace of the state house. He drew laughter at the beginning by saying, "The Giant himself has been here recently," and a loud cheer by asking, "Now what is Douglas's popular sovereignty? It is, as a principle, no other than that if one man chooses to make a slave of another man, neither that other man nor anybody else has a right to object."

The next day he spoke between trains at Dayton, and when they arrived at the station in Cincinnati there was a group of enthusiasts in carriages to escort them to the Burnet House. Mary had a fighting sparkle in her eye; it was in Cincinnati that Abraham had been so ignominiously ignored in the reaper case. They had tea in their own parlor, then Abraham went to the balcony of Kinsey's Jewelry Store overlooking the Fifth Street Market Place to address an assemblage that seemed to consist of the whole city and the surrounding population for a hundred miles.

At eleven the next morning there was a knock on their door. Gibson Harris came in. He now had a wife and a thriving law practice in Cincinnati, but to Mary he still seemed the charming young boy who some thirteen years before had brought her an envelope of money from Abraham's office. They fell to talking about the 1860 campaign. Gibson said:

"It looks like my father may have been a proper prophet after all. Remember, he said we would have to fight a civil war to keep the Union in existence. We're getting closer to that war all the time, don't you think, Mr. Lincoln?"

Mary studied Abraham's face. If he were nominated and elected, would that be the signal for secession and bloodshed? If Stephen Douglas were elected, would that mean no disunion, no fighting on battlefields? Was that the country's choice? For whom would her father have voted, were he alive?

She waited tensely for Abraham to answer. He was a long time in formulating his thoughts, and then his voice was so quiet it seemed as though he were talking to himself.

"Many who are for the Union greatly fear the success of the Republicans would destroy the Union. Why? Do the Republicans declare against the Union? Nothing like it. The south says that if the Black Republicans elect a president they won't stand it, they will break up the Union. That will be their act, nor ours. To justify it they must show that our policy gives them cause for such desperate action. Can they do that? When they attempt it they will find that our policy is exactly the policy of the men who made the Union. Do they really think they are justified to break up the government? If they do they are very unreasonable; and more reasonable men cannot and will not submit to them. If constitutionally we elect a president, and therefore they undertake to destroy the Union, it will be our duty to deal with them. We hope and believe that in no section will a majority so act as to render extreme measures necessary."

The breath came out of her all at once. When Abraham made his decision to work for the nomination it had been predicated on the conviction of a reasonable man that a legal election would not result in an illegal revolt. She had the deepest respect for his judgment. She would remain serene.

Norman B. Judd, who had managed Abraham's campaign in '58, was on his way to New York to attend a meeting of the Republican National Committee. He came to the Lincoln house to explain his strategy.

"The real purpose of this meeting is to set the place and time for our convention," he told them. "Abraham, when do you think is the best time?"

"It must certainly be after the Democrats' Charleston fandango."

"Agreed. Seward, Chase, Cameron and the others who have the best chances will all be angling to have the convention held in their home states. I'll step up guilelessly and say, 'As Illinois has no candidate, why not come to neutral ground and hold the convention in Chicago?'"

The next morning a letter arrived from Iowa which read: "Part of the Iowa delegation will support you for president if you are a candidate, and all of us will support you for the vice-presidency."

"Looks like I may have to be elected vice-president to get into the Senate," Abraham commented.

"You're not equipped by temperament to sit up on the dais making parliamentarian decisions, with no voice," replied Mary.

"But what a wonderful chance to bang with my gavel and say, 'Senator Douglas, you and your squatter sovereignty are out of order.'"

Her eyes flashed fire.

"The only way you can silence Stephen Douglas is to defeat him. If you can't have the first place, you shan't have the second!"

They continued their travels, Abraham taking her to St. Louis where she spent a week visiting with four of her cousins while he went to Kansas, reaching there the day John Brown was executed in Virginia by the government for his raid on Harper's Ferry, in which some seventeen of his own men had been killed in what the south had interpreted as an abolitionist slave uprising. Kansas' political nerves were on edge; it was Abraham's task to convince them that the Republicans were not abolitionists, that they did not approve of John Brown's acts of violence. While she enjoyed a delightful week in the home of Judge John C. Richardson, Abraham made his way across the raw and icy prairies in open buggies, speaking to a handful of people in hotel dining rooms.

When they returned to Springfield Abraham settled in front of the living-room fire, which he kept blazing hot in an effort to forget the cold of Kansas, and set down the autobiography which their friend had asked for a full year before. She was disappointed when he handed her the slim manuscript.

"There seems so little of it, Abraham."

"Well, there's not much of it for the reason I suppose that there is not much of me. If anything is to be made out of it I want it to be modest."

"I know modesty is considered a virtue . . . but couldn't you puff yourself up just the tiniest bit?"

She rose early on New Year's, for she was receiving; as she went into the parlor to fill the silver containers with candies, almonds, Brazil nuts and filberts, she looked out the window and saw Abraham walking up and down the plank walk which connected their house with the Smiths', the Smith baby on his left shoulder, composing the speech he had been invited to give at Henry Ward Beecher's famous church in Brooklyn, New York, in February.

As she walked into the kitchen to supervise the making of the traditional escalloped oysters, there was a jangling of the doorbell. She went to the door to find her cousin Logan wrapped in a huge formless overcoat, his white hair standing up as though frozen.

"I can see Abraham's walking the baby," he commented, "that means he's working on his New York speech."

"I hope he finishes soon: Mrs. Smith is beginning to worry about whether the baby should be kept out so long in the cold air."

"Mary, I'm not able to talk to Abraham about Billy Herndon; I don't like the man any more than you do. But someone's got to stop him. Abraham's the only one who can do it."

She stared at her cousin.

"Stop him from what, Cousin Logan?"

"From creating a rupture between Norman Judd and Abraham. He's making the charge that Judd played Abraham false last year, that because he also led the movement that elected Trumbull, he's out to deceive us again. Herndon says that he's backing a minority movement for Lyman for the presidency, and will emerge from the convention with Trumbull controlling the delegation."

"But Mr. Judd has gone off to New York to try to get the convention for Illinois so that Abraham will have local backing. Why is Mr. Herndon doing this?"

Logan's eyes squeezed half shut.

"My guess? Jealousy. He thinks he should be Abraham's campaign manager. He has already caused considerable ill feeling between Republicans here."

"That's no way to start the new year," she exclaimed.

She seized upon Abraham the moment he came onto the back porch. He listened carefully to the charge, replying:

"Judd did vote for Trumbull against me, and though I've said a thousand times that was no injustice to me, I cannot change the fact and compel people to cease speaking of it. I have constantly labored to have all recollection of it dropped."

"While your charming partner is working equally hard in the opposite direction. Abraham, you've got to tell him to stop this kind of thing."

"Right this very moment? It's mighty cold out."

"Not too cold to walk the Smith baby for an hour! I want our new year to start right."

When he returned he told her, "Billy said he didn't do it; and that he'll never do it again."

By noon the house was thronged; many of their friends and Abraham's political supporters had come in from the surrounding towns to be with them. She was gowned in poplin and Paris velvet of somber rose spotted with gold. The happiness of the day suffused her with gaiety and energy; having just given William a ninth birthday celebration, with sixty boys and girls over for the afternoon, she had thought she would never be able to stare another party in the face. But a party for political purposes was different.

The last two evenings before Abraham left for New York he invited Judge Samuel Treat to come play chess with him. While he played he whistled "Dixie's Land" quietly and tunelessly, to which Treat was apparently accustomed from his games with Abraham in the Melvin drugstore on the square. Abraham played mechanically, rarely attacking, concentrating on his defense and on his New York speech, going over it line for line, testing the sentiment, weighing the judgment, simplifying the prose . . . even though the entire speech was already written.

Funny thing about that speech, she reflected, it was the only one that had not been compounded of a hundred scraps of paper dumped from his hat; this one he had thought out for months and then written as though from the scroll of his mind.

11

THE March 1, 1860, New York *Tribune* reached Springfield with startling news: Abraham's speech had at the last moment been sponsored by the Young Men's Central Republican Union and been transferred from the Brooklyn church to Cooper Union on Manhattan, gathering place of the city's intelligentsia. On the stage behind Abraham sat William Cullen Bryant, the east's literary idol and editor of the New York *Evening Post*; David Dudley Field, the celebrated New York lawyer, who escorted him onto the stage; and Horace Greeley of the *Tribune*, who thus publicly avowed that he would not support New York Senator Seward for the presidency. Greeley wrote: "Since the days of Clay and Webster no man has spoken to a larger assemblage of the intellect and mental culture of our city." The *Tribune* reporter, Noah Brooks, said, ". . . the tones, the gestures, the kindling eye, and the mirth-provoking look defy the reporter's skill. No man ever before made such an impression on his first appeal to a New York audience." These reports compensated for the snide remark of the *Illinois State Register* the day before, on the subject of Abraham's trip east:

Subject not known. Consideration $200. and expenses. Object, presidential capital. Effect, disappointment.

Within a few hours her house was thronged with friends and political associates, and she was serving up food and drink for the men and their wives who kept the two parlors and sitting room full, poring over the five full columns in the *Tribune*, new people coming in as fast as others departed. There was a glow over the men, as though Abraham had done them proud. Plainly he had taken the town: it was a definitive answer to Stephen Douglas's article in *Harper's* in which he had attempted to document the constitutionality of slavery by proving that the founding fathers approved it.

Abraham gave the results of his researches these past years: of the thirty-nine fathers of the Constitution, a clear majority of twenty-three had stated that the federal government had the right to control slavery in the territories; and the other sixteen, though they left no official record, contained such well-known anti-slavery men as Benjamin Franklin, Alexander Hamilton and Gouverneur Morris.

As those fathers marked it, so let it be again marked, as an evil not to be extended, but to be tolerated and protected only because of and so far as its actual presence among us makes that toleration and protection a necessity. Let all the guaranties those fathers gave it, be, not grudgingly, but fully and fairly maintained. For this Republicans contend, and with this, so far as I know or believe, they will be content. . . .

Let us do nothing through passion and ill temper. Even though the southern people will not so much as listen to us, let us calmly consider their demands . . . let us determine, if we can, what will satisfy them. . . .

Neither let us be slandered from our duty by false accusations against us, nor frightened from it by menaces of destruction to the Government nor of dungeons to ourselves. LET US HAVE FAITH THAT RIGHT MAKES MIGHT, AND IN THAT FAITH, LET US, TO THE END, DARE TO DO OUR DUTY AS WE UNDERSTAND IT.

The following day he had left New York for Exeter to visit with Robert, then he was coming straight home. Instead, as she learned from hurried notes and newspaper reports, his trip became a triumphal tour through New England with a dozen speaking invitations pouring in for every one he could fill: Providence, Concord, Manchester, Dover, Hartford, New Haven, Bridgeport. Apparently only Abraham was not reading the newspapers; his letter from Exeter said:

I have been unable to escape this toil. If I had foreseen it, I think I would not have come east at all. The speech at New York, being within my calculation before I started, went off passably well and gave me no trouble whatever. The difficulty was to make nine others, before reading audiences who had already seen all my ideas in print.

Because of his letter she imagined that when the Great Western train pulled in he would be exhausted; on the contrary he was in the best of health and spirits, bringing gratifying stories of Robert's progress at Exeter, and the flattering news that he had been offered ten thousand dollars a year by the New York Central to become the railroad's attorney. When Mary asked what he had answered, he put on a mock-serious face and, exaggerating his own nasal drawl, said:

"What would I do with ten thousand a year? It would ruin my family to have that much income."

She shrugged one plump shoulder.

"I think we could manage to withstand the ruination. But why should you become the New York Central's man when you are doing so well as your own man? That's really what you thought, isn't it?"

The next morning she read short stories to William and Tad from a book called *The Lost and Found, or Life Among the Poor*, which had been presented to Abraham by the author, when Abraham had spoken to a group of abandoned boys and girls at the House of Industry at Five Points. Finishing the last paragraph of "The Little Street Sweeper" as Abraham came in from a caucus, she laid the volume aside and asked how their chances looked. He squinted the wrinkles around his gray eyes before answering.

"Our name is new in the field, and we're not the first choice of a great many. I've tried all along to give no offense to the others, to leave them in a mood to come to us, if they should be compelled to give up their first love. Senator Seward is the very best candidate we could have for the north of Illinois, and the very worst for the south. Bates of Missouri would be the best candidate for the south of Illinois, and the worst for the north . . ."

"Ergo, since the Republicans must win Illinois to win the election, the Honorable A. Lincoln is the best choice for the whole of Illinois?"

"Exactly the right sentiment, Mrs. Honorable Lincoln."

Because of the question Abraham had asked Stephen Douglas in Freeport, which many Suckers still said cost Abraham the senatorship, the senator was having serious trouble with his party; for when he answered Abraham by saying that "Emphatically in my opinion the people of a territory can, by lawful means, exclude slavery from their limits," he had alienated the deep south states . . . as Mary now perceived Abraham had known all along he must.

When the Democratic convention opened in Charleston, South Carolina, in April, the southern bloc demanded that a powerful pro-slavery plank be adopted before a candidate be named. When the northern Democrats refused to pass this kind of platform, eight cotton states withdrew from the convention, naming another time and place to meet and nominate an all-south, all-slavery candidate. Though Douglas had no competition for the nomination, the withdrawal of the southern delegates made it impossible for him to get the requisite two-thirds vote, and the convention adjourned.

"If the south puts up its own candidate," observed Abraham with excitement, "he will be the equivalent of Fillmore in the last election: Fillmore split the Republican vote and elected Buchanan. The south will split the Democratic vote, and elect . . . the Republican! This battle of 1860 is going to be worth a hundred of that '58 campaign!"

At the beginning of May she went with him to Decatur for the state convention. They found the town thronged with delegates, most of them dressed in new broadcloth suits and silk hats which they were trying out for the Chicago convention. When she came across her cousin Logan wearing a new silk hat specially made for him by Adams, Springfield's best hatter, she realized this show was no laughing matter.

They were late entering the dark flimsy tent, built in the shape of a wigwam. The crowd was so dense that half a dozen men raised Abraham up on their shoulders and carried him toward the speaker's stand. At that moment the chairman announced that an old Democrat by the name of Hanks wished to contribute something to the meeting. The delegates cried, "Receive it!" and down the main aisle came two men, each carrying a split rail held high in the air, and on top of it a painted banner which read:

ABRAHAM LINCOLN
The Rail Candidate for President in 1860
—

Two Rails from a Lot of 3,000 Made in 1830 by Thos. Hanks and Abe Lincoln—Whose Father was the First Pioneer of Macon County

She saw Abraham flush and look plagued: a Hanks was like an uninvited guest at the wedding.

The delegates knew nothing of these niceties: they jumped and screamed and howled, throwing their hats and canes, books and papers in the air until part of the roof awning fell down on their heads. It was the wildest fifteen minutes she could remember; when they were over the wigwam was a wreck. But not the delegates: they resolved that "Abraham Lincoln is the choice of the Republican party of Illinois for the presidency, and the delegates from this state are instructed to use all honorable means to secure his nomination by the Chicago convention, and to vote as a unit for him."

There were five days before the convention in Chicago officially opened, five days that passed for Mary in a phantasmagoria of rumors, reports, hopes and fears, estimates, analyses and prayer: Senator William H. Seward of New York, admittedly the leader of the party, had behind him a formidable political machine run by Thurlow Weed, the most astute political boss in the country. Simon Cameron, Republican boss of Pennsylvania, also had unlimited money and resourcefulness, not to mention the powerful Pennsylvania delegation, but his financial and political influence had been acquired at the expense of his reputation. John McLean, Supreme Court justice, had many admirers, but was not seventy-five too old for the presidency? Salmon P. Chase, former governor and senator from Ohio, was reputed to be an abolitionist; Edward Bates of Missouri was respected as a conservative, but Missouri was a southern state. . . .

Abraham? He was called a favorite son, a dark horse; yet could any man be considered a dark horse who had been declared available by such newspapers as the Chicago *Daily Democrat* and the New York *Herald?* The delegations of Cameron and Bates, among others, were reputed to be split; the Illinois delegation contained men like Stephen T. Logan, Leonard Swett, Jesse K. Dubois, Norman B. Judd, David Davis, Orville H. Browning, Gustave Koerner, clever, indefatigable and dedicated to Abraham.

Again the house was filled with people coming and going; from six in the morning until well past midnight the Lincoln home needed only a canvas top to resemble a wigwam. Mary was untiring, infusing everyone with her own radiance.

The convention opened officially in Chicago on May 16, 1860. Every hour brought the Lincolns a new telegram:

WE ARE QUIET BUT MOVING HEAVEN AND EARTH NOTHING WILL BEAT US BUT OLD FOGY POLITICIANS THE HEART OF THE DELEGATES ARE WITH US

PROSPECTS FAIR FRIENDS AT WORK NIGHT AND DAY

DONT BE FRIGHTENED KEEP COOL THINGS IS WORKING

AM VERY HOPEFUL DONT BE EXCITED NEARLY DEAD WITH FATIGUE TELEGRAPH OR WRITE HERE VERY LITTLE

"I am not frightened," Mary commented to Abraham. "But just how does one keep cool?"

They talked late the night before the balloting was to begin, not about politics or the nomination, but reminiscently of their lives together. She fell asleep for perhaps an hour at a stretch; each time she awakened and went into Abraham's room she found him lying with his eyes wide open, staring at the dark ceiling.

They arose early, had a light breakfast and sat together on the outside porch. The morning was bright and warm, the neighborhood beginning to stir. There was a feeling of tenseness in the air. At eight o'clock Abraham put on his coat.

"I guess I'll practice a little law."

"Can you possibly concentrate?"

"Practice makes perfect: a poor pun, but my mind is in Chicago. I'll stop in and see James Conkling; he came back from there last night."

"You'll let me know as soon as there is word . . . one way or the other?"

He kissed her on the cheek.

"I'll bring you the news myself."

She went upstairs, began to strip off the linens, turn mattresses, remake the beds. She knew by the side glances the maid threw at her that she was awkward in her movements, yet she felt calm inside herself, particularly after she went into the guest bedroom where she kept her sewing materials, picked up a dress she had been making, and bent over the intricate work of sewing black beads onto a ball gown.

Her mind plowed backward through furrows of time and memory: she was standing on the bridge at the bottom of the Todd garden in Lexington gazing down into the clear water of the brook while Sandy McDonald was asking her to marry him and offering her the management of his plantation. If she had married Sandy and gone to Mississippi she would now be an ultra-slavery woman hating the north, the Republican party and Abraham Lincoln. Her grandmother Parker had said, "Out there in that wide circle of Kentucky bluegrass, Mary, there is a mate for you." But she had left Lexington and come to Springfield, to a heated political argument in a hot, crowded room, and watched two long legs dangle downward from the ceiling and Abraham Lincoln drop, apparently from heaven, into her life.

Her sister Elizabeth had favored Stephen Douglas, had pleaded with her to give it time so that her liking for Stephen might turn into love. "He's going far," Elizabeth had said. If she had married Stephen Douglas she would be campaigning for popular sovereignty and the Democrats. But she had known that she loved Abraham Lincoln, that he was the man and his was the life she had been searching for. The Edwardses had cried, "He's the last man in the world for you to love, this unpolished diamond; he has the least to offer."

The road had been hard, right from the beginning; there had been years that were barren of meaning and happiness; but others that had been rich in work and companionship. In some ways he still was an unpolished diamond, but what she had to offer from her own high finish she had given wholeheartedly.

She had not heard the front door close, nor his step on the stairs; now suddenly as she looked up from her beading he was standing over her, his face pale yet exalted. There was a telegram sheet in his hand. She gazed at him for a long moment without speaking. He reached down and lifted her up out of the chair, the dress and the hundreds of black beads spilling noiselessly onto the carpeted floor.

"We have the nomination, Mary . . . on the third ballot. I was in the *Journal* office when the telegram arrived. The message reads:

WE DID IT, GLORY TO GOD

I said, 'There's a little woman up on Eighth Street who will be interested in this message,' and I came right home to you."

Cannon started firing from the square, dozens of them, then a hundred bells began ringing all over the town. In the distance men were shouting and blowing bugles. Yet she hardly heard them because of the pounding of her own heart as she was held powerfully against him, his lips on hers.

And she relived their first embrace almost twenty years before. She had known then what she knew now, nor had it taken a hundred cannon or a hundred ringing bells to tell her. No one else had known about Abraham because no one else had loved him. Love had told her everything, with the end implicit in the beginning. She had fallen in love with the last man that any other woman wanted, for she had known him to be the first and finest of them all.

Book VII

MRS. PRESIDENT LINCOLN

1

SHE stood in the sitting room by the circular worktable on which there were trays of sandwiches and two pitchers on a white cloth. Across the hall in the parlor Abraham was replying to the notification committee that had come directly from the Chicago convention. That afternoon a large basket of champagne had arrived from friends to be used as refreshment for the committee.

"We've served no liquor in this house for sixteen years," said Abraham, "and we shouldn't change our habits now. Ice water will refresh their thirst."

"Ice water! My Kentucky ancestors will turn over in their graves!"

Outside the sitting-room window she could see rockets exploding in the sky and bonfires blazing on every corner. Apparently this was true throughout the north, for when her cousin Logan had come from the depot to embrace them, he exclaimed:

"I thought I'd get some sleep on the train last night, but cannon kept firing all along the line and it was like traveling in the sun of high noon, there were so many tar barrels burning."

He had brought back an interesting piece of news from the Chicago Wigwam: Cassius Clay's name had been put in nomination for vice-president to run with Abraham, and had garnered over a hundred votes on the first ballot, only to be defeated by Hannibal Hamlin of Maine because it did not seem advisable to have two native Kentuckians on the same ticket. Abraham was amused.

"Too bad Clay didn't get it, we could have called it the Mary Todd ticket."

"Tease me if you want," said Mary, the excitement of the day filling her with gaiety, "but as Grandmother Parker observed, I've got good judgment . . . in horseflesh."

There was a hubbub of voices in the parlor as Abraham finished his brief acceptance speech. She heard him remark to Mr. Kelley of Pennsylvania, "You are a tall man, Judge. What is your height?"

"Six feet three."

"I beat you. I am six feet four without my high-heeled boots."

"Pennsylvania bows to Illinois," replied the committeeman. "I am glad that we have found a candidate for the presidency whom we can look up to."

There was a burst of laughter, then Abraham announced:

"Mrs. Lincoln will be pleased to see you, gentlemen. You will find her in the sitting room."

Mary smoothed the neck of her dress, smiled warmly as she extended her hand. Having been wined and dined at the Chenery House, the committeemen partook sparingly of her refreshments and stayed only a few moments, but she made the most of the time, speaking with each one, letting them know that the Lincoln home would be an open house for the campaign. As Judge Kelley of the booming voice went out the front door they heard him remark:

"Well, we might have done a more brilliant thing, but we could hardly have done a better thing."

She was happy: they had won their first acceptance . . . on ice water.

The nomination made little difference to Abraham except that he wore his Sunday suit every day and bought a new hat before the old one had properly worn out; but her days were changed totally. Visitors began ringing the doorbell at eight in the morning; she had to be up at six to work with the new servants, including Frances Affonsa, who was now the major-domo, Irish Mary, who had returned bringing a brawny cousin to help, and a silver-haired, quiet-mannered Negro by the name of William, who tended the door. Everyone present at mealtime was invited to sit down at the family board. Several times a week she had to give a more formal party, when Thurlow Weed, Seward's manager, came to Springfield, or the governor of Pennsylvania, or Carl Schurz, the leader of the politically important group of native-born Germans, whom Mary made comfortable in the guest room overlooking Eighth Street.

Since the last of the guests did not leave until midnight she had only the two early morning hours to get the house cleaned, fresh flowers put in the vases, shopping lists assembled, breakfast out of the way and herself dressed to receive the daylong jam of relatives, friends and political admirers. Her sister Elizabeth appeared puzzled but pleased for her; Ninian was restrained because he had committed himself to support Stephen Douglas; Cousin Stuart was proud for the family but confided that he too could not support Abraham's sectional party; Dr. Wallace was deeply gratified, but her sister Frances's congratulations were cool; Ann sent a message that she knew Sister Mary would be busy with guests and therefore would appreciate not having Ann to bother with. Mary noticed that the more distant the relationship the purer seemed to be the congratulations. Her most important assistance came from her cousin Elizabeth Todd Grimsley, the older of Dr. John Todd's two daughters, who had been a bridesmaid at her wedding; Lizzie was tall, with willowy grace, the happiest of all her feminine kin at the Lincolns' good fortune. She shopped for the vast quantities of food that were needed, accomplished the delicate task of cleaning house without sweeping under the soles of people's feet.

The campaign sprang into existence full-blooded and full-blown: a wigwam was built, prototype of thousands throughout the north, marching groups and military companies called Wide-Awakes paraded with kerosene torches, wearing red military caps and blue capes of shiny leather to catch the dripping pitch. The enthusiasm and the crowds throughout the villages and cities surpassed the Fremont campaign of four years before; from the very outset the upsurge for Abraham and the Republicans was infused with a religious fervor amounting to exultation.

For the first time since she had known Stephen Douglas his Democratic organization broke down, and all because of the question Abraham had asked him at Freeport two years before, the cotton south walking out of the Charleston convention because Douglas had replied to Abraham that it *was* possible for the people of a territory to exclude slavery within its limits prior to the formation of a state constitution.

By the time the Democrats assembled in Baltimore a month later, the northern portion to nominate Stephen Douglas, the southern to nominate Vice-President John C. Breckinridge on a slavery platform, the Republicans had had a full month to organize their local, state and national committees, collect funds and flood the north with pictures and stories of *Old Abe, Honest Abe, The Rail Splitter*, and *Friend of the Poor*. Douglas was further bedeviled by the formation of a fourth party, declaring for Union and peace, which nominated John Bell of Tennessee and was drawing support from Tennessee, Kentucky and Virginia. Stephen started on a whirlwind tour that took him from Maine to North Carolina in the hopes of reconsolidating the Democrats.

Abraham remained quietly at home, doing no speaking or campaigning, as was the custom. He spent his days at the governor's office, which had been loaned to him for the campaign, greeting the hundreds of people who poured into Springfield to meet and confer with him. Cousin Logan had arranged this, and Mary was as grateful to him for getting the campaign headquarters out of the filthy Lincoln-Herndon office as she was for the five thousand dollars he raised among ten Springfield supporters to pay their expenses.

William and Tad were curious to see their father behind the governor's desk, so she took them up to the second floor of the Capitol, then along the dark narrow hallway where the crowds pressed back to give them passage. The governor's room was about fifteen by twenty-five feet with a highly colored Brussels carpet and a gas chandelier. In one corner sat a portrait painter trying to get a likeness of Abraham down in oil. At a small desk in another corner under a banjo clock, with stacks of mail before him, sat John G. Nicolay, twenty-eight years old, slender, German-born secretary, impeccably dressed and undisturbed by the motley group of politicians, rough fellows with hats on and lighted segars, pantaloons tucked in boots, others with hickory shirts, some wanting interviews, some just come to shake hands or stare.

She watched Abraham from the doorway, noting how he greeted the visitors, treating each one courteously without giving the information or political commitment they sought. Two youths peered about the room anxiously, then made their way to Abraham.

"Father sent us into town to see if the report that you had been poisoned was true," the older one blurted out. "Dad says you must look out, eat nothing only what your Old Woman cooks for you."

Abraham stole a mischievous glance at Mary, who was dressed in a soft summer-blue dress with her hair brushed straight back under a fashionable leghorn hat, her spirits high. When the boys had left, she murmured:

"I guess you didn't see that article in the New York *Times* today? It states categorically that I am fifteen years younger than my husband."

There was no way to avoid the threats of secession which grew more clangorous every day, leading southern newspapers maintaining that Abraham's election would mean the dismemberment of the Union, charging the north with fomenting "a gigantic servile uprising, when at a given signal the slaves would rise against their masters, burn towns and dwellings, murder their owners and families." Mary knew well the inordinate pride and hot temper of the southern people: did she not share in these qualities? Behind her hours of work and her hope for their success was an omnipresent anxiousness over what the south might do.

"Couldn't you make one last appeal, Abraham?" she asked. "Assure them that you have no intention of interfering with slavery where it exists . . ."

"Mary, what good would it do for me to write these sentiments again to southern newspapers which never bothered to print my speeches in the first place, or when they did, distorted them for their own purpose? A repetition would give an appearance of weakness or cowardice."

Yet if he was refusing to speak, he was watching every move of the campaign, writing to his running mate Hannibal Hamlin in Maine when he heard that there was danger of losing two congressmen in that state: "Such a result would put us on the downhill track, and probably ruin us on the main turn in November. You must not allow it"; and to a Pennsylvania party man, "I am slow to listen to criminations among friends, and never espouse their quarrels on either side."

They had come through some twenty years of politics without receiving personal vituperation; now the floodgates were open and in the opposition press Abraham was called a nullity, an ignoramus, a third-rate country lawyer who could not speak correct grammar, who made coarse jokes, was not a gentleman, looked like a gorilla and walked like a baboon. Mary took none of this seriously, but she resented the high glee in which his supporters throughout the country called him *Old Abe*. When she told Abraham this he replied:

"It's good politics, makes them feel familiar and friendly with me; just so long as they don't start calling my Old Woman Old Mary . . ."

She wrinkled the skin over the ridge of her nose.

"Abraham, what will I be when you are president?"

"Why, the same old fool you've always been."

Red spots flared high on her forehead. She was about to burst out in indignation when she remembered herself whispering through the front window, "Come in, you old fool, don't you know your own house when you see it?" They laughed until the tears streamed down their faces.

The morning of August 8, the day set for the great Illinois rally, dawned hot and clear. It was reported that there were over fifty thousand Republicans in town, come not only from Illinois but from a half dozen neighboring states as well. From her porch Mary saw hundreds of people asleep on the surrounding lawns. At the Fair Grounds there were five separate stands for speaking and gigantic barbecue pits.

"Remember that big Harrison rally back in '40, Abraham, when you were in charge of the pits?" she asked. "You said you might not be a good politician but you were a good chef. To the best of my knowledge you haven't cooked anything since."

In the afternoon she stood with Abraham on the front porch as the parade started past their house. She was dressed in cool cotton and soft kid slippers, Abraham in a white linen suit and black tie. A hundred of their friends and neighbors crowded on the small lawn and steps around them to watch the eight-mile-long procession. First came the companies of Wide-Awakes, spaced between a dozen Illinois bands. Horse-drawn floats depicted a log cabin of the kind in which Abraham had been born, its sides covered with coonskins and deer hides; a complete flatboat, replica of the one in which Abraham had taken produce to New Orleans; a cabin built entirely of split rails and carrying the legend *Vote for Lincoln the Rail Splitter*. Glee clubs chanted:

> "Ain't I glad I joined the Republicans,
> Joined the Republicans,
> Joined the Republicans,
> Ain't I glad I joined the Republicans,
> Down in Illinois!"

The campaign pitch never lessened.

The night before the election, quiet fell, the last of the visitors vanished. Mary let the servants go home, served a simple supper in the kitchen and persuaded the boys to get into bed on the grounds that they would want to be up early the next day. Abraham went down to his office for a final conference with his Illinois committeemen.

When he left she felt alone; after months of high energy and high confidence there came a giant hand striking out of the night, suffocating her. What if they had been deluding themselves again, as they had so often in the past? Suppose they were roundly beaten tomorrow, as Stephen Douglas had beaten them for twenty years? Suppose all the people they had counted on abandoned them, as Mr. Strunk of Kankakee had in 1855 after promising to walk a hundred miles to elect Abraham? Suppose some of the seemingly safe states, fearful of war . . . ?

She undressed, went into Abraham's room and lighted the small lamp by his bed. She knew neither of them would sleep that night.

At the breakfast table she asked:

"What are the soothsayers soothsaying to you this morning, Abraham?"

Good humor was lurking about his clear gray eyes, a smile moved down the long, curved furrows of his cheeks and twitched his capacious mouth.

"If you promise not to tell any of the voters today, I would rather have a full term in the Senate, where I would feel more able to discharge the duties required, and where there is more chance to make reputation and less danger of losing it, than four years of the presidency."

Lizzie came to help her pass the time, never once touching upon the subject of the millions of votes being cast in the tensest election since the founding of the nation. At midafternoon Mary dressed the boys in their dark wool suits and walked them downtown to see the crowds thronging the square, the state house, the sidewalks, the restaurants and the shops, a subdued hush over them all. The largest group stood in front of the telegraph office though there could be no significant reports until night.

She had been invited to join the Republican ladies at Watson's Saloon where they were preparing what they hoped would be a celebration supper when the news came over the wires that Illinois, Indiana, Pennsylvania and New York were safe for Lincoln. There were at least a hundred women in Watson's when she reached there, the big hall brilliantly lighted. She slipped an apron over her cassimere gown and pitched in with the others.

Abraham had gone to the telegraph office to read the bulletins as they came in. At last it was reported that Philadelphia had gone Republican by five thousand votes; Pennsylvania was safe. Then Abraham carried Springfield and Illinois, though he lost to Douglas in Sangamon County. Indiana also was counted secure. It would take only the vote of New York to ensure victory. Mary worked frantically to keep her tension under control.

At midnight Abraham came into Watson's. He reached out a hand for hers, while he shook his head indicating that they still were awaiting the final word.

A few minutes later a messenger from the telegraph office came running. Outside a tremendous shout went up. Mary knew even before Abraham, pale and solemn, passed her the telegram that he had won.

When she looked up from the dispatch he took her in his arms.

2

THIS time when she and Abraham went to Washington they would not have to go to a boardinghouse, or occupy a back room overlooking pigsties and privies; this time she would not have to search the city to learn which was the best section, then locate a house the rent of which she could manage out of her savings, only to have Abraham refuse to move in. This time she would be neither snubbed nor, worse, ignored by the entrenched southern society of the city who had given her no opportunity to get the toe of a slipper inside the door of their rigorous regime.

She caught Abraham in a quiet moment, sat him on the parlor sofa.

"Abraham, since we will be away from Springfield for eight years, don't you think it would be wise to sell the house?"

He bounded up as though angry, then gazed at her with an amused glint.

"Mary, don't you know that presidents are elected for a four-year term?"

"Presidents Washington, Jefferson, Madison, Monroe and Jackson all served two terms. James Conkling says he can get us over four thousand dollars for the house, furnished. Then we wouldn't have to worry about repairs . . ."

"But, Mary, this is our home. The only home I've ever had! I love it. Besides, I've been offered three hundred and fifty dollars a year rental for it, unfurnished. Then, when our work is done, we will have a place to come back to."

"To Springfield? Surely you will want to live in a wider world after the years in the capital?"

"If during all those years in Washington I have no homeplace to think of, I'll be like a man dispossessed. When I went up to the office today I told Billy to let our shingle hang there undisturbed, that if I live I'm coming back and we'll go right on practicing law as if nothing had ever happened."

She was relieved to learn that he was not taking Herndon to Washington.

"The New York Central offered you ten thousand dollars a year to be their counsel, and that was before you were nominated. What would you be worth in New York or Boston after being Chief Executive?"

He continued to go to the governor's office during the day to take the press of people off the house, for the most part crowds of complete strangers come to ask him for a job with the government, but also Republican party leaders come to study the final election returns: while Abraham had received a large majority of the states' electoral votes, he had received only 1,866,452 popular votes, considerably less than a majority of the vote cast, Douglas, Breckinridge and Bell amassing 2,815,617 votes among them.

In their late evening hours together he answered letters from editors, loyal southerners, radical abolitionists, conservatives alarmed over the preservation of the Union.

"It's the cabinet that's worrying me," he confided. "When the convention was meeting I telegraphed Chicago: 'Make no contracts that will bind me.' When I was nominated I thought I was free; now I find that they have gambled me all around, bought and sold me a hundred times. I cannot begin to fill the pledges made in my name: Simon Cameron for the Pennsylvania vote, Caleb Smith for the Indiana vote . . ."

Mary sat opposite him, writing to everyone whom Abraham said she might invite to the inauguration: her stepmother Betsy, her brothers Levi, George and Alexander, her sister Katherine, her sister Emilie and Ben Hardin Helm, all from Lexington; her brothers David and Samuel, in business together in New Orleans; her married sisters Elodie and Martha with their husbands from Alabama; her sister Margaret Kellogg and her husband from Cincinnati. Here in Springfield she invited Elizabeth and Ninian and their two daughters, Elizabeth accepting for herself and the girls, Ninian declining; Lizzie Grimsley, Frances and William Wallace, William accepting and Frances declining. Abraham asked Dr. Wallace to attend the family on the inaugural train; Elizabeth, her daughters and Lizzie would join them in New York. Mary would keep as many with her for the first week of receptions as the White House guest rooms could hold. She passed by her sister Ann, who had not called at the Lincoln house during the campaign or in the days following the election.

Then on December 20 South Carolina seceded from the Union, an act she had been threatening since 1830. In the early weeks of the New Year the legislatures of Mississippi, Florida, Alabama, Georgia, Louisiana and later Texas voted themselves out of the Union, and representatives of the seven seceded states met in Montgomery, Alabama, to form the Confederate States of America, elect Jefferson Davis as president, set up its own government.

Though for four years the southern press had warned the north that it would secede if a Republican were elected, the actual breakup of the Union after eighty years plunged the house on Eighth Street into deepest gloom.

As March 4 grew close there were increasing threats that Abraham never would be inaugurated, that he would be assassinated before he could leave Springfield, that if he ever reached Washington he would be shot down before he could take the oath of office. One morning he received a box containing the mummy of a Negro; Mary was the recipient of an oil painting showing Abraham with a rope around his neck, his feet chained, his body tarred and feathered, hanging from a tree.

Depressed as they were over the turn of events, she was determined that they would not be intimidated. She would not leave Springfield without giving a farewell reception for their faithful friends in Illinois. Abraham brightened when she told him of her plan.

"Yes, do it, Mary. Then when it's over we'll hold a private sale and get rid of some of the furniture. It will be kind of a farewell to this house, too."

While he went to Coles County to bid his stepmother good-bye and to lay flowers on his father's grave, Mary sent out a thousand invitations to their party. On the evening of the reception a group of Springfield women arrived a little before seven, bringing with them a highly ornamented table-style Wheeler and Wilson sewing machine. Mary was touched by their generosity.

She and Abraham stood side by side, Abraham receiving their guests as they entered, the women admiring Mary's white antique silk with full train and small French lace collar. Robert, who had passed his examination and entered Harvard and come home to join the inaugural train, gave his hand to his father, saying, "Good evening, Mr. Lincoln," in reply to which Abraham gave him a gentle slap. By midnight seven hundred well-wishers had thronged the Lincoln home; even their friends among the Democrats put aside their political differences and came to wish the Lincolns Godspeed.

The next morning she learned that her husband's Godspeed and hers were not to be enjoyed on the same train. Because of the threats of violence he had been advised not to take her or the younger boys with him. They would all meet at the Astor House in New York in about ten days. She was furious.

"I have my weaknesses, Mr. Lincoln, but cowardice doesn't happen to be one of them."

"I am not the one who is afraid for you, Mary, it is General Winfield Scott, head of the army. He is responsible for our safety."

"If anyone were intending violence against you, Abraham, wouldn't they be less likely to try it if they knew that your family was along? Shame on you, agreeing to deprive Willie and Tad of this inaugural trip."

Abraham sighed. "There will be excitement enough for all of us in the next four years, never fear."

She threw her head back, fire in her eyes.

"Once I let the army turn me into a delicate old lady who can't be exposed to danger, I'll not be my own mistress any part of the four years ahead."

But in the end she was defeated by the War Department. She decided to go by train to St. Louis the very day Abraham went east, and do some shopping; she had no desire to shop in St. Louis, it would be a face-saving gesture. Friends and neighbors had bought most of the big pieces of furniture: the wardrobe, whatnot, chairs. The rest of their furniture and boxes of papers were stored. She dismissed Frances Affonsa with an affectionate kiss on the cheek, but not until the Lincolns had supplied her with a wedding dress for her coming marriage.

Abraham leased the house, then engaged a suite of rooms at the Chenery House, each with its wood-burning stove and newly installed pull-cords for the servants. On the evening before their departure he roped their big trunks in the lobby. She asked with one eyebrow raised:

"Are you sure this is proper procedure for the president of the United States?"

"President-elect; I promise not to do it any more after March fourth."

She slept fitfully; the day after tomorrow was Abraham's birthday, and she would not be with him.

The dawn was a coal-ash gray sifting down a shaken grate. Breakfast was brought up at seven o'clock and set out in the middle room. Robert felt important because, "I'm going along to be blown up with Father, while you little ones are left behind." Mary said it was too early in the morning for macabre humor, but Abraham laughed. Neither of them could eat, they merely sipped strong coffee. At seven-thirty their carriage was announced.

303

A fine rain was falling. Abraham was cold and pale. He wore a gray wool shawl around his neck and covering his shoulders. When they reached the small brick depot of the Great Western station they were surprised to find several hundred people assembled. The locomotive whistle made its sharp tooting noise. Tad and William clambered up their father's legs and nestled one in each arm. She walked with Abraham to where a little special made up of a smoke-black engine, a brick-red coal car, a baggage car and single coach of the same color with a rear platform protected by an iron grating, was waiting for Abraham to board.

He held her to him for a moment, then went up the steps and stood at the rear railing. Umbrellas were raised against the cold drizzle. He gazed down at Mary and William and Tad, then past them to the silent faces of the friends come to bid him good-bye.

The train was ready to leave. Abraham took off his hat, tightened the shawl about his shoulders, holding it together with his left hand on his breast, began to speak in a quiet voice:

"No one, not in my situation, can appreciate my feeling of sadness at this parting. To this place, and the kindness of these people, I owe everything. Here I have lived a quarter of a century, and have passed from a young to an old man. Here my children have been born, and one is buried. I now leave, not knowing when, or whether ever, I may return, with a task before me greater than that which rested upon Washington. Without the assistance of that Divine Being, who ever attended him, I cannot succeed. With that assistance I cannot fail. Trusting in Him, who can go with me, and remain with you and be everywhere for good, let us confidently hope that all will yet be well. To His care commending you, as I hope in your prayers you will commend me, I bid you an affectionate farewell."

The train pulled away. A path was opened for her to the carriage. She walked with one of her sons on either side. She noticed that many of the men and women standing there had tears in their eyes; she did not know that they were in her own as well.

3

AN hour before she was to leave for St. Louis a telegram arrived from General Winfield Scott ordering her to join the inaugural train the next morning in Indianapolis on the grounds that the president-elect would be safer if he were surrounded by his wife and children. William and Tad were hysterical with joy; Mary was dazed at the sudden reversal.

The inaugural locomotive was waiting with its steam up for her arrival. Abraham received her as she came down the steps of her passenger car. She leaned up to kiss his cheek, murmuring:

"Happy birthday."

A little sheepishly he said:

"You're the nicest present I could have had."

When he led her into their parlor car she gasped with delight: it was a revolution in car building, having been made by a manufacturer of railroad cars in Buffalo expressly for this trip. Her eye took in the rich carpeting, single panes of glass instead of numerous small ones, the carved black walnut furniture and horsehair upholstery, the extra-long sofa for Abraham to stretch out on. There was also a refreshment bar with an assortment of liquors for the party.

The train left the station and soon was traveling through the Indiana countryside at a speed of thirty miles an hour. At every small station there were flags and banners along the track and crowds of people gathered, firing cannons and sending up cheer after cheer; at Cincinnati a hundred thousand people jammed the station, square and streets. In Columbus, Ohio, they were taken to the state capitol for a reception by the governor and the legislature; the next morning they were on their way again by seven-thirty. The skies were overcast and by the time their train had been moving a half hour torrential rains began to fall. Abraham confided to her that he did not mind because now he would not have to make so many speeches; but he was mistaken: neither the rain nor cold nor mud kept the throngs away from the tiniest station, where the train was greeted with bands, songs and the roar of artillery.

The journey was a constant delight for the three boys; Robert spent half of his time with the engineer, the other half at the refreshment bar. Each time the train stopped and strangers came aboard, Tad rushed forward crying, "Do you want to meet Old Abe, the Pwesident?" then would point out one of the other members of the presidential party.

At one station the crowd called for Mary Lincoln. She heard Abraham say, "I'll see if I can get Mrs. Lincoln, but I don't believe I can; in fact I can say that I've never succeeded very well in getting her to do anything she didn't want to do."

She waited until the flush had left her cheeks before joining him on the platform. In another town when she stood by Abraham's side, he said, "Now you see before you the long and short of the presidency."

For Mary the great stop was New York. She took from a valise the silver brushes she had given Abraham for his birthday.

"Abraham, I'm going to fix you up a bit for these city folk."

She parted, combed and brushed his hair, arranged his black necktie.

"Do I look nice now, Mother?" he asked affectionately.

"I'm not sure you're ever going to make anything of the whiskers that little girl and the Republican Committee thought would make you look more dignified. They're still pretty scraggly."

"That's strange, I water them every morning when I wash my face."

They rode to the Astor Hotel in an open carriage, barely had time to clean

305

up before there was a reception, with the Veterans of the War of 1812 parading past in full uniform. Abraham's hand was now so sore and swollen that Dr. Wallace forbade him to shake hands any more. Mary greeted New York society flanked on one side by her sister Elizabeth, on the other by Lizzie Grimsley, feeling exquisite in a steel-colored gown with a black chenille and gold headdress.

Shortly after the flag-raising ceremony at Independence Hall in Philadelphia, Mary saw that something was troubling Abraham, something beyond the growing apprehension of the chaos he would find in Washington. When they reached Harrisburg at one o'clock, though he had confessed to a crowd a few hours before that "I am too unwell to say much to you," he waved aside her demands that he forgo his two scheduled speeches and rest for a few hours before covering the last leg of the journey across Maryland and Baltimore, the only city on the itinerary which was not welcoming the president-elect or offering an official escort across town when the cars were drawn by horses from one station to another. Yet she did not fully grasp how overwrought he was until he burst into her room, his skin dark with anger.

"Where is Robert? He had charge of the gripsack with my inaugural speech in it. If any reporter lays hands on that speech . . ."

"He's out with the Young Republican Club."

"We've got to find him immediately!"

John Nicolay, whom Abraham was taking to Washington as his private secretary, scoured Harrisburg, returning with a bewildered Robert. When his father demanded to know whether the gripsack had been lost or stolen, Robert replied:

"It's with the rest of the baggage downstairs."

Abraham took the stairs to the lobby three at a time, made his way behind an astonished clerk to the stack of luggage and began scattering valises. Mary had come downstairs at a slower pace; she watched until at last he straightened up with his gripsack, examined the lock, beads of perspiration on his forehead.

"Thank heavens! If this speech had been printed in the papers before I had delivered it, I would have been hopelessly embarrassed."

"Come upstairs, the whole lobby is staring at you. And in the future don't send a boy to do a man's work: carry the speech yourself."

He returned to their suite shortly after four o'clock, slumped into a brown mohair chair. Without looking at her, he said:

"Mary, we're going to have to change our plans."

She stared at him in silence. After a moment he continued:

"Seems there's a conspiracy in Baltimore to harm me while our cars are being drawn across the city. Norman Judd hired a detective by the name of Allan Pinkerton to investigate and they told me yesterday in Philadelphia they're convinced a barber by the name of Fernandina, head of one of the secret military societies, plans to kill me."

There was a straight-backed chair against the wall; she pulled it to position facing him, lines of puzzlement screwing up her face.

"Isn't it a bit farfetched to believe that some Baltimore barber is going to be able to assassinate you when you are surrounded by twenty of your friends, and a half dozen military men provided by the army to protect you?"

He hung his head like a lamb in a storm, said, "The men believe this is a genuine danger. They've made plans for me to leave Harrisburg secretly tonight; the regular Washington train will be held in the Philadelphia station and I'll go into Washington on it with no one knowing I'm aboard."

"Should the president-elect slink into Washington?"

"I don't like it any better than you do, Mary," he cried irately.

"Very well," she said, resignedly. "I'll pack at once."

A net of silence encompassed her. She saw the pained expression on Abraham's face.

"Mary, I'm to make this trip into the capital alone, with only one man, Hill Lamon. If you and the children were along it would be impossible to conceal the fact that we are changing our plans."

She sat down weakly on the edge of the bed.

"Oh, Abraham, not again?"

He gazed back at her out of stricken eyes.

"Let me get Norman Judd and Alexander McClure, he's the governor's friend . . . perhaps they can convince you."

He went across the hall. In a few moments the presidential party filed in: Norman Judd, Judge David Davis, Ward Hill Lamon, Abraham's burly partner from Danville, W. S. Wood, who had been sent from the east to direct the inaugural train, four army officers under the command of the white-haired, courtly Colonel Sumner, who had been assigned by Washington to protect Abraham, and Alexander McClure, heavily mustached, pointed-chinned representative of Governor Curtin of Pennsylvania.

Judd was their spokesman. He reviewed the situation in Baltimore: at least half of the city was secessionist and in an ugly temper, the chief marshal of police was sympathetic to the secessionists and would afford Mr. Lincoln no protection, a gang would start a fight at the Baltimore station to distract the few police available and then Fernandina and his secret society would close around Mr. Lincoln, Fernandina either shooting him or delivering a fatal knife thrust. The nation would suffer a great loss if Mr. Lincoln should be killed.

Mary stood at the back of the room facing the twenty-odd who had assembled in a semicircle before her. For an instant she felt trapped.

"Very well, I'll not argue any further against this affront to the dignity of the presidential office; but if you are so sure there is real danger to my husband, then I wish to be with him. Who has more to lose than I, gentlemen?"

"There will be no danger if Mr. Lincoln goes alone," said McClure in a heavy voice; "we're cutting the telegraph wires so that no news can reach Baltimore after Mr. Lincoln's train leaves . . ."

"If you're so resourceful as to prevent anything from happening to Mr. Lincoln, Mr. McClure, I'm sure you can be resourceful enough to keep it from happening to me and my children."

Norman Judd stepped forward; he was a heavy-set man with a florid complexion, flowing gray beard and an unlit cigar between his teeth.

"Mrs. Lincoln, it takes only one demented man with a knife in his hand . . ."

She felt her voice rise out of a deep well of anger.

"And have we no stouthearted men to prevent it? Are we to go through four years in the presidency hiding and fleeing? If this is the best we have to offer to defend the Union, then God help us!"

They stood before her, some of them staring, others with their eyes lowered.

"We will sneak into Washington, gentlemen, but if anything is going to happen to any member of the Lincoln family, it is going to happen when we are all together. Now if you will kindly leave the room, I will finish my packing."

The men started out the door, taking Abraham with them, Colonel Sumner saying as he left, "Mrs. Lincoln, I am going through with the president-elect tonight, and I want to assure you that no harm will befall him." Only Judd and McClure remained.

When the door had closed behind the colonel, Judd said:

"No, Mrs. Lincoln, you are not going with your husband."

She was gripped by each arm, pushed toward the adjoining room and forced inside. Then the door closed and she heard it lock behind her.

She sat up all night, not attempting to undress, hearing the men of the party pace the corridors and talk in guarded tones. In the morning as she was seated in the dining room with her three sons, eating mechanically, word was brought that Abraham was safely in Washington, and that the inaugural train was ready to leave as soon as she and her party boarded.

4

SHE had forgotten, during the intervening thirteen years, how predominantly southern Washington was; she was reminded on her first day in the capital by learning that if the District of Columbia had had the franchise, Abraham Lincoln would have received hardly a handful of votes; that it was not merely the Virginia and Maryland families who felt this way, but almost the entire body of government employees and the business houses that served them. Though she was received with courtesy, the Willards awaiting her in the lobby of their hotel and escorting her up to the luxurious five-room suite on the second floor, she felt an air of standoffishness as she passed through the public rooms.

Already a number of important senators and representatives from the seceded states had made inflammatory resignation speeches and gone home; on their first evening at the hotel a disunionist persuaded the musicians to play "Dixie" while the Lincolns were entering the dining room. Rumors reached her that for weeks the capital had been buzzing with stories of the uncouth manners of the rustic president-elect and his wife, while the secessionist ladies had been amusing themselves with anecdotes of the gaucherie of the log-cabin First Lady.

Whatever chance they might have had for a respectful if not affectionate welcome had been blasted by Abraham's manner of arrival. A reporter back in Harrisburg, awakening to find the president-elect gone and no story to file with his paper, invented the detail of Abraham Lincoln stealing into Washington disguised in a Scotch plaid cap and long military cloak. The cartoons of Abraham in all versions of the Scotch plaid disguise appearing in the press were lethal; even his friends and supporters were ashamed. When she had arrived at the Willard he took her into the far bedroom of the suite, a mirrored wall reflecting his thin, hunched-over shoulders.

"Mary, it was the gravest mistake I ever made. I knew it by the time I reached Philadelphia and received a message from Pinkerton in Baltimore that he was doubtful whether the conspirators had the nerve to attempt the execution of their purpose. But even if the conspiracy had been real, all the more reason to face up to it. From now on, Mary, my decisions will be my own. Never again will I take even the best-meant wishes of our friends as my law. What happened . . . happened . . . because I did not really know who was boss. Now I know. I am the president. No man, no group of men, will ever come between us again."

She reached her hands up and ran them over his cheeks.

"Thank you, Abraham, you have just made me mistress of the White House."

They settled down in the Willard to await the inaugural. Abraham set up a corner table on which to work. Senator Seward, who had accepted the post of Secretary of State in December, had just resigned, ". . . because I want to appoint my choices instead of his," explained Abraham. "He refuses to serve with Senator Chase of Ohio, whom I will have for Secretary of the Treasury. The abolitionists want only men in the cabinet who will declare for immediate emancipation; the conservatives want no abolitionists, but only representatives from the border states; there is almost no man I could appoint who wouldn't be opposed by strong blocs. I can't let Seward take the first trick."

When they had been at the Willard for several days and not one southern woman had called to pay her respects, Mary asked herself:

Are we to be treated as outlanders?

309

The answer came at teatime in the form of beautiful Adele Douglas, attired in green silk trimmed with rose-colored bows, a lace cap and kid gloves. Mary thanked her for coming.

"Mrs. Douglas, surely the women of Washington can't believe that I am the ignorant, gauche frontierswoman they make me out?"

Adele Douglas took Mary's hand, her large brown eyes sympathetic.

"These are political attacks, my dear Mrs. Lincoln, and not personal. Many of our families moved into Washington when it was little more than a swamp. They built homes, brought their books, music, art . . . and all the culture they had been evolving for some two hundred years."

"I have the highest respect . . ."

"Unfortunately, within their high wall they have become inbred. Cruel things would have been said against the wife of any victorious Republican; they fear that their reign and their power are to be ended; but once they come to know you their animosity will vanish." She smiled a bit wryly. "You must be charitable to the vanquished." After a moment she added, "The White House is run down and shabby, not brilliant and glowing as it was during the regime of my great-aunt, Dolly Madison. Make it the most beautiful house in the land, Mrs. President; for we plan to try again. . . ."

Mary ordered tea. With it arrived Abraham and a moment later Stephen Douglas, looking pale. Neither she nor Abraham had seen him since the '58 debate at Alton.

"Mary, you crowned me with a garland of roses that day we walked down to Watson's for an ice cream, some twenty years ago. But I think you always knew that Abraham was going to be crowned with the presidency."

"Wouldn't have married him if I hadn't," she replied with a straight face. "How do you like your tea, Steve?"

"One drop at a time . . . in my whiskey."

They were interrupted by the arrival of Mary's sister Margaret and her husband Charles H. Kellogg from Cincinnati, and just behind them her half brother Alexander, the red-haired boy who had been only eight months old when she left Lexington for Springfield. Betsy was ailing and could not come, Samuel and David said the journey from New Orleans was too long, George said he would not attend the inauguration of a Black Republican, her sister Elodie too had been committed to the secessionist cause, but her sister Martha and her husband, also living in Alabama, put family above politics. Mary's greatest disappointment was over Emilie and Ben Hardin Helm, who had important cases on the docket which could not be put over.

Abraham had not invited a single relative to witness his swearing-in.

She wished March 4 would hurry on so that she could get into their own home; she cared no more for hotel life now than she had in the days of their small bedchamber at the Globe. There was no privacy whatever, with the lobby, parlors, dining room and even the hallway outside their rooms jammed night and day with office seekers who had journeyed from every part of the

Union with folios of papers proving that they should be installed in lucrative offices in place of undeserving Democrats.

Inauguration day dawned cloudy and raw. President Buchanan came into the Willard Hotel at noon, his face white as chalk, his neck swathed in an enormous white cravat. He bowed formally to Mary in the private parlor, then asked Abraham if he were ready. Mary and her three sons went out behind them. When the two men reached the sidewalk the band struck up "Hail to the Chief" and they walked to their open barouche in a procession headed by a marshal with aides in blue scarves and white rosettes.

Mary's carriage was called somewhere near the middle of the procession, after the congressmen, jurists, clergy and diplomats had been cared for. Soldiers marched along both sides of Pennsylvania Avenue, which had been brushed clean even of dust. As her carriage moved slowly toward the unfinished dome of the Capitol with its steel derrick and guy-wire structure fingering skyward, she saw sharpshooters at the windows and on the roofs. Ahead of Abraham's carriage were the heavily armed West Point sappers and miners; massed thick on either side of him were cavalrymen, and following were detachments of the navy and militia. She could hardly see the ailanthus trees for the squads of riflemen protecting the procession; as her carriage passed the intersecting streets she could see General Scott's regulars moving along in a flanking movement.

Four years before, President Buchanan had ridden to his inauguration through flags and crowds of wildly cheering enthusiasts; now as Mary gazed at the faces lining Pennsylvania Avenue she saw that most were solemn, many downright unfriendly. The shutters of the windows were closed and bolted. There was no sound except the boots of the infantrymen and the noise of the carriage wheels on the cobblestones; no bands of music, no cheers, no throngs of happy people giving the president the traditionally tumultuous welcome to Washington. General Scott had described this inaugural parade to them as a "movement" designed not only to protect the life of the incoming president but also to repulse the threatened invasion of the capital.

It was not the way she had dreamed it.

She took her seat in the second row on the platform that had been built out from the Capitol's east portico. Squads of infantrymen had spent the night underneath the boards because of the threat to blow up the stand. On the ground around the stand were blocks of cut granite, cables, sheds and workmen's tools, everything in a state of incompletion and neglect. At each window of the Capitol were riflemen.

Her sons sat on either side of her, Stephen and Adele Douglas immediately next to them. In front of the stand there were probably fewer people than had filled the public square at Ottawa for the opening of Abraham's debates with Stephen Douglas in 1858.

Abraham had selected their friend Edward Baker, to whose defense he had dropped through the ceiling and into her life, to introduce him: handsome, white-haired, red-faced Edward Baker who had migrated in 1852 to start a new life, and had been sent to Washington as the only Republican senator from the Pacific Coast to support the new administration. It was the possibility of this office of senator from Oregon that had made Abraham willing, back in 1849 after the Land Office disappointment, to pull up his roots and make the long trek west.

Abraham came onto the stand. By now his beard came down in a straight line below the ears, the sides of his chin were respectably bushy, but his upper lip and the hollow cheeks still were innocent of growth. There was a scattering of applause. Senator Baker gave a discreetly short introduction. Abraham rose, set on a small table the gold-headed cane that had been given him as a gift, took off his high silk hat and, not finding adequate space for it on the tiny table, was looking about for another when Stephen Douglas leaned forward, took the hat and held it on his lap. He gave Mary a smile of sad wistfulness.

Little space had been left to Abraham to move about. He took the galleys of his speech from his inside coat pocket, laid them on the table, then adjusted his spectacles. The spectators were as silent as the blocks of cut granite scattered on the lawn. When he began to speak his voice was high, a little nasal, the same voice she had heard address countless Illinois audiences. He had spoken only a few sentences before the tension went out of her, and she leaned back comfortably in her chair: for Abraham was delivering his inaugural address as though he had been giving them all his life.

First he tried to reassure the south:

"Apprehension seems to exist among the people of the Southern States, that by the accession of a Republican Administration, their property, and their peace, and personal security, are to be endangered. . . . I have no purpose, directly or indirectly, to interfere with the institution of slavery in the States where it exists."

Next he informed the south that it could not secede:

"No State can lawfully get out of the Union, *resolves* and *ordinances* to that effect are legally void. . . . I therefore consider that, in view of the Constitution and the laws, the Union is unbroken; and, to the extent of my ability, I shall take care that the laws of the Union be faithfully executed."

Then, flinging out his long arms as though to enfold all men throughout the nation, he cried in a voice in which love and anguish were intermingled:

"In *your* hands, my dissatisfied fellow countrymen, and not in *mine,* is the momentous issue of civil war. The government will not assail *you.* You can have no conflict, without being yourselves the aggressors. *You* have no oath registered in Heaven to destroy the government, while *I* shall have the most solemn one to 'preserve, protect and defend' it. I am loth to close. We are not enemies, but friends. We must not be enemies. . . . The mystic chords of memory, stretching from every battle-field and patriot grave, to every living heart and hearthstone, all over this broad land, will yet swell the chorus of the Union. . . ."

The applause, Mary noted, was more enthusiastic than when he had risen to make his speech. The ancient Chief Justice Taney, whose Dred Scott decision declaring that slaves were not human beings had done so much to elect Abraham, stepped forward with a Bible bound in cinnamon velvet. Abraham put his left hand on the open Bible, raised his gaunt long right arm to the heavens, and repeated after the Chief Justice:

"I, Abraham Lincoln, do solemnly swear that I will faithfully execute the office of the President of the United States, and will, to the best of my ability, preserve, protect, and defend the Constitution of the United States."

Dignitaries on the stand crowded around to congratulate him. He turned to Mary, kissed her solemnly. The batteries on the hill began firing, announcing to the world that the United States had a new president.

Mary thought, I hope that's the last cannon I hear to the end of my days.

5

THEY rode up the north driveway to the main entrance of the White House. Ex-President Buchanan shook hands in farewell.

"If you are as happy to be entering the White House as I am to be leaving it, you are the happiest people in the world."

Mary shivered as the sick old man entered his carriage and drove away. Abraham linked his arm through hers. Together they crossed the threshold. They were courteously bowed in by Old Edward, the long-time Irish doorkeeper. Mary could feel her pulse pounding in her ears as she clenched Abraham's arm to help support her wobbling knees.

"Abraham," she whispered, "we're home."

They had taken no more than three steps into the vestibule when General Winfield Scott stepped out of the doorkeeper's sentry room dressed in a resplendent uniform with huge epaulets, gold buttons, yellow sash. He was holding in front of him a sheaf of papers from the War Department.

"Mr. President, this dispatch just arrived from Major Anderson, commander of Fort Sumter in Charleston Harbor. He is encircled by a ring of shore batteries, and the rebels are threatening to blow him out of the water. . . . He warns us that if he is not provisioned by the fifteenth of March he will be forced to evacuate the fort."

Abraham thanked the general. He left. They continued through the drafty vestibule and up the main staircase. Mary turned to Abraham, red spots flaming on her forehead.

"Couldn't General Scott have given us time to find out where we live and wash our hands? Did he have to force a war upon you within seconds of our entering the White House?"

He tucked his hand intimately under her arm, craned his long neck downward and whispered against her ear in gentle irony:

"Mary, we're home."

Their family apartments lay to the right in the west wing, supposedly unavailable from these public stairs which would be carrying the nation's business up to Abraham's office. Stackpole, the White House messenger, met them on the upper landing, guiding them through a series of secretarial offices and waiting rooms before ushering them into Abraham's office, a big, high-ceilinged room scrupulously scrubbed. The south wall had two enormous floor-to-ceiling windows similar to the ones she had loved in the Houghan house, giving a magnificent view over the green lawn, the presidential park, the marsh that went all the way down to the Potomac River, and the most prominent element of the view, the truncated Washington monument, less than half completed. Abraham twitched one corner of his lips.

"Seems like I mostly inherited unfinished business: the open dome of the Capitol, this half memorial to President Washington . . . a federal garrison in a South Carolina harbor encircled by shore batteries that will blow it to pieces if we attempt to reinforce it. Yet I remember myself saying this morning that the power confided to me will be used to hold, occupy and possess the property and places belonging to the government. Sort of committed myself, didn't I, Mrs. President?"

Mary walked to the tall desk with numerous pigeonholes that stood between the two south windows, ran her hand over the massive rectangular walnut table in the center surrounded by a dozen shabby old chairs; on the west wall above a white marble fireplace was a portrait of Andrew Jackson. Gazing at the man whose policies and party Abraham never had supported, she asked:

"What would this other lean long-faced president have done?"

Abraham stood with a grim smile on his upturned face; he had lost thirty pounds since the election, and the bones stood out in his cheeks like jagged rocks in a dark sea.

"Same as he did back in '32 when South Carolina passed a law nullifying a federal tariff law, and threatened to secede if the federal government tried to collect the tariff by force. He dispatched a man-of-war and seven revenue boats to Charleston, then proclaimed, 'No state has a right to secede. The Union must be preserved at all hazards and at any price. The Constitution forms a government, not a league. To say that any state may at pleasure secede from the Union is to say that the United States is not a nation. Disunion by armed force is treason.'"

He brought his eyes down from Jackson's shock of white hair and cadaverously hollow cheeks, turned to Mary.

314

"You see, my dear, I have his words burned into my mind. I never knew, until this moment, how great a man he was."

There was a knock on the door. Stackpole announced that Senator William H. Seward wished to see the president. Abraham motioned Mary to a chair in the far corner. She gazed with interest at the man who was said to be the greatest political intellect in their party, a man of slight build, stooped, with a large head carried precariously on a long slender neck; secretive yet penetrating eyes, a flexible mouth made for talking, a prominent aquiline nose.

"Mr. President," Seward's voice was obstructed by a perpetual cigar clenched in the corner of his mouth, "I wish to tell you that I am deferring to your wishes as expressed in your letter to me, and am withdrawing my resignation."

"Thank you, Senator," said Abraham. "Since you were my very first choice for the cabinet, your withdrawal was the subject of the most painful solicitude to me."

Seward turned to Mary with a courtly bow.

"As Secretary of State, I will give the first state dinner."

Mary too bowed, then replied courteously but firmly:

"Mr. Lincoln is the president. It would seem to me proper that we give the opening state dinner."

Senator Seward's big head leaned over his thin chest as he peered at her, looking as though he were going to resign all over again. Instead he murmured, "Mr. President, Madame President," and was gone.

Mary and Abraham gazed at each other for a long moment, eyelids raised, thoughts racing through their heads too fast to be formed into words. Abraham linked an arm through hers.

"We're just a couple of old fools, Mary, but it looks like we may be the boss around here, after all!"

They walked through the west wing together, assigning the rooms her family and guests would sleep in that night, then went down the family flight of stairs which led from the small reception room to the main floor, recalling how Mrs. Donn Piatt, wife of an Ohio supporter of Abraham, had exclaimed:

"The rooms are furnished more miserably than a family boardinghouse!"

Lizzie Grimsley agreed. "Why, the furniture is so deplorably shabby it looks like it was brought in by the first president. That mahogany French bedstead in my room is split from top to bottom; in case I'm missing in the morning, just have me dug out of the debris."

At that moment John Nicolay came from the executive offices to summon the president. He was a quiet man, thin almost to emaciation, with cool blue eyes, a dark brown mustache and small beard. When she asked how he was faring, Nicolay replied in his circumspect manner:

"We have pleasant offices, Mrs. Lincoln, and a nice large bedroom in the northeast corner; however, I must confess that all of them sadly need new furniture and carpets." Then he tendered her one of his rare, unbending smiles. "Though I suspect all that will be remedied after a while."

Yes, she thought, as she entered the state dining room, which was immediately below her bedroom, all that will be remedied, but not right away; first would have to come the refurbishing of these official rooms where all the world would come to see and judge the administration. They could live like poor relations upstairs for a while until she had turned the official part of the White House into the brilliant mansion that Adele Douglas had said she could.

The state dining room, where she began her critical tour, was a room of good dimensions, but the carpet was dirty, the chandeliers had not been washed for years, the draperies were frayed. She walked through the huge wooden doors into the Red Room and stood before the portrait of President Washington which Dolly Madison had taken out of its frame when the government fled the oncoming British in 1814. In the early years this room had been used for cabinet meetings; it was of intimate size, immediately under Abraham's bedroom, the wallpaper discolored, the massive scuffed furniture inappropriate.

She turned next into the Oval Reception Room, just under their library-sitting room upstairs. She loved it at once for its lyrical grace, and as she sat on the circular settee in the center of the room gazing into the tall mirror over the fireplace, she decided on the blending shades of blue she would use in the new wallpaper, draperies, carpets and vases after she had cleaned the peeling paint off the ceiling.

Next came the Green Room, unused except as a waiting room for guests because the sickly green walls made the ladies look sallow. It was the shabbiest and most neglected room in the mansion. She knew that it had not always been so: Adams, Jefferson and Madison had used it as the main dining room; James Monroe had turned it into a cardroom with glass and gilt chandeliers, rosewood furniture covered with brocatelle. She promised herself to restore the room to its former elegance.

She gasped as she stepped into the great East Room, which ran the entire width of the White House, eighty feet long and forty wide, with four giant fireplaces, huge gilt mirrors over pier tables, great hanging crystal chandeliers. Here the formal receptions and levees were held . . . where in 1800 Abigail Adams had hung out the family wash in long lines. The velvet carpet was worn; she could see the muslin backing through the hangings.

She mounted the family stairs, her head whirling with the amount of work that needed doing; she would have to search for the finest of upholstering materials, French wallpapers, carpets, *objets d'art*. Aside from a conservatory built by Buchanan, little had been spent on the White House for some ten years, not since Mrs. Fillmore had had a coal range installed in the kitchen, and secured five thousand dollars from Congress to begin the first permanent library in the upstairs oval sitting room. Everything was scrubbed and clean, but not even the best efforts of a good staff of servants had been able to keep the mansion from looking as though it belonged to poor folk who had once been prosperous but had come down in the world.

She found Abraham in his office sorting documents at his stand-up desk, began pouring out her plans for the refurbishing. He gazed at her over the rims of his spectacles like a schoolmaster at an excited student.

"Whoa, Mary, whoa, you've just broken the Treasury! Are you sure these times are . . . propitious . . . for redoing the mansion? With seven states no longer contributing funds . . . ?"

"A tenable point, Mr. President, but the opposite is equally true: to leave the White House in this threadbare condition is to confess our uncertainty over the future. If we are shabby, that will encourage the south to treat us shabbily. And what about the diplomats who see us living like poor relations: won't their reports of our poor purse and poorer prospects hurt us abroad when the seceded states look for recognition?"

Abraham chewed on this morsel, found it palatable.

"Basically you are right, we are not a country of paupers and no one in the north would want us to live in genteel poverty . . . any more than they want us to show weakness to the south. So our problems are similar: each of us must use his strength and resources to rebuild what has been neglected and allowed to fall apart. I'll see that Congress appropriates the money for you to do your job."

Together they had dispelled the shadow of James Buchanan.

6

SHE awakened before seven to find sunlight flooding her room, jumped out of bed and stood at the open window in her nightgown facing the beautiful lawn to the south. At the other side of an old canal she could see the Potomac gleaming in the bright sun with small boats sailing its water, and then the green hills of Arlington Heights in Virginia. It was as enchanting a view as anything she had known in the Bluegrass, its only drawback being the insane asylum clearly evident on a none too distant hill.

In a corner dressing room next to her bedroom William and Tad were sleeping on cots, with Robert and Dr. Wallace occupying the upstairs reception room. Across the hall Elizabeth, her daughter and Lizzie Grimsley had the huge Prince of Wales guest room, her other relatives occupying three more chambers. It was like being back in the Todd house in Lexington!

She heard Abraham padding about in his slippers in the next room, put on her quilted cashmere wrapper, knocked and entered. It too was a big room with a high ceiling, adjoining the oval library which Mary planned to use for the family sitting room. In it stood a massive nine-foot mahogany bed that had been built by their friends in Springfield and sent to be installed for President Lincoln's first night in the White House; the back canopy was also nine feet high, enough to crush a regiment if ever it fell.

"Good morning, Mr. President Lincoln."

"Good morning, Mrs. President Lincoln."

"Did you sleep well on your royal couch?"

"Hardly closed my eyes for the joy of roaming around in it. Are you up early to go house hunting?"

She smiled. "My husband found one for me, thank you. Shall I see about breakfast? The inner workings of this hostel are still a mystery to me."

"Give me an hour to look over the War Department file on Fort Pickens, down in Florida; it too will have to be reinforced."

She sat before the writing desk in her bedroom trying to learn just how one practiced housewifery in this combination of business offices, public reception rooms and family apartments. Apparently her overlord was the Commissioner of Public Buildings, who hired and paid the wages of the door-keepers, messengers, night watchmen, furnace men and gardeners, but not of the cook, waiters or coachmen, whose salaries she would be obliged to meet. The commissioner paid for a stewardess, Jane Watt, wife of the head gardener, who supervised the staff of servants, but as far as Mary could fathom she was going to have to pay for the cleaning women and scullery maids. The government would pay the costs of such items as fuel, flowers, soap, table and bed linens, but she must pay for all food and liquors out of Abraham's salary. The government provided a stable, but they would have to buy their own horses, carriages and feed. Nicolay and John Hay, the young assistant he had brought with him from Springfield, a boyish chap, quick to laugh, even quicker to immature judgments, with a talent for name calling, having already dubbed the president *The Ancient* and *The Tycoon*, would be paid by the government but she must make quarters available to them and feed them at her family table . . . as well as feed their horses at the family stable. The government allowed her a modest yearly sum to run the White House, but the actual money would never be in her keep, it would be paid out by the presidential secretaries after they had checked and approved the bills.

The rules and customs had grown up over a period of sixty years and arose from the anomaly of having the presidential residence and the presidential business offices contained within the identical walls: no opportunity would be afforded to set up a private court in a private castle. The president's life and family were public property and they must remain in public view at all times.

Very well, since she was a public character she meant to show the world what a superb job she could do as mistress of the Executive Mansion. She did not think of this family apartment as merely a group of rooms in which she and Abraham and the boys were to live, as they had lived in the house on Eighth Street; she had her own concept of her job as chatelaine of all that

318

part of the White House beyond the vestibule in the first floor, and west of the folding doors at the head of the main stairs.

Now that she had achieved her greatest ambition and her greatest opportunity she was resolved to control her temper and her tongue, to avoid strong likes and dislikes, to be friendly and gracious to all, to eschew her alternating periods of parsimony and sprees of extravagance. People never would be able to say about her that she had been dowdy or inept or unresponsive to her tasks. By the same token she was determined that she was going to be the real mistress of the White House.

Her outstanding surprise was the totally public nature of the White House, which was open to everyone: any person or committee wanting to see the president simply walked in the front door, crossed the vestibule, mounted the main stairs and took their place in line in the upstairs waiting room or in Nicolay's office. Those who were important did not have to sit in the common waiting room but waited in the upstairs hall until the clerk announced them: senators, legislators, clergymen, bankers, newspaper correspondents . . . all waiting for a private audience. The crush of office seekers continued so great that it was impossible for Mary or the family to use the main stairs or front door at all; the broad staircase was packed solid, the vestibule too was full, with the overflow pouring into the corridor and even the Red, Blue and Green parlors. When she wanted to go to one of her sisters' rooms across the hall from her own she was obliged to walk from room to room the three sides of a quadrangle. The noise of the milling, clamoring men and women could be heard through the walls; until she turned the locks even the doors of the family apartment would be opened and strange faces peer in. Nor did the crush end with the workday: after the family supper Abraham would get into a long-skirted dressing gown and his slippers with the embroidered initials, have the gas lighted in his office, a fire in the hearth, and see visitors until midnight.

Late one afternoon he came into Mary's bedroom for a respite, threw himself on a couch, his face gray with fatigue.

"Mary, they have descended on me like a plague of locusts."

She smiled, sat down on the edge of the sofa.

"Tell me, Abraham, how do you like being president?"

He chuckled, asked, "Have you heard the story about the fellow who was tarred and feathered and carried out of town on a rail? When a man in the crowd asked him how he liked it, he replied that if it was not for the honor of the thing, he would much rather walk."

Then he grew serious.

"Frankly, it's like taking over the bridge of a ship in a high hurricane: if I fail to provision Fort Sumter and Fort Pickens, they will fall into Confederate hands. Yet I must do nothing that will lead to the firing of shots. These office seekers make me feel like a man sitting in a palace assigning apartments while the structure is on fire."

Within the next few days she too would be facing her Forts Sumter and Pickens. In launching her first reception the following Friday, her first state dinner three weeks later, she must, in Abraham's words, permit the firing of no shots which would precipitate a war; at the same time she must restrain the southern coterie whose purpose it was to make a laughingstock of the Lincolns in the capitals of the world. If they succeeded the Red, Blue, Green and East rooms would appear abandoned, and the administration as well. By her breeding, her knowledge of protocol, her ability to command the reception, she would give the lie to the gossip and the slanderers, earn the respect of the nation and the foreign embassies. This was the greatest service she could render her husband in these days of crisis.

Knowing that the southern women of Washington were the most richly dressed in America, and that the Todd taste would be under the closest scrutiny, she summoned four mantuamakers to provide gowns for the White House ladies. Mary chose a handsome Negro woman by the name of Elizabeth Keckley to sew her bright rose antique moiré. Mrs. Keckley had only four days in which to work. On Friday evening Mary stood in her stockings, waist tightly laced into a boned corset and many petticoats and hoops, her father's pearls about her neck, roses in her hair, with no gown to wear for her first levee as mistress of the White House. Panic seized her; she turned to her sister Elizabeth crying:

"Mrs. Keckley sewed for Mrs. Jefferson Davis! Do you think she just won't appear?"

Mrs. Keckley arrived a full hour late, but with no apology; and when Mary gazed at herself in the mirror she saw that no apology was necessary: the rose moiré was sumptuous. Her heart filled with pride as she stood amidst her elegant family, Elizabeth in brown and black silk, her daughters in lemon and crimson, Lizzie in watered-blue silk, her sisters Margaret and Martha in ashes of roses and white silk.

Abraham came in at a few minutes to eight in his inaugural suit, polished black boots and fresh white kid gloves. Mary had bought six dozen pairs of white gloves in New York, an extravagant outlay of money, she knew, yet the handshaking at each reception ruined several pair. When Abraham saw Mary's gown he pursed his lips in a silent whistle.

"You look charming."

"Thank you, Mr. President; I quite frankly hope to be the belle of the ball."

"I expect all of us Todds to do Lexington and Springfield proud tonight," he declared.

They went down the main staircase and into the vestibule, where the Marine Band was playing; then took up their station in the center of the Blue Room with its many vases filled with fresh flowers.

At eight o'clock the gates of the grounds were opened. Within a matter of minutes the room was filled with cabinet officers and their wives, members of Congress, army and navy officers in their colorful uniforms, foreign diplomats with bright sashes. Abraham gave his right hand to the men and his left to the ladies; they were then presented to Mary by Dr. Blake, Commissioner of Public Buildings. Mary received as though she were standing in the foyer of the Todd home in Lexington, engulfing everyone in the joyousness of her party mood. With those she recognized either by face or by name she stopped the line for a little chat. The guests responded to the sincerity of her greeting and handshake.

She felt herself being coolly inspected, sensed that her gown was being admired. She stole a glance at Abraham, who stood head and shoulders above the crowd, like Saul over Israel, his figure relaxed, a genial smile on his face, stopping people frequently to remember an incident or tell a story. There could be no doubt that he was enjoying himself.

The reception had been announced for the hours of eight to ten, but at ten the crowd was still thronging in, the entrances so crowded that many men climbed in through the windows. Sometime after ten-thirty, with Abraham whispering to her, "My hand is totally paralyzed," they made their way into the East Room for one final promenade of the vast throng before the Marine Band struck up "Yankee Doodle Dandy," signalizing the end of the reception. At the foot of the main staircase Dr. Blake said his adieus:

"President and Mrs. Lincoln, I am one of the oldest frequenters of the Executive Mansion, and I do not recollect ever to have seen so many people pass through the house at any previous levee." An officer who had served Presidents Pierce and Buchanan added, "Nor was it ever excelled in brilliancy."

Mary thanked them for their kindness. On the way up the stairs she murmured:

"That's Fort Pickens taken care of; now if I can do as well with Sumter . . ."

7

THE next morning she bade farewell to all of her family except Cousin Lizzie, whom she was urging to stay on as her companion, and in the quiet and near loneliness prepared for her second challenge: the state dinner at which it would be her duty to unite in harmony the vice-president, the cabinet members, the general of the army and head of the navy. This was a difficult assignment, for Abraham, in an effort to balance the cabinet between radicals and conservatives, former Whigs and former Democrats, New England and border states, had assembled a crew of men who not only disliked and distrusted each other but were convinced that they themselves should be sitting at the head of the table. Abraham yielded to her plea to serve American wines. She was going to need them!

They received in the Blue Room, Mary welcoming the members of what was to be her official family: William Seward, who eyed her coolly; Montgomery Blair, the Postmaster General, chosen from the border state of Maryland, who had been the counsel for Dred Scott, a tall, lean man with a terrifying temper; Gideon Welles, Secretary of the Navy, from Connecticut, with such a heavy beard and thick brown wig that Abraham had dubbed him "Father Welles"; Caleb Smith from Indiana, Secretary of the Interior, accompanied by his wife, a white-haired, matronly woman whom Mary liked at once. Smith was a cautious, conservative man with a lisp, forced on Abraham by David Davis's pledge at the convention. Simon Cameron, Secretary of War, tall, slight, with gray hair and eyes, an unscrupulous politician, another convention pledge; Salmon P. Chase, Secretary of the Treasury, former senator and governor of Ohio, fifty-three, brilliant, with penetrating blue eyes, accompanied by his handsome young daughter Kate, who was said by all Washington to have only one ambition: to make her father president and rule as mistress of the White House; lastly, Attorney General Edward Bates of Missouri, long-bearded, prudent, a fighter when provoked, who immediately protested the appointment of an unknown lawyer to an important judgeship. Abraham ran his hand through his hair, rubbing his right thigh with an open palm.

"Come now, Bates, he's not half as bad as you think. Once when I had twelve miles to go to court and no horse, the judge overtook me in his buggy. 'Hello, Lincoln, come in and I'll give you a seat.' The buggy struck every hole and stump in the road. I said, 'Judge, I think your coachman has taken a drop too much this morning.' The judge put his head out the window and shouted, 'Why, you infernal scoundrel, you are drunk!' Turning around with great gravity, the coachman said, 'By gorra! That's the first rightful decision you have given for the last twelvemonth!' "

Everyone laughed. The ice was broken. On the way into the dining room Mary found a moment to whisper:

"Those stories of yours may yet prove a social asset. Remind me to invite you to more of my parties."

With the storm clouds hanging over them, no one was in a mood for gaiety, yet there was a babel of small talk. The menu, which she had arranged with Mrs. Watt, was excellent, the bright fires in the two fireplaces gave the room warmth. The guests lingered at the table for four hours, with Mary feeling that at least a beginning spirit of bonhomie had been established. When at length they rose, Abraham murmured:

"I've called a cabinet meeting in my office. Wait up for me."

She went upstairs to her bedroom to slip out of the tight laces and many layers of silk of the rose dinner gown and into a comfortable dressing robe, then sat before the mirror of her dressing table brushing her hair and noting how clear and happy her eyes were. She realized that it was midspring and she had had no return whatever of the seasonal headaches that had so racked her in Springfield. Was this because her ambition had been satisfied? Certainly the scandalmongering about the president's wife was beginning to subside.

She wished this could be true of Abraham too. His adversaries were accusing him of being vacillating because he had taken no action against the rebellious states or to reinforce Fort Sumter; of being too engulfed in what one paper called the "forty thousand office seekers fiddling around the administration for loaves and fishes, while the government is being destroyed."

And somehow Washington could not get used to his appearance: the shambling, loose, irregular gait, the stooping shoulders and pendulous arms, extraordinarily large hands and even bigger feet, the ill-fitting suit of black which put the newspaper writers in mind of an undertaker's uniform at a funeral, the turned-down shirt collar disclosing the sinewy yellow neck, the tie of black silk knotted in a large bulb with flying ends projecting beyond the coat; the strange, homely face and head covered with its thatch of what had been labeled "wild Republican hair." She was doing all she could to primp him, keeping his suits pressed and a supply of white shirts in his bureau, ample for three changes a day if necessary; but she must redouble her efforts, summon the best Washington tailors.

It was midnight before he came into her room. She felt a pang of compassion for him.

"One inconvenience of living in an Executive Mansion," she observed, "is that the kitchen is too far away to get you a cup of tea."

He sank onto a worn armchair.

"We have only a day or two to decide about Sumter. General Scott says it cannot be supplied and we must get out. Captain Fox of the navy, whom I sent down to Charleston two weeks ago, says we can reinforce Sumter by sending troops down on steamers and armed vessels. The cabinet is split the same way: three votes to get out at all costs, three to stay in at all costs, Cameron not voting. The Virginia state convention has been in session since February, they refuse to adjourn as long as there's a chance of our using force against South Carolina. South Carolina knows that the only way to get Virginia into their Confederacy is to start a war, or at least fire a shot. I'm going to offer Virginia a deal: I will evacuate Sumter if they will adjourn their meeting without seceding. A state for a fort is no bad business."

She gazed out the window at the dark, sleeping hills of Virginia. If Virginia seceded Washington and the White House would be within range of rebel artillery.

"I've ordered two naval expeditions to get ready in New York Harbor. The first is for Fort Pickens; if we land our reinforcements there without difficulty, I can then order Sumter evacuated without the government losing caste. . . ."

Two weeks later she was getting ready for breakfast when a messenger summoned her to the president's office. She found Abraham standing before the fireplace, gazing up at Jackson, holding a telegram in his hand. He held out the message. She read:

FORT SUMTER FIRED ON BY REBEL SHORE BATTERIES 4:30 THIS MORNING
APRIL 12 AFTER GENERAL BEAUREGARD DEMANDED SURRENDER OF FORT
AND MAJOR ANDERSON REFUSED FORT SUMTER RETURNING FIRE

She looked up at him, her heart pounding in her breast.

"Abraham, what does it mean?"

He went to one of the big south windows to look out through a storm of rain at the uncompleted monument to President Washington which stood outlined against the hills of Virginia. When he spoke his voice was hoarse.

"I'll have to issue a call for troops . . ."

"Oh, Abraham, a civil war . . . with our own people killing each other . . ."

She felt neither anger nor bitterness, only sadness. She saw from Abraham's dark gray eyes that there was no hatred there either, or desire for vengeance, just profound unhappiness.

"I expect to maintain this contest until successful, or till I die, or am conquered, or my term expires, or Congress or the country forsakes me."

She went to his side, stood with tears in her eyes. In spite of Abraham's conciliatory efforts the shooting had begun. How much blood would be shed, how many lives lost, how much of the country destroyed before Abraham once again would be president of all the states?

She rested her head against his bony ribs, feeling wretchedly sorry for him, and for all the millions of families, north and south alike, both parts her country and Abraham's, both her people and Abraham's. Hate and destruction would rule; but there had to be love, too. Who would have the heart and the humility and the compassion for love while holding reins on a maelstrom?

She looked up into her husband's face, lined, hollow-cheeked, the sunken eyes brimming with tears, the lips trembling, carrying in his bosom all the pain and terror and heartbreak of a sundered nation. Could it be Abraham?

It would have to be.

8

THE reaction to the firing on Sumter and the president's call for seventy-five thousand troops was instantaneous. The border states categorically refused the order, Kentucky saying, "We will furnish no troops for the wicked purpose of subduing our sister southern states"; the governor of Missouri telegraphing, "Your requisition is illegal, unconstitutional, and revolutionary in its object, inhuman and diabolical, and cannot be complied with"; while Tennessee stated, "In such unholy crusade no gallant son of Tennessee will ever draw his sword." But from Illinois came a telegram, "The governor has already received the tender of forty companies"; from Indiana,

"We have six thousand men in camp here and will have eight thousand by tomorrow night"; from the governor of Ohio, "I have already accepted and have in camp a larger force than the thirteen regiments named; without seriously repressing the ardor of the people, I can hardly stop short of twenty regiments." Vermont telegraphed the White House, "Our citizens will respond with great enthusiasm to any call for sustaining the government against the designs of the conspirators," and Iowa's governor telegraphed, "Ten days ago we had two parties in this state; today we have but one . . . for the Union unconditionally."

The patriotic fervor of the north was their only good news. On Wednesday, two days after Abraham's proclamation reached there, Virginia seceded and, as he explained to Mary, with Virginia gone, North Carolina, Tennessee and Arkansas were sure to follow; the south would have the wealth, the talent and manpower to fight. All hope of a peaceful restoration of the Union was gone; Washington was faced across a none too wide river by the most militarily powerful state of the rebellion.

Abraham summoned General Winfield Scott to the White House. Unfortunately the seventy-four-year-old, big-boned, big-brained fearless soldier who was the father of the country's professional army was no longer able to command so brilliantly as he had in the War of 1812, the Indian Wars, the Mexican War. Mary watched him painfully cross the room, hardly able to ease himself into a chair for his gout.

"General, I must put the question bluntly," said Abraham. "Is Washington defensible?"

General Scott closed his tired lids over the yellowed eyeballs.

"Washington is not defensible. All regular troops were sent out west by President Buchanan; my effective force for the defense is twenty-one hundred men. General Beauregard has thousands."

Abraham pushed aside the curtain.

"It does seem to me that if I were General Beauregard, I would take Washington. What a blow that would be to the north, to lose the capital!"

Scott straightened up in his chair, said with dignity:

"No, sir, the capital can't be taken, sir; we can fortify Executive Square: the White House, State Department, Treasury, War and Navy Departments, and successfully withstand a long siege." He turned to Mary. "But I would suggest that Madame President and her children leave for the north at once. . . ."

Mary rose to the majestic Todd height of a little over five feet, clenched her plump fingers into a tight fist.

"Shall I take the portrait of George Washington out of its frame?"

She heard Abraham chuckle.

They had been back in their upstairs library with the family only a few moments when William looked through his telescope and exclaimed excitedly:

"Tad, Tad, come here quick, there's a mortar battery over on the Virginia hills."

"Lemme see." Tad gazed south for a moment. "Papaday, they can plunk cannon balls right into this room, can't they?"

"I shouldn't be surprised," replied Abraham dryly; "get yourself a basket, Tad, and catch them as they fall."

The boys rushed out, returning as breathlessly as usual, Tad crying, "Mamaday, Papaday, come see what we got on the roof."

Mary, dragged by the hand by eight-year-old Tad and Abraham by William, who was ten, went up a flight of stairs to the attic, repository for all the broken furniture and abandoned personal effects of presidential families since 1800, then through a trap door to the roof. There, facing Virginia, the boys had mounted some logs for cannon, and had half a dozen condemned rifles on the parapet.

"Let 'em come," cried Tad. "Me and Willie are ready for 'em!"

Abraham said guardedly:

"Most of our West Point officers are from the seceded states. During the past four years Buchanan has let the south drain us of troops, cannon, guns, ammunition. If we have to start defending ourselves tomorrow, Tad's and Willie's fort will be as well armed as the rest of the north."

Each day dawned with its own disaster: Virginia's secession on Wednesday; on Thursday the blowing up of the arsenal and armory at Harper's Ferry by the federal garrison, which could not hold it, as well as secessionist riots in Baltimore and the burning of a key railroad bridge leading into Washington; Friday, the destroying of the federal navy yard and ships at Norfolk before they could be captured by the south; the attack upon the Sixth Massachusetts Infantry as it moved across Baltimore while changing trains; Saturday, the wrecking of the last railroad lines into Washington by the rebels, cutting the city off from the north not only for supplies and mail, but troops as well; Sunday, the severing of the telegraph lines, depriving Washington of its last communication with the north; Monday, General Scott's report that some two thousand secessionist troops were just below Mount Vernon, erecting batteries, that several thousand more were being brought down-river from Harper's Ferry, while secessionist mobs were marching up from Baltimore and Confederate gunboats were coming up the unguarded Potomac. . . .

At four o'clock she went after Abraham and insisted that he go out for an hour's drive.

"It's the only fresh air you get all day."

But this Monday afternoon she could not extricate him from his nest of generals, so she drove out alone. Pennsylvania Avenue, usually crowded at this promenade hour, was empty; all shops were closed, windows boarded, even the Willard Hotel, jammed with hundreds of guests a few days before, as deserted as though decimated by a plague. Secessionist families were locking their homes and bolting southward, northerners with children had fled the city in carriages, farm wagons, on horseback and afoot. Even the public buildings seemed abandoned, for whole segments of government employees, from file clerk to an adjutant general of the army and commodore of the navy, had resigned and gone over to the rebels. There were sentinels in front of the capital buildings, the Treasury was barricaded with sandbags.

Abraham came to their sitting room a half hour after she had returned. He looked harassed.

"I walked south along the river as far as the arsenal: the doors were wide open, and not even a guard on duty! My God, Mary, southern troops could have rowed across the river and emptied the building without our even knowing it."

"Abraham, what is being done to protect you? Or are you as wide open as the doors at that arsenal?"

"Well, now, General Stone has double sentries posted in the bushes, and there is a guard stationed in the basement. If they kill me, the next man will be just as bad for them; but in a country like this, where our habits are simple and must be, assassination is always possible."

"Forgive me if I can't accept this oriental fatalism," she replied with a touch of asperity. "I don't happen to have a vice-presidential husband who would automatically move up to take your place."

Nicolay announced that some of the wounded soldiers and officers of the Sixth Massachusetts were calling. Mary accompanied Abraham to the Oval Room. When the commanding officer asked where the main body of northern troops was, Abraham replied caustically:

"I don't believe there is any north. The New York Seventh Regiment is a myth. Rhode Island is not known in our geography any longer. You are the only northern realities."

The next morning she awakened before six, found Abraham already gone. When he returned he had little stomach for food: he had been on an inspection tour of the city's defenses, had found Fort Washington on the bank of the Potomac in a complete state of neglect, the gun carriages rotted, the shot piles rusty. The navy yard, though it was well kept up, had lost so much of its personnel that it could not resist an attack; the city's food supply was so low that the military had had to seize stores of flour and grain at Georgetown. Without regiments from the north the capital was doomed; for fifteen thousand rebel troops were reported massed at nearby Alexandria, eight thousand at Harper's Ferry, two thousand at Mount Vernon.

John Hay entered with his usual morsel of gossip: those southerners who had remained behind were predicting that Jefferson Davis soon would be writing orders at Abraham Lincoln's executive desk, and Mrs. Varina Davis sleeping in Mary's bed. When Hay told them of the clergyman who, before fleeing south, had left enough food in the cellar of his house for the cat for three weeks, since that was all the time needed before the preacher would return with the Confederate government, Mary swore:

"By the Eternal, tell somebody to break into the cellar and bring that cat to the White House!"

Abraham smiled wistfully.

"You're right, Mary, that's one convert we can make."

But that was the bottom of the cup: at noon the next day, while she was in her sitting room with the boys, reading aloud from Longfellow, she heard the music of a marching band. Abraham rushed in from his office, his face aglow, followed by General Stone.

"It's the crack New York Seventh! A thousand strong! They've been sitting in Annapolis for three days, then they started marching and repaired the railroad ahead of them. Come to the north portico, they're going to pass by in review."

Mary posted the two boys at the big windows, went downstairs with Abraham to the main portico. The Seventh New York paraded past in their handsome gray uniforms, marching smartly to the music of their own band, saluting the Lincolns with a sharp "Eyes Right!" as they passed the White House. Within a matter of hours the Eighth Massachusetts arrived, and behind them the First Rhode Island . . . and then a flood of newspapers, telegrams, mail from every part of the north.

The seige was ended. Neither her husband nor her children nor she could be forced to flee, or be barricaded in the Treasury or captured by the rebels. She had come as close as a cat's whisker to having the shortest tenure in the White House of any First Lady in the history of the country.

9

PRIOR to Sumter Abraham had been criticized for lacking policy, strength and action; now he was exercising his fullest executive powers: seizure of the telegraph offices, suspension of the writ of habeas corpus, blockading of the southern ports, calling up troops, dipping into the treasury for millions of dollars for the matériel of war, refusing to summon Congress until July 4, thus giving himself time to organize the war before Congress could start its debates. As she watched him sign a staggering pile of parchment army commissions every morning before the first visitors were admitted; study charts and statistics of the manpower and productive power of the sixteen northern states as compared to the eleven rebellious ones; try to bring unity into a cabinet that was torn with personal animosities, irreconcilable political antagonisms and individual ambitions; confer hourly with the army generals who had to whip a mass of green clerks, farmers, mechanics, students and lawyers, most of whom had never shot a gun, into disciplined soldiers; organize a north totally unprepared for war, without adequate shipyards or factories to turn out matériel; and to bring into some kind of working order the hundreds of committees throughout the nation who were trying to buy and produce the countless commodities needed to supply an army, she was delighted to see that he who had maintained that he had neither desire nor talent to sit behind an executive desk had a real skill in handling a multiplicity of detail.

His workday was endless, with a visitation of commission seekers replacing the army of job hunters, and a horde of self-appointed advisers. During the course of one hour that she spent in his executive office, knitting in a chair in a corner, she heard him advised to let the south go, build a wall between the north and south, burn Baltimore, seize and hang all southern traitors, destroy Charleston, force the resignation of his cabinet, raise an army of three hundred thousand men, liberate and arm all slaves.

"Why do you continue to go through it?" she asked, when at last she had got him out of the office and into the library to have his lunch of biscuit, fruit and milk on a tray.

He ran a hand over his eyes, replied:

"I can't do without these public-opinion baths, they keep me in touch with the plain people. Take that fellow this morning who looked like a pious preacher. I was sure I was in for it! But when he shook my hand he said, 'Mr. President, I think you are doing everything for the good of the country that is in the power of man to do. As one of your constituents I now say to you, Do in the future as you damn please, and I will support you!' I was so pleased with him I invited him to lunch tomorrow."

She too was busy. She spent her mornings in the sunny library upstairs with old friends like Edward Baker dropping in to reminisce about the days in Springfield, new friends like Chevalier Wikoff, a fine linguist and elegant man of the world who had been decorated by the queen of Spain and been intimate with the royal family of France, to tell her about life in the courts of Europe; newspaper and magazine reporters dropping in to chat. In the afternoon she received in the Red Room: there were manufacturers and financiers from the east with their beautifully gowned wives sitting next to country people in boots and calicoes; in the evenings she received in the Blue Room, inviting whatever actors, musicians, singers, painters or writers happened to be in Washington, along with Senator Sumner, James Shields, Horace Greeley, Ann Stephens, a lady novelist, Kate Chase, Mrs. Gideon Welles, Mrs. Caleb Smith. Saturday afternoons she welcomed the public in the conservatory, sending each visitor home with a little bunch of flowers.

And now she planned to go with Lizzie to New York to shop for the White House. Abraham asked her to buy an open carriage at Brewster's. She had only six thousand dollars to work with until Congress convened on July 4 and Abraham could get more money for her; aside from sheer necessities such as sheets and towels, blankets and mattresses for their bedrooms, she planned to spend most of her available funds on the state chambers, where its effect would be evident to the public.

They went down the Potomac by boat, then up the Atlantic coast to

Perth Amboy where they changed to the cars for New York, putting up at the Metropolitan Hotel. After purchasing a gorgeous carriage from Brewster's, the money coming out of her own pocket, she began her shopping at Humphrey's, where she bought three hundred yards of fancy matting for the executive offices, and then at Stewart's selected crimson Wilton carpeting for the Red Room, chintz Wilton for the upstairs guest room, G. and O. Wilton for Abraham's office. For the state dining room she ordered from Haughwout's a hundred-and-ninety-piece royal purple and gold china dining service to be engraved with the presidential seal; a porcelain dessert, tea and breakfast service, Sèvres bonbon dishes and punchbowls to match; a seventeen-hundred-piece set of Bohemian cut glass with the United States coat of arms, ten dozen ivory-handled dinner knives, six dozen ivory-handled dessert knives. She next went to William H. Carryl and Brother, the furniture store, buying armchairs, wall chairs, a sofa with a French satin cover and a rich rosewood center table, materials for curtains and draperies, French brocades; a rosewood bedstead, washstands and bureau and purple satin bed curtains for the guest room.

She also managed to find some exquisite French fabrics for new gowns. When Lizzie raised an eyebrow at the amount she was spending, Mary exclaimed:

"I have to spend a great deal of money, Lizzie. The Washington ladies scrutinize everything I wear with critical curiosity. The very fact of having grown up in the west subjects me to more searching observation."

"I didn't mean to criticize, Cousin Mary. I think you should wear only the best, not so much because of the Washington ladies but because Cousin Lincoln likes to see you in full dress."

Everywhere she went she was followed by reporters who inquired into the details of what she was buying.

When she returned to Washington Abraham asked, "Could I see that three-thousand-dollar lace shawl the papers say you bought?"

"Three-thousand-dollar shawl!" Indignation flared on her forehead. "I never bought a *three-dollar* shawl! Abraham, why are the papers so cruel? The reporters literally hounded me . . . some of their stories had me spending fortunes in stores I never even entered."

She was eager for the Washington news, but it wasn't until midnight that he came into her bedroom, where she was reading *Père Goriot* in French, and stretched out his full length beside her: railroad service to the north had been resumed, federal soldiers had taken Alexandria and Arlington Heights of Virginia without a fight, so that they no longer could see Confederate flags or artillery from the White House; but the thousands of troops sequestered in Washington, without sewers or sanitation, getting drunk and unmanageable in their enforced idleness, were making the city uninhabitable.

"John Hay says Washington smells like ten thousand dead cats. Everyone's afraid of a pestilence, but what concerns me more is the collapse of discipline. These men came to fight, not drill and bugle all day, and in their idleness

330

they're quarreling with their officers, firing their weapons just for the sport, committing crimes. . . . If I don't fight them, I'll lose them. . . ."

It was past one when they finished visiting. Before going into his bedroom Abraham kissed her good night, said:

"It's good to have you home again."

She was happy: he had not outgrown his need for her.

10

NOW that Virginia was recruiting troops, Abraham was convinced that the fate of the secession depended on the border states: Kentucky, Missouri, Maryland, Delaware: those states that formed a picket fence between the slave south and the free north, having some slavery within their boundaries but an equal sentiment for the Union. He was particularly sensitive about their birth state, Kentucky.

"I think to lose Kentucky is nearly to lose the whole game," he told her; "Kentucky gone, we cannot hold Missouri, nor, as I think, Maryland. These all against us, and the job on our hands is too large for us. We might as well consent to separation at once. I have some wonderful letters from Josh Speed; he's asking for arms to be distributed to men of proven loyalty; but above all we have to bind their leaders to the Union cause."

Within the hour Mary had sent a dinner invitation to John Breckinridge, former vice-president under Buchanan and candidate of the slave states for the presidency against Abraham, now a senator from Kentucky. He had been an intimate of the Todd household; she counted on their long relationship to help keep him loyal. As dignified, serene forty-year-old Breckinridge finished the last of his poundcake, he turned to Lizzie Grimsley.

"Cousin Lizzie, I would not like to see you disappointed in your expected stay in the White House." His voice had a teasing tone. "So I will now invite you to remain here as a guest when the Confederacy takes possession."

Mary pushed away her dessert plate, feeling that beneath his banter Senator Breckinridge had announced himself. There was an edge to her voice as she replied:

"We will be only too happy to entertain her until that time!"

The next morning Ben Hardin Helm called at the White House. Ben, a West Point graduate with military experience in Texas, had told Abraham before Sumter that he would like to return to the army. Abraham welcomed the young man.

"I have no claim on you, Mr. President," Ben confessed; "I opposed your candidacy . . ."

Abraham waved this away.

"What counts now, Ben, is your loyalty to the Union." He went to the tall desk between the windows, brought a sealed envelope from a pigeonhole. "Here is a major's commission in the paymaster's division, so that you will never use the sword against the people of the south."

Ben ran his fingers through his brown hair.

"You are most generous. . . ."

Mary put her hands on Ben's shoulders.

"Go back to Kentucky and get Emilie and bring her here to the White House. I need her with me, Ben, just as the army needs scholarly, dignified young men like you."

When Ben returned two nights later, internecine war had dug lines of embattlement on his face.

"Mr. President, Sister Mary, I've just been to see my old friend from the army, Colonel Robert E. Lee . . ."

"We have the highest regard for Colonel Lee," Abraham broke in. "General Scott has offered to step down and place the Union army in his hands."

Ben's voice was constricted.

"Colonel Lee is ill because of the decision he has to make, but he says he cannot strike against his own people; the property belonging to his children, all they possess, lies in Virginia. He says he cannot raise his hand against his children . . . he's resigning his commission in the United States Army."

Abraham was the first to recover. His voice was soft.

"It's a bad blow, the Union needs Colonel Lee. But he's a Virginian and Virginia has seceded." His voice grew firm. "This is not true for you, Kentucky has not seceded, it is not getting up an army against us, you would not be called on to strike against your people or your home . . ."

When Ben did not answer, Mary cried:

"Ben, you're not going over to the rebels? There's no reason on earth! You're not a slaveowner, or a plantation owner . . ."

Ben was breathing heavily.

"I'm going . . . to join . . . the Confederate army. . . ."

The room was rent with the piercing lines of unspoken communication. Then, when Mary was about to walk out of the room, Abraham said in a paternal voice:

"I appreciate your coming here to tell us, Ben; it can't have been easy for you. Good-bye, I hope we meet again . . . in happier times."

Ben kissed Mary's cheek with a kiss that burned her skin. Abraham said in profound sadness:

"His sympathies are with the south instead of the north. Why? And if, with all logic on the side of his remaining loyal, he walks out on our offer of a commission, to join the rebel army, how many good and honest souls like himself, sorely troubled in conscience, will we lose?"

To herself, Mary answered, Nearly all my Kentucky family! What I've dreaded has come to pass; we'll be a house divided.

332

The weeks passed in a welter of activity as she brought crews of workmen into the White House to scrape off old paint, wash windows, ceilings and moldings, take down and clean chandeliers, gaseliers, the White House portraits, replace bellpulls, lay the matting and carpets as they arrived from New York. The early afternoons she saved for visits to the ring of army camps encircling Washington, in particular Camp Mary Lincoln, which was the favorite of Tad and William. They returned at teatime usually to find Bud and Holly Taft, two youngsters who lived close by, waiting for the boys, along with their sixteen-year-old sister Julia, a pretty girl with long black curls and crisp taffeta dresses who had become attached to Mary, partly because Mary let her read the novels in the White House library, a pastime forbidden by her mother.

"Why is it, Mrs. Lincoln, that I can discuss things freely with you, subjects like . . . boys . . . and love? You're never too exalted to sympathize with my stories. I would not dare annoy my lady mother with such trivial things."

"Perhaps because I've always longed for a daughter, Julia."

Tad kept the house alive with his laughter and pranks; he was also the despair of the servants, whom he kept in an uproar as he ran the rooms in his baggy trap-door pants buttoned to a waist, looking for ways to liven up the sober routine of the Executive Mansion. Watt, the gardener, called him "the Madame's wildcat." When a visitor gave him a present of a new ball he transformed the spacious vestibule into a handball court . . . promptly breaking a large mirror. William and the Taft boys gathered around the shattered glass in horror.

"I don't believe Pa'll care," muttered Tad.

His pronunciation had improved a little, but mostly he was better understood because people took pains to understand him.

"It is not Pa's looking glass," objected William, "it belongs to the United States Government."

This impressed Tad, but only for an instant; he ran down to the kitchen, returned to sprinkle salt over his left shoulder onto the velvet carpet, then dragged the three boys upstairs to the library to teach him the Lord's Prayer backwards so he would not have seven years of bad luck. When he interrupted an important conference in Abraham's office, shooting a cannon or beating a drum, Abraham would say mildly:

"My son, can't you manage to make a little less noise?" and go on with his discussion.

When the servants complained that Tad and William, having found a bin of visiting cards in the attic that had been accumulating since the John Quincy Adams regime, had thrown them high into the air of all the rooms, pretending they were snow, then ridden across them on a sled made of a chair on barrel staves, Mary replied:

"Let the boys have a good time."

During her ten-day absence Abraham apparently had abandoned the habit

333

of coming to the family dining room for breakfast. She knocked on the door of the Executive Office, walked in without waiting to be bidden. She found herself facing Abraham and his cabinet of seven men, all gazing up at her with interrupted intentness. After a moment's pause Abraham said quietly:

"Yes, Mrs. Lincoln? What can the government do for you?"

"The government can come to breakfast."

"But, Mrs. Lincoln, we are settling some urgent matters," protested Seward in a tone that was intended to send her back through the door.

"Have you had your breakfast, Mr. Seward?"

"Why, yes."

"Then I must tell you that Mr. Lincoln has neither breakfasted nor had a cup of coffee since he rose this morning. Mr. Lincoln must eat if he is going to conserve his strength; you most patently do not want to be interrupted, but I assure you the president won't do you much good dead."

Abraham smiled, dropped his head toward his left shoulder as though to say, That does it! and excused himself from the meeting. She knew from the stares of the cabinet officers that she had convinced them of nothing more than the fact that Mrs. President Lincoln was a busybody.

For that matter, hardly a day passed without some attack being printed against her in the Democratic press, trivial gossip that she was playing favorites among the hostesses whom she invited to social functions, of there being a hundred Todds in Washington all looking for federal jobs; accusations of extravagance, of having spent thousands of dollars in New York with nothing to show for it; charges that she had poor taste, was naïve. Tad came home with a bloody nose because he fought some boy in Lafayette Square who said the Lincolns were mudsills. The Washington *Standard* reported:

Her majesty Mrs. Lincoln is doing much to make King Abraham unpopular. Her conduct is that of an uneducated female without good sense who has been unluckily elevated into a sphere for which she cannot fit herself.

She went to Abraham with the journal in her hand, crying in exasperation:

"Abraham, we simply must answer some of these absurd charges. That one about the three-thousand-dollar shawl has been reprinted in every small town in the country."

Abraham sheltered her.

"Mary, if we were to try to read, much less answer, all the attacks made on us, this shop might as well close for any other business. Let's do the very best we know how, the very best we can; and keep doing so until the end. If the end brings us out all right, what is said against us won't amount to anything. If the end brings us out wrong, ten angels swearing we were right will make no difference."

She was looking forward to the first state dinner for the foreign embassies. The diplomats had been cool to the Lincolns the first time they had been invited to a reception; this time she hoped to make friends among them.

The dining room had been repainted and had a fresh air. She had just finished her final check of the menu with Mrs. Watt, the stewardess, when news was brought to them that Senator Stephen Douglas, after a series of fiery speeches in Springfield's Hall of Representatives on the need for loyalty in the midst of treason, and in the Wigwam in Chicago on the theme that a man could not be a true Democrat unless he was a loyal patriot, had fallen into a high fever in his rooms at the Tremont House, and died after a few days' illness.

Abraham was in his bedroom, his eyes wet with weeping.

"I feel as though I've lost my closest friend," he said; "and yet all our lives we were adversaries. We're going to miss him."

". . . he was like a brother. I didn't meet Steve until I was eighteen, yet I always felt that we were children together. Poor Adele, I'll write at once." She paused. "Will you want the White House draped in black? Shall I send word to the diplomatic corps that the dinner has been postponed?"

"The work of the government must go on . . . no matter who dies."

She was inclined to wear black but Abraham thought it would throw a pall over the party, so she donned a dark green taffeta with a small lace collar, and wore no jewelry or flowers in her hair.

The dinner was delicious, the conversation matched in brilliance the colorful insignia of the ambassadors and ministers, and that of their wives in their exquisite court dresses. She glanced up to find Abraham's eyes resting warmly upon her as she conversed in French with the French and Chilean ambassadors. They exchanged amused smiles as the diplomats and their wives passed snuffboxes about the table.

A few days later she read in the New York *Star:*

> The President, on Tuesday evening, gave a dinner to the Diplomatic Corps which was, in many respects, the most brilliant affair of the sort that has ever taken place in the Executive Mansion. Through the good taste of Mrs. Lincoln, the stiff, artificial flowers heretofore ornamenting the Presidential tables were wholly discarded and their places delightfully supplied by fragrant, natural flowers from the floral riches of the White House conservatories and grounds. The dinner was served in a style to indicate that Mrs. Lincoln's good taste and good judgment had exercised supervision in this department also.

She hugged the paper to her. "We do have to take the bad with the good, don't we, Abraham, and survive them both?"

Abraham peered at her solemnly over the silver rims of his spectacles. "Wisdom is minted out of mortal wounds."

His expression brought to mind Dr. John Ward: she was again standing beside the white-haired wisp of a man at a window overlooking Transylvania University. She had cried out in confusion and pain, "Where does a woman turn?" and Dr. Ward had replied, "This may seem an unsatisfactory solution for one of your ambitions and gifts, but perhaps you will have to create your place in the world through a husband, or a son. Do not despise this approach, if it is all that is open to you."

Wisdom is minted out of mortal wounds, said Abraham.

She would add to that: the wisdom to survive must be minted not only of their wounds but of their love.

11

BY mid-June a suffocating heat had settled over Washington, yet the heat of the weather was nothing compared to the heat of pressures being exerted upon Abraham to make a quick end to the rebellion. Horace Greeley started a campaign in his New York *Tribune* that swept the north like a wild fire across parched foothills:

> ON TO RICHMOND! The Rebel Congress must not be allowed to meet there on the 20th of July! By that date the place must be held by the National Army! ON TO RICHMOND!

Abraham stood before a topographical engineer's map of Virginia on the wall of his office.

"On to Richmond: that's all I hear! I'm afraid the enthusiasm of the north will die down if we don't have a battle." He pointed with a long index finger to Manassas, where the Confederates were reported to have thirty thousand men assembled. "When I asked General Scott why he hadn't ordered a reconnaissance, he replied, 'I have not an officer on whom I could depend for the work. They would fall into some trap, or bring on a general engagement when I did not seek it or desire it.' When I asked General McDowell what he knew about the force and position of the enemy, he complained that he had no trustworthy maps of the country, no knowledge of the enemy's position or numbers. The only one who has come in with an over-all plan for espionage is your favorite detective, Allan Pinkerton. . . ."

He did not pursue the thought, he was in too grim a mood for humor.

"McDowell has no intention of fighting this summer; he says it is wrong to make him organize, discipline, march and fight all at the same time. I told him, 'You are green, it is true, but they are green also. You are all green alike.' General Scott doesn't want this battle at Manassas, he wants to plan a gigantic operation down the Mississippi Valley in the autumn or winter with a final battle at New Orleans, thus sealing off the Confederacy."

He turned to her with anguish in his eyes.

"That might take years; we haven't got years! The cabinet wants the battle to take place, the entire north wants the battle to take place." He stared out the window. "Yes, and I want it to take place. I've become convinced that the quicker we get this war over the less costly it will be to everybody. If we can beat their army at Manassas, then take Richmond, the backbone of the rebellion will be broken."

Finally he brought her the news that the attack was to be launched in ten days. The doors of the Executive Mansion were open day and night. She stopped all entertaining, kept the family rooms uncluttered for those few moments when he might be able to come in for rest or quiet. She left the presidential grounds only to call for Adele Douglas and sit beside the stricken widow in the visitors' gallery of the Senate while the late senator from Illinois was richly eulogized.

When the scheduled day of battle arrived no one was ready: the weather was hot, the mechanics of moving a federal army to the battlefield had not yet unfolded. It was not until six days later that she stood on the north portico overlooking Pennsylvania Avenue with Abraham on one side of her and General Scott on the other, watching a parade of troops headed for the Long Bridge to Virginia: the Fourth Pennsylvania, the Eighth New York, the Thirteenth New York, the First Massachusetts, the Seventy-first New York, the Third Maine, the Minnesota and Wisconsin volunteers; German troops singing "Ach, du lieber Augustin," Scotch Highlanders in their kilts, French immigrants in Zouave uniforms with white gaiters and red culottes, Irishmen of the Sixty-ninth New York with green banners mixed among the American flags.

Suddenly there was a commotion below: a band stopped playing "John Brown's Body," the New York Eighth fell out of step, its soldiers jamming into those in front of them while everyone gaped openmouthed at the Lincolns.

As of one accord they turned about . . . to see Tad waving a Confederate flag over their heads for all he was worth. Abraham pinioned the boy and the flag under an arm until an orderly arrived, and Tad was handed over like a sack of potatoes. Abraham chuckled.

"That was Tad's idea of showing he's neutral."

Washington was pervaded by the confidence arising out of action, long lines of troops, sutlers' wagons and ambulances crossing into Virginia. General Scott announced, "We shall be in Richmond by Saturday!" but as she glanced out of her dressing-room window and saw Abraham hurrying toward the War Department, a felt hat on the back of his head, wiping his face with a red pocket handkerchief, she thought, Indeed he has reason to be anxious: for anybody in Washington could read in the newspapers the precise number of troops the north was using, their line of march and where the battle was to be fought.

She hardly saw Abraham all day Saturday for the crush of people in the White House wanting passes to go through the lines to observe the battle, not only newspaper reporters and such senators as Wade, Trumbull and Chandler, but groups of excited civilians who had engaged every horse, carriage, gig, wagon and hack that was available. The demand for hampers of provisions and wines had increased so sharply that the chefs of hotels had trebled their prices.

She locked herself in her bedroom, sat down in a rocker and picked up

337

her sewing. Her stomach churned, her throat was dry, the thought of people rushing to a battlefield as though it were a festive Sunday picnic made her ill, particularly the stories of congressmen who were lugging heavy navy revolvers and rifles in the hopes of shooting something, women who were carrying opera glasses, the better to see the show.

Everywhere people exclaimed:

"By Monday morning the rebellion will be a thing of the past!"

She fervently hoped so.

She awakened early to a beautiful dawn, the air clear and cool. Before her the Potomac was a broad silver ribbon. At eleven she and Abraham set out in their carriage for the New York Avenue Presbyterian Church. After Reverend Gurley's sermon they drove home through silent streets, the crowds standing in front of the War Department and Treasury building waiting for news . . . and listening to the distant rumbling of guns. They found their two boys and the three Taft children in the library.

Abraham sat down at the table, read the story of Jacob and Esau out of the Bible, explaining to the five youngsters, "Every educated person should know something about the Bible and the Bible stories." When he had finished, Mary asked:

"Why do our boys like to go to your church, Julie?"

"I guess our church is livelier," Julia replied.

"Lots livelier," agreed William; "only it won't be any more. Up to now when Dr. Smith prayed for you, Pa, all the secessionists would bang their pew doors and leave church. This morning a lieutenant was there with some soldiers and he announced in front of the church, 'Ordered by the provost marshal, anyone disturbing this service or leaving it in the middle of prayers will be arrested and taken to the guardhouse.' Pa, why do the preachers always pray so long for you?"

"I suppose because they think I need it," replied Abraham, no longer smiling, but looking sad and worried. He turned to gaze out the window for a moment and said, half to himself, "I guess I do."

The rumbling of the distant cannon grew in intensity. William asked:

"Pa, is that noise the battle in Virginia?"

"Yes, Willie, those are big cannons going off."

"Sound like Ma slamming doors," said Tad.

There was a knock. A messenger from the War Department handed Abraham a telegram. A flash of joy lit his weary features. He handed her the sheet. She read:

BULL RUN THE KEY OF THE ENEMY'S POSITION HAS BEEN TAKEN AND THE ENEMY COMPLETELY ROUTED

At four o'clock Abraham told her he was going to walk over to General Scott's office; he returned in a half hour to report that he had found the

338

general asleep. There was a telegram informing him the secession lines had been driven back two or three miles.

"I feel considerably better now, Mary. Could we order the carriage and go for a drive?"

They returned at six-thirty, refreshed, to find Nicolay and Hay waiting for them at the top of the stairs: Secretary Seward had just been to the White House to inform the president that General McDowell was in full retreat, that the Battle of Bull Run was lost, that he had called on General Scott to summon forth extra troops to save the capital.

Abraham shook his head in disbelief, left immediately for the War Department. When he returned she asked:

"How bad is it, Abraham?"

"It's damn bad. We just had a confirming telegram from McDowell: his troops are in rout, they will not re-form. He is crying for help."

Rain began to fall: the rain that seemed eternally to fall when misfortune struck. A dozen times during the evening Abraham left the White House and walked alone to the War Department.

At midnight she went to his office to see if she could persuade him to come to bed. He was reclining on a couch, listening to Senators Wade, Chandler and Trumbull, Congressman Riddle and several newspapermen pour out their eyewitness accounts of the battle. She stood inside the doorway, listening. First one took up the narrative, then another:

"The battle began with a heavy cannonade; the only sign to the eye were clouds of smoke and the rattle of small arms. We pushed on within the wood and found the Twelfth New York at rest along the highway, beyond which was the Second Ohio. In the distance toward Manassas was a dense cloud of dust said to be the retreating foe. Everybody said the battle was over, the rebels beaten, and our boys were awaiting orders for the approaching end of the day."

"The temporary success at the noon hour was achieved by less than two thirds of the effective force drawn out in a long, irregular, barely connected line, tired and suffering from hunger and thirst. But few officers and men could be rallied for another advance. Towards four o'clock the rebels felt strong enough to take the offensive. Suddenly a small body of cavalry turned the angle of the wood and headed toward us at full speed. Someone called: 'These are the Rebs! Jump out and be ready for them.' They came within fifty yards, fired into our crowd. Rebel cavalry with a battery section commenced shelling the turnpike."

"It seemed as if the very devil of panic and cowardice seized every mortal soldier, officer, citizen and teamster. No officer tried to rally the soldiers or do anything except to run toward Centreville. The farther they ran the more frightened they grew. They threw away their blankets, knapsacks, canteens and finally muskets, cartridge boxes. We called to them, tried to tell them there was no danger, implored them to stand. We put out our heavy revolvers and threatened to shoot them, but all in vain. A causeless, sheer, absolute, absurd panic possessed everybody. We were borne along with the mass, unable to go ahead or pause or draw out, with the road blocked with wagons thundering and crashing on. Members of Congress and civilians abandoned private vehicles and joined the race for safety. The terrified crowds presented a pitiful and humiliating sight."

Abraham slowly raised his head.

"It is your notion that we whipped the rebels and then ran away from them?"

Congressman Riddle replied:

"We ran away, and so were defeated. We were not beaten on the field."

At dawn she and Abraham rode down Pennsylvania Avenue. Rain was falling in torrents. Over the Long Bridge from Virginia came the demoralized Union soldiers, straggling singly and in broken squads, soaked through with the rain, covered with mud, without their knapsacks or crossbelts or muskets, lacking their shoes and greatcoats, many with blood caked on their heads and faces.

All about them men were dropping from exhaustion. Others stumbled blindly, falling onto doorsteps to lie with their faces turned away from the rain. On corners women poured hot coffee for those who could hold the cups, while onlookers stood dazed and helpless, unable to believe the tragic sight.

Abraham got out of the carriage. A soldier began to speak.

". . . how many dead . . . stopped trying to count . . . strewn through the woods . . . stretched on their backs with their caps laid over their faces. I saw men laying in grotesque positions, arms and legs shot off . . . one I dragged under a tree had part of his neck and skull carried away . . ."

Abraham asked questions of the returning cavalrymen slumped in their saddles, learned that some of the retreating troops had stopped on the Virginia side. There was no evidence of General Scott's efforts to bring out fresh troops or to reorganize the old ones.

Back in the carriage, Abraham sat with his head in his hands.

"I can't understand why General Beauregard isn't here already. He must know that we couldn't even put up a fight."

"Abraham, do you think we ought to open the White House to these men, prepare hot food for them?"

He had not heard her; their carriage was passing the railroad station where hundreds of soldiers jammed the cars, men whose three months' enlistment was up, sitting with their heads bowed, eyes averted, wanting only to get out of the capital before the Confederate forces struck.

As they entered the White House Abraham turned to her.

"This day is bitterer than gall; but it must not conquer us. We've got to lift ourselves and the Union out of this defeat."

He put his arm about her shoulders; resolutely they mounted the broad staircase, returning to this job of work and this agony they had so passionately pursued.

340

12

A pall settled over Washington; all roads of censure led through the murky gloom to the White House. As she watched the patchwork of crow's-feet wrinkles extend from under Abraham's eyes down the hollow cheeks, Mary could not decide which was the bitterest pill for them to swallow: General Scott's coming to the White House to cry out, "I am the greatest coward in America: I deserve removal because I did not stand up, when my army was not in condition for fighting, and resist it to the last"; the demand of the Democratic papers that the "effusion of blood" be stopped even if it meant the recognition of the Confederacy; the more than one hundred and fifty newspaper editors signing a petition to end the "present unholy war"; or the letter they received from Horace Greeley, saying:

> If our disaster is fatal, then every drop of blood henceforth shed in this quarrel will be wantonly shed. If the Union is irrevocably gone, an armistice ought to be proposed at once with a view to a peaceful adjustment.

She watched Abraham walk up and down the sitting room, hands behind him, head bent, sighing. She did not know how to comfort him . . . except to be there and to listen when at length he was able to talk.

"We've learned one thing from this defeat: the rebellion cannot be a summer excursion. The north knows nothing of war! We have to learn everything there is to know, and on that knowledge build an army. As commander-in-chief I have no escape from that responsibility; working in the blind is too costly in human lives, the south's as well as our own."

His first move was to summon to Washington General George B. McClellan, who had won two opening skirmishes in western Virginia, to replace General McDowell.

To avoid the suffocating heat of the Washington summer she had planned to move the family out to the Anderson Cottage at the Soldiers' Home, located on a hilltop three miles north of Washington in the midst of five hundred acres of shade trees and green lawns that swept down to the Potomac.

"Then you won't want to be moving out to the Soldiers' Home?"

"We'd best sit right here . . ."

"Oh no," she interrupted, "I won't sit and lick my wounds; if Washington sees us continuing the work on the White House perhaps they'll stop looking through their telescopes for the rebel army."

Armed with the twenty thousand dollars that Congress had appropriated for her use, she hired a crew to repaint the entire outside of the building until it shone in its new white coat, then brought the painters inside to do the woodwork and ceilings. She had the newly arrived wallpapers hung, put white needlework Swiss lace curtains at the long windows, French brocatelle draperies with gold tassels in the East Room.

Hearing that Prince Napoleon was coming to Washington, she summoned Nicolay and Hay and asked them to draw up a list of dignitaries she must invite to a state dinner for him. From the Chevalier Henry Wikoff, who had been awarded the cross of the Legion of Honor by Louis Napoleon, she sought instruction on the protocol in entertaining French royalty.

Secretary of State Seward was bringing the prince and his party to the White House. Having been helped by Mrs. Keckley into her white grenadine gown, Mary went into Abraham's bedroom to find him sitting in a chair by the window, his heels locked into one of the rungs, knees under his chin, reading his mail in the fading sunlight while a servant shaved his upper lip and cheeks.

"Mr. Lincoln, it's half past six, the prince's party will be here in a half hour."

"I have only to put on my shirt and that fine-fitting black coat the tailor made me."

She went into Lizzie's bedroom overlooking the north drive to summon her cousin. Out the window she saw William and Bud playing ball in the driveway. Secretary Seward's carriage turned in from Pennsylvania Avenue. As the carriage drew abreast of William he pulled up to his full height, took off his cap and bowed to the ground in courtierlike fashion, Prince Napoleon and his suite returning the bow ceremoniously. She told Abraham the story as they descended the main staircase to the Marine Band tune of "Hail to the Chief."

"William's got the makings of an ambassador," she told him.

"Good thing it wasn't Taddie," commented Abraham with a laugh, "he'd of had the prince in the driveway, shooting marbles."

She took the prince through the Red, Blue, Green and East Rooms. He exclaimed with delight at the velvet French wallpapers, the Sèvres bonbon dishes. The new presidential china and glassware had arrived, the state dining room was beautiful. After dinner the prince remarked in an eloquent whisper, loud enough for Abraham, just up ahead, to hear, as well as Secretary Seward and Lord Lyons, the British minister, just behind:

"Madame, after enjoying the elegant hospitality of the Executive Mansion, I am forced to confess that Paris is not all the world!"

She flushed with pleasure; but the next day when she sat at the escritoire in her bedroom assembling the bills she was shocked to find that the party had cost nine hundred dollars. She sent a messenger for Nicolay and Hay. They stood in the open doorway of her bedroom as though reluctant to enter.

"Gentlemen, I have here the bills for last night's dinner. Would you kindly pay them out of the White House running fund."

The secretaries gazed at each other for a moment. Nicolay replied quietly:
"I'm sorry, Madame President, but we are not permitted to pay for state dinners out of operation expenses."

"Now, Mr. Nicolay, why should the president be obliged to spend nine hundred dollars to entertain Prince Napoleon and the diplomatic corps when their good will is so important to our government?"

"I agree there is no logic in it, Mrs. Lincoln; I simply haven't the authority to pay those bills."

He bowed formally, half turned, waited for her nod of dismissal, then left with Hay trailing him. She felt humiliated that it was in the power of Abraham's secretaries to refuse her. What fund could absorb these bills? The gardener's appropriation was sizable. When Mr. Watt arrived and Mary explained what she wanted him to do, he shifted apologetically from one foot to the other.

"I would be more than happy, Mrs. Lincoln, but I have to send every bill over to the Commissioner of Public Buildings, and if he finds ten dollars that's not spent on plants and flowers, he sends it right back to me. I just got nowhere I can plant nine hundred dollars without it sprouting all over the place."

She next asked Commissioner Wood, in charge of the White House, if he could not absorb the expenses under the heading of improvements to the grounds. Mr. Wood refused categorically.

Angry by now, she stuck the sheaf of bills into a big envelope and sent them to Secretary of the Interior Caleb Smith, whose department was in charge of all public buildings including the White House, and responsible for functions held in public buildings. The bills were returned with a polite but firm note that the Secretary of the Interior could not authorize his department to pay them.

By nightfall the story was all over Washington of Mrs. President Lincoln's frenzied attempt to get somebody, anybody, to pay the expenses of her dinner for Prince Napoleon. When Lizzie returned from a tea at Mrs. Charles Eames's, a cultural as well as gossip center of the capital, she brought back verbatim Mary's conversation with Nicolay and Hay.

Outraged, Mary left the library, went through two of the clerks' offices and into Nicolay's office, where he was sitting at a desk signing letters, with young Hay sorting the mail.

"Mr. Nicolay and Mr. Hay, I am amazed at your disloyalty and bad taste in carrying tales. The White House may be a business office to my husband, but it is also my home and you are guests in my home. I hardly expected that you would repeat conversations or divulge confidences."

Hay looked with his mouth open at John Nicolay, who had gone pale but had not lost his composure.

"Just what confidences are we supposed to have violated, Mrs. Lincoln?"

"The story of my discussion with you this morning is all over Washington, and in precisely the words we used. If you did not repeat them, who did?"

"I'm sure I can't say, Madame President," replied Nicolay coolly. "But I am a man of honor, and no word that has been spoken to me in this White House has ever passed my lips."

There could be no questioning the sincerity of his statement; nor for that matter, in spite of the near contempt on young John Hay's face, could she fail to perceive that her charges against these two men were unfounded. She stammered an apology, withdrew, sick at heart over having broken her most important resolution: not to lose her temper. But nine hundred dollars for a single dinner!

13

WHEN they entered their carriage for an afternoon drive they found that in spite of Abraham's protestations they were surrounded by a cavalry escort. The jingle of the sabers and spurs made such a racket they could hardly hear each other without shouting. Abraham leaned over to exclaim:

"Frankly, our escort seems so young and unused to firearms, I'm more concerned about injury from a carelessly handled weapon than from an assassin's bullet."

Suddenly what sounded like an entire regiment of cavalry came hurtling down on them at breakneck speed, covering Mary and Abraham with a fine dust. It turned out to be General McClellan, at the head of his imposing retinue of aides-de-camp, making for the general's headquarters across Lafayette Square with the passionate intensity with which McClellan did everything. He had completely reorganized the shattered troops and so instilled them with fighting spirit that the danger of Beauregard's invasion had vanished. He had also cleared Washington of the filth, stragglers, drunkenness and other threats to the city's safety. As Mary watched the magnetic young general disappear down Pennsylvania Avenue she said to Abraham:

"He's a great commanding officer, isn't he?"

Though McClellan was a West Point graduate whom the War Department had sent abroad as an observer of European armies and the Crimean War, Abraham had known him, after he resigned from the army in 1857, as vice-president of the Illinois Central.

"My opinion is, he's an engineering genius. The fortifications he has thrown up for the defense of Washington look impregnable. If he is as good a fighter as an organizer the rebellion should be over in a matter of months."

Reassured about Abraham's state of mind, she planned to escape the heat of August and give the boys a holiday on the New Jersey coast. She wrote Hannah Shearer:

We expect to visit Long Branch, to remain a week or ten days. We have invitations from three different hotels, with suites of rooms offered us in each. We have railroad passes, and the trip will cost nothing, which is a good deal to us all these times. How I want you to lay all difficulties aside, and join us. It will give you strength for a year to come. Bring your boys with you, it will be more pleasant all around.

Your attached friend . . .

She received a favorable reply from Hannah.

Before she could leave Washington the Union forces suffered another severe defeat, this time in Missouri where the able and popular General Nathaniel Lyon, attacking a considerably superior Confederate force on Wilson's Creek, not only lost over twelve hundred men in dead, wounded and missing, but was himself killed by a rifle bullet through the heart.

She offered to cancel her trip but Abraham insisted she go as planned. She gathered together William and Tad, Lizzie, Mrs. Watt to look after the ladies and Old William to keep an eye on the boys and the baggage, met Hannah in the railroad station in Philadelphia, then continued on to Long Branch where the fashionable society of New Jersey gathered.

They had beautiful rooms overlooking the sea. The weather was ideal. In the morning they took the four boys sea bathing. In the afternoon while the boys rode ponies furiously up and down the beach, she and Hannah went for visits to the Coast Guard rescue station or walked on the cliffs above the sea in the brilliant-hued sunsets.

"It was so good of you to invite me, Mary," said Hannah.

"You have no idea how I need a friend, my dear," replied Mary. "One I can talk to in full confidence, even in full foolishness sometimes. I'm surrounded by dozens of people, yet I've found the White House to be lonely. Lizzie has to go back to Springfield. All of my White House friends are as new as the paint on the outside of the building; everything I say has a way of becoming gossip." Mary stopped in her walking. "Hannah, could you and Dr. Shearer and the boys move to Washington, live in the White House with us? If we could get the doctor an appointment . . . ?"

Hannah took Mary's hand as she gently shook her head no.

"The doctor isn't well enough; but even if he were, Washington would resent your moving a whole family into the Executive Mansion. Only the president's family is supposed to live there. That's part of your job, Mary, to live alone amidst the crowds."

Mary stared out over the sea, her lips quivering.

She had promised Hannah a quiet vacation and so she accepted only two invitations, one a formal reception and ball in her honor, the other an informal hop to which the countryside was invited. For the grand ball at the Mansion House she wore the white granadine made for Prince Napoleon's dinner. The guests were presented by former Governor Newell of New Jersey. During the eleven o'clock intermission when she rose for a promenade around the ballroom the guests assumed she was ready for supper and made a dash for the dining room, leaving her party deserted in the ballroom. To Mr. Newell's stammered apologies, she said with an amiable laugh:

"I'm as hungry as they are; let us join them, I'm sure there will be plenty of food for all."

The next day the major eastern newspapers, many of whom had reporters at Long Branch to report her activities, spoke of her tact and of how much her hosts had appreciated her good nature. The New York *Herald* ran a column called *The Movements of Mrs. Lincoln*, compared her to Queen Victoria, wrote, "Mrs. Lincoln looked like a queen in her long train and coronet of flowers," spoke of "the glare of lights, soft rustling of silks, cloud of rich and elegant laces."

She returned by way of New York, buying some recent novels for Julia Taft and sets of Washington Irving, Cowper and Roberts's *Holy Land* for their library.

When she stepped inside the door of the White House, refreshed and ready to resume her duties, she found Abraham caught in a new crisis: word had reached Washington that General John C. Fremont, whom Abraham had appointed to build an army in Missouri, had issued a proclamation that the slaves of all those persons in Missouri who had taken up arms against the government were emancipated and free.

The abolitionists went into frenzies of delight, but Abraham showed her a telegram from St. Louis reading, "There is not a day to lose in disavowing emancipation or Kentucky is gone over the mill dam." A letter from Joshua Speed said, "I have been so much distressed since reading that foolish proclamation of Fremont that I have been unable to eat or sleep. So fixed is public sentiment in Kentucky against allowing Negroes to be emancipated, that you had as well attack the freedom of worship in the north as to wage war in a slave state on such a principle." The northern newspapers declared that although they would support with their very lives a war for the preservation of the Union, they would have no part in a war against slavery.

He paced the full length of his office.

"For my part, Mary, I consider the central idea pervading this struggle is not slavery but the necessity that is upon us to prove that popular government is not an absurdity. We must settle once and for all whether in a free government the minority have the right to break up the government whenever they choose. If we fail it will go far to prove the incapability of the people to govern themselves. Taking the government as we found it, we will see if the majority can preserve it; that is what we must never forget: that this new and marvelous democratic form of government, our last best hope on earth, shall not be destroyed. It may seem selfish to put the Union ahead of freeing the slaves; yet if democracy is destroyed, there will be no way for any people anywhere to achieve freedom."

He pulled down a map from the spring roller above the lounge, pointed to the border states. "Look at this whole country that we lose by such an act!"

346

"You can rescind General Fremont's order," she offered tentatively, "you're his commander-in-chief."

"Yes, but he is a good man. I don't want to undermine him. I'll send him a confidential note and ask him to rescind the order himself."

The tranquillity she had garnered on her vacation was drained by the tension inside the White House during the next days, for General Fremont refused to take the president's suggestion. Abraham was forced to revoke the order himself. Abolitionist senators cried: "Only a person sprung from 'poor white trash' could have behaved that way"; Senator Sumner of Massachusetts declared, "We cannot conquer the rebels as the war is now conducted"; preachers denounced him from their pulpits, editors of the abolitionist press and Republican party leaders of New York and Boston swore that Fremont would supplant Lincoln as Republican nominee in 1864.

But it was not until a letter reached them from Springfield, detailing William Herndon's attack on Abraham, that she saw him throw up his arms in despair; for Herndon had said:

"Good God! What is Lincoln doing? This people has got to meet this Negro question face to face now or at some future time. Does he suppose he can crush, squelch out this huge rebellion by popguns filled with rose water? He ought to hang somebody and get up a name for will or decision —for character. Let him hang some child or woman, if he has not courage to hang a *man*. If I were Lincoln I would declare that all slaves should be free and stand emancipated. I would be this age's great hero."

Abraham winced.

"Even my partner turns against me! Can't he see that an emancipation proclamation at this time will lose us the border states, the war and the Union, perpetuate the very thing they're fighting against? Once the Confederacy becomes an independent sovereign nation, no one will rout slavery out of there for a thousand years! Only by keeping the south in the Union can we ultimately prevail on them to rid themselves of slavery."

That same day she heard that Mrs. Keckley's only son had been killed in a skirmish in Missouri. Mary sat down and wrote the Negro mantuamaker a letter of sympathy. Mrs. Keckley came to the White House with eyes red from weeping.

"You can't know what your letter meant to me! To think that the busy Mrs. President Lincoln would take time to feel sorry for me and my boy . . ."

"Sons are very precious, Mrs. Keckley; only a mother can know what his loss would mean."

Mrs. Keckley turned away for a moment, then said, "You are a good woman, Mrs. Lincoln, you have a kind heart. But you have enemies. You must be careful."

"What do you mean?"

"One morning a woman drove up to my rooms and gave me an order to make a dress. When her dress was ready she remarked: 'Mrs. Keckley, you know Mrs. Lincoln very well. Now listen; I have a proposition to make. I

347

have heard so much of Mr. Lincoln's goodness that I should like to be near him. My dear Mrs. Keckley, will you not recommend me to Mrs. Lincoln as a friend of yours out of employment, and ask her to take me as a chambermaid? It may be worth several thousand dollars to you in time.'"

Mary was aghast. "Thousands of dollars! What could she hope to do here that would be worth such a sum of money?"

She had been home only a few days when the rain of printer's ink which had drenched Abraham after Bull Run, and after the revoking of Fremont's emancipation, descended in a cloudburst of black hail upon her own head. She perceived that the *Herald* articles had a purpose in calling her another Queen Victoria, writing of her being surrounded by a royal court at Long Branch, of being swathed in elaborate gowns and exquisite laces: for now the newspapers of the small towns and farming areas, where people of modest means worked so hard for their living, began criticizing her for an unconscionable display of wealth. She was called a wastrel and an unfortunate example to have in the White House in time of tragedy, charged with disgracing the north and weakening their cause, spending money that the Union needed for guns and medicines; being wantonly frivolous in the face of defeat and death . . . unworthy of being First Lady. One letter from a northern mother was published in the *Express* even before it reached her:

Shall the inanities of a Ball Room be now the order of your life? When anxiety for the loved imperilled by war is dimming the eyes of the worthiest of the land, shall you be cheating time and thought by the laugh of the festal group and the buzzing soulless insect life of those who find in these things scope for their hollowness? Are there no lessons of self-sacrifice, of Republican simplicity to be taught when bankruptcy, poverty, and distress stand appalling the homes of thousands in our once prosperous land?

The attacks reached into a new field: she was accused of interfering with the president in the making of appointments. True, she had secured the consulship at Dundee for the Reverend James Smith, their minister at Springfield, a paymastership for Dr. William Wallace, the postmastership for a cousin in Lexington; and a new government job for the father of the Taft children when he was fired from his department and was going to have to move away from Washington; but she had had nothing to do with a hundred other hirings that were charged against her, including the colonelcy for Edward Baker. It was Abraham who had yielded to Senator Baker's request, since Baker had had a fine record in the Mexican War.

Abraham had literally thousands of appointments he was obliged to make, and he saw no reason why he should not appoint qualified friends: Ward Hill Lamon as district marshal of Washington, D.C., Norman Judd to the legation in Berlin, Simeon Francis as paymaster at Fort Vancouver, Dr. Anson Henry surveyor general of Washington Territory. Why should she not express her opinion? Was not her estimate of character and ability as good

348

as the estimate of the thousands of strangers who had thronged the vestibule and main stairs for months, trying to get appointments for themselves or friends?

A letter she had written to General Meigs now made the rounds:

I make a special request, the only one I've ever made of you, to authorize the purchase of five hundred to a thousand Kentucky horses belonging to a special friend of mine in Kentucky. He is a strong Union man and it would be a particular pleasure to me to have, as Kentucky is my native state, some horses from there on the battlefield.

The barrage of criticism was devastating.

"Apparently we can do no right, Puss," said Abraham. "It is hard to wake up every morning and find the air thick with bullets, but until this rebellion is put down we have to serve as foot soldiers." He brushed the hair back behind her ears, kissed her hot tired eyelids. "We're like the travelers who were lost in a wild country on a pitch-black night. A storm raged. Suddenly came a crashing bolt and the travelers dropped upon their knees. 'Oh, Lord,' prayed one of them, 'if it's all the same to You, give us a little more light and a good deal less noise.' "

She laughed, felt better.

14

AT the end of September she came down with chills, what Washingtonians called malarial fever. General McClellan sent her a box of grapes from Cincinnati, Senator Sumner sent her bouquets of autumnal flowers, Mrs. Caleb Smith brought her a handsomely bound set of poems, Kate Chase came calling with two French novels just off the boat. After she had spent ten days in bed, Abraham took her for a drive, showing her how General McClellan had put his entire army into uniform blue, how smartly they marched and drilled in review for their idolized general, whom they called *Little Mac.*

"Abraham, I'm tremendously impressed. When does he fight?"

There was a constrained silence.

"That is the rub. He says he's not ready . . . rebels outnumber him. By the by, he has brought Allan Pinkerton to Washington to organize a spy system. It's Pinkerton who tells him he is outnumbered, though for the life of me I can't see how."

"I would imagine that anything Pinkerton reports about the enemy bears the same relationship to truth that I do to Cleopatra of the Nile."

"I am not going to force McClellan to fight before he's ready. I had a visitation from the three abolitionist senators who came to Washington ahead of the Senate to help me run the war, accompanied by my old friend Lyman Trumbull, who doesn't seem to think too much of me any more. They told me I had to fight, right now, today, because a defeat is no worse than a delay. They don't have to take the responsibility for defeats; I do. The rebel armies don't have to attack us or win battles; all they have to do is defend themselves against our attacks. Their sole purpose is to gain strength so they can function as a separate nation."

If she and Abraham were finding life in the Executive Mansion something less than Utopia, their sons were enjoying their new home. They were constantly receiving gifts; the ones they loved best were two goats, Nanny and Nanko, which they hitched to carts and drove through the wide-open spaces of the White House main floor. Tad took Nanny to bed with him at night. When Nanko escaped, the entire White House had to search until he was corralled in a flower bed, having dug up some of Mr. Watt's favorite bulbs. Watt was furious; only a few days before Tad had picked and eaten all the strawberries he was forcing as a special treat for a state dinner.

"Now what made you do that, Tad?" his mother asked.

Tad kicked the leg of his chair. "I won't do it any more, Ma, I give you my after-David."

The next afternoon she was summoned to the attic by Julia Taft to see a circus before an audience of soldiers, sailors, gardeners and servants, all of whom had been smuggled up the back stairs after paying a five-cent admission charge. Mary sat in the front row between the cook and an upstairs maid. Tad came from behind the sheets, a pair of silver-rimmed spectacles on his nose, began singing:

> "Old Abe Lincoln, a rail splitter was he,
> And he'll split the Confederacee."

Mary interrupted in a stage whisper, "Tad, are you sure you should be singing that song?"

"Pa won't care. Besides, everyone in the world knows he used to split rails."

John Hay broke in, looking miffed.

"Have one of you boys got the president's spectacles? He can't see to read some official papers."

"Tell Pa I got them," said Tad, "and he's to come up and see the show."

"He can't, he's with the generals."

Tad reluctantly peeled the spectacles off his nose, handed them to Hay, saying, "Tell him to come as soon as the generals go away."

In a few minutes Abraham appeared in the attic, paid his five cents, squeezed in between Mary and the cook, laughed heartily at the boys' jokes.

"I don't know what I'd do without Willie and Taddie," he commented, "they always manage to cheer me up."

The boys organized a military company called Mary Lincoln's Zouaves. Abraham wangled them some discarded uniforms. When Mary heard wailing and moaning coming up from the garden, she cried, "What's that?" to Julia Taft, who was reading in the library with her.

"The boys must be burying Jack again, he's that Zouave doll. Practically every day they court-martial him and sentence him to be shot. Then they dig a grave among the roses and bury him."

"Julie, they must not dig holes in the roses. Watt says it kills his young plants."

They found the boys surrounding a freshly dug grave in which lay Doll Jack. Watt got there at the same moment. He looked at the grave in helpless anger. Suddenly his expression lightened.

"Boys, why don't you get Jack pardoned?"

That appealed to Tad. "Come on, we'll get Pa to save him!"

In his office Abraham considered the argument with mock gravity.

"It's good law that no man shall twice be put in jeopardy of his life for the same offense, and you've already shot and buried Jack a dozen times. I guess he's entitled to a pardon."

Turning to his desk, he wrote on a sheet of paper and handed it to Tad. The boys clattered out of the room. Abraham said to Mary a little sadly:

"I wish they were all that easy. Right now I'm being criticized for pardoning a young boy who fell asleep at his post and who was ordered shot by his commanding general, the order upheld by General McClellan. The enemy is killing enough of us, I just can't bear for us to be destroying our own. I told them to let him fight instead of shooting him. It makes me feel rested after a hard day's work if I can find some good excuse to save a man's life."

Mary patted his shoulder. "I once heard you say, 'I don't believe it improves a soldier any to shoot him.' That makes good sense, particularly to the mothers of the boys you save."

If Tad was the laughter of the White House, William was its love: an affectionate child who unabashedly hugged and kissed his parents whenever he came upon them. Frequently when Tad would disappear for days on end, eating and sleeping at the nearby Taft home because he tired of the public scrutiny at the White House, William would spend his hours in the library with Mary, curled up in a chair in the morning sunshine, his hair parted sharply at the left side and combed meticulously over his big head, his eager eyes devouring the pages of Irving, Longfellow, consuming Bunyan or *Favorite English Poems*, writing stories and verses of his own.

William thoroughly enjoyed Tad's funmaking, but at the same time he lived his own life, each morning setting out his program of study, piano practice, work with his tutor because the southern-run schools of Washington were shut down. Mary was proud of William's sensitive and studious nature; he is so much like Abraham, she thought, in his slow careful way of thinking out problems in his mind. Perhaps William would become a poet or a novelist? She flushed with joy at the prospect.

It was good to have the children to create warmth and life, for the days were filled with sadness: their friend Colonel Edward Baker, while leading a detachment across the Potomac toward Leesburg, had been attacked at Ball's Bluff by a well-concealed Confederate force, driven back to the river, with hundreds of Union soldiers killed and captured and drowned in the Potomac. Colonel Baker too was dead. The first important engagement since Wilson's Creek, it was once again a terrible defeat for the Union army.

The north was stricken; chagrin and anxiety turned to fear and despair: Bull Run, Wilson's Creek, Ball's Bluff . . . were all the battles to be lost? Were all the Union soldiers to be killed until there was no one left to fight, and no Union to fight for? The abolitionists in Congress accused Abraham of putting only Democrats into the roles of commanding generals: Stone, a Democrat, had purposely sent out Colonel Baker and his troops to be slaughtered; McClellan, a Democrat, had a concealed objective never to fight a battle against the Confederates, so close by in Virginia that once again their batteries could be seen from Washington.

The accusations had a tart taste in Abraham's mouth: having forced him to remove General Winfield Scott from command of the Union army by insisting that it was General Scott who was preventing him from fighting, General McClellan, now supreme commander, was still confining his efforts to fortifying Washington.

The family went to watch one of the general's vast reviews. Loud cheers went up from the soldiers as General McClellan passed at the head of the reviewing staff of some eighteen hundred hand-picked cavalrymen; a loud silence greeted President Lincoln. The general turned to his aides and said:

"How these brave fellows love me, and what a power that love gives me. What is there to prevent me from taking the government in my own hands?"

That evening Abraham told Mary he was going to McClellan and insist that he divulge his plans for the coming campaign, that the plans be reviewed by the cabinet and general staff. He was back in less than an hour, a baffled expression on his face.

"I certainly am in no temper, but I am annoyed some: to all my questions the general replied: 'If the president has confidence in me, then it is not right nor necessary for him to trust my designs to the judgment of others; but if your confidence is so slight as to require the commanding general's opinion to be fortified by those of other persons, then you ought to replace me by someone who fully possesses your confidence.' I noticed this morning that the *Herald* has changed his nickname from *Little Mac* to *Little Napoleon*; how does one answer Napoleon?"

November passed, but still there was no plan for the "drive on Richmond" which the northern press and the public demanded of Abraham. When the last week of the month opened with gray skies and portents of winter in the air, Abraham saw Senators Wade, Chandler and Trumbull coming across the president's park. He called Mary to the window.

"Once when I was attending an old field school, and we were taking turns reading from the Bible, a little towheaded fellow mangled up Shadrach and Meshach woefully, and went all to pieces on Abednego, for which he was punished. The reading went round again, when suddenly the towhead let out a pitiful yell. 'Look,' he cried, pointing to the next verse, which he would have to read, 'there comes them same darn three fellers again!'"

He went into his office, stayed a long time with the committee. When he came back to the sitting room, looking tired and harassed, he said:

"I've got to go over to McClellan's headquarters. I'll take Tad for company, and pick up Secretary Seward on the way."

It was Tad who told the story when they returned several hours later. They had gone to McClellan's house and been informed that the general was at an army wedding. They had waited for an hour, after which time McClellan had returned and, being told in the hallway by the servant that Mr. Lincoln was waiting to see him in the parlor, had gone upstairs without presenting himself. Abraham and Seward waited for another half hour, then sent the servant to inform the general again that the president and Secretary were waiting for him. The servant came downstairs, stammered that the general had gone to bed.

Mary was shocked.

"Abraham, surely you gave him his comeuppance!"

"I will hold McClellan's horse if he will only bring us success," Abraham replied quietly; "nothing is to be gained by making points of etiquette and personal dignity. My opinion is that he has built us a superb army."

"For fight or for show?" She was fuming over the affront to Abraham, her cheeks a flaming red. "He stages magnificent reviews, but the whole country is demanding a decisive battle. We're supposed to have two hundred thousand men in arms and ready to fight . . ."

"Mr. Pinkerton has reported to General McClellan that the Confederates have ninety thousand men at Manassas; McClellan says he can only put seventy-six thousand into action. He says he needs more men, and when they are ready, he'll be prepared to fight."

"But we so desperately need a victory, Abraham; even a little one . . ."

The next morning snow fell, and with it the severest blow since Ball's Bluff: General McClellan ordered his men to cut down trees and build their winter encampment. His army would not fight until spring and good weather. Abraham was cast into the deepest gloom. The rebels would have another four or five months to learn how to recruit armies, supply them, organize their railroads and communication lines, tax their citizens, run the northern blockades with cotton for Europe and bring back supplies they needed. Each day their government grew stronger, more solidly entrenched; they were arranging to send diplomatic representatives to the capitals of Europe, to secure recognition of themselves as a sovereign nation, to float European loans, buy arms and ammunition, build their own ships, arsenals. With the war a year old come April, could the rebellious states ever be brought back into the Union?

He turned to Mary, said quietly, "The verdict is now in: my old friend and supporter, Lyman Trumbull, has just told people in Illinois that I might have been a successful president in ordinary times, but that the present crisis is too much for me."

"A mere trifle," she replied. "You haven't seen Senator Wade's reply to my invitation to a reception. Says Senator Wade, 'Troops have been drained from the northwest to enable Mrs. Lincoln to pursue without interruption her French and dancing.' Oh, Abraham, what sins have we committed that our own people should be more merciless than the so-called enemy?"

He slipped an arm about her waist, walked her to the window where the two boys were watching the first snowfall.

"I hope it comes to the top of the fences!" Tad exclaimed.

William stared out the window, said with near tears, "Pa don't have time to play with us any more; I'm not so sure it's good to be president. . . ."

Abraham turned to the boys.

"Come, Willie, we're going to find sleds and spend the day coasting down hills. According to all the evidence I can scratch up, the government'll run much better without me. Coming, Mary?"

15

A number of federal soldiers, who had been captured at Bull Run and exchanged, returned to Washington with stories of a "fat and savage Confederate lieutenant" in charge of the prison in Richmond.

The jailer's name was David Todd.

As the newspapers of the north made abundantly clear, he was the brother of Mrs. President Lincoln.

She simply could not believe the stories she read against David. She had spent wonderful hours with him, horseback riding and walking through the woods around Lexington and Buena Vista. He had been a fine and lovable boy. Could a war so quickly turn quiet decent men into savage beasts? She did not believe so.

But the north did; it had no reason to question. Once started, the newspapers informed the Union that three others of her brothers, Alexander, Samuel and George, were officers in the Confederate army; that her brother-in-law Ben Hardin Helm was a colonel of the First Regiment of Kentucky Cavalry, which he had recruited and trained for the secessionists; that Mrs. President Lincoln had eleven second cousins in the Carolina Light Dragoons, that her sister Elodie was married to Colonel Dawson and her sister Martha to Captain White, both of the Confederate army; that her mother was living in Alabama with her secessionist daughters. Articles were written about her southern birth and education, told of her father's being a slaveowner, of having sold slaves on the public block. Prior to this time the criticism of her had come from the opposition press; now the Republican newspapers described her as:

Two thirds secesh, one third pro-slavery.

Stories began circulating from mouth to mouth, letter to letter, big-city newspaper to small-town journal that Mary Todd Lincoln's sympathies were with the south, that she wanted the Confederacy to win the war. Now at last the truth was revealed:

Mrs. President Lincoln was a spy!

She was accused of maintaining an espionage system for the southern armies, receiving mail from Confederate generals and sending information on federal army strength and proposed invasions, of using her vantage post at the heart of the government, in the White House itself, to ferret out the secret and confidential plans of the president, the cabinet, the army, in order that the south might defeat the north.

Could not this explain the defeats at Bull Run, Wilson's Creek and Ball's Bluff? The fact that no attack had yet been made by General McClellan's army?

The letters addressed to her at the White House grew violent. There was no slanderous name she was not called. She was made responsible for the Union dead at Ball's Bluff just now being fished out of the river under the Long Bridge. She should be court-martialed, shot, hanged, whipped out of the White House.

William Stoddard, a twenty-six-year-old secretary who had been added to the White House staff, came to speak to her. He had been a newspaper editor in Illinois during the debates of 1858, and had worked tirelessly for Abraham's election in 1860. Mary found him the most sympathetic of the executive office staff.

"Mr. Stoddard, you seem upset."

"That rascally clerk who does the paper folding, Mrs. Lincoln, got at a lot of your letters and opened every one of them. I caught him before he had had time to read them, but I'd like to know what I am to do about him."

Stoddard's implication was clear: the clerk had been rifling the letters for information and gossip.

"Mr. Stoddard, I wish you would read every letter that comes to me. You've seen many of them, so you must know why I feel this way."

"Indeed I do, Mrs. Lincoln; and I would like your permission to drop the abusive ones into the wastebasket. Nicolay and Hay are doing that with the president's letters now, you know. I see no more reason for you to read these poisoned letters than to eat poisoned food."

She was moved by the kindness of this young man.

"Please do that, Mr. Stoddard. I would be so grateful."

Stoddard walked to the window, pushed aside the curtains, looked out across the White House grounds.

"Perhaps you will let me help in one more matter? You have been distressed over happenings reported in the newspapers that could have been known only to people inside the White House. I'm quite sure I know who the leaky vessel is, I've caught him several times half listening outside doors. He has been a welcome visitor here from the beginning."

Mary's face flamed.

"A friend of ours, reporting our personal conversations?"

"Yes, Mrs. Lincoln. It's Henry Wikoff."

"Wikoff! I can't believe it! Why, he's an accomplished man, with a private fortune . . ."

"I am convinced that if you will drop a few fictitious hints of important events in his presence, when he is the only one who could betray the confidence, you will catch him in a matter of a week."

Stoddard was right: she caught Wikoff red-handedly reporting to the New York *Herald* two stories which she had concocted for the purpose. Only then did she learn that he had been planted in the White House by Mr. Bennett of the New York *Herald* for this very purpose. Her early unpleasantness with Nicolay and Hay could be laid at the door of this man whom she had welcomed as a friend and counselor.

The blow upset her emotionally. She retired to her room, called off her appointments, could hardly bear to see anyone outside of her immediate family.

Then, a week after the reconvening of Congress at the beginning of December, she stopped being sorry for herself, for her husband needed her full commiseration: a group of abolitionists headed by Benjamin Wade and Zachariah Chandler pushed through the Senate and then the House a bill authorizing the organization of a Congressional Committee to Inquire into the Conduct of the War. Though it was not their avowed purpose to assail the administration, but only to promote the vigorous prosecution of the war, they immediately began an investigation of the military defeats at Bull Run, Wilson's Creek and Ball's Bluff and, as a corollary, of the commanding officers, voting themselves the right to question the military officers and to be informed about all impending plans for conquest. Abraham now would have on his back what he described to her as "a hysterically irresponsible committee which was willing to achieve emancipation at the cost of the Union."

Broad as were the powers of the committee, Mary did not learn how much authority they had taken unto themselves until William Stoddard heard through a friend that the group was to meet that very morning in a room in the Capitol basement to investigate Mrs. Abraham Lincoln.

"But on what grounds?" she cried.

Stoddard continued with difficulty.

"Giving important information to secret agents of the Confederacy. They claim as their justification that if the stories they hear are true, it fastens treason upon the president's family in the White House. Something must be done at once, if they are to be stopped."

Scalding tears trickled down her cheeks. Stoddard withdrew. This was the most searing humiliation she had ever known: the United States Senate accusing her of treason! No wife or relative of a president ever had been subjected to such disgrace in the history of the nation. It would be the end of her; there would be no chance to serve any good or useful purpose during the rest of Abraham's regime. She could no longer be First Lady. She would have to pack up herself and her children and return to Springfield.

She had withstood the slanderous stories about her lack of background and culture from the southern contingent of Washington, they had been defeated and bitter; she had withstood the scurrilous reports about her Confederate sympathies and lack of sympathy for the Union dead on the part of the Democratic press, after all, this was the opposition; she had withstood the daily outpouring of hysteria and violence addressed to her in her home, such people were ill, she could be forbearing; she even had withstood betrayal by a friend and intimate . . . But how did she withstand this official action by her own government?

Her breath came short, she felt a familiar hollowness in her chest, a dull, throbbing ache in her throat. She clenched her teeth to fight the nausea rising within her, gripped the arms of her chair to restrain her emotion. When she had quieted she sent for her husband.

Abraham's eyes became pits of black fury. He stamped out of the room, put on his heavy wool coat and left the White House, his head craned forward, every fiber of him bristling. From one of the north bedrooms she watched him go out the driveway and down Pennsylvania Avenue; in her misery she had the compassion to pity him: surely this was the loneliest man who ever walked in solitude?

She stood at the window in a trancelike state until she saw him coming back down the driveway, his head under the soft felt hat held high in the air.

She went to the sitting room to wait. He came in, kissed her paternally on the cheek.

"Mother, you need never worry about this nonsense again. It is over."

Without another word he turned and left her.

She awakened early on January 1, 1862, to find the day bright and mild. She had an early breakfast, laid out new suits and linen for the boys, cautioned Abraham to give himself plenty of time to dress for the traditional New Year's reception that began at noon. Mrs. Keckley arrived at nine to help her with her headdress, weaving flowers and jewels through her hair, now thoroughly dark from brushing oil into it. How many years ago was it that she first noticed her hair darkening and resolved to ask Abraham if he preferred it chestnut?

She concealed her nervousness while Mrs. Keckley helped her into the petticoats and steel hoops she wore under her gray silk; for this reception would be the most crucial of her ten months in the White House. Did the people of Washington believe the attacks on her integrity and loyalty? They had heard a great deal about her extravagance but had not had an opportunity to see the redecorated White House. How would they respond?

Abraham came in a few minutes before twelve, drawing on white kid gloves, his face tired. This reception was a test for him too: just how popular was he with the people of Washington, and with the north on this New Year's Day? How successful had he been? When he was inaugurated seven states had rebelled, now the Union had lost eleven of them; when he had taken his oath of office there had been no physical conflict, now the two halves of the Union were at war on battlefields from Virginia to New Orleans. When he had entered the White House, Europe was respectful; now England was threatening war because the north had seized two southern envoys off a British ship, France was irate because the blockade kept her from southern cotton, and might ally herself with England. When he had become president the Treasury was solvent, the nation's business good; now the Treasury was empty and had to print a new kind of paper money called "greenbacks." Abraham was spending a million dollars a day for armies that did not fight, the nation's business was at a standstill; charges of inefficiency and corruption could no longer be denied, for Secretary of War Cameron had given contracts to men who had provided the army with guns that would not shoot, horses that were diseased, uniforms and boots that disintegrated in the first rain, meat that was tainted.

They descended a moment before twelve to the music of the Marine Band, stood at the entrance of the East Room to receive the officers of the army and navy, the cabinet, the foreign ministers and their attachés. At one o'clock the gates were thrown open. The people thronged in.

On all sides she heard exclamations of approval and delight alike from newcomers and those who had known the White House for years. Mrs. Donn Piatt, who had come down on the train with her from Harrisburg and stayed several nights in the White House, exclaimed:

"Mrs. Lincoln, it is an astonishing change! You have turned a shabby and tired old house into an exquisite jewel!"

Mary squeezed Mrs. Piatt's hand in gratitude. Adele Douglas, garbed in black, who had not been out in public save for the Senate eulogy of her husband, said:

"Mrs. Lincoln, I was confident you would make the White House into something brilliant." She paused for a moment. "And I know you have done it under trying circumstances."

When the party was over they retired to Mary's bedroom to soak their aching hands in bowls of hot water, and to exchange happy thoughts of the day. Abraham told her of the high praise he had heard for her taste and judgment.

"My father would have liked to hear that," she murmured pensively. "He taught me."

The time had come to bring up a problem she had been concealing these past two difficult months. She drew a deep breath, then said in what she hoped was a tranquil voice:

"I'm glad you approve, Abraham, because it cost a lot of money."

"Let's see, six thousand to start, another twenty thousand from Congress . . ."

"I'm sorry, Abraham, but I couldn't have done over this entire house for twenty-six thousand dollars, not without compromising with inferior materials. . . ."

He looked up sharply. "What does this mean, Mary?"

"There is one bill that has not yet been paid; it is the last, but it combines many things."

He jammed his hair forward as he did when he disapproved.

"You mean you've gone over the appropriation?"

"Yes. By $6858.80. All owed to Mr. Carryl."

"But, Mary, there is no more money to pay it with. Why did you do this?"

"Because that's how much it cost for the full job. Here, look at the bills yourself, you'll see that it is for many of the things that were most highly admired."

He took the account, held it out at a distance from him, then began reading aloud:

" 'Papering four rooms and private apartments: president's room, $432.50; Mrs. Lincoln's room, $254.45 . . .' " He looked over at her with a ghost of a smile, said, "I see you're only half as expensive as I am. 'East Room paper selected in Paris, $832; Red Room, $392; Blue Room, $399.50; gilt molding, $200 . . .' "

"These items were authorized by Mr. Wood last summer. It took this long to get them here from France, and to put them up. I couldn't know how much the total would be until the work was finished. I've gone to the records, Abraham: Andrew Jackson spent forty-five thousand dollars on White House renovations, that's twelve thousand more than I've spent, and Martin Van Buren spent sixty thousand dollars, twice as much as I've spent. Franklin Pierce, who did no entertaining, still found it necessary to spend twenty-five thousand dollars on the house for refurbishing. Mr. Jefferson must have spent a full thirty thousand dollars on the wings he added; Mr. Monroe completely refurnished the White House with pieces brought over from France. This is not money wasted, Abraham, or that vanishes, it will keep the White House beautiful for many years."

His expression had lightened considerably as she detailed what other presidents had been obliged to spend.

"I'm not insensible to what you've accomplished, Puss, but I can't go to the Congress now and ask them for more money; we have too many opponents who will use it as another excuse to criticize us. I'll pay it out of my own purse."

He rose, went through a series of rooms into his office, returned with a handful of salary warrants. When he had added them up, he said, "I haven't deposited any of these yet, there's almost thirteen thousand dollars in wages. We can afford to pay the sixty-nine hundred."

"By the Eternal! I won't let you spend three to four months of your earnings on a house that doesn't belong to us! There were enough congressmen here today who expressed pleasure with the redecoration to carry the appropriation."

There was a moment of silence, then he asked plaintively:

"Is this the end? We won't have to ask them for any more?"

"Not for another dollar; that is, unless the roof falls in. I give you what Tad calls his after-David."

"Very well, if this is the end, I'll find the right moment to ask Congress for the seven thousand dollars. But I'd better wait until the army has won at least a skirmish . . . or they're likely to revoke our lease."

16

THE first visitor to the White House after the New Year was William Herndon; her sister Elizabeth had written telling her that all Springfield believed Herndon was coming to Washington to secure from his law partner the position of minister to the kingdom of Italy. At noon when Abraham came in from his office visit with Herndon he was chuckling.

"I know you've been worried that I might appoint him minister, but what he wants is for me to help him get a new wife. His old one died a few months ago."

"A new wife? Are you what our friend Dr. Isachar Zacharie calls a shad-chan?"

The image of himself as a matchmaker amused Abraham.

"Herndon's courting the belle of Petersburg. His hoped-for brother-in-law has promised that if Billy can get me to appoint him to what he calls 'a lucrative and adventuresome federal position,' he'll help the match." He hesitated. "I sent him over to Secretary of the Interior Smith . . . and invited him for dinner tonight; we can't do less, Puss."

She sat up in her chair, swallowed hard.

"I suppose not."

By the middle of January she was faced with the obligatory series of three state dinners. They would cost her three thousand dollars out of the family funds. Worn by the attacks upon her, she would have been willing to forgo all formal entertaining; but oddly enough there was now considerable pressure by the wives and families of the northerners in the Congress for her to give a big party because Washington was so funereal, with General McClellan locked into winter quarters and Abraham declaring gloomily that "the bottom is out of the tub." Everyone was depressed, Abraham, the cabinet, Congress, War and Navy Departments, government employees. If Mrs. President Lincoln could find it in her heart to create a little gaiety, perhaps official Washington would take another hitch in its belt.

She waited until Abraham came into her bedroom that night at eleven for a chat before retiring, then told him of her idea of giving one large reception and scratching the state dinners from the program.

Abraham draped himself over a chair.

"Mary, I'm afraid. It is breaking in on the regular custom."

"These are war times, Abraham, and old customs can be done away with."

"Yes, but we must think of something besides economy."

She flushed, added quickly, "Public receptions are more democratic than state dinners. For the same thousand dollars that it would cost us for thirty guests we can have a reception, ball and midnight supper catered by Maillard of New York, they're the best now. That way we can invite the cabinet, the Supreme Court, the Congress, heads of departments, judges, the entire diplomatic corps, generals, admirals, governors . . . There are a great many strangers in the city, foreigners and others we can entertain at our receptions whom we cannot invite to our state dinners."

He pursed his underlip.

"You argue the point well, Mary . . ."

"Secretary Seward asked if we would make the next reception an invitational one. We'll send out five hundred invitations; everyone will have room to promenade and to dance comfortably."

The protest was immediate: from those who resented the abandonment of the state dinners, from members of the press who had not been invited to the reception, from private people who felt they should have been included. William Stoddard explained that this was an official affair, but the articles in the press became so acrimonious that Mary had to send out several hundred more invitations, knowing full well that the White House would be so jammed with widely hooped crinolines that no one would have room enough to fall down, let alone dance.

She was unprepared for the eighty rejections sent to her by the abolitionists in the Congress, spearheaded by Senator Benjamin Wade's note:

Are the President and Mrs. Lincoln aware that there is a civil war? If they are not, Mr. and Mrs. Wade are, and for that reason decline to participate in feasting and dancing.

She groaned, inwardly.

Rain filled the end of January, with the streets running rivers of mud. It reminded her of those bleak winter weeks when she and Abraham, Robert and Edward were cooped up in one rear room of Mrs. Sprigg's boardinghouse. February 1 was a particularly raw and rainy day; it was exactly twelve years since Edward had died. She asked Julia to come down to the Red Room and play the piano for her.

"I feel so brokenhearted at the return of these anniversaries."

When last she saw William and Tad they were headed for their playroom in the attic, but late in the afternoon they came in drenched from having ridden their ponies down to the Potomac. By bedtime they were sneezing; in the morning they were permeated with cold. She was scheduled for an informal reception that afternoon in the family library and another in the evening in the Red Room, but she canceled them both and stayed with the boys.

When the next morning showed no improvement, she sent for Dr. Robert K. Stone, a native-born Washingtonian who had been president of the Board of Health of the District of Columbia; local opinion said he was the finest doctor in Washington. Dr. Stone was a bald man with curling whiskers under his chin; he examined the boys, assured Mary and Abraham that it was just a cold, but added:

"I recommend that you separate the boys, it's never good to have them near each other's illness."

Mary had a fire lighted in the huge Prince of Wales Room, the sheets were warmed with bed warmers, then Abraham picked William up in his blankets and put him in the center of the guest-room bed. She and Mrs. Dorothea Dix, superintendent of women nurses for the army, stayed up all night, alternating between the two sickrooms. When Abraham came in at dawn Mary said:

"These are pretty sick boys. I would like to withdraw the cards of invitation."

Abraham was thoughtful.

"Well now, Mother, there are some eight hundred passes out. My opinion is, they shouldn't be withdrawn. However, let's ask Dr. Stone."

Dr. Stone was disappointed that William's fever was continuing to mount but saw no reason to cancel the party. Mary spent the night in front of the big fire, watching William, whose breath seemed to be rasping in his chest. Tad slept.

In spite of the fact that she now had been sleepless for two nights, she went downstairs to work with Maillard who had arrived at the White House the day before from New York with his own retinue of cooks and waiters and a prodigious supply of food. She then made the rounds of the rooms with Mrs. Watt and a number of the White House servants, making sure everything was in order, the flowers spread profusely, the vases and bonbon dishes filled.

At dusk Dr. Stone examined both boys, said that Tad could have something to eat, that he saw some improvement in William. Reassured, Mary went into her dressing room with Mrs. Keckley, began the elaborate preparations for her formal appearance: she had a long hot bath to rest her, then sat before the mirror in her dressing room while Mrs. Keckley brushed her hair and arranged a wreath of black and white flowers through it. Mrs. Keckley helped her into her white satin gown with low décolleté and long train.

At eight o'clock she went into William's room; Abraham was standing before the fire, his hands clasped behind his back, gazing down at the flames. He heard the rustling of her gown, looked up.

"Whew, our cat has a long tail tonight. It is my opinion that if some of that tail was nearer the head it would be in better style."

They received in the East Room. After the incoming guests had shaken hands they passed into the Green, Blue and Red parlors. The Marine Band played in a corner of the corridor. Abraham need not have issued the injunction against dancing, for by nine o'clock the crowd was so dense no one could move.

Three times she made her way up the back stairs to William's room; in between her visits Abraham went up twice. The boy was whimpering in his sleep, but Mrs. Dix said there was nothing he needed.

When Mary and Abraham reached the state dining room at eleven o'clock they found that the steward, having kept the door locked during the evening, had misplaced the key. As the crowds filled the Red Room and then the Blue Room behind that, someone cried, "I am in favor of a forward movement!" and a second wit exclaimed, "An advance to the front is only retarded by the imbecility of the commanders!"

When the doors finally were opened Mary gasped with delight at the table, decorated with large pieces of ornamental confectionery, the center object representing the steamer *Union* armed and bearing the Stars and Stripes, on a side table a sugar model of Fort Sumter provisioned with game. A Japanese punch bowl was brimming with champagne punch; nougat water nymphs held up a fountain; down the length of the festive board were roast sliced pheasants, hams, turkeys and ducks, partridges and venison; and on the ends, beehives filled with charlotte russe for dessert.

The last of the guests did not depart until three o'clock. It was declared the best White House party in years.

Mary made her way up to her room, exhausted.

Tad slowly gained his strength. William grew thinner and more shadowy. An extra bed was brought into his room and she and Abraham took turns sleeping by him.

The days dragged by. Only the presence of Bud Taft could perk up William. In spite of the grueling watch she did not become seriously alarmed until Dr. Stone confided to them that the illness was beginning to assume a typhoid character. With Dr. Stone's approval they called in Dr. Neal Hall for consultation.

On February 19, Stoddard came to her bringing a copy of a wrapped newspaper.

"Mrs. Lincoln, this is marked *Personal and Private*; since it comes from a small town near your home I thought it might be from a relative, so I didn't open it."

She thanked him, tore the paper band, and took out a folded copy of the Menard, Illinois, *Axis*, dated February 15. Under the name of John Hill, the editor, was a two-column-long editorial marked in the margin with ink. It was a story about Abraham, telling of his early life in New Salem; then came a paragraph that had been heavily underlined:

> He now become an actor in a new scene. He chanced to meet with a
> lady, who to him seemed the height of perfection. He could think or

dream of naught but her. His feelings he soon made her acquainted with, and was delighted with a reciprocation. This to him was perfect happiness; and with uneasy anxiety he awaited the arrival of the day when the twain should be made one flesh.—But that day was doomed never to arrive. Disease came upon this lovely beauty, and she sickened and died. The youth had wrapped his heart with her's, and this was more than he could bear. He saw her to her grave, and as the cold clods fell upon the coffin, he sincerely wished that he too had been enclosed within it. Melancholy came upon him; he was changed and sad. His friends detected strange conduct and a flighty immagination. They placed him under guard for fear of his commiting suicide.

She sat rigid, unable to think . . . or to understand. Her eyes went back to the heavily scored paragraph: *He could think or dream of naught but her . . . when the twain should be made one flesh . . . saw her to her grave . . . wished he could be enclosed within it.*

Her first thought was, How low we have fallen! This story could be nothing but the sheerest fiction. Had not Abraham told her she was the only woman he had loved? To whom could it be referring? Abraham had never loved Mary Owens, nor had she died; she had rejected him and moved away. Once there had been a girl who lived near the Lincoln farm in Kentucky whom he had liked, but whom he unblushingly confessed had run away from him because he was the homeliest boy in the neighborhood. He had told her about a pretty little girl called Kate Roby in his blab school whom he had helped win a spelling bee by pointing to his eye at the proper time in the word "defied." Neither he nor anyone else ever had mentioned a young lady with whom he had been in love, who had loved him, to whom he had been betrothed, and who had died, sending him into . . . what did the article say?

Melancholy came upon him; he was changed and sad. His friends detected strange conduct . . .

She rose with the newspaper in her hand, made for the door leading to Abraham's office. But as she stood with her hand on the knob, her head bowed, a constricting pain in her chest, she realized that she could not talk of this to Abraham, not now. . . .

Even as she turned from the door her mind flooded with anger at the bad taste of a man, purportedly writing a eulogy of Abraham, to start a canard about an early and tragic love which could accomplish nothing except to embarrass the president's family!

And what charming, anonymous friend had gone to all the pains of mailing her this issue of the *Menard Axis*, the offending paragraph underlined so that she would have no chance of missing it?

She hid the paper in a locked compartment at the back of her desk, went into the sickroom.

William was terribly weak. She tried to feed him some broth that Mrs. Keckley brought, but he had difficulty in swallowing. She remained calm, kept up her hopes, did not permit herself to weep at the sight of the pale and wasting boy, not until the afternoon when William whispered to their minister from the New York Avenue Presbyterian Church:

"Dr. Gurley, please give the money in my savings bank to the missionary society for the Sunday school."

Dear God, what could this mean? That William knew he was going to die? She caught a bleak look on Abraham's face. Had he no hope left for the boy's recovery? She would not give in to such feelings!

The next morning the executive office never opened. Abraham remained with her at the boy's side. At a little after noon William died. Mary fell to her knees by the side of the bed, buried her face in the covers. The last thing she heard was Abraham saying:

"My boy is gone, he is actually gone."

17

A storm broke overhead, beating against her exhausted body and her feverish brain. Dimly she heard voices: Abraham's trying to soothe her, Mrs. Keckley's as she washed her face with a warm cloth, the nurse's. Orville Browning, who had been named as senator from Illinois to replace Stephen Douglas, came in with his wife; Abraham had sent a carriage for them. It was good to have someone from home with her, someone who had known them in the years before they had been married, who had known William from the time of his birth.

Suddenly Robert too was in the room, down from Harvard. Her oldest son stood by, pale, very still.

She slept. It was morning. Abraham was sitting by her bed, leaning over her with grief-stricken face.

"It was hard to have him die," he said in a half whisper, "but it's harder on us, Mary, to be alive without him. The Reverend Gurley is holding services in the East Room. All our friends will be there . . . Willie's friends . . ."

She closed her eyes, buried her face in the pillow. He did not press her.

She awakened to the sound of someone walking back and forth, back and forth, with slow heavy tread. She recognized the sound as that of Abraham pacing his room. The footsteps stopped, she heard uncontrollable weeping.

She laid back the blankets, put her feet into a pair of slippers, gathered a robe over her quaking shoulders, then went through the door connecting her bedroom with her husband's. Sitting in a chair, his face gripped in long bony fingers as he rocked up and down, was Abraham. The draperies were drawn, the room dark. She went to him, slipped onto his lap, took his hands gently away from his face, kissed the wet cheeks and eyes.

"Abraham, you mustn't . . . you mustn't . . ."

"This is Thursday, just a week since . . . It's hard, hard to have him die."

"My dear, don't you remember what you told me when Eddie died? *The Lord giveth and the Lord taketh away.* If you believed it then, you must believe it now."

But even as she said the words she realized the basic difference: then they were young, they would have other sons to take Edward's place. Now there would be no more children.

"It's not only Willie, it's all those boys on the battlefields . . . Bull Run, Ball's Bluff, others to come . . . dying so senselessly, so needlessly. Mary, do you think if we had stayed home in Springfield, if Stephen Douglas had moved into the White House, there would be none of us parents losing our sons . . . ?"

She held her cheek against his until at last he was soothed. He bathed his face with cold water in the big bowl on his dressing stand. There was a quiet knock on the door. Abraham opened it to find Nicolay standing there.

"Forgive me for intruding, Mr. President, but the representative of the king of Siam is in my office for the third time this week. He insists upon knowing whether you will accept the brood elephants the king wishes to send you."

Abraham gave Mary a grim smile.

"Please inform the king of Siam that I respectfully decline, having a very large elephant on hand just now which occupies all my attention, and which the assembled wisdom of the nation don't know what to do with."

She had helped her husband; but how did she help herself? Now that she was alone again in her bedroom she pulled the blankets over her head and wept, paroxysms that devastated her. She had loved William so deeply, and he had loved her with all the warmth of his tender and affectionate nature. How did she live through the dread hours ahead, the long grief-stricken days? How did she get out of bed, dress, run her home, attend receptions, be a wife?

At nine that evening Browning came in with Elizabeth Edwards. The sight of large-boned, gray-haired Elizabeth of the strong face and calm manner was heatening; she relived the day she had been summoned home from the picnic where she was listening to Henry Clay's speech: everybody was acting strangely, Grandmother Parker was weeping; eleven-year-old Elizabeth had put an arm about her shoulders, said: "Come, Mary, I'll take you upstairs to your room"; and from that time had taken the place of their dead mother. It was Elizabeth who had summoned her to Springfield, told her she had a "vacancy."

Elizabeth sat on the edge of the bed, holding her sister while Mary wept hysterically, then sank back on the pillow, spent.

When she was able to get out of bed she could not bring herself to enter the Prince of Wales Room where William had died; the door was locked. Nor could she go into the room where William had lain in state. She canceled all receptions; of a late afternoon Elizabeth would receive people who wished to present their condolences. When the Marine Band played on Saturday afternoon in the president's park, with all of Washington out in the fine spring weather to stroll arm in arm, she asked Abraham to stop the concerts. He urged her not to give in to her feelings, yet on March 4, when his secretaries came into the library to offer restrained congratulations, Abraham repeated slowly:

"The fourth of March? I have been president of the United States just one year, and if either of you thinks it is a nice thing to be president of the United States, just let him try it."

With spring she suffered headaches of such blinding intensity she had to avoid all bright light; sudden noises made her quiver from head to foot. Frequently she would be overcome by a lassitude such as she had not known since the twenty months in Elizabeth's home when Abraham had disappeared from her life. There were days when she could not get out of bed, when she was racked by grief. There were other days when she could dress in the mourning gowns Mrs. Keckley had made her, walk through her daily chores, preside as mistress at table; but she never knew which day was arriving on the morrow.

At the end of the first week in April the biggest and bloodiest battle of the war was fought at Shiloh in Tennessee, with the Confederates catching General Ulysses S. Grant by surprise. Grant re-formed his troops and counterattacked, driving the rebels from the field. It was the first major victory of the war, but the White House was appalled at the more than thirteen thousand Union soldiers killed, wounded or missing. The north too was horrified, turning on General Grant as having been responsible for the slaughter.

Abraham confided to Mary that Governor Curtin of Pennsylvania, one of his staunch supporters, was sending Alexander K. McClure from Harrisburg to persuade him to remove General Grant. McClure was ushered into the library by Hay. Neither he nor Mary greeted each other. He launched into a lashing attack on Grant, called him a butcher and a drunk whose dismissal the north demanded.

It appeared to Mary that McClure was not asking the president to dismiss Grant, he was telling him. Would Abraham take this order? He was sitting deep in thought, his head lowered; then he raised his head slowly and said:

"I can't spare this man; he fights."

That night she saw that Elizabeth had something on her mind. Elizabeth took a deep breath.

"It's best you learn from me: our brother Samuel was killed in the battle of Shiloh . . . fighting against Grant. . . ."

". . . Sam dead . . ."

Pictures of her brother flooded back: handsome, bright-faced Samuel, all fun and fire like herself, sitting a horse with reckless grace . . . Then the images faded; Samuel was gone; as grief flooded over her, she said to Elizabeth:

"Death must be my friend, he is so much with me."

She was ill again. The month of April saw her out of bed almost not at all. On those rare occasions when she looked into a mirror she saw the deep purple rings under her eyes, and behind them the stranger who had taken possession. She did not know what she would have done without Elizabeth's ever capable hands to help her.

It was finally Tad's loneliness which penetrated her isolation.

"Ma, I'm tired of playing by myself. I want to play together."

"Poor Taddie, you do miss Willie, don't you? We'll go out to the stables and arrange to have hutches built for your rabbits."

She loved Tad the more deeply for the fact that his loss had been as profound as her own. She had not been spending much time with Tad, they had only to look at each other to think of William; but Abraham had been good for Tad, he spent much time working at a little desk in Tad's room, signing his documents there, telling his son, "When I sign my name for the public I have to sign *Abraham Lincoln*, but I like best the A. *Lincoln*." Tad was happier when his father was doing his work close by.

May passed, then June was on them, and the heat of summer. She knew little of what was going on about her except that the war still was a stalemate, that Abraham still was not able to persuade General McClellan to strike because no matter how many men, guns or horses the Union had, the general was convinced that the Confederacy had a greater number.

There were days, sometimes even weeks, when her grief was unassuageable, when she wept for long hours in her room. Abraham spoke kind and patient words to her, yet she was unconsolable. A tall skinny woman by the name of Bonpoint wrote articles on spiritualism for the newspapers, which were devoting more and more space to the subject since so many people after the beginning of the war had started going to séances. She tried to persuade Mary to accompany her.

"Come with me tomorrow afternoon to Mrs. Laury's in Georgetown. She can get directly in touch with your William, and tell you about his life in the next world. If you believe hard enough, she can bring William back to you."

Mary declined, but she went sleepless through the night. When Mrs. Bonpoint persisted in seeing her the next morning, Mary had no strength with which to resist. At Mrs. Laury's she sat hand in hand with strangers around a table in the darkened room and heard ghostly noises interspersed with the sound of beating on a drum and the tingle of distant bells. Intimate details of William's life were revealed. Could Mrs. Laury be speaking with William's spirit? Mrs. Laury asked questions and repeated William's answers: he was with Edward; he was sorry to see her grieving; that night he would come to her in her bedroom at the White House.

She went to bed immediately upon returning home, was prevailed upon to eat some supper at sundown, fell into a sleep of exhaustion. Some hours later —she knew only that the night was pitch-black and silent—she half wakened to feel rather than see a light at the foot of her bed. There stood William with the same sweet smile he had always had.

368

She bounded up from her pillow. The light faded. William was gone. Shivering from head to foot, she fumbled her way out of bed, donned robe and slippers, made her way into Abraham's room. She found him awake and reading the Bible. She cast herself upon his bosom in an uncontrollable rush of joy.

"He lives, Abraham, he lives! He can come to me every night, if only I'll believe."

Abraham put her under the covers, wrapped the blankets about her shoulders to stop her shivering, then held her securely in his arms.

"Mary, you must not give way to this kind of thing. These people victimize the lonely and sick at heart. This willingness to believe in spiritualism is part of your illness. Promise me that you'll give no more credence to it?"

She did not answer. The next morning, when he came into her bedroom and found her at the window, her eyes red and puffy, he put an arm about her waist, said:

"Mary, you see that asylum up on the hill? Many of its unfortunates are there because they have been unable to control their feelings."

She turned from his grasp; his warning seemed to have been spoken as much to himself as to her.

"This afternoon I'm visiting the Judiciary Square Hospital. Suppose you come with me?"

She wore a black dress with a long crepe veil. They walked around the tables in the dining hall, shaking hands with those getting well, asking questions about home and family. Then they passed into the wards; here there was no handshaking, for dried blood and death hung heavy on the air, fetid with festering wounds. Young men with pale bone-ridged faces, arms or legs or parts of the head shot away, burned with fever. She stopped at each bed, talking with those who could talk, touching the coverlet of those of parched lips and parched eyes who could not speak.

When they returned to the carriage she said, "I'm ashamed of all the tears I shed at my own loss; I should have been shedding them for these sick and dying boys, and for their mothers who can't be here to comfort or care for them."

"Do not reproach yourself, Mary; there are tears enough for all."

That night she prayed for the living instead of the dead.

She went into the conservatory, asked Watt to cut her all the flowers in bloom and returned to the Judiciary Square Hospital to spend the afternoons in the wards, laying fresh flowers on the pillows of the sickest, pouring forth words of hope and encouragement to the so desperately young and lonely boys, far away from home, in their fawnlike eyes the fear of dying before having lived.

She made the rounds: to the Douglas Hospital on Minnesota Row and I Street, already known as the surgeons' hospital, to the Union Hotel Hospital, with the smells of damp corridors, kitchens and stables permeating the forty-bed ward in the ballroom, the men covered with dirty blankets; to the hospitals organized in churches and factories, to the museum of the Patent Office where each alcove had been converted to a ward, the marble floors scrubbed and covered with matting by the housewives of the country who had come in to be nurses.

Each day she went unaccompanied to a new hospital; no one knew she was coming, in few instances was she recognized. When she learned that the patients were starved for such little luxuries as candies, cakes, jellies, she stripped the White House of its incoming gifts of sweets and liquors, urged the cooks to bake all the extra cookies their time would allow.

When she found that no provision had been made for special dinners on Sundays, she emptied the White House larder of its chickens and turkeys, then finding that this was only a meager start, took a hundred dollars of her own savings and ordered enough chickens for every hospital patient in Washington for that week end.

The joy on the faces of the boys as she came into the gloomy wards brought her heartbroken happiness. Soon she knew the name, home place, family history of hundreds of the wounded; she began carrying a dispatch case and each afternoon wrote a dozen or so letters home for boys who were unable to write:

My Dear Mrs. Berdin:
   As I am sitting by the side of your dear boy, I will write you for him. He is sick and wounded, but he is getting along nicely. He says don't worry about him as he will come out all right.
                                        Yours in love,
                              Mrs. Abraham Lincoln

A grizzled old doctor, who had come out of retirement to help in the crisis, took her hands in his gnarled ones.

"So this is the woman the papers say shows excessive grief! Mrs. President, I wish more of our Washington ladies understood the nature of grief, these homesick boys would get well sooner."

The only friend she met on her rounds was Mrs. Caleb Smith, wife of the Secretary of the Interior; the white-haired matronly woman was on identical errands of mercy. They joined forces in those projects which were too large for one woman to handle, such as a supply of oranges and lemons which the army did not consider necessary to the sick but the doctors felt were urgently needed. When there was no other way to get the supplies she purchased them out of her own purse, no longer bothering to keep track; and then, mysteriously, she began finding sums left in her sewing basket in the family library.

Her helper and confidant in the White House was William Stoddard, ever loyal and discreet, who somehow had got it into his head that protecting the wife of the president was tantamount to serving the president, the administration and the Union. One morning when she was reading some of the eastern newspapers, noting the criticism against her for omitting all White House entertaining and for preventing the Marine Band from playing during the summer, Stoddard said in his friendly voice:

"Mrs. Lincoln, you are losing opportunities by not taking outside company with you to the hospitals. If you were worldly-wise you would carry newspaper correspondents with you, of both sexes, every time you went, and you would have them take notes of what you say to the sick soldiers, and what they say to you. Noah Brooks, the reporter for the Sacramento *Union*, says that if you would then bring the reporters back to the White House and give them cake and coffee, you could sweeten the content of many journals . . . and certainly of my wastebasket!"

She put her middle finger on Stoddard's rough wool coat, replied with a wistful smile:

"If I had something to gain from all this, beyond my happiness in giving, it would lose meaning for me. Besides, so many of my troubles I bring on myself. That's the nature of true tragedy, isn't it, not what happens to us from the outside, from external fate, though heaven knows that can be bad enough; but what, through our own character, we make happen to ourselves. But not a word to the newspapers, Mr. Stoddard."

A few days later Stoddard rushed into the library with a copy of the New York *Tribune*, spluttering:

". . . swear I didn't do it . . ."

Mary took the paper from his hands, read:

Mrs. Lincoln has contributed more than any lady at Washington, from her private purse, to alleviate the sufferings of our wounded soldiers. Day by day her carriage is seen in front of the hospitals where she distributes with her own hands delicacies prepared in the kitchen of the White House.

She thought of what she had told young Stoddard, and of Dr. Ward, who had tried to reassure her about the future by suggesting that in the unfolding of a human life the certainties of character were more important than the accidents of fate. He had been right: with the exception of the death of her two sons, everything that had happened to her for good or evil had arisen from her own needs and nature.

It was true, as the Greeks said, that the gods of fate came shod in wool; yet how delicately perceptive was one's hearing when one had knowledge of self!

18

HER old interests revived. She set out to learn the important things that had been happening during the past months. Abraham was happy to have her to talk to again.

He told her the good news first. The Union had won certain victories: on

April 25 a naval expedition had captured New Orleans, landed troops and new controlled the Confederacy's largest seaport. He had gone himself to Fortress Monroe on Chesapeake Bay, just opposite Richmond, ordered gunboats to attack Confederate batteries, chosen the landing spot for the Union troops who then captured Norfolk, taken six thousand prisoners and forced the Confederates to blow up their first steel-plated ship, the *Merrimac*, which Washington had long feared would steam up the Potomac and reduce the capital to rubble. At the battle of Fair Oaks, General McClellan, though he could not be induced to attack, successfully withstood an attack by the main southern army.

Abraham had rid himself of Secretary of War Simon Cameron, without losing the support of Cameron's Pennsylvania organization, by giving him the post of minister to Russia that Cassius Clay no longer wanted; and had appointed the fanatically honest, able martinet Edwin Stanton. When Mary learned that Stanton was the lawyer who had ejected Abraham from the McCormick-Manny reaper case in Cincinnati she shook her head in amazement: since everyone said Stanton was the best man for the job, Abraham would hold Stanton's dispatch case if the new Secretary of War would bring him victories.

And Abraham had signed a bill forever freeing the slaves in the District of Columbia, though he had insisted that their owners be compensated out of federal funds. Never again would visitors to the capital of a people's government see coffles of bound men moving into Georgia Pen.

Then he felt constrained to relate the bad news: there had been more defeats than victories, more blows than progress. His continuous efforts to have the loyal border states accept compensated emancipation, in an attempt to solidify the north, had been summarily rejected. When the Confederates had abandoned Manassas it was found that the heavy artillery that had frightened McClellan into winter camp and kept him from attacking were nothing more than logs painted black to look like cannon, exactly like the logs William and Tad had mounted on the roof of the White House; that Pinkerton's reports of the Confederacy's superiority in numbers had proved to be equally ludicrous. Stonewall Jackson, lightninglike commander of a highly mobile Confederate army, had defeated the Union troops at Winchester, Cross Keys, Port Republic, despite Abraham's frantic plans to surround Jackson and annihilate his force. When Abraham ordered McClellan to move on Richmond by the overland route, McClellan had countered with a plan to go by a water route. Abraham still could not make him take the offensive.

"I had to take away his supreme command, leave him just the Army of the Potomac," said Abraham. "He must be less than five miles from Richmond now; if he fails this time we'll both be in a bad row of stumps."

Now, at the end of June, eleven months after the Union rout at Bull Run, General McClellan wheeled his men into position to attack. From the beginning the news was bad, for General Robert E. Lee struck first at the hesitant McClellan at Mechanicsville. It was the first of the Seven Days' bloody fighting at Gaines's Mill, White Oak Swamp, Frayser's Farm, Malvern Hill, with McClellan always on the defensive, burning and abandoning huge stores of supplies, at one point in danger of having his army annihilated. None of the Union objectives was achieved; not any; and when the north learned of the staggering casualties, the failure of the highly organized and well-supplied army of McClellan either to crush Lee's forces or capture Richmond, its morale sank to a new low of despondency.

No one escaped censure: General McClellan was called a moral and physical coward, Secretary of War Stanton a fool, Secretary of State Seward a meddler . . . President Abraham Lincoln a weakling who was slowly but surely destroying the nation.

Mary was in Abraham's office late at night while he worked silently at his desk. Their old friend Orville Browning came in, said solicitously:

"Mr. President, you're under such terrible pressure, you shouldn't be working late at night, you need rest."

Abraham looked up from his papers, said in a tone that challenged the importance of such an observation:

"Browning, we must all die sometime."

Mary gazed at his careworn face, silently prayed, Dear Lord, don't let anything happen to him.

He had been in office for sixteen months and was considerably farther from the end of the rebellion than the day he had taken office, with England and France threatening war. What they had hoped would be a family argument that could be settled or compromised without serious damage to either side now looked like a massacre that might not end until every building and state of the nation had been destroyed.

For Abraham, she knew, it was also the bottom of the pit, for New York, Pennsylvania, Ohio, Indiana and Illinois, all of which had gone Republican in 1860, would vote Democratic in the October and November congressional elections, thus disavowing the Republican administration and President Lincoln. The Democrats would take over the Congress, sue for peace, officially ratify the Confederacy as a sovereign nation. The Union would be a dead thing.

He paced the floor, deeply agitated.

"Mary, I am cornered."

"And this is what I yearned for," she said sadly; "to bring you to Calvary."

He wheeled about at the window end of the room, came to stand before her chair at the center table, his eyes flashing fire.

"Nobody knows better than you, Mary, that my paramount object in this struggle has been to save the Union, and not either to save or destroy slavery. In spite of my oft-expressed personal wish that all men everywhere could be free, it is my official *duty* to save this Union. If I could save the Union without freeing *any* slave I would do it, and if I could save it by freeing *all* the slaves I would do it; if I could save it by freeing some and leaving others alone I would also do that."

His voice became high, almost soaring.

"We have asserted our physical strength, it has not been enough; now we must put forth our spiritual strength. It means the utter ruin of the south, a thing I have spent sleepless nights and frantic days trying to avoid. Yet it is too late to try to think of saving the south, we are going down with her."

Mary's heart skipped a beat.

"Abraham, you are going to proclaim emancipation!"

"Yesterday would have been too soon; the border states are tied to us now, with federal troops stationed on their soil. Tomorrow will be too late. Now the north will never be able to abandon the war, even if the Democrats win the next election: for the war and the Union and the freedom of the Negro will be bound together."

His voice became quiet; a radiance in his eyes lit the homely face with an inner beauty.

"We will yet prove that men are capable of governing themselves."

Beyond her feeling of sadness and sympathy for the south, for her friends and neighbors who had been good masters and good citizens, who had everything they owned tied up in plantations and the slaves, fine people who had not invented slavery but who had inherited it as a way of life, and who now would be ruined; beyond her sympathy for them lay an almost uncontainable joy: this would be the end of what Cassius Clay had called the "ultimate evil." Never again would a little girl stand on the lawn of her grandmother's house and from across Mechanics Alley hear the soft moaning of slaves crowded into pens; nor see Negroes lashed across the back; nor watch children torn from their parents on the town auction block. Never again would decent men like her father be obliged, because they were in a business world, to sell slaves in the public square and thus be guilty of perpetuating slavery.

Abraham was speaking softly.

"Victory won't be achieved soon; many more young men will have to die, many parents suffer the ultimate loss. But something noble will be achieved to compensate us for our tragedy."

He sat down at the big central desk, dumped a number of scribbled papers from his pockets onto the table, one corner of his mouth twitching in a little smile.

"You see, Mary, I am up to my old tricks."

She sat opposite him as he picked up his pen, returning the little smile.

"Be lucible, Abraham."

VIII

WHOM HAVE I IN HEAVEN?

1

SHE stepped out onto the porch of the Anderson cottage at the Soldiers' Home, three miles from the White House, where they had come to escape the intense summer heat of the city. The air was pungent with the odor of fresh-cut grass. Stars arching above her lighted the cobalt sky. A clock in the parlor spoke of eleven; Abraham should be home any minute now. She sat on the bottom of the stoop, took off her shoes and stockings, walked about on the grassy knoll. At the crest of the hill she threw herself down to gaze at the lights of Washington; Abraham often returned to the White House after dinner, riding on a gray army mare named Old Abe by Ward Hill Lamon. She did not mind being left alone, it was peaceful here. Abraham had work that could be cared for in these evening hours; it was difficult for him to tear himself away from the dispatch office, and frequently friends from Springfield and the Eighth Circuit, Joshua Speed, Ward Hill Lamon, Orville Browning and a dozen others, gathered round him in his office to tell tales. He needed this laughter and companionship.

On July 11 Abraham had named to the command formerly held by General Winfield Scott, General Henry W. Halleck, who promptly ordered McClellan's Army of the Potomac to move north by water and join forces with General Pope's freshly organized Army of Virginia. But Confederate Stonewall Jackson struck first, at Cedar Mountain, badly defeating General Pope's army.

It was now a month since Abraham had written his emancipation proclamation and read it to his cabinet. Secretary Seward had maintained that the proclamation should follow a military victory rather than defeat, otherwise it might appear as an act of despair. Since the weeks that followed had brought only additional defeat, the proclamation still lay dormant in his desk.

She heard Old Abe coming up the hill, rose and made her way toward the path. A shot rent the quiet night, then the sound of a horse galloping at top speed. She ran past the house to the stable.

"Abraham, what was that shot?"

". . . not a shot, dear, just a loud noise. Scared Old Abe here out of his wits."

"Where is your hat?"

". . . hat? Oh . . . Old Abe bounded forward so fast that it knocked off my eight-dollar plug. I'll find it in the morning."

"We'll find it now."

Some fifty yards down the road she picked up his dusty black stovepipe, discovered a bullet hole halfway up its side. She turned to Abraham, her eyes wide.

"Two inches lower, and your head would have followed your hat!"

"It's just a stray rifle ball fired by some bushwhacker." His complexion had turned a trifle green, belying the conversational tone. "Let's be careful this doesn't get to the press, shall we? No use getting everybody alarmed."

"Abraham, you must let that cavalry company escort you back and forth to the White House. And please don't tell me that it would never do for a president to be surrounded by guards with drawn sabers, as if he fancied himself an emperor."

They turned out the lights in the impersonal parlor with its bare furniture and stale air, went up the angular staircase to a brown-plastered bedroom furnished with a mahogany bed, bureau and washstand. Abraham dropped his coat on the bed, walked to the front window and gazed southward over the Potomac.

"It's almost midnight. Come get some sleep," she counseled.

He turned his back on the window.

"All right, Mary, I'll come to bed. But even when I sleep I don't rest. Nothing seems to touch the tired spot."

They were up at six the next morning in order for Abraham to be back at the War Department telegraph office by seven. The sun was already hot. As he picked up his Sunday hat, Mary announced that she was moving back to the White House; this would avoid the lonely trips home at midnight.

He was having difficulties not only with General Pope, who had been defeated, and McClellan, who had allowed precious days to slip by without breaking camp, but also with his new Secretary of War Edwin Stanton, who was running the War Department with such ferocious efficiency that stepped-on toes made their way to the Lincoln apartment daily to complain about Stanton's dictatorial methods.

Congressman Owen Lovejoy of Illinois came to lunch to recommend that the eastern and western troops be intermingled; Abraham sent him to Stanton with a note of approval. Mary, Abraham and Tad were still at table when Lovejoy returned, red in the face.

"When I showed Secretary Stanton your letter he said, 'The president is a damn fool!' "

Mary and Tad were offended. Abraham only grinned.

"Well, if Stanton says so, I reckon I must be, for he is nearly always right."

That afternoon Stanton called at the executive office. His route back to the War Department lay across the south lawn where Tad was playing with the gardener's new spray nozzle. When Stanton got within range, Tad turned the nozzle on him, hitting him in the face with the stream of water, then playing it up and down Stanton's full figure.

Sopping wet and quivering with rage, Stanton brought the boy to Mary and Abraham.

"I teached him not to call my father a damned fool!" Tad cried.

His parents exchanged a meaningful glance. Abraham turned to his Secretary.

"Stanton, you'd better make peace with Tad. You're getting yourself disliked on all sides by fuming and swearing at everybody, and Tad isn't the only person who resents some of the things you say to and about me. If you can make this boy your friend, you will be better able to win the war and save the Union."

Two days later Stanton came to the family apartment, presented nine-year-old Tad with a commission as a lieutenant of the United States Volunteers, and a Union uniform with epaulets. The latest White House skirmish was resolved.

The air in Washington was stiflingly fetid from the swamps, but not nearly so suffocating as the blanket of silence that had fallen upon the capital: during those rare moments when she could entice Abraham into the family apartments for a cool lemonade or to stretch out for a brief rest, he confided that General Pope's forty-thousand-man Army of Virginia was lost south of Bull Run; there had been neither telegraphic nor courier message from him for three days. General McClellan, who finally had moved his army to Aquia Creek, some twenty-five miles south of Bull Run, would come no closer to the Army of Virginia until assured by General Halleck that he, rather than Pope, would be in command of the combined force.

"I spend half my time trying to locate the generals," Abraham groused, "the other half trying to get news from the front."

Now, toward the end of August, they learned why all communication had been cut off: a rebel force had moved between Pope's army and Washington. All day Friday they heard cannonading. Mary hoped to divert Abraham by making him walk with her in the conservatory, showing him the glowing reds and purples of the late summer blooms.

He said abstractedly:

"I can't tell colors, that's why I never cared much for flowers."

All the next day muffled thunder could be heard coming from beyond the Virginia hills. In the afternoon as the wind veered the smell of powder and smoke drifted into the White House. At midnight, while they sat in the library using their fans to ward off the myriad of bugs that flew in the open windows, John Hay came to report from General Halleck that the greatest battle of the century was being fought, that Halleck had sent every man to reinforce Pope, and that there should be glad tidings at sunrise.

377

When she awakened a few hours later she found Abraham standing over her, his face ashen.

"Mary, we are whipped again! General Pope's army is driven from the field."

She sprang up.

"But how could that be? McClellan's army was just a short march away."

"McClellan never joined Pope. What I feared, happened: General Lee brought his army northward with tremendous speed, joined Stonewall Jackson, and cut our men to ribbons. It's a second disaster at Bull Run."

They made for the wharves at Sixth Street where the white riverboats were bringing in the wounded, their whistles piping the melancholy news of arrival. From the riverbank Mary saw the forms of the dead in the prow, under sheets. The boats moored in silence, the hospital workers went noiselessly aboard with their stretchers, careful not to step on the wounded who were laid out on every inch of the deck, coming off with their gaunt and green-faced cargo, each ambulance making for its appointed hospital.

"Those poor fellows," said Abraham, tears in his eyes. "This suffering, this loss of life is dreadful. I cannot bear it."

Thousands fled the capital, riding trains, carriages, wagons, even as they had in April 1861. Again there were bags of cement in front of the Treasury, horsemen carrying away important War Department documents, clerks from the civil departments drilling in the streets.

Mary spent her time in the Lincoln General Hospital, bringing what comfort she could to the wounded. Soldiers lay on blankets in the hallways, in operating rooms where surgeons were amputating arms and legs, digging bullets out of backs and viscera. She thought, Death is the only victor: we work and hope and pray and fight; we win a little; but death takes all.

She reached home at dusk to find Abraham pacing his office in anguish. When he heard her enter he cried:

"McClellan wanted Pope to fail; he's so scared at what he's done he's down with diarrhea. General Halleck is in bed with a nervous collapse. Secretary Chase says we can't raise any more money. Secretary Stanton says Pope is a disgrace. Our armies are beat, our generals discredited, our money gone. I just don't know what to do, Mary, I don't know what to do."

She contrived a ghost of a smile.

"We'd better have some food or we'll be in poor form to receive General Lee when he rides up to the White House to accept our surrender."

He straightened his hunched shoulders.

"They'll put the iron in our soul before they have done with us, won't they?"

She thought of the dead lying under sheets on the prow of the ambulance boats.

"Sometimes I think that's all we have left: no souls any more, only the iron that has replaced them."

378

Sleep was unthinkable; they padded back and forth in bare feet to each other's bedrooms. At dawn she dressed, loaded the carriage with all the spirits and viands and flowers in the White House, then emptied her savings from the locked drawer of her escritoire into a shopping basket and went abroad to buy additional supplies. In front of the Judiciary Square Hospital the naked dead were stretched out in orderly rows on the ground while carpenters sawed and nailed planks into coffins. Past her went carts and farm wagons loaded with coffins, headed for the cemetery at the Soldiers' Home.

Pope had lost fourteen thousand men, Lee nine thousand. The evidence piling up against McClellan was overwhelming: his telegram to Abraham suggesting they "let Pope get out of his own scrape"; the outcry of the commanders of twenty thousand troops who had been spoiling for battle, when told that McClellan had claimed they were not ready to fight.

Abraham was silent at the family breakfast table. He had reports from the War Department of General Lee's advance into Maryland, giving the Confederate general an open road to Pennsylvania. For the first time a rebel army had invaded the north. The question was no longer whether the north could conquer the south, but whether the south might not capture the north. Abraham dropped his coffee cup into its saucer.

"I have no choice. We must use what tools we have. There is no one in the army who can man these fortifications half as well as he can. He excels in making others ready to fight."

Mary stared in astonishment.

"Surely you can't be talking about McClellan?"

"I am going to his house now and ask him to take over Pope's troops. It's our only hope of saving Washington."

She sat rigid on her chair. The Union press was outraged at McClellan, the members of the cabinet were excoriating him; she could guess the fury that would lash Abraham when he reported his decision.

Yet Abraham proved to be right; McClellan, distressed at the open hostility to him, performed a miracle of reorganization. Within forty-eight hours he had sent an advance corps to search for General Lee, the next day he put his army on the march. Once again Mary went out to the north portico to stand with Abraham and review a Union army moving out to end the rebellion.

Abraham cried: "I make a solemn vow before God that if General Lee is driven back from Pennsylvania I will crown the result by a declaration of freedom for the slaves. Public sentiment will sustain it."

"Amen," she said softly.

A week later a message arrived that McClellan had intercepted a rebel courier with General Lee's instructions to General Jackson. The two vast armies clashed head on at Antietam Creek in Maryland, the first battle to be fought on northern soil. At the end of the day twenty thousand men of both armies lay dead and wounded in the orchards and ripe cornfields. Badly hurt, General Lee would have to pull his army back into Virginia.

379

"The time has come, Mary," said Abraham. "I wish it was a better time. I wish that we were in a better condition. But I'm going to fulfill my promise."

2

THE Emancipation Proclamation was released to the press; it was to become the law on January 1, 1863. They gathered the nation's papers about them of a Sunday afternoon to judge its reception, Abraham sprawling on the floor to read the editorials. Horace Greeley bannered: "God Bless Abraham Lincoln!"; the Chicago *Tribune* said: "The President has set his hand and affixed the great seal to the grandest proclamation ever issued by man." Most people of the north took courage from it, feeling that once the war had been won there could never again be slavery to shame or convulse the nation.

But the Democratic press condemned him as a fraud for having dragged the country into war on the pretext of preserving the Union, when his hidden purpose had been to free the slaves. The New York *Herald* accused him of "throwing a sop to the abolitionists," the New York *World* declared him "adrift on a current of radical fanaticism"; the local Washington paper, the *National Intelligencer*, editorialized, "We shall be only too happy to find that no harm has been done by the present declaration of the Executive." The cruelest cut came from the London *Times*, an attack widely reprinted throughout the United States: "Is Lincoln a name ultimately to be classed among the catalogue of monsters, the wholesale assassins and butchers of their kind?"

Abraham sat with his hands holding his knees under his chin, gazing at her perplexedly.

"Do you know the question that comes to mind? 'Abraham Lincoln, are you a man or a dog?'"

"A man, I hope; if you're a dog, I hate to think what that makes me."

That struck his funny bone.

He left for Antietam to visit McClellan's army: McClellan had not pursued Lee, and Lee had been able to withdraw his army safely across the Potomac. The war was no more over than it had been before Antietam. When Abraham returned, his cadaverous face was twisted into lines of torture, his left iris stuck high in its socket.

"I got the hypo," he announced dully.

Her searching glance took in the introverted look on his drawn and colorless face, his eyes deathlike in their gloomy depths. He half staggered to his desk and sat down, speaking in sepulchral tones of the hard times and agony ahead, of how the war would be long and bloody, with no sign of encouragement anywhere on the horizon.

She shivered inside herself; in spite of the succession of military defeats and the unceasing pressure of numberless groups and individuals, this was the first time he had succumbed to his dread ailment.

She asked William, the servant, to fill the green tub in the basement with tepid water, laid out fresh linen, had a plate of quartered oranges taken to him from the adjoining kitchen. He came upstairs clean and shaved, but he could not bring his eyes into focus. When she asked how he had found the Army of the Potomac, he muttered darkly:

"You think it's the Army of the Potomac? It is General McClellan's body-guard. I said I would remove him if he let Lee get away from him. I cannot bore with an auger too dull to take hold. But who do I put in his place?"

That was the last word he uttered. He was sunk deep in melancholia. All night she heard him moving about his bedroom. In the morning his office door was closed and had a locked look. For a second day he spoke not a word. Her own nerves were beginning to get on edge as she tried to tell herself that this would pass in a day or two.

The news grew worse: state elections brought defeat and repudiation, the Democrats sweeping New York, Pennsylvania, Ohio, Indiana, New Jersey, all of which Abraham had carried in 1860. The Illinois legislature too went Democratic; her cousin John T. Stuart, running as an independent, defeated Abraham's Republican friend, Leonard Swett, for Congress; the new governor of New York, Horatio Seymour, was a Democrat who had consistently opposed Abraham. Mr. Lincoln, elected as a minority candidate, was now more in a minority than ever.

William came to the little reception room at the head of the family stairs where she was keeping her hands busy sewing lace on gift handkerchiefs.

"Mister Lincum not eaten, three days now. Beggin' your pardon, Madame Lincum, but cook has food on the table; if you could fetch him, someaway?"

She went into the main hallway, made for the executive suite. In Abraham's office the cabinet was assembled about the big table, Abraham silent, the air rent with controversy as Secretaries Seward and Chase glared at each other. She went to Abraham's side.

"Abraham, William tells me you haven't touched the trays of food I sent in. I shan't leave the room unless you come with me."

Abraham rose, said hoarsely, "All right, Mary."

She started for their apartment with Abraham immediately behind her. At the door he picked her up by the elbows, deposited her on the outside, pulled the door to.

That afternoon she received a letter from Lexington, telling her that her brother David had been mortally wounded in a battle on the Mississippi. In the same post was a copy of *Harper's Weekly* for November 8 informing the country that Mrs. President Lincoln's brother, who had just been killed in battle, was the one who formerly had been the jailer of the Union troops at Richmond, that . . .

. . . It is probably this division of sentiment which has given rise to the gossip and scandal respecting the views of the lady who presides over the White House.

Chills swept over her. When Mrs. Keckley got her under covers the tears came, tears for David, for whom she could only weep clandestinely; for Abraham, sick with anxiety.

Mrs. Keckley brought hot senna tea.

"I don't know what I should have done without you, Mrs. Keckley," sighed Mary. "Some of these periods will launch me away. . . ."

A few mornings later Abraham awakened with the headache gone, his eyes in balance. He came into Mary's bedroom with a warm smile, kissed her.

That day she and Mrs. Caleb Smith began their work of providing the hospitals with Christmas dinners; they had been collecting funds for several months and had ample cash to buy a large supply of chickens, turkeys, cranberries, fresh butter, cakes and puddings.

An important part of Abraham's recovery was his renewed hope based on the appointment of General Ambrose E. Burnside to the command of the Army of the Potomac. Sitting in her bedroom with her that evening as she worked on her hospital allotments, he outlined Burnside's plan for a campaign against Richmond. Burnside had promised to move immediately providing General Halleck, in charge of supply, would get him the pontoon bridges necessary to cross the Rappahannock River.

A week later Burnside had not moved his army because the pontoon bridges had never arrived; General Lee had been given sufficient time to entrench his troops on the heights above Fredericksburg, halfway down the main route to Richmond. Burnside believed he could cross the Rappahannock safely on pontoons he would build himself, and with his army of one hundred and ten thousand men drive Lee's army of seventy-two thousand before him.

Abraham could not sleep; she stayed up all Friday night with him, for General Burnside had said he would attack Saturday morning at dawn. Dispatches reported the two armies engaged in full strength. In the afternoon she walked with him to the War Department where the telegraph instruments were clicking at full speed. "The battle rages furiously. Wounded are arriving every minute." "The roar of musketry is almost deafening." "Nothing definite in regard to progress of the fight." At six, a little after dark, came word, "The firing has ceased," but no clue as to how the battle had gone.

Sunday there was silence: no telegram or courier from the battlefield, not even the ringing of bells, so many of the churches having been converted into hospitals. The family apartment was quiet. There were no callers. At nine that night when word reached them that Henry Villard of the New York *Tribune* had been seen at Willard's, giving an eyewitness account of the battle, Abraham sent for him. He came at once, in the dusty, sweaty clothes he had worn on the battlefield. When he was brought to the upstairs reception room Abraham said:

"I am much obliged to you for coming. We, Mrs. Lincoln and I, are very anxious, and have heard very little."

Mary went to a chair by the window, leaving the two men facing each other across the table. It was a dread story she heard: General Burnside had hurtled his troops across fields covered by Lee's artillery, then up open slopes where they had been slaughtered by the entrenched rebels. There were more than twelve thousand Union dead and wounded.

Governor Curtin of Pennsylvania burst into the sitting room, told of the waves of Union troops plunging themselves with magnificent courage into the hell of shrapnel and rifle bullets.

"Mr. President, it wasn't a battle, it was a butchery!"

Abraham swayed on his feet. Mary rushed to him. He was trembling from head to foot. Governor Curtin quieted his own agitation.

"Mr. President, I am deeply touched by your sorrow, and at the distress I have caused you."

All night she heard the slow, heavy tread of Abraham's feet pacing up and down in his room. A man's tread might well be heavy, she thought, when there was such a load upon his shoulders and heart.

The next evening she heard the funereal whistles of the boats coming into the wharf. Every ambulance in Washington was waiting, their backs lined to the wharf, the horses standing motionless with heads down. Members of the Sanitary Commission held torches to light the eerie scene. She heard the cry, "Steamer in sight!" and another boat came out of the rain with its cargo of misery and death. All night, all the next day, all the next night . . . thousands of men shot down in the fields, the drainage ditches, the sunken roads and the open slopes of Fredericksburg.

The north became a Fredericksburg, with the shrapnel and bullets sprayed thick over the fields and ditches and open slopes of Abraham's administration. The Committee on the Conduct of the War summoned General Burnside, questioning him so secretly that Abraham had to wait to read the evidence in the New York *Tribune*. He was accused of "placing the army in the hands of its enemies."

Abraham sat beside her, too stricken for comfort. He held her fingers tightly in his cold hands.

"I appointed Burnside; I allowed him to attack under his own plan. The failure is mine; all the failures must be mine."

"Then the ultimate triumph must be yours too," she said encouragingly.

3

SHE now had the task of apportioning the Christmas foods to the superintendents of the hospitals, spending her days in the cool damp basement which smelled like a country tavern, seeing that each hospital's wagon drove away with an ample supply. On the day before Christmas the cellar storehouse was swept clean. She was exhausted, but there was still the New Year's reception to be held. She recalled how eagerly she had given her first New Year's reception to show Washington how beautifully she had redecorated the White House. Now gloom and censure covered Washington like a battered army tent. She had little taste for entertaining.

She was not pleased with the look of her face in her dressing mirror on New Year's morning: it seemed hard and set, older than her forty-four years, her eyes lackluster on this gray and cheerless day, a dark patch shadowing the skin under her left eye. She laid aside her mourning clothes, put on a gown of black velvet trimmed with thread lace, went downstairs with Abraham to greet the diplomatic corps, the army and navy, the judiciary, members of the Senate and House. At eleven the gates were thrown open and the public came in, jamming the corridors and the public rooms, many pausing a moment in line as they shook hands with Abraham and then with her, to proffer an encouraging word. She saw that she had been wrong in not welcoming the reception: in spite of the sadness and the underlying tensions, this gathering of the government was a symbolic act, a rededication.

At midafternoon Abraham led her up the main staircase, followed by a dozen men of the cabinet and Congress. From a pigeonhole in his stand-up desk he took the copy of the Emancipation Proclamation he had had William Stoddard set down the night before, and into which he had inserted that morning the names of the states in rebellion to whom the proclamation would apply.

He sat down in his accustomed central chair at the big table, the men grouped behind him, Mary at his side. She read:

> Now, therefore I, Abraham Lincoln, President of the United States, by virtue of the power in me vested as Commander-in-Chief, of the Army and Navy of the United States in time of actual armed rebellion against authority and government of the United States, and as a fit and necessary war measure for suppressing said rebellion, do, on this first day of January, in the year of our Lord one thousand eight hundred and sixty three . . . order and declare that all persons held as slaves within said designated States, and parts of States, are, and henceforward shall be free. . . .
>
> And I further declare and make known, that such persons of suitable

condition, will be received into the armed service of the United States to garrison forts, positions, stations, and other places, and to man vessels of all sorts in said service.

And upon this act, sincerely believed to be an act of justice, warranted by the Constitution, upon military necessity, I invoke the considerate judgment of mankind, and the gracious favor of Almighty God. . . .

He dipped his pen in the inkpot and held it aloft in a hand swollen from the hours of continuous handshaking. He could not quiet the pen.

"I never in my life felt more certain that I was doing right than I do in signing this paper," he said, "but if my hand trembles when I sign it, people will say, 'He hesitated.'"

"With slavery dead," she observed, "the people you free are not likely to worry about how your signature looks."

He gazed up at her, unsmiling.

"Anyway, it is going to be done."

He steadied his hand, wrote slowly but firmly:

Abraham Lincoln.

Out of forbearance the men behind him did not offer to shake his hand, tendering congratulations instead. When the last of them had left the room he turned to Mary and said severely:

"I do not agree with you that slavery is dead. We are like whalers, who have been long on a chase—we have at last got the harpoon into the monster, but we must now look how we steer, or, with one flop of his tail, he will yet send us all into eternity!"

"According to the legend you inscribed in my wedding ring, in eternity there is love. Oh, Abraham, when this war is over, do you think there will be world enough and time for love?"

General Mud took over. The armies went into winter quarters. The armistice extended to the White House where, taken off target, Abraham began to recover from the defeat at Fredericksburg. Mary too began to feel well again, knew that she would soon look better, the darkness fade from beneath her eye.

There were snowstorms in February, followed by an early spring with thrushes singing in the presidential park and the flowering shrubs making a colorful border to the fresh green lawn. Neither she nor Abraham had ever lost their love of the theatre; during the first year of the war few players had come to Washington, and Abraham would have been too preoccupied in any event. Now she took him to hear performances of Gounod and Verdi operas, planned parties to see James H. Hackett play Falstaff in *Henry IV*, and John Wilkes Booth, announced for a Shakespearean repertoire at Grover's Theatre.

She also let friends prevail upon her to give a reception at the White House for the famous midget, Tom Thumb, star of P. T. Barnum's circus. When Robert, who was between terms of college, came into her room, she said:

"Dress and come downstairs with us, Robert."

"No, Mother, I do not propose to assist in entertaining Tom Thumb. My notions of duty are perhaps different from yours."

She wheeled around on her dressing chair.

"What's wrong with entertaining Tom Thumb and his bride? They've been the honored guests of English and French nobility, the highest society of New York attended their wedding, they received gifts from the Vanderbilts and the Belmonts."

"I think the affair is in bad taste."

"All of Washington has accepted our invitations: cabinet members, congressmen, generals, they're bringing their families; even Kate Chase is coming."

"This kind of side show makes us lose face. I won't come."

They stared coldly at each other from across a chasm.

In early April Abraham proposed the first family outing since they had moved into the White House: a week's trip to the Army of the Potomac. Their old friend from Springfield, Dr. Anson Henry, was in from the Washington Territory of which he was surveyor general. Abraham invited him along.

They left on the little *Carrie Martin* from the navy yard. Snow fell all the next day. At Aquia Creek, which was a vast Union storehouse for the Army of the Potomac, they boarded a freight car fitted with plank benches and decorated with bunting and flags; at Falmouth they transferred to two wagons and, surrounded by an escort of cavalry, were carried to the headquarters of General Joseph Hooker, who had replaced General Burnside. The next day "Fighting Joe" Hooker staged an enormous review, with Abraham in a high silk hat riding horseback alongside the general. Tad rode with the cavalry, his gray cloak flying behind him.

The weather turned warm. Though Abraham had replied to Dr. Stone, when advised to take a vacation, "Two or three weeks would do me no good; I cannot fly from my thoughts," she saw that he had grown cheerful, was telling funny stories. Learning that the Confederates across the Rappahannock had called to Union pickets, "Have Abe and his wife come yet?" Mary and Tad insisted upon seeing the "butternuts" who had become so friendly with the "bluebellies" as they called the Union soldiers, exchanging newspapers, knives, tobacco, coffee. When Tad heard the pickets calling to each other, he asked:

"Why do they have to fight, when they're friends?"

"Out of the mouths of babes," commented Mary, and hugged her son.

At the end of six days the Lincolns returned to Washington, refreshed. When Secretary of the Navy Welles reported to Mary that the public wanted the Marine Band to resume its Saturday afternoon concerts, she consented. Abraham believed that his superbly outfitted army would at last defeat Lee, if only General Hooker would use it to its best advantage.

On May 1 the Army of the Potomac went into action to capture the same Fredericksburg where Burnside's troops had been slaughtered. It was a plan of attack conceived by General Hooker, who informed the White House that he would be striking too hard and fast to send dispatches. At the end of six days and nights news of the battle was at last brought to the Executive Mansion: Hooker's attack had started out successfully, but General Lee had counterattacked, General Hooker had been injured slightly, his judgment had collapsed, Stonewall Jackson had cut his flank, and General Lee, with half the troops at Hooker's command, had forced Hooker to a full retreat. Seventeen thousand of the federal troops, whom Abraham and Mary had watched pass by in review, their heads and hopes high, now lay dead and wounded in the dense forest and tangled underbrush about Chancellorsville.

Abraham whispered hoarsely:

"My God, what will the country say, what will the country say?"

July 2 dawned hot on the knoll of the Soldiers' Home, where they had again sought refuge from the stifling June heat. Abraham had not come home until almost three o'clock that morning, and by seven he was on his way back to the telegraph room of the War Department: for General Lee had invaded Pennsylvania. Abraham had appointed General George G. Meade to replace Hooker, and the day before the two armies had met head on at a little town called Gettysburg. She was anxious to reach the White House to learn the latest developments.

Jehu, the coachman, brought the open barouche with the matched black horses. The movement of the carriage down the hill created a refreshing breeze. It was near ten o'clock when Jehu led the horses into the short cut across the open lot near the Mount Pleasant Hospital. She was fanning herself and gazing at Columbia College when she heard a sharp metallic snap; one end of the coachman's seat rose as though projected by a spring, the seat and Jehu somersaulting through the air. The horses took fright, bolting across the lot.

She made a swift survey: if she waited she ran the risk of having the carriage overturn; if she jumped wide so that she did not get caught in the wheels . . . She sprang out, holding her cotton skirts high in the air.

For two or three steps she retained her running movement, then fell. Her head hit something hard and sharp. It was as though all the Fourth of July fireworks she had bought for Tad were being shot off in her brain. She put a hand to the back of her skull, brought it away covered with blood. She heard voices, was picked up and carried across the lot into the Mount Pleasant Hospital. Inside the front door a man identified himself as a surgeon.

"Bring her into the operating room."

She opened her eyes; she was being set down on a table in the center of a

387

clean odorless room; beneath her was a scrubbed rubber cloth, in front of her she could see mahogany boxes of surgical instruments. The doctor standing behind her said reassuringly:

"There don't seem to be any bones broken, Mrs. Lincoln. I'll have to cut away a little of your hair in order to clean out the wound on the back of your head. We'll send a messenger for President Lincoln . . ."

"Don't do that, Doctor, you would only frighten him."

"As you wish, Madame President. I'm going to have to sew up the cut, it will probably hurt. . . ."

She watched him, a blond young man in spectacles, take a needle and thread out of an instrument box, wet the thread in his mouth, roll it to a sharp point between his fingers. She had the physical sensation of a needle going through the skin of her scalp; the only pain came from her shoulder, which burned like fire. The surgeon covered the wound with wax, bandaged her head, helped her into a waiting carriage.

With the surgeon supporting one arm and the coachman the other, she made it up the family stairs and to her bedroom, putting on a pink silk nightcap which concealed the ugly bandage. She then sent word to the surgeon, who was attending in the hall, to bring the president.

Abraham came rushing, so deeply solicitous that it was almost worth the misadventure to watch him fuss over her. The voices of Abraham and the doctor began to recede. She felt herself falling into sleep. . . .

4

ONE lid fluttered open. The room was black. She tried to move her head. The second lid fluttered.

Where was she? Home in the Main Street house in Lexington? Then where was Ann's bed? No, it must be the house on Eighth Street. She pushed up on one elbow, looking for the walnut wardrobe. There was nothing familiar here. Who was that sitting in a chair in the middle of the room, sleeping? Why did her head feel so strange, as though it were not docked permanently onto her neck?

She fastened her eyes on the woman sleeping in the chair. Who was she? Now she remembered: it was Superintendent of Nurses Dorothea Dix. She was here to nurse William. Then why was she sitting in her room? Probably William had fallen asleep. Mrs. Dix had come to sit by her, knowing how worried she was about William.

Now she knew where she was. She was in the White House. She was preparing for her big February 5 reception; Abraham had not liked the idea of replacing the three state dinners with a catered reception, nor the issuing of passes, but she had convinced him. She had had to send out an extra three hundred invitations; the women's crinolines would suffer mercilessly.

But no, wait! William and Tad were both ill. They had ridden their ponies down to the Potomac and been drenched. She had better watch Tad, his chest always had been weak; Dr. Stone was frankly worried about the boy. Perhaps she had best cancel the invitations?

Tired, she turned off her thoughts. When she awakened again there was a cream-colored gray in the sky.

Abraham did not want her to cancel the party. After all, it was a government affair. The boys would be better by tomorrow.

Then what was this anxiety gnawing at the pit of her stomach? Something had shaken the very base of her well-being. What was it? Then, in an instant, her mind flooded with indignation: what kind of man would write such an article? Pretend that he was eulogizing the president, only to make a mockery of his marriage and his wife? She would take the article to Abraham and he would tell her there was not a syllable of truth in it.

What was it that awful man had said? *He awaited the arrival of the day when the twain should be made one flesh.*

The physical image of Abraham and another woman, though faceless and nameless, made her ill. She must find out who this girl was, assuming there ever had been such a person. She would ask all of the people who had lived in New Salem or who had known Abraham then, the Orville Brownings, to whom Abraham had written his letter about Mary Owens, her cousins John Stuart and Stephen Logan, the Simeon Francises.

Her thoughts veered to William. Tad had recovered, but William was very sick. She slipped out of bed, went across the hall, stood in front of the Prince of Wales Room. Why was it locked? She got the key, returned and unlocked the door.

The room was empty. William was not in the big canopied bed. Abraham, who had been sleeping on a cot for the past few nights, was not there either.

Her head began to throb. She heard a voice behind her. A nurse came to her side.

"Mrs. Lincoln, you shouldn't be walking around like this. The doctor says you must stay quiet."

Why must she remain in bed? True, she was exhausted for want of sleep, having stayed up several nights with the boys; but it was morning now, and there was so much work to be done, the caterer Maillard was arriving from New York with his cooks and waiters.

Her knees began to wobble. She allowed the nurse to take her arm, guide her back to bed again. As she laid her head on the pillow she felt an excruciating pain. Was it spring? The time when she had these bad headaches? Strange, she couldn't remember what time of the year it was.

The throbbing grew more intense, moving outward in circles until it filled her entire cranium. She slipped into unconsciousness.

When she awakened she felt the oppression of the July heat. She knew now why she had not been able to find William: William was dead, the dearest of all boys had been taken away from her. How could she live without William? Face the endless months of anguish and loneliness?

As for John Hill and that mendacious article about Abraham's early love, what would be the use of showing it to Abraham? He would deny the truth of it, say with a shrug, "Let it alone, Mary, it will die of its own accord."

Just then Abraham came into the room, with a broad smile and a story from one of the morning papers that reported her as fatally injured. He joshed her about having deliberately misled the reporters. She matched his light tone.

"You'd better telegraph Robert that I'm all right, or he'll come rushing down for the funeral."

She was not all right. Dr. Stone assured her that the wound was clean and healing, but warned of the possibility of a linear fracture. Certainly the force of the blow seemed to have filled her brain with strange whirring movements that dislodged the habitual processes of thought. It was not merely that concentration was difficult, but rather that something had taken possession of the inside of her head: a quite independent commander who shifted her back and forth in the realm of time and space and reverie so fast she never could be altogether certain which house or year or crisis she was living in.

Tad wandered in and out of her bedroom disconsolately, sat on the floor by her bedside whittling on sticks with the new penknife Abraham had given him. Though he was past ten, he could neither read nor write; Mary kept the tutor on, both for company and because the boy had the capacity to absorb learning by being shown or talked to. She ran her fingers through his thick brown hair.

"Tad, why don't you make a theatre out of the little bedroom across the hall? I'm sure Father will let you have a carpenter to build a stage."

Tad threw his arms around her neck and kissed her, then ran headlong for Abraham's office.

Robert arrived the next morning, having taken the first train home after receiving his father's telegram.

"Father said you were very slightly hurt, but I read in the paper that you had struck your head on a rock. I wanted to be here with you."

"Thank you, Bobby."

It was the first time she had used his childhood name since he had left for Exeter, four years before; but then, she realized, this was also the first solicitude she had known from her oldest son, who now demanded every tiny detail of the accident. He insisted upon having dinner with his parents in Mary's bedroom, told of the decision he had made: when he was graduated from Harvard the following year he was going to enter law college. Abraham put down the knife with which he had been cutting his roasted beef.

"You'll be a better lawyer than I was, Robert. All I learned I had to glean from the books I could borrow from Cousin Stuart. Read most of them on the twenty-mile walk to New Salem from Springfield."

A zigzag pain flashed through her head at the mention of New Salem.

"You didn't do badly for a country lawyer," she essayed, but the humor was lost in the constriction of her voice.

Since she seemed upset, Abraham recounted his twin pieces of good news: General Meade's troops had dug in on Cemetery Ridge behind Gettysburg, and in the largest artillery and foot-soldier battle yet fought in the United States had repulsed General Lee's attack, wiping out nearly half of the Confederate army. General Grant had captured Vicksburg and taken thirty-eight thousand prisoners, putting the entire Mississippi in Union hands.

She was grateful for her hour of clarity, but she paid a price for the concentration, lying awake all night in pain, rolling her face from one side to the other in the pillow to stifle the groans she did not want Abraham, listening in the next room, to hear. Dr. Stone had left her a sedative which she mixed in cold water; as the pain drained out of her head it filled her bosom, as though she were pouring from one jug to another.

In the morning she sent for Isaac Newton, a white-haired Philadelphian who had made a fortune from an ice cream saloon, bought a farm with which to provide himself with cream, and been appointed head of the new Agricultural Bureau. He had been kind to her after William's death, letting her weep on his shoulder after everyone else was weary of her weeping. Newton went frequently to Mrs. Laury, the spiritualist, in Georgetown; she asked him to take her with him, but not until she had sworn him to secrecy.

After each séance she awakened in the middle of the night to see William standing at the foot of her bed. Mrs. Keckley told her:

"The other ladies I make gowns for in Washington, they tell me the best medium here is a man by the name of Colchester. My ladies go heavily veiled, you would not be recognized."

In midafternoon she went to a house on the outskirts of Washington where she sat in a darkened room with other women and heard taps and scratches, the noise of bells and banjos. Colchester, whom she found to be a man of charm and persuasiveness, learned that she was present. The next day he came calling, begged for a chance to give a demonstration of his powers in the White House. Mary agreed. She invited Mrs. Keckley and, as William Stoddard was out of the city, asked Noah Brooks, a newspaperman whom both she and Abraham trusted. He respectfully declined.

She set the meeting for an hour when Abraham was habitually at the War Department telegraph office. Colchester darkened the sitting room, established contact with the next world. The following day she received a note from the medium in which he demanded that she "procure for him from the War Department a pass through the lines; if she refused he would have some unpleasant things to say to her." She sent for Noah Brooks, showed him the note. Brooks shook his head in disbelief at the man's impudence.

"When you invited me to attend this session here with Colchester, my curiosity was aroused, so I invested one dollar to attend one of his sittings.

After we were seated around the table the silence was broken by the thumping of a drum and the ringing of bells. I rose and grabbed a very solid and fleshy hand in which was held a bell that was being thumped on a drumhead. I shouted, 'Strike a light!' When the gas was lighted I found that I had grabbed the hand of Colchester. Send for the rascal and let me confront him."

Abraham returned from the War Department. First he reviewed the recent happenings: General Meade had not pursued General Lee's shattered army, allowing Lee to cross the Potomac and return to the safety of Virginia. Instead Meade had congratulated his troops on "driving the enemy from our soil."

"This is the same notion that moved McClellan to claim a victory because 'Pennsylvania and Maryland are safe.' Will our generals never get that idea out of their heads? The whole country is our soil."

He rolled up the map he had been studying, then turned to her with a look of dumb, gulping patience.

"Mary, it's bad enough that you go to these meetings, and that you delude yourself into thinking Willie can come into your room at night; but how could you let that rascal hold a séance in the White House? It will look as though the president believes in spiritualism and approves it. This is not our house; we are not private citizens. We must do nothing that will bring discredit upon the office of the president, or upon the Executive Mansion."

She thought, He sounds like Robert, scolding me.

In the beginning of August her red-haired brother Alexander was killed at the battle of Baton Rouge. She had carried the infant Alexander around on her shoulder during the months prior to her leaving Lexington for Springfield. Alexander had been the only brother to come to Washington for their inaugural, proud and happy for his sister. When she heard the news she locked her bedroom door, fell on her knees weeping.

"Oh, little Alex, why did you too have to die?"

A dark mood came over her. She was filled with anxieties: their furniture that had been stored with friends in Springfield was being neglected; her sister Ann was spreading unkind stories about "Queen Mary," who was too royal to invite her younger sister to the White House for a social season. She no longer had the patience to direct the servants with whom she had worked so well, giving her orders abruptly; she quarreled with Kate Chase, who held her own little court at Mary's receptions. She also quarreled with Nicolay and Hay over the hundred dollars a month salary available to a steward, a job no longer filled, when she asked the secretaries to let her use this salary for White House supplies and entertainments. Nicolay replied:

"That money has to be paid to a steward or revert to the government."

John Hay added, "Mrs. Lincoln, the money simply isn't ours to disperse for any other purpose than that laid down by the law."

392

She did not like being lectured by this smooth-cheeked boy.

"For two perfectly strange men whom I have been obliged to keep in my home, it does seem to me that you are behaving in an arbitrary fashion."

The next day the secretaries moved to a hotel. Abraham did not like to see them go; in the evening they had frequently returned to the office to catch up on their mail. Abraham enjoyed going in and reading them funny chapters from Artemus Ward or Petroleum V. Nasby.

A few nights later there was a special reception for visiting groups of women from Boston and Manhattan. In spite of the hearty cordiality of Mary's greeting, the Boston contingent, dressed severely in plain black up to their throats, looked askance at the décolleté of her deep crimson gown. She was glad when the New Yorkers arrived in their vividly colored silks and glittering diamonds, diverting the critical attention from herself. When it came time for the promenade about the East Room, she stepped up to Abraham, took his arm and said:

"For two and a half years now you've been selecting a lady to lead the promenade with you. This custom is absurd. The president takes the lead in everything, and as your wife I should take the lead with you."

Abraham raised his eyebrows but did not dissent.

A small dinner party was scheduled; she scrutinized carefully the list of women guests. She had come through years of purgatory with Abraham; she was not going to let some young and beautiful woman become important by laughing gaily at the president's jokes and gazing adoringly up into his face.

One morning she opened the door to his office: in the middle of the room was Abraham, before him an attractive woman on her knees, her arms flung about his legs.

"Well, of all the sights I've ever seen!" she exclaimed.

The woman rose, stood blushing furiously.

"Mrs. Lincoln, I was just imploring the president to help me collect my claim against the government . . ."

"What makes you think your claim looks any better from the floor?" she asked icily.

The woman left. Abraham turned to Mary.

"Now, Mother, don't pull those gas globes down over our heads: I only saw her as a favor to the congressman of her district. Surely you are not jealous? Of the homeliest man in Sangamon County? The one none of the girls of the Pedestrian Club would walk with, except greathearted Mary Todd?"

The "greathearted" mollified her, as he knew it would.

She held her finger ends to the throbbing nerves in her head.

Oh, Abraham, tell me it isn't true, tell me it's all a lie, about that girl back in New Salem. Tell me that I'm the only woman you ever loved!

Abraham saw the distress in her face. He put his arms on her shoulders.

"Why don't you and Tad and Robert go up to the mountains of Vermont

393

for a vacation? You'd gain back your calm. I'll come to visit with you."

"Is that a promise, Abraham? Because I would like to get away from the heat and the bugs and the . . . unhappiness. If you're sure you'll come?"

All arrangements were made. She had only to gather her sons, enter the carriage and then the train for New York. News of their arrival had been published in the New York papers; when they reached the Metropolitan Hotel they found a delegation of admirals from the Brooklyn Navy Yard asking if Mrs. President Lincoln would journey out to the Yard the following day to receive the wives and officers on the *North Carolina*.

As she walked across the deck she saw spread between herself and the receiving dais a Confederate flag. There was no way to walk around the edges. Noting her hesitation, Captain Richard W. Meade of the *North Carolina* asked:

"Is there something wrong, Madame President?"

"I don't think it right to walk across a flag."

"It is the enemy's flag, Mrs. Lincoln."

"The president says we must not think of them as our enemy," she replied with dignity. "Too many fine southern boys have died, even though in an erroneous cause, for me to wipe my feet on what they have been willing to die for. Captain, I must ask that you take this flag up, otherwise I cannot reach the dais to receive your officers and their wives."

Had it been a trap? Had whoever thought of it known that no matter what she did, it was bound to cause criticism? Why should anyone want to put her in such a difficult position? Or was it sheer thoughtlessness? She preferred to believe it was the latter; but the strain of the contretemps brought the blood pounding to her head. She wished she could apply heat or cold to the wound to quiet the vibrations.

She had wanted to add: Too many of my brothers have died in this cause for me to step on what they so deeply believed in. She restrained herself; yet the inner conflict intensified her suffering. How much longer could she go on, having the war fought not only on battlefields but on her bosom?

5

SHE was enchanted with Manchester, the leading summer resort of Vermont, partly because the little New England town reminded her of Lexington, with its colonial houses and white-pillared porches set far back across smooth lawns from the elm-boughed streets. Tad was fascinated by the sidewalks of sawed marble slabs.

If anything could cure the movements and rushes in her head this clear-scented mountain air, with nothing to disturb her, surely should be the medicine. Abraham wrote often:

Executive Mansion, Washington
August 8, 1863

My dear Wife:

Tell dear Tad, poor "Nanny Goat," is lost; and Mrs. Cuthbert & I are in distress about it. The day you left Nanny was found chewing her little cud, on the middle of Tad's bed. But now she's gone! And has not been heard of since.

The weather continues dry, and excessively warm here.

The election in Kentucky has gone very strongly right. . . . Upon Mr. Crittenden's death, Brutus Clay, Cassius' brother, was put on the track for Congress, and is largely elected. But enough.

Affectionately
A. Lincoln

Tad found playmates of his own age, was off and running the entire day. Robert was solicitous, taking her for drives through the Green Mountain forest with its spruce, maple and birch, sitting with her on the porch overlooking Mount Equinox. She surrounded herself with books on the nation's capital and for an hour or two each day read the history of the Executive Mansion.

How sad a domicile it had been for most of its occupants: Andrew Jackson, whose wife Rachel was slandered to death in the campaign of 1828, spent eight lonely years inside its walls. William Henry Harrison died there after only one month of residence. The wife of John Tyler, who succeeded Harrison, moved in as an invalid, dying shortly after of a paralytic stroke. Zachary Taylor died in the White House after a year and a half of the presidency. Mrs. Millard Fillmore suffered from ill-health during her entire tenure and died at the Willard Hotel only three weeks after leaving the Executive Mansion, people said from the strains and exhaustions of her social life as First Lady. Mrs. Franklin Pierce, who succeeded Mrs. Fillmore, had been in a railroad wreck only three weeks before coming to Washington, and saw her son, the last of three children born to her, killed before her very eyes when the coaches fell down an embankment. She never recovered from the shock of the tragedy, was unable to serve as mistress of the White House. James Buchanan was a bachelor; during most of his four years the White House had stood dark and cheerless.

As the last of August passed, the communications from Abraham became fewer. He said nothing about joining her. There was little in his telegrams but war news:

Executive Mansion,
Washington D.C.
Aug. 29, 1863

All quite well. Fort-Sumpter is *certainly* battered down, and utterly useless to the enemy, and it is *believed* here, but not entirely certain, that both Sumpter and Fort-Wagner, are occupied by our forces. It is also certain that Gen. Gilmore has thrown some shot into the City of Charleston.

A. Lincoln

Washington, D.C.
Sep. 6. 1863

All well, and no news, except that Gen. Burnside has Knoxville, Tennessee.

A. Lincoln

Robert returned to Boston, leaving her alone with Tad. Abraham's telegrams now consisted of three words, *All going well*. The weeks of rest and recovery were disrupted by the gnawing fear that Abraham no longer needed or wanted her near. How changing were love and marriage: now warm and bright with the sun, now cold and dark with the night, beset by all the ills the flesh and spirit were heir to.

It was close to the end of September, with the weather turning cool. She caught cold. She would go to the Fifth Avenue Hotel in New York where she would be closer to home, and wait for Abraham to bid her return. She had been wrong to give in to her illness, to let the confusion in her head lead her into unpleasantness. She must straighten herself up, fix a smile on her face, never again mention the ugly word "pain" . . . nor let that pain trap her into emotional upsets. If she did not have the courage to take the *Axis* article to Abraham because this involved the risk of having him admit that there was a germ of truth in the story, then she must keep her jealousy under control. She must make herself beautiful again, be gay, tell herself that it was better to laugh than to sigh.

She had been in New York only a couple of days when she received a letter from the White House stewardess, Mrs. Cuthbert, conveying a message from the president that "Washington is sickly and you should on no account come." She was hurt, then remembered her resolve. The following day came a telegram:

Executive Mansion, Washington,
Sep. 22, 1863.

Mrs. Cuthbert did not correctly understand me. I directed her to tell you to use your own pleasure whether to stay or come; and I did not say it is sickly and that you should on no account come. So far as I see or know, it was never healthier, and I really wish to see you.

A Lincoln

She felt wanted again. She telegraphed Abraham when to have the carriage at the station for her.

She was about to leave the hotel room when another telegram was brought to her. It was from Abraham, telling of the battle between Union General Rosecrans and Confederate General Bragg at Chickamauga.

Sep. 24 1863

The result is that we are worsted, if at all, only in the fact that we, after the main fighting was over, yielded the ground, thus leaving considerable of our artillery and wounded to fall into the enemies' hands, for which we got nothing in turn. We lost, in general officers, one killed, and three or four wounded, all Brigadiers; while according to rebel accounts, which we have, they lost six killed . . . including your brother-in-law, Helm.

Ben, Emilie's husband . . . to whom Abraham had offered a major's commission in the Commissary, so he would not have to fight or kill . . . Now he had been killed. Emilie, her beloved little sister, was a widow.

She stifled a cry. How many brothers have I already lost? Samuel, Alexander, David, Ben. How long will it be before we are all dead, all?

She set a smile on her face, walked through the crowd in the lobby to her carriage.

She sat in her bedroom in a white cashmere dressing gown she had brought from New York. Abraham sat beside her, on the table in front of them a bowl of fruit and a box of candy. The oil lamps were turned low; in the half-light Abraham did not look bad, his face was thin but with a touch of color. Her own cheeks were glowing. The vacation had invigorated her; she was happy to be back in her bedroom at the White House, to have her husband beside her, feel the reassuring, companionable pressure of his hand, hear the rich nasal twang of his voice as he reviewed the happenings of the past two months.

"I was asked by your mother for a pass to go to Atlanta and bring Emilie and her two little daughters home to Lexington. I am sending it."

"Thank you, Abraham," she murmured, "you have always been good to my family."

The military situation was still the sorest trial. Rosecrans's substantial defeat had been once again the result of bad judgment: after taking Chattanooga without a fight he had pursued Bragg southward and fallen into a snare in which Bragg had the advantage of a strong defensive position.

"I am going to have to remove Rosecrans," he sighed. "We have only one general who will fight and who will win: that is Ulysses S. Grant. I am putting him in command of the new Division of the Mississippi."

One day toward the middle of November Abraham came into their sitting room munching on an apple left over from lunch, a faraway look in his eye.

"Senator Sumner brought me a letter from a prominent Boston businessman who maintains that I ought to find an occasion to tell the people about the purpose of the war. There's to be a dedication of a cemetery on the nineteenth, and I've been invited to speak. I haven't spoken in public for a long time, but this might be the right place and the right time. I have most of it worked out in my mind."

He sat down at the big table, took up a piece of Executive Mansion stationery. He filled the first page, scratched out a phrase at the bottom of it, wrote a half dozen lines on the second page.

"It's short, but it's all I have to say. I'll have a chance to rewrite it going down on the train."

He passed the two sheets of stationery to her. She read:

397

Four score and seven years ago our fathers brought forth, upon this continent, a new nation, conceived in liberty, and dedicated to the proposition that "all men are created equal"

Now we are engaged in a great civil war, testing whether that nation, or any nation so conceived, and so dedicated, can long endure. We are met on a great battle field of that war. We have come to dedicate a portion of it, as a final resting place for those who died here, that the nation might live. This we may, in all propriety do. But, in a larger sense, we can not dedicate—we can not consecrate—we can not hallow, this ground. The brave men, living and dead, who struggled here, have hallowed it, far above our poor power to add or detract. The world will little note, nor long remember what we say here; while it can never forget what they did here.

It is rather for us, the living, ~~to stand here,~~ we here be dedicated to the great task remaining before us—that, from these honored dead we take increased devotion to that cause for which they here, gave the last full measure of devotion—that we here highly resolve these dead shall not have died in vain; that the nation, shall have a new birth of freedom, and that government of the people by the people for the people, shall not perish from the earth.

She looked up, said quietly:

"It's deeply felt, Abraham."

The next morning he left for Gettysburg. When he returned home the following midnight, she was waiting up for him. His face was peaked.

"How did it go?"

He was thoughtful.

"Fairly well, I suppose. Edward Everett, the famous orator from Massachusetts, spoke for two full hours and moved the audience to practically every emotion in the books. Mine only took two and a half minutes, so I guess I was through before the crowd settled down. There was a little applause, not much. I'm feeling strangely tired, I don't know why."

Dr. Stone first called it a cold, then bilious fever, then when a rash appeared, scarlatina; but it turned out to be varioloid, one of the lesser forms of smallpox. Abraham looked up at Mary with a weak grin.

"Now at last I've got something I can give to everybody."

He was wrong: the minute the news was published, the White House was abandoned. He worked in bed, reading telegrams which told of General Grant's victories south of Chattanooga, where he had replaced General Rosecrans and immediately defeated Confederate General Bragg. While she and Tad kept him company in the last stages of his convalescence, another telegraphic report was brought concerning her mother and Emilie: when the two women reached Fortress Monroe on Chesapeake Bay, Emilie had refused to take the oath of loyalty to the Union which was required of everyone before they could be admitted into Union territory from the south, saying that to take the oath would be treason to her dead husband.

398

"Poor child, she is unhappy and confused," said Mary; "but her courage has not faltered."

"No southerner's courage ever faltered," replied Abraham grimly; "if it had, we might have been able to get this war over by now." He picked up a telegraph form, wrote:

Send her to me.
A. Lincoln

Mary went into the Prince of Wales guest room for the first time since William's death, brightened the room with new yellow flounces. Emilie arrived, pallid, in trailing black crepe: Emilie, who only a few years before had been so beautiful, with rosy cheeks, a happy laugh on her lips. She had her four-year-old daughter with her, Betsy having taken the younger child to Lexington.

Mary ordered dinner served for just the two of them in her bedroom before the fire, learned that Emilie was in the family way. They were overjoyed to see each other, but it was a sad reunion. Emilie said, "The present is a fresh and bleeding wound, and the future seems empty of everything but despair." When they spoke of old friends in Lexington, Mary exclaimed:

"I have a forty-fifth birthday coming next week—oh yes, I'm getting old, Emilie! I think I'll have a quiet party, just for close friends; I do want you to see the White House when it is happy with guests."

After dinner she took Emilie downstairs, had the lamps lighted in the Red, Blue and East Rooms, related tales of the White House and the story of the redecorating.

The next morning was cool. When the sun broke through in the late afternoon she took Emilie for a ride in the closed hammercloth coach to show her the sights of Washington. She summoned every ounce of delicacy to keep Emilie from fresh reminders of her grief, yet that was more than she could do for herself, for the north was distressed at the idea of Mrs. President Lincoln's sister, who had refused to take the oath of loyalty, being summoned to the intimacy of the Executive Mansion as her reward.

The newspapers once again dwelt on Mary's southern birth, questioning her loyalty. When she came upon a Confederate newspaper and found that it too was calling her a traitor, demanding to know why she did not return to the south where she belonged, she cried:

"Kiss me, Emilie, and tell me *you* love me. I seem to be the scapegoat of both the north and the south."

They heard Abraham's long shambling gait in the outside hall. Mary put on a bright smile. Emilie drew back in astonishment. Mary explained:

"I mustn't let him see me in tears, he has burdens enough."

When Abraham had bade them good morning and gone to his office, Mary asked:

"Oh, Emilie, will we ever awake from this hideous nightmare?"

"No, Sister Mary," said Emilie thoughtfully, "there are parts of it we'll never awaken from; yet there are fine things in it too, like the solicitude you and Mr. Lincoln have for each other. Only this morning Brother Lincoln said to me, 'Little Sister, I hope you can spend the summer with us at the Soldiers' Home. You and Mary love each other. It is good for her to have you with her. I am worried about Mary. She cannot hide from me the strain she has been under, both mental as well as physical.' "

They were interrupted by the arrival of Cousin John Stuart, the newly elected congressman from Springfield. He and Mary embraced warmly. That evening they all had dinner *en famille*, then went into the Red Room. Tad sat on a rug before the fire with Katherine, Emilie's daughter, showing her photographs. He picked up one of his father, handed it to his four-year-old cousin and said:

"This is the president."

Katherine shook her head with considerable emphasis.

"No, that is not the president. Mr. Davis is the president."

Tad shouted, "Hurrah for Abe Lincoln!"

Katherine cried with equal vigor, "Hurrah for Jeff Davis!"

A card was brought by the messenger that General Daniel Sickles, who had lost his leg at Gettysburg, was in the vestibule with Senator Ira Harris of New York, and that he particularly wished to see Mrs. Helm. The general came stumping into the room.

"I told Senator Harris that you were at the White House, Mrs. Helm, just from the south, and could probably give him some news of his old friend, General John C. Breckinridge."

"I am sorry, General, but I have not seen General Breckinridge for some time."

Senator Harris asked Emilie about the armies of the south, how their enlistments were going and provisions holding out. Emilie replied quietly that she knew nothing of such matters.

"Well, we whipped the rebels at Chattanooga," shouted Harris, "and I hear, madam, that the scoundrels ran like scared rabbits."

Emilie, her voice choking, replied:

"It was the example, Senator Harris, that you set them at Bull Run."

Senator Harris turned on Mary.

"Why isn't Robert in the army? He is old enough and strong enough to serve his country."

She felt the blood drain from her face.

"Robert is making preparations now to enter the army, Senator Harris; he has been anxious to go for a long time. If there is any fault here it is mine: I have insisted that he should stay in college until he graduated, as I think an educated man can serve his country with more intelligent purpose."

Senator Harris pointed a long finger at Mary.

"I have only one son, and he is fighting for his country!" Turning to Em-

400

ilie, he added, "Madam, if I had twenty sons, they should all be fighting the rebels."

"And if I had twenty sons, Senator Harris," Emilie replied, "they should all be opposing yours."

She jumped up, made her way from the room.

General Sickles protested to Abraham about Emilie's conduct. Abraham turned to John Stuart and said with a twinkle:

"Emilie has a tongue like the rest of the Todds."

Abraham's attempt at humor infuriated General Sickles, for he brought his fist down on the table and cried in a loud voice:

"You should not have that rebel in your house."

The general had gone too far.

"Excuse me, General Sickles," said Abraham sternly, "my wife and I are in the habit of choosing our own guests. We do not need from our friends either advice or assistance in the matter. Besides, the little 'rebel' came because I ordered her to come; it was not of her own volition."

The next morning at breakfast Emilie said:

"Sister Mary, Brother Lincoln, I have been here a week now; last night proved that I can only be an embarrassment to you. I should so like to stay with you, Sister Mary; but you understand that I must go?"

Mary could not speak. Abraham said softly:

"We understand. I'll have your papers made out giving you safeguard."

That afternoon they took her down the family staircase and through the family dining room to the north portico, helped her into their carriage. As they watched her black-creped figure going out the driveway, Abraham put an arm about Mary's shoulder.

"I feel as though I shall never be glad any more. If to be the head of hell is as hard as what I have to undergo here, I could find it in my heart to pity Satan himself."

6

THE turn of the year 1864 brought a new emphasis to the political situation; both parties would be holding their conventions and nominating candidates for the presidency. The Democrats had grown stronger with the successive military defeats, as well as with the growing apprehension of the north that the rebellion never could be put down. The Democrats talked of nominating their strongest, most popular man, General George B. McClellan, on a peace-at-any-price platform; they would have an excellent chance of carrying the election.

Secretary Chase of the Treasury had entered Abraham's cabinet with the firm belief that he would be the next Republican president of the United States. It was his daughter's politicking that had caused the breach between Mary and Kate Chase. Chase's supporters circulated a pamphlet, signed by Senator Pomeroy of Kansas, which made it manifest that Secretary Chase was the only man who could save the nation. The circular found its way into the newspapers and so embarrassed Chase that he felt constrained to offer his resignation.

Mary and Robert, who was home for the holidays, were in the sitting room when Abraham came in with Chase's letter and an amused smile.

"I hope you are going to accept the resignation, Abraham?" said Mary.

"You will when you see this Pomeroy circular," added Robert.

"I'm not going to read it, Robert," his father replied. "I want to know just as little about such things as my friends will allow me. Mr. Chase has made a wonderful Secretary of the Treasury. I certainly shall not accept his resignation for personal considerations. And I shall do nothing in malice. The issues I deal with are too vast for malicious dealing."

When Mary drew up the invitational list for the traditional state dinner at which the members of the cabinet were to be guests of honor, she thought, I am not going to invite Secretary Chase or his daughter; if we must have vipers in our bosom, I see no reason to feed them at the family board.

Apparently there was a reason; circumspect John Nicolay presented it with considerable force.

"It's my duty, Mrs. Lincoln, to check the guest lists for these state dinners. I see that you have omitted the Chase family. You cannot do that: it would be a violation of protocol. There are certain obligations which the First Lady must fulfill. I beg you to reconsider."

"I will not reconsider."

Nicolay bowed coldly, withdrew.

For the next two nights she did not sleep. In the middle of the third night she admitted to herself that she had been wrong. She rose early, sent invitations to Secretary Chase and his daughter, also a message to John Nicolay asking him to breakfast with the family. Nicolay came, polite but reserved.

"Mr. Nicolay, I offer my apologies. I've already sent invitations to the Chase family. I sincerely hope that you will show your forgiveness by attending the state dinner yourself."

"Thank you, Mrs. Lincoln, I accept with pleasure. I knew all along that you would do what is demanded of the president's wife."

Demanded of the president's wife? Yes, that was what she must always do. But how did one achieve the nobility of an Abraham who, betrayed by a member of his most intimate official family, could say in all humility, "I shall do nothing in malice. The issues I deal with are too vast for malicious dealing"; who, when an opportunity presented itself to be revenged on one of his bitterest opponents, said:

"Not since the day of that near duel with James Shields have I knowingly planted a thorn in any man's bosom."

402

She could not achieve such greatness of spirit herself, but how proud she was of her husband! How magnificently he had grown, borne the buffeting of a thousand pressure groups pushing him in every direction until nearly every inch of his body and brain was black and blue with bruises. How earnestly she yearned to be worthy of him.

The early spring weather was bad. They took advantage of the quiet on the war fronts to attend Ford's new theatre, built after his remodeled Baptist church burned down; there was a spacious presidential box from which, the winter before, they had seen Maggie Mitchell in *Fanchon, the Cricket* and John Wilkes Booth in *The Marble Heart*. Grover's redecorated theatre also had its presidential box, where they now went to see *Der Freischütz* and *Martha*.

Her regular Tuesday night receptions were well attended. On March 8 the Blue Room was crowded with guests when suddenly at the door stood a short man in a dusty battle-worn uniform, clamping a cigar in the corner of his bearded mouth, a stumpy awkward-gaited man who pitched with the movement of a ship. As he stood clasping hands with Abraham she realized that this must be Ulysses S. Grant, come to Washington to be officially appointed lieutenant general of all the armies of the United States. Secretary Seward brought General Grant to her. She gave him her hand.

"I am happy to see you here, General."

"Thank you, Mrs. Lincoln. I would not have come had I known there was a party . . ."

"Oh no, General, you couldn't have come at a better time. Look at these people: every one of them wants to shake your hand."

The guests shouted and cheered. Grant began to blush like a schoolgirl; a vein stood out red and powerful on his forehead, perspiration poured down his brown whiskers. He turned to Mary:

"This is a hotter spot than I have ever known in battle."

Learning that Grant would be in Washington for four days, she planned a dinner for Friday evening, inviting the twelve leading military men in Washington. Shortly before the guests were due to arrive, Abraham came into her bedroom looking sheepish.

"I'm sorry, Mary, but we have lost our lion: he has gone to the station to take the train west. I told him that Mrs. Lincoln's dinner without him would be *Hamlet* with Hamlet left out. He told me he appreciated the honor, but time was very important now and that we would have to excuse him."

Color flared into her cheeks, but she held her tongue.

The White House and the north were soon in high spirits, for General Grant was reorganizing the Army of the Potomac and putting it in position to begin a giant offensive against General Lee; while General William T. Sherman, one of the most successful of the Union commanders in local campaigns, was starting a drive through Georgia.

Regiments from the north moved through Washington to join Grant's Army of the Potomac; then on May 4, Grant moved that army across the Rapidan and plunged into the wooded wilderness in which General Lee had chosen to make his stand. For three days the battle of the Wilderness was waged and for three days there was no word from Grant, with Abraham sleepless, foraging about the capital for news.

"General Grant has crawled into the wilderness, drawn up the ladder and pulled the hole in after him. Everybody will have to wait until he comes out," he conceded finally.

"Then suppose you crawl into bed and pull the blankets in after you?"

At the end of eight days of fighting it was reported that Grant was bogged down in mud; he had inflicted grievous losses on General Lee but had not succeeded in either encircling him or driving him out from behind his breastworks. Grant lost almost a full third of his army, yet he held on doggedly, telegraphing:

"I propose to fight it out on this line if it takes all summer."

Abraham was grim but reassured.

"Grant is the first general I have had. I am glad to find a man who can go ahead without me."

On June 3, Grant attacked Lee nine miles northeast of Richmond. He warned the White House that Lee had once again been able to select a strong defensive position; but even Grant was surprised at the terrible slaughter of the Union troops, some five acres of men lying dead, packed close together, the stench unendurable, with Grant refusing to ask for a truce in order to bury his dead.

"Can't you stop him, Abraham? He'll kill off every able-bodied man in the north if you don't," cried Mary, as the charge of "Butcher" rang through Washington.

"No, I can't stop him. If I do, we have no way to end this war. Do you hire a man to do your work, then do it yourself? It is true our losses are shocking, but he is hurting Lee worse in proportion to the men that Lee has left. Our General Butler has been bested at Drewry's Bluff, General Sigel has been whipped in the Shenandoah Valley, Banks was almost annihilated on the Red River; Sherman is driving on Atlanta, but slow, slow. If I stay with Grant, he'll win for us."

General Grant swung south of Richmond, attacked Lee's supply lines in order to force Lee to meet him in the open; but General Lee dug in behind hilly field fortifications at Petersburg. Grant would have to lay siege to the town.

The spring activities of Secretary Chase's promoters and the unappeased abolitionists failed to create a division in the Republican ranks. The Republican convention meeting in Baltimore in early June renominated Abraham Lincoln on the grounds that "it was not best to swap horses while crossing a stream."

"I predicted in Springfield that you would be the first president since

Jackson to have a second term," exclaimed Mary, as Abraham brought her the news from the War Department dispatch office.

"Whoa, Mary, whoa, I'm not elected, only nominated. A second term would be a great honor, but it would also be a great labor."

Exhilarated over the convention's vote of confidence and the renomination, Mary planned a trip to Boston for Robert's graduation from Harvard, began drawing up plans for a remodeling of the Anderson Cottage so that they could have an attractive home in which to spend the summer months, celebrated with an informal supper party for their closest friends, after which they went to the theatre. Abraham accepted Secretary Chase's resignation from the cabinet over a disputed appointment.

General Lee continued to outmaneuver the best Union military brains; early in July he sent General Jubal Early around Grant's army and northward to attack Washington. General Early cut the railroads and the telegraph lines; the capital filled with panic-stricken families from the villages of Maryland; every able-bodied man was mustered into the District of Columbia militia and drilled through the streets as long as daylight lasted. Firing could be heard clearly in the Executive Mansion, doubly so in the summer cottage, which was only three miles from the battlefield.

She drove out with Abraham in an official party to Fort Stevens. They stood on the parapet of the fort watching General Early's troops charge. A Union officer standing within a few feet of them was felled by a bullet. A young officer shouted at Abraham:

"Get down, you damned fool, before you get shot."

Two Union regiments met the Confederate force, sent it retreating across the fields. The Union troops did not pursue. Secretary Stanton said to Mary:

"I intend to have a full-length portrait of you painted, standing on the ramparts of Fort Stevens overlooking the fight."

"That is very well," replied Mary, "and I can assure you of one thing, Mr. Secretary: if I had had a few *ladies* with me the rebels would not have been permitted to get away."

Abraham turned so that Stanton would not see his grin.

On July 18 he issued another call for a half million men. The north rose in angry protest, draft riots threatened in New York. By the middle of August, with Grant still stalemated in front of Petersburg, leaders of the Republican party informed Abraham that his election was an impossibility. Thurlow Weed said, "Nobody here in New York doubts it, nor do I see anybody from other states who authorizes the slightest hope of success." Henry J. Raymond, editor of the New York *Times*, wrote that the tide was setting strongly against him, that if the election were held then, Abraham would be beaten in Illinois, Pennsylvania and Indiana.

"Isn't there any way you can get out and earn votes?" Mary asked.

"No, I cannot run the political machine; I have enough on my hands without that. It is the people's business. If they turn their backs to the fire and get scorched in the rear, they will find they have to sit on the blister."

"We'll be nothing but blisters," she said forlornly.

"The Democrats are undoubtedly going to nominate General George McClellan, so I am going to write a note to the cabinet which I will seal, and ask every member to sign."

When he had finished, he handed the note to her:

Aug. 23, 1864

This morning, as for some days past, it seems exceedingly probable that this Administration will not be re-elected. Then it will be my duty to so co-operate with the President elect, as to save the Union between the election and the inauguration; as he will have secured his election on such ground that he can not possibly save it afterwards.

She looked across the table at him.

"Then on March fourth you will ride in a carriage to the Willard, pick up General McClellan and take him to the Capitol to be inaugurated. And you and I will ride away from the White House just as pale and sick and cynical as Mr. Buchanan was?"

"Pale and sick I'm sure we'll feel; but I don't think there is need to be cynical. We've done our best and no one can ask more of us."

"What do we do after that?"

"After that?" He raised his eyebrows. "Go back to the house on Eighth Street, return to the old law office . . ."

"Not Lincoln and Herndon again!"

He shrugged.

"I have to earn a living. The law is my trade."

The full Todd pride and fighting spirit flooded over her. She sprang to her feet, walked quickly to his side.

"I don't believe a word of it. I don't believe the people of this country could be so blind. They'll never order you to hold McClellan's horse! You've been a good president; you've held together all the warring factions in the government, met problems the country never has had to face. It's not your fault if you can't get generals to win battles; you're not a West Point graduate."

"No, I'm just a blab school graduate."

Her eyes were blazing.

"You can tell me all of the Thurlow Weed predictions you like, you can read me Mr. Raymond's letter from the *Times*, show me all the opinions from Indiana and Illinois . . . but when the people go to the polls in November you are going to be re-elected: they'll never turn you out of this office in defeat."

"Well, Mary," he replied mildly, "we have been in office nearly three and a half years and even the best friends of the Union admit that these are the darkest days of the war. In the north they are saying 'there are no Lincoln men.' Greeley says I am beaten already. There is a movement in New York

406

whose purpose it is to ask me to withdraw from the nomination because I can bring the Republicans nothing but defeat."

He smiled at her.

"All I have on the other side to support me is your determination that I shall not be beat."

It was the Union generals who put sinews into her intuition: on September 2, General William T. Sherman occupied Atlanta, on September 19, General Philip H. Sheridan decisively defeated General Early in the Shenandoah Valley. General Grant so effectively nailed down Lee's army at Petersburg that he could give no help to those Confederate armies being beaten and removed from the conflict.

The Lincoln opponents scrambled onto the bandwagon, Horace Greeley trumpeted, "I hate McClellan," Thurlow Weed and his Republican committees went to work with money, energy and enthusiasm; and at last Abraham did something in his own behalf: he made sure that General Sherman gave his thirty-odd regiments leave to go home and vote.

The campaign was bitter, with fortunes being spent on newspaper, pamphlet and oratorical attacks on President Lincoln and his wife, the Republican failure to end the war, the Emancipation Proclamation; for the northern Democrats realized that the only hope for the continuation of slavery was a presidential victory for General McClellan, who would declare an armistice, repeal Abraham's Proclamation, grant the south its independence. By the same token all Republicans, even those who stated publicly that "the administration has been politically, militarily and financially a failure, and its necessary continuance a cause of regret for the country," had to vote for Abraham or find the Union and the four years of bloody strife irretrievably gone.

Election day dawned gray and cold. Strong winds blew rain through the deserted streets. Abraham and Tad stood at one of the south windows watching the White House guard casting their ballots. At lunch Mary asked Abraham how he felt.

"Uncertain. It's a little singular that I, who am not a vindictive man, should have always been before the people for election in canvasses marked for their bitterness."

After supper Abraham and John Hay walked across the wet grounds to the War Department telegraph room. About ten o'clock she received a batch of telegrams showing Abraham in the lead in Indiana, Massachusetts, New York, though the voting was close. She asked the messenger whether the president had sent any word.

"Yes, ma'am," replied the messenger with a grin, "he said, 'Hurry these dispatches over, Mrs. Lincoln is more anxious than I.'"

She got Tad to bed at eleven. It was three in the morning before Abraham returned. The War Department had provided fried oysters at midnight. By now it was clear that he would carry every state except New Jersey, Delaware and Kentucky. Mary could not resist exclaiming over the defeat of a relentless enemy in Maryland. Abraham replied:

"Perhaps I have too little personal resentment, but I never thought it paid. A man has no time to spend half his life in quarrels. If any man cease to attack me I never remember the past against him. The same goes for the south: we must give them a friendly and helpful peace, so that they can get back on their feet as quickly as possible."

Mary reached up her arms to him in a jubilant victory embrace.

"It's all clear to me now, Abraham: you be the saint in the family, I'll be the prophet."

7

THE weeks following the election were among the busiest she could remember. General Grant, who had lost such a large part of his army in the summer and autumn campaigns, was seasoning green troops in preparation for the drive against Lee with the coming of spring; Sheridan was cleaning out the Shenandoah Valley so that he could join Grant after the turn of the year; Sherman, after capturing Atlanta, started down the full length of Georgia without provision or supply, in an effort to remove that state from the war and close the critically important port of Savannah.

Abraham worried about Sherman, for the Confederate press reported that his men were ragged and starving; but all other news from the south was heartening: the Confederacy was growing destitute from its nearly four years of heroic effort to hold off an opponent many times its size in wealth and manpower. The Union navy blockaded most of her ports; the Mississippi was in federal hands, with the supply of food which had poured across from Arkansas, Louisiana and Texas shut off; Lee's army was on short rations, reports drifting into Washington that his soldiers on the picket lines came in frozen with cold; desertions were riddling his army, soldiers slipping away at night to return to their homes to protect them against Sherman.

Before, there had been defeat after defeat; now there were messages of victory: Union General George Thomas so destroyed Confederate General Hood's army in Nashville that it could never again be effective. A telegram arrived on Christmas night from General Sherman, saying, "I beg to present you as a Christmas gift, Savannah." Sherman had left a wake of destruction behind him, burning down practically every building and plantation on his way. Georgia was out of the war, and Sherman was free to swing north through the Carolinas to join his seasoned troops to Grant's.

The rising Union hopefulness was reflected in their New Year's reception on Monday, January 2, 1865, far and away the vastest crowd that ever thronged into the White House.

Abraham's greatest drive, now that the termination of the rebellion was in sight, was to replace his own emergency war measure with an amendment to the United States Constitution which would make Emancipation the permanent law of the land. He had helped guide a thirteenth amendment through the Senate, only to have it defeated in the House. At its next session she was amused to see him once again become the Sangamon County politician, gathering up three reluctant Democratic votes by offering one of the men a federal appointment for his brother, another, assurance of support for his contested seat, the third, friendly votes for the railroad which he represented and which was facing constraining legislation.

On January 31 the Thirteenth Amendment passed the House. A hundred-gun salute was fired over Washington. News reached the Executive Mansion that Maryland, Arkansas and Louisiana had abolished slavery. A procession came to the White House to serenade and thank President Lincoln. Abraham stood with Mary on the portico, waving to the crowd. When there was a lull in the music, he turned to her and said matter-of-factly:

"As affairs have turned out, it is the central act of my administration and the great event of the nineteenth century."

Back inside he paced the library, head on his chest, thinking. She bent over her sewing, waiting for him to speak.

"You know, Mary, I've always believed that all our states share in the responsibility for slavery. If the south would end the hostilities tomorrow, and voluntarily abolish slavery, I think the federal government should indemnify the owners. I've figured out the sum roughly: some four hundred million dollars would do the job."

She said without looking up, "It would give the people of the south money to get on their feet again . . . start working their plantations with employed labor. But with the war so nearly over, would the north be that magnanimous to a defeated foe?"

"I'm going to propose it to the cabinet in the morning."

He came to their sitting room the next day, after his cabinet meeting, crestfallen.

"Not a chance: they voted unanimously against the idea. We could have saved more battles and bloodshed, done much to eradicate the hatreds. . . . They were so bitterly opposed that I asked them to say nothing of my proposal."

She did not know whether it was this disappointment, or the letdown after the years of anxiety and overwork, but the following day, just before his fifty-sixth birthday, she heard angry voices coming from his office, entered in time to hear Attorney General James Speed, brother of Joshua, castigate Abraham for having pardoned a large batch of Union soldiers charged with desertion. Abraham jumped up from his desk, shouting:

"If you think that I, of my own free will, will shed another drop of blood . . ."

409

The blood drained from his own face as though from a great gash. He slumped back into his chair. He had fainted.

Mary helped put him to bed. By the time Dr. Stone arrived, he had regained consciousness and was practicing a thin smile. Dr. Stone turned to Mary:

"I've been warning the president that his nerves were nearing exhaustion. You must keep him in bed for a day or two, Mrs. Lincoln, and then oblige him to cut down on his work schedule."

She spent several quiet days in Abraham's bedroom, reading, writing letters to Hannah Shearer and Lizzie Grimsley, interceding for Adele Douglas's brother, who was about to be cashiered from the army. Abraham amused himself with the humorous sketches of California life by Phoenix.

Time flew so fast she could not keep track of the passing days and weeks. Before the second inauguration she went to New York for a vacation, splurged on amethyst and pearl breastpins, pearl and diamond rings, clocks, vases, coffee and ice cream spoons, silver bouquet holders and a gold card case for the White House. She felt she could afford the extravagance, for they had saved some seventy thousand dollars out of their first term's salary.

She rose early on March 4. Mrs. Keckley helped her into her new black velvet trimmed with ermine. She had hoped that this second inaugural, with no need for vast military display or sharpshooters at the windows, would be a joyous one; instead it had rained most of the night, Pennsylvania Avenue was a slough of mud, the sky overcast, a cold shifting wind blew a drizzle now into the faces and now onto the backs of the spectators standing in inches of mud on the sidewalks.

At eleven o'clock she entered her carriage at the White House with Robert, Senator Harlan of Iowa and his pretty young daughter Mary, the first girl in whom Robert had shown any sustained interest. They were detained at the west gate in a mass of would-be paraders who were wet and mud-covered and defeated by the weather. After watching the swearing in of Vice-President Andrew Johnson of Tennessee, a thoroughly embarrassing performance in which Mr. Johnson, who appeared to have been drinking, gave a pugilistic speech, Mary stepped out of the Capitol doors to the inaugural stand. At that moment the sun came from behind the clouds, bathing the waiting crowd in a strong clear light.

Abraham rose at the front of the stand, dressed in black suit and frock coat. He was sworn in by Chief Justice Salmon P. Chase, whom he had appointed to head the Supreme Court when Roger Taney died. Mary glanced at Kate Chase sitting on the other side of her father, her expression dour.

The crowd fell silent, its face turned upward. Abraham began speaking. He reviewed the progress of the Union arms, the difference between this inaugural address and the one he had made from this same stand four years before:

"While the inaugural address was being delivered from this place, devoted altogether to *saving* the Union without war, insurgent agents were in the city seeking to *destroy* it without war—seeking to dissolve the Union. Both parties deprecated war; but one of them would *make* war rather than let the nation survive; and the other would *accept* war rather than let it perish. And the war came.

"Neither party expected for the war, the magnitude, or the duration, which it has already attained. Neither anticipated that the *cause* of the conflict might cease with, or even before, the conflict itself should cease. Each looked for an easier triumph, and a result less fundamental and astounding."

Then, throwing both arms out wide in a gesture she remembered from four years before, as though to embrace the crowd before him, as well as the sundered nation, he concluded:

"With malice toward none; with charity for all; with firmness in the right, as God gives us to see the right, let us strive on to finish the work we are in; to bind up the nation's wounds; to care for him who shall have borne the battle, and for his widow, and his orphan—to do all which may achieve and cherish a just, and a lasting peace, among ourselves, and with all nations."

She sat with her eyes closed, thinking, I have been married to Abraham for almost twenty-three years, and I am convinced he is not a lawyer, he is not a politician, he is not even a statesman. He is a poet. I believe that is all he ever wanted or meant to be.

There was no room for exultation at the reception that evening, when some fifteen thousand men and women swamped the White House, crowds of people whose faces and mood they had never seen before: walking on the furniture, breaking vases, carrying away *objets d'art* as souvenirs. When at the end of four hours the last of the guests had been herded out, Mary and Abraham went through the rooms; they looked as though a regiment of rebel troops had been quartered there with permission to forage. A yard-square piece of red brocade had been cut from the window hanging in the East Room, another piece from a drapery in the Green Room; floral designs from the lace curtains had been cut out with penknives. The reception rooms were a shambles. Abraham was aghast.

"Why should they do it, Mary? How can they? After all, it is their own property, their own White House."

"Perhaps that's why: they feel it is theirs to do with as they will. You had better issue a call for the Congress to convene here tomorrow and see the damage: I'm going to need an appropriation to repair this vandalism."

8

SHE had thrown all of her energies into the reception and the inaugural ball which followed, designing for herself a shimmering white silk and lace gown with an elaborate fan and headdress which cost almost two thousand dollars, then entertaining large groups of the Republican party, family and friends. Now she was tired.

At this moment Julia Baker, her sister Elizabeth's daughter, who had come to Washington with her husband for the inauguration and was occupying the Prince of Wales Room across the hall, scandalized Washington by riding out at daylight with a gentleman in a closed carriage while her husband remained asleep in the canopied bed. The next night Mary awakened to see Abraham standing over her in his long nightgown.

"Mary, I hate to waken you, but it's two o'clock. Julia is still in the library carrying on so loud I can't sleep."

Mary put on a robe and slippers, went into the sitting room. The gentleman with Julia was not her husband. Mary invited her niece to return home to Springfield.

Ninian, who had urged Abraham to appoint him commissary of subsistence because he was in straitened circumstances, was reported by reliable friends in Springfield to have amassed a fortune by giving out war contracts to the Democrats, particularly those who were avowed enemies of the administration, and who were providing the troops with worthless goods. Abraham summoned Ninian to Washington, weighed the evidence, shifted him to the Chicago quartermaster's division where he would have no power to grant contracts.

Immediately on the heels of Elizabeth's outraged protest came a problem with her sister Ann's husband, Clark Smith. Abraham stormed into her bedroom late one afternoon waving a letter under her nose.

"Listen to what your brother-in-law has the nerve to write me: 'If you could at the proper time give me a little notice or a hint that things was likely to be brought to a close in our troubles, I could unload my several hundred thousand dollars of merchandise before a drop in prices comes. I will keep the information strictly confidential, you can send the letter to a private address in New York. No one will ever know . . .'" He put the letter down, his face flaming with indignation.

Then the crowning blow came from her sister Martha, married to Confederate Captain Clement White, who asked if she could visit Sister and Brother Lincoln in Washington. Abraham acceded to Mary's request for a pass. When Martha returned through the lines on her way to Richmond, the New York *Tribune* published a story which charged her with refusing to have her luggage searched, boasting that her trunks were filled with contraband, and that the president had forbidden anyone to open them. For weeks the press of the country ran stories of Martha White carrying back to the rebel armies her weight in quinine, a drug sorely needed, of having made dupes of President and Mrs. President Lincoln.

"I'm beginning to understand why there was no member of your family at either inauguration, Abraham," said Mary apologetically; "why you've never appointed any one of them to even a minor post, or had a family visitor at the White House. I've had family enough for two."

Abraham smiled a little ruefully.

"Oh, my cousin Dennis Hanks came up here once, wanting trading permits for his sons-in-law." He gazed at her sheepishly. "I granted both requests; but I never told you about it."

The blinding headaches returned: now she felt pressure upon her brain, with a burning sensation on the surface of her scalp. Her vision became blurred, and there was a feeling of constriction. For days she could speak to no one, not even Tad, who wandered in and out of the bedroom forlornly. When William Stoddard came down with typhoid, and left Washington, she lost her staunchest friend in the White House. She became depressed.

"I've got the hypo," she murmured.

She forced herself to go downstairs one evening because a number of guests were coming, but ended by quarreling with Senator Sumner, who was unwilling to give the southern state governments back into the hands of the men who had led them out of the Union. Sumner left the White House in a huff; the next morning she had to apologize:

> Words are scarcely an atonement for the inadvertent manner in which I addressed you yesterday. Therefore, I pray you, accept this little peace offering for your table: a few fresh flowers brought up by the gardener.
> Trusting that your kind nature will excuse me, I remain,
>
> *Respectfully,*
> Mary Lincoln

Abraham was planning to go to the battle front, hoping to be present for the fall of Richmond and the surrender of General Lee. She remembered her trip to the Army of the Potomac in the spring of 1863, how considerably it had refreshed her. Tad could go along, and they would all see Robert, for she had prevailed upon Abraham to get an appointment for Robert on Grant's staff.

Abraham approved her idea.

On March 23 they pulled away from the Sixth Street dock in the *River Queen*. Mary and Abraham had the captain's room, Tad and Mrs. Keckley adjoining cabins. The following night at nine they reached City Point with the varicolored lights of the boats in the harbor, the little town wandering its way up the bluffs from the shore, and on top the lights of General Grant's headquarters.

The next morning Robert boarded in his captain's uniform, direct from General Grant's headquarters, to tell his parents of a sharp fight at dawn resulting from an attempt of the Confederates to slash through the Union lines and reunite two segments of their army.

An hour later Mary and Abraham boarded a military transport coach behind a slow-moving, smoke-belching locomotive which took them over the supply railroad to the front. When Mary descended from the coach she froze in horror at the sight of hundreds of Union and Confederate soldiers lying dead and wounded on the field, with the gravediggers digging, the Union Sanitary Commission giving aid to the wounded, the gray Confederate hospital corps working under a flag of truce to bury its dead. She felt ill.

General Grant's secretary, Adam Badeau, helped her and Mrs. Grant, a heavy-featured woman with a squint, onto the seat of a half-open carriage, then took the seat facing the two ladies. Abraham and the other men of the party rode horseback. The road was a continuous line of mudholes which knocked them about. Mary put her hand to her head, which had begun to throb. Adam Badeau said:

"I think there is a decisive battle coming up very shortly now: all wives of army officers have been sent back home. The only exception is the wife of General Charles Griffin, she got a special permit from the president."

Mary leaped up from her seat.

"What do you mean by that, sir? Do you mean to say she saw the president alone?"

Badeau stared at her with a sickly grin.

"That's a very equivocal smile, sir. Let me out of this carriage. I will ask the president if he saw her alone."

Badeau sat silent. Mrs. Grant said in a mollifying tone:

"Mrs. Lincoln, we will be at the front with the president in a few moments. Please sit back and stop distressing yourself."

They reached the reviewing ground. General Meade came up to help Mary alight from the carriage. He linked an arm through hers as they walked a few paces.

"General Meade, did Mrs. Griffin secure her permit to remain here with the army from the president?"

General Meade gazed at her troubled face, replied quietly:

"That would be quite impossible, Mrs. President Lincoln; her permit to remain at the front came directly from Secretary of War Stanton, to whom she appealed."

Mary returned to the carriage, said triumphantly to Mrs. Grant and Badeau, "General Meade assures me it was not the president who gave Mrs. Griffin her permit, but Mr. Stanton."

In the silence that followed she saw that they were embarrassed, not for themselves but for her. She shook her head sharply, as though to clear her thoughts; she must keep better hold on herself.

That evening she and Abraham had a quiet supper in the cabin of the *River Queen*. The next morning when she went on deck she found that the cold winter winds had died down; the sun was warm, the air thin and fragrant. The harbor where the Appomattox and James rivers came together was filled with fighting boats, sailboats, transports and passenger boats. The *River Queen* left its pier and went down the James in the morning sun. On the bank were Union soldiers from Sheridan's army swimming, bathing, watering their horses, laughing and singing like children out of school. The *River Queen* went through a flotilla of Union boats, all draped with flags, men cheering as Abraham stood at the rail with his arm linked through Mary's, dressed in his long-tailed black frock coat and his high silk hat, the ends of his cravat blowing in the breeze.

Across the river from City Point they disembarked; this time a carriage with springs had been provided, to make the journey to the review grounds of the Army of the James, under command of General Ord, easier for Mary and Mrs. Grant. Adam Badeau again was in the carriage, accompanied by a Colonel Porter.

At a road fork the driver lost his way; they came to the end of what was little more than a trail in the woods and had to double back. The mud had not yet dried, the pace was slow. Nervous now because they might miss the review for which they had come, Mary decided that she would do better by walking the several miles to the review grounds. She ordered the driver to stop, but when she got one foot out of the carriage she saw that she would be wading in mud up to her knees. She settled in a corner of the carriage, gnawing her lip.

They reached the review grounds almost two hours late. The giant review of the Army of the James had been completed, but she arrived in time to see Abraham, with Generals Grant and Ord, riding between the columns to the music of the bands, the soldiers drawn up at present arms. Riding next to Abraham there was a woman.

Mary turned to the officers on the front seat.

"Who is that woman riding next to President Lincoln?"

"Why, that's Mrs. Ord, wife of the commander of the troops under review."

"What does she mean by riding by the side of the president? What right has she to pretend that she is the wife of the president?"

"Oh, I'm sure that she isn't trying to pretend that, Mrs. Lincoln," replied Mrs. Grant. "Everyone knows who you are. It's just that we were too late for the review . . ."

At that moment Major Seward, a nephew of the Secretary of State and frequenter of the White House, came riding up with a grin.

"The president's horse is very gallant, Mrs. Lincoln. He insists on riding by the side of Mrs. Ord."

So! The talk would be in all the newspapers of how Mrs. President Lincoln had been relegated to a back seat, with Mrs. Ord chosen to ride alongside the president. This would be the beginning of another one of those miserable rumors like the one that had run in the *Menard Axis*.

Mrs. Ord, having seen Mary's carriage drive up, detached herself from Abraham and General Ord and came riding to Mary's side.

"Mrs. President Lincoln, I am so happy you have arrived. The general thought I ought to take your place, since you had been so unfortunately delayed."

"You take my place! May I inform you, Mrs. Ord, that no one takes my place. In the future I'll thank you not to impersonate the wife of the president."

Mrs. Ord burst into tears.

Mrs. Grant said, "Mrs. Lincoln, I don't think you ought to speak that way to Mrs. Ord, she meant no wrong, she was simply following her husband's instructions."

"I'll thank you not to defend her. Your loyalty should be to me as the First Lady. I begin to believe that this whole thing was a conspiracy."

There was silence. Mrs. Ord and Major Seward rode away. Mrs. Grant excused herself, leaving Mary alone in the carriage. She ordered the driver to take her back to the *River Queen*.

The return journey was a nightmare in which she was only half conscious, burning inside herself at the humiliation she had suffered. Everyone was against her. If they had the power they would relieve her of her post as First Lady and fill the breach themselves. But she would not allow it. She had suffered too long and endured too much to be made a laughingstock. Neither was Abraham free from all blame; he could have waited the parade for her, he owed her that much.

She locked herself in the cabin, threw herself face down on the bed, her head a torment. It was dark before Abraham came back; he knocked on the door several times.

"Mary, are you there? May I come in?"

She opened the door. He stood crouching over, an expression of guarded melancholy on his face.

"Mary, I'm terribly sorry about the driver losing his way. It was unfortunate, but the division had been standing at parade rest for hours. I felt it wasn't fair to keep the men waiting any longer."

"So you chose another woman to ride alongside of you! Abraham, how could you? That was my place and no one else's! You led the troops to think she was the wife of the president. Every newspaper will make a story of it."

Abraham was genuinely surprised.

"But why should they make a story of such an incident? Those troops have seen Mrs. Ord before. She has a permit to be at the front. The Lord knows we've been subjected to every attack conceivable to the human mind, but certainly no paper has linked my name with any other woman's."

She flushed; shafts of pain shot like bullets through every angle of her head. She would not tell him; this was the one humiliation she would never let past her lips. Abraham raised her up from the pillow.

"Wouldn't you like to dress now? We're entertaining General and Mrs. Grant and his staff for dinner. They're bringing a band on board."

"Mrs. Ord will be there?"

"General and Mrs. Ord will be there."

"Then I'll not come."

She could contain her pain and anxiety no longer; she burst into tears, burying her face in her arms while she wept. Abraham stood above her, patting her hair.

She decided to return to Washington.

Back in the seclusion of her own apartment in the White House she realized the enormity of what she had done. Dear God, how could she forgive herself? What was she to do about this pain in her head which left her open to every passing temper, pushed aside her judgment, laid waste the years of resolve and discipline?

Abraham sent her telegrams as though nothing had happened, messages giving her the details of battle just as, for four years in the White House, he had discussed with her the strategy and results of the campaigns.

> Head Quarters Armies of the United
> States, City-Point,
> April 2. 7/45 1865

Mrs. A. Lincoln,
Washington, D.C.

  Last night Gen. Grant telegraphed that Sheridan with his Cavalry and the 5th. Corps had captured three brigades of Infantry, a train of wagons, and several batteries. . . . This morning Gen. Grant ordered an attack along the whole line.

> A. Lincoln

A few hours later another telegram from City Point:

Mrs. Lincoln: At 4:30 P.M. to-day General Grant telegraphs that he has Petersburg completely enveloped from river below to river above, and has captured, since he started last Wednesday, about 12,000 prisoners and 50 guns. He suggests that I shall go out and see him in the morning. . . .

> A. Lincoln

The next day she received word that Petersburg had been evacuated by General Lee; within a matter of hours General Grant took possession of Richmond, which also had been evacuated by Confederate troops and government. But there was alarming news as well: reports were brought to her from the War Department that, in the bitterness of defeat, a plot was being hatched to assassinate Abraham. She wrote notes to the provost marshal of the Washington police asking that two officers who had been recommended, Joseph Sheldon and John F. Parker, "be detailed for duty at the Executive Mansion." The extra guards reported that night.

Abraham returned, overjoyed that while he was en route General Lee had surrendered to General Grant. As soon as General Johnston surrendered the rest of the Confederate army to General Sherman, the war between the states would be over.

9

SHE awakened on Good Friday, April 14, the day Abraham had proclaimed as one of general thanksgiving throughout the north, to find the spring morning clear and beautiful; exactly four years before, Major Robert Anderson had been obliged to haul down the American flag at Fort Sumter. Today he was raising the identical flag above the fort.

The city had been wild with joy since the previous Sunday when General Lee had surrendered to General Grant at Appomattox; so many celebration cannon had been fired that windowpanes were broken throughout the city. Church bells rang, business houses closed, thoroughfares were jammed with people, buildings were covered with flags, bunting strung across streets. At night Washington was ablaze with glory, every house, shop, hotel and public building illuminated with thousands of candles and ropes of lanterns strung along walls, with brass bands marching through the streets playing at the top of their trumpets, fireworks going off on every corner.

It was seven o'clock when she arose. Abraham was already at his desk. He had invited General and Mrs. Grant to see Laura Keene in *Our American Cousin* with them that evening at Ford's Theatre.

At eight o'clock she and Tad took Abraham downstairs to the family dining room to breakfast with them. Captain Robert Lincoln came in, his uniform soiled and dusty, a three-day beard on his face. He kissed them all.

"You were with General Grant at Appomattox," said Abraham proudly. "Tell us of General Lee's surrender."

Abraham had requested of Grant that Lee and his men be treated generously. Robert's report proved that Grant had followed the president's orders: the starving southern soldiers had been fed with Union rations, allowed to return home after signing a paper that they would not fight for the Confederacy any more; the officers carried home their side arms and personal baggage, the soldiers kept their horses and mules for plowing.

"I brought a picture of General Lee back with me," concluded Robert. He handed the portrait to Abraham, who laid it on the table before him.

"It is a good face," said Abraham with deep feeling. "It is the face of a noble, brave man. I am glad that the war is over at last."

Mary looked across the table at her husband; he had shaved early that morning, there was color in his cheeks, his hair and whiskers were neatly combed, he had on a freshly pressed suit.

"You must be expecting company this morning, Mr. President," she said in a bantering voice. "Is it to be the singer, Patti, or Laura Keene?"

Abraham's eyes sparkled to see that she could make jokes again about other women.

418

"Oh, nothing quite so lovely, Mary: Schuyler Colfax, the Speaker of the House, is coming in at nine, then Senator John A. Creswell of Maryland, who wants me to set free a friend of his who is in a Confederate prison camp. Our old friend Richard Yates, who has just been elected to the Senate, is bringing in Colonel William Kellogg, who he thinks should be appointed Collector of the Port of New Orleans. John Hale, the new minister to Spain, is coming for his instructions. There is a batch of senators and representatives who have an appointment to discuss the governments to be set up in Virginia and Louisiana. Aside from that I have only to get over to the War Department very quickly now to make sure that General Johnston has surrendered to General Sherman, then I must get back to my office for an eleven o'clock cabinet meeting in which General Grant is joining us."

She rose, kissed him.

"Your usual idle morning. Robert, you're free this evening. Wouldn't you like to come and see *Our American Cousin?*"

"Thank you, Mother, but I haven't slept in a bed for two weeks, I'd like to turn in early."

"Mama, can I come in Robert's place?" cried Tad.

A messenger arrived from Grover's Theatre, inviting a presidential party to see *Aladdin, or The Wonderful Lamp.* Mary told Tad something of the story, adding, "Taddie, I think you and your tutor would enjoy that play much more than *Our American Cousin.* Suppose you be Mr. President Lincoln tonight?"

She lunched downstairs with the two boys; Abraham was still in his cabinet meeting. Later he came into the sitting room, told her that Major J. B. Merwin of Connecticut had missed his appointment, and could she have some lunch for the two men brought up here? He wanted to hear Merwin's plan for having Negro troops dig a canal across Panama.

She dressed slowly in a black wool street dress with a deep collar effect created by white braid and fringe looping across the bosom. A little before four Abraham came into her room bringing a visitor, Irish Mary, the Springfield servant who had been so faithful during the months of the 1860 campaign. Mary shook hands warmly.

"I'm glad to see you. I trust the president has given you an order for your husband's release from the army?"

"Oh yes, Mrs. Lincoln, he surely did; but he is always such a nice man."

Mary picked up a basket of fruit which had arrived as a gift the day before, presented it to the girl. She curtsied, left.

Abraham took Mary's hand, pulled her down beside him on the sofa.

"There's only one thing I am worried about; it's the abolitionists in Congress who want a harsh peace and severest punishment of the south. If we are wise and discreet, we will reanimate the states and get their governments in successful operation, with order prevailing and the Union re-established, before Congress comes together in December. There are men in Congress who possess feelings of hate and vindictiveness, in which I do not sympathize and cannot participate."

He rose from the sofa, walked to the window overlooking the president's park, the Potomac, the lovely rolling hills of Virginia.

"I hope there will be no persecution, no bloody work. There is too much of a desire on the part of some of our very good friends to be masters, to dictate to those states, to treat the people not as fellow citizens. There is too little respect for their rights. We must extinguish our resentments if we expect harmony and union."

"You must win the peace, Abraham, just as you won the war."

The doorman came to inform them that the carriage was waiting. They went down the main staircase into the vestibule. At the bottom of the steps stood a one-armed soldier. He said:

"I would almost give my other hand if I could shake that of Abraham Lincoln."

Abraham grasped the soldier's hand, asked his name and regiment, commended him for his bravery.

As they stepped out onto the portico they found that the sun had gone behind the clouds. Abraham told the driver to take them into the country, past the Soldiers' Home. They rode through the suburbs, Abraham holding Mary's hand in his.

"I feel very happy, Mary, because I consider this day the war has come to a close. We must be more cheerful in the future; between the war and the loss of Willie we have been very miserable."

"We've been in a bad row of stumps," she replied.

"We have laid by some money, and during this term we will try to save up some more. Then we'll go back to Illinois, and I will open a law office at Springfield or Chicago."

"But we'll have a nice long vacation before we do that, won't we, Abraham?"

"Yes, Mary, we are going to have the vacation in Europe that you dreamed about all your life."

She looked up at him, saw that he was in earnest. A trip to Europe, what a glorious fulfillment!

As they turned in to the White House they saw two of their Illinois friends going across the lawn toward the Treasury.

"Come back, boys, come back," shouted Abraham.

She smiled to herself. They were all boys to Abraham.

The family dined alone. She was disappointed to learn from Abraham that General and Mrs. Grant had declined Abraham's invitation to go to the theatre with them. She sensed the rebuff; well, she would find her own way and her own time to make peace with Mrs. Grant. She sent an invitation to Senator Harris's daughter and her fiancé, Major Rathbone, to accompany them instead.

She dressed in a full-skirted black silk gown with a pattern of widely scattered tiny white flowers, adjusted the white quilted satin bonnet trimmed in black and white lace over her carefully dressed hair. When Abraham returned from a last trip to the telegraph office he showed signs of fatigue.

"Mary, I feel inclined to give up the whole thing."

"Very well, if you'd rather not go; you've had a full day."

"It's been advertised that we will be there and I cannot disappoint the people. Besides, if I stay home, there will be people in the whole evening long, and I will have to shake hands and talk to them and I will get no rest at all."

It was time to leave for the theatre. Speaker Colfax and George Ashmun were waiting in the Red Room for a conference. She sent a messenger down to summon Abraham, but as he came upstairs he was caught by Senator Henderson of Missouri, an ally on reconstruction for the south. When she went with Abraham into his bedroom to help him get an overcoat, cards were brought in from Senator William Stewart of Nevada and Judge Niles Searles of New York. He sent the message, "I am going to the theatre with Mrs. Lincoln. It is the kind of engagement I never break. Come with your friend tomorrow at ten, and I shall be glad to see you."

Mary put on her black velvet cloak, picked up her fan and opera glasses in their black case lined with red.

They were now a half hour late for the curtain.

They got into the carriage. Up above, holding the reins, was the coachman, Francis Burns, while Abraham's valet, Charles Forbes, stood by the door to help them in. They drove quickly along the cobblestone streets to pick up Clara Harris and Major Rathbone, then made directly for Ford's Theatre on Tenth Street between E and F. Forbes dropped down to the sidewalk, opened the door, helping Mary, Abraham and Miss Harris onto the wide plank platform which carried them safely across the muddy gutter in front of the theatre. John Parker, the guard she had had assigned to the White House, was waiting for them.

The lobby was deserted; it was eight-thirty and the play had been on for a half hour; an usher who had been posted to wait for them led them up a flight of stairs, then down a sloping aisle to their box. There was a white door into an anteroom, then another door which opened into the box proper.

Mary led the way, stepping into the carpeted compartment with its red-flowered wallpaper. At the front, hanging from a support at the top and all the way down to the floor, were curtains of closely woven Nottingham lace which gave them almost complete privacy. Yet they were seen; there was applause and some few cheers from the audience; the players stood momentarily, then continued with their lines.

Inside the box were comfortable armchairs, a small sofa, a rocking chair for Abraham. Mary took her seat in an armchair at the front of the box, with Abraham in the rocker at her left side behind the curtain and in the corner so that he could not be seen from the audience. Miss Harris sat next to Mary in the right corner, Major Rathbone behind his fiancée. Parker took up his station outside the anteroom; Forbes, who drove with the family so often to the theatre, had permission to sit at the back of the box and watch the show.

They had seen the play before, but Abraham was amused by the English description of Americans as seventeen feet tall, with black hair reaching down to their heels, carrying tomahawks and scalping knives. Between acts they laughed and chatted without leaving the box.

After the opening of the third act it grew cold and drafty. Mary suggested that Abraham put on his overcoat. He rose, put on the coat, then sat down again in the horsehair rocker. Mary leaned across his lap, resting her elbow on his knee, gazing at him with a smile.

"What will Miss Harris think of my hanging on you so?"

Abraham smiled indulgently.

"She won't think a thing about it, Mary."

10

THERE was a loud noise behind them, like an explosion. She jerked upright from Abraham's lap. The box filled with white smoke.

She saw Abraham's eyelids slowly close, as though he were falling asleep. The affectionate smile faded into weariness as he swayed backward. The rocking chair, which had been leaning forward in intimacy as they whispered to each other, moved away from her. His head, high above the back of the chair, fell to rest against the wall behind him.

A scream was wrenched from her throat.

For the first time she was aware of another man in the box: black hair, black suit, the face familiar, the eyes wild, lids distended over the whites, staring down, first at Abraham then at her.

Major Rathbone hurtled himself from his chair at the other end of the box, struggled with the dark stranger so close to her she could feel the violence of their movements. She rose from her chair, her hands pressed to her heart. There was the gleam of a knife, a slashing movement, a groan from Rathbone.

The dark man pushed between her and Abraham, jumped up on the railing of the box. Rathbone lunged past her, grappling for a hold. There was another slash of the long knife, then the dark man jumped to the stage below. Rathbone shouted:

"Stop that man! Stop him!"

She fell to her knees in front of Abraham, reached up, took his face in her hands.

"Abraham, where are you hurt? What is it? Tell me!"

422

His head fell forward into her hands. He did not speak or open his eyes. She felt his body begin to sag. She wrapped her arms about him, held him upright in the chair. His head fell onto her shoulder. She held him to her breast so that he could not fall. She could scarcely feel his breathing. She heard Rathbone calling to the audience for a surgeon.

"Abraham, speak to me, tell me where you've been hurt."

The door to the box was opened. A man in uniform rushed to her side.

"Mrs. Lincoln, I'm Dr. Leale, surgeon from the General Hospital."

"Doctor, take charge of him."

Dr. Leale and Rathbone, bleeding profusely from an arm wound, lifted Abraham from the chair and laid him on the carpeted floor. She stood above them, her heart pounding so loudly in her ears that she had to strain to hear Dr. Leale.

". . . clot of blood on shoulder . . . may be a stab wound . . . slit the coat and shirt . . ."

The box filled with people: Laura Keene, trying to comfort her, another of the actors bringing water, a young man who introduced himself as Dr. Charles Sabin Taft, Julia's brother, still more doctors. She watched Dr. Leale trying to breathe air into Abraham's lungs, pour a little brandy down his throat.

"Can't we take him home?" she pleaded. "It would be so much better for him there."

"I'm afraid not, Mrs. Lincoln; the president would die before we got him to the White House."

Die! Abraham die?

She sank to her knees, put an arm under Abraham's head, raised him to her. Where her right hand held his head firmly against her, she felt something wet and sticky. She brought it up slowly, saw a blotch of blood. She stared at it in silence, uncomprehending, then raised her eyes to the doctors who were watching her. After a pause Dr. Leale said:

"I'm sorry, Mrs. Lincoln. The president was shot . . . in the back of the head."

Four soldiers who had been in the audience, and three doctors, picked up Abraham, carried him out of the theatre. Mary followed, supported by Major Rathbone. The crowd in Tenth Street, across which was a row of family residences, was now so dense that an army captain had to clear a way with his sword. Abraham was being carried feet foremost, sagging in the middle. More soldiers joined the cortege to hold him under the hips.

Overhead, the moon was covered by dark gray clouds.

The house immediately opposite, to which Dr. Leale was taking Abraham, was closed. A man standing with a lighted candle in the open doorway of the next house beckoned to them. They went up a half flight of stairs leading to the front door, down a long hall, past two doors. There was a room with a bed in it. The soldiers left. The throng of stricken, as well as curious, who had followed into the house, were put out. A chair was drawn up to the bed for her. She sat on the forward edge, holding Abraham's hand.

The bed was too small for him. Abraham had to lie with his knees up. The doctors tried to remove the footpiece of the bed; they could not. Dr. Leale moved him so that he lay diagonally, the way he had slept in Springfield.

Cushions were put under his head. The bed was pulled into the center of the brown and white wallpapered room so that Abraham would lie immediately under the flaring gas light. Dr. Taft stood at the head of the bed, holding his hand on the wound.

The room was filled with doctors. She heard their whispered consultations, though not the words. Abraham still had on his heavy leather boots and long frock coat. Dr. Leale told her they wanted to undress Abraham and search for further wounds. Would she mind going into the next room?

Clara Harris helped her up; she went back down the hall to the front parlor. It was dark. The fragrance of lilacs was so heavy in the air, she could not breathe. She asked that Robert be sent for, also Dr. Stone, Mrs. Keckley, Mrs. Welles. She sat in a chair, her face in her hands.

Dr. Taft came in, said she might return to the president's side. Abraham was now under blankets. He was still unconscious. Occasional sighs escaped his lips. Clean napkins had been put over the pillow to cover the bloodstains. She stood over him, cried:

"Abraham, live, you must live!"

The Reverend Gurley arrived, went on his knees between Mary and Abraham and began to pray. Dr. Stone arrived, was given an account of the wound. Brandy was poured between Abraham's lips; he did not swallow it.

Men continued to come in: the cabinet, Senator Sumner, who put an arm about her shoulders, Speaker Colfax, another half dozen doctors, until the room was crowded to suffocation. A window and door admitting to a porch were opened for air.

Robert came running, started for the bed, was taken aside by Dr. Stone, told something that started the tears streaming down his face. He came to his mother, put his head in her lap like a child, wept. She stroked his hair, gazing over him at Abraham's face, now beginning to twitch on the left side. When the doctor pushed back his lids she saw that now, as in all crises, his eyes were in imbalance, the left iris contracted and pulled high in its socket.

The doctors decided to probe for the bullet. Once again she was asked to leave the room. Robert helped her into the front parlor. When she was permitted to return she saw that Abraham had taken a turn for the worse: his left eye was dark and swollen, his breathing irregular. She wanted to fling herself upon him, cover his eyelids and mouth with kisses, pour her overburdening love and life back into his frame. She turned to Robert.

"Bring Tad, he will speak to Tad, he loves him so."

There was a pause. Someone said no. She burst into tears.

"Oh, that my little Taddie might see his father once more."

424

No one moved.

She sat with Robert in the parlor. The gas light had been lit. Its hissing was the only sound. She sat, as the night hours spun themselves out.

She returned to Abraham's side. His features were now distorted, the breathing stertorous. The doctors were standing around the bed, doing nothing more to help him, heads bowed. Senator Sumner was sitting close to Abraham, holding his hand, sobbing.

In a swift instant her eyes took in the room: the two dozen black-frocked and uniformed men; the picture on the wall just beyond Abraham, Rosa Bonheur's *Horse Fair*; the bureau, wood stove, washstand; the brussels carpet beneath her, which she did not see until she had fallen halfway to the floor in a faint.

Her senses returned. Dr. Stone was applying a restorative. All discipline and self-control were gone. Abraham was dying, and they were doing nothing about it. If only she could make him hear her voice.

She stood with her lips almost upon his, cried out:

"Love, live for but a moment! Speak to me once! Speak to our children!"

She listened for his voice; there was no sound in the room except that of men weeping; of Secretary of War Stanton giving orders, endless orders.

A piercing cry escaped from deep within her. She fell supplicatingly to her knees by Abraham's pillow, sobbed with all the force and tortured despair of her nature. Then she heard a voice say sternly:

"Take that woman out and do not let her in again!"

It was Secretary Stanton.

She had only time to think, I'm "that woman" now, with Abraham unable to defend me. Oh, Abraham, Abraham, what will I be without you?

Hands lifted her from the floor, helped her grope her way along the hall to the sofa in the parlor. She wept silently. Twice she rose, tried to go in to Abraham. Twice she was restrained.

The minutes ticked away. The hours. She lost count of time and circumstance. The world receded from her consciousness. How much was she dead, how much alive? She did not know, did not care.

Then it was morning, a gray grim morning. Robert came to fetch her. He led her by the hand, down the dark hall to the bedchamber. She stepped inside. The men turned away. She looked at Abraham.

He was dead.

She flung herself upon his bosom, covered his face with kisses.

"Oh my God, and I have given my husband to die."

11

SHE could not bear the familiarity of her own bedroom. She went to bed in a little guest room.

There was movement past her door, men going and coming, hushed voices, those of doctors. Abraham had been brought back to the Prince of Wales Room.

On Sunday morning the sun came out brightly.

"How can the sun shine," she asked aloud, "with Abraham dead?"

Tad was the only one in the room.

"It's a sign Father is happy in heaven. He was never happy after he came here. This was not a good place for him."

Waves of weeping shook her to the depths of her being. When she raised her head from the pillow she saw Tad cowering at the foot of the bed, his face an agony.

"Don't cry so, Mama, or you will break my heart."

She held out her arms to the boy.

"Tad, today is Sunday; bring me paper and pen, I'll send a note to Dr. Gurley, ask for the prayers of the congregation."

She wrote the note. The effort to hold clarity exhausted her. She fell into a delirium of tangled, frenzied images that made a chaos of her mind.

There was a shot. She bolted up, screaming. Mrs. Keckley was in the room. She put her back in the bed.

"It's the carpenters in the East Room, Mrs. Lincoln; they're hammering nails."

"Every nail that's driven comes up here like a pistol shot. Can't you stop them?"

Robert had come in quietly.

"It's for the services, Mother. They're building the . . . catafalque. . . ."

All day footsteps went down the hall to the Prince of Wales Room. Robert brought in cards from people wanting to pay their respects.

"I'm too ill to see anyone, Robert."

It would be good to have Elizabeth with her; but Elizabeth sent no word. Dr. Stone kept her under sedatives.

She slept, awakened. Cannons were firing. Washington was under siege. Then it had been a hideous nightmare, Abraham was still alive . . .

Robert was sitting in a chair by her bed.

"Mother, it's time for the . . . for services. Dr. Gurley is giving the sermon. Mrs. Keckley and Mrs. Welles will help you dress. Won't you get up now, let us take you down to the East Room?"

Church bells began to ring over the city, funereally. She shook, slowly at first, only her hands; then her arms, her shoulders, her bosom and innards, until every part of her was shaking convulsively. She pulled the blankets over her head.

The house was still. Mrs. Keckley was sitting in a corner. The door opened. It was Dr. Anson Henry. She threw her arms about his neck, held herself to him fiercely while she wept. Then she related the story of the last day. The telling relieved her.

Noon. Again there were church bells. Minute guns were fired. It was the time.

She rose from the bed, went in her nightgown to the window overlooking the north drive and Pennsylvania Avenue. Six gray horses left the portico pulling a draped and canopied hearse. People lined Pennsylvania Avenue, solid, in trees and on rooftops. Regimental bands played the death march. The army marched in slow time, behind.

She was dry-eyed now. She felt only a consummate hollowness. She remembered the first moment they had crossed the threshold of the White House; she had taken Abraham's arm, said, "Abraham, we're home."

How many times had she stood at a window watching him make his way across the lawn, to the War Department, the Treasury? Now he was going through the gate, for the last time.

In Springfield she had cried, "If I must be destroyed, why can't it be on the plane of high tragedy, where at least I might sacrifice my happiness for some great and noble cause?"

I cried out too loud, she thought. The gods heard me.

Robert entered.

"I telegraphed Judge David Davis to come to Washington. He is taking charge of our affairs. He and I and Orville Browning, we think it best that Father be buried in Springfield. It's where Father started, where he made his career . . ."

"There are too many memories for me in Springfield. I prefer some other place, Chicago, perhaps. I want Willie taken out of the vault, buried with Father . . ."

"Yes, Mother. The cabinet spent all day arranging for the funeral train. They plan to take Father home on the same route he came to Washington. In each city he will lie in state: the City Hall in New York, Independence Hall in Philadelphia . . ."

She stiffened. She never had been able to gaze into the face of death. Now poor Abraham would be dragged from city to city, lying defenseless while millions of strangers stared down at him.

"Father is too tired. He must not be dragged over two thousand miles of rails, through city streets. Death is not a show. Tell them I do not want a funeral train."

He returned in an hour. His face was haggard.

"They say Father doesn't belong to us any more. That he belongs to the ages."

427

Mrs. Keckley washed her face with a warm cloth, brushed her hair, propped pillows behind her. She asked after Tad.

"This morning I found him asleep under Mr. Lincoln's desk in the executive office. When I woke him and asked if he wouldn't like to come downstairs for breakfast, he answered, 'Pa is dead. I'll never see him again.'"

"Bring him in to me. If not for little Taddie, I would pray to die, I am so miserable."

Tad came in. His face was pinched, his eyes two dark hollows, like Abraham's when he was stricken. She saw a man in the hall.

"Who is that?" she asked Mrs. Keckley.

"The guard, Mr. Parker."

"Tell him to come to me."

Parker entered, a heavy-faced man with half-closed lids. He trembled.

"Why were you not at the door to keep the assassin out?" she asked fiercely.

Parker hung his head.

"I have bitterly repented it. But I did not believe that anyone would try to kill so good a man in such a public place. The belief made me careless. I was attracted by the play, and did not see the assassin enter the box."

"You should have seen him. You had no business to be careless." She fell back on the pillow, covered her face with her hands. "Go now. It's not you I can't forgive, it's the assassin."

"If Pa had lived," said Tad, "he would have forgiven the man who shot him. Pa forgave everybody."

Letters of condolence poured in, touching letters from strangers who wrote how much they loved and esteemed their dead president. There were letters too from Betsy and Emilie, Levi and Dr. Wallace, Lizzie Grimsley and Hannah Shearer. Elizabeth never came, or any other member of her family.

Robert asked:

"Mother, are you feeling better? Because we have to start packing. It's a week now, President Johnson and his family have the right to move in."

"Robert, I'm still so ill. How can I get up, pack, move? I don't even know where I'm going."

"We'll go to the Eighth Street house."

"I can't go back to Springfield. I would be overcome by memories."

A reprieve came from John Hay: he had gone to an influential senator who was close to Andrew Johnson, urged him to obtain from the president a word that Mrs. Lincoln need not feel rushed in moving. President Johnson sent the message.

Hay had left on the funeral train. She wrote, thanking him for this last act of kindness.

On May 4, almost three weeks after Abraham had been killed, Robert sent her word that Abraham had been buried at Oak Ridge Cemetery in Springfield.

His burial marked an official end to the Lincoln regime.

428

No one came into the White House. It had the feeling of being abandoned. Guards and servants left, unable to stand the silent melancholy.

In the deep night she heard noises, subdued voices, running feet. Mrs. Keckley explained: vandals were stripping the public rooms, cutting open sofas and chairs, tearing down lace curtains, stealing vases, silver and diningware, carting away pieces of furniture.

"They say it's your fault, Mrs. Lincoln. They say you fired the steward years ago, and there's no one here to oversee."

Indignation flamed in her cheeks.

"Secretary Stanton has a whole army in Washington. All he needs to do is to assign one squad of soldiers . . ."

Mrs. Keckley gazed at her, stolidly.

"They say you overstay your welcome. They say you must get out and let President Johnson move in, so he can carry on the nation's business, protect the White House."

She lay back. Tears pooled in her eyes.

Mrs. Keckley helped her to dress. She went across the hall to her bedroom for the first time since Abraham's death, staggered back as though struck, then entered.

She ordered up all the trunks and boxes to be found in the basement, began working as though possessed, assembling everything the Lincolns had brought with them from Springfield or accumulated over the four years in the White House.

She could not bring herself to go into Abraham's bedroom. She had his clothes and personal effects brought to her, giving them away to friends and associates and servants who had loved him: a gold and onyx initial sleeve button he had worn the night he was assassinated to Dr. Charles Sabin Taft; a cane to Charles Sumner, another to Slade, a messenger; the hat he had last worn to Reverend Gurley, the comb and brush he used to Mrs. Keckley.

Of her own things, she could give nothing away, nor leave behind the oldest of her dresses. She treasured the bonnets, purses, shawls, furs, laces, gloves, the tiniest scrap of material or yarn, ribbon or button: for she was afraid she would not have enough money to support herself and her sons. And so she filled the boxes and trunks, combining, fitting, packing from early morning until late at night, deriving energy from the task at hand.

Robert disapproved.

"It makes no sense to take away all these old scraps. You must have fifty to sixty boxes here, not to mention the dozen trunks. What are you going to do with this torn dress?"

"Never mind, Robert, I will find use for it."

"You won't. People are beginning to talk: they say you're the one who's stripping the downstairs of the valuables, packing them in these boxes to take away with you."

She was aghast.

"How cruel they are! I've taken nothing that belongs here, only Father's stand, the one he kept his brushes and razor on. He loved it so, he agreed I could take it with us when our second term was over, providing I replaced it. I'm only taking it for Taddie."

He was out of patience.

"How many more days are you going to spend on all this, when everyone wants us out? I hope to heaven the car which carries all these boxes to Chicago catches fire and burns up your plunder!"

"Plunder? Why do you call my personal possessions plunder?"

"Because it's . . . it's irresponsible . . . crazy! If you don't stop packing all this worthless stuff, I shall simply have nothing more to do with it. It's bad taste, as well as bad judgment."

Bad taste, bad judgment, plunder . . . ? This rose antique moiré in which she had received for the first time as First Lady, and elicited the approving glances of the scoffing Washington ladies? This white flowered satin and matching headdress with which she had impressed the diplomatic corps?

She threw back her head. The two spots flamed on her forehead. Robert stared at her coldly.

"I think you've said quite enough, Robert. Would you mind leaving my room?"

The packing was finished, hers and Tad's. She gathered together the formidable sheaf of bills of her past few months' purchases, sent for Dr. Henry.

"Would you be so kind as to pay these bills for me, as reasonably as you can? They're for things I bought in New York. Here is seven thousand dollars. I think they'll settle for that."

Her train left at six for Chicago.

It was five weeks since Abraham had died.

She sat stiffly in her heavy black mourning dress and black veil. But she knew she could not go without one last look at Abraham's bedroom, one visit to their sitting room, to Abraham's office.

Her legs could hardly carry her through the rush of memories, the four years as President Abraham Lincoln and Mrs. President Lincoln: their first hours in this executive office, with its view of the Virginia hills, the portrait of Andrew Jackson and Abraham's vow to hold the Union together; the call for troops; the anguish of Bull Run, Fredericksburg, Antietam, Gettysburg, with all the young men dying; the big mahogany table, and Abraham sitting across from her writing the Emancipation Proclamation, giving it to her to read, seeking her approval . . .

Abraham's bedroom, with its massive bed, the tramp of his heavy feet when their son had been dead a week, and she had come in here to comfort him. Their library-sitting room where she had worked out her plans for the refurbishing of the White House, making it glow proudly as the seat of the government . . . in which she and Abraham had spent so many companionable, confiding hours . . . She would be so terribly lonely without him. . . .

Tad came to her side.

"Ma, it's time to go. The carriage is waiting."

They went down the main stairs, out the front door to the portico. She stood on the top of the steps, overlooking the lawn, the driveway.

Her heart was cold and dead within her. She was half blind from crying. How could she face an indifferent, a hostile world? She wanted to die, right then and there, on the top of these steps.

She raised her left hand, slipped the wedding ring off her finger. Slowly out of the blindness and the unseeing, the well-worn words of the inscription came forth to her, standing clear and strong, the living and ultimate truth:

LOVE IS ETERNAL

This, then, was what she had left: her love for Abraham. His love for her. She took Tad's hand in hers. Together, they went down the steps.

ACKNOWLEDGMENTS

THIS book would have been infinitely more difficult to write and authenticate had it not been for the untiring efforts of the Lincolnians in its behalf. Whatever credit there may be for the book's historicity I most gratefully share with the dedicated group of writers and researchers in the Lincoln vineyard; the interpretations of character and happenings are my own, as are whatever errors may remain.

Dr. Harry E. Pratt, Illinois State Historian, guided my efforts for two and a half years, drawing maps of early Springfield, making special studies of the Lincoln neighbors and contemporaries and answering endless technical questions about the Lincolns and their times. Mrs. Marion Pratt made the voluminous files of the Abraham Lincoln Association available to me, and corrected galleys. Margaret Flint, Reference Librarian, put at my disposal the magnificent resources of the Illinois State Historical Library, researched obscure problems. In Springfield I am also indebted for special material to Virginia S. Brown, V. Y. Dallman, Helen Blankmeyer.

In Lexington I was helped by William H. Townsend and J. Winston Coleman, Jr., who guided me to all the Todd landmarks, sketched maps of the city for 1839, indefatigably searched the Kentucky records for my special needs. Dr. Thomas D. Clark helped with a Kentucky bibliography.

I was aided in the uncovering of needed books, records, documents, costumes, unpublished letters, memoirs, theses, by Paul M. Angle of the Chicago Historical Society, Roy P. Basler of the Library of Congress, Elsie Bergland of the Library of Medical Science of the University of Illinois, Norma B. Cuthbert of the Huntington Library, Robert L. Kincaid of Lincoln Memorial University, Stanley W. McClure of the National Park Service, R. Gerald McMurtry of Lincoln Memorial University, David Mearns of the Library of Congress, Ralph Newman, of the Abraham Lincoln Bookshop, James N. Primm of the University of Missouri, Willard L. King, Virginia Stumbough and Justin Turner, all devoted Lincoln students. Benjamin Thomas made available to me his *Abraham Lincoln* prior to its publication; The Rutgers University Press did me the great kindness of providing galleys of its su-

433

perbly edited and printed *The Collected Works of Abraham Lincoln* almost a year before its release.

For source material the most valuable magazine publications were *The Journal of the Illinois State Historical Society; Transactions of the Illinois State Historical Society; The Abraham Lincoln Quarterly; Abraham Lincoln Association Papers; Lincoln Herald*, Lincoln Memorial University; *Lincoln Lore; Lincoln Centennial Association Papers; Papers in Illinois History*.

Specialized publications used include *The American Journal of the Medical Sciences; Illinois Bar Journal, Chicago Bar Association Lectures; Iowa Journal of History; Farm and Fireside*. Among the newspapers of the times used are: Lexington *Observer*, Lexington *Gazette, Sangamo Journal* which became the *Illinois State Journal, Illinois State Register*, Chicago *Tribune*, Chicago *Times*, Cleveland *Plain Dealer*, Washington *Evening Star*, Washington *Chronicle*, New York *Tribune*, New York *Herald*, New York *Ledger*, Boston *Traveller*, Taylorville *Semi-Weekly Breeze*, Cedar Rapids *Evening Gazette*, Ottawa *Republican Times, The Crisis*.

I had access to the unpublished letters of Mary Todd Lincoln and Robert Todd Lincoln, and to the collections of unpublished papers of Orville H. Browning, Jacob Bunn, Mercy Levering and James C. Conkling, David Davis, Ninian W. and Elizabeth Edwards, Benjamin and Helen Edwards, C. H. Graves, Elizabeth Todd Grimsley, Reverend Phineas D. Gurley, John J. Hardin, Emilie Todd Helm, William H. Herndon, Stephen T. Logan, John Todd Stuart, Dr. John Todd, Dr. William F. Wallace.

I wish to express my gratitude to the libraries who made their resources available: the Illinois State Historical Library in Springfield; the Lexington Public Library; the Los Angeles Public Library; the Library of the University of California at Los Angeles, which also borrowed rare books from all over America. My thanks are also due to the libraries of the Universities of Chicago, Illinois, Kentucky, Missouri, Transylvania; to the Huntington Library and the Library of Congress, as well as to the Historical Societies of Chicago, Illinois, Iowa and Wisconsin.

I wish also to thank William H. Townsend for permission to use the oil painting of Mary Todd Lincoln in his collection.

BIBLIOGRAPHY

THERE are over five thousand published books on Abraham Lincoln. I have listed below only those volumes important to the construction of this novel:

MARY TODD LINCOLN: Gamaliel Bradford, *Wives*, 1925; William E. Barton, *The Women Lincoln Loved*, 1927; Katherine Helm, *Mary, Wife of Lincoln*, 1928; William H. Townsend, *Lincoln and His Wife's Home Town*, 1929; W. A. Evans, *Mrs. Abraham Lincoln*, 1932; Sandburg and Angle, *Mary Lincoln*, 1932. Among the more important magazine articles and pamphlets on Mary Lincoln are: Elizabeth Todd Grimsley, "Six Months in the White House," *J. Ill. St. Hist. Soc.*, October 1926; Virginia Kinnaird, *Mrs. Lincoln as a White House Hostess*, Papers in Ill. Hist., 1938; William H. Townsend, *The Boarding School of Mary Todd Lincoln* (pam.), Lex., Ky. 1941; Pratt and East, "Mrs. Lincoln Refurbishes the White House," *Lincoln Herald*, February 1945.

ABRAHAM LINCOLN: Biographies: J. G. Holland, *The Life of Abraham Lincoln*, 1866; Ward H. Lamon, *The Life of Abraham Lincoln*, 1872; *Recollections of Lincoln*, 1895; William O. Stoddard, *Abraham Lincoln*, 1884; Noah Brooks, *Abraham Lincoln*, 1888; Isaac N. Arnold, *The Life of Abraham Lincoln*, 1891; Ida M. Tarbell, *The Life of Abraham Lincoln*, 2 vols., 1895; Nicolay and Hay, *Abraham Lincoln*, 9 vols., 1904; Alonzo Rothschild, *Lincoln, Master of Men*, 1908; Francis F. Browne, *The Everyday Life of Abraham Lincoln*, 1913; Herndon and Weik, *Abraham Lincoln*, 1913; Lord Charnwood, *Abraham Lincoln*, 1917; Nathaniel W. Stephenson, *Lincoln*, 1922; Jesse W. Weik, *The Real Lincoln*, 1922; Carl Sandburg, *The Prairie Years*, 2 vols., 1926; *The War Years*, 4 vols., 1939; Albert J. Beveridge, *Abraham Lincoln, 1809–1858*, 2 vols., 1928; Raymond Warren, *The Prairie President*, 1930; Emanuel Hertz, *Abraham Lincoln*, 2 vols., 1931; Edgar Lee Masters, *Lincoln the Man*, 1931; William E. Barton, *President Lincoln*, 2 vols., 1933; L. Pierce Clark, *Lincoln: A Psycho-Biography*, 1933; John G. Nicolay, *A Short Life of Abraham Lincoln*, 1938; J. G. Randall, *Lincoln the President*, 2 vols., 1946; *Midstream*, 1952; Benjamin P. Thomas, *Abraham Lincoln*, 1952.

SPECIAL STUDIES: A. K. McClure, *Abraham Lincoln and Men of War-Times*, 1892; Ida M. Tarbell, *He Knew Lincoln*, 1907; *In the Footsteps of the Lincolns*, 1924; *A Reporter for Lincoln*, 1927; Edwin E. Sparks, *The Lincoln-Douglas Debates of 1858*, 1908; Francis T. Miller, *Portrait Life of Lincoln*, 1910; Joseph F. Newton, *Lincoln and Herndon*, 1910; F. Lauriston Bullard, *Tad and His Father*, 1915; William E. Barton, *The Soul of Abraham Lincoln*, 1920; Charles T. White, *Lincoln and Prohibition*, 1921; Russell H. Conwell, *Why Lincoln Laughed*, 1922; John W. Starr, Jr., *Lincoln's Last Day*, 1922; *Lincoln and the Railroads*, 1927; Daniel K. Dodge, *Abraham Lincoln, Master of Words*, 1924; William H. Townsend, *Lincoln the Litigant*, 1925; Wayne Whipple, *Tad Lincoln*, 1926; Louis A. Warren, *Lincoln's Parentage and Childhood*, 1926; Rexford Newcomb, *In the Lincoln Country*, 1928; Albert Shaw, *Abraham Lincoln, His Path to the Presidency*, 1929; *Abraham Lincoln, The Year of His Election*, 1929; W. J. Ferguson, *I Saw Booth Shoot Lincoln*, 1930; Julia Taft Bayne, *Tad Lincoln's Father*, 1931; Paul M. Angle, *Lincoln 1854–1861*, 1933; *Here I Have Lived*, 1935; *A Shelf of Lincoln Books*, 1946; *The Lincoln Reader*, 1947; Milton H. Shutes, *Lincoln and the Doctors*, 1933; Blaine B. Gernon, *The Lincolns in Chicago*, 1934; Benjamin P. Thomas, *Lincoln's New Salem*, 1934; *Lincoln 1847–1853*, 1936; *Portrait for Posterity*, 1947; Albert A. Woldman, *Lawyer Lincoln*, 1936; William Baringer, *Lincoln's Rise to Power*, 1937; *Lincoln's Vandalia*, 1949; Otto Eisenschiml, *Why Was Lincoln Murdered?*, 1937; *In the Shadow of Lincoln's Death*, 1940; Emanuel Hertz, *The Hidden Lincoln*, 1938; David H. Bates, *Lincoln in the Telegraph Office*, 1939; Helen Nicolay, *Personal Traits of Abraham Lincoln*, 1939; Harry E. Pratt, *Lincoln 1840–1846*, 1939; *Lincoln 1809–1839*, 1941; *The Personal Finances of Abraham Lincoln*, 1943; *Concerning Mr. Lincoln*, 1944; Henry C. Whitney, *Life on the Circuit with Lincoln*, 1940; Lloyd Lewis, *Myths after Lincoln*, 1941; T. Harry Williams, *Lincoln and the Radicals*, 1941; Henry Villard, *Lincoln on the Eve of '61*, 1941; George F. Milton, *Abraham Lincoln and the Fifth Column*, 1942; Carmen and Luthin, *Lincoln and the Patronage*, 1943; William F. Petersen, *Lincoln · Douglas, The Weather as Destiny*, 1943; Meserve, Hill and Sandburg, *The Photographs of Abraham Lincoln*, 1944; Jay Monaghan, *Diplomat in Carpet Slippers*, 1945; Montgomery S. Lewis, *Legends That Libel Lincoln*, 1946; Edgar D. Jones, *Lincoln and the Preachers*, 1948; Donald W. Riddle, *Lincoln Runs for Congress*, 1948; Norma B. Cuthbert, *Lincoln and the Baltimore Plot*, 1949; Robert S. Harper, *Lincoln and the Press*, 1951; Colin R. Ballard, *The Military Genius of Abraham Lincoln*, 1952; David C. Mearns, *The Lincoln Papers*, 2 vols., 1948.

OTHER PEOPLE: Stephen T. Logan, *Memorials of the Life and Character of Stephen T. Logan*, 1882; Adam Badeau, *Grant in Peace*, 1887; Carl Schurz, *Henry Clay*, 2 vols., 1887; Clark E. Carr, *Stephen A. Douglas*, 1909; Horace White, *The Life of Lyman Trumbull*, 1913; Jesse R. Grant, *In the Days of My Father*, 1925; Paxton Hibben, *Henry Ward Beecher*, 1927; W. E. Woodward, *Meet General Grant*, 1928; Lloyd Lewis, *Sherman, Fighting Prophet*, 1932; George F. Milton, *The Eve of Conflict* (Douglas), 1934; Catherine Gilbertson, *Harriet Beecher Stowe*, 1937; Bernard Mayo, *Henry Clay*, 1937; Philip Van Doren Stern, *The Man Who Killed Lincoln*, 1939;

Townsend and DeVries, *Lives of the Presidents*, 1940; Eckenrode and Conrad, *George B. McClellan*, 1941; R. Gerald McMurtry, *Ben Hardin Helm*, 1943; Irving Stone, *They Also Ran*, 1943; Fawn M. Brodie, *No Man Knows My History* (Joseph Smith), 1945; Burton J. Hendrick, *Lincoln's War Cabinet*, 1946; David Donald, *Lincoln's Herndon*, 1948; Helen Nicolay, *Lincoln's Secretary* (John G. Nicolay), 1949; William H. Hale, *Horace Greeley*, 1950.

WASHINGTON, D.C.: Mrs. E. F. Ellet, *Court Circles of the Republic* (no date); *Queens of American Society*, 1867; F. B. Carpenter, *Six Months at the White House*, 1867; Mary C. Ames, *Ten Years in Washington*, 1874; Laura C. Holloway, *The Ladies of the White House*, 1881; Ben Perley Poore, *Reminiscences*, 2 vols., 1886; W. O. Stoddard, *Inside the White House in War Times*, 1890; Noah Brooks, *Washington in Lincoln's Time*, 1896; Mrs. John A. Logan, *Thirty Years in Washington*, 1901; Rufus R. Wilson, *Washington, The Capital City*, Vol. I, 1901; Anne H. Wharton, *Social Life in the Early Republic*, 1902; Gaillard Hunt, *The First Forty Years of Washington Society*, 1906; William H. Crook, *Through Five Administrations*, 1907; *Memories of the White House*, 1911; Esther Singleton, *The Story of the White House*, Vol. II, 1907; Helen Nicolay, *Our Capital on the Potomac*, 1924; Allen C. Clark, *Abraham Lincoln in the National Capital*, 1925; Edna M. Colman, *Seventy Five Years of White House Gossip*, 1925; Ethel Lewis, *The White House*, 1937; Charles Hurd, *The White House*, 1940; Margaret Leech, *Reveille in Washington*, 1941; Bess Furman, *White House Profile*, 1951; Joseph Leeming, *The White House in Picture and Story*, 1953; Ann D. Brown, *The White House* (bibliog.).

MEMOIRS: William H. Russell, *My Diary, North and South*, 1863; Elizabeth Keckley, *Behind the Scenes*, 1868; Princess Felix Salm-Salm, *Ten Years of My Life*, 1877; Usher F. Linder, *Reminiscences of the Early Bench and Bar of Illinois*, 1879; Anna L. Boyden, *Echoes from Hospital and White House*, 1884; Cassius M. Clay, *The Life of Cassius Marcellus Clay*, 1886; Allen T. Rice, *Reminiscences of Abraham Lincoln*, 1888; Albert G. Riddle, *Recollections of War Times*, 1895; Samuel C. Busey, *Personal Reminiscences*, 1895; L. E. Chittenden, *Recollections of President Lincoln and His Administration*, 1901; H. Augusta Dodge, *Gail Hamilton's Life in Letters*, 1901; Henry Villard, *Memoirs*, 2 vols., 1904; William T. Sherman, *Memoirs*, 1904; Thomas J. McCormack, *Memoirs of Gustave Koerner*, Vol. I, 1909; Isabel Wallace, *Life and Letters of General W. H. L. Wallace*, 1909; Marian Gouverneur, *As I Remember*, 1911; Gideon Welles, *Diary of Gideon Welles*, 3 vols., 1911; Frank E. Stevens, *Autobiography of Stephen A. Douglas*, 1912; Henry B. Rankin, *Personal Recollections of Abraham Lincoln*, 1916; *Intimate Character Sketches of Abraham Lincoln*, 1924; Orville H. Browning, *The Diary of Orville Hickman Browning*, 2 vols., 1925; Howard K. Beale, *The Diary of Edward Bates*, 1933; Tyler Dennett, *Lincoln and the Civil War* (Letters and Diary of John Hay), 1939; Rufus R. Wilson, *Intimate Memories of Lincoln*, 1945; *The Diary of a Public Man* (anon.), 1946; Marquis Adolphe de Chambrun, *Impressions of Lincoln and the Civil War*, 1952; Allan Nevins, *Polk, the Diary of a President*, 1952.

CIVIL WAR: Wood Gray, *The Hidden Civil War*, 1942; Marjorie B. Greenbie, *Lincoln's Daughters of Mercy*, 1944; Bruce Catton, *Mr. Lincoln's Army*, 1951; *Glory Road*, 1952; *A Stillness at Appomattox*, 1953; T. Harry Williams, *Lincoln and His Generals*, 1952.

ILLINOIS: Timothy Flint, *History and Geography of the Mississippi Valley*, Vol. I, 1833; Eliza W. Farnham, *Life in Prairie Land*, 1847; *History of Sangamon County, Illinois*, 1881; John Moses, *Illinois Historical and Statistical*, Vol. I, 1889; Governor Thomas Ford, *A History of Illinois*, 2 vols., 1945; *Counties of Illinois*.

KENTUCKY: Lucile N. Clay, *The Lexington Theatre from 1800 to 1840* (Thesis in University of Kentucky), 1930; J. Winston Coleman, Jr., *Slavery Times in Kentucky*, 1940; Thomas D. Clark, *The Kentucky*, 1942; *A Description of Kentucky*, 1945; *A History of Kentucky*, 1950.

HISTORIES: James F. Rhodes, *History of the United States*, 4 vols., 1896; Benson J. Lossing, *Harper's Encyclopaedia of United States History*, 10 vols., 1906; Edward Stanwood, *A History of the Presidency*, 2 vols., 1928; *Dictionary of American Biography*, 20 vols., 1928; James T. Adams, *Atlas of American History*, 1943; William E. Baringer, *A House Dividing*, 1945; Allan Nevins, *Ordeal of the Union*, 2 vols., 1947; *The Emergence of Lincoln*, 2 vols., 1950.

GENERAL: John Forbes, *The Cyclopaedia of Practical Medicine*, Vol. II, 1854; Allan Nevins, *American Press Opinion*, 1928; Ruth E. Finley, *The Lady of Godey's*, 1931; George C. Odell, *Annals of the New York Stage*, Vol. VI, 1931; Catron and Masters, *Edwards Place* (pam.), 1945.

LINCOLN'S OWN WORDS: Anthony Gross, *Lincoln's Own Stories*, 1912; Gilbert A. Tracy, *Uncollected Letters of Abraham Lincoln*, 1917; Nathaniel W. Stephenson, *An Autobiography of Abraham Lincoln*, 1926; Emanuel Hertz, *Lincoln Talks*, 1939; Roy P. Basler, *Abraham Lincoln: His Speeches and Writings*, 1946; *The Collected Works of Abraham Lincoln*, 8 vols., 1953; Robert D. Richardson, *Abraham Lincoln's Autobiography*, 1947.